The Gospel According to
Ben Elton

Ben Elton is one of Britain's best-known stand-up comedians. He writes his own material and is a successful television writer whose credits include *The Young Ones* and *Black Adder*. He has written three successful West End plays, *Gasping*, *Silly Cow* and *Popcorn*, and collaborated with Andrew Lloyd Webber for the musical *The Beautiful Game*, and with Queen for *We Will Rock You*. He is the author of the bestselling novels *Stark*, *Gridlock*, *This Other Eden*, *Popcorn*, *Inconceivable*, *Blast from the Past* and *Dead Famous*. When not touring, Ben Elton lives in London.

The Gospel According to
Ben Elton

This Other Eden
Popcorn

POCKET
BOOKS

LONDON · SYDNEY · NEW YORK · TOKYO · SINGAPORE · TORONTO

This Other Eden first published in Great Britain by
Simon & Schuster UK Ltd, 1993
Popcorn first published in Great Britain by
Simon & Schuster UK Ltd, 1996
This omnibus edition first published by Pocket Books, 2002
An imprint of Simon & Schuster UK Ltd
A Viacom Company

1 3 5 7 9 10 8 6 4 2

Simon & Schuster UK Ltd
Africa House
64–78 Kingsway
London WC2B 6AH

www.simonsays.co.uk

Simon & Schuster Australia
Sydney

A CIP catalogue record for this book is available
from the British Library

ISBN 0-7434-6798-1

Typeset by Palimpsest Book Production Limited,
Polmont, Stirlingshire
Printed and bound in Great Britain by
Bookmarque Ltd, Croydon, Surrey

The Gospel According to
Ben Elton

This Other Eden

For Sophie

Chapter One

In which a much-loved man pursues the elusive green light

A rat's tale.

A rat feeds greedily on rotten meat . . .
   A rat feeds greedily on rotten *human* meat. A rotting, human limb, attached to a living body.

The desperate man knows it will be easier to detach the limb from the body than the rat from the limb. The diner is stronger than the dinner, for the diner has no drug to numb its pain. The rat's head is buried deep in the silver green flesh, its claws hidden beneath the blackened skin. Only its plump body and twitching rump can be seen as it pushes deeper and deeper into the decaying muscle. The desperate man knows that the hungry rat will never let go. Yet if it remains, how long before it or its friends and relations discover the living meat beyond the putrid thigh? Not very long, surely, and even a rat must prefer fresh meat to foul.

If one is to die, then there are better ways than being eaten alive by enormous flea-ridden rats; even in his weary, drifting state, the man can see that. Swallowing two sparkling capsules, the only bright thing in his dull world, the man waits for the drugs to rush his brain and then takes up his big knife. The knife is blunt, but the flesh is rotten and falls apart before the blade, as if it has been braised. In a moment, man and leg are parted. His mind on other things, he pulls himself away, leaving the rat to its refreshment.

This is how it will be in the century to come. No savage biker tribes, no lone still-human heroes, no Mad Max millennium, only ill, old people and large hungry rats eating them.

Those who love you hurt you most.

Nathan knew it was good; it was the best work he'd ever done. That was why he so desperately wanted the job. This was more than just a bit of seriously good copy. This was prophecy, this was the truth.

But telling the truth is never easy. Nathan was drained. The night Los Angeles re-ignited, as it did at regular intervals these days, he had been a prisoner in his hotel room for a week. Held captive not by a gunman or a sex criminal or even the fantastical illusion that the room service he had ordered in a previous life might one day arrive, but by a great and terrible desire to please.

There were people in that town who loved Nathan and he had to justify that love. He knew they loved him, for they had told him so many times, and they had also sent a limousine to collect him at the airport, when they might easily have suggested that he take a cab and keep the receipt. For a man used, as Nathan was, to the finances of British radio this was big love indeed.

Sometimes though, mere love is not enough. In Hollywood one can be embraced and rejected with equal fervour and integrity by the same people and at the same time. This, over the years, had led to movie people getting something of a reputation for craven hypocrisy. But there is nothing disingenuous about combining love with rejection. It is quite possible, and indeed reasonable, to like and admire, yes, even love somebody without wishing to commit hundreds of millions of dollars on the strength of their script.

Every day, all over town, writers faced producers, producers faced bigger producers, bigger producers faced studio heads and the same tortured mantra was heard: 'You are a great artist and we all love you. Speaking personally, yours is the kind of talent that was the reason I came into this business in the first place. Will we be picking up your project? No, I don't think so, but that's about us, it isn't about you.'

Nathan understood his position. They loved him, but he frustrated them for, try as he might, Nathan had so far been unable to produce a scenario in which the plot *curved* sufficiently or in which the characters possessed heart, moral worth and, above all, warmth.

'It's no good this guy dying, one-legged in a polluted world,' the men who loved Nathan would tell him, 'if we don't *care* that he dies.'

Nathan understood what was required of him. He returned to his room and tried to make the people who loved him care; for if they cared, then so would Mr and Ms America, and if Mr and Ms America cared then it was a reasonable presumption that the whole world would care. That was Nathan's brief, to make the whole world care. If he could achieve that then he would truly have justified the faith which Plastic Tolstoy had placed in him. With this thought Nathan turned wearily back to his computer. For when Plastic Tolstoy placed faith in you, it was wise to justify that faith. For Plastic Tolstoy was the most important man in the whole communications industry. It was his job to market the end of the world.

Everything is fascinating when you should be working.

All week Nathan had moped from his bed to his desk to his bathroom and back to his bed. Trying to think of ways to make those who loved him, Mr and Ms America, the world in general and above all, Plastic Tolstoy, care. But everything is fascinating when you should be working, and Nathan had also spent his week fighting the desire to stare out of the window, leafing through magazines and flicking through the endless permutations available on the in-room entertainment system.

The Hitler trial was reaching its climax. That sad, grey monster stood before the cameras every day, his shocked and baffled face devoid of any real understanding of the crimes they told him he had committed. Under normal circumstances DNA cloning was banned; the world was overcrowded enough without people re-growing the dead. However, when a lock of Hitler's hair had been unearthed, the World Court ruled that an exception might be made, the general feeling being that Hitler was one villain for whom being dead should not prevent justice being done. Besides, the UN was as always hugely in debt and the TV rights to the trial were worth a fortune.

Nathan carried on through the news channels. They were all pretty similar which, considering they were all owned by the same company (Plastic Tolstoy Communications System), was hardly surprising. The daughter of the British king had been videoed turning tricks in Piccadilly, although a lot of people said it was just a clever hologram. Jurgen Thor was to address the European parliament yet again, on the subject of banning or at least massively taxing Claustrospheres. A new fish had been developed that was capable of surviving in the dead waters of the Atlantic; a fish which had the added advantage of being so radioactive it could cook itself while the busy house-spouse prepared a salad.

Under normal circumstances Nathan would not have dreamt of watching a news item about marine research. Nor would he have allowed himself to get sucked into a public forum-style chat-show, where victims of pedestrian-dog faeces encounter were brought together with dog-owners, in order to come to terms with their anger. But everything is fascinating when you should be working.

Making them care.

Nathan snapped the TV off, as he had done a hundred times that week. He dragged his hand angrily from deep within the great plastic sack of Bacon Cheezos on his lap. He resisted the colossal temptation to spend twenty minutes staring at the wall and scratching his balls. He avoided the Virtual Reality helmet beckoning him from the coffee table. He must concentrate, he must focus. He had to make those who loved him care.

'What I need,' Nathan mused to himself, 'is a kid . . . a cute kid who is in some way relying on the dying man who chops off his leg . . .'

Nathan grabbed his Voice to Screen DictaType Transmitter. Suddenly, after all the waiting and prevaricating, inspiration struck. The words tumbled out.

'All right, so the man has a child . . . a tiny little girl who peeks out from her hiding place amidst the mountain

5

of rotten garbage . . . rotten *stinking putrid* garbage . . . Uhm . . . she's dirty and thin . . . but cute, very cute . . . the dying world has yet to dull her bonny beauty . . . nice sentence, *good* sentence . . . OK, so somehow we know that the half-dead man with the big knife is the little girl's father . . . a signet ring? Maybe the same haircut? . . . Or else we see her mouth the word "Daddy" . . . yes, that's it, she mouths the word "Daddy" so we know he is her father, her last chance, her only protector. Then we see him drug himself into oblivion and cut off his own leg . . . beautiful, that is *great* . . . So the gorgeous little girl knows that she is now in deep doo doo . . . Uhm . . . her sparkling eyes fade to dull despair as her dad . . . no, as her *last best hope* drags himself away to die . . . Then what happens? What's the punch?' . . . Nathan paused for a moment, willing his little flight of fancy to see him through to some stunning conclusion. Yes! He had it. Breathlessly he spoke again into the DictaType microphone: 'The little girl retreats back into the rotting garbage which provides the only warmth available to her now . . . and the rat is left on its own, eating her dad's leg . . . great image, hold on that a moment . . . Then the rat's head emerges from the severed leg . . . its snout all twitching and gruesome . . . uhm . . . The white fangs show amid the soft maggoty meat bulging in its mouth . . . good sentence, good sentence, keep that . . . So why has the rat stopped eating? Because it's *heard something*, that's why! . . . Something tempting . . . something exciting. The evil rat turns and stares towards the place in the garbage where the tiny child is hiding. Freezeframe . . . Cue Voiceover . . . Doesn't your child deserve a better tomorrow? Invest in Claustrosphere today.'

Nathan turned off his DictaType machine.

'It's good,' he told himself. 'They've *got* to pick it up.'

And as the flames which a few hours earlier had burnt only in the hearts of an angry people began yet again to engulf large sections of one of the world's premier cities, Nathan sat, hand clamped unconsciously on his crotch, hoping that those who loved him, who had failed to care about a dying man, might now care about a threatened little girl. Hoping that his assuredly fine treatment for a Claustrosphere commercial, his unquestionably brilliant vision, would also now have that all-important factor, 'warmth'. That those who loved him might love him all the more, love him, perhaps, even enough to suggest to Plastic Tolstoy that his project be green-lighted.

Nathan did not resent the compliant, entirely reactive nature of his creative endeavours. That was the town, he thought, and, indeed, as the flames danced outside his window, he was right.

If I should get lost in development, think only this of me. That there is some corner of the US entertainment industry that is for ever England.

Nathan was British, but despite this, he did not suffer from that terrible anger that many Brit artists who visit Hollywood feel. That private shame that comes from the knowledge that *you* have come to *them*. That, for all your babble about seeking a more vibrant culture, about fleeing the anally-retentive, small-minded snobberies one encounters at home, they know and you know that the only reason you have come is because they have more money. Much, much more money.

Brits in Hollywood divide largely into two categories: the ones who are living there and the ones who would like to live there. The ones who are living there tend to be aggressively Yankophile, partly taking on the character-istics and language of the town. When they say things like 'if we pass, it's my arse', 'pass' still rhymes with 'farce', as it used to in Kensington and Soho, but 'arse' now rhymes with 'mass'. They will say, 'If we parce, it's my ass'. They wear loafers, or smart deckshoes, sometimes without socks, and drink Lite beer and dry martinis, ordering them by brand name. 'Get me a Beefeater martini and a twist please.'

The visitors, on the other hand, affect an exaggerated Britishness as a defence against the obvious fact that they are on the make. They ask for tea and are gently amused when it arrives with the tea-bag still in the cup. They order obscure malt whiskies, secretly hoping that the bar won't stock them. They tell their hosts that the thing they like most about LA is the paper toilet-seat covers. When they get home to Britain they speak wittily of toothy but empty smiles and glib, automised admonishments to 'enjoy'. They claim firmly that it is a fine place to visit but they could never live there, which translates, of course, as nobody has asked them to.

Nathan made no such pretence at indulgent distaste. He thought California was lovely. He enjoyed the toothy smiles. He thought it was nice to be greeted cheerfully.

'But for God's sake, they don't *mean* it,' a disaffected independent producer from Fulham had said over an Isle of Locharno McClaymore the Bonny single malt in the hotel bar. 'They don't care if you live or die.'

'Since when have good manners been a matter of sincerity?' Nathan replied. 'You wish me "all the best" every time I see you, but you wouldn't lift a finger to make it happen.'

'Look, I was taught good manners, not vacuous hypocrisy,' snapped the producer, who had that day failed even to be loved very much, let alone green-lighted.

'Exactly,' said Nathan. 'You were *taught* to say please and thank you, not because anyone wished to indoctrinate you with a false sense of goodwill, but simply because it is important to show consideration. Is the Californian "have a nice day, enjoy your life, die happy and come back as something wonderful" any different?'

The producer from Fulham moodily ordered another drink. He thought that Nathan would sing a different tune when Plastic Tolstoy's people knocked back his Claustrosphere ad and put him straight on a sub-orbital back to dirty old England. Then he'd be badmouthing the Yanks along with all the other unloved Brits.

But Nathan had no intention of getting knocked back; he was going to be green-lighted. Because he was prepared to bet that, with the addition of the scared little girl, his scenario about the end of the world would be the warmest scenario about the end of the world that Plastic Tolstoy's people would have seen all week.

An idea that's time has come.

Everybody was talking about the end of the world these days. It was a very big subject, not perhaps quite as big as sport, or the love-lives of the British royal family, but none the less very big. Some people, like Plastic Tolstoy, were trying to market it. Others, like Jurgen Thor, the Great Green Warrior, were trying to prevent it. Some people were, of course, causing it. Whether by accident or design, every day countless incidents, both large and small, were hastening the Earth's untimely demise. One such event, a rather large one as it happened, was shortly to occur off the coast of Alaska. There, whilst Nathan awaited the studio's reaction to his heart-warming vision of catastrophe, would be found images of Earth death every bit as chilling as those he had invented. Not *quite* as chilling, perhaps, for in real life the plot rarely curves and people are often less inclined to care.

Chapter Two

A loose-fitting coffin in a watery grave

A view from a cliff.

The mess was indescribable. Yet it would have to be described, as always, described in yet another of the pointless reports that had to be written. No report could ever adequately convey what a mess it really was, though. As Judy, the investigating officer on the scene, often said, you had to be there.

'You know how with babies,' Judy would say, 'you can never quite believe what a state they can get things into, until you find out for yourself? Well, it's the same with supertankers.'

Everything was as it always was on these occasions. Judy sometimes wondered why anybody bothered turning up at all. As far as the eye could see, the boiling ocean was black. The cliffs and rocks were black. The dead creatures were black. The emergency operations personnel were black from head to foot, as they got their emergency operation underway in the usual totally inadequate manner.

'Tanker disasters are like the first snows of winter,' Judy would explain to friends. 'You remember how we used to have snow? Well, year in, year out the stuff would fall, and every time it was like the first time, it was like nobody had ever had to deal with snow before. The roads would get clogged up, the trains would stop, the pipes would burst. Nothing was ever ready. Well, it's the same when a billion litres of crude hits a coastline. People think the authorities know what to do. They don't. We all just shrug our shoulders and get down there with a spade and a bucket like we always do.'

Judy was standing on the highest cliff overlooking the disaster with the coastguard people and a couple of local cops.

'Well, guess we'd better go get the captain. I hear he's drunk,' said the chief coastguard with the weary sigh of a man who had left a good dinner to come and bear witness to an event which would follow its tragic course, whether he was there to watch it or not.

'Are you going down on to the bridge?' Judy inquired.

The coastguard turned disdainfully to look at Judy.

'I don't see any reason to discuss my plans with you, nerd,' he said.

A boy named Judy.

Judy was a man even though he had a woman's name. He was called Judy because he had been unfortunate enough to be born during the time of the great gender realignment. A period when it was a commonly held belief in the university common-rooms of the world that all single-sex imagery was oppressive. This was a time when men were strongly encouraged not to grow beards, which were seen as visual assertions of gender, whereas it became fashionable for women to be as hairy as possible, in order to blur the margins. The idea was that if everyone could pretend to be exactly the same then no one could be held back by being different and hence, it was argued, the individual would be in a position to prosper.

That was how Judy came to be called Judy. One morning before he was born, as his father waxed his face and his mother applied mascara to her legs and upper lip, it was decided.

'If it's a boy we'll call it Judy,' they said, 'and if it's a girl we'll call it Hercules.' In this manner the margins were not blurred, and Judy got dead-legged every day at school for sixteen years.

When Judy reached his majority he astonished those who knew him by not changing his name. He had, of course, always intended to do so the moment he got the chance; but when that chance finally came around, he had suffered so much at the hands of bullies that there seemed little point in bothering. Children are much crueller than adults, Judy reasoned, so he had already weathered the worst of it. He was, of course, wrong. At college, the coarser element laughed at him and pushed him around every day, and as an adult he rarely turned his back without hearing a snigger.

It was not just that Judy was a boy with a girl's name; his problems were further compounded by the fact that he was the least prepossessing of men. He had one leg slightly shorter than the other and something of a stoop. His glasses were thick and his hair always greasy. He was what the Americans call a nerd and since Judy was an American, nerd became his middle name. He was a textbook nerd. It was almost as if he had been deliberately designed that way. In terms of appearance there was quite literally nothing about him that was not nerdy. If they gave out air-miles for looking ineffectual and inadequate, Judy could have been the first man on Mars.

If he had been a stupid nerd Judy might simply have been ignored, but he wasn't: he was a clever nerd, very clever indeed, which was of course something of a red rag to the bullies. It was bad enough, the bullies reasoned, putting up with someone who was such a dork, without that dork having the gall to be cleverer than they were.

Occasionally, in his younger days, Judy had considered having a physical rebuild, or at the very least getting his face done. But as he grew up he came to rather resent the idea of paying a surgeon to attack his body simply because people did not find it attractive. Besides which, he could not have afforded a really decent operation. The cosmetic surgery industry had become fearful of creating a world filled with semi-identical, plasticised, doll-like figures. They had therefore introduced a system which they called 'financial discrimination', which meant that only very rich people could turn themselves into semi-identical, plasticised, doll-like figures.

Therefore Judy remained as nerdy as the day he was born and suffered the consequences. It was probably because of this discrimination that a clear sense of what was right grew strong in Judy's heart, and he determined that he would spend his life fighting intolerance and injustice. To this end, he employed his considerable intellect to win himself a place with the FBI, reasoning that he would certainly find plenty of intolerance and injustice in the FBI.

He was right. Nothing changed. Judy irritated the nastier element amongst his new colleagues no less than he had irritated the bullies at school and college. He continued to look stupid and talk smart, a combination almost guaranteed to bring out the bully in anyone who was even remotely so disposed. During his training the oafs and toughs continued to beat him up as they had always done. He was shouldered aside on the firing range and wet-towelled in the showers. Many of his colleagues were, of course, nice to him, but a kind smile does little to mitigate the pain of being held down and given a Chinese burn, or of having a Magnum .44 suspended by a piece of string from your scrotum.

The passage of years had not tempered Judy's sense of injustice and the resentment he felt at being constantly dismissed remained undiminished. Therefore, when the coastguard on the polluted clifftop called him a nerd, he drew himself up to his full height, which was either five-five, or five-five and a half, depending on which leg he put his weight on, and prepared to confront yet another nerdist.

'My name is Judy Schwartz,' he said. 'I am an FBI agent and I demand that you take me with you on to the bridge of this stricken tanker. Otherwise I shall devote the rest of my life to finding out who your mistress is and then revealing her identity to your wife.'

Dead hand at the tiller.

The little coastguard helicopter stood with its engine idling on the roof of the ship's bridge, while Judy, two coastguards and the local chief of police went inside and surveyed the scene.

'Well, he sure saved us a lot of trouble,' said the police chief.

'Did the decent thing, I reckon,' a coastguard added.

They were referring to the captain of the stricken

tanker who was dead, killed, apparently, by his own hand. There he sat, slumped across his bloodied charts, a bottle in one hand, a revolver in the other and his brains in the wastepaper basket on the other side of the room.

It was déjà vu for Judy. He had seen this scene before, on another bridge in another storm. In the midst of a different disaster he had seen a ship's master dead over his charts. Dead before he could explain why he had allowed his ship to get so close to shore in such inclement circumstances.

Outside on the enormous deck, which was listing at an angle that made standing up extremely difficult, the crew were being winched to safety. Apart, that is, from the captain, who was dead, and the second in command, a competent looking woman named Jackson. She was standing near the bridge, awaiting any further instructions from the coastguard before following the crew off the ship. Judy wandered outside into the gale and spoke to her, shouting, to be heard above the wind and the rain.

'Did you order the abandon ship, Ms . . . ?' he asked.

'Jackson. Barbara Jackson. No, I did not, sir. The captain ordered abandon ship and most of the crew got away in the boats before the situation deteriorated to necessitate coastguard helicopters.'

'So the captain discharged his duties and then killed himself?'

'That is the case.'

'Was that like him?' Judy asked.

'Was what? Discharging his duties or killing himself?'

'Killing himself.'

'Well, he didn't make a habit of it,' Jackson responded angrily. 'But then he didn't make a habit of losing ships.

Certainly not like this. We went down like a stone, holed both sides. The captain would have known what the consequences of that would be. This coast's finished for three hundred miles, the fishing, the wildlife, everything. Would you want that on your conscience? He was a decent man. I reckon he'd have been dead inside before he pulled the trigger.'

'Holed both sides, you say?' Judy inquired. 'Seems rather unusual, doesn't it? The rocky coast is only on the one side.'

'There's plenty of channels, we must have got caught in one.'

'And yet the captain was a good seaman?'

'As good as I've sailed with . . . They say he'd been drinking.'

'Did he often drink on duty?'

Jackson hesitated. She was a loyal crew member, but did not wish to lie to the FBI.

'He may have touched it. But, as I say, he was a good seaman. I never saw him even remotely drunk on watch.'

Judy was lost in thought for a moment. The captain was a drinker, that much was clear, which could certainly make him the culprit . . . but it could also make him a very convenient scapegoat.

'Do you think he got drunk and ran the ship aground?' he asked Jackson.

'I suppose he must have done,' she replied.

Inside, the coastguard and police chief, having completed their perfunctory investigation, were preparing to leave.

'Can I see where the ship's ruptured?' Judy asked hurriedly.

'Sure, if you're a fish, they're both below the waterline,' Jackson replied.

'But the ship's listing, eventually the port-side rupture will emerge.'

'It might,' Jackson conceded, 'if the ship hasn't broken up by then, which it probably will have, the way this storm's blowing.'

But Judy was insistent, he wanted to see the hole in the side of the ship. The coastguard people were astonished, and informed him that if he wished to risk his neck on damn fool errands he could do it alone. Then they left in their helicopter without him. Jackson, despite Judy's protestations, elected to stay, arguing that Judy would have no hope whatsoever of finding his way into the ship's hold without guidance.

Judy thanked her and radioed the helicopter, which had by now winched the crew aboard, requesting it to stand by overhead. The pilot was not overjoyed.

'Lieutenant Schwartz!' the pilot called back. 'We're getting blown all over the damn sky! What the hell are you *doing* down there?'

Judy replied that he was conducting the fullest investigation possible into the source of a major environmental catastrophe before the principal piece of evidence was lost to the elements.

'Something,' Judy added angrily, 'which the coastguard has signally failed to do. Now shut your face and do your job or I'll give your address to the Mormons.'

Hidden depths.

With one side of the ship shuddering slowly upward and every inch of the vehicle screaming and groaning and loudly announcing its imminent break-up, Judy and Jackson edged their way below. It is not easy trying to descend a ship's stairway at the best of times, but when those stairs are leaning over at an angle of forty-five degrees it is very nearly impossible. Particularly if you are extremely conscious of the fact that at any moment the entire million-tonne ship is going to snap in two and hurl you into a freezing vortex of oil, rock and toxic seawater. It was also pitch-black, of course, the ship's emergency lights having given up at the first sign of an emergency. Jackson led the way with a flashlight.

They found the breach in a vast container dock still half-filled with oil and water. There was no way they could actually reach the great tear in the side of the ship, because the flood stood between them and it. Judy played the flashlight around the edges of the rupture.

'Notice anything strange about this hole?' he inquired, shouting himself hoarse above the crashing of the sea outside and the huge booming and creaking of the ship itself.

'Only that it's pretty big. I didn't think we'd done that much damage. If the hole on the other side is as drastic, we'd better get out now. I don't give this hulk five more minutes.' But Judy continued to play the light around the edges of the hole, or at least those parts that the torch beam could reach.

'It is strange, though, isn't it?' he said, almost to himself.

'I can't hear you,' Jackson shouted. 'Give me the flashlight. We have to leave!'

Judy took no notice. He was still thinking, his mind elsewhere. His body was in danger of being elsewhere shortly, too. The ship was shuddering its last and it was a question of get out now or go down with it. Fortunately for Judy, Jackson was much stronger than he was. As he mused, she wrenched the torch from his grasp and let them both out of the huge half-kilometre chamber that could so nearly have become a rather loose-fitting coffin.

As they ascended the stairs, Judy could not resist taking one last look back despite the danger.

'It *is* strange, though, don't you think?' he said.

But Jackson was way ahead of him.

Chapter Three

On a drive through Hollywood

The city that Liz built.

Before you can be green-lighted or knocked back, you have to make a pitch, and it was Nathan's day to pitch. The biggest day of his life.

The riots were dying down as he drove his hire car through Century City; the city, legend had it, that Liz Taylor built. Nathan had heard the story a number of times in various versions. The facts seemed to be that the whole area had once been the back-lot of Twentieth Century Fox. It was here that in another, more innocent age they had re-enacted great wagon trains, built medieval castles and re-fought the Pacific battles of the US marines.

Anyway, the story went that Fox lost so much money on Liz Taylor's movie *Cleopatra* that they had to sell most of the back-lot to real estate developers. This débâcle was a direct result of the curious Hollywood belief that equates gossip column inches with potential ticket revenue. The extraordinary idea that, just because the public is interested in who some celebrity is screwing, they will go and see them in a movie is a delusion that nearly cripples the industry regularly.

So Fox sold their back-lot, and a mighty city of steel and glass skyscrapers grew up, and was subsequently burnt

21

down as a result of the civil unrest that became part of day to day life in the LA area. It was through this urban strife that Liz's city gained a far more significant claim to fame than as a mere monument to the fiction of the star-system. For it was here that pollution was first used as a means to facilitate social engineering.

Environmental protection.

The problem was a serious one. Every time the city was rebuilt, the disaffected have-nots would come up from the badlands to loot it and burn it down again. This, obviously, was a source of considerable irritation to the civic authorities. Even more galling, though, was the fact that these regular acts of vandalism were perpetrated under the protection of top quality filtered sun and the very cleanest air, for which the victims of the attacks were paying.

Century City, by dint of its great wealth, boasted a state-of-the-art municipal eco-defence system. Its sun was UV-filtered by the satellite method, whereby a solar screen was placed in orbit over the city. The air was kept reasonable by the simple blow system, where huge fans prevented smog from gathering by blowing it away into other parts of the city.

All this safe sun and clean air made life in Century City very pleasant. Unfortunately, it was as pleasant for the visiting vandals, as for the legitimate residents. The outrageous fact was that honest citizens were paying local tax, so that the people who robbed them might be protected from skin cancer and lung disease. Something had to be done.

Something was. The world's first pollution-based security system was installed. The orbital sun-shield was sent spinning away to join the ever growing slicks of debris caught in the gravitational pull of other planets and the giant fans were silenced. The sun-screen was replaced by a solar cell intensifier which acted in the manner of a vast UV magnifying glass. A deal was done with the electricity people, who stopped pumping their exhaust out over the Pacific and let it out on the Avenue of the Stars instead. Parking lots were connected to buildings via BioTube, so that the legitimate citizen could step from the safety of his or her car directly into a sealed environment. Anybody without BioTube access was in big trouble.

The effect was dramatic. Signs went up on the freeways entering the district: 'WARNING. This Area is Environmentally Protected!! Even short-term exposure to the Century City environment will result in serious illness leading to death! Stay in your car and keep moving unless you have access to a BioTube.'

By this simple method, unfiltered sunlight and industrial smog were transformed from problems into solutions. Pollution became a saleable commodity.

Fame is the spur.

Nathan eased his car to a halt. He lowered his windows only very slightly because the atmosphere outside was pretty foul. He would have liked to have dealt with the guards via his car-roof air-lock, but that might have appeared furtive, and the last thing you did with the Beverly Hills Perimeter Private Police Force was appear in any way furtive.

Looking furtive was crazy behaviour and, as far as the Beverly Hills Perimeter Private Police Force was concerned, crazies were the principal targets of their profession. Beverly Hills was the home of the stars and hence attracted crazies like bees to honey. Crazies would queue up in line to get a chance to try and murder the object of their love and admiration. There were hot-dog stalls and cheap hotels all over the surrounding area, set up purely to cater for the number of unbalanced sad-acts who flocked to Hollywood in pursuit of this vicarious and violent brush with celebrity.

How Hollywood had changed. There had been a time when every bus that pulled into LA had ten kids on it, all desperate to be a star. Suddenly it was ten kids, all desperate to kill one.

The problem, as always, was one of celebrity. Just about everybody seemed to want it, but not everybody could have it. Celebrity could be achieved by becoming a star, but that was a very tough call. The crazies had discovered an easier way. Why, they argued, spend years going to acting and improv' classes, exhaust oneself moonlighting as bar-staff and waiters, suffer the endless auditioning for adverts and pleading for bit-parts in exploitative cheapo vids, torture one's conscience wondering whether to sleep with producers or not, generally fritter one's life away looking for that million to one break that would make you a star? Why do all that when you could get just as famous by finding some idiot who had already done it, and shooting them?

It was this kind of remorseless logic that had led some people to ask themselves who were the crazies.

Agencies had sprung up to deal with what had become a major part of the industry. The life of a star-killer was big news; there were the book rights, the movie rights, the exclusive interviews, the exclusive photos. These things needed careful handling.

'Lock up your past,' was the first thing an agent would tell a hopeful young crazie who approached them for representation. 'If you get lucky and waste a biggy, every childhood photo of you becomes a gold mine. Believe me, the press will have stripped your ol' mama's home clean before the gunshots die away. You have to have every document, every picture relating to you hidden away, ready for me to sell the first day you go on trial. We need to do exclusive interview deals with all your old pals and school teachers *before* you kill your star. Believe me, even your own family will start seeing dollar signs once they realise what you're going to be worth.'

By the time Nathan arrived in Hollywood, the worst excesses of stardom via murder were over. At its height, though, people were walking out of prison straight into talk-show host jobs and six-picture deals. A vicious circle developed. Scarcely would the ex-murderer have time to adjust to his or her new-found celebrity when they themselves would be shot, and so the dreadful cycle continued.

Some agencies who represented both genuine stars and crazy stars (and of course crazy stars who had become genuine stars) even discussed the possibilities of mutually profitable deals between both parties, whereby a star who was in big financial trouble might do a deal with a crazie, whereby the crazie only wounded the star and they split all revenues that ensued. These deals never really took off. For one thing, there was a distinct whiff of insider trading about the whole thing. Besides which, in the midst of all the wheeling and dealing, it was easy to forget that the crazies involved were, by the very nature of their profession, crazy, and could rarely bring themselves merely to wound a target.

All in all, the Beverly Hills security guys had reason

to be nervy. Being a mad gunman was one of the best paid jobs a talentless nobody would ever get and fame is universally recognised as the spur. Certainly, in order to get the fame, you had to be caught and imprisoned, but then the objects of your murderous careerism were also forced into prison, living as they did behind wire and guns and leather-clad security men. Yes, their prisons were more comfortable, but they were prisons none the less.

The market force.

Nathan could see that the private cops thought he was a crazie.

'I'm not a crazie,' he said, 'I'm a British writer named Nathan Hoddy.'

The cops' demeanour stiffened noticeably. They fingered their armaments conspicuously. If crazies were a little crazy, writers were dangerous lunatics; embittered socially dysfunctional grudge-carriers who had spent so long in development that they had come to believe that they and their scripts were the only real things in the world and that everything else was irrelevant fantasy. The private cops had lost count of the number of writers who had come their way, armed to the teeth, having decided that the only way to get their projects through development was to shoot any reader, editor or producer who stood between them and a green light.

'A writer, huh?' the first guard sneered. 'Ain't no casual labour hired here, son. I believe they're hiring pump attendants at the gas station 'bout a mile back.'

The guards sniggered at the joke. It is a curious facet of the Hollywood obsession with success and pecking orders that literally everybody in the town, from studio head to studio cleaner, harbours the same snobberies and prejudices.

'I hear Hank Wank's new picture didn't open,' one tramp will remark to another. 'Overspent and overblown, the studio lost its shirt.'

'What a schmuck,' the other tramp will reply. 'Always had that guy picked for a loser.'

Nathan hastened to establish his legitimacy.

'Yes, all right, I'm a bloody writer, but I am a writer who has an appointment with Plastic Tolstoy.'

Nathan could not help but be pleased as the guards' manner changed yet again. A crazie was just a crazie and a writer was of course something which you scraped off your shoes, but Plastic Tolstoy was a man of stratospheric importance. If, as is said, power is the ultimate aphrodisiac, Plastic Tolstoy could have teased an erection out of a concrete monk. The man was an industry legend. Not only did he own a large percentage of the global media, but his company held the Claustrosphere account and had done since almost the very beginning. Claustrosphere was the world's biggest industry, and it was Plastic Tolstoy who had made it so. Through ruthless, attrition marketing, he had made hermetically sealed BioSphere environments the biggest single consumer durable of all time. Bigger than cars, bigger than hamburgers, bigger even than wars. Because every time Plastic Tolstoy made a sale, he sold a whole world – only a little one – but a world none the less. A world that some lucky group or individual could forever call their own.

Plastic Tolstoy marketed the future, which, of course made him the enemy of the present. He was PR man for history's most irresponsible idea. The idea that it was possible to survive the end of the world.

Chapter Four

The life of a salesman

Communication breakdown.

The stricken tanker story was on the news. Nathan had heard it on his car radio as he drove up towards Beverly Hills. Plastic Tolstoy saw it fifteen times all at once, standing before the vast fibre-optically fed information wall that he had had built in his kitchen.

First the news, then the adverts. Plastic sipped his coffee and watched.

The first ad was for snack-food: 'You know that feeling when you're hungry as a horse but you're also fat as a pig? Donut Heaven understands, which is why we're now offering free, on the spot liposuction to any customer who eats twenty Donuts or more, plus extra frostings! So if you're feeling hungry *and* fat, why not get down to Donut Heaven . . . You fill your face, we'll suck your butt.'

Plastic Tolstoy was watching one of the channels on his own Plastic Tolstoy Communications System. Despite this, his grim, angry expression suggested that the thing which he had hoped to see had not materialised. Long before the Donut advert was over, Plastic Tolstoy had patched a multi-call through to his media co-ordinators and programme controllers.

'What, in the name of my mother is happening, excuse

me!' he barked. 'An oil tanker has sunk and what do I see first up on the break? On one of my own damn networks, no less! Donut ads and liposuction! After an *oil tanker has sunk*! You're supposed to be ready for this kind of thing!'

What Tolstoy was upset about was the failure of a classic piece of cross-promotion. Tolstoy marketed Claustrosphere and he had a policy that, whenever there was an environmental disaster, the news would instantly trigger a buying programme within his own media mainframe. The theory behind this shameless abuse of influence was this: whenever planet death lurched a small step closer, the vast Tolstoy worldwide audience would be instantly hit with Claustrosphere adverts playing in heavy rotation. That was the theory; it appeared not to have worked.

'We're up next break, Plastic,' an anguished employee spluttered over the line. 'The Donut people had the space booked and threatened to sue if we shifted them. They think the end of the world will make people reach for comfort food.'

Plastic Tolstoy looked back at the screens. Sure enough, the current Claustrosphere campaign was now showing. A gorgeous sun rising over a geodesic dome and the simple slogan: 'Claustrosphere. Who are you to deny your kids a future?'

'You see, Chief! You see,' the anguished employee pleaded. 'Right there, second slot. Personally, I think that's a better placing. More impact.'

'Listen, man with no brain, shortly to become man with no job,' Plastic shouted, 'when there's a disaster we take first slot, OK! Not second, not third, ever. First. Donuts, for chrissakes! I'm selling people the future here!'

Tomorrow's man.

It wasn't a new idea, the Rat Run mentality with which the human race ushered in the third millennium and which Plastic Tolstoy marketed with such enthusiasm. It was not the first time people had taken a good square look at Armageddon and decided that they would prefer it to happen to somebody else. Ever since Noah built the Ark, the seductive notion that it is possible to opt out, to stand on the sidelines whilst global cataclysm passes you by, has exercised a strong pull. Prior to the First Great Green Scare of the 1980s, it had been nuclear war which seemed most likely to carry off the human race. Then, people had built fallout shelters, as they now built Claustrospheres. Although admittedly, not on quite the same scale.

It was Jurgen Thor, the man whom many people considered to be the last sane person on Earth, who had coined the phrase the 'Rat Run' to describe that hypothetical time when people would take refuge in their Claustrospheres. He had appeared on numerous TV chat-shows, condemning the very idea of Armageddon survival. Sitting on couches wedged between pop singers and popular authors flogging their books, he would thunder that Claustrosphere was a terrifyingly dangerous illusion, a kind of global death-wish madness. He, in his capacity as head of Natura, the World Environmental Party, had taken a civil action against Claustrosphere all the way to the US Supreme Court, attempting to question the very legality of marketing a product which, he claimed, encouraged planet death. It was then that Plastic Tolstoy and Jurgen Thor had first crossed swords. Jurgen Thor had called Plastic Tolstoy a salesman of doom. Plastic Tolstoy had told Jurgen Thor to lighten up.

'Hey, survival is a commodity,' Tolstoy had said. 'People should be allowed to buy it just like anything else.'

Claustrosphere won the case.

Plastic's mother.

Plastic Tolstoy was named Plastic by his mother, who thought that plastic was the most beautiful material on Earth.

'Wood will always be wood and stone will always be stone,' she would say. 'But plastic can be anything, anytime, anywhere.'

'It's cheap and it's common,' grumbled her husband.

'So am I,' Mrs Tolstoy would reply. 'So is rock'n'roll.' Then she would peer down at her son, asleep in his cot, and say again, as she always did, 'Plastic can be anything, anytime, anywhere, my darling. And so can you.'

Mrs Tolstoy was Professor of Popular Culture at the University of Disney World in Florida. It was there that she had developed the thesis for her best-selling book *The King is Not Dead*, which demonstrated conclusively that Elvis did not die. He could not have died, Mrs Tolstoy asserted, because he had in fact never existed. The meticulous detail with which she documented and then disproved every single sighting of the King between the years 1935 and 1977 (the period of his supposed 'life') obsessed the nation for nearly a whole morning.

Mrs Tolstoy used the revenue from her book to set up a school of modern art, dedicated to the principle that the Barbie Doll was greater sculpture than the Venus de Milo, and that a reproduction of a great painting was of more value than the original. As she explained, with an original all you got was a painting, whereas a reproduction could also be a tablecloth, an apron, indeed, anything one cared to print it on.

Don't judge a book by its contents.

Plastic was his mother's son, but his eye was better than hers. Whilst she worshipped populism via its products, he saw that the real beauty lay in that which surrounds the products, the marketing. It was a lesson he learnt early on, as he often explained to the numerous documentary film-makers who were endlessly doing documentary films about his life.

'I was at this kid's party, you know? With the clown and cakes and the abuse therapist and stuff. Anyway, we all got a present of a toy gun. Brand new, still in the box, right? Well, let me tell you, those boxes were big! And the picture on them? Wow! A marine blasting away with an M16! We were in heaven. So we open the boxes, right? And of course there's this tiny, shitty little toy inside and all the other kids think they've been ripped off. But not me, I didn't think so. All I could think of was how beautiful that box was! It looked so big and exciting, it had fooled us all. I lost the toy that same day, but I kept the box a long time.'

Plastic had realised the great truth. A truth he would later embody in his First Law of Attrition Marketing. That law said that almost everything anybody ever buys is crap: instant noodles, four-wheel drive-trucks with huge wheels, vaginal deodorants. Anyone can produce any amount of crap, Tolstoy would later explain, in his famous educational video entitled *Selling: My Soul*, the clever part is to get someone to buy it.

'Listen,' the video explained, 'the world is one big

marketplace full of people buying and selling useless, shitty stuff that nobody ever dreamt they wanted. So why do they buy it? Because, while the product may be ugly, the marketing is beautiful. You don't believe me? Turn it round, consider trying to sell a truly great product but with useless, shitty marketing. You couldn't do it, right? The message is the only thing that counts.'

At the age of twelve Plastic Tolstoy made his first million. He had been pondering the delight with which his friends searched for the little snap-together toys hidden in their cereal boxes.

'Toys in cereals, that's great,' the boy Plastic thought, 'but timid.'

So he wrote to the manufacturers, suggesting that they reverse the ratio and market boxes full of snap-together plastic toys with a free cornflake hidden amongst them. Kids went crazy for it.

Plastic always considered himself fortunate to have been young and impressionable when the great Cola wars of the 1990s erupted on screens and in shopping malls. He watched with childlike wonder as two nearly identical drinks made of carbonised water and flavoured with vegetable extracts indulged in a worldwide orgy of aggressive saturation marketing which became *in itself* a multi-billion dollar industry. The name was sold, the image was sold, the history was sold. Eventually, people actually began to forget about the drink because *the marketing had become the product*. Young Plastic watched in starstruck awe as Pepsi and Coke actually marketed their own marketing. It was beautiful.

The only thing that could be more beautiful, the boy Plastic thought, was if both companies were owned by the same people.

It would be well into the twenty-first century before the truth about that emerged.

Advertainment.

All kids love TV, but it irritated young Plastic intensely. Years later, in *Selling: My Soul*, he would recall his youthful anger.

'I kept wondering why there had to be commercial breaks. You know? Insulting little ghettos where the marketing got crammed in any old how? As if the adverts were some kind of embarrassing necessity, instead of the very thing that was paying everybody's damn wages! And I'm thinking, one day I'm going to change all that. But I knew even then that, to do it, I'd have to control not just the imagery but also the *means of communication*. I vowed then on my mother's memory, except, of course, at the time she wasn't dead, that one day I would own a network and on that network the insulting division between entertainment and adverts would be banished for ever. The shows, the ads, even the news would all be mutually complementary. Sure, everybody knows that now, but one time I was a pioneer! I conquered an American frontier, I'm the guy who invented Advertainment.'

Often when *Selling: My Soul* was being screened at marketing seminars, the eager young salesmen and women would burst into spontaneous applause at this point, such was the passion and conviction of Tolstoy's message.

'Let me remind you of something incredible,' the video Plastic would pontificate with evangelical zeal. 'There was a time when they made films just so that people might watch and enjoy them. You hear what I'm saying! Then gape in awe, why don't you? Let your jaws drop in disbelief. For decades, Hollywood created entertainment from which the only source of revenue was the price people paid to see it! You got millions of people sitting silently in cinemas, their attention completely focused and *not being sold anything*! A hundred million Americans went to the cinema every week, and what did they see? A stupid movie! A story, nothing else! No subliminals, no product identification, nothing! People actually went to all the trouble of telling a story simply in order to tell a story! It makes me sick to my stomach.'

Even the most committed students of marketing were sometimes a little surprised at the passion with which Tolstoy spoke of his contempt for the likes of *Gone With the Wind*, *The Grapes of Wrath* and *Casablanca*. To Plastic these were not classic works of art, they were sterile self-indulgences. Pointless, egotistical displays of imaginative power and technical skill, nothing more.

'It's like a tennis player without a sponsor,' he would say. 'Take the name plugs off the guy's shirt and what have you got? Some rich brat hitting a ball around with a bat, and that's *all* you've got. Which is nothing.'

Of course, even in Plastic's childhood, things were changing. He well remembered and spoke glowingly of seeing *Batman* as a tiny child, and noting with great satisfaction the extent to which the film was in fact a colossal advert for the spin-off paraphernalia which accompanied it. But the product still followed the story: the film came first and the marketing developed out of that. It was Plastic who finally put things in their proper order.

'The Second Law, boys and girls, is that the marketing is the product, and vice versa.'

Ben Elton

Selling the future.

Some people say that the hour produces the man.

'That's bullshit,' Plastic Tolstoy would answer. 'You have to make your own history in this world, ain't nobody going to make it for you.'

Perhaps the truth lies somewhere in the middle. Certainly Tolstoy was no scientist and he never designed a Claustrophere. On the other hand, by his late twenties be had built up a communications empire which put him in a position to pitch for what would become the biggest sales campaign in history. When it began to dawn on people that the Earth was dying, Plastic Tolstoy was perfectly placed to take up the portfolio.

The Second Great Green Scare was sparked off when it was revealed that the governments of the world were using BioSphere technology (i.e., the research into self-contained, self-supporting environments) to construct bolt-holes to be used in the event of the Earth becoming unable to support life. The powers that be had recognised that planet death was a possibility and they had begun to sink bunkers from which they might administer the world's death-throes. The argument was the same as had been used during the Cold War. The responsibilities of the civil authorities remain unaffected by global catastrophe. Though the public might be dead, their interests would not go unrepresented.

Concerned individuals the world over reacted in horror to this revelation. If those in power were actively anticipating and preparing for life after Eco-death, then the situation was clearly horribly serious. Even the most complacent began to realise that the Earth was in terrible danger, and a vast and furious groundswell of public opinion grew up. The immorality of those in power, preparing to survive Eco-death rather than prevent it, was clear to all. The fact that BioSpheres cost millions of dollars to construct, hence placing them beyond the reach of all but governments and the most stupidly rich, fuelled righteous indignation.

This was the chance the Environmentalists had been looking for: clear proof that those in control accepted the reality of the approaching catastrophe.

'When the rats prepare to leave, you can be sure the ship is sinking,' thundered a very young Jurgen Thor in his first appearance as leader of Natura. It was a speech which rang round the world.

'These despicable individuals are preparing their escape! Their rat runs!' the big Norwegian declaimed. 'Having first destroyed the Earth by their greed and irresponsibility, these human rodents seek to escape the dreadful consequences of their actions.'

Such was the horror this idea engendered, that people finally began to demand real action on the environment. Sustainable development became politically fashionable and for a time it seemed that, as if out of evil (the BioSphere alternative) had come forth good, the craven self-interest of the few had spurred the many to action.

Then the price of BioSphere technology began to drop. It always happens. Pocket calculators started off as luxury items; a decade later they were giving them away with petrol. One day, the first back-garden Claustrosphere went on the market and the Earth was in big trouble. At first the threat seemed small. The unit was still pretty pricey and its life support systems basic and uninviting. It required a quarter of an acre of good firm land under a sixty-metre geodesic dome. It could provide water and air and recycle human waste, but that was all. It didn't offer a night and day cycle and nothing could be grown. The food supply was just a hundred years of military 'C' rations. Hardly an appetising prospect.

It didn't take long though.

Techno-research that had been sold to the public as pertaining to some future trip to Mars was employed on Earth. A five-year secret development was undertaken in the Arizona desert. When the pioneers emerged from their exile with a tray of hot muffins freshly baked from BioDough, raised within the dome, the first true Claustrosphere was ready to market.

Plastic Tolstoy called it Eden One.

The initial ads were a teaser campaign. They featured Rodin's thinker pondering an apple, and the caption was a simple, bald statement: 'Think about it.'

Plastic loved an enigmatic little come-on.

'Think about the Earth, think about the apple, think about Eden, think about the future. It's all there in the one image. It's brilliant, though I say it who shouldn't.'

Next came an apple that was also a globe. 'The Earth is in danger!' screamed the caption, 'Recycle! Join Greenpeace! Buy a Claustrosphere!' That had been Plastic's strategy in the early days; to equate Claustrosphere with the concerned individual. One per cent of the cover price of an Eden One went directly to the Worldwide Fund for Nature.

All that had been nearly forty years ago. Now, both Claustrosphere and Plastic Tolstoy were huge on a scale which the multi-nationalists and media moguls of the twentieth century could only have imagined. Tolstoy had fulfilled his dream, and he owned the very news and entertainment services which delivered his messages.

At heart, though, he was still just a salesman. Which is why, big though he was, he was standing in his kitchen, watching a stricken oil tanker on the news and personally bawling out his staff for allowing some donut commercial to get between him and the proper exploitation of an environmental disaster.

Chapter Five

A spy unmasked

The man who talked too much.

Judy was being hoisted off the stricken tanker. Nathan was stuck with the private cops outside the Beverly Hills Fortified Village. Tolstoy was in his kitchen, giving his people hell, and Rosalie Connolly, a Mother Earth unit leader, or terrorist, as Tolstoy would have called her, was standing in a California desert.

An Irish girl of twenty-five, she carried great responsibilities on her young shoulders, for it was her job to save the world. Not on her own, of course. Mother Earth was a large organisation and, despite being a unit leader, Rosalie was by no means particularly senior. None the less, saving the world is a big job, even if you have help, and the romantic, slightly mystical girl who had joined Youth Natura at the age of ten had grown into a tough and cynical individual. Rather tougher and more cynical than she would have liked to have been had the world been different.

But the world, of course, is never different. Nothing ever is, and Rosalie had a nasty little job to do before she and her team could depart in the large personnel-carrying helicopter that stood waiting for them.

Shackleton, her tough ex-marine second in command,

was priming the charges on the detonators when Rosalie approached him.

He nodded at her, she nodded at him, there was a pause, then she put a gun to his temple.

'Mr Shackleton, I believe you are an FBI spook and I think I may have to kill you.'

Rosalie was right. The man was an agent, although in a very different mould to Judy Schwartz. This man's name was Cruise and he was tall and tough and rugged and handsome. He was also one of the bullies who had tormented Judy, having been in the same training team. Cruise and the guys had regularly given Judy and the other nerds surreptitious dead-legs during forensics classes and compared their dick sizes unfavourably with a .22 slug from a ladies' handgun.

Rosalie, of course, knew nothing of this, but had she done so, she would have liked Cruise even less, which was saying something because she did not like him at all. She had suspected him from the day he had joined them, ostensibly fresh from service against loggers in South America. The man had just talked too bloody green.

'Sometimes I think it's my own environmental impotence that makes me most angry,' Shackleton (or Cruise) would say as they sat around the fire at night, while everyone else was trying to talk about sport or sex.

'I mean, the logging is ten times worse than the press admit and the defoliants are so deep into the water table they're never going to come out . . .'

The man was a complete bore. Greener than green, whiter than white and holier than thou. It was like he'd found God, started therapy and given up smoking all on the same day; he just wouldn't shut up.

'God, Shackleton goes on, doesn't he?' other members

of the team would remark to one another. 'I don't think I can stand it much longer, let's turn him in to the Feds.'

But Rosalie was beginning to fear that Mr Dull *was* a Fed.

Most Mother Earth activists had been in environmental politics so long they never discussed it. What was the point of talking about planet death? It was too depressing and everybody felt the same way about it anyway, so why go on? There was nothing worse than a bunch of self-righteous zealots sitting round the bean casserole, all nodding in agreement and going, 'Yeah, doesn't it make you so angry? I mean it's just *unbelievable*! Don't you think?'

At one point, the problem of endless talking about the environment had actually begun to have a seriously destructive effect on the whole Environmental Movement. People were forever getting trapped into spending entire evenings agreeing with each other. It was beginning to affect recruitment. The syndrome became known as 'green discussion fatigue' and so many potential fighters had drifted away as a result of it that eventually it became an unwritten rule within the Environmental Movement that you did not discuss the environment. Therefore, when an ostensibly experienced activist turned up in her unit, stating the bloody obvious about Eco-Armageddon over and over again, Rosalie was immediately suspicious.

And then there was Shackleton's endless references to Mother Earth funding. Of course, everybody would love to know who was putting up the cash, but it had been a secret for thirty years and was certain to remain so. Rosalie herself had been an activist since leaving college. She was moderately well-advanced in the Movement, yet completely ignorant about the greater part of Mother Earth's financial affairs. The FBI and indeed every other law enforcement agency in the world were endlessly probing and investigating, trying to get to the heart of it. But they never would. It was the big secret and, had Shackleton been the experienced fighter he pretended to be, he would have known not to mention it.

The clincher came when Shackleton got on to the subject of Jurgen Thor. He professed to worship the man, quoting that old chestnut about him being called the last sane person on Earth. That did it for Rosalie. Nobody who had been around Mother Earth long thought Jurgen Thor was sane, and nobody worshipped him. The people who dodged the bullets did not have much time for a personality cult egomaniac who would try to screw a tree if it had a dress on. Jurgen Thor was immensely talented, hugely charismatic and absolutely crucial as a spokesperson to the wider world. At the sharp end, however, the general impression was that he was a bit of a big hairy git.

Rosalie began to investigate the history of the man who called himself Shackleton.

On the surface it all looked fine. An American named Shackleton had been assigned to join her active service unit after seeing action under cover in Argentina. But anyone could switch a body, Rosalie thought. She had the Mother Earth database modem her up a photo of the real Shackleton. That checked out too, but since, if you had the money, you could get a temporary cosmetic rebuild done in an afternoon, that was also non-conclusive. Eventually Rosalie took a scroll of the man's fingerprints from an organic carrot juice container that he was carrying around until he could find somewhere to recycle it.

The result was great news. Shackleton was a spook. Nobody would have to listen to him whine on about the environment ever again.

Rosalie continued to hold the gun to his head.

'What did you do with our man?' she inquired. 'The real Shackleton.'

'We've got him, that's all, he isn't hurt,' replied Cruise. 'How did you see through me?'

'You just didn't talk about the environment enough,' replied Rosalie, 'it just didn't seem like you cared at all.'

Cruise was mortified. He had studied so hard, he had felt he could spout green crap in his sleep. He had got the majority of his environmental bilge from that asshole nerd Judy Schwartz. Cruise made a mental note to kill Judy at the next reunion.

'Where's your tracer implant?' asked Rosalie. The spy glanced down at his arm. 'Do you want us to cut it out or do you want to do it yourself?'

'Hey, listen . . .' Cruise protested nervously. No matter how tough you are, you still don't relish having a hole cut in your arm.

'Oh, come on! You know all about today's hit,' snapped Rosalie impatiently. 'If we leave you wired up you'll send out an alarm. Your pals will come and get you, you'll tell them where we are and we'll be blown out of the sky. Now you know very well that we either have to shoot you or cut out your tracer, so which is it to be?'

Reluctantly the FBI man offered his forearm. Rosalie drew her Swiss Army Knife. There was a brief hiatus while she tried to find a blade. She searched through the scissors, the toothpick, the digital video camera, the miniaturised two-way communications system, the

BioShield umbrella, the thing for getting stones out of horses' hooves . . .

'Christmas present,' Rosalie said apologetically. 'Stupid, really. I never use any of these things.' Finally she found the knife, only the little one, but it would do. She advanced upon a rather scared Cruise.

'Now you might feel a bit of prick,' said Rosalie. And she was right, he did.

Chapter Six

When two stars collide

Fortune's child.

It was still the same morning. Nathan was negotiating with the thugs at the Beverly Hills Fortified Village. Plastic was in his kitchen, watching Judy and Jackson get winched off the stricken tanker on fifteen different screens. Rosalie was in a helicopter with the Mother Earth direct action team, heading for a spot of terrorism and, back in the desert, Cruise, who has little further to do with this story, was nursing a bleeding arm.

Max had problems too. Problems, that is, in addition to his usual one, which was that of being a screw-up. Admittedly, at present he was a rich and famous screw-up, a colossally popular screw-up. The screw-up, in fact, of the moment. But Hollywood is a place where the distance between being a celebrated screw-up and a despised, pitied casualty doing underwear ads is a short one. Something in the very back of Max's addled brain was telling him that the time was coming to pull himself together. At twenty-six he had been a very big star for over eight years. A celebrated 'brat', to be found drinking, partying and getting into fights all over town. What's more, he was the real thing, a genuinely naughty boy. Not one of the amorphous mass of pouting pretty things who got puke drunk once on their eighteenth birthday and spent the next five years telling *People* magazine how they kicked their booze hell. Max was adored not only for the wild, confused characters that he played on screen and inside Virtual Reality helmets, but also for the wild, confused character that he clearly was.

The Good Fairies that had attended Max's birth were many and generous. They gave him great charm, tremendous acting talent and a fine, powerful, if rather small, physique. They gave him wonderful looks, which included ice-blue eyes set against dark Mediterranean colouring. Also, and perhaps most importantly of all, they gave him James Dean eyebrows which slanted upwards in a sad, little-boy-lost manner whenever he frowned. All this did the Good Fairies give to the baby Max, who laughed and gurgled as befitted the carefree, devil-may-care, sunny personality which was also their bequest to him. The Bad Fairy, on the other hand, gave Max only one gift, but it nearly killed him. For the Bad Fairy decreed that at the age of seventeen, Max would, without any warning or preparation, become hugely famous as the super-cool teenager in a Levi's ad.

Some high school kids, faced with suddenly becoming the most celebrated and drooled-over adolescent on the planet, might have handled it with calm detachment and genteel reserve. Max was not such a kid.

'Max, last week you were shooting hoops with your pals in Burbank, now you're on the cover of every magazine in the store. Do you worry about what you will do when the adoration ends?' a motherly chat-show host had asked Max in one of his very first celebrity interviews.

'No way, little lady dude, babe,' young Max had replied.

'For I hereby vow to party myself to death before the dumper beckons me.'

The advert that shot Max to superstardom was a co-sponsorship deal between Levi and Claustrosphere. It was set in the future, on the day of the Rat Run. Eco-death had ostensibly arrived and everyone was fleeing in terror for their Claustrospheres. Max's character, the cool teen, refuses to join his fleeing, terrified family until his jeans come out of the tumble dryer. The memorable caption being: 'Without your Levis, eternity will seem like a very long time.'

Ever since that famous last shot, when Max had set a billion hearts fluttering as he rushed towards the Claustrosphere's closing door, pulling on his faded jeans whilst his mother screamed, Max had been front-page news. He still was, but behaviour which is cute in a lad of twenty is a bit pathetic in a man of thirty. Max was twenty-six and getting rather bored with himself. It would not be long, he reasoned in his occasional lucid moments, before he began to bore everyone else. Some-day soon, he kept promising himself, maybe not today, but someday soon, he would get himself together.

Morning head.

There were, however, more immediate things to con-sider. Where was he and what time was it?

It was, in fact, nearly time to meet Rosalie and for his life to change for ever, but of course he did not know this. What he did know was that he had a mouthful of carpet. By this he deduced that it must be morning. He always started a day like that. Of course, it wasn't always carpet; sometimes it was tarmac, or paving stone, garbage, quite often, occasionally even a pillow. Max slept face down and breathed through his mouth, so whatever he collapsed into the night before was what he would find his tongue stuck to when he woke up in the morning. He could generally tell where he was without opening his eyes.

Carpet, thought Max, not bad. Things were looking up already. Police cells did not have carpets, nor did streets. Max reasoned from this that he was neither under arrest nor in immediate danger of being so. The carpet was also clean, that was a surprise. Max could not remember the last time he had tasted a clean carpet but this seemed to be one. He could detect no booze nor vomit beyond that which traditionally adorned his person when he awoke in the morning. Where was he? They had carpets in brothels and low bars, but you tended to stick to those carpets and this one was definitely non-adhesive. Max wondered whether maybe he had made it home. It seemed unlikely, he had never made it home before. As a matter of fact, Max was only vaguely aware of where his home was. On the morning of his mother's latest marriage he had woken up in the surf on Malibu. He had had to buy a tourist map of where the stars lived, just so he could get home for half an hour on his bathroom stomach pump and grab a change of clothes. Max never went home unless he absolutely had to. Home was dull and Max was wild.

Max decided he did not care where he was. Whatever, wherever, it was OK by him. The carpet tasted good. This would be a good day. Max could not see how being crashed out in some place with a nice clean carpet could get him into trouble. It was not worth a spread in the tabloids, it was unlikely to land him in court and it would not give his mother an excuse to get back on the chat-show circuit claiming that she blamed herself.

Cautiously he opened his eyes and raised his head a little. It took a moment or two to focus, and maybe another half a moment for all the vague confidence he had been feeling about the clean carpet to evaporate before his bloodshot eyes. He had made an asshole of himself again. Stretched out on the carpet before him was a naked woman. A gorgeous naked woman. The sort of woman who looked great on the front of scandal magazines.

Even in repose her natural instinct to adopt the position of a centrefold had not deserted her. She lay on her back, slightly propped up against a few silk pillows, one arm thrust gently behind her neck, supporting her head, the other soft against her belly. A knee was slightly raised, exposing a firm, flawless thigh, whilst the other leg stretched long across the floor, culminating in a ballet dancer's point, the delicate toes so close to Max's head that it might easily have been the foot rather than the carpet which he had found in his mouth that morning.

What a magnificent creature she was! Mother Nature and plastic surgeon working together in perfect harmony! Her breasts stood out firm and separate against her taut body. Despite their generous size and obvious weight, they still pointed defiantly heavenwards, as if invisible threads tethered her nipples to the ceiling. The woman's crotch had been waxed by a fanatic. It was virtually bald. Smooth and shiny as a car bonnet, almost as if it had been laminated. There was one tiny fringe of pale soft hair hovering above the cleft. This was a vagina with a mohican.

Max felt depressed. How had he ever allowed his life to

arrive at a point where such a gorgeous woman could be a problem to him? Yet she was a problem. The problem being that Max was married. Very publicly and very recently married to a fellow movie star. Max was a man of certain principles. He valued his honour. Certainly he fought and he drank, that was fine, what he did not do was publicly humiliate his wife.

Irresponsible use of drugs.

Fidelity, or at least a decent pretence at such, was a major pose on the coast, it had been for years. The place was stuffed with mega-stars assuring journos that they had found true bliss in marriage and that their hell-raising days were over.

AIDS was still around. There was still no cure and no vaccine, no vaccine available to the public, that is. It had, in fact, been possible to immunise people against the disease for many years but the drug had been suppressed. The reason for this being that the vast chemical conglomerate that had isolated the vaccine had found to their dismay that it was extremely easy to copy and reproduce, a simple compound, made from the cheapest and most basic ingredients. Ingredients that a child could reconstruct from a junior chemistry kit and a bag of household groceries. The conglomerate concerned realised that, were they to market their new drug, its secret would instantly be wrested from it. That done, in defiance of copyright, the recipe would be published in every scabrous, alternative publication in the world. Faced with this wholly unacceptable prospect, the vast chemical conglomerate had taken the only course open to it. This was, after all, business. There was no point in them developing a drug from which it was impossible to profit. They had therefore decided to withhold the drug until such time as their chemists had been able to develop a sufficiently complex molecular disguise for it. They would secrete their simple little miracle drug deep within some intricate atomic structure that was fantastically difficult to break down, and near impossible to reproduce. This way their patent would be protected and a reasonable price could be charged.

Expensive bodywork.

Max looked at the slumbering woman. How the hell had this happened? How had he ended up crashed out on a carpet with a naked woman? He wasn't even the sleeparound type. What Max liked to do was get off his face, act like a rich asshole and fall over. Certainly he liked to flirt, but screwing around was stupid. Getting caught was stupider. Could he get away with this? Not easily, he thought, and certainly not cheaply. The woman stretched out before him had not spent the countless dollars she clearly had spent getting a body like that in order to hand it out gratis. That body was a career move.

It was too perfect, too calculated, not one centimetre of it had been left to chance. This was a body that would almost certainly be featuring in next year's Coscars (Cosmetic Surgery Awards). Max searched in vain for signs of human frailty. Just one dimple of cellulite on the extraordinary limb stretched out before him might have given him hope that here was a straight-shooter. A woman who would wake up and say, 'Wow! That was fun and so unlike me, now you go back to your life and I'll go back to mine.' But there were no dimples of cellulite, not the tiniest stretch mark, hair or crease to suggest that this was a real human being.

The leg pointing at Max seemed to be singling him out, accusing him. 'There's the jerk,' its stern posture seemed to say. 'There's the guy I'm going to be talking about on every chat show for the next ten years. The asshole who's going to make me a celebrity.'

Max never understood why he got married. His wife Krystal, herself a huge star, was no clearer about her own motives. It was almost as if they'd been forced into it to feed the Max and Krystal industry that had grown up around them. Like a king, Max lived in a world where everything he did was deemed to be important. If he got drunk it was important. If he hit a journalist it was important. His notorious decision to have a penis *reduction* ('I owe it to the women I sleep with') had made the cover of *Premiere* and the number one news item on MTV. This, despite the fact that MTV now had a core audience in its fifties, twice Max's age.

The problem was that, like most kings, Max began to believe that what he did was important. There are few Canutes in the entertainment industry, people with the strength of character to turn their face against the tide of popular obsession and say, 'I am not even one millionth as interesting a person as I'm cracked up to be'. Certainly, Max could not resist the endless seduction of self-importance. It was a short step from throwing up on request to getting married on request.

Since then, both Krystal and he had assured the world that they had been tamed by love and that their hell-raising days were over. But they weren't. Krystal had continued to paint the town at night and have her body reconstructed in the morning, while Max had kept right on drinking, punching people, getting punched and waking up face-down, not knowing where he was. Now it seemed he'd got sufficiently off his head to make a real idiot of himself. Max did not love Krystal but he had no desire to insult and embarrass her on the front page of the *National Enquirer*.

The woman stirred.

'Max, I want a divorce,' she said.

Max was surprised. He squinted his aching eyes to focus.

'Krystal?' he said.

'What?' she replied.

Max fell silent. He felt ashamed. It was all very well being a complete screw-up, but not recognising your own wife was just gross. Certainly she had had a number of faces since he married her, but a husband is supposed to keep track of these things.

'I want a divorce, Max. Last night at Simone's we got treated like yesterday's news. I felt like an old married lady. Well I'm not an old lady, I'm just twenty-four and I want a divorce.'

'OK,' said Max.

'Don't you have anything else to say?' Krystal asked.

'Well . . .' Max thought for a moment. This was his wife and yet he scarcely knew her. This beautiful woman was a stranger to him. The aimlessness of his existence swept over him. For a moment he saw himself clearly and he saw nothing, for there was nothing to see. His whole life was a pointless charade. Fortunately, for Max, introspection was a passing thing.

'Any chance of a final jump?' he said.

Krystal never could resist a bit of romance.

'Oh, go on then.'

Max crawled forward across the carpet and up along Krystal's astonishing body.

'I don't think my breath's too sweet,' he confessed. 'You didn't see anyone taking a leak in my mouth last night, did you?'

Krystal always had her disinfectant at hand. She sprayed Max's mouth and then her own, for she had dined on pepper vodka and garlic corn chips the previous evening. Stretching across to her handbag she produced an altogether more formidable looking aerosol.

'OK. Stand up and drop them,' she said. 'You may be my husband but I don't know where you've been.'

'I don't think I can stand up, Krystal. Going anything higher than carpet before I've had some coffee gives me vertigo.'

'Stand up and show, Max, or you can whistle for a wriggle,' said Krystal, who had very strict views when it came to sexual hygiene. Max knew that nothing blew a screw quicker than resisting the precautions, so he staggered to his feet and dropped his jeans. Krystal sprayed his crotch, coating his dick in spermicidal stretch laminate.

'The spray-on condom has to be the greatest invention since inflatable handguns,' said Krystal as she blew on it to help it dry.

'I like this bit,' said Max. 'I hope you have some solvent, though.'

Max spoke from painful experience. The spray-on condom was a triumph of synthetic fibre engineering. It could be applied to a flaccid member and would then stretch and move like a second skin. Obviously, with a conventional condom there is a teat on the end which

Ben Elton

provides somewhere for the ejaculation to go. With spray-on jobs the laminate simply stretched to accommodate whatever was necessary. It would stretch, but it would not break, ever. This was fine for the containment of a bit of sexual effluvia, but less convenient if you needed a wee and you had no solvent. Max, like most men, had experienced the pain and embarrassment of driving to the chemist with a big balloon of piss hanging off the end of his dong.

Krystal drew Max down on top of her. They embraced and she kissed him long and hard. In a town where good kissing was the norm, Krystal was a star. It was said that if you had had a cosmetic lift you should not kiss Krystal for at least six months, because she would suck your face right off. This rumour began when Krystal was just sixteen. She had been a child star and, having been through sex, drugs, college and fully diagnosed media dependency, she had married an ageing star, a man with the career of a seventy-year-old and the face of a thirty-five-year-old. At least, he had the face of a thirty-five-year-old until his wedding night with young Krystal. Loud screams were heard from their hotel suite in Aspen, Colorado. A paramedic Cosmetic Surgical Rapid Response unit was scrambled from Cedars Hospital LA, and the ageing star was not seen in public for four months.

'Ate the old boy's face right off,' the gossips assured each other.

'I heard they had to cut his teeth out of the back of her throat. That little girl nearly choked on her old man's dentures.'

Krystal was now giving Max the benefit of her plunger-like skills, but despite administering a kiss that could have

56

unblocked a drain, she could feel that the fire was not getting lit.

'I'm not stretching your laminate, am I, honey?' she inquired gently.

'It isn't you, Krystal, it's just early, you know? I had a gutful of booze last night and . . .'

'Hangover hanging over, is it?' she said. 'Let me show you something I had fitted last week.'

Krystal rose to her feet and glided across the room. It was a walk that had made a hundred million Virtual Reality helmets steam. Crossing to her dressing-table and perching herself gently against it, she looked down at the prostrate Max.

'Like what you see?' she inquired, and Max would have had to have been made out of granite to demur. What's more, it would have had to have been granite which was probably gay, anyway. Krystal was an extraordinary vision of market research generated design perfection. She looked as if a Japanese porn artist had just created her from computer graphics. Certainly it was a little soulless, but as her body sculptor often said, 'Krystal, there are tits men, and there are ass men, the only soul men I ever knew were musicians'.

'You think this is good, huh?' Krystal pouted. 'Watch.'

She took up a thin tube that was attached to a little cylinder in her vanity case. Max watched in astonishment as she removed what he had imagined was a tiny mole deep within her cleavage. She attached the tube to the spot where the mole had been, there was a hiss and Krystal's already generous bosom began to expand. Max gaped, he had never seen anything like it. Krystal laughed at his confusion.

'Neat, huh? It cost an awful lot,' she said. 'Great

for the career, though, so it should pay for itself. You see, now I can do big girl parts and little girl parts. Versatility is so important for a serious actress, don't you think? I've had the skin elasticated so it won't stretch either, and they go down after a couple of hours. You like?'

Well, as it happened, Max wasn't particularly into big ones, but it seemed churlish to say so when a woman had just gone to the trouble of inflating her body for his benefit. Besides, Max's libido was finally beginning to struggle through the fog of stale booze and old smokes that had so far kept it down and Krystal was a woman who would look good in any proportions. He definitely wanted to get horizontal with her. The problem was getting the message through downstairs.

Max had had trouble with hard-ons for years. It was that age-old problem, erection awareness. The minute he started thinking about them, boof! they were gone. It was not a physical thing, it was purely mental. As every man knows, the penis is a paranoid portion. If it knows you're worrying about it, it heads south. Fortunately there is a solution. It is a matter of getting one's mind off the subject. Max's method was to indulge in a discreet fantasy, in order to transport his libido away from the current pressurised circumstance. However, Krystal would not have felt put out had she been a party to Max's secret thoughts for it was not other women of whom he thought, but of himself. Not sexually, but professionally. Max was an actor and the most exciting thing in the world to him was just how *bloody good* he was. He thought of the triumphs, the tears, the quirky little workshop productions he still got involved in because, despite being a megastar, he was first and foremost an artist. He thought about how great he looked warming up in leg warmers and an old torn T-shirt . . . and there it was, a great big proud upstander, all present, correct and ready for action.

Krystal was pleased. As far as she was concerned, her inflatable tits had worked their magic.

'So you do like,' she purred, giving them a jiggle.

'Sure I like, Krystal,' Max said. 'Just so long as they don't go pop and you end up being blown all round the room like a balloon.'

Raunchy sex scene.

Max had already dropped his jeans and underpants in order to receive the laminate. Now he kicked off his moccasins, advanced across the room and stood before her, smouldering for a moment. Without taking his eyes off hers, he pulled off his T-shirt to reveal the taut, tanned torso beneath. He was naked, and looking great.

Apart from his socks.

Socks are terrible things. There is no way you can take them off in a sexually charged manner. Shoes, you can kick . . . T-shirts, you can pull . . . underwear you can drop . . . But socks, you have to hop around on one leg, tugging at. A few years previously, someone had attempted to market socks that dissolved under the heat of passion, but since the temperature of most people's feet drops by about forty degrees the moment they get into bed with anyone, the idea was a flop.

Having disposed of his socks as quickly as possible, Max gathered Krystal up in his arms and carried her to the bed. Max was a small man, but he was strong and wiry, and at just twenty-six the booze and smokes had yet to reduce his strength. They fell upon the bed together with the usual, slightly ungainly thud and tangle of arms and legs that traditionally accompanies this move. They both laughed a little, as if to acknowledge the moment, then they clinched into an embrace.

It is an irony which only movie stars can truly appreciate that sex is not like in the movies. Here were two international icons of popular entertainment, who had delivered more sensational sauce in their time than Mr Heinz and yet, when it came to actually having it off for real, they were as dodgy as anybody else.

'Your arm's on my hair,' Krystal said gently. 'It's pulling my hair.'

Max whispered an apology and shifted, making them both yelp loudly because their skin had got stuck together and it hurt when Max moved his arm. Returning to the business at hand, Max placed his mouth gently on Krystal's and began to tease her tongue with his. Moments later, like all couples, they had to stop for a moment to fish the hair out of their mouths.

In all the countless shows that Max had starred in, movies, Virtual Reality Reactive Scenarios, Direct Input home entertainments, all the times he had been called upon to plant huge lippy kisses on flaxen-haired beauties, never once had he fished a hair out of his mouth.

He and Krystal returned to their embrace. There was another yelp.

'Do you think perhaps you could take your watch off?' Krystal inquired. 'It's in danger of amputating one of my buttocks.'

Max's watch was a fully-equipped home entertainment centre with a library of ballgame mini-vids and a six-pack of Dehydrated Budweiser. He took it off.

'Thanks,' said Krystal.

'No, I should have remembered,' said Max, smiling his sweetest smile.

'Oh, my God,' Krystal said, 'what's happened to your mouth? . . . Oh no, hang on, it's just my lipstick.'

On-screen, of course, Krystal spent almost entire shows with her gums round some guy's plums and still had impeccable lipgloss when she came up for air. Off-screen, however, like any other woman she could smudge it eating a banana.

Slowly the romance returned and the two lovers began to work their bodies against each other until Krystal opened her thighs and allowed Max to slip between them.

'For old times' sake, huh?' she whispered.

Max could not actually recall any old times but he was happy to believe there had been some, and with one smooth, gentle motion, he entered her.

Except of course he didn't. That was what he did in the movies. In the movies, one lover can gently enter another without so much as a guiding hand; without even breaking the embrace, they just slide in. This is, of course, virtually impossible. For a penis to simply glide into a vagina, whilst the lovers involved continue a passionate embrace, would actually require a funnel. In real life, people have to probe a bit.

'Almost,' Krystal breathed. 'Down a bit, that's it, nearly, no, up a bit, yes, a bit more, nearly . . . No! Not there! Get out of there!'

Max jerked back like a startled rabbit.

'Sorry, sorry, sorry, sorry!' he gasped.

The misunderstanding over, Krystal guided Max to the correct orifice and they began, finally, to make love. And it was good. She gasped, he gasped, they both gasped. Then they squelched.

It was the old problem. When a man is on top of a woman and the sweat begins to flow, the woman's cleavage will often start to blow raspberries. It never happened in movies, of course. Max had pumped his body up and down on top of countless gorgeous actresses, Krystal had gasped and sweated beneath numerous bits of thespian beefcake. Yet never once had a single cleavage so much as squeaked. In the real world, however, it was a noise that had intruded on many an ecstatic moment. It's always a difficult decision, whether to refer to it or not. Krystal always did.

'Your chest is making my tits fart,' she said.

'Yeah, I know,' replied Max.

'I could let some air out of them, maybe.'

'No, that wouldn't work, it happens with little ones too. Try to forget it, OK?'

'Yeah, OK.'

So they returned again to the matter in hand. Soon their passion began to take control again. The gasping returned. He grunted, she squeaked. She squeaked, he grunted. She arched her back, he plunged his hands under her buttocks.

'Yes,' she said. 'Yes, yes, yes!'

'Oh!' he said. 'Mh! Ah! Oooh!'

Krystal's body was dissolving, making ready to orgasm. As she got warmer and wetter, Max thrust with ever greater passion. The inevitable happened. There was a squelch that made Krystal's cleavage sound positively polite.

'Damn! I hate it when my crotch makes that noise,' said Krystal. 'Sorry.'

'It's me, too, I'm creating the vacuum,' Max observed reasonably and nuzzled up to Krystal's ear. 'Try not to think about it. It's beautiful.'

'Beautiful! My crotch is blowing reveille and you're saying it's beautiful!'

'Well, it is.'

Krystal liked Max's attitude. She held him tighter, and gasping and squelching away, they rushed towards climax and astonishingly it looked as if they were going to reach the tape together. Nearly. Nearly. Gasp, squelch, squelch, gasp. Sadly, at the last moment, as Krystal began to come and Max drew back for a last glorious plunge . . . it came out and he banged it into her thigh, bending it double and making him screech in pain.

'Yes!' said Krystal.

'Ouch,' said Max.

And so the brief marriage ended, amicably, painfully and messily. Afterwards they had a cup of coffee and discussed the upcoming divorce.

'Who shall we sell the story to?' Krystal asked.

'Well, I'm having lunch with my agent at the studio. I'll have a talk with her about it, she'll get us a good price.'

So Max headed into Hollywood for lunch at the DigiMac Studio commissary. Which was, as it happens, where Rosalie and her team of Eco-terrorists were heading in their helicopter.

Meanwhile, far away in Europe, where the morning was early evening, the man often celebrated as the last sane person on Earth was addressing the European parliament on the subject of environmental destruction. To emphasise his arguments, live footage of the Alaskan oil tanker disaster was playing on screens hung about the Grand Chamber. The same disaster which Plastic

Ben Elton

Tolstoy was watching in his kitchen and above which Judy Schwartz was hanging on a winch, still puzzling over the surprising nature and extent of the ruptures in the tanker's sides.

Chapter Seven

A gunpowder plot

The house that Jacques built.

Jurgen Thor stood, massive and imposing, behind the marble podium inside the magnificent European Federation Parliament building in Brussels.

The place had only been open a week. It had been scheduled to open fifteen years ago but, having been designed by a committee of architects from all thirty-six Federal States, it had overrun somewhat. Also, and for the same reason, there were no toilets. No country was prepared to take responsibility for so mundane an area. No proud Euro Head of State was going to be the one who had to stand before that great, imposing repulsive marble palace and say, 'Our man did the bogs.'

There were no cloakrooms either, no kitchens, no committee rooms and no offices, just thirty-six Grand Chambers. Everybody had wanted to design the Grand Chamber and in the end everybody did. The Palace of Peace and Profit (for such was the Euro building's name) was almost three square kilometres of Grand Chamber. Thirty-six Grand Chambers contained within an edifice of such striking horror that children ran crying in fear to their mothers' arms after a single glance at it. If an infinite number of monkeys were given an infinite amount of graphic design equipment, never, in an infinite number of years, could they have designed such a stupid and repulsive building. But then that could have been said about most of the new buildings in the thrusting modern Europe.

The Palace stood in the centre of what had been beautiful Brussels, mile upon mile of marble and precious hardwoods almost entirely obscured from view by the ring of Portaloos that surrounded it. As it happened, the Portaloos were not really necessary because there were so many statues, fountains and frescos symbolising the Euro ideals of peace, liberty and buggering the rest of the world's trade, that it was a simple matter, even for female delegates, to find some large symbolic lump behind which to relieve themselves.

Jurgen points the finger.

The European Federation had invited Jurgen Thor to address the opening session of the Palace because it wanted to demonstrate to the world Europe's continued commitment to defending the environment. It was, after all, a lot cheaper to give a platform to a green politico than to legislate against polluters.

Jurgen was, as always, pulling no punches.

'When you buy a private Claustrosphere!' he thundered. 'When your taxes help build a municipal Claustrosphere! By that very action you accept as fact the dreadful possibility that we are about to destroy the Earth! In essence you yourself destroy the Earth! You commit planetary treason!'

The various delegates, lobbyists and Euro MPs listened in uncomfortable silence. They were uncomfortable, partly because the seats of the particular Grand Chamber in which they were sitting had been designed for purely aesthetic purposes. They *looked* all right. The architect (a Latvian) had attempted to create a prismatic effect, making all the seats out of perspex pyramids, and when the room was empty, light bounced from seat to seat, creating a dazzling effect. However, when the room was full of delegates (which was, after all, what it was there for) the effect was merely one of lots of people wincing because they had hard plastic points up their behinds. The Euro delegates were also uncomfortable, however, because of what Jurgen Thor was saying. It was horrid to be accused to planetary treason, particularly if secretly you felt the accusation to be a fair one. There was not a person in that huge chamber, with the probable exception of Jurgen Thor, who did not own a Claustrosphere. Everybody had of course agonised over buying one, but what could you do? Everybody knew that the Earth was half dead and that there was every possibility of it going the whole hog at any moment. A person would feel something of a fool standing outside some pal's Claustrosphere, explaining with their last gasp that the pal had hastened the situation which was about to kill them. It was, when everything was said and done, all very well having principles, but no principle was worth sacrificing your children for, was it?

'You tell me you have to protect your children!' Jurgen Thor beat his mighty fist down upon the lectern. 'Will your children thank you for bequeathing them a rat-hole in exchange for a paradise?'

Jurgen Thor was, as he had done a thousand times in the previous twenty years, demanding immediate legislation against Claustrospheres. He might as well have gone to Texas and demanded immediate legislation against a man's right to buy a machine-gun in a service station.

Jurgen was not stupid. He knew his argument was unwinnable; it was riddled with inherent contradictions. You could not, on the one hand, say, as Jurgen often did, that world eco-degradation was at the point of going critical, that we were all about to die horribly with bubbling flesh and phlegm-choked lungs, then on the other hand seek to deny people a small sealed, self-sustainable environment in which they might survive this unpleasant prospect. All the same, he kept plugging away. Endlessly pointing out that, by purchasing an alternative to Earth health, one gave up on tackling pollution.

'Not so,' the Euro delegates said. 'If you buy a burglar alarm, does it mean you've given up on crime?'

'Yes,' cried Jurgen Thor, 'yes, yes, yes! You stupid Euro delegates! Crime is a very pleasant and perfect metaphor! The world is staggering towards violence and anarchy and what do we do? We lock our doors! Employ guards! Buy guns and hide! We *have* given up on crime, and we've given up on the environment also! What is air, yes, if you can't breathe it, huh? What is food, I don't think, if you can't eat it?'

Jurgen was a Viking. His first language was Norwegian and when much moved his English lapsed into the Euro-American MTV-speak of his youth, that strange language which seems to be a constant series of questions.

'I'm going to save the world, yes?' he had said in one of his first interviews, decades previously, before Natura, the world political party of which he was principal spokesperson, had even been formed. 'I am the champion for all living things, OK? You dig it?' he had said and, hopeless though his battle sometimes seemed, the world could not have had a more convincing champion.

Green God.

Jurgen Thor was almost too good to be true. From his great mane of shaggy golden hair to his enormous sixteen-hole, tan leather Timberland workboots he was more god than man. His gimlet-sharp clear grey eyes could puncture a politician across a hundred-metre conference room. They were more than just piercing, they were armour-piercing, and a thousand women had felt the prick.

Jurgen was huge. It was as if when the Almighty was making him He (or She) had always intended to make two, perhaps even three, environmental activists, but had decided to save time by making one big one. Muscles coiled like serpents about his colossal frame. His chest was a giant's chest, the nipples were in different time zones: this was a chest that exerted its own gravitational pull.

Legends of Jurgen's strength and physical powers rang around the world. Stories abounded of his days with the Mother Earth direct action group, before he had renounced terrorism. It was said that he had once plugged a shallow water toxic outfall with his own body, withstanding the immense pressure for many desperate hours whilst a team of activists had made good the sabotage with steel and cement. People whispered in awe about how the great man had once personally dragged a stranded pilot whale from a polluted beach and swum it out to sea. His body was pockmarked with scars from numerous bullet wounds he had received during attacks on Claustrosphere factories in the early years. It was said that, on the occasional times when his vast consumption of chilled peach schnapps got the better of him, Jurgen's party trick was to crack walnuts with his foreskin.

Concerned constituents.

'Mr Thor, what can you tell us about the activities of the terrorist group Mother Earth?' Colin Carper, the MEP for Essex, England and a paid Claustrosphere lobbyist inquired.

'As I have said many times, although I support their intentions, I do not support their methods,' Jurgen answered.

'But surely you were yourself once a terrorist, Mr Thor?'

'I do not accept the term terrorist, sir. Yes, I have committed acts against local laws, you know? In pursuit of a wider justice, yes? However, in my capacity as principal spokesperson for Natura, I, of course, acknowledge that it is not acceptable to take the law into one's own hands.'

'Oh, come now, Mr Thor. Enough of this pious bunkum,' Carper sneered.

'Bunk up? What is this bunk up, please?' Jurgen replied.

'Bunkum, Mr Thor! Bunkum! It is common knowledge that you are still a Mother Earth activist and that Mother Earth itself is nothing less than the armed wing of Natura.'

'Sir! If the European parliament is to be reduced to a forum for the perpetration of gossip, suspicion and innuendo, OK? Then let me say that you, matey boy, are internationally recognised as a place man and paid lackey of the Claustrophere conglomerate . . .'

The odious Carper reddened visibly at this outrageous slur.

'If I seek to make the case for Claustrosphere, Mr Thor, that is because ninety per cent of my constituents own them, and the others are protected by municipal arrangements! –'

'The majority of your constituents also have vermin and rat infestations. Do you see it as your duty to end-lessly represent those interests too?'

People occasionally noted, with some surprise, that Jurgen Thor's English could be as articulate and perfectly formed as the King's, when he wanted. Those in the know knew that he put the Norwegian inflections and stumbling, half-Americanised word formations into his speech for effect. He felt that it gave him a vulnerable air, which was useful in debate and also made women want to sleep with him. This latter was a goal that Jurgen Thor was rumoured to treasure even more highly than an eco-friendly world.

'Mr Thor, who is funding Mother Earth?' Carper demanded.

'What has this question to do with me, Mr Carper?'

'Oh, for God's sake, Mr Thor, your attitude insults this house! The Mother Earth direct action group has colossal resources. Its activities become ever grander and more daring. It has an air arm, a small navy; it has been able to operate effectively in space, destroying countless commercial launches. Anti-satellite ballistics cost billions of dollars, Mr Thor. Who the hell is providing that sort of cash! I say that it is you, Mr Thor! I contend that it is the saintly Natura party which funds this murderous terrorism!'

'Natura, Mr Carper?' Jurgen laughed. 'We are a political party, not Fort Knox Incorporated, OK, yes, you foolish dude. We exist by private donations and membership fees. We have less money worldwide than either of the two main parties hold in the US alone . . .'

Colin Carper's exasperation was getting the better of him.

'Claustrosphere factories have been attacked countless times, Mr Thor! Causing billions of dollars in lost revenue! My constituents have a right to know who is funding these outrages . . .'

It is a particularly gruesome characteristic of parliamentarians worldwide that, in order to legitimise their own prejudices and self-interest, they place them in the mouth of some shadowy collective constituent. Thus they lobby the cause of those who pay them in the guise of voicing the fears of those who vote for them. Jurgen was in fact about to point this out, but at that moment an enormous bomb went off.

European disunity.

The marble cracked and the chandeliers shattered. The blast was truly terrible. Repulsive sculptures and meaningless murals were found hundreds of metres away. Metal shapes representing the Euro ideals of peace, diversity and a strong currency were still landing in the suburbs of Brussels minutes after the initial explosion. A vast silk collage entitled 'Vive La Différence', which had been commissioned to represent the twin Euro goals of cultural diversity and keeping out penniless refugees from the

East, could be seen flapping in the wind, skewered on the spire of the secular chapel. Great blobby sculptures, which looked like huge, fat, multi-cheeked bottoms, but were in fact symbolic of the smaller European states, were sent rolling across the Euro Piazza and off down the busy shopping streets of the capital. All was chaos and confusion, a nightmare of smashed modern art mixed up with dead and dying delegates.

There were dismembered corpses everywhere. It was a harsh irony that only in death could those earnest European representatives find the unity of body and soul that had eluded them in life. The arms of staunch Flemish fundamentalists were to be found embracing the torsos of die-hard Norman separatists. The brains of Sicilian secessionists could be seen spread across the faces of Ulster unionists. Bits of socialists from Schleswig embedded themselves in bits of their sworn enemy, the socialists of Holstein. Christians were plastered over Muslims. Communists blended with Fascists. Jews, or at least parts of them, mingled freely and unchallenged throughout the chamber. For one shining moment, all creeds and nationalities – both real and dreamt of – became one nation. Croats, Serbs, Basques, Cornish separatists, Slovak nationalists, all puréed together in one grand multi-limbed, multi-brained, amorphous delegate. In the short period after the dust settled and before the finger pointing began, Europe was, in a strange way, and for the first time, unified.

When the finger pointing did begin, the directions in which it pointed were as many and varied as the special interest groups that were doing the pointing. Everyone was convinced that the dreadful carnage had been caused by the secret agents of those whom they most despised. But as it happened, the bomb was not in fact planted by a secret agent at all. It was planted by an advertising agent. The bomb was a marketing ploy.

Chapter Eight

Dangerous investigations, a broken heart and a terrorist attack

Getting your head round the news.

Plastic could almost feel the great black glutinous movement of the sea as it beat against the ruined shore. He had forsaken conventional screen-fed communication for Virtual Reality television. From inside the helmet he was able to accompany the news teams as the full horrors were revealed. It was not a type of broadcasting that appealed to everybody. The three-dimensional images which surrounded the viewer tended to induce a certain degree of motion sickness. However, it suited Plastic's purposes. He wanted to get a feel of the disaster.

The rupture was complete; the oil was out. The booms were already being breached, the detergents washed about pathetically on top of the impenetrable slick. There could not have been a worse mess if it had been created by a giant two-year-old with bad hand and eye co-ordination, instead of responsible adults. Adults with awesome technical skills and a wealth of bitter experience to guide them.

They just don't learn, do they? thought Plastic, as he

watched the last two people being winched off the fast disintegrating tanker.

On the horizon he could see the Natura ship approaching at speed.

'Wow, those Natura protest people got on the case fast,' the news reporter said, and inside the VR helmet it seemed as if he was addressing Plastic personally.

'They sure did,' Plastic murmured in reply, ruefully comparing their performance with that of his own sales team, who had let a donut ad get between them and their target.

Further investigation.

Judy Schwartz was also marvelling at the rapid appearance of a Natura protest vehicle.

'How the hell did those guys get here so quick?' he remarked to Jackson as they swung together on the line hanging from the coastguard helicopter.

'They've been trailing us for days,' Jackson replied.

'Interesting, isn't it?'

'What?' snapped Jackson. She was getting a bit tired of Judy being interested in everything.

'That they've been trailing you. There are literally thousands of supertankers at sea at the moment, and Natura just happen to be hanging around the one that goes down.'

'Tankers sink all the time,' Jackson replied. 'There's so much oil in the Atlantic, you could use it to make french fries.'

At that point, further conversation was cut short because they had to clamber into the helicopter and be disconnected from the wire that had winched them up.

'Well, Agent Schwartz,' the pilot said sarcastically, 'if you've seen everything you wanted to see, perhaps we might go home now.'

Judy did not answer. He was watching the Natura ship through the open door of the helicopter. He turned back to Jackson.

'How well did you know your crew?' he asked.

'Not well. It was a short trip. Why?' Jackson replied.

'So they were all new to you?'

'Not all, there were some faces from previous trips. What are you getting at? You think one of us deliberately ran the ship aground?'

Judy looked around the interior of the helicopter, and wished Jackson would keep her voice down. There were some very tough types lining the walls of the craft, and he didn't want them to think he was accusing them of being saboteurs.

'Give me a break, will you?' he said. 'I have to write something down in my report, don't I? Who recruits the crew?'

'The oil company, of course.'

'Not the captain?'

'Well, obviously not. He doesn't pay the wages, does he? If the captain isn't happy with a sailor then he can ask the company to change him. That's all.'

'And the captain was happy? I mean, apart from killing himself, obviously.'

'It was a good ship and a good crew, OK?' Jackson was getting angry.

'Until you ran aground.'

'OK, mister, that's it. I don't know what you're getting at and I don't care. Maybe you think we sank our own ship, I don't know, but I'm fed up with your questions and if you know what's good for you, you'll shut up. Because you're looking at one lady who's getting ready to throw you out of this helicopter and there's twenty-five witnesses here who'll swear an oath you tripped.'

Dressed to kill.

Meanwhile, Nathan was still negotiating with the private cops at the gates of the Beverly Hills Fortified Village.

'So you're meeting with Plastic Tolstoy, huh?' they said, not really wanting to believe it. 'OK, writer, let's just check this one out.'

They strutted back to their little hut, positively sparkling in their gleaming black BioTech flak suits. Their shiny boots crunched on the ground in a tough aggressive manner. Not for the first time, Nathan reflected on the dubious value of allowing policemen to dress up like Nazis.

They wouldn't look so tough if they took off all their guns and stuff, he thought. Which was true but, since they were not likely to, rather irrelevant.

Cops had not always looked like this. Once upon a time, when policemen were first invented, they had looked rather stupid in a cosy sort of way. In Britain they wore top hats and frock coats and often sported enormous side whiskers, in which it was possible for small criminals to hide. On the continent of Europe their brother officers strutted about the place in shiny breastplates, big hats and any amount of plumes and feathers. Streets had to be widened in the Paris of Napoleon III, simply to make room for the epaulettes.

It was a wonderful system whereby those in authority

were brought face to face with their own human frailty by being made to look very silly. It's rather difficult to act like an arrogant bully when you're dressed like a complete twerp. Sadly, things changed. First, a leather jacket appeared. Next, a peaked cap, then a pair of shades. Slowly but surely, over the years it became commonplace to see those in whom the community were expected to place their trust decked out like a cross between a Hell's Angel and Heinrich Himmler.

Nathan resented it deeply. Before leaving Britain he had actually recorded a Whinge about it for the Boring Channel. *Whinge* was an open access programme, where members of the public (preferably university lecturers) were invited to whinge for fifteen minutes on a subject of their choice. Nathan had chosen to pontificate on police uniforms.

'Those entrusted with power and authority should not be encouraged to strut around the place getting a great big stiffy about it,' he had argued earnestly. 'I mean why do people become police officers?' he asked. 'There are basically only two reasons. It is either because they want to serve the community or because they like being paid to look tough and push people around. The latter should not be encouraged with fascistic paraphernalia.'

Nathan demanded that police uniforms should be changed. That all officers, male or female, should be required to carry out their duties in stripy lycra tights, pink dresses and enormous leprechaun hats with shiny silver buckles on them. According to Nathan, the effect would be immediate. Cops would feel too self-conscious to intimidate people, crooks would not be able to bring themselves to shoot such jolly looking officers, victims of crimes would suddenly feel relaxed about approaching the police, witnesses would come forward. The whole community would rise up in support of such brave men and women, who were prepared to uphold the law no matter how stupid they looked.

Nathan extended his idea to include the military.

'While I accept the need for some form of collective security,' he said, 'I object strongly to the constant glamorisation of something which is, when all's said and done, an unpleasant necessity. I mean, calling ships things like HMS *Indomitable* is just silly.'

Nathan argued that there was something dangerously seductive about giving weapons tough macho names. Nothing made a politician happier than being able to announce, 'HMS *Indomitable* was deployed today in the Gulf, carrying officers and men of the Second Armoured Division'. Would it not be better to rename these things? A politician pandering to jingoistic public opinion would find it much less tempting to deploy 'HMS *Dubious Use of the World's Resources*, carrying officers and men of the Very Small Penis Division'.

The programme format of *Whinge* allowed for a right of reply by anyone taking issue with the speaker. Strangely, nobody from the police or armed forces took up the offer. The entertainments industry, however, sent along a spokesperson to object in the strongest possible terms to these pernicious efforts to undermine their livelihood. Geared, as it is, to providing entertainment exclusively for mentally challenged teenage boys, film and television programme makers found the idea of policemen dressed as clowns and battleships called the *USS Stupid* entirely unacceptable. There was simply nothing exciting about a Terminator in a dress.

Fool in Paradise.

The guards checked their list. The clipboard and ballpoint pen seemed curiously anachronistic in the hands of these distinctly high-tech bobbies. The reason for such archaic communications technology was, of course, that, unlike with computers, it was very difficult to hack into a Biro. If you want to change a name that's been written on a piece of paper in ink, you have to scribble it out and write another one over the top. A subterfuge that even the stupidest goon could recognise.

Finding that his name was indeed on their list, the guards waved Nathan through the huge electric gates. As he let his window down and let in the clean, filtered air of the Fortified Village, Nathan's mood lightened.

Beverly Hills! he thought. He was driving through Beverly Hills on his way to play tennis and make a pitch to the most powerful communications mogul in the world. It didn't get any bigger than this. He was inside the oyster, inside the *pearl*. What would Flossie make of it?

Damn! He'd done it. He'd let his mind wander and of course it had wandered straight back to Flossie, as it always did. Nathan had to be constantly vigilant because the moment he let his guard drop, the little devils that lived inside him would put that big heavy piece of lead in his stomach again.

'Screwed it up, didn't you?' the little devils would whisper in his ear. 'You had a beautiful, perfect girl and you screwed it up ... and why did you screw it up?' they asked, although they already knew the answer. 'Because you're a complete git, that's why. What are you?'

'I'm a complete git,' Nathan whispered to himself. Then louder, 'I'm a complete git. A complete and utter git!' His voice rose to a shout and he banged his head on the steering-wheel as he drove.

Suddenly his car was surrounded by Beverly Hills private cops. They leapt in droves from out of the lush plastic vegetation that enclosed the quiet road. Shouting at yourself, and banging your head on a steering-wheel was crazy behaviour in anybody's books. The Beverly Hills Private Cops were certain that they'd caught themselves a live one.

Some say love is blind but in fact it doesn't see half that well.

'Why were you shouting to yourself and banging your head against the steering-wheel?' the first leather-clad gunman demanded of Nathan.

Nathan faced a positive sea of ballistics. One wrong move and he'd be vaporised. He decided honesty was the best policy.

'Because I spent two years trying to leave my wife, under the impression that I didn't love her and also because I wanted to screw other women. Then one day *she left me* and I realised that I did love her madly, and ever since then my life has been a pointless joke.'

The cops considered this for a moment. Weighing their response. Eventually their leader spoke.

'You have to fly to her,' said the tough, hard-bitten cop. 'You have to fly to your beautiful lady and smother her with wild, burning kisses. You have to put a cartload of flowers on her bed and say, "Hey, sexy pants, I made you a meadow, get in it so I can bang you till your ears rattle". That's what you have to do. Otherwise, you ain't even a man.'

Nathan thanked the officer for his advice, adding that this course of action had not occurred to him before, but now that it had been pointed out, it was certainly what he would do. Secretly, however, he suspected that these were not tactics which would work on his beautiful Flossie.

His beautiful Flossie! Ha! Nathan had not called her that twelve short months before. No, then Flossie's charms had been lost to him. They had been together for eight years, and for the final two Nathan had wanted out. He had wanted to sleep with other women. He had wanted to sleep with just about every woman he passed in the street. What's more, he had wanted to sleep with women who put the top back on the toothpaste after they had used it. He had wanted to sleep with a woman who always left her keys and money in the same place, and hence was able to find them again when they were next needed. Flossie never knew where her keys were and Nathan had hated it. Most of all, he had hated it when she stole his and lost those too. Nathan always *always* put his own keys back in the same place, so he always knew where they were. Unfortunately, so did Flossie, and it was a source of constant irritation. She never put the milk or the butter back in the fridge after using them either.

Nathan often reflected that the God of Love was at best a fickle, indecisive type and at worst a total raving schizo and bastard. When Nathan had first known Flossie he had been obsessed with her sexuality. Later he grew indifferent to her charms and now here he was again, desperate to take her to bed. How could such conflicting passions exist within the same person? Every aspect of his attitude to Flossie had swung like a pendulum. It was absurd that a woman's personal habits could appear cute one day, utterly irritating the next and back to cute again the day after. Nathan, who only a year before had thought Flossie's lifestyle bordered on the disgusting, now longed to see her knickers flung anyhow on the bathroom floor and to discover his special bedroom nail clippers in the larder. Flossie never finished a cup of coffee; she always left it half-full to be knocked over at a later date. There was a time when this habit had wrenched Nathan's guts with frustration. Now he looked back upon it as the most endearing of characteristics.

Yes, the God of Love was fickle, and he had turned Nathan upside-down. A year ago Nathan had almost hated Flossie. He was sick of her and their relationship. He had moped through his life, cold and distant, wondering how he could get away from this woman whom he no longer loved.

'Do you love me?' Flossie would ask.

'Of course I love you,' Nathan would reply.

'It doesn't seem like you love me,' Flossie would insist and, although Nathan denied it, he knew she was right. A combination of sexual frustration and domestic irritation had convinced him that he wanted out.

Every day he had tried to think of a way to leave. He didn't want to hurt her and he didn't want to have a row about who owned the house, but he had to get out. The months went by, while he continued to assure her that he loved her . . . and continued to try to figure out a way of escape. He was a coward and he could not face the unpleasantness, but he knew that he would do it soon.

Then, one day, Flossie had announced that she was

leaving him for another man and from that second onwards he had loved no one but her.

Terror hit.

As Max drove into the DigiMac Studios for lunch with his agent, having left his beautiful, nearly ex-wife Krystal (who will play no further part in this story) slumbering on their satin bed, he too was reflecting on affairs of the heart. Although he did not feel quite as desperate as Nathan, he could certainly take no satisfaction from his position.

Being asked for a divorce by a wife whom he did not even recognise had really brought it home to Max just how aimless his life had become. It was all very well being a great big star, but if you were also a sad drunk whose idea of a long relationship was making it to the second screw, then surely something was wrong. There was a hollow feeling inside him which he could not place. Was he hungry? Starting a cold, perhaps? No, it did not feel like either of those things. It was sort of empty and melancholic. Max arrived at the studio gates and drove through on to the main boulevard. There he saw two young lovers strolling arm in arm inside the sidewalk BioTube. The scene touched a nerve. That was it! He had it now. Max recognised the hollow sensation. He was feeling lonely.

Inside the commissary, Max's agent, Geraldine Koch, was waiting to have lunch. She had great news; news that instantly returned Max to his customary good humour.

'You have a meeting with Plastic Tolstoy at three forty-five today.'

Max's eyes widened with excitement and Geraldine could not restrain a grin of triumph from spreading across her face. A face which was usually so sour, people's jaw muscles prickled just looking at it.

'He wants to put you together with a British writer called Nathan Hoddy. I believe he has a feature in mind.'

'You mean a full-length commercial?' Max asked, trying not to get over-excited.

'No, I mean a feature, Max. He's planning a huge advertainment around the theme of the battles between Claustrosphere and the Green Movement. I've convinced his people that you're mature enough now for major adult leads.'

This was just the kind of break Max needed. He and Geraldine had been discussing for months how he was going to make the difficult transition from idol to icon. There were some stars who were merely of the moment and some, a few, who became stars for life. Despite his huge celebrity, in many ways Max was still the Levi's guy. That all-important leap from being a fashion to being an institution had so far eluded him and the sands were running out. Working for Tolstoy would change all that. It would confirm Max as a proper, grown-up mega-star and place him on an exalted level from which he could never be knocked.

As Geraldine was giving Max the details of the meeting, Rosalie and the terrorists arrived. Not at the table; they landed on the translucent BioDome roof of the commissary with a loud thudding. Everybody looked up at the shadowy figures moving about on the dark blue tinted filter-shield. Most people, including Geraldine, were rather scared, but Max loved any kind of excitement and found the scene exhilarating.

'Look at those guys,' he said. 'They certainly know their stuff.'

'The security people should shoot them,' Geraldine replied.

Max watched, fascinated, as above him the five masked figures in green fatigues mined the BioShield with well-rehearsed efficiency. They laid the charges at five-metre intervals across the great domed canopy whilst their helicopter clattered above them.

'What are they doing!' asked Geraldine.

'I think they're going to blow a lot of holes in the roof.'

And before Geraldine could respond to Max's calm observation, there was a series of bangs as Rosalie detonated the charges and fragments of BioShield rained down on the screaming diners below.

'What are they doing!'

'I guess we'll find out in a minute,' said Max excitedly.

And of course they did. Rosalie attached a grappling iron to the largest hole in the roof, and then she and the rest of the team climbed back into the helicopter.

'I think they're going to try and pull the roof off,' observed Max. They could see the shadowy blue shape of the terrorist craft pulling slowly away from the canopy. Thirty feet above the roof, however, the helicopter stopped, hovering in mid-air, tethered firmly by the grappling rope stretched taut below. The mighty engines roared and tugged, but the roof was tougher than the terrorists had allowed for in their otherwise flawless planning.

Downstairs Geraldine laughed. They all laughed. They could see that what was clearly a plot to expose their pristine epidermises to killer Ultra Violet sunshine had gone wrong.

'Roof's too strong, huh?' they shouted upwards. 'Fuck you, green assholes.'

Up in the Mother Earth craft there was consternation.

'We'll have to cut her free,' the pilot shouted above the scream of the labouring engines. 'I give the cops another two minutes.'

But Rosalie was having no such defeatest nonsense. This was the DigiMac Studio, a world famous location in the middle of the most public town on the planet. Mother Earth could not be exposed as incompetent fools in such a dazzlingly high-profile arena. Grabbing her bag of detonators, Rosalie launched herself down the straining grappling rope and back on to the commissary roof. Quickly she laid a second line of charges close to the gaping holes. Down below, people did not know whether to scatter or stay put; most opted for cowering under their tables. Only Max remained calmly seated, although his heart was pumping. He was trying to make out the face of the woman crouching high above him.

Rosalie finished laying the new charges and ran back over the blue-grey dome to the straining rope which attached the roof to the helicopter. Grabbing it, she activated the detonator. Her idea was that as the terrorist chopper rose into the air, taking with it that detested symbol of eco-complacency, the BioShield, she would be hanging on to the tow rope. She would then be whisked away to the comparative safety of a life of international terrorism. Unfortunately, the roof came away with such a jerk and the helicopter lurched upwards with such violence, that Rosalie lost her grip on the rope and she was thrown through the great jagged hole in the BioShield, of which she was the principal creator. She fell fifty feet into the dining-room below, landing with great good fortune in Rupert's cake.

Chapter Nine

The dream factory and the dead sea

Rupert's cake.

Fortunately for Rosalie, even in such elevated surroundings as the commissary of DigiMac Pictures, the
dreaded birthday interruption could occur. As hazards of
dining out go, the birthday interruption is not the worst.
It is not as bad as being poisoned by the seafood or getting
a table next to fifteen blokes on a stag night, but it's
still a pain. One is in the middle of one's meal, in the
middle of a conversation, maybe even in the middle of
suggesting that coffee be skipped in favour of screwing
all night like crazed rabbits. What is more, rabbits who
have grown tired of life and lettuce and decided to
fuck each other to death instead. Then suddenly the
lights dim, 'Happy Birthday' (or one of the groovier
pop options) is cranked up on the sound system and
a mound of whipped cream and sparklers is brought in
and plonked in front of whoever's birthday it is. This is
always a pretty gruesome affair. The self-conscious smiles
of the recipient and pals; the scarcely veiled hostility of
the other diners; the show-off waiter letting it all go on a
bit too long. The occasion at the DigiMac commissary was
rendered even more horrid by the fact that the birthday
person was a child star. Hence everybody had to profess

themselves absolutely delighted that this youngster, who had everything, had got just a little bit more.

Rupert, who was only eleven, accepted the ten-foot-tall cake with the practised grace of a true professional. He was a wonderful actor, one of the studio's hottest properties, and he had been a huge hit in the *Child Star* Virtual Reality games. In these incredibly popular entertainments, the player is faced with a fictitious juvenile Hollywood super-celebrity, played by Rupert. The player is then allowed to punch, throttle and, if he can, run over the Child Star with a truck.

The game was already in its twelfth mutation: *Child Star 12: The Première*. In this version, the player inside the VR helmet encounters the Child Star at the opening of *Smirk*, the Star's latest kiddy picture. The Star does an interview, in which he goes on about how his mom only gives him ordinary pocket money like the other kids and how neat it is to get to meet all those big stars, etc. At the point at which the Child Star says, 'I'm just a regular kid. I guess I like to do what all kids do,' the player has fifteen seconds to throttle him before the minders arrive. The player must kill the Child Star immediately, because with each throttling the Child Star survives, the more obnoxious the interview gets: 'I'm just a regular kid, I eat pizza, go to movies and hang out with the guys in the mall. Girls are cool but I don't have a regular date.' Eventually, if the player has failed, the Child Star, still grinning his endearing grin, gets awarded a special juvenile Oscar by Mickey Mouse.

Surprisingly, Rupert himself was popular in actual reality as well as Virtual Reality because he was, in fact, a nice child. Whilst the trend for many decades had been for pint-sized little shits to play witty, decent, inventive boys and girls, Rupert, who was actually a fairly well-adjusted young person, had made a hit playing a pint-sized little shit.

Cross-dressing.

As she fell, Rosalie caught a momentary glimpse of the terrible pandemonium she had created. Sunlight was pouring in! Pure, unscreened, naked sunlight! Not one square inch of flawless white skin in the room had felt such a harsh glare in years. It was a beautiful bit of terrorism. The sort of witty, brutal protest for which Mother Earth was justly notorious. To pour sunlight on the beautiful people of the Golden State and watch them run screaming for their BioShield parasols was to remind the world yet again just how far people had drifted into simply accepting eco-degradation.

Rosalie was in and out of the cake in a moment. It was as if she'd been falling into and leaping out of cakes all her life. However, one glance showed her that it was out of the frying pan and into the fire. Or in this case, out of the cake and into the arms of the studio security officers. Five of them were closing in on her, although they were making heavy going amongst the upturned tables and panicking beautiful people. Rosalie scanned the room for a means of escape. The ladies' room was only yards away; she made for it. Rushing in, she surprised a beautiful young starlet at the basin. The starlet had no idea what had been happening, having been re-stapling a chin tuck whilst all the excitement was going on . . .

'Get your dress off!' shouted Rosalie, already stepping out of her cake-covered green dungarees.

The starlet wondered. This could be her big break.

True, the casting couch was a coin to be spent sparingly. If you dropped your drawers every time anyone with a two-picture development deal on the outer edges of the lot suggested it, you might as well leave them off altogether. On the other hand, this woman in dungarees had a pretty commanding presence. A lot of gay girls made pictures these days; a couple were even production heads. The starlet thought that perhaps now was the time to swallow her pride.

'Hey, listen, you're real nice, I like you,' she said, trying to hedge her bets. 'But, you know, I don't want you to think I get it on with just anyone, you know?'

'Get your dress off now, you repulsive little bitch or I'll kill you.' The wire-strippers Rosalie found in her belt gleamed inches from the girl's face.

The starlet was thrilled. This woman had power attitude. In Hollywood, the more powerful you are, the ruder you can afford to be, and this lady was rude enough to be a production head, maybe even a studio chief. The wire-strippers were a bit of a worry but nobody ever said a career in movies would be easy.

'OK, but you can't hurt me, all right? Like, I don't do that at all, OK?' the girl said, slipping out of her dress. 'No pain, just fun stuff, right? Are we going in a cubicle?'

'Gimme the shoes,' said Rosalie, kicking off her own boots.

'My name's Tori Doherty. I'm an actress,' the starlet said, feeling that she really ought to get the business side of the transaction sorted out, but not really knowing what the procedure was. 'Uhm, maybe you can help me, I don't know, some advice perhaps or . . .'

'My advice is separate all your garbage, avoid plastic containers and insulate your loft.'

Rosalie pulled off her woollen hat, letting her hair fall to her shoulders. Then, dressed in Tori's frock and high-heels, she ran out of the toilet screaming. The security people had only just arrived at the ladies' lavatory and Rosalie pushed past them, shouting, 'There's a weirdo in the rest-room.'

As the guards ran into the room, Rosalie dived into the panicking crowd. Within moments she was out of the commissary and trying to find a way off the studio lot.

Lost in Development.

Rosalie was running along the little sun-drenched lanes looking for an exit. The UV was ferocious and the skimpy dress she had taken from the starlet was specifically designed to let just about anything through. Rosalie could feel her skin burning, but she could not afford to get trapped in a sidewalk BioTube. She blessed the fact that she had only recently had her pores reblocked. They'd hold for an hour at least, and if she wasn't out in an hour, she wasn't going to get out. On she ran through the blinding sun, between rows and rows of little pale bungalows. She turned one way . . . there were little pale bungalows. She turned another . . . there were little pale bungalows. She was in a maze of little pale bungalows.

'Where's the exit?' she said to a strange, distracted-looking fellow in glasses who was loitering beneath a kerbside shade.

'Why?' he replied, a weird tinge of panic in his high voice. 'Is something happening at the exit? Do you have a *deal* at the exit?'

Rosalie had no time to confer with weirdos. She ran on. Two people, a man and a woman, were emerging from a little pale bungalow. Rosalie accosted them before they could get into the BioTube.

'I need the exit,' Rosalie demanded.

'We can give you that,' said the woman with a desperately ingratiating smile. 'In fact, we have a whole bunch of ideas around the theme of exiting. Death, departure, decay. We have a treatment right here.'

'But funny,' the man chipped in. 'Death meets funny. It's about what's happening now, today.'

The two dazed people wandered off into the sunlight together. Rosalie feared that she had stumbled into an insane asylum, but she was actually somewhere far more confused and paranoid. She burst into the bungalow which the two people had just left.

'Where's the exit?' she blurted to the lady behind the desk, a forceful looking woman of about fifty, cut up to a fairly convincing thirty-five. Her name was Shannon.

'If your treatment is on micro, leave the chip in the bucket. We accept no other formatting,' Shannon said.

Rosalie had had enough. The studio security staff would not take long to work out that she was wearing somebody else's dress. She had to get out.

'OK, love, I don't know what kind of loony-bin I've wandered into here, but you listen to me and you listen hard.' Rosalie was employing the kind of look and tone that had cowed whale murderers on the bridges of their own ships and unmanned SWAT teams in the bowels of nuclear power stations. 'This is very important.'

But Rosalie wasn't on the bridge of an illegal whaler, nor was she attempting to interfere with a nation's civil domestic nuclear capacity. She was in a little pale bungalow on a back-lot in Hollywood, facing the most formidable attack beast ever developed. The producer's secretary.

'Everybody's treatment is important, dear.' Shannon's smile never left her lips, but the voice was honeyed steel. 'Everybody's idea is an idea that's time is now. Just place your micro-chip in the bucket provided, dear, and I'll see that –'

Rosalie lunged forward, intending to grab Shannon's lapels and shake the information out of her. Instead, she found herself staring down the barrel of a stun-thrower. She had not even seen Shannon move.

'You know, dear, I can't tell you how much I miss the days when writers went off and killed themselves instead of trying to kill me.'

'I'm not a bloody writer,' Rosalie shouted. 'I'm a terrorist.'

'I never met anyone on this lot who didn't think there was something special about themselves, dear. Take a hike.'

Rosalie stumbled out of the little pale bungalow.

Where ideas go to die.

In the midst of Hollywood, the dream town, Rosalie had stumbled upon the place where there were only nightmares. For in those quiet little buildings the desperate met the scared. Desperate writers and scared producers. Writers, desperate to be used; producers, scared of making the wrong decision.

The place where ideas went to die.

There are two ways for an idea to die in that sunny bungalow world; fast and slow. Fast is easier. Fast is when it gets rejected outright. Of course, even then the idea only dies for the studio; for the writer it will never die, but since the writer is one of the living dead anyway, that's irrelevant. The slow way for an idea to die is in development. This happens when a person inside a bungalow takes an interest in an idea. This special privilege is reserved for very few ideas indeed. These are special ideas and for them a very special form of torture has been devised: they will be discussed to death. Considered from every possible angle by as many people as the producer can afford to employ until nobody can remember what was good about the idea in the first place. Then somebody will say: 'I think we've gotten real complex here. We need to get back to first cases,' and slowly the idea will fade and die.

There is a haze which hangs over Los Angeles. Many people say it's pollution, others say it's something to do with what happens when cold water meets warm air out over the ocean. The truth is that it is the haze of a million ideas slowly fading away.

A way out appears.

Rosalie knew she had to get out, not merely because she had just perpetrated a violent act of terrorism and the forces of the law were closing in on her, but also because she could sense something strange and terrible about the place in which she had found herself. Rosalie was born and brought up in Dublin; she was fourth-generation hippy and had listened to poetry and song all her life. She knew when a place had bad karma and this one had it. She was not a writer nor an actor. She had nothing to do with the entertainment industry, but quite suddenly she knew she was surrounded by lost souls and unhappy spirits. The ghosts of a hundred years of unrequited artists, all of whom had died in development.

She began to run, sensing that if she stayed much longer she would never leave. A strange sensation was beginning to overtake her. She felt a desire to buy the daily trade papers, to attend improv' classes, to talk to kindred spirits about which heads had rolled at the majors, to drop a mention or two of a potential meeting over at Fox . . . She ran, up one avenue, down another, past sound stages, more bungalows . . .

A car pulled up beside her.

'Jump in,' said Max.

Max had followed Rosalie out of the commissary. Her disguise had not fooled him for a moment. He was a good actor and he knew a performance when he saw one. Also, the girl who had originally owned the dress had only a few moments previously approached Max at his table and mentioned that she admired his work. Max remembered the dress and he remembered the girl. Now there was the dress again, but on a very different girl. A much more interesting looking one. Max had watched, fascinated, as the strange woman in the stolen dress made her escape. He was hugely impressed. Here was somebody who clearly had a purpose. Somebody who had worked out what it was they wanted to do and was doing it. What's more, that thing was nothing to do with show business. To Max, this was quite incredible. He wanted to know more about this woman. That was why he had followed her out and was now offering her a lift.

For a moment, Rosalie thought about punching Max out and taking the car. However, reflecting that she still had absolutely no idea how to get off the lot, this did not seem like a very clever move. Besides, Rosalie may have been a green terrorist, but she read magazines and went to the pictures. This was Max Maximus. If she ever got back to Dublin, this would make for great gossip down at Flannagan's. 'So there I was, driving about in Hollywood with your man Maximus himself. Would I lie to you?'

She got into the car and Max headed for the studio gates.

Horn of a dilemma.

Once they were out on the public highway Rosalie asked Max something she had wanted to know for months.

'Why did you have the horn done?'

'I'm getting rid of the horn.'

Max hated that horn. Why the hell had he done it? Drunk, that's why, drunk enough to get a stupid, dumb, simulated-bone spike grafted to the front of his head. Doctor Rock said he could take it off again in about a month and it wouldn't scar, but then Doctor Rock was a Bioquack and a casualty. Doctor Rock's principal source of income was doing dick extensions for porno stars that fell apart if you so much as gave them a slap.

At first, having a horn had felt great. Nobody had had a horn before. Krystal had liked it and Geraldine his agent thought it was a terrific idea.

'Sure, a horn, why not? It goes with the whole wildman thing and it kind of resonates solidarity with endangered species. Like Rhinos. Do they still have Rhinos, by the way or did they get Dodoed?'

Rhinos had definitely got Dodoed some fifteen years earlier. What's more, a drunk movie star with an imitation horn surgically grafted on to his forehead was not going to bring them back. Still, it did look pretty wild. Geraldine had immediately organised a major stills photo-shoot which had gone over big. Max had looked great. Torn jeans, slashed open at the fly to reveal a flat hard stomach rising to a lean, wiry torso. Arms spread wide like Christ. The expression on his sweetly handsome face that of a wounded beast, sad, tortured, noble and come-fuck-me all at once. And atop it all, that majestic spike, thirty centimetres of smooth clean imitation bone. What a pose. Eight pages in *Vanity Fair* plus the cover. The teens had gone crazy for it. Within a week the shops had been full of plastic stick-on horns and Max got twelve per cent of all the marketing. Of course, as always, some kids went too far and Max had to go on the TV and try and look responsible; not an easy thing to do with a horn grafted on to your head.

'Mr Maximus,' the talk-show guys had said, 'how do you feel about reports of kids whose parents can't afford decent sub-cellular surgery getting cheap horn jobs from backstreet BioQuacks and ending up scarred and maimed and totally socially dysfunctional for life?'

Max had been very firm on this one. 'Don't do it, kids,' he had said. 'The easily removable, glue-on "Horno Maximus" is available at any K-Mart, so you can look keen and stay safe.'

But all that was weeks ago. Now Max was sick to death of the thing. He couldn't wear a hat, toughs had started throwing ring donuts at it in bars, and it banged against the fawcet when he was in the shower.

'I'm having it removed next month,' Max said to Rosalie and changed the subject. 'So what do you do, then?'

'I kill people who murder planets.'

'That sounds pretty radical. Did you ever think about trying to talk to them first? You know, put love out to them and keep it there?'

Coincidence considered.

The stricken tanker was a stricken tanker no more; it was a wreck. Only the port bow of the forward section could now be seen above the water. It stood out like the tombstone that it was. A tombstone for a dead sea.

The water surrounding the wreck was a mass of activity. The coast defences had been scrambled and the 'clean up' was underway. 'Clean up' was of course a strange description for a process which really consisted of nothing more than spreading the mess about a bit. Worse, the detergents and chemicals used in the pointless operation were in themselves dangerous pollutants. Basically, the whole effort was entirely cosmetic and a cynical world knew it. The reason that they knew it was largely because of the constant efforts of Natura to put the facts before the public. For more decades than anybody cared to remember, Natura had battled against terrible and dangerous odds to get to the heart of environmental disaster. Their aim was always to expose the cover-up efforts of those who profited most from those disasters, or at least from the industrial and economic activities which made such disasters inevitable.

The Natura scientists were hard at work as the little coastguard launch, upon which Judy Schwartz had hitched a lift, approached their ship. Once aboard, Judy and the other authority figures were met with the cold hostility they had come to expect from any encounter with green activists. As far as Natura were concerned, the FBI, the coastguard and all other law enforcement agencies were there to protect the interests of the polluters.

'You see this!' an irate biology professor from Princeton said, addressing the news cameras that had also arrived at the ship. 'Now the coastguard turn up! Coastguard! That's got to be the sickest joke on record. Did they guard this coast? I don't think so, because this coast is now dead. So what do they do now? Subpoena the people that created this hell? No, they come and hassle us!'

'Your ship is impeding the clean-up operation,' the chief coastguard said, employing that stiff 'only doing my job' manner that cops of any description adopt when they find themselves in front of a camera. 'You have no authority to sail in these waters.'

'The clean-up operation is a crock of shit and these waters are not waters, they are a porridge of oil, heavy metals and dead fish,' the Princeton professor stated, addressing both coastguard and cameras. 'As regards who has authority to be here, Natura is a world party and claims the moral authority to be wherever Eco-death is being covered up and sanitised.'

One thing was for sure, Judy noted. They might be losing the environmental war, but Natura certainly won all the propaganda battles. The little confrontation which he was witnessing would play heavily on all the news broadcasts. Judy drifted away from the group. As usual, he was able to do this because of his appearance. He looked so harmless, the casual observer would certainly have picked him for a greenie rather than a Fed. Judy reasoned that although the activists on the ship would know each other, extra personnel would now be arriving on board to help cope with the disaster. He decided to see how far he could get before he was challenged.

'Looks pretty bad, doesn't it?' he observed to a couple of scientists who were drawing up buckets of polluted seawater for analysis.

'Worse than I've seen for a while,' said one of the scientists, clearly very upset. 'It'll dilute a little, further out to sea, but what's it going to dilute into? It's shit out there too.'

'Still,' said Judy. 'Kind of fortunate in a way, though, isn't it? I mean, not fortunate, but sort of, well . . . you know.'

'What the hell are you talking about? Fortunate? What do you mean "fortunate"?'

'Just that the Natura ship was here and everything when it happened. You know, to exploit the propaganda value of it and all. It's a lucky coincidence.'

'That's a damn strange way to look at things. Who the hell are you, anyway? I don't know you.' The scientist turned to his companion. 'Do you know this guy?'

'I do.'

There was a voice behind Judy which he thought he recognised. Turning round, he found himself facing an old adversary, a man whom he had first encountered during a Mother Earth blockade of a leaking nuclear facility.

'Hello Pierre,' Judy said. 'How are you? Any tumours yet?'

The man called Pierre was in no mood for comradely reminiscences.

'You have no jurisdiction here, Schwartz,' he said, making no attempt to conceal his hostility.

'We're in US coastal waters, Pierre. Sorry,' Judy reminded him.

Pierre changed his tack, although not his manner.

'Well, you'll get no co-operation from us . . . This man is an FBI agent!' Pierre loudly informed the scientists working on the deck. 'Offer him no assistance, answer no questions, show him nothing unless he produces a warrant.'

Judy glanced around. Suddenly he was the focus of attention. Angry, hostile faces glared at him wherever he looked.

'I have no warrant,' he said. 'This is a peaceful Natura protest ship, why would I need one?'

'Exactly,' said Pierre.

'So what are Mother Earth terrorists doing here?' Judy asked.

Pierre did not reply. Instead, with calm deliberation he spat on the deck at Judy's feet.

The scientist whom Judy had first approached spoke up.

'A whole sea is dying, so what do they do? They send the FBI. Brilliant.' The man's voice shook with anger and contempt.

Judy turned and walked away. He knew that he would learn nothing more, now that he had been unmasked as an agent. None the less, his trip had not been wasted. He had made an important discovery: Mother Earth terrorists were present at the scene of the disaster. Judy felt they would have done better to keep themselves hidden.

Chapter Ten

Holistic bullets, robotic needles and Cupid's arrow

Script conference with God.

Nathan peered over the top of his knees. He was in Plastic Tolstoy's study, seated on quite the softest, lowest couch he had ever encountered. It was like sitting in a luxuriously cushioned hole. On the table in front of him stood a glass of fizzy water, but he could not reach it, not without a rope to haul him out of the couch. His shoulders were at a lower level than his knees and his head was sunk deep into his chest. Where his neck had gone, Nathan did not know. He presumed it would reappear when he emerged from the couch, should he ever find himself in a position to do so. He did not need his neck at the moment, anyway. At the moment he cared for neither neck nor water. All Nathan cared about was how Plastic was reacting to his treatment.

This was the biggest break it was possible to have. Nathan was past every hurdle, every script reader, every consultant, every vice president in charge of development. He was pitching direct to the man. It was unheard of. To pitch direct to Plastic Tolstoy was a writer's Holy Grail. This man owned the largest communications empire on Earth. He commissioned more copy than everybody else in advertainment put together. He took a direct personal interest in probably no more than one in a thousand of the projects his companies developed for production. Writers would plead to be allowed to compromise every artistic principle they ever had just to eat in the same commissary as the lowliest of Plastic's people. A few years previously, before it was made illegal, some Harvard undergraduates had isolated Shakespeare's DNA and fast-grown another Bard of Avon. Plastic's office had not even bothered to return the guy's call.

Nathan watched nervously as the great man paced about. Plastic spoke without looking up from the synopsis that Nathan had prevaricated over for so many lonely nights in his hotel room.

'So the rat's going to go eat the kid?' he said.

'Yes,' said Nathan, 'I thought that might make us care . . . in a warm way.'

'You want me to put a rodent carnivore about to orally defile a cute little girl on prime-time?'

Nathan sensed some criticism in Plastic's tone.

'Well, I don't know about orally defile . . . I mean . . . eat, yes.'

'Did your mother reject you?' Plastic inquired with bitter sarcasm. 'Were you denied the breast? Is that where the sicko stuff started? You think a *rat* eating a sweet little girl is not a defiling thing? You think that it is somehow *nice*!'

The combination of power and indignation was terrifying. Nathan sank so far into his seat that he was in danger of disappearing altogether. Plastic towered over him, shaking the few pathetic pages.

'Here's an idea – why doesn't the rat *screw* the kid first? Yeah, that's right, he could screw her, *then* eat her. Would that be sick enough for you? Huh? What is it with you English guys? Is Disgusting Pervert on the syllabus at Eton? Can't you even pitch a script scenario without flaunting your sado-masochistic paedophile obsessions?'

Plastic had been in California for about a thousand years, but he still spoke New York Media Jewish. Rhetorical questions and heavy-handed sarcasm were his conversational armoury and he was always at war. He did not really mean to hurt. In fact, what he really liked to do was amuse. Plastic loved to get a laugh, and if none was forthcoming from his audience of cowering employees, he was always happy to provide his own. He certainly had to do his own laughing in this case, for Nathan could not laugh. He was too horrified, terrified and bent double inside a couch.

'We don't actually see the rat eat the girl,' Nathan murmured. 'It's implied.'

'Oh, it's *implied*!! I'm *so sorry*, Jeeves, old boy! I missed the sub-text, don't you know, what ho and pip-fucking-pip!' Plastic's English accent was no less biting for the fact that it sounded about as English as the Statue of Liberty.

'*Implied*! Don't give me your fucking English fucking subtlety.' He seemed almost in despair. 'What are you? T. S. Eliot? You think a prime-time vision bite gives you time to indulge your obscure pretensions? You think people who clean cars and wait tables want to spend their precious leisure dollar trying to work out some up-its-ass limey bullshit?'

Nathan gulped in fear and confusion, something to be avoided when folded in half with your ears resting on your shoulders and your knees forced against your chin.

It was an action almost certain to bring on the hiccups, and it did.

'Why stop there with your pretentious fucking subtlety? How about this, how about we don't even *have* a little girl?' said Plastic, who, as always, liked to milk any comic theme he found himself developing till its tits squeaked. 'Maybe we should have a packet of Pop Tarts that *represents* a little girl, so ten years from now, when we're all on welfare because our product stank, some fag English professor from UCLA can tell the world that the whole thing was actually a masterpiece, if only we coulda worked out what was *implied*!'

'Hic.'

'What, are you going to puke on my couch now?' asked Plastic.

'No, I have hiccups,' said Nathan, and with a monumental effort he rocked himself forward far enough to grab the bottle of water on the table before plunging back into the bottomless couch.

'Like, I want to hear about your hiccups. Like that *really* interests me. You know what the Claustrosphere advertainment budget is each year, Nathan?' Plastic asked. 'Twenty billion minimum, in the US alone. Work out how many dollars just got spent so you could tell me about your damn digestive problems. We brought you here . . . we sent a *limo* to the damn airport! So you could pitch. So pitch!'

'Uhm . . . hic . . . do you think perhaps, hic, we might show something of the little girl's fate, but tastefully, you know, avoiding the more graphic details.'

'"Do I think perhaps hic"!' Plastic quoted Nathan with such withering sarcasm that all the pot plants died. 'Do *I* think! *I'm* not the damn writer! *You're* the damn writer.

I'm just the moron who *pays* the damn writer.' Plastic punched his intercom. 'Sarah! You know that outrageously inflated sum Nathan Hoddy's agent demanded for her client's pathetic services? Get her on the line and tell her since Mr Hoddy seems to desire me to do half his work would she object to me taking half his fee.'

Nathan hiccuped miserably.

'You think I'm being hard on you, don't you? You think I'm being unnecessarily negative,' said Plastic.

Nathan did not reply. He had nothing to say but hic.

'You want to see negative!' barked Plastic. 'This is negative.'

Suddenly Plastic pulled open a drawer of his mighty desk and took out a gun. Nathan could not have moved had he wanted to, being stuck in a couch as he was, but there was no time anyway. It was over in a second. Plastic took two steps towards him, pointed the gun into Nathan's astonished face and fired. Three shots, point-blank range. The gun flashed, the noise in the confined space was deafening, the glass rattled as acrid smoke filled the room.

'Have they gone?' Plastic inquired mildly.

Nathan could not reply; you cannot talk when your heart is in your mouth.

'The hiccups, have they gone?' Plastic asked again. 'All that eerk-eerk-eerk was making me nauseous. Thought I'd try this out on you.'

The gun disappeared and in its place Plastic held a small tube with a switch on it.

'It's a holographic projector,' Plastic explained. 'We're going to give them away at gas stations. Look.' He held the tube as if it was the butt of a pistol, flicked the switch and the three-dimensional image of the pistol reappeared in his hand. 'Did it cure your hiccups?'

'Yes, they've gone,' whispered Nathan.

'OK, let's play some tennis.'

'All right,' said Nathan, struggling out of the couch.

'We'll play in the Claustrosphere.'

Play? In the Claustrosphere? Play *tennis* in a Claustrosphere? Nathan thought Plastic must mean table-tennis, but he didn't. Set in the grounds of Plastic's house in Beverly Hills was quite the biggest Claustrosphere Nathan had ever seen. In fact, it wasn't really set in the grounds, it was the grounds.

'Hey, who wants a damn garden?' Nathan said. 'At least in a Claustrosphere your grass don't die.'

Nobody likes it but what can you do?

They walked down the connecting BioTube and through the EcoLock into the central dome.

Nathan was stunned, he had never in his life encountered such opulence. The thing must have covered well over four acres, and contained everything: living quarters, gardens, a little stream. The air was fresh and sweet, birds chattered in the upper reaches, butterflies fluttered over a small field of wheat, fish went 'glop' in the pond.

'Of course it's all BioMechanically generated,' Plastic explained. 'A genuine eco-cycle is impossible on such a small scale. This whole cycle is kept functioning with sub-cellular protein concentrates and fast-grow organic engineering. It'll work for at least a hundred years though, so who's complaining? This is the kind of development that Mother Earth have been trying to knock out for years. Stupid Luddite schmucks, always bombing the wrong labs.'

Nathan had of course been aware, as everyone who read a Sunday colour supplement was aware, that Bio-Sphere technology had improved; but he had not quite realised how good it had got. Plastic's dome made his and Flossie's ancient old backyard job look like exactly what it was: a poxy little eco-shelter. A bog standard Eden Three, no frills. It had water rotation and a basic food cycle. It could break down and reconstitute human waste and it could maintain a breathable atmosphere. It had come with a free gift miniaturised bonsai tree rain forest, but that was about its only luxury. Even the video library was manual . . . you actually had to eject the micro-tapes yourself. Flossie and Nathan had debated whether to purchase the optional day and night cycle, but had decided that they couldn't really afford it. Those eye guards you get for sleeping on aeroplanes would be just as good anyway.

The truth of the matter was that they had both been rather reluctant to buy a Claustrosphere at all. They had not been the first of their friends to do it, but they were not the last, either. They had, in fact, wrestled with their consciences for about the average amount of time taken by most middle-class liberal couples before buying one. Nathan often reflected that his generation seemed to have spent its entire adult life sitting round dinner tables drinking red wine, eating Tuscan bean soup, and trying to justify the morality of buying a Claustrosphere.

'I mean you don't *want* to do it, for God's sake. Do you?' they all said.

'Nobody *wants* to do it.'

Of course, as students they had all been deeply opposed to Claustrospheres. Natura was big on campus and when their parents had slowly begun to think about buying an Eden One they had all reacted with horror. Referred to their dear old mums and dads as 'Pollution Fascists' and 'Planet Traitors'. However, when they themselves reached maturity, the situation looked a bit different.

Dying of consumption.

The Earth just wasn't getting any healthier. How could it? The one single and abiding criterion by which the success of countries is judged is in terms of their 'growth'. Each year the great nations agonise over how much they have 'grown'. How much more they have made, how much more they have consumed.

Consumer confidence is actually considered a measure of a country's relative economic strength. When a load of poor deluded sad-acts are down at the shops running up debts on their credit cards, finance ministers claim that the economy is 'growing' and start celebrating. Recessions are deemed to be over the moment people start spending money which they don't have on things that they don't need. Consumption is synonymous with 'growth' and growth is good. It is always good, whenever and wherever. Hence, clearly consumption is good, all consumption, anywhere, anytime. Judged by the logic of world economics, the death of the planet will be the zenith of human achievement, because if consumption is always good, then to consume a whole planet must be the best thing of all.

Acting sensibly.

And so, faced with the fact that the world was growing to death, slowly but surely people began to buy their Edens. Just as their grandparents and great-grandparents had moved out of the dirty inner cities into the countryside. Nobody wanted to do it, but on the other hand, things were as they were and privately martyring yourself was not going to change things.

Every night Jurgen Thor and all the other self-righteous greenies were on the TV, banging on about planet death. What were you supposed to do? It was obvious: send Greenpeace a donation and start digging the foundations for your Claustrosphere.

It was, of course, self-perpetuating. The more people bought them, the more difficult they were to resist. Those who had taken the plunge became Claustrophere's most passionate advocates. Every time another tanker sank or a nuclear power station went pop, they would silently congratulate themselves on having made the right decision. They scarcely liked to admit it even to themselves but there was almost a grim satisfaction to be had out of the daily worsening eco-statistics.

'I see that two-fifths of Russia is no longer habitable,' they would say to each other over breakfast. 'I knew getting a Claustrosphere was a sensible decision. I mean nobody *wants* the Earth to die, but you only have to look at the papers . . . I wonder what Mr Holier Than Bloody Thou next door will say when it's two-fifths of the bloody Home Counties you can't live in? I know what he'll bloody say. He'll say, "Any room in your Eden for me and the wife?"'

The question of what non-Claustrosphere owners would

do in the event of planet death added considerable piquancy to the delicate social politics of the whole issue. In the early days those who owned a 'Sphere were in the minority and they had looked rather selfish and anti-social, but as Claustrospheres became more and more common, the moral balance switched. So that it was those without a shelter who began to appear selfish. Once it came about that there were only a few houses left in any street without a Claustrosphere, the majority became obsessed with what those people would do if the Rat Run was announced. More and more, those who held out (be it for moral or financial reasons) began to look like the irresponsible, anti-social ones. In many communities, those who were neglecting to take due precautions to ensure a future for themselves and their families in the event of Eco-death, came to be held in contempt.

'It's all very well being green, we're *all bloody green*,' people would say. 'But they'll be banging on my door trying to get in when the Rat Run starts. I know they will.'

These debates were even more heated when it came to flat dwellers. Many people in communal living situations had begun to band together to purchase land out of town and commission larger, group Claustrospheres. The question of who was in and who was out divided previously friendly neighbourhoods.

Finally the whole community became involved in the issue as politicians began to plan for mass, public Claustrospheres, for the use of the broader population. They claimed that they were concerned for the wellbeing of all citizens in the event of Eco-Armageddon, but the real reason was of course fear of the mob. If you have a nice back-garden Claustrosphere, just right for you and your family, and up the road there is a housing estate containing thousands of people with no eco-cover whatsoever, then you're going to get a little nervous about what all those people are going to do on the day of the Rat Run. Therefore, in order that the rich might feel confident about using their Claustrospheres unmolested, some arrangement had to be made for the poor. Right across the industrialised world, borders began to be reinforced and legislation passed to make it a local government responsibility to provide basic eco-cover. The Community Claustrosphere became as much the responsibility of City Hall as the roads and the police.

Everyone could see which way this type of thinking was leading. It didn't need a Jurgen Thor to spot it. The more effort that went into what would happen *after* planet death, the less effort people were putting into preventing that death. Coupled with which, the Claustrospheres themselves consumed colossal Earth resources in their actual production. The extraordinary irony was clear to all but the stupidest. The world was actually hastening its own destruction in order to survive it.

Some people like Nathan and Flossie agonised over this paradox; other people said, 'Shit happens.' Everybody made sure they had access to a Claustrosphere.

Discussing death.

As Plastic Tolstoy led an astonished Nathan into his palatial Claustrosphere, Plastic's most public and bitter enemy, Jurgen Thor, was being sewn back together after the explosion of the European parliament.

Jurgen allowed only local anaesthetics to be used. This was partly because he wanted to keep his mind clear to consider the implications of the outrage, and partly because the press were outside the room and he wanted to look tough. It never does a politician any harm to be seen showing physical courage, and also it helps when trying to get laid.

'I tell you, this was a company job, and we go public with the story.'

Jurgen was addressing a small group of senior Natura officials, announcing his theory that the bomb blast had been aimed at him as part of a seasonal Claustrosphere marketing push. He spoke through gritted teeth as the laser surgeons worked to sew his massive limbs back on. 'Hey, take it easy with that,' he shouted as his colossal Nordic penis was unpacked from the ice and prepared for surgery. 'It's the basis of my legend.'

'You're lucky we saved it at all,' the surgeon said. 'It landed in the *smörgåsbord* at a reception given by the Norwegian fisheries people. It was a chilled plate and the rollmops kept it cool.'

'You mean my prick's been saved by the whaling lobby!' Jurgen roared with laughter. 'Imagine what all the earnest little hippies who vote for us would think? Jurgen Thor had his dick in a whaler's *smörgåsbord*. Ha, ha! Maybe I won't get so lucky with all the "right on" girls! What will they say?' Jurgen affected a high squeaky tone, 'No, Jurgen, you cannot rumpy-pumpy me! Your wang has the blood of innocent whales upon it!'

Jurgen's great frame shuddered with amusement at his own jollities. The chief surgeon looked up from her delicate work.

'Mr Thor, I am trying to sew your penis back on, here. Could you kindly lie still?'

'Ha! Doctors! You pretend you are such special people!'

Jurgen laughed. 'We all know the Robo-surgeon does the difficult bits.'

'Even Robo-surgeons have to be programmed, Mr Thor. I would hate for you to walk out of here with your penis disappearing up your backside.'

Jurgen felt this was a good point and decided to stop cracking gags for a minute, much to the relief of all concerned. The brief respite gave a chance for Natura's Chief of Press Liaison to observe that Jurgen's theories regarding the source of the bomb were unsubstantiated slander.

'The police say the blast could have been planted by one of any number of nationalist groups. What on earth makes you so sure that the company tried to hit you, Jurgen?'

'Hey, groover, two things for a start. First, as a rule of your thumb, right? Whatever the Belgian police say, you take the opposite. Right? OK? Ciao, baby, wake up and smell the flowers. Second, the bomb was indiscriminate, no? Too big by far to have been targeted at any one group. In fact every group suffered casualties, right? You think people plant bombs to kill themselves? I don't think. No, the bomb was designed to breach the security screen which protects the speaker. The speaker was me, OK, babe? But I was lucky, the screen was strong, and so am I. All that happens is my love pump got a little damaged.'

'It certainly did,' said the surgeon, again looking up from her work, 'Look, there are burn marks on it.'

'Hey, baby,' Jurgen smiled. 'Those burn marks didn't come from no bomb, OK? Right? You know what I'm saying here!'

Jurgen rarely failed to make a strong impression on

women and this occasion was no exception. The micro-surgeon would have liked to have taken that big long fat dick of which Jurgen was so clearly proud and throttle him with it; but she was a professional and so she returned quietly to her work, making a mental note to put it about that she had actually seen the great Jurgen Thor's legendary appendage and it was tiny.

'I'm telling you,' Jurgen continued, 'that bomb was meant for me.'

'Well, maybe,' conceded the Chief of Press Liaison. 'If it was, you sure are lucky they installed such a tough screen.'

'Oh yes, that's for sure and certain, OK? They designed it for when the British hold the presidency . . . everyone in Europe wants to kill them, right?'

'But the company?' The press officer protested. 'It would be pretty audacious, I mean, it could easily back-fire. Killing you could provoke a green backlash.'

'Not if I got killed by someone else's bomb! Look, it's simple, man. Claustrosphere want me dead, right? They always have, but they know that if I die, bang! Immediately I'm a martyr. The Guevara syndrome, right? OK? Unless, of course, I die stupidly, like getting blown up by someone else's bomb. Then it's kind of a stupid, embarrassing way to die, like those people who get sucked into airline toilets. So what do they do? Wait till I'm addressing the European Federation, bomb capital of the damn Universe, Goddamn and damnit, and hit me with a bomb so big that every nationalistic zealot will be crying foul. They want me dead! I am more than a mere man, I am an idol, an inspiration, a prophet! In many people's eyes I am just too wonderful to be allowed to live.'

The surgeon raised her head from her work again.

'I can certainly understand people wanting to kill you,' she said.

'Exactly. Of course the Claustrosphere Company will kill me if they can do it safely. Believe me, babe, I am lying here today in fourteen separate pieces because Claustrosphere *have added murder to their marketing strategy*. I want you to knock up a press release explaining our opinion. They won't sue, I'm telling you.'

'But it seems so wild, I mean . . .'

'Listen, man, ask yourself this: if one of our people got the chance to knock off Plastic Tolstoy. Wouldn't they take it?'

A meeting to kill for.

'Hey, how would you like to meet Plastic Tolstoy?' Max asked Rosalie. It was a last-ditch attempt to interest her.

Max was already halfway smitten by Rosalie. She was exciting. She had purpose. He wondered whether her sweet face and pale, slightly freckled skin could possibly be real. It wasn't that she was perfectly constructed like Krystal or anything, far from it, but Max was aware that some girls deliberately had slightly flawed, kooky face-jobs done, so that people would think it was natural. Having lived in Hollywood all his life, Max was only vaguely aware that there was a big world outside where people did not have themselves routinely reconstructed to suit their clothes.

He had asked her to lunch. He had suggested a drink, a swim in his pool, a trip to the BioDome-enclosed beach at Venice; but all this Rosalie had politely declined. She reminded him that she was an international terrorist who had just tried to give a whole crowd of media stars a dose of cancer and was now on the run from the forces of justice. So could he kindly drop her at the airport so that she could make her escape before her description got circulated.

That was when Max suggested introducing her to Plastic Tolstoy. Max occasionally caught the news, and he had a vague idea that Mother Earth and Natura people considered Tolstoy a figure of some significance.

There was a pause. Rosalie was wondering if this was a joke, or perhaps a trap of some kind. 'You can get me in to see Plastic Tolstoy?' she asked warily.

'Sure, I have a three forty-five at his place in the Hills . . . You green guys have kind of a down on him, don't you?'

'Oh, well, you know,' said Rosalie, 'these things get blown out of proportion.'

'He's actually a pretty cool person. I think you'd like him. You know, you're both kind of energetic "in your face" type of people. You get things done. He's a legend in the industry . . .' Max put on his most impressive tone of voice. 'He wants me for a picture.'

They were manoeuvring through the traffic which was, as usual, gruesome. But for once Rosalie did not go into her traffic-jam rant. For once she was appreciative of the delay. She needed time to think. Despite her tough talk, Rosalie was not a killer. She *had* killed, in an indirect sense. During Mother Earth actions she had often been fired upon and had occasionally returned fire. She might have hit someone, she didn't know. She had never hung around long enough to find out. Also, she had blown up a lot of things around and about the world; polluters, Dodo-makers (as the traders in near-extinct species were called), Claustrosphere showrooms. There must have been casualties then, she supposed. Her own side had certainly suffered many losses, so she presumed that the enemy must have had them too. She had, however, never specifically or deliberately killed anyone.

Could she do it now? Should she do it now? Rosalie's mind was racing. Plastic Tolstoy was not, after all, directly responsible for the dead seas and extinct species. Except in a small way he was. He was, after all, the prophet of the alternative to saving the planet . . . But that was stupid. If there was no Plastic Tolstoy there would still be Claustrospheres. He had not invented them, what's more somebody would still be selling them. It was people who were destroying the Earth, not any single person . . . But then again, Tolstoy did encourage them. Every day, he cynically tempted people to neglect their true responsibilities . . . History was full of leaders and Plastic Tolstoy was definitely a leader and an incredibly powerful one at that. More so than any politician. It wasn't politicians who shaped the world any more, it was the marketing people, the people who perpetrated and justified the myth of consumption. Plastic Tolstoy was the biggest marketer of all.

'I don't think you heard me,' Max interrupted Rosalie's reverie. He was very disappointed that his news had not gone over bigger. 'Plastic Tolstoy wants me for a picture! Have you any idea what kind of huge shit that is?'

Rosalie was anxious not to arouse Max's suspicions. She pretended to take an interest.

'Why is it so special? You're a big star, everyone knows that. I've read that you could work with anyone you wanted to.'

'Anyone but Tolstoy. He's so far ahead of everybody

else he's an industry in himself, he *is* the industry. No matter how big you are, you're still small compared to him and if I play my cards right, he's going to make a picture with me!'

Not if Rosalie could help it he wasn't.

Chapter Eleven

Career opportunities

The games people play.

Plastic and Nathan were not playing tennis in the conventional sense. Big though Plastic's 'Sphere was, it did not actually contain a court. It did not need to. It was equipped with state-of-the-art games suits which offered a tennis court, a baseball diamond, in fact, any pitch the player desired. The suits were Virtual Reality body stockings which the player wore whilst suspended, weightless, inside a vacuum tank. One could run, kick and jump in them without going anywhere. You could play any sport, either against a great player of your choice, via computer or against a real person whose suit was linked to yours. Thus, Plastic and Nathan played two hard sets of tennis involving some pretty impressive serving and net-play, and yet all an outside observer would have seen was something akin to two frogmen squirming and writhing in a big fish-tank.

'That's the kind of leisure accessory that is going to make New Generation Eden absolutely irresistible,' Plastic remarked over a glass of fruit punch as they sat relaxing under the great geodesic dome on the edge of the desert, next to the rain forest. 'Inside one of those suits you can join any team you ever dreamt of playing for and play against any team you ever wanted to beat. Some great match you think your team should never have lost? Join the side, play it again and see if you can make the difference. Many times I've come down here on my own, got in that tank and shot hoops with the 1980s LA Lakers when Magic was playing. Of course, your average guy couldn't afford one of these suits if he saved for a thousand years, but the price will come down, it always does.'

Nathan was quite interested, but only quite. He didn't want a game, he wanted a job. He guessed that, despite Plastic's rough treatment of his synopsis, he must still be in some kind of contention or he would not still be in the great man's company. All he could do was sit and wait. Eventually Plastic returned to the point.

Marketing lesson.

'Your treatment is good,' said Plastic. 'The rat is going to eat the kid, that moves me. It's a little down, a little sombre, maybe, but it's good.'

Obviously, Nathan, not being privy to Plastic's sense of humour, was a little surprised, considering what had been said in the office, but he was happy to take his luck where he found it.

'But, with respect, I would contend that it *has* to be down,' he said, launching into his pitch. 'You market a product which will protect people from the death of the Earth, surely the best way to do that is to push the total planetary screw-up we're in. Environmental degradation is the best sales tool you've got. You can't talk it up enough.'

Plastic smiled at Nathan's naïve enthusiasm.

'Oh, like, and that never occurred to us, right?' he said, returning to his favourite tone of aggressive sarcasm.

'Well, I just thought –'

'Like, there's all us dummies sitting around here in Hollywood without an idea in our heads, just waiting for some genius Englishman to come and reveal the dazzlingly obvious to us. Thank you, Mr Einstein, thank you for striking the scales from my eyes. I feel so stupid my dick has shrunk.'

Nathan was at a loss.

'The reason that we have avoided the scare advert for nearly thirty years, you feeble-minded jerk,' Plastic shouted, 'is because we market a product that shames us all, that's why! Jurgen Thor and the Natura guys are right. It's absolutely disgusting that people are investing in post-Armageddon life insurance. Jesus! We should all be putting every penny we have into saving what we've got.'

'Well, yes, of course but –'

'But nothing! Shut up and listen. Claustrospheres are the thing everybody says they wish they didn't have to have. It's like private education! People would like to support the state system; on the other hand, they don't want their kid getting shot for his eraser. Now if we'd been playing the doom card all these years we'd have looked like we were exploiting a terrible situation. Like we were *happy* the Earth is screwed – which of course we are – but if we say that, we look tacky, right? We've had to be positive and up-beat! We've had to say *"Because we hope you'll never need it"*. If we had said "your kids will die unless you buy our product", people would have smelt a rat, and the rat would have been them. Nobody likes getting the mote in their eye shoved in their face.'

'So you don't like my treatment, then?'

'I just said I liked it!'

'But then you said –'

'Listen, Nathan, just let me do the talking here, OK? You shut up and maybe we'll get somewhere. The situation has changed. Just about everybody in the developed world has a Claustrosphere. You have one, right?'

'Well, actually it's part of a property dispute with my ex-wi –'

'Like I should care? Nathan, please. We will be here all day. Everyone has a damn Claustrosphere, the market is drying up, right? We've been so damned successful we have consumed our consumers. Now this ain't a new thing, right? Producers have faced the problem before, like everybody has a freezer, a car, a semi-automatic weapon. The point is that with other products you get round the problem with built-in obsolescence. You just make a damn freezer that falls apart after two years, it's easy. Unfortunately, built-in obsolescence would rather defeat the object of a Claustrosphere. By definition, it's got to last at least a couple of generations. So what's the solution?'

Nathan decided not to risk attempting an answer. He knew that whatever he said Plastic would twist it so that he was wrong.

'We gotta get people to upgrade, that's what. People have to realise that their present units, Eden Ones, Twos and Threes, are crap. What are you and your wife fighting over?'

'A Mark Three with a bottled rain forest.'

'Exactly. Crap. A bolthole, nothing more. Sure, it'll keep you alive but who wants to live like that? I'll bet the video library doesn't even have Virtual Reality.'

Nathan could only nod at this casual exposure of the woeful inadequacy of his arrangements.

'The point is that all the time people have been sort of presuming that in the end they ain't actually going to have to use the thing. You know, it's been like insurance. Nice to have it there but you hope you'll never have to claim it. What we need to do now is change the emphasis. We have to make people believe that *they're actually going to have to use their Claustrosphere* which, let's face it, they probably are. People have got to realise it's a pretty good bet that they're going to spend the rest of their lives inside a geodesic dome, existing off a Biosphere technology. We've got to have them asking, "Hey, do we fit new carpets in the house? Or do we stick a rain water simulator in the 'Sphere?" They've got to say, "Well, hell, where are we likely to be five years from now?" That's what we've got to do, Nathan, we've got to get people to upgrade their Claustrospheres before they change their cars. It is finally time to play the doom card – the one which you seem to be under the impression you're the only person who's thought of!'

Consumer control.

'So you're going to make my ad, then?'

'Yes, I'm going to make your stupid little dumb advert,' Plastic replied irritably. 'But that wasn't why I asked you up here. You think I ask every pen-pushing little scribbler I commission into my private 'Sphere to play tennis? Let me tell you, under normal circumstances I *shit* you kind of people. I actually shit little guys like you and then use another little guy like you to clean my ass. Understand?'

Nathan nodded.

'I brought you here because I think you can write and I want to make a movie. A real movie, a centre-piece to the new campaign. I want a real old-fashioned advertainment and I want you to work on the words, OK?'

Nathan was stunned. A proper movie! So few were made these days. To be asked to be involved in one was to join an echelon so upper it gave Nathan vertigo.

Only a few years previously it had seemed as if nobody would ever make a real movie ever again. Not one with actors and a proper fixed plot, that people had to go to a cinema to see. A series of technical innovations seemed to have made the genre obsolete. The feeling was that technology was more interesting than art, and that if you didn't need a million dollar helmet to watch a show then it wasn't worth seeing.

Interactive entertainment became the miracle ingredi-ent that was going to revitalise a depressed industry. The consumer was going to be put in control.

'Like the consumer knows anything!' Plastic and a few like-minded visionaries had complained at the time. 'Remind me because I forget, did the consumer write *Oliver Twist*? Or Beethoven's 'Fifth'? No, I don't think so. As I recall it was *artists* who did those things, people with special talents. And what did the consumer do? The consumer *consumed* it, didn't he? Sucked it right up and went away with his life enriched.'

But for a while the revolution was unstoppable. It was presumed that since the technology existed by which an audience could be presented with an infinite number of possible solutions to a drama, then that must be what they would want. Likewise, since it was now possible for a viewer to don a helmet and a suit which would enable them to enter the action along with their favourite heroes, then it was presumed that the public would jump at the chance.

Plastic still felt bitterly about the way art had been hijacked by technology. He ranted at Nathan as if it had been Nathan who was responsible for the development of interactive entertainment.

'The public *always* had the technology to get involved with the action if it wanted to. Right back to the Greeks. All they had to do was get up on stage and join in. But they didn't do it, did they? Weird, huh? Maybe, just maybe, they kind of guessed that it would completely screw up the show. The public could *always* choose their own endings when they read books. All they had to do was get a damn pen and write in that Scrooge never got nice and Moby Dick was a chipmunk. But they didn't, and why? Because the public don't pay for entertainment in order to have to provide it themselves. The whole damn nightmare was a conspiracy by scientists and computer brains to make everyone in the world as boring as them.'

But now the tide was turning. The public were returning to more traditional forms of entertainment; movies, in particular, and it seemed that Nathan was being commissioned to write one. What is more, Max Maximus, who was just driving up to the house with Rosalie fidgeting nervously at his side, was going to star in it.

Stormy meeting.

'Here's what I want,' said Plastic. 'I want a straight megabuck advertisement to sell new generation Claustrospheres.

It's got to be the biggest hit of the year. I want everybody to go and see it and I want it to star Max Maximus, OK?'

The BioLock entry-screen leapt into life. An electronic voice announced that Max and a friend were outside. Max and Rosalie appeared on the screen.

'Come on up, Max. We're in the Claustrosphere,' Plastic said. The screen went dark and he turned to Nathan. 'Can you believe this guy, brings a chick to a meeting? I've got a good mind not to put him in the picture. Chicks always distract things. Am I right?'

Plastic was about to find out how right he was.

Max and Rosalie emerged through the BioLock.

'Hi, Plastic. Great 'Sphere, cool,' said Max, like an over-eager schoolboy visiting a much respected master at his home. 'Wow, you have a mini-mountain,' he said, referring to a hundred-metre-high rock structure complete with snow on its upper reaches. 'I've been thinking of putting one of those into mine, but I'd have to extend. I don't have the height for a split-level climate.'

If Rosalie had been having trouble making her decision, that was behind her now. The sheer obscenity of what she was looking at confirmed her resolve. She did not consider herself Plastic's judge and jury. That task lay with all the dead animals and sick dying people she had encountered in her years of struggle. The devastated areas where peasant populations skulked in the shade, nursing their tumours, waiting for night to fall so they could harvest their mutated crops. *They* had tried and convicted Plastic Tolstoy. It was merely Rosalie's job to carry out the sentence. Of course, she knew it wasn't all his fault, but there he was, inside a private paradise that he had built for himself in a doomed world, and Rosalie was in no mood to make excuses for him.

'So, who's your little pal?' Plastic said, turning to Rosalie only to find himself staring down the barrel of a gun.

'Plastic Tolstoy!' Rosalie announced, her hand trembling on the trigger. 'I am a Mother Earth activist. Dedicated to the principle that the ultimate human responsibility is to the planet which supports us. The idea that we can exist separate from the planet is treason. You are the principal perpetrator of this fiction and therefore, on behalf of the planet Earth and all the people, animals and plants that live on it, I am now going to execute you . . .'

Rosalie had never been so lucid in her life. Conviction lent her eloquence. Plastic Tolstoy was dead. She knew it, and he knew it. Rosalie's finger tightened on the trigger.

It was pure ambition and naked careerism which saved Plastic.

For a moment, both Max and Nathan had simply watched in horror whilst Rosalie announced her sentence of execution. Then, separately and simultaneously, it dawned on them that this mad bitch was about to murder the biggest break either of them had ever had. For Nathan in particular it would be an unbearable fate . . . to be commissioned to write a screenplay by the top producer in the world, only to have that producer murdered, minutes later. People spent their whole lives looking for a break like this. Nathan couldn't let it go now. The planet was all very well, but this was a *movie*, for God's sake!

Max was in a similar position. He needed Tolstoy

badly. Yes, he already had a huge career but, as his agent Geraldine never tired of pointing out, it was trend-based. He was the current big thing, a teen idol. He had to move on from that; he had to mature and become a genuine star. A Tolstoy project was his chance at real longevity.

For both Nathan and Max, saving Plastic Tolstoy was a career move, pure and simple. Hence, just as Rosalie's finger began to tighten on the trigger, the two of them launched themselves at her, and as the gun fired, all three collapsed together on to the ground. As she fired, the gun flew out of Rosalie's hand. The bullet went wild, missed Plastic, bounced off the geodesic wall and rebounded, killing a rare breed of domestic pig which was feeding on supa-grass concentrate by the pond. The noise of the shot rang round the dome, causing a cloud of airborne wildlife to rise in fear above the canopy of the rain forest and an androgynous self-breeding bull/cow to emerge from its stable and tread on all the chickens.

Around the world in eight minutes.

Rosalie was up in a moment but Plastic, who had had to defend himself before, already had the gun.

'OK, stay where you are, young lady,' he said as two armed servants appeared at the mouth of the BioLock.

But Rosalie had no intention of staying where she was. Instead, she dived into the dense vegetation of the rain forest. In a moment she had disappeared within its generous foliage. The two muscular servants plunged in after her, trampling down millions of dollars-worth of Tuf-Plant. Tuf-Plant was greenery genetically engineered to withstand pretty much anything, although not, as it happened, a couple of fifteen-stone armed thugs jumping all over it.

'Watch out for the fucking rain forest!' Plastic shouted, 'And don't kill her. Dead babes look bad!'

Rosalie plunged on through the jungle which covered about a third of an acre of the whole Claustrosphere. Plastic tried to run around it to cut her off on the other side, but was prevented from doing so by the babbling stream.

'Nathan,' Plastic yelled over his shoulder. 'You're a writer, make a note. I have to have a bridge built.'

Rosalie emerged from under the dark canopy of the rain forest and jumped into a small field containing various giant Hi-Yield cereal crops. Pushing through that, she leapt over a small mangrove swamp and started to skirt around the rocky outcrops at the bottom of the mountain.

'Where is she?' shouted Plastic, as the two servants thrashed their way out of the forest.

'I think she headed for the hills,' one of them replied.

Rosalie continued skirting the mountain, the foothills of which lay at the very edge of the Claustrosphere, right up against the walls of the geodesic dome. As she crouched behind a large rock she could hear her pursuers circumnavigating the foot of the mountain from both sides. Her only option was to head upwards. As she broke cover to scramble up the scree which lay all about on the lower slopes, one of the servants spotted her. He fired a couple of warning shots, hitting a small herd of geep.

'Mind my geep! You asshole!' Plastic shouted.

Geep were one of the most successful products of a genetic engineering revolution which had been going on in deadly secrecy for years. The original genetic project had been started by a group of very rich men who had been hoping to breed a camel that would fit through the eye of a needle. They spent years on it, until one day it occurred to them that it would be easier and cheaper to simply build an enormous needle. They got out of genetics immediately, selling their research to the Claustrosphere company.

Geep were a cross between a sheep and a goat. They were incredibly hardy, living for over a hundred years, and all the while provided wool, milk and, quite astonishingly, meat. So resilient were these creatures that you could cut glamb chops out of their hind quarters for supper and the animal would have healed up by the next morning. This Kwik-Heal flesh was developed out of DNA isolated from those insects that grow another leg if you pull one off. Therefore Plastic Tolstoy need not have worried about his geep. The bullets scarcely made them flinch. They had been the result of such brutal grafting and cloning experiments, that being shot at was just like the old days in the lab to them.

Rosalie reached the snowline and looked back. Seventy-five metres below, in near tropical conditions, she could see one of her pursuers beginning to climb up after her, whilst Plastic and the other guard doubled back round the base of the mountain, clearly planning to cut off her descent. She had no choice but to press on. She breasted the summit and began to run back down the opposite slope, hoping to arrive at the bottom before Plastic came around through the foothills. It was a tough descent, with alpine conditions for the first twenty feet. Almost inevitably, she slipped on a glacier and fell into a mini-gully. Fortunately, nothing was broken, but she was pretty winded and it slowed her down. So much so that, by the time she had completed her descent, the first of her muscular pursuers was emerging round the mountain with Plastic Tolstoy puffing behind.

'OK,' said the pursuer, by way of a warning, 'I don't want to hurt you.'

'Whereas I do want to hurt you,' replied Rosalie.

She had taken the precaution of picking up a fist-sized boulder on the lower slopes of the scree and she smashed this into the face of her assailant, causing him to offer no further opinions. Plastic arrived next, just in time for Rosalie to deal him a mighty kick in the balls before running for the BioLock.

Career decision.

Unfortunately for Rosalie, by now, the second of the muscular types had descended the mountain. He charged after her, covering the entire desert in four strides before bringing her down with a flying tackle. The man was an Akido master and, despite Rosalie's formidable fighting skills, he was easily able to fix her in a body-lock. Crushed as she was by a large martial arts expert, Rosalie knew that the game was up.

Max had to make a career decision. This woman had just tried to murder the most powerful producer in the world, a producer for whom Max very much wanted to work. On the other hand, this same woman was very attractive indeed, and her announcement of execution had contained some extremely valid points. What to do? Max usually left difficult decisions to his agent but he knew that she would have been in no doubt. There was no point even calling her to ask. Max knew what her answer would be, 'Stand back and let the girl be taken,'

Geraldine would have said, 'and just pray Tolstoy forgets you were the one who brought her here.'

Yes, that is certainly what Geraldine would have said. Then, again, Geraldine was not in full possession of the facts. For one thing, she did not fancy the girl. In fact, to the best of Max's knowledge, Geraldine had not even met her, and had she done, Max doubted that she would have found something wild and compelling about the girl's behaviour. Max certainly did. Everything about Rosalie spoke to Max's very soul. She seemed to throw his own pointless and dissolute existence into shameful contrast. Max was by nature both romantic and a bit mad. It was these two factors which led him to decide to lay professional considerations aside and be romantic and a bit mad now. Except that he did not really decide; he just did it, because, as has already been pointed out, he was a bit mad. Running over, he took a huge kick at the Akido master's head. Rosalie rolled the unconscious man off her and leapt to her feet.

'Here,' said Max and threw her his car keys.

'Thanks,' said Rosalie.

Max would love to have believed that there was a poignant glance, a meeting of eyes, an unmistakable moment of understanding, and perhaps even affection between them. But there wasn't. She just grabbed the keys and fucked off.

'See you sometime,' he murmured as Rosalie flipped the switch on the BioLock and disappeared into the tube which led to the car-port.

Max turned to face Plastic, who was staggering to his feet in some considerable pain. Plastic had, of course, witnessed Max's craven disloyalty. What is more, that disloyalty was not over yet. As the BioLock closed behind Rosalie, Max marched over to Plastic.

'I don't want you to call your security people, Plastic. I want you to let the girl go.'

Max gulped, Nathan gulped, even Tolstoy gurgled slightly. None of them could quite believe that Max was aiding and abetting the escape of someone who had just kicked the most powerful person in Hollywood in the balls. Everyone knew that Max was a bit mad, but this was insane.

'You want me to let her go?' Plastic inquired.

'Yes,' said Max.

Plastic could see that Max was clearly determined. He also knew that Max was young, fit and very strong. He shrugged.

'Looks like she's going to get away then.'

There was a pause in which nobody made a sound except the numerous mutant animals which were still voicing their protest at the sudden disturbance.

'Uhm . . . listen, Plastic . . . Mr Tolstoy,' Max mumbled, reason returning to its throne, 'I hope this incident won't affect our working relationship.'

'You hope it won't affect our working relationship?'

'Yes.'

'You take sides with a woman who tries to execute me and you hope it won't affect our working relationship?'

'If that's OK by you.'

'All right then,' said Plastic, ever the pragmatist. 'I don't know what we would have done with her if we'd caught her anyway. The last thing I need is to be seen dragging some cute little greenie through the courts. You can bet your best dollar she'd get all the sympathy. Just as a matter of interest, though, may I inquire why you brought this homicidal lunatic along to a creative meeting?'

'I just met her at DigiMac . . . I thought you might be interested. I didn't know she was going to try and execute you.'

'Thank you. That's nice to know. Are you porking her?'

'Well, I . . .'

'Good, because it's a connection we can use. Nathan here is going to write me a movie for you to star in. A movie about the battle between Mother Earth and Claustrosphere. He's going to write about how those decent but misguided souls in the Green Movement learn that, far from threatening the survival of the human race, Claustrosphere is in fact ensuring it. Isn't that right, Nathan?'

'That's exactly the type of plot I had in mind,' Nathan said hastily.

'Good.'

Broadening the campaign.

After Max and Nathan had left, Plastic returned to his communications room in the house. A marketing strategy has to be many-levelled. You can't just make a decent ad. A well-designed packet alone is not enough. A marketing strategy has to set the agenda for consumption. A perfect marketing strategy not only provides the product, it also identifies and promotes the need. All his life Plastic Tolstoy had known that the easiest market to exploit is the one which you create yourself.

Chapter Twelve

The paranoid conspiracy theorist

Trapped nerd.

Judy was cornered and he knew it. There were two of them outside the cubicle. What is more, they were armed, and Judy was not. Normally in these circumstances, when an agent is trapped in a toilet cubicle, there is a convenient back window through which to make an escape. This time, however, there was no window and probably a good thing too, considering that the lavatory was on the 190th floor.

'Come on out, man.' The tone was violent, with the hint of a sneer. 'Unless you want them to find you with your pants down.'

It was a point, thought the terrified Judy. If one has to fight, best not to have to do it with your trousers round your ankles. He pulled them up and readied himself for the inevitable. Outside they were laughing; they had their man and they knew it. Judy desperately tried to recall his training. It was a while since he had found himself in a combat situation and, in truth, he had never been very good at it anyway.

'Make a plan,' he said to himself. That was what he had been taught. If your opponent is confident, then he is at his most vulnerable. The idea being that an assailant who thinks he has the attack in the bag will move sloppily, he will make mistakes. This is the point where clear thinking and properly planned actions can turn the tables.

OK, thought Judy, there are two men outside the door, which is my only exit. They are bigger and tougher than I am, they are also armed. Clearly they are going to be feeling confident. Hence, according to combat training, they are at their most vulnerable.

Judy's plan was simple. He knew from the voices that one of his assailants was standing directly outside the cubicle door and that the other was slightly off to one side. What Judy would do was kick the door open with all his might, slamming it into the face of the first of his enemies. He must then follow through instantly. He must be out of the cubicle before the first man's nose had even started to bleed. Having emerged from the cubicle, he must immediately stick his fingers in the eyes of the second man, the one who was off to the side. He would have to move fast enough to give the second man no time to raise his guard. Then, with both assailants briefly disabled, he would run out of the toilet. He would not pause, he would make no witty cracks, he would simply run, for his foes would surely not take long to revive. So that then was the plan. One: kick the door open. Two: emerge and stab eyes with fingers. Three: run away. In this manner, Judy, a weedy man of five-foot-five with one leg slightly longer than the other, would get the better of two enormous, armed thugs.

Very gently he edged open the lock of the door, a necessary prerequisite for kicking it open. It was a tense moment. If they heard the bolt slip, he was dead. They didn't and Judy had the door unlocked. Holding on to the toilet paper dispenser, he drew his foot back against the lavatory bowl, getting ready for the mighty kick.

'Are you still out there?' he inquired, attempting a casual tone.

'That's right, and now we're coming in to get you,' the thug replied, thus establishing to Judy's satisfaction that the first assailant was still in the same position.

'Good,' said Judy, and with all the force that fear and loathing could summon up in his small body, he drove his boot against the cubicle door.

Sadly, the door was an inward opener. The whole cubicle shook with the impact, and pain shot up all the way from the tip of Judy's toes to deep within his bollocks. From there, the pain proceeded upwards through his agonised body, finally coming to rest at the back of his head and making his eyeballs rattle. Judy sank back on to the toilet seat as the two thugs burst in and started to beat him with rolled up magazines.

'Please, please, guys!' Judy screamed as the blows fell about his head and shoulders.

'Repeat after me,' said Cruise, beating Judy all the while, 'I am a stupid little queer and a disgrace to the Bureau.'

Agent Cruise had been nursing a deep resentment for Judy ever since Rosalie had cut his arm open in the desert. The humiliation of being cut up by some freaky little green chick had weighed heavily on him in the weeks since his return and he had come, irrationally, to blame Judy for the failure of his mission. Somehow he felt there must have been something in the environmental briefing he had been given that had been inadequate. Cruise concluded that Schwartz had stitched him up. Therefore, when Judy returned from his adventure on the stricken oil tanker, he found Cruise waiting for him and looking for trouble.

'I am a stupid little queer and a disgrace to the Bureau,' Judy shouted.

'And don't you forget it,' said Cruise, administering a final swipe with the magazine.

'Hey,' said Cruise's companion. 'It's nearly noon, we'd better get into the meeting, you know what Klaw's like if you're late.'

The man was referring to the monthly meeting of the FBI's Environmental Department, which all three of them had been on their way to when the ambush had occurred.

'OK,' said Cruise. 'Looks like you're off the hook for now, Schwartz, but you'll be back next month and I'm going to get you all over again.'

But by now Judy had had a moment's breathing space to size up his opponent and prepare a counter-attack.

'No you aren't,' Judy replied, 'because in the meantime I'm going to devote my life to hacking my way into your file and compiling a comprehensive list of every single bar-tab, taxi ride and hotel room you have ever claimed on expenses. Then if you hit me with a rolled-up magazine again, I will send that list to one of the numerous congressmen who got elected by promising to cut waste in government, so they can use your name in their personal crusade to haul in big spending federal agencies like the FBI.'

It was a complicated plan, but Cruise for one could see how effective it might be.

'Yes, well . . .' he said after a moment's thought. 'Just watch it, that's all,' he added rather weakly, and with that they all went into the meeting.

Dark suspicions.

The departmental meeting was not going very much better for Judy than the meeting in the toilet.

'You're saying you don't think the captain of the stricken tanker killed himself.' The voice of Judy's boss, Bill Klaw, was heavy with sarcasm.

'That is correct, sir,' said Judy, trying to sound firm.

'You find the guy, a known drunk, I might add, dead in his sinking ship, a bottle in one hand, a smoking gun in the other, his brains in the trash basket and you don't think he killed himself?'

'I've looked into his background, sir. I've found nothing that suggests a suicidal personality.'

'Oh, I see. In that case, of course there's *no way* he could have killed himself,' Klaw said, showing his exasperation to the whole room, in which thirty or so equally exasperated field officers were assembled. It was nearly lunchtime and nobody was interested in Schwartz's paranoid investigations . . . 'Brilliant deduction work, Schwartz.' Klaw continued in this withering vein. 'The captain never tried to kill himself *before*, so why should he now? Did you by any chance discover whether the guy had ever *lost a billion-dollar tanker and destroyed three hundred miles of coastline* before!! And if not, did it not occur to you that this might have been a factor in dampening his normally sunny disposition!'

'I don't think he killed himself, sir. I believe his ship was sabotaged and that the captain was murdered to prevent the discovery of that sabotage. I inspected the hold of the tanker, sir, accompanied by the ship's number two, a woman named Jackson. I have her testimony here . . .' Judy could see that Klaw was losing patience. He pressed on quickly . . . 'The condition of the ruptures in the walls of the ship were not conducive to the reasons given by the coastguard for the wreck, sir. I noted that the lip of the tears were predominately curling outwards, sir, which, you will agree, is very strange. A ship holed externally by treacherous rocks would have shown damage caving inwards, which it did, to a certain extent, but not entirely. Some of the damage distinctly suggested pressure from within. The kind of pressure which could only have been caused by an internal explosion.'

'What is this, Schwartz? The coastguard are satisfied that the ship got caught in a rocky channel. Are you moonlighting for the insurance company or something?'

'Insurance is not an issue, sir. There is no claim because the captain is presumed to have been drunk.'

'In that case, there's no possible motive for anybody wanting to sink the damn thing now . . .'

'What about the close proximity of the Natura ship, sir?'

'What about it? They're always there, aren't they? The little cockroaches.'

'Exactly, sir. In every case we've heard today, the Natura people were on the spot before even the emergency services. I've been studying the files, sir. It's happened numerous times; nuclear meltdowns, toxic leaks, Dodo syndromes, conveniently placed disasters occurring where no one could have predicted them, and with no one left to say what happened –'

'Schwartz, that's what happens with disasters, they pop up and they kill the people who are around.'

'And every time Natura are there to extract the maximum propa –'

'Are you saying these people are being tipped off?

That these well-meaning and highly-respected greenies are somehow being *used* by nastier, more sinister, less principled people?'

'I think it's possible, sir.'

'Who?'

'Mother Earth, sir,' said Judy firmly. 'They were definitely present on the Natura ship that approached the stricken tanker. I know, I encountered an activist on board. We've heard today from other agents who have detected a covert presence at similar disaster scenes. Agent Thompson,' Judy addressed a colleague sitting behind him, 'is it not true that Mother Earth were present at the scene of the most recent Five Mile Island meltdown?'

'Of course they were, it's in my report,' said Thompson testily. 'It was they who first alerted us to the leakage. They discovered it.'

'Oh, they "discovered" it, did they? Isn't that rather convenient?' said Judy. 'Sir, I believe we may be facing the nastiest piece of black propaganda in history.'

'OK, that's lunch,' said Klaw, closing his file.

As people began to leave the room, Judy approached his boss.

'Something strange is happening, I swear it. If I could just infiltrate them, get inside the organisation. Please. I've made numerous requests.'

'I know that, Schwartz, it's me that keeps knocking them back . . . Listen, Judy,' said Klaw, for a moment trying to be nice. 'You're keen, I like that, but you're not a cool, glamorous spy and you never will be. You're a shitty little assessment officer whose job is to compile shitty little assessments. That's it, no more. Now in words of one syllable, get the fuck out of my face.'

Despite his best intentions, Klaw just simply was not very good at being nice.

LFS.

The next day, Judy's luck changed. He was summoned to Klaw's office and shown a series of photos of the recent Mother Earth raid on the roof of the DigiMac Studios.

'Yes, I read about that,' Judy admitted. 'Pretty audacious stuff, eh? The leader escaped via a birthday cake, didn't she?'

'Yes, she did,' Klaw replied. 'And we're getting a lot of heat to make an arrest. The studio wants blood. It's getting sued by just about everybody who was at the damn restaurant. There's a full LFS developing.'

'That bad, huh?' Judy was impressed.

LFS or Litigation Frenzy Syndrome could leave families and communities divided, it could destroy vast corporations, it could leave grand and respected institutions broken in the dust. Studies had suggested that, left unchecked, LFS could eventually develop into civil war. LFS was, however, always checked eventually, due to the first law of legal dynamics. The first law of legal dynamics states that litigation will expand to absorb the amount of money available; a corollary of this law clearly being that all litigation will cease when the money runs out.

The LFS which was consuming the DigiMac Studio, and hence causing so much concern to Klaw, was a textbook example. A potentially dangerous situation of some kind had occurred, in this case, exposure to sunlight. Medically a very simple problem, legally a potential minefield. The moment the first rays of light had fallen on the beautiful people in the DigiMac commissary the

145

anguished cry had gone up, 'For God's sake, somebody phone a lawyer.'

Within minutes, the streets approaching the studio had been jammed with Rapid Response Litigation Teams. Over the years this type of development had become a major headache for the emergency services. It was not uncommon in the aftermath of an accident for the fire and ambulance people to find themselves unable to get to the scene because the roads were blocked with lawyers. As it happened, the DigiMac disaster required no medical assistance because the UV exposure had been so brief. This was great news for the law firms, it being recognised that the absence of specific injury was a classic catalyst in the development of LFS. With no actual physical problem to get in the way of vague speculation, the leap to the fantastical was much more easily made.

The first claims were obvious. Compensation would be required for the emotional stress caused by the *potential* damage via exposure to sunlight. The studio instantly recognised the danger it was in and mobilised its own damage control teams to counterclaim, their assertion being that their reputation as a responsible and caring employer was being irrevocably damaged by such wild accusations. Also, that the mere fact of being beautiful and famous meant that the litigants had set themselves up as terrorist targets, so in real terms, the attack had been their fault and they should pay for the roof.

All this had happened within minutes of the attack. A legal meltdown was occurring even before Rosalie had escaped from the building. Faced with the studios counter-attack, the original litigants hit back furiously. The second phase began, as claims were made on behalf of the children of the litigants. Children whose homelife would be rendered dysfunctional by the suffering caused through fear of their parents getting cancer. The logical knock-on from this, of course, was phase three: representations made on behalf of the as yet unborn and indeed unconceived offspring of the litigants, notional children whose future existence would be adversely affected by the case, should they ever materialise.

It was the acceptance in the courts of the principle of cross-generational suffering that made LFS such a terrifying phenomenon, because once it was accepted that a hypothetical future child could be affected, then clearly so could future grandchildren and indeed great-grandchildren. Presuming a reproductive rate of two children per adult, a lawyer who extrapolated a mere ten generations into the future could find him or her-self representing over a thousand hypothetically injured hypothetical parties, all of whose costs would be awarded against the plaintiff should their case prevail. This was, of course, presuming that the original litigant had only one family, something extremely rare in Hollywood. Then, inevitably, there were all the claims from friends and relatives (plus *their* future offspring) whose lives had also been adversely affected due to stress caused by knowing somebody who might have been exposed to dangerous sunlight.

All in all, it was a classic case of Litigation Frenzy which, within a year or two, would certainly destroy a mighty studio unless it could be contained. Obviously the money would run out in the end, and the first law of legal dynamics would apply, but that was scarcely a contingency to be desired. This was why an arrest was required. If a conviction could be secured against a person or group directly responsible for the outrage, then all other actions would go on hold for fear of prejudicing the case. The trial with all its appeals and counter-appeals would hopefully carry on long enough to dampen the worst excesses of LFS, possibly extinguishing them altogether.

Target.

'So we need to make an arrest,' said Klaw.

'How can we arrest anyone? They got away. I mean, we're the FBI. Investigation's not really our strong point, is it?'

'Don't get smart with me, Schwartz. We know who one of them is.' Judy was shown a series of photos of a woman falling through a Biodome roof into a cake and then running into the ladies' lavatory.

'We took these stills from the security video tape.'

'She's a bit blurred,' said Judy, stating the obvious.

'I know that, jerk, but not when she comes out of the john.' He held out another series of pictures of a small, pale woman in a saucy little dress rushing out of the ladies'.

'That's her, she took the dress off a bimbo in the toilet.'

'Very clever.'

'Sloppy security work. In these situations the only way to avoid suspects escaping is to shoot everybody. I tell these people till I'm blue in the puss, but do they listen? Like hell they do.'

Judy studied the photos.

'She's a unit leader,' Klaw continued. 'Agent Cruise was on to her but his cover was blown.'

'Yes, I heard about that,' confessed Judy. 'You know, I think he rather blamed me.'

'Of course he blamed you, you were the briefing officer.'

'Yes, and I also sabotaged his parents' gene pool, so that they'd give birth to a complete dickhead.'

'Shut up, Schwartz, and stick to the point. The girl's Irish. She works out of the Dublin Natura office. We've had her marked for a year or so, always hoped if we tailed her we might get something on Jurgen Thor. But now we've got to bust her. DigiMac and the city want an arrest, so the chick gets thrown to the scheisters.'

'You do know that we're not allowed to bust people in Ireland, don't you, sir?' Judy had often noticed a tendency in certain Federal agencies to presume that since America was the world's policeman then the planet was their precinct and US law applied.

'Yes, I know that we can't bust people in Ireland, you little fuck!' Klaw replied. 'But we have an extradition treaty with Europe on terrorism. The Garda will arrest her and hand her over to you for escort back to the US.'

'Why me?' asked Judy.

'Because she's a cute little girl, concerned for the planet, and we are the FBI which is slang for Satan to the liberal press. If she gets off a plane in cuffs with some big hairy thug bearing down on her, *we* look like the bullies even though *she's* the terrorist. I was going to send a woman, but then I thought, no, Judy's the one. Christ, you're such a nerdy little shit, people will feel sorry for you.'

'Thank you, sir. That's a lovely thing to say.'

Judy decided on this occasion to let what was clearly a palpable bit of nerdism go unchallenged. For he could see that, if he played his cards right, he would get what he wanted; a chance to infiltrate Mother Earth.

Chapter Thirteen

Astonishing vegetables and other surprising developments

City of the night.

D ublin was a night-time city. Not in the traditional, Parisian sense of an exotic world that occupies the town after dark, but in a literal sense. Dublin had become a night-time city. Most cities had. It was all a question of money. If a municipality could afford orbital filters like Up-Town LA, or if they had the money to enclose their pavements in BioTubes, then some semblance of traditional day-time activity could be maintained. But Dublin had never been rich, and so most activities now took place at night. It had begun gradually. For years people had simply put up with the inconvenience of ozone depletion. As the sun's rays became ever more deadly they had dodged from doorway to doorway and borrowed each other's BioBrellas, perhaps having their pores blocked as a special treat at Christmas.

Slowly, however, all over the world, it began to dawn on people that there were a good eight to ten hours in every day when the sun wasn't around at all. When it was possible to walk down a street or kick a fluorescent ball around a park without fear (from the sun, that is – you still had to breathe, of course). At first, in many western cities there was a strong objection to switching to night-time. It was thought of as something that only mutated peasants did in far away places.

'We'd look like a piss poor little fourth world cock-up country,' people said to each other, flattering themselves that they did not look that way already.

However, good sense eventually prevailed, and shops and offices began to open after sunset. The whole structure of the day changed. Twilight became morning, and people started to go to work at around six in the afternoon. Their evening's leisure time began at about four a.m. and the pubs closed sometime towards noon.

Of course, the European Federation had been promising to locate orbital shields for years, but they never did. Not over the cities, anyway. As always in Europe, agriculture came first. Hundreds of billions of ECUs had been spent sun-screening large patches of the countryside. This was so that quaint old ladies dressed in black could continue to bend their backs in tiny, chemically saturated fields whilst their husbands pissed it up in the local bar. In this manner, traditional country life was maintained. Also, vast quantities of semi-poisonous crops were produced that were then piled up into enormous food mountains, whose only use was that they provided some shade.

'What about us?' the city dwellers' representatives would occasionally ask. They would have liked to have asked more frequently, but they could not normally get past the near-constant demonstrations organised by the farmers. It was an accepted feature of European government that it existed under a state of siege and that mad farmers in huge combine harvesters would spend their lives blockading the various buildings designated for democratic debate and terrorist attack.

The representatives of the Euro city dwellers knew that their requests for BioShields were useless. Euro administration was entirely crisis-led. Every time the coffers in Brussels were deemed to be sufficiently full to start thinking about sun-screening cities, another civil war would break out. These wars smouldered endlessly across the vast continent from Lisbon to the Urals and could break out at any time, meaning, of course, that all the cash had to be spent sending soldiers to observe the genocide and say very firmly how horrid it was.

The European Federation's budget priorities were quite clear and had been for over half a century: first, the bureaucratic apparatus itself; second, the agricultural subsidy; third, observing genocide whenever it occurred and making a point of saying what a bad thing it was; fourth, everything else. Sadly, there was very rarely any money left for fourth, so any city that wanted an eco-defence was forced to pay for it from its own local taxes.

Hence, some of the countryside was on day-time, but not all, and some of the cities were on night-time, but again not all of them. The situation was much the same in America and South East Asia. It was of course far more confused in Russia where the whole thing changed on a twenty-four-hour basis and, indeed, from street to street. It was quite possible for a Russian to get out of bed, ready for a full eight hours' work, walk five minutes up the road and arrive in time to clock off at the end of the working day. By this means it was possible for people to rack up vast amounts of overtime and still spend upwards of twenty-three hours out of twenty-four in bed.

An actor does his research.

Max and Nathan were sitting in the bar of the Dublin Shelbourne Hotel at about three-thirty in the morning, watching the office workers drift in for an after-work refresher. They were waiting for their drinks. It had already been half an hour, but that is nothing at all if you have ordered Guinness. It is an article of faith for bar-staff in Dublin that a pint is not worth drinking unless it has taken about an hour to pour and another hour to settle. Those with any experience in these things ring the pub and put in an order before leaving home, but Max and Nathan hadn't worked that out yet.

They had been in Dublin for three days, searching for Rosalie, and had so far drawn a blank. The reason for trying to locate Rosalie, apart from the fact that Max had developed a crush on her, was in order to use her to research the movie that Plastic Tolstoy had commissioned. They wanted to get inside a Mother Earth unit. Actually, it was Max who wanted to get inside a Mother Earth unit. He was thrilled with excitement at the idea. Nathan would quite happily have made the whole thing up. He was not big on research.

'Shakespeare had no experience of the Roman Empire but he still wrote *Julius Caesar*,' he was fond of saying. In Nathan's opinion, if you took the experience and reality theory to its proper conclusion, he could only ever write about emotionally shattered middle-class Englishmen who had screwed up their lives and lost the only person they had ever loved.

'Exactly,' said Max. 'And that's just about all most English writers do ever write about. I admire that, it has integrity . . . it's dull, but it has integrity.'

Max believed that artists had to inhabit the thing which they wished to portray.

'You have to live the experience. *Be* the experience. If you're lying to yourself, then you'll be lying to the audience and, believe me, they'll know.'

'Oh, for God's sake, Max,' said Nathan. 'The last thing I wrote, a bloke cut off his own leg because a rat was eating it.'

'Then you should have cut your leg off,' said Max piously. 'My last role was about this guy who is indulgence-obsessed, right? It was a harrowing drama about a man addicted to having a great time. All he does is eat, drink and screw beautiful women. The guy's a hollow shell, right? His existence is empty and pointless. Do you think that scared me off? Do you think I shirked confronting the debilitating properties of excess? No way, man. I did my research! I went out and ate and drank and screwed around like some jerk trying to party himself to death. That's the point, man. I have commitment. Without commitment you're Jack Shit.'

'OK, so what about *Yellow Ribbon*, when you played that POW who got tortured and put in solitary for twenty years?'

'I researched that.'

'You did?' Nathan was surprised.

'Sure. The thing I figured was that the horror of the guy's situation had to lie in his *back history*, right? Back history is the whole thing for an actor. I thought, the guy gets tortured, right? So what? A lot of guys get tortured. How can I make this torture different? How can I make it *special*? Then it hits me. I think, if this man has lived a life of unadulterated luxury, that would make his suffering more acute and more ironic. You see what I'm saying.

To give the characterisation depth, in my own mind I needed to juxtapose his present torture and loneliness with a previous life of . . .'

'Eating, drinking and screwing beautiful women?' Nathan inquired.

'Exactly. I felt if I could get that side of things right, the suffering would develop naturally from there.'

Picked up by the greenies.

A sweet-looking little old lady approached Max and Nathan at their table.

'Mr Maximus?' the sweet old lady inquired.

'Sure, it would be a pleasure,' said Max, producing a pen and paper. 'Whom shall I dedicate it to?'

Although Max was disguised, he was still being recognised and always gave autographs when asked. This was partly because he was a nice person who did not like to disappoint people and partly because he was normally followed around by ten or fifteen journalists, waiting for him to refuse to sign an autograph, so that they could write stories about how rude and arrogant he was and how he had forgotten the people who made him what he was. On this occasion, however, Max need not have worried.

'I don't want a fucking autograph,' the sweet-looking little old lady said. 'You've been making inquiries at the Natura shop about a friend of mine. Follow me.'

They walked outside into the darkened, bustling street. In the park opposite the hotel some kids were playing a game of fluoro-soccer. The bright, glowing shoulder sashes danced about in pursuit of the moon-like ball. Max and Nathan stood on the pavement whilst the sweet old lady made a signal. Up the street a large car pulled into the traffic and across towards the hotel entrance. It was a big new Japanese limo, a real Eco-car, greener than green, as befitted a Natura vehicle. So copious were its filters that it emitted not one single poisonous gas of any sort. You could have put a flatulent elephant on the back seat and nobody would have been any the wiser.

Not for the first time, Nathan wondered where the hell these people got their funding. Natura always had the best transport. Mother Earth always had the best assault choppers. Whilst the IRA and the Basque separatists were making bombs out of fertiliser in their back garages, Mother Earth bought the best, direct from British and German businessmen, paying top dollar.

'Nice car,' Nathan observed. 'How many tin rattling volunteers does it take to buy one of those?'

'Get in,' said the woman, as the hotel doorman opened the back door for them.

They got in the car, Nathan experiencing his never-ending hotel dilemma of whether to tip the doorman or not. Max, of course, had no such problem. He was so rich and famous it would not have occurred to him to do something so mundane as tip a person. Max had people to do that for him. In fact, he was so big and special that even his people were too important to tip, they too had people to do things like that. It is a strange fact of power, fame, riches and general celebrity that the more you have, the more you get. Real celebrities never pay for a ticket to a show. They endlessly eat for free, it being generally assumed that, by simply gracing an event with their presence, the mega-sleb is making contribution enough. It is, in fact, possible to be so rich that you have no need for money at all.

Nathan tipped the doorman the price of a pint for five seconds' labour that he would have preferred to have done himself, and they got in the car. Once inside Nathan noticed that the rear windows were all blacked out. Max did not notice because, despite it being night-time, he was wearing shades. The sweet-looking, foul-mouthed old lady did not join them and they were left alone as the big limo pulled away. They could not see the driver because there was a screen between the front and the back of the car. Max lifted the screen. There were two men in the front.

'Hey guys,' he said. 'Where are we going?'

The front passenger pointed an automatic pistol in Max's face.

'Put the blind back down. If you lift it up again, even once, I'll kill you.'

Max put the blind down and looked at Nathan. Nathan was white with fear and shock. Max pulled the blind back up again. He and the gunman stared at each other for a few very tense moments as Nathan struggled to maintain control of his bowels.

'Ha! I knew you wouldn't do it,' Max said and dropped the screen again. 'You have to call guys like that,' he said to Nathan. 'It's a point of principle.'

They drove for at least three hours. First along straightish roads, then on what they guessed were winding country lanes and finally along what were clearly dirt tracks. Nathan passed the time by continuing to dwell on the cruel irony of his longing for Flossie.

'You see, I know now that I've always loved her. How could I not have known it then? I suppose, in a way, I made my biggest mistakes early on in the relationship, when I thought we were still happy . . .'

Max wondered whether, if he lifted the blind again, he could persuade the gunman to shoot Nathan.

The little stone cottage.

Max and Nathan were led blindfolded into a room filled with a wonderful smell. They heard their captors retreat and the door close behind them. The two men stood for a moment, unseeing and, they thought, alone, breathing in the splendid aroma.

'Cool smell,' ventured Max.

'Yes,' Nathan replied.

Something about the smell struck a chord in Nathan's memory. It took him far back to his childhood. Back past years and years of tired, joyless, fantastically expensive media lunches in Soho, back to an almost forgotten time when he had still enjoyed food. A time when the only connection between the words 'eating' and 'meeting' was that they rhymed. A time before irradiation, before menus featured 'lite alternatives' and butter carried a government health warning. Yes, that smell took him back. It also plonked him right down in the present. He was hungry, very hungry.

'Stew,' he said out loud. 'Stew with dumplings.'

'That's right, it's nearly ready,' they heard a soft, female voice say. It was an oldish voice with a strong Irish accent. 'You can take your blindfolds off now, boys.'

The two men removed their blindfolds and found themselves in the kitchen of a little stone cottage. An old lady was sitting at a wooden table. A very old lady. Max would have put her at a hundred and fifty plus. Her hair was grey and there was far too much skin on her face, enough skin, in fact, for two faces, Max thought, maybe three. This wasn't age, this was disease. Max felt a little ill just looking at her. What sort of horrible affliction could cause such deformity? Was the woman a leper? Whatever it was, Max sure didn't want to catch it. He moved a step back towards the door.

The woman was peeling a pile of strange brown lumpy things, stranger even than she was. They looked like tumours hacked from the body of a fourth world nuclear power worker. Beside the tumours, spread out on a bit of newspaper were some weird, bent, orangy long things with hairs growing out of them and knobbly bits sprouting out at various angles. Neither Nathan nor Max had ever seen anything like these ugly-looking lumps. Instantly, the hunger which they had been feeling so keenly vanished. They did not want tumours with their stew, no matter how nice the smell. Nor hairy lumps. Perhaps it was eating the tumours and lumps that had made the old lady look the way she did.

'Where are we?' Nathan asked, wishing he was somewhere else.

'Well now,' the old lady replied, 'we're hardly likely to be going to the trouble of bringing you here in darkened cars, blindfolded and all, just to tell you where you are the minute you arrive, are we?'

There was a brief silence, then Max asked the question that was actually foremost in both their minds.

'What the hell is that stuff on the table?'

'Potatoes and carrots,' the lady replied.

'No way,' said Max. 'I've seen potatoes and I've seen carrots, and they aren't anything like that stuff. That stuff looks like dogs' balls. In fact, it looks like something you'd cut off a dog's balls.'

'I don't wish to hear language like that in this house, young man,' the old lady said.

The money.

Max was rather taken aback. He was so rarely ticked off by anyone that he did not know how to react. If you are a star and you live in LA, you will literally never be contradicted.

In movie language, a star is known as 'the money'. This is because it is very difficult to get a project financed without a star attached. In any industry, money is virtually all that matters. Hence in the entertainment industry, stars are virtually all that matter. Their power and influence are awesome and far outstrip any talent or ability they might have. This is not to say that stars have no talent, many are fine actors. It is just that it is not physically possible to be talented enough to justify the kind of money that really big stars earn. God simply does not make human beings that good. This is why stars are not measured by ability, but by what they earn.

'Hey, granted, the guy's screen presence was hewn from a block of solid teak, but have you any idea how much he *earns*?'

The star is not an actor. He or she is the money. Hollywood is an industry town. Everyone has a script to be read or a portfolio they want looked at. You do not get those sort of breaks by badmouthing the money. Hence, no star is ever contradicted.

Back in the cottage.

The old lady, however, (whose name was Ruth) did

not have a script she wanted reading, or a portfolio to be looked at. It was years since Max had met anyone like that.

'You don't walk into a person's kitchen and start being foul about her veggies,' Ruth said. 'What on earth would your mother think?'

Max considered a moment.

'My mother wouldn't mind,' he said. 'She likes foul. In her case, foul is a life-style choice. She just did a centrespread in *Penthouse*, split beaver, the lot.'

Now it was Ruth's turn to be taken aback. She raised an eyebrow as if to say 'it takes all sorts' and returned to her peeling. The door opened and an old man entered. He had clearly contracted the same disease as the old lady, for his face too was baggy and creased. If anything, he seemed to have the plague worse than her, for there were great sacks under his eyes, red veins all over his nose and great tufts of pubic hair coming out of his ears. Max was nearly nauseous.

'This is my husband, Sean,' the old lady said, putting the chopped potatoes and carrots into boiling water. 'My name's Ruth. We're Rosalie's grandparents. She'll be along in a while. Meanwhile, will you have something to eat? It's nothing much, stew with dumplings, 'taters and carrots.'

Both men hesitated.

'Those potatoes?' Max inquired.

'These are what spuds actually look like, you know,' Ruth said. 'The knobbly bits and the eyes, that's a real potato.'

'You're kidding me,' said Max.

Ben Elton

The great visual food joke.

But the old lady was right. Generations ago, before the great visual food joke had been perpetrated upon the public by supermarket owners, potatoes had eyes and carrots had hairs.

Unfortunately, real food is notoriously volatile. Filled as it is with endless bacteria and trace elements, it is delicate to grow and goes rotten easily. This is a bugger for accountants trying to use shelf-space cost-effectively. What the food suppliers needed was to get the public to accept vegetables and meat which were entirely anaesthetised and uniform. Anaemic, tastless crap of a constant shape and size that would be easy to grow and transport and would last a long time. The joke was that it turned out that the public actually preferred their food this way because it looked nice. People were attracted to small, hard pale red tomatoes and small, hard pale yellow potatoes, they looked clean and fresh, with no horrid bits to have to cut out.

Only two groups objected: the blind, obviously, and the makers of magazine-style, public involvement TV programmes. The programme makers' problem was that they had, of course, lost their best visual gag. With uniform-shaped vegetables there were no longer any to be found that were shaped like genitalia. The vegetable nob gag was a hardy annual which had kept generations of television viewers amused. People had vied with each other to send in the rudest shaped carrots and the most suggestive marrows. Sadly, the great visual food joke had put an end to the laughter.

Revelation stew.

Max and Nathan could not believe their tastebuds. The meal was a sensation. Never had they imagined such carrotyness or potatoeyness. The lamb in the stew tasted as though a thousand lambs had been blended into a single chop. The onions and herbs created an orgasmic richness that left their tongues lying at the bottom of their mouths, exhausted, satiated and saying, 'That was wonderful, darling'.

'We still farm organically here,' said Sean. 'You can't do it entirely properly – the water table's as poisoned for us as for everybody else – and we have to use artificial sun. But we do all right.'

'You do fantastically,' said Nathan, mopping up the gravy with bread. For a moment he almost felt happy, then he remembered that Flossie didn't love him any more and reminded himself that he would never feel happy again.

'And that's not all,' said Ruth, having modestly received Max and Nathan's unstinting praise. 'Look at this!' and from her apron pocket she produced a carrot that looked exactly like a big dick with two little bollocks. 'I just couldn't bear to cut it up until I'd shown it to Sean,' she said, her eyes damp with laughter. 'Isn't it a scream?'

They all agreed that it was indeed a scream and, after they had stopped laughing, Max and Nathan had second helpings. When they had all finished eating, Max felt so kindly disposed to the two old people that he decided to bring up the subject of their illness.

'Listen, guys,' he said nervously, 'I don't know what's wrong with you, but I'm sure I could recommend someone who could help. You know with your . . . faces.'

Ruth and Sean were clearly not following Max's gist, so he attempted to explain. 'You know, all the flaps of skin and the ear hair and . . . well, there are doctors who can . . . Ouch!'

He said 'ouch' because Nathan had kicked him under the table. Nathan understood that there was nothing at all wrong with Ruth and Sean. They were just old. Although, even to Nathan, who lived in a far less cosmetically adjusted world than Max, the old couple did look weird. Just about everybody had *something* done when their faces began to fall. A little tuck, a touch of electrolysis, a hint of colour, but these two had absolutely left nature to take its course.

'There's lots like us, you know,' said Sean.

Max hoped not.

The meal over, they sat around with a glass of beer and chatted. They could have talked about anything. Between them they had a world of experience. However, within thirty seconds Nathan had worked the subject around to him and Flossie.

'People say I'm just experiencing classic jealousy, but I don't agree. You see, Ruth, I love her, I truly do, I know that now . . .'

Fortunately for Nathan, just as Max was about to strangle him, they heard a truck outside. Dawn had not yet broken but when Ruth crossed nervously to the window she could make out a familiar shape. Moments later, Rosalie had joined them in the cottage.

'Hello again,' said Rosalie to Max as she entered, hanging up her beret and gun.

Max did not know what to say. What he felt like saying was, 'Hubba! Hubba! Hubba!', which was the preferred method by which he and his friends at school had informed each other that they had met the girl of their dreams. If Rosalie had spoken to the depths of Max's soul before, now she was shouting through a loudhailer. To see her in the wild country (anywhere out of town was wild for Max) with a beret and a machine-gun, was to see a vision, a vision of strength and sauciness. Max thought about asking her to marry him, but he recognised that this might be considered a little presumptuous on only their second meeting. Anyway, he had only been divorced a few days, and did not wish to appear flighty. Particularly in front of his future granny-in-law.

'Hi,' he said, feeling that he could have done better.

'Well now,' said Rosalie. 'Who's your friend?'

'His name's Nathan Hoddy.'

'I'm a screenwriter,' said Nathan, 'and I thought I didn't love my wife but then she left me and it turned out that I did love her after all. Actually, you and I met at Plastic Tolstoy's, when you tried to kill him and had to hide in the rain forest, but you probably don't remember.'

The long arm of the law.

Outside, the Garda, as the Irish police are known, were surrounding the cottage. They were acting on a request from the FBI who wanted, as Judy had learnt from Klaw, to bring Rosalie back to the United States in order that she might face trial for the DigiMac hit. Had the FBI not wanted Rosalie the Garda would have happily left her alone. Europe was full of terrorists. If a police officer really felt like busting one, they could be picked up in the local pub. There was certainly no need to schlep all the way across the country to do it. Particularly if it meant creeping about in the damp grass. 'For Christ's sake, will you stop your complaining,' the Garda sergeant said to his constables. 'Some coppers have to work for a living, you know, and it's not as if this is going to tax your powers as police officers.'

The sergeant was right. It certainly did not look as if it would be a difficult arrest. The truck that had brought Rosalie had left, as had the limo in which Max and Nathan had arrived. The cottage was entirely undefended and the occupants were on their own.

We are talking about a movie here.

Inside the cottage, Nathan was making his pitch. Pitching in the only way he knew how, desperately. As if he was in that terrible land of pale bungalows where ideas went to die.

'We see this picture as committed, ideology-wise, it will be *very* committed. Bimbo pic, this is not. *No way* are we in the business of compromise. Principle is a big word to us, prin-see-pull, three *very* important syllables. But we want to be number one. Of course we want to be number one. We don't *know any other numbers. We* want to be number one and *you* want to be number one because nobody remembers the guys who came sec –'

'Excuse me,' said Rosalie, who had never been pitched at before and hence was unused to such copious quantities of bullshit. 'Would you mind leaving aside the crap at all?'

'Of course not, no way! Let's leave the crap aside,' Nathan agreed.

Nathan always agreed. He was a writer and so during any pitch he simply agreed on instinct. The only way a writer can get his ideas across is through a process of aggressive agreement. The process is simple. The writer states his or her idea and then waits for the executive's objections. Having heard and considered them, the writer then fervently agrees with everything the executive has said, adding that he or she feels a complete fool for not having seen it himself. The writer then repeats his or her idea as if it were a summation of all the executive's points, thanking the executive for making it all so clear.

It sometimes works, but only if the writer is talking to an executive. Rosalie was not an executive and she was deeply unimpressed.

'Will you let me get this straight?' she said. 'You say that your man Plastic Tolstoy wants to do a movie about Mother Earth, and you want me to let you join my active service unit so that you can get all the details and the atmosphere down perfect. Am I right?' she asked.

'Exactly,' Nathan agreed, 'I *think* that's what I was trying to say, but I did not see it so clearly until you explained it.'

'You do recall, I'm sure, that I'm the woman who just tried to shoot the very fellow you want me to work for?'

'Ah, but that's the point,' Max chipped in. 'Plastic thinks he's going to use you, but really you're going to use him. We're in the driving seat! I'm the star, I have veto on any director, Nathan here will write it. Don't you see? We're in control. We can do a movie that makes you people look great, that makes *you* look great. A real hero.'

'I never heard such nonsense,' said Rosalie, and how Max loved the way that she spoke. 'I'm sure I don't know much about Hollywood, but I do know that the only person in the driving seat on a Plastic Tolstoy film would be the man himself.'

'Fillum?' asked Max. 'What's a fillum?'

'Film,' Nathan translated, 'Rosalie means a Tolstoy movie.'

'Oh, right . . . Well, sure we'll have to put the case for Claustrosphere a little in the fillum too,' Max conceded, 'but balance is good.'

'I like balance. Balance is sexy,' Nathan agreed.

'Damn balance,' Rosalie said, adding, 'Sorry, Granny.'

'I agree with the point Rosalie just made about balance,' said Nathan, 'I don't think we need it. I'm sure Granny agrees with me on this one.'

'Of course we need balance,' said Max.

'Exactly,' Nathan agreed furiously. 'We need balance, we don't need balance. It's a both ways thing, it *has* to be.'

'That's right,' said Max. 'Balance shows what big people Mother Earth are. People who are not afraid to see the other guy's point of view. Vulnerability is very big right now.'

'It's huge,' Nathan agreed, 'believe me, Rosalie. Vulnerability is huge. There was a new fillum premièred last month: no vulnerability, it *died*. Complete turkey. You could smell the gravy and the Brussels sprouts from outside the theatre.'

'You're both completely out of your little minds.' Rosalie picked up her mobile phone. 'I'll give the fellows who brought you here a call – they're only in the village. They'll take you back to Dublin.'

'What? Now?' asked Max.

'Certainly, now. The sooner you complete idiots go away and stop wasting my precious time the better. And I might add that I don't care if I never see or hear from either of you again.'

'So it's a "maybe" then?' said Nathan.

'Rosalie,' pleaded Max, seeing his chance to get to know her better slipping away. 'We are going to make you into a national hero!'

'We are talking about a *fillum* here,' Nathan added.

Neither he nor Max could begin to comprehend Rosalie's attitude. They thought it must be a joke. In the world in which they lived, a green-lighted movie with the budget in place was *the* life goal. Nobody turned it down.

'Mr Hoddy,' Rosalie asked, 'if this *movie* goes ahead, how long before it gets shown?'

'From now? Ideally eighteen months. Realistically two years tops.'

'Yes, well it's my belief that there may not be a world to show it to in two years' time. Perhaps everyone can take a little video of it into their Claustrospheres when the Rat Run happens! Good heavens, Mr Maximus, when I heard you were looking for us, I thought perhaps you genuinely wanted to join us.'

'I do! I do!' Max exclaimed.

'No, you don't! You just want to use us, that's all. It's a damn shame, that's what it is. A figure like you could have helped us with getting through to younger people and . . .'

Rosalie's voice trailed away. She scarcely liked to admit it even to herself, but she had been rather excited about seeing Max again. What is more, not for merely professional reasons. She had liked him the day they met at the DigiMac Studio. Liked him, even considering that he had had a horn grafted to his head at the time. He had also, of course, saved her from Plastic Tolstoy. Rosalie liked men who did that sort of thing. Yes, there was no doubt about it, Rosalie had been a bit taken with Max Maximus. Now it turned out he was just another shit who was working for Claustrosphere.

'I wouldn't let you near one of my operations if you were Jurgen Thor himself.'

Max could see that he had a lot of ground to make up. He was just about to start the process when events overtook them.

Chapter Fourteen

A standing ovation

Under siege.

Outside, the Garda were in position. The Inspector of Police in charge of the arresting party fired his revolver into the air and informed the occupants of the cottage via megaphone that they were surrounded. The Inspector added that he and his men were there in order to arrest the woman known as Rosalie Connolly. If she came out quietly nobody would be hurt and no other person would be arrested.

Inside the cottage there was silence for a moment. Rosalie's eyes burned into Max. She was wondering why the Garda had come now. Did this American and this Englishman have something to do with it? Rosalie did not mind Yanks, but she was not big on the Brits at the best of times, and it did seem strange that the Garda had followed so hot on the heels of the two movie men. Max shrank under Rosalie's gaze. He was a fine actor, he had made a career out of communicating a thought with just a look. He could also read the thoughts on other people's faces. He knew what Rosalie was thinking.

'Rosalie, I swear I –' he started to protest his innocence, but Rosalie's gran cut him short.

'This has nothing to do with you. So shut up, keep your head down and you won't get hurt.'

Her husband was sweeping china ornaments from the beautiful old chest that stood in the corner of the room. Having cleared the top, he opened it to reveal a stash of arms.

'If you fight,' said Max, 'I fight too.'

'What!' Nathan gasped.

Ruth too was surprised, but she was not about to look a gift horse in the mouth.

'Can you use a gun?' she asked. Max gave her a pitying glance.

'Ruth, I come from LA. Most times it's a question of trying to remember how *not* to use a gun.'

Sean thrust an automatic rifle into Max's hands. He offered one to Nathan.

'We are here to pitch a *movie*,' Nathan pleaded in horror.

'Not any more!' cried Max. 'We're defending the homestead!'

Max was terribly excited. He loved to do mad things and they did not come much madder than this. In fact, the only thing he loved more than doing mad things was doing mad things in front of beautiful girls. Particularly beautiful girls with whom he would dearly love to spend long romantic evenings, drinking wine, talking and eventually screwing for an inordinately long time and in a variety of interesting positions and different domestic locations.

Nathan could see that trying to reason with Max would be useless, and dived under the kitchen table. He could think of nothing better to do.

Ruth and Sean were both armed now. Sean ran out of

the kitchen to cover the back of the cottage, whilst Ruth knocked out one of the kitchen windows and prepared to fire. Max, taking his cue from the gun-toting granny, also knocked out a window and then inspected his weapon. He wanted to ensure that he fully understood its working and would not be fumbling to reload when the heat got hot. Rosalie too had got her weapon from the wall and for a moment she seemed ready to start shooting, then however she stopped and her face fell. She stood dejected in the middle of the kitchen.

'Gran,' she said, 'this is stupid. We're trapped, we can't shoot it out, they have us cornered. Besides, we don't want to kill a load of innocent coppers. I mean, that's no good, is it?'

'But, sweetie,' said her gran. 'The stuff they've got on you, they'll put you away for ever. You'll do thirty years.'

'There aren't thirty years left, Gran.'

'Exactly, darling, which is why you have to be free to fight.' The old lady's knuckles were white over the trigger. 'No copper ever stopped your mother and father getting shot outside Sellafield, did they? The police may just be innocent boys, but their job is to defend the things that are killing us all.'

Sean shouted from the other room. 'Your gran's right, Rosalie! They mustn't take you. The trail bike's all ready in the sheep shed. If we cover you, you can get along the stream gully to the dry-stone wall and be away!'

'Sure, and have my own grandparents tried as cop killers.'

'We don't have to hit them,' Max interjected. 'We just use our fire to pin them down.'

But Rosalie was adamant. The place was surrounded

by armed police and, as far as she was concerned, she was nicked. Outside, the Inspector of Police reacted to the clear signs that the cottage was preparing to defend itself. He informed them in no uncertain terms that they were hugely outgunned and that any threat to his officers would be met with the full force at his disposal. The Inspector's point was basically that Rosalie was cornered good and proper so why should anybody have to get killed? Rosalie agreed with him and decided to give herself up.

Inside the cottage Max started to take his clothes off.

The actor prepares.

Max's plan was simple. He was, he reminded them, short and slim and also a brilliant actor. It was still only half-light outside and, as far as anyone knew, none of the Garda had ever seen Rosalie personally. Yes, they had probably seen her arrive, but it would have been at a distance and in the dark. Even if they had used night-sights, they would really only have been able to make out her clothes. Max explained all this whilst stripping down to his underwear before the startled group.

'Come on, come on,' he snapped. 'Give me your clothes! They'll have seen your clothes.'

'Don't be bloody stupid. You don't look a bit like me.'

'Hey lady! This is my bag, OK? My space. I know what goes down . . . It's dark, it's cold, the cops want to bust some ass and go home. So, let them bust my ass. Believe me, acting is about bluff. If you do it with chutzpah people will buy it, no matter how unconvincing you are.' Max spoke with conviction, having recently attended an Arnold Schwarzenegger retrospective at the American

Film Institute. 'If I go out there with your beret pulled over my ears, a little bit of make-up and a dress they won't think Jack Shit about it. Get real, Rosalie, what are the chances of an American movie star walking out of this cottage dressed as a babe terrorist? Zilch. The cops wouldn't believe it even if I showed them my dick. They saw you go in, they'll see you come out . . . Besides which, what have you got to lose . . . to be sure my little darling?' This last, Max delivered in a good approximation of Rosalie's Irish accent. He also raised the pitch of his voice a little, not a great deal, just enough. Not all women have high voices by any means and there is nothing less convincing than a man squeaking to sound like a woman.

Rosalie wavered no longer. She pulled off her jumper and dress.

'What do I have to lose? If they suss you, which they will, so what?'

'Exactly,' said Max. 'But they won't.'

'They will if you say "to be sure",' said Ruth. 'I don't think I've ever heard an Irish person say that in my life.'

'I'll need the bra, I'm afraid,' said Max, unable to stop himself glancing appreciatively at Rosalie's body . . . It seemed so, he didn't know, real . . . 'and something to stuff it with.'

'You won't need much, I'm not one of your Hollywood types.'

She turned her back to him and took off her bra, replacing it with a T-shirt that her gran handed her from the clothes-horse by the fire.

Max began to construct his character. He had shaved only a few hours earlier at the hotel, and, by adding a little powder that Ruth supplied, he managed to conjure up an acceptably smooth skin. Some lipstick and a tiny nod towards eyeliner changed him out of all recognition . . . although, of course, he still did not look a bit like Rosalie. Rosalie had been wearing big walking boots with her dress, long woollen socks, a greatcoat over it all and her chestnut hair tucked into a black beret. Max's hair was nearly shoulder-length so he was able to get away with that and, having borrowed a pair of farmer's boots from Sean, the magic was beginning to work.

'You know something, Max,' said Nathan, who had emerged from underneath the table, 'you might just get away with it.'

'I don't know any Max,' replied Max in his gentle Irish accent. 'Jesus, you know I'm still half-tempted to shoot it out with these Garda bastards.'

Nathan couldn't believe it. Max had only just popped the frock on and he was already doing the usual actor crap. Nothing in the world frustrates writers more than when actors claim to be getting 'inside' a role, and refuse to drop it. This is because the writer, who has normally created the character, suddenly finds him or herself being told that they understand nothing about it, that only the actor can truly inhabit the soul of the part. Nathan had no such investment in Max's current characterisation, but he still hated the way actors tried to imply that acting was 'real' and not just pretending.

Max squatted down and did some deep breathing. He stood up and did some stretching. He stood on his head. He lay on his back and hummed, the hum growing into an articulated note . . . 'mmmmmmaaaaAAAAHHHHH.' He got up. He was ready. He walked to the window.

'If I come out,' he shouted in his Rosalie voice, 'will

you be after leaving my Ma and Pa be?' Rosalie winced somewhat at his choice of language, which seemed to be rooted somewhere in the nineteenth century, but she could not deny that the accent and voice were good.

'We're not interested in the old couple,' the Inspector of Police replied. 'You're all we want, Miss. We'll bring a truck up, you can walk out, we'll put you in it and be gone.'

'All right,' Max shouted. 'I'm coming out. If you break your word now, the sweet Holy Virgin Mother of God and Jesus will know about it.'

Max turned away from the window. Rosalie decided to venture a bit of advice.

'Maybe a bit less of the Irish stuff,' she whispered.

Nathan could have told her it was madness. You just did not criticise an actor mid-performance. Max may have been falling in love with Rosalie, but an actor is always an actor first and a human being second. He turned on her with a look of such ferocity and contempt that she actually backed away.

'Look, *babe*!' he hissed, '*I'm* the poor bastard who's actually got to make some sense of this crappy little part! *I'm* the *dumb schmuck* who's actually got to get out there and *fucking do it*!'

'Sorry,' Rosalie whispered. 'Actually, I think it's brilliant. I really do.'

She was catching on fast.

Max collected himself. They could hear a truck drawing up outside.

'Just go out there and *fucking enjoy it*,' Nathan murmured under his breath.

Max picked up his automatic rifle and, holding it above his head, kicked open the cottage door and stood, silhouetted in the dawn light. He paused for a moment and then cried, 'Before God I surrender my worthless body to you, but my immortal soul you shall not have! That I keep for myself and the Earth which bore me. And I tell you now, you agents of immoral laws, better men and women shall follow me and a new law will prevail! A law for life and for the planet! A law for children! A law for the future! You cannot stop us, for we are the Earth and all that lives upon it!'

With that, Max hurled his gun down and stepped forward towards the truck where the Inspector of Police was waiting, visibly moved.

'Miss,' he said, 'I have to take you in, but let me say it grieves me to do so.'

'You must do your duty as you see it, Inspector,' said Max and, walking past him coldly, he climbed into the back of the Garda truck, handling the dress like he'd been born in one.

From the cottage they watched as the Garda pulled away, police gunmen retreating from behind every bush and rock.

'All I hope,' Rosalie said, 'is that when I do go, I go one half as well as that.'

The sign of a good performance.

God he had been good.

As the Garda truck pulled away from the tiny stone cottage and began to bump slowly along the rutted dirt track, it flooded in upon Max just how good he had been. The performance of a lifetime! Had such a triumph ever been presented at the New York Met or by the Royal Shakespeare Company? Max thought not. He had successfully hoodwinked armed police into accepting that he was a wanted green terrorist, a *female* wanted green terrorist. And the show was not over yet, the fat lady was a long way from singing the 'Star-Spangled Banner'. Here he was in the back of a truck, with two constables and an inspector not three feet from him and still his extraordinary characterisation continued to utterly encapsulate his audience. He had them eating out of his hands.

God, he was good.

But theatre is a bitch of a mistress, as they say. She always wants more, more! More! She won't let go until she's handcuffed you to the bed, spanked you hard and made you plead for mercy. Max knew he must focus! Concentrate and focus! That was all great acting consisted of, concentration and focus, and good bones, of course. Good bones were terribly important, but fortunately Max had been amply blessed in that department. Concentrate! Mustn't lose it now, must *focus*. Max discreetly checked that his knees were right . . . not glued together, just gently side by side, an unaffected, girlish, athletic grace was what was required, not some tarty come-on pose . . . Perfect, the legs were perfect. Now, hold the body firm, don't slouch, you're Joan of Arc, not some used-up bar girl. Proud bust. 'If you've got it,' Max thought, 'flaunt it.' Don't thrust, though! Make the bosom work for *you* not vice versa. Now the head. Chin turned slightly away, let it drop, sullen, but defiant. The tiniest gap between the lips, short, angry breaths . . . And the eyes! The eyes are everything. 'If you get the eyes right,' Max's old triple-M (movement, massage, meditation) tutor used to say, 'you can play the part in a tutu and rubber waders and people will believe in you.' Let the eyes blaze. Fire and defiance. A cornered dog. A wild thing trapped.

Max's spirits soared. How long could he maintain the pretence? To trial, perhaps? Could he actually get himself imprisoned? The theatrical possibilities were mind-boggling . . . and when the story came out! He would be the toast of Hollywood. A play would be written. A movie made! There would be personally sponsored VR games . . . 'Max Maximus asks "Could you act well enough to kid the cops and save the world?"' Max had struck a blow for all actors! He had proved that their very special and delicate talents could be used to protect the environment. That they were not just a bunch of neurotics who liked dressing up, but crack assault troops in the battle of life. Max was positively tingling with his triumph.

Not physically, of course. As far as the policeman and woman sitting opposite him were concerned, he was not triumphant but defeated. His whole body suggested a wild woman chained and captive. Except for one bit. One bit of his body suggested neither a woman nor captivity. For unbeknownst to Max, his private excitement was beginning to show. Just as it had done on his last morning with Krystal, Max had often teased a reluctant appendage into action by dwelling upon his enormous talent, and on this occasion the process was underway without even being prompted. The Inspector and the woman constable watched in astonishment as a bulge appeared in their captive's lap. Whilst inwardly discreetly congratulating himself on his brilliance, outwardly Max was taking a standing ovation. The Garda could not believe their eyes as the bulge strained at the cloth of the dress and thrust itself ever upwards. Growing right there in front of them, reaching up to the feminine chin that rested in the delicate cupped hands above it. '*J'accuse*,' that straining bulge seemed to be saying, '*j'accuse*. This woman is not a woman and I, a proud, full-blooded erection am here to prove it.'

Busted.

Back at Ruth and Sean's cottage, Rosalie was just getting ready to leave when the Garda returned.

It was a cruel blow. Moments before, they had been celebrating Max's extraordinary success. Rosalie knew that she owed him a favour and she promised Nathan that if he remained in Dublin she would re-establish contact the moment Max reappeared.

'They won't keep him long.' Rosalie was sure of that. 'The last thing the Garda want is the papers telling the world that a famous American Virtual Reality star tricked them into believing that he was a wanted Irish girl. There's enough jokes about the Irish as it is.'

She had just finished pulling on a change of clothes when they heard the roar of trucks hurtling back up the dirt track. There was no time to voice the disappointment they all felt. Rosalie moved as if she had to escape from armed police every day. She grabbed her automatic rifle and, pecking her granny and her grandad on the cheek, she ran out of the cottage and made for the outhouse where the trail bike was hidden. She was just kicking the machine into life as the Garda arrived. In the cottage, Ruth and Sean made ready to fire at the police vehicles. Nathan returned to his position under the table. There was the high-pitched rev of an over-tuned engine and Rosalie roared out of the shed and headed for the gully of the little stream by the dry-stone wall.

It was over in moments, the Garda did not even leave their armoured trucks. A single stun-shell from the riot cannon mounted on the front of the lead vehicle blew the bike out from under Rosalie and she landed heavily in the stream. Nothing was broken and she was on her feet in an instant. Peering out of the gully, she considered running, but what was the point? They'd got her and she knew it.

'Granny! Grandpa! Don't shoot,' she called as she emerged from the stream, her hands held above her head. 'No sense us all going to prison.'

Poor Ruth and Sean had to watch helplessly through the broken window as their granddaughter was nicked. Nathan tried to look elsewhere, furiously studying a magazine he found on a shelf. It is never a socially relaxing situation, being a guest in the house of people you do not know, as they watch a beloved relative get charged with numerous acts of terrorism and start what will almost certainly be decades in captivity.

'Don't you bastards understand!' they could hear Rosalie shout as she was handcuffed. 'The Earth's being fucked rigid. We've got to do something.'

'I have to tell you, Miss,' the Inspector of Police said, 'this poof here in the dress made a much prettier job of getting arrested than you're doing.'

Angry eyes.

They sat opposite each other in the back of the Garda truck, retracing the journey that Max had made so triumphantly a few minutes before. How different were things now! His costume, which previously had been his armour, his triumphal robe, was now just a stupid dress. Max had been hauled in by the law on many occasions, but this was the first time he had done it wearing women's clothes. He hated it. Still, in a way he was lucky. At least you don't get thirty years in the slammer for wearing lippy and wasting police time. You did, however, for a five-year career as a terrorist, and both he and Rosalie knew it. She was going to watch the world die, helpless to stop it, from behind prison bars.

'How did they suss you?' she asked.

Max was ready for this one.

'Oh, you know, performance is a myriad of subtleties,' he said earnestly. 'You get one gesture or expression out of place, even a thought, one tiny nuance, and the edifice crumbles. A single tiny moment misjudged and the whole house of cards collapses.'

'Your man here got an erection,' the policewoman said cheerfully.

'An erection!' Rosalie gasped in astonishment.

Max was mortified. With every moment he was becoming more and more attracted to Rosalie. And now this! Shame covered him as if it had been mixed with custard and poured on his head. He loved this girl, he knew that. He had felt it from the first moment they had met. He loved her soft Irish voice. He loved the tough things she did. He'd seen her in her underwear and he loved that too. What he wanted most in the world was to impress her, and he had a sneaking suspicion that the manner of his exposure was unlikely to do so.

'I couldn't believe it,' the policewoman continued happily. 'A big whopper, right there in his lap. I nearly hung my cap on it!' She was having a lovely day, this WPC. You didn't often get a chance to arrest movie stars in drag on the west coast of Ireland.

'That's enough of that, Constable,' the Inspector admonished sternly and silence fell for a moment.

Rosalie looked round. Searching for the source of the stiffy. There were two policemen and a policewoman. Rosalie knew that Max was not gay, not only from his reputation, but also from the way she had noticed him looking at her. That left the WPC. Rosalie was not one to judge a person by their appearance, but this girl did not look the sort to provoke uncontrollable trouser-based excitement. Particularly in a man who had recently been married to one of Hollywood's sexiest stars. The policewoman was large and rather dumpy . . . very attractive in many ways, no doubt, lovely hair, but scarcely an instant erection trigger.

'How come you got a hard-on then?' Rosalie asked Max finally, fixing him with her steady, unblinking, green eyes. Eyes that Max usually found drop-dead gorgeous, but at the present time found intrusive and frankly intimidating.

'Uhm, well . . . I just couldn't help it,' he replied.

'I presumed you couldn't help it,' Rosalie snapped. 'I didn't think you'd sat there and induced the damn thing. Why couldn't you help it?'

Somebody had once told Max that honesty was the best policy.

'Look, Rosalie . . . It was amazing, you know? My performance. To pull it off like that, to trick all those cops. It was like a career triumph, like winning an Oscar or something . . .'

Rosalie's eyes said it all. Whoever had told Max that honesty was the best policy was wrong.

Parting of the ways.

By the time the police convoy arrived back in Dublin, Max was almost tired of those gorgeous green eyes that he had found so fascinating since the first day he had seen them. They had glared at him in silent fury for the entire journey. They were so fierce and strong that Max was actually beginning to fear that their impact might by now have left permanent marks on his face.

The reason for Rosalie's fury was not just that Max's vanity had been the cause of her being about to spend the rest of her life in a cell. She was a reasonable woman and aware that the Garda were clearly on to her, and that she would have got nicked whether Max was there or not. No, her fury went much deeper than that, for it was fuelled by a wounded heart.

She liked Max. He had already saved her life once, in Plastic Tolstoy's Claustrosphere, and she had liked him then. Even tough, no-nonsense terrorist fighters have a romantic side, and Rosalie's was very well developed indeed. She was a wild country girl raised on fairy tales and ancient myths. If gorgeous handsome men wanted to risk their lives on her behalf, then she didn't mind a bit. Rosalie had wondered from the start whether Max might not be a little sweet on her, from the way she had caught him looking at her. However, she was not a vain woman, and thought it unlikely that such a colossal and rich star could be showing anything other than a passing interest. Therefore, when for a second time he had offered to save her bacon, she had been deeply moved. Rosalie had been brought up to believe that when you love someone you'll do anything to look after them and protect them. That certainly seemed to be what Max was doing. After all, aiding the escape of serious criminals was a pretty big crime in itself and Max had walked into it without a murmur. Now it turned out the whole episode had just been about an actor's vanity, a vanity so great that it had eventually ended in Rosalie getting arrested anyway. He didn't like her at all, he had just used her as an opportunity to show off. She hated him. She hated him because she had started to fall in love with him, and now she would never see him again.

The little Garda convoy eventually pulled up in the courtyard of Dublin's Central Police Station. Max was removed first.

'Rosalie, I'll –' he started to say.

'I wish I'd never met you at all,' she said, her eyes no longer fierce and strong, but liquid with sadness. 'And I never want to see you again.'

'You won't, love,' the Inspector assured her. 'They don't put men in women's prisons, not even transvestites.'

Chapter Fifteen

Unlikely saviour

Exit pursued by love.

Max was deported the next day. Nathan met him at the airport and was with him when the Garda escorted him to the plane. Except, of course, they did not get as far as the plane, not for quite a while anyway. Dublin Airport Authority, like all airport authorities, seemed to see it as their principal duty to herd passengers as far down the departure process as possible, before informing them that there will be a two-hour delay. They do not inform you that you are passing the last lavatory or the last bar or the last newspaper shop. That is something you discover for yourself once ensconced in a place called a departure 'lounge', which is defined as a room in which the sole facility is an inadequate number of plastic seats.

They stood, leaning against the wall. Nathan, Max and the two cops. For once it was Max's mind that was utterly preoccupied with affairs of the heart. All Max could think about was those green eyes staring at him and then filling with tears. Astonishingly, Nathan was not, for the moment, thinking of his beloved and unattainable Flossie. When you are talking about a movie, even love sometimes has to take a back seat.

'I have this great idea for the plot of our film,' he had said to Max when they met.

'If it's anything to do with cross-dressing, forget it. I'll kill you if you ever breathe a word of what happened,' Max snapped, 'and believe me, I know how to kill.'

'No, no, it's a bigger thing, a thematic curve.' Nathan was very, *very* excited. 'I am very, *very* excited,' he said.

'I don't care, I'm not interested. The world is a hollow and empty place and I am the hollowest and emptiest thing in it.' Max turned to the officers who were escorting him. 'Listen, guys. I have let down a woman I think I am in love with. I have to make it up to her, please unlock the cuffs.'

The officers did not move. Max pressed on.

'Please, guys. Try to forget for a minute that you're tough, hard, ball-breaking peace officers and get in touch with the child inside you. Ask that child what he would do.'

'We're doing you a favour putting you on a plane, son,' the first officer replied. 'If you start a relationship by apologising to a bird, you'll be under the thumb all your life. Jesus, you'll be after asking permission to go and get pissed in the pub.'

'That's right, pal. You have to be tough, forceful,' the second officer added. 'If you love this little lady, then ring her from the States and say, "All right, so I fucked up. So what? Do you have a problem with that, darling?" Tell her that and if she does have a problem with it, then tell her that she can fuck right off. There's plenty of birds in the world that aren't so fucking choosy.'

'That's right,' said the first officer. 'Besides which, you're better off sat in the pub anyway. At least your money's your own.'

'Thanks, guys. You've been real,' Max said, and the group lapsed into silence. The Irish cops' attitude reminded Nathan of the cops he had met at the Beverly Hills Fortified Village. He wondered whether this relaxed attitude to romance was common to all policemen. Maybe if he joined the police he would get over Flossie. Damn! He had let his mind wander on to Flossie again. Now he was as sad as Max.

Protective custody.

After Max had parted from Rosalie she had been taken to an interrogation room and asked a lot of questions about Mother Earth. She, of course, had told the police nothing. Partly because she would rather have died than sing, and partly because, like all members of even vaguely efficient secret organisations, she actually knew very little.

She did not, for instance, know where Mother Earth's detailed knowledge of the next environmental hot-spots came from. And she could not have told the police, even had she wanted to, how her unit and others like it were always able to be at the heart of the action so quickly.

'The intelligence people look after that stuff,' she told her interrogators. 'We just go where we're told.'

'So who pays?' they had asked, as they always did in such circumstances, Mother Earth finances being so notoriously shadowy.

'Rich green fellas, I guess,' Rosalie replied, and she knew no more than that. She had, of course, heard the rumours, as everyone had, that some megabillionaires were finally beginning to see sense. That they were turning the funds they had acquired destroying the Earth to the job of saving it. Rosalie did not, however, have any better idea than the police as to whom these dubious philanthropists might be.

'Oh, come on!' barked the policeman. 'The kind of equipment you people carry doesn't materialise out of thin air! That automatic rifle you were caught with is a state-of-the-art weapon. Our men don't have anything as good as that. Who the hell is supplying all that stuff?'

'I don't know, gentlemen, and if I did I certainly would not be after telling you now, would I? Now if you're going to torture me, will you please do me the courtesy of getting it over with?'

The chief officer adopted a slightly offended but still censorial tone.

'Sorry to disappoint you, Miss, but contrary to hysterical rumour we do not torture people. Not unless you count the food. Take her down, Constable.'

'When do I get to see a lawyer?' Rosalie asked as she was hauled to her feet by a tough WPC.

'You can see a lawyer in America. Good day, Miss.'

And to Rosalie's surprise, she discovered that she was not to be tried in Ireland at all, but handed over to the FBI for extradition to America. There she would face trial for the DigiMac Studio raid. Her departure was set for the following day. A magistrate had already issued the appropriate authorisation and there were no avenues of appeal. In vain did Rosalie protest that this was completely illegal, that they could not just hand over a European citizen to the American authorities. The truth was, of course, that they could do what they liked and were going to. The European Federation was so utterly plagued with terrorists (terrorism having taken over from car theft as the number one crime) that they were absolutely delighted when another country offered to take one off their hands. The head of the Irish Special Branch of EuroPol had actually phoned the US ambassador to tell him that they had hundreds more suspected terrorists awaiting trial, and the FBI were welcome to as many of them as they wanted. On behalf of the Bureau, the ambassador had politely declined the offer.

What kind of G-man are you?

The following evening, the Garda handed Rosalie over to the custody of the American authorities, embodied in this case by Special Agent Judy Schwartz.

'Hi, I'm Special Agent Judy Schwartz,' said Judy, offering Rosalie his hand. She kept hers, which were handcuffed together, firmly in her lap.

'You're a G-man?' she said. 'You don't look like one.'

'Oh, well, I can explain that. What happens is, when there's any rough stuff, what I do is I rush into a telephone box and put on fifteen stone of pure muscle and I get so handsome and cool it's terrifying.'

Judy didn't know why he bothered really, it never changed. No matter how many times he tackled nerdism head on, it never got any better. Ever since he had arrived in Dublin and met his opposite numbers in the Garda Special Branch he had been aware of the sniggering that followed him about. Judy sort of understood. The media had decreed many decades before what a secret agent should look like and it just wasn't like Judy. Judy realised that it was not really the fault of the people who laughed at him. It was society in general. After all, if you're a policeman and you're told that the FBI are sending an agent to pick up a terrorist, you do not expect somebody with one leg shorter than the other, thick glasses and crooked teeth. Judy *sort* of understood, but it still hurt, even after all these years.

Judy would have been pleased to know that on this occasion his little anti-nerdism joke did at least hit home. Rosalie nearly apologised, but then stopped herself. This man was, after all, going to haul her off for trial in the States. On reflection, she didn't care if she had offended him or not.

'I'll take charge of the prisoner now,' Judy said to the officers who were flanking Rosalie, but they did not move away. Instead, one of them snapped open one of the cuffs on Rosalie's wrist and locked it on his own.

'You're still on European soil, Agent Schwartz. We have to escort you and the prisoner to the airport and put you both on the plane.'

'Yes, of course,' Judy said. 'Well, I'm afraid I'm going to have to insist that, in the interests of security, the suspect is handcuffed to me.'

Judy met the surprised look of the big policeman steadily.

'This case is extremely important to the Bureau,' he explained. 'Ms Connolly is an experienced criminal, known to be shrewd, resourceful and tough. I cannot take any chances on us losing her.'

It took some guts to say it. There were four Garda officers in the room, and any one of them, including the woman constable, could have just about put Judy in their pocket. They laughed at him, of course. Even Rosalie could not help sniggering at the man's front.

'So what you're saying, Agent Schwartz,' the Inspector

asked, 'is that, in the event of the suspect playing silly buggers, you feel that you will be better placed to prevent her escape than my officers? Is that it?'

'I have been very highly trained, sir. No offence is intended.'

The Inspector just laughed again and instructed his man to handcuff the suspect to the American, if that was what he wanted. Judy asked for the key but was told perfunctorily that it was not Garda policy to leave the key with the man wearing the handcuffs. Judy could have it when they were on the plane.

And in this manner they left for the airport, Judy, Rosalie and two Garda officers. It was pretty much at the same time that Max and Nathan were heading out the same way. Rosalie, however, was destined to miss her plane.

Riveting viewing.

Judy and Rosalie stood apart from the queue as one of the officers checked them in for their flight. There were, as in all airports, numerous television sets hanging from the ceiling and attached to the walls. Some offered flight information, others offered what could loosely be called 'entertainment': cable music video channels, local morning TV and interactive games.

Many years previously, it had been decreed by the moguls of media and marketing that the human race was so utterly devoid of originality and creative powers that it was incapable of getting through even the simplest activity without some electronically delivered stimulus. Hence, shopping malls were suddenly suffused with tinny renditions of classic pop songs, wafting hither and thither amongst the discarded litter, dried up fountains and utterly repulsive sculptures. It was possible for old people to stand for ever on escalators that had never worked and die to the sound of 'Wonderful World'. Lifts, shops, even buses, all began to sing. When people rang up for mini-cabs they were forced to sit through fifteen minutes of commercial radio before being told that there was a three-day wait for cars at the present time. Noise joined the dazzling pot pourri of pollutants that the industrialised world was devising in order to make the fact of being alive ever more unpleasant.

Nor was it just aural 'entertainment' that was forced upon people who had previously been capable of doing their shopping without having to listen to orchestral arrangements of Beatles' hits. Televisions began to appear everywhere. The logic was that, because people liked to watch the television in their living-rooms, then they would surely like to watch it in all other circumstances. Coaches, shops and particularly pubs and bars were invaded. The appearance of TVs in pubs was surely the cruellest blow of all, for a pub is above all a place of social intercourse. It evolved out of a natural human desire to go out, meet other people and talk to them. A telly has no place in a pub. People do not have beer-taps in their living-rooms. A telly utterly destroys all possibility of conversation, for it is a physical property of all televisions that *the eye is inevitably drawn to them*. Its hypnotic powers know no bounds. If a telly is on in a public place, people cannot avoid staring at it. The sound does not even have to be on. No matter how boring the programme, and no matter how interesting the conversation one is having at the time, the eye will slowly drift over to the television and have to be constantly dragged back.

TVs can now be found in post offices, banks and police stations. Surely it is only a matter of time before they appear in operating theatres, which will mean a lot of wrong bits get cut off.

Handling the handlers.

Socially disastrous though these electronic intrusions usually are, they were good news for Rosalie, although she did not yet know it.

Judy had been waiting for his chance and now he saw it. One police person was checking them in, the other was momentarily transfixed by the silent broadcast of a morning shopping show being presented on a wall-mounted television nearby.

'Hope the flight's on time,' Judy ventured.

'Mmm,' the policeman replied, his attention else-where.

'I'll bet the VR helmets on the plane don't work,' Judy mused.

'Mmm,' replied the distracted policeman.

'Would it be OK if Rosalie and I were to jump across that empty check-in position and disappear through the rubber curtains on to the luggage belt?' Judy asked in a bored voice.

'Mmm,' the policeman replied.

Fortunately Judy had squeezed Rosalie's hand to get her attention, for she too had been staring at a TV set.

'Thanks,' said Judy. 'Let's go, Rosalie.'

And, handcuffed together though they were, they jumped across the check-in bay and pushed themselves through the rubber curtains.

'What in the name of goodness is going on?' Rosalie

cried as they began to glide along the conveyor belt with all the luggage.

'I don't think now is the time to explain,' Judy answered.

Up ahead of them, the baggage handlers were performing their duties as laid down by the airport authority. These consisted of flipping one catch open on every fourth bag, sprinkling red wine and bits of broken glass on everything and loosening one wheel on each baby carriage.

'Airport cops behind us,' Judy shouted at the baggage handlers.

He was pretty sure what their reaction would be, and he was right. The idea that the airport police had been set upon them yet again was a red rag to a bull for airport baggage handlers. They are notoriously easy to offend. Baggage handlers know that everybody hates them. They know that every individual passenger feels personally victimised by them, believing that their own particular bag has been deliberately held back. They know that everybody firmly believes the lengthy time it takes to get the bags to the carousels is caused by the handlers trying to decide what to steal. They know that the tatty, forlorn little unclaimed suitcase which seems to have been bolted to every carousel by the manufacturers is taken by the public as evidence that the handlers remove only one bag at a time from the aeroplanes and refuse to get another until that one has been claimed. All this the baggage handlers know and they do not like it. They believe it is the public who are the unreasonable and indeed immoral ones. They believe that the public deliberately fill any excess spaces left over after they have packed with lead ballast, in order to ensure that an adequate level of spinal injury is inflicted upon the handlers. They believe that it is the public who neglect to fasten their luggage properly, so that the bags explode in a flurry of dirty knickers on the conveyor belt. The handler is then expected to restuff them whilst all the while an inadequately wrapped granite boulder is bearing down upon him.

The public hates handlers and handlers hate the public. It is a universal truth and cannot be altered. If there is life elsewhere in space then it may be safely presumed that there are little green men and women exchanging horror stories about how their cases ended up in the wrong solar system.

'What aliens must think of our planet when they visit I just don't know,' the little green creatures will declaim loudly to each other as they mill aimlessly around the baggage collection transporter rooms. 'When we can't even beam down a few damn cases from the mother ship.'

All this antagonism has led to a sullen touchiness on the part of baggage handlers worldwide. It was these feelings of persecution that Judy was attempting to exploit when he announced that the two figures emerging through the rubber curtains behind them were airport police. He had judged the situation well.

'Right, that's it,' the handlers said to each other and turned off the conveyor belt. 'Yet again, we're being harassed by the company. Yet again, we're being categorised as a bunch of thieving job's-worths who have to be constantly spied upon in case we try to pinch a plane.'

And so a strike was called, which left the two Garda minders stuck on the stationary belt, struggling to follow Judy and Rosalie, whilst angry handlers expressed their antagonism to authority by heaping luggage in their way.

A not very alert security alert.

Outside in the arrivals hall alarm bells were ringing and police and soldiers had started to run around all over the place. This was all to the good, as far as Judy was concerned. For the airport, like all European airports, was on hair-trigger alert for terrorist attack. Every day, the authorities planned in meticulous detail where every soldier and every police person should run to the moment the alarms went off. They held a full dress-rehearsal once a week with smoke and blank bullets and everything. There were also regular false alarms which occurred when old ladies forgot to inform the authorities that they had packed a small handbag mounted mortar for personal protection. All this training meant that when the alarms went off, the soldiers and police at the airport operated with machine-like efficiency . . . only, however, if there was a terrorist attack underway. If, for instance, two handcuffed people were trying to slip quietly out of the airport together, the activities of the security forces were not merely irrelevant but actively counter-productive.

'This way,' Judy instructed Rosalie and, jumping off the conveyor belt, he pulled her towards the next set of rubber curtains along the line.

'But that's back into the check-in area,' Rosalie protested.

'I know,' said Judy, trying not to resent her for acting as if he was an idiot. 'Do what I tell you and we may get out of this . . . OK?'

Rosalie had nothing to lose.

'OK,' she said.

'Good. Now when we go through the curtains, hold up your arm so that everybody can see the cuffs, right? And shout out that it's all right, you've got me and everybody should be calm. All right?'

'But . . .' Rosalie attempted to interject.

'Look! You're a tough, beautiful Irish girl, right? I'm an American nerd. In terms of bluffing our way out of Dublin airport, who do you think should play the good guy?'

Rosalie could see the logic. She dragged him through the rubber curtains, emerging behind an Aer Lingus check-in girl who was in the process of telling everybody to be calm. The whole hall was a mass of confusion.

'Garda Special Branch,' Rosalie shouted, holding their arms aloft. 'It's fine. I have him.' And with that she thrust herself forwards past the Aer Lingus desk and into the astonished line of travellers. For a moment the crowd did not part, and Rosalie experienced a split second of panic as she thought the bluff had failed.

'Make way now! Clear a path,' she shouted, pushing on, dragging Judy with her. Rosalie need not have worried. The momentary hesitation on the part of the crowd in front of her was merely due to the fact that, even during a terrorist attack, the first instinct of a person in an airport queue is to protect their place. The nagging suspicion that everything that happens is a ploy by some other traveller to push in dies hard. Fortunately, Rosalie's natural ability to command and the inherent dignity of her bearing won through.

'Get out of the fucking way, all of you! I've got a killer here,' she screeched, flailing her free arm about and the people parted. They did more than part, they cheered and clapped. Judy had again judged the psychology of the situation to perfection. The sight of a pretty little local girl with flashing green eyes capturing such a nasty looking foreign weasel of a man filled the crowd with a sense of romance and pride.

'Death to all papists!' Judy shouted in his broadest Southern US accent. 'The Elitest Church of Christ the Crew-cut is the one true faith.'

Judy knew that Ireland is a country that has suffered more than most from religious bigotry over the years, and he reasoned that people would be pretty happy to see a bigot busted, particularly a Protestant one. He reasoned correctly. How they cheered as their brave girl cop escorted the evil zealot across the arrivals hall. People from other queues heard the commotion and walked across to see what the fuss was about. In a few moments, a large crowd was celebrating the victory of law and order over bigotry and violence.

'OK, let me through, this is isn't a freak show,' Rosalie shouted as the crowd pressed in. Judy began to regret inflaming the crowd, but help was on its way.

'Get back there, sharp now!'

The voice was that of an army sergeant who, seeing that a capture had been made, was following statutory instructions to facilitate an orderly arrest. Before they knew it, Rosalie was escorting Judy up an avenue of soldiers who, whilst grinning broadly, were holding back the cheering and rapidly growing crowd. People usually felt so helpless in the face of terrorism, that to see it temporarily vanquished was a massive thrill for everybody at the airport, soldiers and public alike.

'Good on you, you little darling,' they shouted. 'Hang the bastard.'

As Rosalie and Judy arrived at the exit the sergeant

marched up to them. He stamped and saluted in his proudest manner.

'Well done, Sergeant,' Rosalie said. 'You moved very quickly.'

'Thank you, ma'am,' the proud sergeant replied, 'and on behalf of the lads, may I congratulate you on nabbing the little shit.'

'That's very kind, Sergeant. Thank you. Now if you'd just hold this door for a moment while I get my man here into the Special Branch car, I'd be grateful.'

And whilst the army held back the crowd Rosalie and Judy went out and caught a taxi.

Chapter Sixteen

The loneliest girl in the world

Bitchin' pitchin'.

'OK, it's like this,' said Nathan, attempting to sound dynamic.

He was back in Plastic Tolstoy's office, perched on the very edge of the bottomless pit which Plastic called a couch, nervously gripping his empty soda glass and making his pitch. Nathan was at the crunch point. That point which must be faced in every pitch. The point when the pitcher knows that he or she can prevaricate no longer and that the actual idea must be stated. It is always a nerve-racking moment, because so often it is the last moment before ignominious failure. Nathan, therefore, like all pitchers, had put it off for as long as possible, spending a full ten minutes lucidly repeating the principles of his original brief.

'You don't want a story that slags off the greenies,' he had said in about six different ways. 'The greenies hold the high ground, we have to accept that. What you want your story to do is acknowledge the moral position of the Environmentalists, whilst showing the Claustrosphere company in a great light. Right?'

Plastic Tolstoy was losing patience.

'Nathan. I know this. *I* told *you*,' he replied testily. 'You think I'm renting you a house off Sunset to be told back what I told you already? Is that how things get done in England, huh? Jesus, excuse me! No wonder you guys lost an empire.'

'Yes, yes, no, fine. Just re-stating our position,' Nathan agreed hastily. 'You know, checking we're both coming from the same place.'

'Well, don't because we ain't. You're coming from being poor, and I'm coming from being rich, which means *you* have to impress *me*, which, I would like to tell you, so far is not happening. No impact is being made. I am looking around my office here and it is an impact-free zone. There is no zing in the air, no pow! No ideas bouncing off the walls. All there is, in fact, is nothing, and nothing, as the dead white guy said, comes of nothing. Certainly not enough to justify the exorbitant amounts of money –'

For just one moment, Nathan saw red.

'Oh, for God's sake, you smug bastard, will you shut your stupid face for a minute so I can explain my idea!!'

It was out before he could even believe he'd said it. Nathan went white with fear. He had shouted at Plastic Tolstoy. He had called Plastic Tolstoy an arrogant bastard. He had told Plastic Tolstoy to shut his stupid face. It is sometimes said that when a person is dying their whole life passes before their eyes. When you die in Hollywood your whole future passes before your eyes. The beach house you won't own, the waiters who will not be crawling to you, the twenty-seven page profiles which will not be being commissioned about you for *Vanity Fair*. All this and more passed before Nathan's eyes as the realisation of what he had done sank in on him and the dark shadow of Shepherds Bush fell upon his soul.

(Shepherds Bush being that place in West London where what was left of the once mighty BBC still lived.) A dark, shadowy place of plastic cups, underfunded projects and memos querying expense claims for a taxi ride and a sandwich. This was what Nathan was going back to and he would never see the Californian filtered sunshine, the swimming pools, or the money ever again.

Then Nathan noticed something strange. Plastic Tolstoy was still talking.

'I don't know, maybe I'm the only idiot in this town who pays for writers to tell me what he just said. Maybe it's a special talent I have . . . "that Tolstoy", they all say behind my back, "he pays for an echo". They're laughing at me . . .'

Nathan realised that the man had not even heard his outburst. Plastic Tolstoy had just kept right on going, happily developing his little comic theme, wallowing in the glorious sound of his own voice. As far as Plastic Tolstoy was concerned, Nathan only even existed when Plastic wanted him to.

'OK, so we've established what I want,' said Plastic, having finally exhausted the particular well of sarcasm from which he had been drawing. 'Now maybe we can find out what *you have*.'

'OK,' said Nathan, momentarily emboldened by his close shave. 'Mother Earth are always attacking the Claustrosphere Company because they claim that Claustrosphere people are hastening the end of the world. What our movie has to say is that Claustrosphere want exactly the same things that all those greenies want, they just happen to be a bit more responsible about it –'

'This I *know*!' said Plastic, but Nathan barged on before Plastic could get going again.

'The biggest mystery about the Mother Earth lot is where they get the money from, right? I mean, I've seen these people, they have limos, incredible tasting potatoes, everything. Some shadowy philanthropist is clearly bank-rolling them, but he just won't take the credit. Well, how about this? How about *we take it*! We say in our movie that it's *Claustrosphere that is providing the funding*! . . . I mean, what a great twist, right? All the time you've got these greenies attacking the very people who are paying for them to do it! But the Claustrosphere people just keep on paying, because they believe in the future of the Earth more than anybody and think Environmental protest is important.'

Plastic Tolstoy stared at Nathan and for once he did not speak. He was thinking. Nathan blethered on, as writers do when met by producer silence.

'I mean it is *the* greatest plot twist, don't you think?' he said, trying not to sound desperate. 'Like all through the picture, the greenies are trying to kill the head of Claustrosphere – we'll fictionalise him, of course – meantime, they're blessing this mysterious guy who makes it possible for them to continue the fight. Then at the end, they realise it's the same person! That Claustrosphere is part of the Green Movement! That's when they learn the error of their ways. I mean, irony or what? You've got to admit it.'

For a moment, Plastic Tolstoy seemed to be far away.

'It's an extraordinary idea,' he said finally. 'You told anybody else about it?'

'Have I, hell! There are more plagiarists in this town than at an Elvis convention.'

Maybe it was the mention of the name Elvis, that hallowed and imperial American name upon which his mother's fortune had been based, that decided Plastic. He seemed to snap out of his reverie all at once and make a decision.

'OK. We'll run with it. It's a good idea. It's a great idea. Go write the script.'

Factory town.

Nathan virtually floated out of Tolstoy's mansion. Even the thought of Flossie could not puncture his delight. He nearly sang to himself as he touched his sports coupé into action. His idea had been accepted! He was going to be allowed to write the initial script for a genuine fully-fledged feature. He knew it would only be the initial script, for it is a foregone conclusion in Hollywood that any feature will be written by more than one person. It has to be this way . . . so that the producer may remain in control.

Many artists working in Hollywood resent what they see as the factory mentality of the town. They consider it crass and wicked that their creative juices are seen as merely one ingredient in a cocktail which somebody else is mixing. They forget that Hollywood *is* a factory, and pretends to be nothing else. It has no sponsors, it receives no government money. Like a producer of canned food, it exists solely on the income it can generate in the marketplace. The Royal National Theatre of Great Britain may proudly commission plays that people don't like, written by tired old playwrights who don't like people, because it is generally considered to be a function of government to subsidise national culture. The New York Metropolitan Museum of Modern Art may be in a position to purchase an obscure arrangement of wire and pebbles from a talentless drug addict because some rich industrialist wants to cloak his brutal legacy with a veneer of culture. This is all well and good and no doubt much to be encouraged, but Hollywood can count on no such indulgences.

When somebody commissions a film in Hollywood they are spending money that somebody else has invested in order to make a profit, and, unless the artist is a committed Marxist, then he or she has no real grounds for complaint. They may moan about artistic freedom, financial censorship, making room for ideas to grow, but in other industries the creative elements do not expect such indulgences. The chefs at Heinz do not consider it outrageous that their bosses aren't interested in a fascinating new recipe they are working on for anchovy-flavoured baked beans.

The Director Monster.

Some film writers accept these financial arguments, but still plead with producers to be given a chance to see a script right through to production. They promise that they will make the end product even more profitable than if the script were produced by committee. They are wasting their breath. If scripts written by individuals rather than a succession of hired hands were ever accepted, the writer's vision would be seen to have at least partially shaped the movie.

This can never be. For the ego of the Director Monster must be fed.

It is this gargantuan appetite that has come to shape the pecking order of the film industry. The self-esteem of the writer must be sacrificed, along with that of everybody else involved (barring that of the star, if very big) to satisfy the Director Monster's insatiable gluttony for credit and control.

The Director Monster, or Director as they were once called, is the bloated Queen Bee at the centre of an army of drones. It was directors who invented probably the most arrogant billing in the annals of human endeavour. It is they who, not content with the mere words 'directed by so and so' at the end of a film, decided to insist on the phrase 'a so and so picture' at the beginning of the film. The beginning of a film, it must be remembered, which will have involved the artistic commitment of literally hundreds of people. No other command figure feels the need to grab credit in this all-encompassing way. The President of the United States does not insist upon the words 'a so and so country' prefixing any mention of the USA. The battle of El Alamein is not remembered as 'a Rommel and Montgomery battle'.

Clearly there have been many great film directors of vision and ability. Some, perhaps, who actually deserve the credit they get. That said, a film must of course have a script. It also requires actors, who will wear costumes that must be designed and made. Those actors will perform within selected locations and on specially designed and constructed sets. The film will require a cinematographer to shape the pictures and lighting designers to provide the atmosphere. There will be sound engineers, special effects wizards, also an editor, the person who actually pieces together the thousands of disconnected shots to create the whole.

Of course, the director is in charge of all these things, but he or she does not actually *do* any of them. The director does not even have to ensure that the actors exit through the right door and look to the correct side of camera during their close-ups. They have a continuity person to do that.

None of this is to run down the director's contribution. He or she is the boss, and since movies began the director has been rightly respected as the principal *auteur* of any picture. But the cult has got out of hand. Ask some directors what they would like to be written on their gravestone, and the answer will be, 'A so and so life'. What else?

Happiness is a temporary thing.

None the less, despite the knowledge that his script, when finished, would be handed on to other writers, Nathan was happy. Even though his self-respect would eventually be forcibly taken from him, he was thrilled. Yes, his vision would be pulverised and distorted . . . yet he was deliriously happy, for he had been green-lighted to write a script, and for a writer in Hollywood, breaks do not come any better than that.

'Yes,' Nathan thought, 'I am happy.'

Then, of course, he remembered Flossie, and realised that he could not be happy because he was unhappy. The little demons inside him re-inserted the lead weights into the pit of his stomach and reminded him that to pretend that one was happy when one was, in fact, unhappy was a contradiction in terms.

Pulling herself together.

As it happened, Flossie was thinking of Nathan. She had

just had a very unpleasant experience and it had led her to ponder her life somewhat.

For Flossie had just lived through the day of the Rat Run. The day on which the peoples of the world had acknowledged that normal life on Earth had finally become unsustainable and had hence retreated to their Claustrospheres. Although on this occasion it had not actually been the people of the world that had acknowledged this horror, but merely the people of Great Pew, a tiny village in Oxfordshire. A village in which Nathan and Flossie had once lived, and in which Flossie now lived alone, her brief, post-Nathan affair having ended some time before.

Flossie had awoken that morning with no suspicion of the momentous events which were about to unfold. What she had awoken with, however, was something of a hangover. Her supper on the previous night had consisted of a bottle and a half of red wine and an entire packet of chocolate biscuits. She was definitely feeling a bit rough as she staggered into the kitchen, still dressed in her night clothes . . . a big nightie, baggie tracksuit pants and large furry slippers. The half-full bottle of wine stood on the kitchen table where she had left it but Flossie resisted the temptation to take a slug, and instead made herself a cup of tea.

The kitchen was a bit of a mess. The kitchen was, in fact, a lot of a mess. There was a huge pile of used tea-bags on the edge of the sink, which had some mandarin peel in it. There were old newspapers and old tea-towels. Empty frozen food cartons, frozen food cartons with a bit of lasagne still left in them, frozen food cartons with a bit of lasagne and also a couple of old tea-bags, some mandarin peel and a cigarette end in them. On the floor, beside the bulging kitchen bin, there was a pile of pizza boxes. These would stay on the floor for ever, because they would not fit in the bin, even had it not been bulging. There were some mouldy crumpets and a ketchup bottle which had all its ketchup on the outside. The floor needed sweeping and the washing-up needed washing up.

It was not merely because she now lived alone that Flossie was living this dissolute existence. She had always been completely slack, domestically. But fag-ends in the lasagne? A whole packet of choccie biccies for supper? Still in your nightie at eleven in the morning? Flossie feared that she was becoming a touch gross.

Sitting down with her cuppa, Flossie decided that she really had to pull herself together. Of course, if Nathan were still around, he would have told her that. What is more, she would have been infuriated by his prissy attitude. She would have told him that the world would not come to an end just because a girl did not put her socks in the dirty clothes basket. Sometimes she had wanted to throttle him, the way his whole body had twitched with agony if she so much as made a ring with her coffee cup, or left the newspaper folded inside out, the way he seemed to follow her about with a damp cloth.

Now she felt differently, now she would have rather liked Nathan to have been around to tell her what a state she looked. After all, it was not much fun looking a state if there was nobody there to tell you how beautiful you were, even when your hair was greasy. The bitter truth was that nobody was bothered whether Flossie looked a state or not. She could scum around the house all day in yesterday's knickers and an old nightie and nobody would care. She could go naked if she wished, daubed only in cold lasagne and fat scraped from the bottom of the grill-pan. Flossie had only herself to please, and she hated it.

She decided that she needed to inject a little dynamism into her life. She would pull herself together. She resolved to have a bath, put on some proper clothes, eat a proper breakfast, including fruit, and then do some work, which in her case was dress-making.

Just then, just at the very moment when Flossie had definitely decided to get her life in order, pull herself together and damn well get things sorted, the world came to an end.

Midnight.

The Rat Run had started. That moment which had been talked about for so many decades, around so many dinner-tables and on so many talk-shows had arrived. The doomsday clock which scientists had long used to illustrate the Earth's close proximity with Eco-Armageddon had finally struck midnight.

Flossie first heard about it from her radio. People still listened to the radio, despite the numerous technical innovations which, it was regularly announced, would supersede it. Radio, despite being well into its second century, remained the only medium which one could enjoy whilst doing other things. At the moment the Rat Run started, the other thing which Flossie was doing was pouring another cup of tea. This being the first part of the process of prevaricating by which she would put off the moment when she would begin getting her life in order, pulling herself together and damn well getting things sorted.

The music that had been playing on the radio suddenly stopped and a stern voice announced an urgent newsflash, adding that all listeners should stand by for information of the utmost importance. Momentarily Flossie was pleased. Here was justification indeed to put off pulling herself together. The radio had actually told her to, and you couldn't get a much more official excuse than that. She sat down with her tea. Almost immediately the announcement came and any sense of wellbeing which Flossie may have been harbouring instantly left her. The news was truly and hugely terrible. The unthinkable had happened. The Rat Run was beginning.

It seemed that the mosquito infestations which had become such a familiar feature of the British summer had taken a dramatic turn for the worse. Years of exceptionally hot and wet weather, combined with ever-expanding swamplands and increasingly ineffective insecticides had produced breeds of mozzie with jaws like tigers, who could suck the sap out of a tree, massive, body-building insects who drank DDT for breakfast and which one did not so much swat as wrestle. It used to be said that you could not get blood out of a stone, the truth was that these terrible airborne vampires probably could.

Now it seemed that they had decided to take over the Earth. The radio informed Flossie that there had been a sudden and catastrophic explosion in the insect population and that they had swarmed. Vast clouds of virtually invulnerable blood-sucking monsters had appeared all over the Northern Hemisphere. It was a plague, similar in many ways to the plagues of locusts which crop up so regularly in the Bible, except whereas the locusts ate only crops, these mosquitoes ate people, a few drops at a time.

Within an hour or so, the announcement said, the Home Counties would belong to the insect world, soon all Britain and Europe. Therefore, it was suggested that everyone should get inside their Claustrospheres immediately and not come out until the following year, when the mosquitoes would have been destroyed by their own weight of numbers.

Flossie sat for a second as the message was repeated. She could not move, it was all too much. One second she was thinking about having a bath, the next, it's get in your Claustrosphere for a year or have all the blood sucked out of your body by billions of fist-sized mosquitoes. A siren outside in the street jolted Flossie into action. She went to her front door and saw an army half-track beside which stood an officer with a megaphone.

'Get in your Claustrospheres! Get in your Claustrospheres!' he shouted, as soldiers in protective suits rushed from door to door. One of them ran up the garden path of Flossie's little cottage.

'Haven't you heard?' the soldier shouted through his mask.

'Yes, but –' Flossie responded weakly.

'Then get in your bloody 'Sphere, you stupid cow! Quick! They'll be here in an hour! Norfolk's black with them, carpeted from the sea to the broads.'

Flossie's next-door neighbour was at her door, nearly hysterical.

'But my husband's at the office!' she cried.

'Can't help that, madam,' the soldier shouted. 'He'll find a place in a municipal shelter all right. It's only a year, you can find each other then! Now get in your Claustrosphere!'

With that, the soldier ran on to the next house, where some of his comrades were helping an infirm old couple.

Feeling completely stunned, Flossie went back into her cottage, took up the half bottle of wine and made her way into the back garden. She did not need the booze, there were plenty of drugs and dehydro wine in the 'Sphere, but she took it anyway. She tried to think of something else she might like to take, but couldn't. What was the point? The Claustrosphere was fully equipped, that was what it was for. The urgent commotion in the street was getting louder. Flossie could hear it even standing in the back garden.

'This is the last warning,' the commotion said. 'This environment will be lethal in approximately fifty-five minutes!'

Dressed in her nightie and slippers Flossie went inside the Claustrosphere and closed the BioLock.

The black hole of Great Pew.

The geodesic shell of Flossie's Claustrosphere was non-transparent. All Claustrospheres were like that, the reason being that the outer surface of the dome was its energy source. Sunlight so dangerous that it could kill people was still a valuable source of solar power, and it was this solar fuel which made the BioCycle viable. There were not even any windows. So delicate were the ecological rhythms of existence within the dome, it was thought that the intrusion of a natural light cycle might imbalance the process. Besides which, no transparent material had yet been developed which could be guaranteed to filter all the harmful elements of naked sunlight. Many Claustrosphere psychologists argued that windows would be a bad thing anyway. They felt that, to the occupant, their Claustrosphere *was* their world and to be able to look out at another might lead to them denying their new reality and failing to come to terms with their own world.

Therefore, once inside, Flossie was completely alone. Claustrospheres had no phones. The very fact of Bio-Sphere technology was based on the presumption that all life outside was over. Therefore, any factor which required maintenance, power or organisation from outside the Claustrophere was, by its very nature, untenable. Some richer people had invested in expensive radio and solid state land-line networks between small groups of friends, but any intrusion into the structure of the geodesic shell was frowned upon by the manufacturers. The whole principle worked on complete enclosure. A world apart. They refused to guarantee shelters in which the dome had been punctured. 'Once you're in, you're in' was the cheerful slogan employed by the companies marketing the numerous Claustrosphere accessories that ranged from Virtual Reality sex-suits to worry beads. Flossie was in.

Now she knew how much she missed Nathan. She missed him, to coin a phrase, with all her heart. In fact, with all her heart and all of the rest of her body. She shook with how much she missed him. She wept and she wept. She was weeping when she realised that a light was flashing and a recorded voice was speaking to her.

'Please activate LifeCycle immediately, please activate LifeCycle immediately.'

Flossie knew what that meant. She had to start the damn thing up. Claustrospheres produced their own oxygen and if the occupant did not start the generation process within approximately half an hour of closing the BioLock, the available natural oxygen would be exhausted and the occupant would suffocate.

Flossie seriously thought about ignoring the warning. Why not? She was alone in a Claustrosphere! Alone, without Nathan, in the Claustrosphere that they had built together after endless debate and hand-wringing. True, it was only for a year, but a year alone in a Claustrosphere? Could she hack it? She looked around at the big TV screen and the miniature rain forest which would be her only companions. She could not even turn the lights off because she and Nathan had decided that they couldn't afford a night-time cycle.

It was the thought of Nathan that made her turn on the LifeCycle. If she loved him, and she knew now that she did, she could wait a year. Where was he, she wondered? In America; that was in the Northern Hemisphere, wasn't it? Of course, it was. Would he make it into a Claustrosphere? He had faxed her a message to say that Plastic Tolstoy himself had rented him a house off Sunset. It would have a Claustrosphere, surely? Of course it would. There was not a house in the US without one. Flossie tried to think of Nathan, sitting in some American Claustrosphere. She wondered if he was alone. She hoped not, for his sake. Flossie found her own solitary prospects rather daunting. On the other hand, she rather hoped there wouldn't be any women with him. It could happen, if he had been forced to retreat into an LA municipal. He was a man with a development deal, possibly about to spend a year amongst secretaries, waitresses and wannabe actresses. Flossie decided not to think about it.

The banging.

Flossie drank the rest of her wine and tried to adjust. She stood, she sat, she stuck an old film into the entertainment centre. She could not settle, however, and the moments crept by. Without any light changes she had only the clock to tell her the time and she was sure it was slow. She would look up at it, convinced that an hour had passed, to discover that only five minutes had gone by. Then only one minute. At this rate she felt it would not be long before time would stop altogether and then she would never get out. What if time started to go backwards? she asked herself. Would that mean that she could get out before she got in? Or would it only be going backwards in her world? Would the world outside carry on without her? These were the thoughts of a woman all alone in the universe with only half a bottle of wine for company. They were big thoughts but they did not take long to think. Scarcely any time at all seemed to have passed.

The clock was getting slower. The silence was oppressive. Afters three or four hours, Flossie began to wish that she had not turned on the oxygen.

Then the banging started.

Flossie nearly jumped out of her skin. The banging was certainly worse than the silence. She should have been expecting it, of course, but somehow it had slipped her mind. There could be no doubt that this was the noise of those terrified, dying people trapped outside. Every Claustrosphere brochure warned of this development. It was obvious that there would be those who either did not have access to a 'Sphere, or who got caught too far away from home and, ignoring the municipals, had tried to make it back. These were the people who were now hammering in terror upon Flossie's door. But she could not open it. The stern warning given out by the police and the Claustrosphere company alike was that, once you had closed your BioLock, under no circumstances should you open it again. If the poisons which were killing the desperate souls on the outside should once upset the delicate eco-balance on the inside, then no one would survive.

After about twenty minutes, Flossie could hardly stand it.

'Go away,' she shouted. 'I can't open it! You're not supposed to! I can't.'

But she knew they could not hear her. The sound of a voice would not travel through the dome. The banging continued. Flossie could not bear to imagine the scene which was being played out in her own little back garden. Choking, dying people, gasping their last on her astroturf. It hardly seemed possible. Perhaps there were children? Some of the bangs seemed less hard than others. This thought was too much for Flossie, and she resolved to open the lock. She could not live with herself for a year, imagining the skeletons of tiny children clawing at her door outside. The little Eden Three which she and Nathan had bought could support four people, and she was only one. That was not right. Flossie felt that she must try and share, whatever the risk. Of course, the people outside might be a gang of adults, in which case she would perhaps die. She had no weapon and if a desperate crowd wished to eject her then there would not be much she could do about it. None the less, she resolved to open the door. She could not in all conscience take up four Claustrosphere places whilst people, possibly children, died outside.

Ben Elton

BioSting.

As Flossie opened the door of her BioLock, the police officers outside were just fixing a charge of dynamite with which to blow it open. Claustrospheres were extremely tough, but if you had the right explosives, you could get into them.

'Good afternoon, Mrs Hoddy,' said the head constable. 'Glad you opened up. You're not supposed to, you know, but it did save us ruining your Claustrosphere.'

What had happened made the news worldwide. It was a bio-sting. A beautifully conceived and executed crime. Great Pew was a very wealthy village. A couple of rock stars had built studios in the surrounding manor houses and all the residents were London media people. The place simply dripped with money. It was also very self-contained. There was only one road in and out, meaning that a simple diversion sign ensured privacy for at least a little while.

The moment the residents of the village had been hurried into their Claustrospheres, the thieves had removed their army uniforms, switched off the radio jammer that they had used to intrude on the local air waves and robbed all the houses. They were in and out in under an hour; it took another two for anybody to notice anything amiss and it was mid-afternoon before the police began to blast people out of their 'Spheres.

'What a beautiful idea,' said Judy to himself when he heard about it later. 'I'm amazed that nobody thought of it before.'

Chapter Seventeen

The difference between Virtual Reality and actual reality

Delegation.

P lastic Tolstoy made at least a hundred major decisions an hour. His colossal empire required a never-ending succession of split-second judgements. When he moved he had to move fast, and he was always moving. This required delegation. Tolstoy was constantly giving orders. He was a general with a whole army of foot solidiers who scurried about the world, day and night, doing his will. He had development people, money people, management people, marketing people and he was in virtual constant communication with all of them. Just occasionally, though, Plastic Tolstoy put them all on hold and gave orders to his killing people.

Boring door knockers.

The process of prevarication began anew. While Flossie was wandering around her Claustrosphere, Nathan was wandering around the nice little house off Sunset that Plastic Tolstoy had rented for him. He sat down at his computer console. He got up again. He walked around. Had a cup of coffee, played with himself. He flicked through the news input channels. Jurgen Thor had fully recovered from the explosions at the Euro parliament. Hitler's lawyers had pulled off a plea bargain whereby he admitted to the lesser offence of using intolerant and inflammatory language, and the court agreed to drop the six million murder charges. He got a hundred hours' community service.

Eventually Nathan wrote something.

'Scene one.'

It was a start.

Then the prevarication began again. What style of computer font to employ? What type size? Word processing had increased the opportunities for writer prevarication considerably. Nathan was still playing around with his computer mouse fifteen minutes later, when the doorbell rang. He jumped up in delight. Here was a genuine diversion. Nathan had no idea who it might be, for he had told no one of his new whereabouts except Max, and of course Flossie in England, but it didn't matter. Anyone would do to get him away from his computer.

The world is full of quite awesomely boring people who knock on doors. Often they are religious zealots, sometimes political representatives, occasionally market researchers. Normally, the reaction that these sad door knockers provoke is one of brusque dismissal. Most people make it quite clear that they resent the intrusion on their privacy and that they neither wish to be told what to think, nor asked what they think. Indeed, so thankless is the lot of the average boring door knocker that it is a mystery how they keep going. The truth, of course, is that every job, even door knocking, has its occasional rewards. Every now and then, not often, very rarely, in fact, but sometimes, the boring door knocker knocks on the door of somebody who is pleased to see them. Somebody who, on being asked the question 'Where will you be spending eternity?' will actually be prepared to give the matter some thought. Somebody who does not shout, 'Rover Kill!!!' when faced with the announcement 'Hi, we're talking with people today about faith.' Somebody who is actually prepared to express an interest in current proposals to turn the high street into a one-way system and pedestrianise the north end. It is these seemingly generous, open-spirited souls who keep the boring door knockers going, for in them exists the great door knocker's illusion. The illusion that somebody out there appreciates them. Appreciates the fact that they have chosen to devote their lives to irritating other people with their fatuous prejudices or public-spirited obsessions. Alas, it is only an illusion. For the people who encourage them do so out of purely selfish reasons. For they are writers merely seeking further justification to prevaricate. Desperate people, every one, who would welcome a burglar into their homes as a happy diversion from having to sit down and do some work.

Welcome visitor.

Nathan was in for a pleasant surprise, for the person at the door was Max, which meant that he could put away the idea of work for the rest of the evening.

'I don't know, I just thought I'd come and say hi,' Max said, walking in. 'I know you're working so I won't stay above a minute,' he added, putting two six-packs of beer and a litre of Jack Daniels on the coffee table.

'No, that's fine, stay as long as you like,' said Nathan eagerly. The arrival of a superstar definitely absolved him of all obligation to write. Particularly a superstar who was going to star in the film he was supposed to be working on.

'Nathan,' said Max, cracking open the beer and the rye, 'I've never felt like this before.'

Max had been thinking about Rosalie. He just could not get the girl off his mind. Nathan was the only person he knew who had met her (unless you counted Tolstoy) so Max naturally gravitated towards him. Besides, Nathan too was unhappy in love, he understood how obsessive it was.

'I tried to get a lawyer in Dublin to send her a message and it turned out that she'd escaped. Can you believe that? Already! What a woman. I just *have* to see her again.'

'Even if you knew where she was, she doesn't want to see you. She said so.'

'Girls say stupid things. All I have to do is find a really good reason to speak to her again. I need something to get back in her confidence. Like, if I could do something for her, you know? Like, if I could steal the plans to a nuclear plant or something and place them at her feet.'

'They have all that stuff already, Max,' Nathan said sympathetically. 'That's part of Mother Earth's mystery, they're so well-informed. I don't think there's much you can offer in the green stakes that would impress a girl like Rosalie.'

'How about money? Supposing I got word to her that I wanted to fund all her bombs and shit?'

'They have money too,' said Nathan. 'You know that. Actually, it's the funding thing that our movie's going to be about.'

There was an evangelical light in Nathan's eyes which

Max had seen in the eyes of writers before. It meant that they were about to explain their idea.

'Nathan, I don't want to hear your movie idea right now. Please don't tell me about your idea.'

'All right,' said Nathan.

But he could not be stopped. Despite Max's protests and efforts to get the conversation back on to the subject of Rosalie, Nathan explained his idea. It was understandable really, he was far from over the excitement of being green-lighted by Plastic Tolstoy himself. When he had finished, Max could not help but nod with approval.

'It's neat,' he said. 'And you say Tolstoy liked it?'

'Well, at first I thought, "Hello, it's turkey time." The room seemed to simply reek of Brussels sprouts and gravy. Tolstoy went all thoughtful and didn't say a thing, which is a bit rare for him, you must admit. But it turned out he was just having a mull, because he's told me to go ahead and write it.'

'A full green light?'

'Absolutely, so I'm holed up here like a monk until it's done. No going out, no parties. I've only told you and Flossie I'm even here . . .'

At the mention of Flossie, Nathan's face fell. He remembered that he had forgotten to remember that he was unhappy. Max could see what had happened and tried to cheer him up.

'Hey, looks like we're going to make a Tolstoy picture together, partner,' he said and they chinked glasses and drank. Then they did it again, and again, and for a moment they were both happy. Then the little devils that now lived inside both their stomachs reminded them both that to be happy when you are unhappy is a contradiction in terms.

They both sank back into love sadness and poured more drinks.

'She's so strongwilled,' they both agreed. 'That's what I like about her, I suppose,' they both assured each other. 'Fucking women, eh?' They clinked glasses in a positive orgy of mutual understanding. The booze flowed.

'You know something, Nathan,' Max slurred, 'you are the greatest guy, you know that? I mean, do you *really* know that?'

'Listen, mate,' the Englishman replied, 'I love you, no, I mean it, I really do, I bloody love you, mate.'

Where truth and fiction merge.

About two thirds through the JD they decided to have a wrestle. This was not done in the old-fashioned method of grappling round on the floor and bear-hugging prior to being sick on the carpet. You did it via a Virtual Reality link-up which would even be sick for you if you liked. Max had picked up a couple of disposable helmets at a Hyper-Mart when he'd got the beer and rye.

'Let's fight it out, old pal,' he said drunkenly, handing Nathan a helmet.

The game was called 'Trial of Strength' and it enabled a person to find out who was better at fighting, them or their mates, without getting hurt. What you did was put on a helmet that was linked to your opponent's. These helmets read the abilities of the people wearing them, and your pal's computerised likeness would become your adversary in a series of combat situations.

Half drunk, they shook hands, put the helmets on and prepared to fight each other to the death from opposite easy chairs.

Inside the helmets they could both see two masked fighters facing each other. One was Max, the other Nathan. The first situation was unarmed combat. There was no contest, Max's hologram, imbued as it was with Max's strength and training, utterly pulverised Nathan's hologram which was, of course, as weedy as its controller. The Nathan figure thrashed about helplessly whilst the Max figure chopped it up, punching it, throwing it, stamping on its head.

From their respective easy chairs the two real people rocked with laughter at the thrashing Nathan's thinkalike was receiving. The disparity in their abilities was so great it was comical. When the first round was over a little voice inside the helmets announced that Nathan had better be better with a Ninja stick, or his ass was dead.

Nathan giggled, feeling for his drink in the real world, whilst inside the helmet his hologram picked up the unfamiliar weapon of two sticks connected by a chain. Max laughed, because it was clear how reluctant to fight the Nathan hologram was. Max made his thinkalike demonstrate his powers with a stunning display of Ninja training, whirling and slashing the sticks about his head. They both roared with laughter and swigged at their drinks as Nathan's hologram did the only thing the real Nathan would have been capable of doing, which was to throw his sticks at the Max figure and launch a massive kick at its balls. The Max figure simply avoided the kick, spun round and in a single sweeping movement hit Nathan's man so hard that the head was actually partially severed.

'Fuck! I bloody felt that,' Nathan shouted out loud, laughing, although of course he could not hear himself inside the helmet.

'Looks like the English guy's a wimp,' the little voice inside the helmet said. 'Maybe he could use some fire power.'

And inside the helmets the two holograms reappeared in a bar-room situation, both armed with handguns. The two real men laughed as the Max figure raised his gun and fired. The Nathan figure shuddered with the impact and was propelled backwards over a table and on to the floor behind. Max walked his hologram forward to finish the job as the Nathan hologram screamed. With one hand Nathan's figure grasped its wound, holding the other one up towards Max's figure, as if pleading with it to stop.

'These helmets are fantastic!' the real Max said into the real world. He was getting a genuine feeling of pain and panic from Nathan's figure. 'OK, kid, say a prayer,' he said, shouting the way people do when they have earphones on.

Inside his helmet Max made his figure raise its gun as the wounded Nathan hologram desperately tried to crawl away, whimpering in agony.

'You're really scared, aren't you?' Max laughed to himself. 'Well, I can cure that.' But as Max's hologram took aim, the prostrate Nathan figure shuddered horribly. It seemed to be convulsing and twitching with pain. Max laughed hugely at the writhing figure, took another pull at his bourbon and poured computer graphically generated fire into the hologram on the floor inside his helmet, finally putting it out of its misery.

'Eat lead death, limey redcoat colonialist scum,' Max laughed. 'That's for Yorktown. I'm a Yankee Doodle Dandy.'

Then the holograms suddenly faded and strange visions began to appear. There was a sudden wash of colour, mainly deep red but with some purple in it, which seemed to fill the whole of Max's helmet. Max felt as if it almost filled his head. Half-formed images appeared and started to swirl about inside the colour. Max could vaguely make out a woman's face and a little boy running, then a house. There were many much less clearly defined shapes. Max thought they might have been people, or perhaps animals . . . he could not make out for sure because all the time flashes of the harsh red and purple kept intruding on the vision. Max felt a great compulsion to understand the shapes, almost, he thought, to *remember* them but he could not . . . the red kept getting in the way. A red which, although it filled Max's whole helmet, still managed to give the impression of being somehow jagged.

'Cool,' Max murmured to himself, appreciative of the way the game makers had programmed such an intense and innovative graphics package with which to end the first part of the game.

The red wash began to throb. Max wondered if it was throbbing to the beat of his pulse, it rather felt that way. It was a sort of undulation, a very intense one, also very uncomfortable but none the less extremely compelling. The jagged quality of the colour intensified as the woman and the other figures began to fade away. Max was sorry to see the shapes go. Although he had not understood them, they had felt very warm, nostalgic even. Max felt sad, he wanted to see them again. He knew that he could do this by simply re-starting the programme. And yet, somehow he felt that he couldn't, that the shapes or memories had gone for ever, far beyond recall. As they faded away completely, Max felt an irrational sense of loss. Something was coming to an end. He knew, of course, that it was just the graphic programme, but it felt like something much greater than that. Then, suddenly and with shocking violence, the face of Plastic Tolstoy burst into the helmet, the image one of blinding clarity. That is not to say that the face which filled Max's helmet and mind was a perfect likeness of Tolstoy, it just *was* Plastic Tolstoy. For a moment, the helmet almost seemed to *be* Plastic Tolstoy. But only for a moment . . . the face disappeared as quickly as it had come, but while it had remained there had been a palpable sense of outrage inside the helmet. The Tolstoy face wasn't outraged itself, it was more that it was surrounded by outrage and suffused by it. Tolstoy and outrage seemed to be part of the same thought. Max felt the outrage inside himself, deeply and personally, also a sudden surge of furious anger. Then immediately after that, so quickly, in fact, as to be almost at the same time, the sadness returned, a kind of desperate, hopeless sadness that brought tears to Max's eyes, which he hoped would not short-circuit the helmet.

The red throbbing returned, but now it was faded and slow. It went from crimson to pink and then, on a moment, it was gone altogether, although as it went Max felt again the face of the woman that he had seen when the display began. After that he knew that it was over.

'Intense, man. That was *weird*,' said Max out loud.

He sat back in his chair and waited for the next combat situation which was scheduled to be machine-guns in a cityscape, although he doubted that anything could beat the display which he had just seen. Nothing more appeared, however, and the helmet informed Max that his opponent had wimped out and was now disconnected, hence Max was the champion.

With a whoop and a holler Max dragged off his helmet and let his eyes readjust to the mundane reality of the room. Nathan was not in his chair. Max presumed he must be in the lavatory or something. He called out but received no answer. Then he realised that he could smell gunsmoke. He had smelt it inside the helmet and thought it was part of the sensual graphics package. But it was still there.

Then he saw Nathan's foot, it was poking out from behind the chair. He jumped up and ran across the room. There behind the easy chair lay Nathan, face down in a pool of blood. Almost exactly as the hologram Nathan had been.

'Shit! I killed him,' Max whispered, desperately trying to unfuddle his brain. Max could see an exit wound at Nathan's shoulder and an entry wound in the back of his neck. Nathan had clearly been knocked over the chair by a bullet in the chest and had been trying to crawl away when the second bullet in the neck had killed him.

Actual reality.

Max sat for a while thinking. Sobering up and thinking. He had not killed Nathan, Virtual Reality was not actual reality. Nathan had been alive when he had put the VR helmet on and he was dead now. Max had not moved from his chair in that whole time. At first he was tortured with vague fears that somehow, in the heat of the game, he had in some way managed to get hold of a real gun and had instinctively fired it. But there was no gun, and besides, Max had certainly not pursued Nathan across the room and shot him in the neck.

Max knew that there was only one explanation. Nathan

231

had been murdered whilst playing the VR game. The murderer, or murderers, had entered the house whilst Max and Nathan were preoccupied inside their helmets, and Nathan had been killed without ever removing his. He had not seen the murderers. He had died not knowing who had killed him, or why.

Max could remember the way the hologram had writhed and shuddered. That must have been the computer attempting to transmit an image of the thoughts Nathan was having whilst being shot and propelled backwards over the chair. Then the holographic figure of Nathan had jerked and slumped, which was clearly the computer's mind picture of Nathan being shot a second time whilst blindly and desperately crawling away. It was then that Max had made his hologram fire imaginary shots into Nathan's hologram to finish the game.

After that had come the visions. Those were the thoughts that Nathan's helmet had been transmitting, and which Max's helmet had attempted to visualise, after Nathan had been shot in the neck. At that point, the killers, whoever they were, must have known that Nathan was breathing his last.

Max had actually watched a computer graphic representation of Nathan's mind as he had died.

Chapter Eighteen

Reading a dead man's mind

New recruit.

Rosalie sat looking at Judy. They were in the cellar of a Mother Earth safe house on the outskirts of Dublin.

'So how do I know you're not an FBI plant?' she inquired.

'Do I look like an FBI agent?' replied Judy, who was quite capable of using his nerdyness to his advantage, if it suited him. One of the few genuine perks of being a member of an oppressed minority is that you can choose when and when not to play the card. One minute, objecting to being defined by one's religion, race or whichever orifice you choose to take it up. Then the next minute, claiming special debating rights at dinner parties on the very same grounds. Sometimes this trick can actually be pulled off in the space of a single sentence.

'As a Bhuddist cat-shagger, I deeply resent the way you seem to constantly categorise people by their religion or sexuality.'

Hence Judy, who had spent his life challenging the idea that weedy looking people are crap, was now attempting to turn this prejudice to his advantage. Unfortunately for

Judy, Rosalie did not suffer from quite such knee-jerk prejudices as most of his colleagues.

'You got me away from the airport,' she remarked. 'Awfully impressive, I thought. Maybe you really do turn into Superman when you get in a phone-box.'

'Look, I've told you, I'm a clerk with the Bureau, I have been for fifteen years. I do the green stuff . . . Other clerks cover commies and God-botherers, I do green. I'm the guy who writes your diary. I know about everything Mother Earth ever did, and why you do it. Like, how about this? You remember the guy you knew as Shackleton? You cut a transmitter out of his arm in the middle of Death Valley before you hit DigiMac? I briefed him. All the environmental stuff he knew? I told him.'

Rosalie sat silent. She was in two minds about this fellow. Not so her colleague Saunders, who was pacing about behind Judy. He wanted none of this inconvenient little American.

'Look, I don't know why we're even talking to this bloke, right?'

Saunders was a tough Liverpudlian who wore a bag over his head after having lost his face through radiation exposure. Saunders claimed that the exposure had been so bad that he could not have his face replaced, due to the need for constant treatment. There was, however, some suspicion amongst other Mother Earth activists who knew Saunders well, that he had rather got to like carrying such gruesome battle-scars.

'He might be straight, he might be a plant, right?' the scouser stated. 'Either way we'll never be sure, so let's dump him now.'

'If you dump me I'll get picked up in hours and I'll do fifteen years minimum for saving your team boss here from twenty-five to thirty in a US jail,' Judy said angrily. 'Listen, I didn't plan this, I just did it. They sent me over here with the actual agent to ensure Rosalie Connolly's identification. Like I say, I'm the expert on you guys. Well, I've been thinking about changing sides for years . . . For Christ's sake, I know more about how close we are to Eco-Armageddon than even you people do.'

Judy paused to consider the reaction he was provoking. Saunders was openly hostile, Judy could not tell about Rosalie. One thing was certain, though. Like Max before him, Judy would be very glad when those fierce green eyes were drilling holes in somebody else.

He persevered.

'You can't look at what's happening to the planet every day like I have to without being affected. Eventually, you get to thinking that maybe you're on the wrong side . . . Ever since I heard they were going to pull Ms Connolly here in for the DigiMac hit, I'd been kind of feeling bad about it, and when they put me on the assignment . . . Well, I didn't know what I'd do, but in the end what I did was drug the agent stupid in his hotel and pick you up myself. And that's it, I'm a criminal now. I can't go back and I don't want to. I want to join you, I'm switching sides and I reckon I've earned a place in your team.'

'Earned a place!' Saunders shouted, his big fists clenched in anger. '*Earned* a place! Jesus Christ, you don't earn a place with us typing letters for the FBI. I'll show you how you earn a place with us, mate!' And with that, Saunders whipped the bag off his head to reveal his complete absence of face. The man's eyes bulged out of the livid pink flesh, his teeth stood forward, stark within the lipless hole that had been a mouth.

Judy would have liked to have greeted this sudden revelation with a cool and steady stare. He nearly pulled it off. Apart from being instantly and hugely sick, he showed almost no emotion whatever. It wasn't that Judy was particularly squeamish, he had seen many shocking things in his time as an agent, it was just the shock. Judy had presumed that Saunders was wearing a mask for security reasons and to be suddenly presented with what was to all intents and purposes a living skull was something of a surprise.

'Ha! Wants to fight with us!' Saunders sneered. 'The man's been sick on his shirt.'

'Oh, for heaven's sake, Saunders!' said Rosalie. 'You really are the giddy limit sometimes. Now put your bag back over your head and shut up, or I'll have you counting dead seabirds in the Shetland Isles.'

Saunders, although a decent enough chap at heart, was a colossal embarrassment to Rosalie and indeed her whole unit. He seemed to see the entire environmental destruction of the Earth as nothing more than global justification for him to stamp about the place, proving how tough he was. It was very difficult to sack a person, though, who had given their face for the cause. Besides which, Saunders was a dedicated and brave fighter, and that had to be respected. Still, Judy was not going to be over-concerned when he got himself shot, as he inevitably would sooner or later, being such a complete lunatic.

'Look,' said Judy, after he had cleaned up the sick a bit. 'I know one hell of a lot about your organisation. I also know plenty about the FBI and its attitude to you. I think I can be of use. Besides which, as I say, I rescued you, Ms Connolly.'

Rosalie studied Judy for a long time. Judy thought to himself that just because she could go for ages without blinking, it did not intimidate him, but this was not true.

Finally she said, 'If you're lying to me, I shall find out and I shall definitely kill you.'

'And I'll kill you as well,' said Saunders, which completely ruined the effect.

Telephone voice.

The phone rang, jerking Max out of his reverie. He had been sitting deep in thought for a long time. All the bourbon was gone, but Max could not remember finishing it.

Nathan's Ansafone clicked into action. Max listened briefly to the voice of the dead writer. Ansafones had been around since before anybody still alive had been born, and yet people still felt the need to offer the age-old instruction 'nobody's in, leave a message', etc. Max had never realised quite how English Nathan sounded, except, of course, that this was just his telephone manner. The English always adopted a telephone manner, Max thought. As it happened, so did Max, except that instead of effecting a more 'proper' voice, like Nathan, he instinctively tried to appear laid back. His own Ansafone message was a low growly drawl, sounding as if nothing really mattered and life was something of a drag anyway.

'Ugh . . . Hi, yeah . . . OK, it's the machine, right? But you knew that. Listen, uhm . . . leave a message, don't leave a message . . . live, die, it's all the same dream, right? . . . Bye' and you can't get much more telephone-mannered than that.

It was a woman on the phone. Her voice followed Nathan's recording. It was another English voice, but lighter and more relaxed than Nathan's rather stilted message.

'Nat,' the voice said. 'Nat, it's me.'

And Max knew that he was listening to Nathan's gorgeous and unobtainable Flossie.

'Look . . . I don't know, I think we should talk. I got all your letters, but I haven't rung before because I've been thinking a lot . . . You know, about us . . . something happened today, it was just so weird, anyway I want to . . . Oh hell, look I'm not going to discuss it with your bloody machine . . . but phone me . . . soon . . . I really do think we should talk. Bye.' There was a pause and then, softly . . . 'I love you, Nat. Glad you still love me.'

Well, irony did not get much more painful than that. If the poor dead bastard behind the chair could have just stayed alive another hour he would have got his girl back. On the other hand, Max reflected, three months from now he'd probably have been just as annoyed about the knickers on the bathroom floor as he'd ever been.

Chasing girls.

Max decided to leave. He was very sorry for Nathan, but there was nothing he could do for him now. It was best to get out. With the exception of the murderers, who were unlikely to come forward, Max was the only person who knew that anyone besides Nathan had been at the house that evening. Max would just walk away. He had no desire to get caught up in the police investigation. Besides which, he was going back to Ireland. He had something to tell Rosalie.

Max had decided that Plastic Tolstoy had ordered Nathan's murder. His reasoning was clear. Nothing had been stolen, and Max, who had been in the room when the attack happened, had been spared. Whoever it was, wanted to kill Nathan Hoddy and Nathan Hoddy alone. No complications, like dead movie stars, just an unknown, unattached British writer, dead, a long way from home. They knew what they wanted to do, they had done it and left. But who had sent them? It had to be Tolstoy. Nathan had only moved into the house the previous day, no one even knew he was there. All he had done since returning to Hollywood was pitch his idea to the great man.

His idea! That had to be the key. Nathan must have stumbled upon the truth! It was the only explanation for his swift, clinical dispatch. Max pondered the story that Nathan had forced upon him only a few hours earlier. He had not really listened very hard, because writers telling you their ideas is generally a pretty dull experience. He remembered the basic point, though . . . it was such a wild idea he could scarcely forget it. The idea that the Claustrosphere Corporation was funding green terrorism. This was the thesis which Nathan had pitched to Plastic Tolstoy and which Tolstoy clearly did not with to see developed. This was the thesis which, Max believed, had killed Nathan.

Max knew that he was not the first person to draw this conclusion either. In his final mortal moment, Nathan had instinctively guessed at the identity of the man who had ordered his death. It was Plastic Tolstoy's image which had come in fury into Nathan's mind and which had from there found its way into Max's helmet. Outrage at Tolstoy had been Nathan's last thought on Earth, excepting for perhaps a fleeting sadness, when Flossie had re-entered his mind at the point of extinction.

There was only one conclusion to be drawn from this. Nathan's idea was more than fantasy. Max could not imagine why, but the Claustrosphere Corporation was funding Mother Earth. Rosalie was in Tolstoy's pay.

Max wished he had not drunk so much. His head was spinning with the size of his suspicions. It was madness. Even Max, who had little time for current affairs, knew that if Mother Earth could close down every Claustrosphere in the world then they would do it in an instant. They would blow them all to bits, and kill the people who made and sold them. For Claustrosphere to fund Mother Earth was like the chickens feeding the fox.

Max was suddenly filled with a sense of purpose, which was a strange sensation for him. A point seemed to have arisen in what was becoming an increasingly pointless life. The old drunk, silly, dilettante Max was being replaced by a new Max, a Max who wanted to know what Tolstoy and Claustrosphere were up to and why Nathan had had to die. A Max who, more than ever, wanted to talk to Rosalie. He had been looking for a reason to see her again, now he had one. How would she react to his suspicions? Could she possibly know already? Of course not, she hated Claustrospheres more than anything, all Mother Earth people did.

Max knew that he had to disappear. He could not be sure how Plastic Tolstoy would react to the news that he had been at Nathan's house on the night when the murderers had done their bloody deed. Would the killers have recognised him under the helmet? He did, after all, have a very fine and distinctive chin. All in all, Max decided that he would like to be away from

Hollywood for a while. Ireland seemed as good a place as any.

Except for the fact that he had of course, only thirty-six hours earlier, been ignominiously ejected from that country and had his visa revoked.

Max was thinking straighter than he had done in nearly a decade. Before leaving Nathan's house, he took Nathan's passport from where it lay on the desk. He also brought a knife from the kitchen and gently scraped a little of the congealed blood from the corpse's neck into a small envelope. He did not like doing it. No amount of Virtual Reality blood had prepared him for the real thing – it was much stickier for a start. However, he had no choice. He had to get past passport control and he intended to use a trick that had been employed by a character he had recently played. Max hoped it would not turn out to be just the stuff of fiction.

Lost in LA.

Max drove home and raided his make-up box for a few small items of disguise: facial hair, nose putty, latex. Max was rather proud of still owning his own make-up box, despite enjoying the services of the best facial synthesisers in the business. Like all actors, when he wasn't dwelling on how wonderful and different being an actor was, Max liked to think of himself as nothing more than a worker, an artisan who did an honest day's labour for an honest day's two or three million dollars.

'It's a craft, that's all,' he would say, 'and these are the tools of the trade.'

As it happened, the only time Max ever used his

make-up box was when he wished to avoid being recognised, which, since he was an actor, was not very often. However, as he ordered a cab to take him out to the airport, Max felt that on this occasion some effort at disguise would be sensible.

This was not because he was fearful that the holographic photograph in Nathan's passport would give him away, but merely because he knew that he had to travel incognito. Nobody ever looked at the photos on passports any more, the DNA cellular print was foolproof. The traveller inserted his or her passport into a scanner followed by the forefinger of either hand. The machine then took a single-cell-thickness laser scrape from the finger and checked that the DNA from the scrape matched that listed on the passport. The system could not be cheated, unless, of course, a passenger happened to have an envelope full of dried blood belonging to the person from whom he had stolen the passport, in which to dip his finger before sticking it into the machine.

The cab took nearly five hours to reach the airport. This was not because Max instructed the driver to dawdle, or visit the fleshpots, but simply because that was how long it took for the man to stumble upon the correct destination. London is the only city in the world which really takes its taxi driving seriously, and considers it a genuine profession for which a person must be trained. All other cities treat the art of people-moving with various degrees of contempt, ranging from mild to utter. In Los Angeles it goes beyond that. It is almost as if being completely lost all the time is a qualification for the job.

In truth, the only actual job qualification to be a cab driver in most cities is being able to drive (ish). If you can drive a car, you can drive a cab. That's it, no special skills are required. In LA, people often take up the profession on their first day in town, simply in order to get in from the airport. It's a curious situation; no other profession takes such a relaxed view as to what is required to enter its ranks. The fact that a person is able to work a stove does not mean they can readily find employment as a chef. Most people are capable of lifting a scalpel and, no doubt, would be equally capable of plunging it into somebody else's flesh, yet this is not generally considered sufficient justification for allowing them to practise as surgeons. But cab driving insists on no such niggling restrictions. If you've got a car and can turn it on then you're away.

By luck, endless references to the map, appeals for help over the radio and shouted suggestions from passers-by, Max's driver eventually managed to get him the six miles from one of LA's premier residential districts to the airport. Max always gave cab drivers the same tip.

'You're in America,' he said and entered the departure hall.

Into Africa.

The passport trick worked at LAX and after the rigours of the cab-ride, Max hoped that he was finally on his way. Unfortunately, the flight took a little longer than expected. It was a sub-orbital, which normally involved a vertical take-off, a brief suspension in the stratosphere whilst the Earth spun beneath it, followed by direct dropdown to one's destination: two hours on the schedule. But as Max's flight commenced its descent into Dublin it got hit by a pressure drop and blown out of alignment.

This sort of thing happened all the time. The weather hadn't been right since they replaced all the real forests with acidic little fern numbers. Billions of Christmas trees just didn't get the job done. Areas of high and low pressure drifted all over the place and the average conventional flight was punctuated by more altitude variations than a roller-coaster. Passengers would, without warning, find their planes dropping thousands of feet in seconds, causing their backsides to shoot upwards and hit the lockers above them. Some aeronautical experts claimed that there had been instances where terrified passengers had actually managed to crap on top of their own heads.

Anyway, a huge squall over Europe meant that nothing was landing for a while and Max's flight got diverted into North Africa to wait out the weather. It was a bad day to land in Addis. Sensational news had just been leaked. The locals had discovered that the vast debt-funded constructions to the north of the city which, it had been popularly presumed, were hospitals, power plants and food research centres, were nothing of the kind. What had in fact been built was a vast armoured Claustrosphere complex, into which the government and its business friends would scurry should the Rat Run ever occur.

This type of centralised Claustrosphere 'town' was becoming increasingly common in the poorer countries of the world. Countries where there was no question of universal eco-cover, but still plenty of rich and powerful people around who didn't want to die. Obviously, in the event of Earth death, isolated elite eco-shelters would be extremely vulnerable to terrified dying people. The answer was, of course, collective security.

The Ethiopian president had tried to reason with the angry crowds. He had been disarmingly frank.

'Come *on*!' he said, his voice full of genuine surprise. 'What's the problem? Some of us are rich, some of us are poor. What's new? I've got a car, you haven't. I've got enough food, you haven't. That's always been the case, it didn't make you riot then. Why riot now? It's bloody obvious that anybody who can afford a Claustrosphere is going to get one. Just the way anybody who can afford decent housing and medical care has always got it. There's no difference. What's all the fuss about?'

It was a powerful argument. The furious masses paused for thought and the president pressed home his point.

'Besides which, the honkies and the Japs won't lend us any money unless we use it to buy their products. Well, we don't want any more dams, do we? The ones we've got turned the country into desert. We've got enough guns and helicopter gunships, surely? So I bought Claustrospheres. What did you want me to do? Turn *down* the money! Say no to billions and billions of dollars and ECUS and Yen? Are you stupid or something?'

The disturbances did not actually reach the airport where Max's sub-orbital was waiting. The populations of the poor countries had been so decimated by decades of ever-encroaching land-death that there weren't that many of them left to riot, and those who did were not over fit. In the latter parts of the twentieth century, world leaders had been greatly worried about what they saw as the ever increasing population. They predicted that pretty shortly there would be tens of billions of people wandering about the world wondering why they should be the ones who were starving to death. Great barriers were erected in anticipation of the day when the majority of the world's population would arrive uninvited at the door of the minority of the world's population and ask to stay for dinner. The Mediterranean Sea became a battle-line, all guns facing south. The Panama Canal was similarly armed, as were the Ural Mountains and the borders of the nations of the Pacific rim. In the end, however, the problem never arose. Deforestation, salination and desert growth provided a solution. As large areas of the Earth died, so did the population who had lived upon it. The much feared south-north population shift withered on the vine.

Scenic route.

When Max finally arrived in Dublin, he hired a car and drove straight out of the city, heading north-west.

He had, of course, only the vaguest idea of where he was going. If only he had taken a little more notice of the journey he had taken with Rosalie in the back of the Garda truck. On that occasion, however, Rosalie's stare had absorbed his entire attention and his one clear memory of the trip was a pair of fierce green eyes drilling into his soul. Beautiful and splendid though those eyes were, they were of little use as a landmark, and Max had little else to go on. The only thing he could remember for sure was that Ruth and Sean's cottage was about three hours' drive from Dublin, and that the route ended in a dirt track.

Sitting in the plane on the tarmac at Addis, Max had tried to get his thoughts together. He made a rough guess that the police convoy would have averaged about thirty-five to forty miles an hour over the entire journey, which suggested a distance of between 110 and 120 miles from the city. Max had studied the map of Ireland which he found amongst the perfume ads at the back of the unbelievably dull airline magazine. Ireland was a fairly small place and it was clear that unless the Garda had driven by an extremely tortuous route, which seemed unlikely, Max's goal lay on either the west coast or in the south-west of the country. He knew he could dismiss the North, because it had been the Garda who had arrested him, not United Nations' forces. Due to the powerful Irish Catholic lobby in Congress, all Americans, even party-heads like Max, knew that the UN kept the peace in the Six Counties, or attempted to, and had done for decades.

Taking up the little vanity bag with which he, as a first-class passenger, had been presented, with compliments of Aer Lingus Orbital, Max removed the drawstring. Using the scale on the map (one centimetre to ten kilometres) he measured the string to approximate the 120 mile radius which he guessed would be the area of his search. Then, tying a pen to one end of the string and pressing the other end on to Dublin with his thumb, Max drew a semi-circular line on the map. The line ran approximately from Sligo in the north-west of Eire, down through Galway and then Limerick, ending up in Cork on the south coast. Max resolved to begin at Sligo and weave his way down the country along this line, in the hope that he might pick up a clue or landmark that he recognised.

At the airport, a nice Avis car-hire lady asked Max where he was off to.

'Sligo,' he replied, suddenly feeling rather daunted by the task he had set himself. Certainly, Ireland was small compared to the USA, but it was pretty big compared with one not very large person. For a little while Max's spirits drooped and as he negotiated Dublin's urban sprawl he pondered whether he might not be on something of a fool's errand. He did not even know whether Rosalie was still in the country . . . she was on the run, after all, and he himself had met her in California. On the other hand, Max was pretty certain that if she wasn't in Ireland, her grandparents would know where she was.

Once he got away from the city, Max felt better. The bulk of the countryside still operated under 'day-time', on account of the European-funded orbital sunscreen and despite the ravages of acid rain the landscape still looked green and blooming. What was more, the winds coming in off the porridge-like Atlantic created a real (albeit false) impression of fresh air. Max, who had lived all his life in a riot-torn super-city had scarcely realised that real green pastures existed anywhere outside of old movies.

'Now this is cool and indeed righteous,' he said to himself as he drove along with the roof down. Had he happened to have a Geiger counter, he might have felt differently. But what the eye doesn't see, the heart doesn't grieve over, not until fist-sized tumours start popping up all over it, anyway.

Having arrived at Sligo and mooched around the bay for a while, Max headed off slowly towards Galway. He did not really know what he was looking for as he traversed hither and thither along the little roads of West Ireland. He hoped that perhaps something he saw might trigger some recognition. At first, he had presumed that people who looked as disgustingly old as Rosalie's grandparents would be pretty notorious, but as he drove through village after village he realised that craggy faces and hairy ears seemed to be quite fashionable that year amongst the more mature citizens.

Suddenly though, Max no longer felt in any particular hurry. Despite all the global ructions which had become a part of daily life on Earth, there was something about this part of the world that soothed the soul. It was possible to relax amongst the ancient villages and hills. Max discovered new delights, like lunch, for instance. Max could not remember the last time he had eaten lunch, merely for the simple and private pleasure that could be got from it. In Max's world, lunch was a thing with which you cloaked your real intentions; getting laid, getting a job, firing a close friend. To rediscover the delight of lunching *alone* was a pleasure indeed. To be simply sitting with some bread, cheese and pickle, pondering the trivia quiz on the back of a beer mat was a genuine thrill. The pace of life was so much slower than in LA, although Max wondered whether in the long run any less actually got done. Probably, he thought, which was a very good thing.

Of course, not everything about the Irish countryside is so relaxing or idyllic. Socially, things can sometimes get a little more pressurised. It is not so relaxing in this quiet world if you happen to want an abortion, or a divorce, or to screw somebody other than your lawful spouse and perhaps adopt a position other than the missionary. Max fell into none of these categories as he meandered from one gorgeous view to another. Certainly, he would have liked to have screwed Rosalie, and in any and every position she cared to favour. However, since he was not in a position to do this, he confined himself to drinking, eating and enjoying the scenery, and, hence, was made welcome wherever he went. This was Max's kind of country. You could get a pint of beer in a post office and the licensing laws merely served to confirm the Irish reputation for writing good fiction.

'What time do you close?' Max had inquired on his first evening in Galway.

'Well, we close on the dot of midnight,' the landlady had replied, 'but you'll be all right for a drink until three or four.'

The pub lock-in is a grand old tradition in rural Ireland, which the Garda often seem to see as their duty to protect. As Max was shown out of the back via the cabbage garden, he wondered whether he might not have found his spiritual home.

Chapter Nineteen

Sexual situations

Rendez-vous.

In the end it was not Max who found Rosalie but, as before, she who found him. Gossip travels fast in the country and on Max's fourth day back in Ireland, Rosalie's grandparents heard word that a rich, mad American was driving from village to village, asking about an old couple called Ruth and Sean who had great taste in vegetables. They of course guessed who it must be and sent word to Rosalie.

She found him in a bed and breakfast in County Cork.

'Will you get up now, Mr Kennedy?' (for such was the name Max was travelling under) 'It's half past eight already and there's a young person to see you.'

The voice of his landlady brought Max struggling to consciousness and it was a struggle, for this was a big hangover. He conducted his usual morning reconnaissance, moving his tongue about to see what he had slept in. Crisp, fresh, linen. Not bad, he thought. A sheet, that sounded hopeful. Then a worrying idea occurred to him. Maybe it was a shroud. No, it couldn't be a shroud, he was face down, they don't bag you up, face down, surely, not in a Catholic country. No, Max decided, he definitely wasn't dead, although he felt as if he *had* died and was now being unceremoniously dug up. He tried to recall where he was, and more importantly where he had been. A linen sheet, that must mean a bed. Slowly it all began to come back to him. The fiddler and the bloke with the weird drum that you hit with both ends of the same stick . . . the singing, his spirited rendition of 'Yankee Doodle Dandy' . . . the eight pints of Murphy's and eight Paddy chasers. That's right, he was in Cork, and he was looking for a beautiful girl.

'What in the name of goodness have you come back for! Shouting about my granny and grandad all over the bloody county? I ought to shoot you where you sleep, that I should, you stupid American bastard.'

That beautiful soft lilt. Music, even on a hangover. He'd found her.

Rosalie walked into the bedroom and closed the door behind her. The landlady had been slightly scandalised about letting her go up, but short of physically restraining Rosalie there was not a lot she could do. Max turned over under the quilt to face her as Rosalie drew back the curtains. The light was blinding.

'Please, you'll rupture my pupils,' Max protested, grabbing for a pair of shades. Rosalie threw open the windows.

'Jesus, the stink of booze in here is disgusting.' She stared down at him with a pitying expression.

'You still mad at me then?' Max inquired.

'Of course I'm still mad at you. Gracious, you make me think you've saved me from the cops and then it turns out you've completely messed it up. Wouldn't any girl be angry?'

But despite herself Rosalie could not restrain a smile.

He did look cute, she thought, lying there in bed, blinking behind his shades like a startled rabbit. The fact that she had so far escaped prison had rather softened Rosalie's attitude to Max's disastrous attempt to help her elude the Garda. He had *tried*, after all.

'My God, the state of it,' she continued. 'Can it think? Can it talk?'

Max found her tone a little patronising and felt the need to assert himself.

'Excuse me, but it takes more than eight pints of stout and eight Paddy's Scotches to leave me without the use of my faculties.'

He had said the wrong thing. The process of European Federation had quickened the already relentless pace of cultural conformity, and Rosalie was big on maintaining Irish icons.

'Paddy's is not a Scotch, you ignorant philistine. Paddy's is an Irish. Scotch is Scotch and Irish is Irish, and if you can't tell the difference then you should stick to whatever foul designer poisons they call drinks in Hollywood.'

'Well, pardon me and six Hail Marys.'

Max lit a cigarette. One of the smaller ironies of the complete degradation of the environment had been the revival in the fortunes of the tobacco companies. It was extremely difficult for health experts to get over-concerned about the long-term prospect of lung cancer when the mere fact of breathing was giving people respiratory disorders. Besides which, lung cancer held few fears for anyone with even a modest income, since a new lung could be bought virtually for the price of installation. The development of 'zipper surgery' plus the fact of millions upon millions of people starving around the world had meant that the price of 'dual organs', i.e. those of which the body is supplied with two, had dropped to a pittance. Solo items had, of course, maintained their price. It is difficult to persuade even a desperate person to part with their heart. A human kidney, however, could often be obtained more cheaply than properly force-fed duck liver.

'You've no idea how revolting that cigarette smells, mixed up with the foul fug you seem to produce naturally.'

'Listen, it's morning, I've been on the booze. If I smelt good it would be weird.'

Rosalie decided to let it go.

'I asked you why you were here.'

'Well, it's partly social, you know? I thought we were starting to have fun.'

Rosalie let this go. 'And the other part?' she inquired.

'It's kind of connected with what we were talking about before,' said Max.

'I've told you,' Rosalie snapped, 'I wouldn't get involved in your stupid pal's stupid film script if you were to –'

'Nathan is dead,' Max interrupted, rather expecting the drama of the situation to pull Rosalie up somewhat.

'Who's Nathan?' Rosalie replied, putting paid to the drama.

'He's my stupid pal. The one who hid under the table at your granny's place.'

'Oh,' said Rosalie. 'Well, what's that got to do with me?'

It was not that Rosalie was a callous person, but she had seen many things die and she could scarcely even remember what the film writer had looked like.

'Just before he was killed, he pitched a screenplay

concept to Plastic Tolstoy. I think Tolstoy had him killed because of what that concept was.'

'I heard that films was a cut-throat business,' said Rosalie drily.

'Nathan was going to base his story on the idea that it is the Claustrosphere Corporation who secretly funds Mother Earth.'

During the previous few days, Max had often wondered how Rosalie would take this idea. He had feared that she would laugh right in his face. Had she done so, he had planned to take her through his reasoning, explaining how Nathan had died, how only Tolstoy could possibly have arranged it, how only Tolstoy had heard Nathan's idea, how Tolstoy had been the object of the final, furious thoughts in Nathan's life. But Rosalie was not laughing. She was thinking. A bell was ringing somewhere far away in her memory. A bell which she did not wish to answer.

'Sounds awful stupid to me,' she said, but hesitatingly. 'I wouldn't pay to see a thick film like that.'

Max could see that he had hit a nerve.

'What's so stupid, Rosalie? Nobody knows who backs you. It's been thirty, even forty years. You'd think somebody would have taken credit by now, wouldn't you?'

Pick up.

Rosalie was remembering a night five years previously. A night she had spent with Jurgen Thor . . .

She was twenty and had joined Natura two years before that, after failing to turn up for her first lecture at Trinity College. It was not long before her qualities of courage and intelligence were noticed, and she had been discreetly recruited into Mother Earth. There followed a gruelling eighteen months of training, towards the end of which she had met the great man.

She and fifteen other trainee combat activists were attending a secret political briefing at which Jurgen Thor was speaking and he picked her up, it was as simple as that. There were seven young women in the group. Thor had chosen her and she had let him. She hated to admit it, but her role in it had been that passive. The moment Thor entered the room he was clearly deciding which of the girls he was going to screw and he had picked her. All women know when they're being eyed up and Jurgen Thor made virtually no attempt to cover it. As the world's premier environmentalist he was often accused of wearing his heart on his sleeve. Anyone who had ever met him knew that it was another organ altogether.

Rosalie was rather irritated by this casual, arrogant sexuality and when, after the briefing, one of Thor's aides told her that the boss would like to see her, every instinct said she should tell him to stuff it. But she didn't. She was completely thrilled. Jurgen Thor was the Green God. The man to whom all environmentalists looked for leadership and inspiration. The one person with the authority to face down the world's leaders and get things done. Ever since she was a girl Rosalie had admired Jurgen Thor above all people. She had also, like millions of other women, wondered what it would be like to make love to him. She still wondered. He was the strongest, most handsome man she had ever seen, and even though he came on like sleaze, he still had more sex going for him than a brothel on Watership Down. Rosalie did not normally fancy big men, but Jurgen Thor was not just big, he was magnificent.

And so, when her weekend leave came up, instead of going home to Ireland to see her grandparents as she ought to have done, Rosalie flew with Thor in a Natura helicopter to his magnificent home in the Swiss Alps. A home perched on a cliff so high it actually still had snow and ice upon it, despite the disappearance of such stuff elsewhere in the mountains.

Icy passion.

The stairway down from the rooftop heli-pad led straight into Jurgen Thor's bedroom, where a bottle of schnapps was warming over a candle. Rosalie was utterly knocked out. It was a room of such splendid sexiness, just being in it could have dropped the knickers on a concrete nun. The room occupied the entire top floor of the house and every wall was glass. For 360 degrees all that could be seen was mountain range. The huge snowy white bed stood dead in the centre of the room, and from there it was possible to make love on top of the world.

'I do not bring many women here, yes?' Jurgen Thor had said. 'This place is very special to me.'

'I'm not surprised,' Rosalie had replied, looking about in awe.

Jurgen was an expert. He enfolded Rosalie in his arms and seemed almost to kiss her clothes off. At least, she could not remember him unbuttoning her blouse, taking off her shoes or undoing her trousers and yet there she was, lying on that huge bed in her underwear as Jurgen Thor knelt beside her, looking down and smiling. Even on his knees he towered above her.

'Jurgen, you'll take it easy, won't you? . . . I'm new to this.'

'It is perhaps . . . the first time?' Jurgen inquired gently. Rosalie did not reply, and Jurgen knew that it was.

'There is no need for the worrying, please,' he assured her calmly. 'For me there is only pleasure in the pleasure of the woman. I make love to make women happy. That is the only reason I do it.'

He meant it too. Nothing feeds a man's soul the way a woman can feed his soul by telling him that he just made her eyes roll and her loins melt. Jurgen understood that the greatest thrills could be found, not in losing oneself, but in inducing abandon in another. To take a woman to the peak of pleasure, to see her forsake her control. To see her hovering between ecstasy and despair. To hear her *plead*. That was sex. Domination by breathless consent was what turned Jurgen on. To be the catalyst, whereby a strong woman or a nervous girl or indeed, as in Rosalie's case, both, surrendered her body to his passionate manipulation. Here lay the route of his relentless sex drive. He was a sensual imperialist. Any fool could bend another to their will by force or payment, but to make a woman beg you to do as you please, to have her offer herself up that you might take her and keep her as long as you wished, now that was worth going to bed for.

Jurgen took especial care with Rosalie. A virgin's sigh was tribute of the highest order. No better proof could be found of a man's sexual and spiritual power. To overcome her pain and bring her to a celebration of her abandonment, that, truly, was a triumph of lasting splendour. For she would always remember that first sigh, and all other men would be measured against it. In a way, whoever could do that for a woman would own a part of her for life.

Such was the logic of love to a control freak. Jurgen tolerated no moment of abandon in himself. He could not bear for a woman to begin to work *her* wiles upon him. Should she start to stroke or touch his body beyond the simple return of his kiss, he would clasp her tight until again it was he who was charting the course of their passion.

At twenty years old, and dazzled by his power and glamour, this was all fine by Rosalie. Seldom can a woman have been deflowered under such splendid circumstances. Long before he actually entered her, Jurgen's skills had induced a climax of an intensity that was new to Rosalie. His smooth, smooth face between her thighs (Jurgen always waxed his chin for special occasions such as this) made her back arch with joy, and when the time came to fully consummate the night, big though he was, Jurgen had made her ready.

Afterwards she lay exhausted on the bed for some time. Jurgen Thor got up and, taking his drink, sat naked on some cushions and watched as the sun dipped behind the glorious mountains outside the window, and turned his body to a silhouette. It was then that the full splendour of the situation enveloped Rosalie, and for a moment she almost swooned, an experience she had never had before or since. She did not swoon, however, because something was preventing her from fully glorying in the luxury of the situation. Something felt very strange, in fact, felt wrong.

'Jurgen,' she said.

'My darling, you were wonderful,' he said, still staring at the setting sun.

'Thanks, but that wasn't what I was going to ask.'

'What, then?'

'Who pays for all this?'

There was a tiny pause.

'It's not so very expensive.'

'A house built on top of a mountain with a heli-pad. That's *quite* expensive.'

Jurgen turned to her. For the first time, there was a touch of irritation in his manner.

'We have friends who believe that what we do is of some worth. What *I* do is of worth.'

'I know that, Jurgen.' Rosalie pulled a sheet over herself. 'I was just saying that this is pretty amazing, that's all.'

'I'm a world leader, you know that, don't you? A *world* leader.'

'Of course I know that, Jurgen.'

'Natura fights elections in every democracy on Earth. Do you begrudge me some trappings of office? A house, a helicopter? Perhaps I should arrive at summit meetings by public transport.'

'Well, maybe you should.' Rosalie was now a little annoyed herself. 'We all know what the private car is doing, if everybody in the world used public transport that alone would probably save the –'

'I *know* that, little Miss Idealist! I knew it before you were born, damn it all, man! But there are practical considerations for a man in my position. People try to kill me, you know! I am also a bit too busy to be waiting for buses!' For a moment Jurgen Thor seemed almost hurt. 'Oh, my sweet naïve little almost virgin, how I would love the luxury of your innocence. To be twenty and to judge every little thing by what is right. But I have to lead and it is the leaders who have to take the tough decisions, yes, and then live with themselves afterwards.

You could not imagine the awful truth of some of the compromises I have taken in pursuit of what I believe. So be careful what you ask, tiny girl. You might get the answers which you don't want to hear!'

Jurgen stopped, the fire in his eyes dying as suddenly as it had been kindled. He got up and, big and naked though he was, his expression was that of a little boy. He crossed back to the bed, his tone suddenly sad and conciliatory.

'Forgive me, little funky beautiful babe. Sometimes even I get tired, you know? It's a tough game you're going to be playing. You must be careful that your dreams do not betray you. Idealism is a wonderful thing, it got you into this, but it is pragmatism that will keep you alive. There are many things we have to do that we don't like. Compromises that must be made. When we let off a bomb, we do not like the damage it does, but we like even less the thing which we seek to destroy. Let's not talk any more. I spend half my life talking.'

And he, of course, spent the other half fucking, which is what he proceeded to do until both he and Rosalie fell asleep.

Later though, and for some time afterwards, Rosalie thought about this conversation. He had seemed so moved, he had actually been hurt and angry. She could not escape the feeling that Jurgen Thor had been talking about more than his house and his helicopter.

Further adventures in cross-dressing.

'Hey, you want to get a coffee or something?'

Max's voice intruded upon Rosalie's thoughts. Bringing her down off that mountain in Switzerland and back across the years. Jurgen's bitter little speech had occasionally returned to her, tainting the memory of what had been a wonderful night. What had he meant about compromises? Why had he seemed so sad? So angry? Surely what Max was suggesting could not be true? Claustrosphere funding Mother Earth? The idea was insane. Then again, the fact that the human race was happily destroying the planet on which it lived was insane, everything was insane. But this? It was impossible.

'Max, I have personally led teams that have destroyed four plants which make Claustrosphere components. We attack them all the time. They can't possibly be funding us.'

'All I know is what I've told you. Maybe it's all bullshit, but Nathan definitely got knocked off after meeting Tolstoy, in a house hired by Tolstoy and it was a professional and clinical hit with no robbery involved. I can't think of a single motive other than the one I've suggested.'

'Maybe he had other enemies?'

'Come on, he'd only ever spent two weeks in LA, in a hotel room. Who's going to kill him for that? Besides, nobody but me, Tolstoy and his wife in England even knew where he was.'

'It's insane.'

'Well, maybe it is. I don't know. Why don't we go ask your pal Jurgen?'

Just then the beeper that Rosalie was wearing went off. She stepped to the window and looked out.

'Garda . . . Oh dear.'

Down in the single street which was all the village consisted of, Rosalie's lookout had been arrested. By an unhappy stroke of poor luck the local Garda were being particularly vigilant at that time, looking for Republicans from the North who were believed to be lying low in the area. Rosalie's comrade, hanging about as she was, had been routinely DNA-scraped by a constable and immediately identified as a member of a Mother Earth unit known to be led by Rosalie. Instantly, the Garda had dropped all thoughts of boring old Republicans. Rosalie was an escapee, somebody who had seriously embarrassed the force. If she was in the village, she would make a grand catch indeed. This was why the Garda were now knocking on doors at both ends of the street and a helicopter was clattering above the houses.

'They're searching every house,' Rosalie said from her vantage point at the window. 'My God, why did you have to come back? They've got me now for sure.'

Max was thrilled. Here was his chance to redeem himself.

'Look,' said Max, 'I know I didn't do too well last time but –'

'Don't tell me you want to pretend to be me again. That story will have been all over the force – they're hardly likely to fall for the same trick twice.'

'Variations on a theme, man. Will you trust me? Ask the child inside.'

Rosalie had little choice; there were no avenues of escape remaining to her. As far as she was concerned, within ten minutes she would be under arrest.

'What did you have in mind, then?'

'On the dressing-table, there's a moustache and some cosmetic putty – bring them over here.'

Rosalie nearly just gave herself up there and then.

'I will not. If I'm to be arrested, I shall do it with dignity.'

'Rosalie! We've only moments left,' said Max and, leaping out of bed, he grabbed his make-up bag. Rosalie would have protested further, but she found it difficult to speak because Max was sticking a false moustache to her upper lip.

'This time you get to be a man,' he said.

'Max, you're insane! I have a bosom.'

'Not by Hollywood standards, you haven't . . . You said you'd trust me, well, trust me! What do you have to lose?'

He pulled Rosalie's hair back tight into a ponytail.

'OK, you'll have to strip, completely, I'm afraid. Come on, come on, we don't have much time.'

'Max, I'm a *woman*!'

'I *know* that. Now strip!'

Scarcely knowing why, Rosalie stripped naked and Max instructed her to lie on the bed, her head propped against a pillow. He draped a crumpled sheet casually across her breasts, but left the rest of her body exposed.

'OK now, legs together . . . casual, come on, you're drunk, you've passed out, you're asleep.' Max raised one of her knees slightly, whilst making sure that her thighs were still clamped together. Then, even as they heard the Garda outside in the street, Max rolled the fleshy putty into a small sausage.

'I don't believe . . . !!' gasped Rosalie, looking down.

'Lie still!' Max barked. 'You're out to it! You've got to *think* out to it. You've got to *act*! A lot of people think acting is easy, but it isn't, it's *a damned tough trade*. Now remember, you are not a wild woman on a mission to save the planet, but a drunk Californian homosexual on holiday with his lover, OK? It's complex, it's delicate, it's *acting*!'

'Well, what do I do then?'

'Just close your eyes and try to snore a bit.'

And with that, Max gently buried one end of his little putty sausage into the mound of Rosalie's pubic hair and draped the length of it delicately across one of her thighs. Rosalie's legs twitched at his touch.

'Keep them together, for Christ's sake,' Max urged, 'I can't do balls at this speed, I'm not Michel-fucking-angelo.'

Rosalie's legs lay still. Max could hear the landlady conversing with the Garda downstairs. He knew he only had moments left. Rosalie already had the slightest downy snail-trail running up from her pubic hair towards her belly button. Max took some ash from the ashtray and darkened the hair slightly, considered attempting a shadow on her chin but knew he would smudge it in the rush. There was a half-empty Paddy bottle on the bedside table, and he laid it on the bed placing the neck of the bottle in Rosalie's hand. He checked again that the sheet across her chest was sufficiently rumpled to disguise the small rise of her bosom, then he gathered the undersheet together on either side of her thighs in an attempt to disguise the feminine curve of her hips. Rosalie's slim waist, he could do nothing about. It would just have to do, acting was down to bluff, and that was up to him. He whipped off the jockey shorts, which to his shame he had been wearing in bed, and just as the Garda began to hammer on the bedroom door he draped himself completely naked across the bed, his head on Rosalie's stomach.

'Open the door!' a stern voice demanded from outside.

'Ugh!' Max moaned as if from a deep sleep.

'Open the door or I shall kick it open!' the voice shouted.

'What? . . . Heh, who the hell is . . . ?' Max knew how to act semi-off his face, he was that way most mornings. The door burst open and two uniformed officers rushed in. Max gave them a split second to take in the whole scene before jumping up, naked, drawing their attention with him.

'My God! Oh no! *Scream*!!' he shouted, affecting a fey campness which would not have gone down very well with those members of the homosexual community who object to such stereotyping.

'Nathan, wake up! It's a bust! Don't tell me boy love is still illegal in this country! It's not! I know it's not! I checked with the travel agent. How dare you burst in here . . . you . . . you damn cavemen! Wake up, Nathan! . . . Oh, my God!' Max pretended to notice Rosalie's nakedness for the first time. Giving the Garda officers just a moment with which to follow his gaze and see again the pale, soft, feminine, but unquestionably equipped with penis, body on the bed, Max grabbed a coat and hurled it over Rosalie, before seeming to notice his own nakedness for the first time and cover himself with a towel.

'We were told there was a woman in here,' the constable stuttered, not knowing what to think.

'A woman! Don't be *disgusting*!' Max screeched.

'The landlady said there was a woman in here.' The policeman was getting out of his depth.

'Darling, I fear that in Mrs Mop's tiny world, when two people are fucking like rabbits and making the china shake in the best room, they are, by definition, a man and a woman. No other couplings would occur to her. Wake *up*, Nathan . . . !' Max shouted at Rosalie's prostrate form as he marched over to the dressing-table and grabbed both his own passport and that which had once belonged to the actual Nathan. 'Look. There's our IDs, I'm American, he's British and we're both *men*, thank you very much. I can assure you, I would know! . . . Wake *up*, Nathan!!' The officer flicked nervously through the two passports. Max, fearing the man might study the photos, attempted to partially obscure Rosalie's face by bending over to shake her, taking care not to disturb either the moustache or the rumpled sheet over her breasts. Rosalie, who was beginning to believe that Max might pull this off, groaned and dribbled, distorting her features as much as she felt she could get away with.

'My God, that Paddy's *Scotch whiskey* is *lethal*,' Max shrieked.

Max had judged his man well. The constable shuddered slightly. He was not a great fan of the love that dare not speak its name at the best of times, but when the homosexual in question also turned out to be a complete whoopsie who thought that Paddy's was Scotch, then the less time spent with him the better.

'Well, sir, as I say, I was informed that you had a woman with you, but since it's a fellah, I suppose . . . that's all right, isn't it?'

Max allowed his eyes to moisten and his voice to quiver with emotion.

'Officer, may I remark that that is the single most lovely thing I have ever heard a policeman say.'

'Yes . . . well . . . sorry to have bothered you then.' The policeman had got himself a little confused. 'Uhm, I hope your . . . friend . . .'

'Lover.'

'Yes, well, I hope he recovers . . . Good day to you, sir . . . and sir,' and with a slight nod at Rosalie's prostrate form, the constable and his companion left.

As she heard the door close Rosalie opened her eyes and they shone with wonder and excitement. In all her experience of living the life of an outlaw, in all the daring stories of escape she had heard around camp fires – or whilst bobbing about in inflatable boats, or sitting waiting in the bellies of helicopters, none had ever come close in audacity and flair to the trick of which she had just been a part.

Max was at the window.

'They've drawn a blank . . . I think they're going to chuck it. Don't break character yet, they may decide to bring their pals up for a laugh at the gay guys.' He stood watching for a while, watching the cops in the street, while Rosalie watched him.

'They're bringing their truck up . . . Man, they're going!' Max spun round to face her, completely thrilled, triumphant. 'We did it!'

'You did it, Max.' Rosalie was a fair-minded girl and gave credit where it was due. 'I can't believe it, but you did. What a concept! What a performance! You saved my neck and you were completely bloody wonderful.'

Yes, he had been wonderful. Max could scarcely demur, it had been a masterpiece of aggressive bluff, and what, after all, was great acting, but bluff?

Rosalie's eyes, which had been fixed upon Max's face, dropped slightly. She could not help but notice that Max was reacting to his own brilliance in his customary manner. Max followed her gaze. Beneath his towel was a stiff you could have flown a flag off.

'Oh dear,' said Max, genuinely embarrassed. 'I'm not

really such a vain guy . . . honestly, not in normal life . . .
It's just, when I do a really great show I . . .'

'Hey, Max,' Rosalie said, and her soft, soft Irish voice
would have made lush green pasture of a desert, 'don't
apologise. You were great, and if anyone's entitled to a
celebratory hard-on, it's you.'

This was it, and they both knew it. The excitement of
being so nearly busted, the adrenaline rush of escape. The
intimacy that the need for survival had already forced
upon them. It was so right. They were even already
naked, Max would not even have to take his socks off.

'I've got a laminate spray in my bag. Would you get
it?' Rosalie said, and as the gentle music of her voice
drifted out of the open window and into the street all
the milk in the village turned into rich butter. Max found
the spray.

'I use it to seal my gun in wet weather,' Rosalie
added.

'No woman should ever apologise for carrying protection,' said Max.

'Yes, well that's all very well, but as a rule spontaneous
love-making is not my style.'

'Nor me,' said Max, spraying on the stretch laminate.
He sort of believed himself too, for he had given all that
up now. He made a mental note to tell Rosalie about his
past some time, but not now.

He got into bed. They embraced.

'Would you mind removing your moustache?' Max
inquired.

Rosalie removed the offending disguise and they
embraced again. Max's hands stole down Rosalie's naked
body.

'Would it be OK if I took your penis away as well?' he

said, having encountered the little putty tube that had served them so well.

'OK, but don't spoil it,' Rosalie said. 'I want to keep it. No prick has ever done me better service.'

Max knew he could not equal that, but he resolved to do his best, and he and Rosalie made love.

It wasn't like in the movies, there were still elbows to get stuck under backs and hair to get in mouths, but suddenly that didn't matter. There can be few things better on Earth than to go to bed with the someone you have been dreaming about. Someone for whom you have been yearning. Max had imagined himself kissing and touching Rosalie's small soft but hard body a hundred times. Rosalie, although otherwise occupied, and somewhat less of a drip than Max, had also been thinking of him. Scarcely even realising it, they had fallen in love, and now, in each other's arms, they acknowledged it.

Chapter Twenty

New lovers, old lovers and screams from beyond a rocky grave

Limping out.

Jurgen Thor sat naked on his cushions, sipping his peach schnapps. The sun was dipping down behind the mountains and his tanned blond skin was growing shadow dark. A young woman lay on the bed. She too was naked, her body as near perfect as Jurgen's. A golden couple, silent in the setting sun. It was as it had always been. The stunning surroundings, the young, starstruck beauty. The man, great and good, unlocking the door to her heart and letting the passion out. It was as it had always been, a thousand seductions, a thousand grateful girls. Just the same. Except it was different. More different than Jurgen could ever have imagined, for instead of the sounds he usually heard emanating from the bed on these occasions – sometimes breathless, coy, half-finished sentences filled with wonder, sometimes gentle sobs as emotions became too much – instead, Jurgen heard something he had quite literally never heard before.

'Please don't worry about it,' the young woman said, 'I hear it happens to all guys sometimes. Really, I don't mind.'

Jurgen struggled to maintain his self-control. That this *little girl* should be trying to comfort him! Assuring him that she did not *mind*!

'My penis was recently blown off by a bomb, you know,' he said, trying to seem casual. 'That bitch of a surgeon must have sewn it back on wrong.'

'Yes, that's it,' said the girl, whose name was Scout. 'She must have sewn it on wrong.'

But they both knew that the surgeon had not got it wrong. Jurgen had been fine and upstanding during the protracted foreplay. He had undressed Scout in his usual accomplished manner, her clothes disappearing as if by magic. He had deposited her near-naked upon his great bed. Stayed her hand as she made to remove her bra, because, as with all things sexual, he liked to do it himself ... the removal of underwear being something which he particularly liked to dwell over. Yes, everything had been running along familiar lines. As usual he had knelt down on the bed beside her, feasting his eyes upon her whilst he spirited away her flimsy final garments and all the while the surgeon's work appeared to be holding up superbly. His erection was as proud and vertical as it ever was, you could have chucked horseshoes at it. Scout's eyes had grown wide with nervous but eager anticipation as she contemplated the miracle of natural engineering upon which she was about to allow herself to be impaled.

'Good Lord,' she had remarked, her voice betraying a childhood spent at a posh English girls' school. 'You will take it easy, won't you, sweetie? The last time I saw anything hung like that, it had just won the three-thirty at Epsom.' Scout snorted with laughter. She was a jolly

girl and like many English girls of her class found demon-
strative passion a bit foreign and embarrassing. She found
sex altogether easier to cope with if it was treated as
something of a joke. This could, of course, be rather
disconcerting for any poor fellow nervously attempting
to engender an atmosphere of lustful abandon. Nothing
spoils a grunting, groaning, bed-wobbling approach to
climax like a loud giggle followed by the comment . . .
'Sorry, I was just thinking how *funny* we must look from
behind.'

But Jurgen had encountered slightly gauche English
girls before and it was not horsey giggles which had
led to his surprising sexual collapse. Far from it. He
usually liked this type. He knew very well how a really
grown-up rogering could quickly wipe the silly grin off
these girls' faces. He had, in fact, been hugely looking
forward to seeing Scout's nervous jollity turn to that look
of complete surprise which comes when a girl realises
that all of her inhibitions have been expertly removed
and are now lying in distant corners of the room along
with her knickers and her hairclips.

'There is no need for the worrying,' Jurgen assured
Scout, as he assured all the girls. 'For me, there is only
pleasure in the pleasure of the woman. I make love to
make women happy. That is the only reason I do it.'

'Oh, don't worry about me,' Scout said with a jolly
snort, 'you just carry on. The only place I ever get an
orgasm is in Louis's Pâtisserie in Hampstead.'

But it looked as if tonight was going to be different.
Because as Jurgen applied his considerable skills, Scout's
body began to respond in a manner entirely new to her.

'Oooh,' she said as Jurgen played delicately with her
breasts. Stimulating them in a manner that was very

different to the maulings that chaps had given them in the past. So different, in fact, that had Scout not been absolutely sure, she might have imagined that Jurgen was caressing a completely different pair of tits altogether to the ones she normally wore to bed.

'Gosh,' she gasped as Jurgen's smooth jaw slid down between her thighs, his lips upon hers. How she shivered as he kissed her where previously she had only been gobbled, and even then, rarely, since Scout had always harboured a vague feeling that vaginas were things into which no chap had much business sticking his face.

By the time push came to shove, so to speak, Scout could not have been any hotter if Jurgen had set fire to the bed.

'Go on, then, screw me,' she astonished herself by saying. Up until now, the most passionate comment she had managed at this stage of the game was, 'I suppose I don't mind if you really want to'. Now, however, she wanted to be screwed and she said so. Jurgen Thor needed no further prompting. He sprayed on the laminate and plunged in.

'Wow!' Scout shouted in gay abandon, unaware that she had such hidden depths . . . and then only moments later, a muted, 'Oh'.

The seemingly impossible had happened. For the first time in his life, Jurgen Thor had gone the way of all flesh. For a moment, confident in his conquest, he had allowed his mind to wander. Having realised that his mind was wandering, Jurgen had reflected that he had better concentrate on the job in hand or else the unthinkable might happen. At which point, of course, the unthinkable did. Jurgen discovered, later than most men, that once you start worrying about it, you've lost it.

Reflections on erections.

Jurgen sat on his cushions in moody contemplation. His mind had wandered. Why? It had wandered a lot of late. He was becoming more and more distracted and he did not really know why. Except, perhaps, that times were changing and even his legendary energy, both physical and mental, must surely ebb some day. It was a curious sensation for Jurgen to be so bothered about something. Very little affected him emotionally in his life, nor had much done so for years. He had lived for so long with a full and profound knowledge of the real extent of planet death that conventional emotion had been rather lost to him. Every single day, he was confronted with statistics so terrible that he had become numb. Jurgen found it difficult to care about anything very much. But he did still value his sexual powers. To Jurgen, virility was a symbol of life in a dying world, and now even that was collapsing. A sense of mortality cloaked him like a contraceptive laminate. The end was nigh. Even his beloved mountains had changed for ever. There was no snow or ice at all on them now, not even on the highest peaks. The last ice had melted five years ago and it would never return.

Dirty snow.

Jurgen had always loved the cold. Snow and ice appealed to him far more than sun and sand. But it was gone. The only ice remaining lay at the poles, and Jurgen knew better than most how soon that too would disappear. It was not because of the famous greenhouse effect that the ancient ice was finally giving up the ghost, but by dint of something much less complex. Straightforward dirt was in the process of liberating four-fifths of the world's fresh water. Airborne pollutants had begun to dirty the shimmering white that lay at the hub of the world. Darkened as it was, it no longer reflected the sun's rays with the efficiency it had once done. Soon it would actively absorb them, and soon after that it would be possible to go surfing in Surrey.

The Claustrosphere Company, recognising the problem, had begun to fit 'Spheres located in low-lying regions with diving gear. Being hermetically sealed, a Claustrosphere could offer complete protection against submersion as long as one did not open the door. This was fine for a while, except that the whole point of the Claustrosphere was that the human race would survive to walk again on the surface of the planet. It would be a shame if one's children's children were to emerge from their long captivity and immediately drown. Hence the scuba tanks.

Jurgen was distracted from his sombre musings by the distant sound of an approaching helicopter. He was at once on guard. He had invited no other guests and as the world's premier greenie, he had many enemies. Jurgen suggested that Scout get dressed and, calling to his servants to arm themselves, he took his gun and climbed up the spiral staircase that led to the heli-pad.

The sound of the helicopter grew louder.

An old lover was returning.

From Galway to the Alps.

After leaving the little village in Galway where they had had so much excitement, Rosalie and Max had rejoined Rosalie's unit in the mountains, where they were preparing for their next action, an assault on the toxic waste convoys that converged in Belgium on their way to Britain.

Saunders, Rosalie's bag-headed colleague, was his usual inhospitable self.

'So now we've got a bloody poncey actor to add to our FBI man,' he had sneered through the hole in the front of his bag.

'This man saved my bacon in that village raid,' Rosalie snapped. 'We lost Hilary down in the street and without Max here, I'd have been caught as well for sure.'

'Oh, so he saved your bacon, did he? So now we have to cart around *two* Yanks who've saved your bacon, do we?' Saunders said, referring to poor Judy who was sitting under a tree, wrapped in a blanket. Judy looked miserable, which he was. He was not well-suited to the life of a guerilla fighter and was missing his duvet and hot malted chocolate. The sneer which Saunders directed at Judy's bedraggled form could be felt even through his bag. 'Jesus Christ, Rosalie, if we have to take on every bastard that saves your bloody bacon it looks like we're going to end up quite a crowd.'

But Saunders did not really mind. He was actually quite impressed to have someone as famous as Max Maximus join them for a spell. He had long thought that *The Man With No Face* would make a terrific subject for a movie and here was just the person to talk it over with.

'What I was thinking, right,' the scouser said, button-holing Max, 'was that you could play me before I got contaminated and I could play me after. That way we could save money on make-up. What do you think?' and with that, Saunders whipped his bag off.

'Potentially, it's huge. I'd suggest we did lunch but I don't think I could keep it down.' Max looked around, hoping that Rosalie would come and save him from the Liverpudlian lunatic. Rosalie, however, was nowhere to be seen. She had asked Judy to accompany her on a little stroll and they had wandered off together out of earshot. They were now sitting on some rocks, deep in conversation. At least Rosalie was sitting on the rocks. Judy, who suffered occasionally from piles, was trying to avoid sitting on any cold damp surfaces, which is rather a difficult thing to do if you happen to be living on the side of a mountain.

Rosalie was questioning Judy about Mother Earth funding.

'Surely the FBI must have investigated it?' she asked.

'I'm sure they did, but either they drew a blank or else they covered up their findings, because I asked many times. Not one of my superiors admitted to having any idea whatsoever about where your cash came from.'

'What about you, did you try to find out? Did no hint ever come out in all the files you had to work on?'

'I never saw the slightest thing. It's too well-laundered. Sometimes I wonder whether even Jurgen Thor himself knows who pays.'

But Rosalie felt that he did know. The memory of Jurgen's tired cynicism on that night in his sex den all those years ago kept returning. Rosalie knew that Jurgen Thor held the only key to the mystery.

Sad reflections.

Despite the absence of snow and ice the Swiss Alps still

presented an awesome sight when viewed from the air, and as she and Max approached Jurgen's lair in the helicopter Max had hired, Rosalie was remembering the last time she had flown over those mountains. On that occasion she had been filled with excitement, nervously anticipating the adventure which she had let herself in for. Now she felt a strange sense of foreboding. She could not explain it, but the mountains which had appeared so inspiring before, with their glittering peaks, now seemed sombre and unforgiving. Of course the sun was setting and the great craggy shadows which blackened the landscape would surely have dampened the lightest of spirits, but it was more than that. Rosalie could not shake a strange sensation of defeat and sorrow. Her spirits were sinking with the sun.

Perhaps it was because it had been amongst these mountains that she had first begun to lose her innocence. Not sexual innocence, although she had lost that here too; Rosalie attached no great significance to virginity. She knew that there was a first time in life for all things, and a last. Rather it was her spiritual innocence which had been so sadly eroded since she had last left these mountains. Since then she had seen so much horror. Horror which she had never dreamt of as an idealistic girl. Dead forests, dead lakes, dead species, dead communities. Everything she ever saw or touched was dead or dying. Rosalie was a naturally spiritual person and the planet's agony was her agony. She honestly believed that she felt it, just as some people's bones ache when the weather changes.

As Max piloted the helicopter through the gloomy sunset (he had starred in the fourth remake of *Apocalypse Now*) it dawned upon Rosalie that it was here that she

279

had first begun to understand how unutterably and indescribably sad humankind was. Jurgen Thor's little lesson in compromise had proved horribly prophetic. She was a terrorist in a terrible world and, like a black crow struggling in a stormy sky, she could not be distinguished from the environment in which she did battle. The passion which had brought her to the struggle against planet death had been replaced by what was merely a grim refusal to take the inevitable lying down. Only a fool could have seen the things which Rosalie had seen and remain an idealist. She had long since given up any thought of fighting for a better, more beautiful world. All her life meant now was struggle, to prevent the most gruesome excesses of a situation which was, and always would be, disastrous.

'Anything wrong?' Max asked.

'People are shit, the world's dead and everything is pointless.'

'Oh, good, I was worried something was bothering you.'

Rosalie smiled wearily.

'I was just thinking, that if your theory about Claustro-sphere and Mother Earth is correct, my entire adult life has had no point whatsoever.'

'Well, you're only twenty-five. Plenty of time to jack it in and do something else.'

'Perhaps I should.'

She wanted to turn round. She was losing her nerve. All they had, after all, was the stupid hunch of one dead screenwriter, and an English one at that. On the strength of this they were preparing to invade the great man's privacy, entirely uninvited, and confront him with the extraordinary suggestion that the forces of environmental protection were in fact in the pay of the planet's number one enemy.

'He'll laugh at us,' said Rosalie as Max manoeuvred the craft down on to the heli-pad.

'Laughter would be fine,' Max replied. He could see Jurgen and a couple of minions waiting on the deck, heavily armed and ready to shoot.

The pragmatist concludes his lesson.

'We have to speak to you, it's important,' Rosalie said as the clatter of the helicopter blades began to subside.

'Why not?' Jurgen shrugged. 'It must be pretty important, OK, for you to interrupt your preparations for the toxic convoy raid. Yes, babe?'

Jurgen loved to show how he was party to all Mother Earth actions. He knew Rosalie as an activist, he also recalled their previous intimacy. Max Maximus, he recognised, of course, but if he was surprised at the arrival of a famed media star, he did not show it. Jurgen of course mixed constantly with world leaders in every field, he was more than used to celebrity. Besides, he himself was a bigger star than any Hollywood actor.

Dismissing his servants, Jurgen led Max and Rosalie downstairs into the house. They descended through the bedroom which, as Rosalie recalled, covered the entire top floor of the house and offered the only access to the heli-pad. Scout was still there as they passed through and Rosalie experienced a small sense of déjà vu. Pausing for a moment on the spiral stair, she took in the proud, slightly defiant face of the pretty young woman and glanced at the huge white bed and crumpled sheets.

Jurgen Thor made his excuses to Scout and led Max

and Rosalie down into his study. There on the wall, they were astonished to find the mounted heads of animals belonging to several species which were basically extinct, except of course, for a few genetically recreated specimens in zoos. There was a tiger, a lion, even an elephant, its expression one of inconsolable sadness . . . as indeed it might have been, considering its head had been cut off and stuffed with straw, its natural habitat had been totally destroyed, and its race had disappeared from the face of the Earth. Jurgen noted the surprise and indeed revulsion that convulsed the faces of his guests as they took in his macabre interior decor.

'They keep my anger alive,' he said, by way of an explanation, although it fell a long way short of convincing either Max or Rosalie. They could not help feeling that there were perhaps more sensitive ways of maintaining one's commitment to wildlife than displaying the severed heads of dead lifeforms above your writing desk.

'So what is it that is so important that you fly all the way to the highest mountain to talk to me about?' Jurgen inquired.

Max had convinced Rosalie that, if Nathan's idea was correct, the only hope of getting Jurgen to come clean about it was to catch him off-guard, to confront him directly and with confidence. It was a risky plan because if they were wrong, Rosalie, in particular, was going to look something of an idiot. She was, after all, an environmental activist and it was pretty big stuff to accuse the biggest green hero of all of sleeping with the enemy. Max, however, was confident that they were not wrong.

'Mr Thor,' he said. 'We have come here because we

know that the Claustrosphere Corporation funds Mother Earth and we want to know why.'

Jurgen could not prevent a flicker of shock from crossing his handsome, granite-like face. He had not expected this and for a moment it seemed that he would hurl their accusation back in their faces. Then he sighed. He had been feeling that events were beginning to approach their end. This surely was just one more symptom.

There was almost a hint of relief in his voice when he said, 'You ask me why? I would have thought the answer was patently obvious.'

Despite his sombre mood, Jurgen enjoyed the effect he had on Rosalie. He might have failed to get it up Scout, but he was certainly still capable of making a beautiful woman gasp and roll her eyes.

'How did you find out?' he added, casually stroking the head of a monkey, whose jaw served as a tobacco pouch.

'It isn't true!' Rosalie shouted. 'Claustrosphere pays us! Pays me! It's madness, they're the enemy. They hate us . . .'

'Of course, they hate us, and we hate them. That doesn't mean that we can't do business, does it?'

Rosalie was speechless. She could not begin to imagine what Jurgen Thor was talking about. It was nonsense, it had to be. Except, of course, that it wasn't, it was just business, as Jurgen went on to explain.

'Think about it, Rosalie. Why do people buy Claustrospheres?' Neither Max nor Rosalie offered an answer, which was fine by Jurgen, the floor was his and he was holding it. 'Because they fear that the Earth is dying, of course. And who is it that tells them every single day that they are right? That the Earth *is* dying!

Why, us, of course! It is Natura and Mother Earth whom people look to for the truth, and my God, do we give it to them. We tell them the truth. We show them the truth. You, Rosalie, personally risk your life most days to confront people with the truth. And the truth is that the planet is getting dangerously close to being incapable of supporting human life. We tell them this in the hope that people will wake up! That they will start to nurture their planet. That they will adjust their lifestyles. Boycott the products of polluters, lobby their politicians, *save the Earth*! That is why we tell them the truth. But what do most people *actually* do when confronted with the unanswerable evidence that we hurl before them every day?'

'Buy a Claustrosphere,' said Max. 'I know I did.'

'Exactly. Buy a Claustrosphere. Of course you did,' said Jurgen. 'It would be madness not to. If the dear conscientious, idealistic old greenies are right and planet death is upon us, *which it is*, what else can one possibly do?'

'Yes, but . . .' Rosalie blurted, but for the time being she could do no better than that. Her mind was reeling.

'Exactly,' said Thor. 'Yes, but . . . what? Yes, but nothing, darling, OK! I have spent half a lifetime searching for that elusive "yes, but" and not one sniff of it have I had. We are trapped by our own beliefs. Prisoners of the truth that we must tell. We say that to own a Claustrosphere is in itself the greatest act of planet treason one can commit, because by owning a Claustrosphere, a person accepts that the death of the Earth is survivable. How, then, are we to stop people taking this terrible step? We must warn them of the consequences of their actions! So we shout that buying a Claustrosphere will hasten the demise of the Earth. And what does that warning make people do?'

'Buy a Claustrosphere,' said Max.

'Exactly.' And for a moment Jurgen Thor even seemed to smile. 'Everything that we do sells Claustrospheres. We are their greatest advert. No wonder they fund us.'

Rosalie spoke as if in a dream. 'But what you're saying is that it would be better for us to do nothing, to say nothing.'

'Believe me, I have often considered it,' Jurgen continued. 'Because if every environmentalist on Earth shut up then Claustrosphere sales would plummet. But if we did that then planet death would surely occur without even a protest, without even a small effort to stop it. That must never happen, we will not die on our knees! And so we are caught, Rosalie, caught between the devil and two hard places, you dig? If we are silent the Earth will probably die, if we are the shouters the Earth will probably die. I am a man of action and so I prefer to be a shouter.'

'But that Claustrosphere should pay for it!' Rosalie was struggling not to give way to despair.

'Who else would support us so generously? Who else would supply us immediately and without question with everything we need? Once I have decided to fight I would be a fool to deny myself the best weapons simply because I did not like the arms dealer. I don't like any arms dealer. Would you like me to turn them down, to say, no, I will blow up this waste ship with a poorer, cheaper but somehow cleaner bomb?'

'You don't have to have such a nice bloody house.'

Suddenly Rosalie was furious. It was the calm logical way he described it, and he did seem to do so damn well out of it.

'Why the hell should I not have a bloody nice house, God damn!' Jurgen too was angry all of a sudden. 'I'm happy to spend as much of their money as they care to give me. I once told you, Rosalie, pragmatism in all things. Would one less Claustrosphere be built if I denied myself beautiful things? Will one more flower grow? No, of course not, I would be cutting off my nose just so I could have some spite on my face.'

'That is a totally corrupting argument.'

'I *am* corrupt, Rosalie. The nature of leadership requires that I be corrupt. If I were not corrupt you would have no guns! The nice ladies who send out our mailshots would have no envelopes. My corruption pays your wages.'

'No, I don't believe it, we have subscriptions, fund-raisers.'

'Jam and bazaars while the enemy has the combined wealth of total world exploitation. Would you have our people face a lion with the shooter of peas?'

It was an unfortunate image. There was a lion, or at least a part of one, silent witness to their debate. Rosalie felt an overwhelming sense of revulsion, against Jurgen, against herself, against the mere fact of being alive.

'I'm going to blow the whistle. This is wrong, it can't go on.'

'If you do that you will sell another 10,000 Claustro-spheres in an hour. If once the dreadful truth emerges, that the human race is so utterly damned that its only defence must be financed by those who seek to destroy it, then surely there will be a panic of the soul. Even those who still hope, who still harbour some small semblance of responsibility to themselves and others, will give it up. They will say, if even Mother Earth is part of the process of planet death then it is over, the planet *will* die. I saw it in your own face a moment ago. It's hopeless, you thought! What is the damn point, you thought! Well if that is your reaction to the truth, to the natural logic of human madness, then how will the less concerned react, the less *pure*? What do you think they will do the day you tell them that Mother Earth sups with the devil?'

'Buy a Claustrosphere,' said Max.

'Stop *saying that*!' Rosalie shouted at him. Her eyes were filling with tears for she knew that Jurgen Thor was right. On learning the truth, a terrible dark fiend of despair had taken her by the throat and brought her to the ground. She had been utterly overwhelmed by the hopelessness of hope. Anything other than bitter cynicism seemed completely naïve. Others would feel the same, and worse. The truth would provide the ultimate justification for cynicism. That must never be. She could not tell. In order to continue to fight for the truth, she and Mother Earth must continue to live a lie.

'Why doesn't the Claustrosphere Company itself blow the whistle,' asked Max thoughtfully, 'if it would shift so many units?'

'In the short-term it would, but the shock would wear off. People would learn to live with this revelation of human frailty as they have with all the others. With us green fools gone, Claustrosphere would lose their greatest propaganda tool. They would have destroyed us, but in doing so they would cripple themselves, and the Earth would stagger towards death with neither defenders nor exploiters. For without environmental protest how can they market the end of the world? We are the shit against which they must kick.'

'*Market the end of the world*! My God, listen to your-self! You sound like Plastic Tolstoy.' Rosalie could not bear the way Jurgen Thor seemed to glory in his pragmatism.

'You pay me a handsome compliment.' Jurgen smiled. 'For Plastic Tolstoy is a genius. It was he who first understood what a splendid marketing tool we are for Claustrosphere. It was he who approached me with the offer to fund us. Believe me, if we could market ourselves with the skill with which he has marketed Claustrosphere, the planet would be healthy indeed.'

'You can't market responsibility! It's not a packet of fish fingers.'

'Exactly. What we offer is painful truth and difficult decisions, both of which are bloody difficult to sell, you dig? Which is why I take Tolstoy's coin. No one but he would support such a hopeless cause with such generous commitment.'

Rosalie sank into a chair made out of stag antlers. She was drained and weary.

'So what am I supposed to do?' she asked eventually.

'Do? Why, nothing. You continue as before. You go back to your unit and organise the raid on the toxic waste convoy. Very few people know what you know. Myself, some senior figures in the movement and of course our opposite numbers in the Claustrosphere Company. If you ever did decide to break the confidences I have shared with you, I would of course deny them utterly. If necessary, I would have you silenced permanently, because if you were believed then Mother Earth and Natura would be finished and the last barrier between us and the Rat Run would be gone.'

'I won't tell,' said Rosalie in a hollow monotone. 'As you say, it would do more harm than good.'

'Remember what I once told you, Rosalie,' said Jurgen.

'Be careful what you ask, tiny girl. You might get the answers that you don't want to hear.'

There was nothing more to say.

'Come on, Max, let's go,' said Rosalie wearily. 'Thanks for being so honest with us, Jurgen.'

'It was nothing, baby, OK?' Jurgen replied. 'My congratulations at having discovered the truth for yourselves. Every day I expect the whole world to wake up and figure it out, but they never do.'

Jurgen offered them dinner but they declined politely. Rosalie didn't want to talk any more, she just wanted to leave. One thing was still bothering her, though.

'If the Claustrosphere Company are your friends, how come they tried to blow you up in Brussels?' she asked as they made their way up to the heli-pad.

Suddenly all Jurgen's masterly charm deserted him. His face flashed with fury. Rosalie thought that he would hit her.

'They are not my damn *friends*, you stupid fucking bitch!! Haven't you been listening to anything? I take their money because I hate them! I take their money because I want to fight them with the best weapons I have. I take their money because if I do not stop them they will destroy the Earth. They pay me, and I try to kill them. It's a simple business transaction.'

'And they try to kill you.'

'Of course they do. At the moment, I am the leader of our movement but there are others, there will always be others. Perhaps one day you, Rosalie; you are very highly thought of in our movement. I am valuable, but expendable. That is why they tried to kill me. Why they try to kill me now.'

'Why now?' Now Max was curious.

'Because Claustrosphere is in a mini-slump. Everybody already owns one. Tolstoy must mount a new marketing drive. He wants to institute a massive and completely pointless upgrade of existing technology. My death would be a tremendous boost for him. Can you see the headlines? Green God Dead! Last Sane Man On Earth Murdered! Environmental Movement In Turmoil! It would sell ten million units. Tolstoy has been saving me up for this.'

Rosalie was about to enter the helicopter. She turned and looked at Jurgen.

'So they pay us, we work for them, our goals are diametrically opposite and we want each other dead.'

'Of course, isn't it obvious?'

Dominant fantasy.

Jurgen Thor watched as the helicopter containing Max and Rosalie disappeared into the distance. They had been lucky, he thought. Really, he should probably have killed them for what they had discovered. But somehow, he preferred to let Rosalie stew in it. He knew she would not tell and Jurgen rather enjoyed the knowledge that beautiful, dedicated little Rosalie, one of the prides of Mother Earth, should have been tainted by the terrible truth. Or at least a part of the terrible truth. Jurgen could not really explain it to himself, but he felt that by sharing at least some of his dark secrets with Rosalie, he had somehow *soiled* her, and that made him feel good. It made him feel strong and bad. He had forced that sweet, pure little girl to descend partway into the mess of compromise and deceit that he lived in every day. She was dirty now, like him, and he had made it so.

One day, perhaps he would tell her the whole truth, then she really would have something to cry about.

Within his loins Jurgen felt the stirrings of the erection that had eluded him earlier in the evening.

'How do you feel now, little virgin?!' he shouted after the lights of the distant helicopter. 'Now that you're in Jurgen Thor's world? Do you feel good, huh? I said, do you feel good?' But Jurgen knew that she didn't feel good, he knew that she felt sad, and compromised. He could picture her, sitting in the passenger seat of the helicopter, miserable, small, confused and . . . dirty. That made Jurgen happy. It filled him up and satisfied him. Except it didn't, because now he wanted to screw her. If only she hadn't brought that shitty little movie star, he told himself, he would have screwed her too.

Then he remembered that Scout was still in his bedroom. Now there was a treat indeed with which to end his sad, dark day. Why not? he had earned it. He would go downstairs and fuck that young idealistic little idiot's brains out . . . what brains she had, anyway. There would be no collapse of manhood this time, Jurgen told himself. For he was Jurgen Thor and he was standing on top of the world. The chill wind of the night whipped at his long blond hair as he glared angrily into the darkness. His chest thrust out, his legs four square and his face set with ugly defiance. It was if he was challenging whatever God watched over him to damn him for the things he had done. For the things he had still to do.

Before retreating to the bedroom for his reward he watched until the lights of the helicopter disappeared completely.

Yes, one day he might give himself the pleasure of

telling sweet little Rosalie the whole truth and she could come with him to hell.

Fatal idealism.

Jurgen Thor turned and went back down the staircase into his bedroom. There would be no protracted foreplay this time, no gentle pursuit of the female orgasm. Jurgen Thor intended to tear the clothes off young Scout and bang her till he was finished, that was all. Then he would drink all night and bang her again as the dawn came up.

His fantasies of domination were brought to something of an abrupt conclusion, however, when he found himself facing the barrel of a gun.

'You disgust me,' said Scout, her lips trembling with emotion.

'Excuse me, baby?' Jurgen inquired, genuinely shocked.

'Don't "baby" me, you limp-willied hypocrite!' Scout shouted. 'I was listening at the door to everything you said when you were downstairs.'

'You listened?' Jurgen Thor was a little concerned by this.

'Of course I did! Coo, you don't get many chances to hear Jurgen Thor talking with huge movie stars. I thought it would be exciting, a bit more exciting at least than things have been with you so far, anyway. I thought it would be inspiring, that Max Maximus must be a secret activist and that I'd hear wonderful things about the fight against Claustrosphere. What do I hear? The most disgusting compromise there could ever be. I still can't believe it. You, me, all this, paid for by Plastic Tolstoy! It makes me bloody sick. I've wasted two whole years of my life training to be a hyprocrite and I think it's absolutly off.'

'Give me the gun, Scout,' Jurgen said.

'Like hell, I will. Crikey, you've got some nerve, still thinking you can hand out orders to me.'

'So what is it you want, then?'

'I'll tell you what I want, chum. I want a full confession from you on video tape. This bloody charade has gone on long enough.'

Scout was just too young and idealistic to swallow the kind of pragmatism with which Jurgen had per-suaded Rosalie to maintain her silence. She had not gone through the five years of pointless struggle that Rosalie had gone through, had not watched everything she tried to defend die. She was still a young girl who believed the world could be saved by people acting decently. She also believed fervently in that old Mother Earth dictum that Claustrosphere was planetary treason – in fact, she had a poster of Jurgen Thor on her bedroom wall which said exactly that. How often had she lain on her bed, staring into those gorgeous eyes, dreaming of how one day she would follow the Green God into battle against Claustrosphere. Now it turned out that those eyes had lied, that Jurgen Thor and Plastic Tolstoy were just two sides of the same coin. Scout was too young to accept that nothing was sacred and that even idealists must make compromises. She was discovering all at once just how wicked the world was and what a terrible thing it was to be human. She could not take it.

'I don't care what it does to Mother Earth, I'm going to make this nightmare public,' she said. 'In the long run you can't build anything lasting and decent on lies.'

'That is not so, my love. Lies are as important as truth, for without lies, the truth is worthless,' said Jurgen.

'Now that's just bloody twaddle and you know it. You don't like being called a hypocrite, that's all. But that's what you are and I'm going to tell, so just get downstairs, you must have a video recorder in your study.'

And so Jurgen Thor returned to the study where he had been so recently conversing with Rosalie and Max, only this time he was not the masterful one, secure and in control. This time he was the prisoner of someone he considered scarcely more than a child. That was what Scout thought, anyway. As it happened, Jurgen was about to regain control in spectacularly brutal fashion. He did not want to kill her, so he made one last attempt to reason with her.

'Scout, you're making a big mistake here. No good can come of this, for you or the Earth. Are you catching what I'm saying here, babe?'

'Listen, Mr Thor, either you're going to tape a confession about Claustrosphere and Mother Earth or I'm going to shoot you and hang the consequences. I feel sick of everything and I don't care any more.'

'So be it,' said Jurgen Thor sadly.

It was a simple matter for Jurgen to manoeuvre Scout into the position he wanted. She was maintaining the maximum distance she could from him, so in order to get her to stand against the wall he required, he merely had to stand against the opposite wall himself. Of course he could have disarmed her. Jurgen was as sure as anything that Scout would not shoot if he called her bluff. But what then? He could scarcely let her go. This was one girl that he could not guarantee would keep her mouth shut. She would blab and blab and blab and even though no one would believe her, hers was a story that Jurgen simply did not want told.

The house was built on the actual peak of the mountain. The top floor, which made up the bedroom, was parallel with the mountain-top, and the lower floors were built out from the steep rock that fell away from the summit. This meant that underneath the bottom floor, which was Jurgen's study, there was nothing but the supporting poles which jutted out of the rockface. In order that these support poles might be periodically maintained, there was a trapdoor in the study floor. It was over this trapdoor that Scout now stood.

Jurgen Thor had always loved that trapdoor. He sometimes opened it at night and sat at the edge, dropping lighted coals into the dark chasm beneath, watching as the bright embers disappeared into a grim crack in the rock hundreds of metres below. He had even had a trapeze fitted. His friends could scarcely credit it, but Jurgen Thor sometimes *swung* from beneath the trapdoor. With no safety harness or line of any sort, he would hurl himself through the air, back and forth, back and forth, nothing but rushing air between him and the chasm below.

'Scout,' he said, 'you are about to experience something truly strange and unique. Something I have always wondered about. Try to stay conscious and aware as it happens, for it will be a fine and a triumphant end for a brave but stupid girl.'

Even as a moment of nervous doubt and concern flitted across Scout's face, Jurgen crossed to his desk in a single stride and pushed a button. The trapdoor fell away beneath her feet and with no more than a gasp of surprise, she disappeared into the cold darkness.

Jurgen went to the edge of the deadly hole and peered out. There was nothing to be seen, Scout was long gone and the velvet night had enveloped her. She could still be heard, though. The scream, which had found its voice moments after Scout's deathly descent began, rang around those dark and terrible rocks, invisible in the blackness, but awesomely present all the same.

Scout screamed for a moment or two, even after she died. The drop was a long one and the speed of sound is no respecter of the dead. As the last echoes of her short life faded into the stillness, Jurgen Thor closed the trapdoor. To his surprise, he found that he was crying, as much for himself as for Scout. He was truly sorry that he had had to kill her. Repentance would do him no good, though, he knew that. If there was a God, then Jurgen Thor was damned and a few idle tears would not wash away his sins.

Chapter Twenty-One

Betrayal and disaster

Traitor in the midst.

The police could only stand back and watch as the first of the mighty tankers pulled on to the grand mosaic-covered piazza at the front of the European parliament.

In a Land Rover leading the lethal procession, squashed in between Rosalie and Saunders, sat Judy, his mood swinging from misery to elation with every bump in the road. He was miserable because he was cold and wet and his backside was sore. Judy had loathed camping and adventure holidays as a child, and the intervening years had not changed his attitude at all. The lifestyle which Mother Earth had chosen for themselves was one which, as far as Judy was concerned, they could keep.

Despite the cold and the damp, however, he was also feeling pretty pleased with himself. Here he was, at the very heart of a major Mother Earth action. He had infiltrated further into the organisation than he could have dreamt possible, further indeed than any of his more favoured colleagues had managed in a very long time. True, he was acting entirely on his own initiative, and had deserted whilst in the line of duty in order to do it, but Judy hoped that if he achieved the result he was looking for, then all would be forgiven.

He shifted uncomfortably in his seat.

'Keep still, will you!' barked Saunders, the man with no face.

'Sorry. I was just thinking that I may have developed piles.'

'Ha! You hear that, Rosalie?' Saunders sneered. 'A noble wound, eh? Give the man a Purple Heart, he's got a sore arse. Some of us have got *real* battle-scars.'

One of Saunders's hands left the steering-wheel and began to tug at the buckles that secured his head-bag at the neck.

'Leave it alone, Saunders, and drive the bloody car!' snapped Rosalie.

She too had a lot on her mind. Despite the fact that the raid had so far been a colossal success, Rosalie could take no pleasure in it, knowing as she did that the whole thing had been financed by Tolstoy . . . who was, to all intents and purposes, the anti-Christ. She was certainly in no mood to deal with Saunders's bombast.

'Don't even think about taking off your bag, Saunders,' she went on. 'I'm in no kind of mood for it. Just leave Schwartz alone to worry about his bum.'

It was not, in actual fact, haemorrhoids that had made Judy shift uncomfortably in his seat. His reflections on how successful he had been so far had reminded him of the unpleasant fact that his success had been obtained at the expense of deceiving Rosalie. Judy was not at all happy about this. He admired Rosalie, and knew that it was only because of her recommendation that the Mother Earth leadership had agreed that he remain with the unit at all. Let alone be allowed to take part in a mission.

'He saved me from a life sentence,' Rosalie had said

whilst pleading Judy's case. 'That means prison for him if we throw him out. I think we owe him the benefit of the doubt. Besides, if he is what he says he is, then he could be very useful indeed. Let me keep an eye on him, I'll answer for it.'

Judy was keenly aware that Rosalie had chosen to trust him and that he intended to repay that trust by betraying her. This did not make him feel good about himself. However, it was Judy's opinion that Rosalie was about to commit a ruthless and wicked crime which he had to stop. He did not doubt that she would be acting in accordance with her own sense of what was right and just, but then every murderous zealot in history had claimed to have God on their side.

Celeb status.

Rosalie had also sought to get Max on to the team, but at this, a line had been drawn. It was felt that famous media stars could prove something of a liability whilst trying to hijack toxic waste shipments. Autograph hunters would only get in the way.

'If he wants to join Mother Earth,' the leadership had said, 'he can start at the bottom, just like anybody else.'

Rosalie could see their point. Terrorist raids were not social events, lovers and boyfriends could not be included. Max was less understanding. In fact he was mystified.

'But I'm a *major celebrity*, man!' he had exclaimed. 'Most people kill to have my puss in their hood.'

'Max, Mother Earth is a guerilla army, not an LA nightclub or a video launch. We don't get better results because we have famous people along.'

Max said that he understood, but he didn't really

believe it. He had lived for too long in a world in which fame was the ultimate credential. A world where there was literally no activity, neither business nor pleasure, which was not deemed the better for having a celebrity attached to it.

'OK, OK,' he said, trying not to sound offended. 'I'll just sit on my butt in Paris and get wasted. You know, really get in touch with my excessive side. That's what I like to do anyway. Party, right? Your mission is to save stuff, mine is to party. I was only trying to be cool.' There was a pause, then Max gave himself away by adding, 'You're *sure* you told them it was me?'

'Yes, I did, Max, I'm sorry, but I think that made it worse.'

Now Max knew there had been a mistake. He attempted to absorb what Rosalie was suggesting but he simply could not, it was too alien a concept. His name had made things *worse*? Impossible.

'Listen,' he said, 'it's kinda clear there's been a balls-up at their end, but don't you worry about it, OK? Just let it go. *Walk away.* I'll have my office check it out with these droogs and we'll have the cruddy little no-names crawling to us on their knees in a day or two.'

Rosalie took Max's advice and let it go. Reminding herself always to remember that even though hers and Max's worlds may have collided, they were still worlds apart.

Waste disposal unit.

The mission, on which Max would not be going, was to hijack the convoy of waste which regularly crossed the English Channel from mainland Europe for what was inaccurately called 'disposal' in Britain. Then to

take the captured convoy to the centre of E
administration in Brussels and dump it.

Britain was Europe's waste disposal unit, and in
the world's. Anything that could not be illegally dumped
in the poverty nations, Britain took. As far as Britain was
concerned, dumping other people's crap, or 'processing
and disposal', as it was called, was actually a desirable
industry that had been quite deliberately developed over
many decades.

'Waste is an inevitable by-product of growth, and what
is growth?' the Prime Minister had inquired of the faithful
at a recent Party conference.

'Growth is good!' the faithful had thunderously replied.

'How often is it good?' the Prime Minister shouted.

'It's always good!' came the nearly evangelical answer.

'Exactly,' said the PM, calming down. 'And we should
be proud of the amount of deadly poison lying around
in Britain, as it is proof of our important role in the
growth cycle.'

There was much to be proud of. Every nook and cranny
in the British Isles was crammed to bursting point with
hamburger boxes, old condoms and nuclear waste. From
disused mine shafts to condemned housing estates, the
waste 'disposal' companies proved endlessly ingenious
at finding new ways to 'dispose' of the undisposable.
And they needed to, for more kept arriving every day.
Sometimes the rubbish was comparatively benign. Many
American cities, for instance, banned from using up any
more of their own environment as landfill dumps for
domestic rubbish, payed the British to take it off their
hands. Often, though, the rubbish was more sinister.
Nuclear waste 'disposal', for instance, was a major industry in Britain. Every day the thousands of power stations,

301

with which the French kept the European Grid alive, produced copious quantities of radioactive waste which the British then 'disposed' of. They did this by sealing it in concrete tombs. Tombs which they then covered in alarming symbols, in the hope of dissuading as yet unborn civilisations, thousands of years hence, from tampering with that which would surely kill them.

Such is progress. The Egyptians left tombs which thousands of years later yielded up treasures of indescribable beauty, testimony to the glory of their civilisation. The British, who have produced so many things that could serve as splendid witness to a great society, leave only deadly poison to be remembered by.

Target.

Then there were the industrial toxins. Those embarrassing by-products of economic activity which could kill a river or poison a sky. Toxins which were taken once a month by convoy from the industrial centres of Europe to be 'processed' in Britain. It was these toxins which were to be the target of Rosalie's raid.

The convoys had long been the focus of much peaceful protest. The Natura argument was that at any point in the lengthy 'disposal' process, a terrible disaster could occur. The authorities argued that such a disaster could not occur because the safety precautions employed were foolproof. Eventually the Natura leaders decided that this complacent attitude must be exposed. It was decided that Mother Earth should demonstrate the convoy's vulnerability by hijacking it before it reached the Channel Tunnel and diverting it to Brussels.

'We will mount a terrorist raid and capture the whole

thing,' the Mother Earth strategists had said at their secret planning meeting, 'in order to demonstrate how easy it would be to mount a terrorist raid and capture the whole thing.'

Once the convoy had been taken to Brussels, the plan was that the entire cargo would be dumped outside the thirty-five-chambered Palace of Peace and Profit. (The thirty-sixth chamber had been destroyed by the bomb attack on Jurgen Thor.)

'We will see just how dangerous those Euro bastards think this stuff is when they have to climb over it to get to their cars!'

The Founding Beardies.

That Rosalie's group should have been chosen to carry out the hijack showed the great respect in which she was held at Mother Earth. It was an enormous responsibility, towards which Rosalie would normally have been looking with a thrill of excitement. However, she could not get the grim discovery of how Mother Earth was financed out of her mind. Jurgen Thor's little lesson in pragmatism had changed her attitude to her work entirely, and it was with weary resignation that she had made the final preparations for the action at hand.

The hijack was, in fact, to be Rosalie's first direct action as a unit commander, or 'Group Facilitator' as the rank was known within Mother Earth. To have become a Group Facilitator was a tremendous leap for Rosalie. There were only fifteen Groups worldwide, and Rosalie would be the youngest Facilitator by far. Rosalie did not like being called a Facilitator, any more than her second in command like being called a 'Facilitator's Friend', or her superior liked being called a 'Team Enabler'. These rather horrid titles were generally felt to be a total embarrassment. They could not be dropped, however, because they were part of the Mother Earth tradition, and held dear by the very oldest activists, veterans who had been so over-exposed to toxicity during the early days of struggle that there was really very little left of them any more but false teeth, boring anecdotes and a seemingly insatiable desire to inform people of how things had been in the early days.

Before Jurgen Thor had formed Natura, there had been a terrible period when mainstream environmental politics were the preserve of naïve, idealistic old hippies and, perhaps even more gruesomely, witches and 'new pagans'. Greenies, who were nice (some of them, anyway) but a bit stupid, firmly believing that if they and their friends pretended that something was so, then it would be so.

'If we want to change the world, we must first change ourselves,' earnest people with beards and big jumpers and the occasional pointy hat assured each other. 'You cannot destroy a structure by creating a structure.'

'But surely this makes no sense and could in fact be described as bollocks,' the odd brave soul would say, only be told that their hostility proved the point.

The bearded and bejumpered ones (the ones with pointy hats having by this time walked out in disgust and gone off to celebrate a convenient solstice) claimed that, since it was power structures which maintained the polluters in their positions of authority, then those structures should not be copied.

'We will not caricature the methods of those we wish to destroy!' they said. 'We will reinvent a non-exploitative structure, to bring about a non-exploitative world. We must *be* what we stand for! Otherwise we will be hypocrites.'

Whether they were hypocrites or not was a matter of opinion, what was beyond dispute, however, was that they very soon became a complete joke.

Having rejected the concept of leadership, their position was presented by an ad hoc committee of occasional speakers, which meant of course that they completely failed to communicate with the outside world. The truth (as everybody knew but no one had the guts to admit) was that an argument, no matter how good, if delivered by an ad hoc occasional speaker was always going to be less convincing than an argument, no matter how bad, delivered by a fiery and charismatic media star.

'If you consume a resource without making provision for its replacement, it will eventually run out,' mumbled an occasional speaker.

'So what? Let's party,' shouted the well-oiled, highly-geared media campaign, organised by those who profited from resource exploitation.

When Mother Earth was formed, it was recognised even by the stupidest Big Jumper that you can't have an army without commanders. However, the Founding Beardies, as they were already becoming known, remained opposed to aping the structures of the forces against which they would be called upon to fight. Hence, Mother Earth soldiers were called 'activists', which was fine as far as it went, but who was to tell the activists what to do? The answer the Founding Beardies came up with was 'catalysts'. Catalysts would tell activists what to do and would be the rough equivalent of sergeants. Unfortunately, as the command structure grew larger and more complex, the Beardies soon ran out of credible alternative terms to describe the various posts that were being created. Rosalie had risen to the rank (or NHL which stood for non-hierarchical level) of Catalyst by the age of twenty-one. Since then, she had been a Suggester (whose 'suggestions' had to be obeyed by both catalysts and activists) a Co-ordinator, a Facilitator's Friend, and now she was a Facilitator. If the Earth and she were to survive long enough, Rosalie might eventually hope to rise to the exalted Non-Hierarchical Level of Number One Equal Person, which was Jurgen Thor's post and meant Commander-in-Chief.

Nice work if you can get it.

The hijack took place at Lille in Northern France, which was the *rendez-vous* point for all the great toxic convoys of Europe. It was here that the colossal transports coming from the industrial regions of Germany met up with those arriving from Italy, France and Spain and made up a super-garbage convoy which would then make its way on up to Ostend. It was at Ostend that the mouth of the third (and least leaky) of the Channel Tunnels was located.

Taking control of the convoy had been absurdly easy. Even the terrorists, who had only embarked upon the hijack in order to prove how stunningly easy it would be, were stunned at how easy it actually was. They just walked in, pointed a gun or two, and drove the tankers away. Of course they should not really have been surprised at the ease with which the crime was executed, the world was far too overloaded with poison for governments to get very excited about its transportation any more. For well over a century, the stuff had been shifted round the world endlessly, on trucks, boats, railways. It was, as they say, as common as muck.

'I don't know, I thought they'd have hidden guards or security locks or *something*,' Rosalie's Facilitator's Friend had remarked to her as they took control.

Someone to watch over us.

The fact was, that the cynics in Mother Earth had been as naïve as everybody else in the world about the nature of government. The basic presumption of modern society is that 'they' (that vague, catch-all term for the powers that be) are at least *attempting* to look after our best interests. That there is a logical and at least partially benign force which watches over us and for which we pay our taxes. Certainly, we all think that 'they' are, in the main, a bunch of hypocritical bastards on the make, but deep down we presume that at heart they want what's best for us. 'Surely "they" wouldn't let us drink polluted water?' we say to ourselves. 'Surely "they" would tell us if the food was poisonous. Surely "they" would never stitch people up for crimes those people did not commit and put them away for twenty years without appeal?'

But most of the time of course, either out of malice or incompetence, 'they' would do these things. They would also, and have always, left nuclear missiles lying around behind wire fences, allowed radioactive materials to travel on ordinary trains and, as in the case of the Lille convoy, allowed toxic waste to be trundled round the public highways, protected by poorly regulated private security companies whose only reason for being in the 'business' at all is to make a profit from it.

The dreadful suspicion.

And so the terrorists drove the tankers away. Brussels was only about forty minutes' journey from Lille and by the time 'they' (in this case the police) knew that anything was wrong, the convoy had already arrived in the suburbs of the capital city of Europe. At this point there was nothing much that the police could do. They could not risk confronting or attacking the tankers, for every one of the transports was a Pandora's Box, filled with hellish poisons. The only course of action open to the bemused police was to wait for the hijackers to stop and do whatever it was that they planned to do.

It was very late at night and so there was little traffic as Rosalie led her cargo of death through the streets of the city. Brussels, being home to all the politicians, had an orbital filter, so of course it still operated on day-time. In the darkness of the cab, Judy was trying not to shift about too much on his piles. He did not wish to provoke Saunders's anger, partly because he was scared of Saunders, and partly because Saunders was very noisy when roused, and Judy needed peace to think.

He was very tense. He knew that at some point he would have to act, but he did not know when. For Judy was convinced that Rosalie planned to poison the heart of Brussels and he knew that it was his duty to stop her. It all fitted, the same sequence of events that he had followed on so many previous occasions was happening again. Except that this time Judy was not piecing it together after it had happened, he was actually there, right at the heart of it. He could prevent it.

Judy believed absolutely that this operation would not be a mere demonstration, he knew that Rosalie's team would not simply dump the convoy at the Palace of Peace and Profit and then disappear, as they had said they would. Judy believed that there would be a far, far more spectacular protest than that. There always was.

Stealing a glance at Rosalie, he reflected on how little one could ever tell about a person from their appearance. Rosalie did not look like a villain, like a person capable of coldly murdering hundreds, perhaps thousands, of people to further her own political agenda. Not that Judy doubted Rosalie's aggressive commitment to the environmental cause, but it had seemed to him that her principles were based on a love of life and a respect for other living things. She seemed an unlikely murderer. Yet unless Judy had made the most monumental miscalculation, Rosalie was about to render Brussels, and possibly the whole of Belgium, temporarily uninhabitable; and Judy knew that he had not miscalculated. The disasters always occurred where Natura were best placed to exploit them, and the shadowy hand of Mother Earth was always detectable. It was the same as before, all the elements were in place.

This was why Judy had infiltrated the radical green movement. He had become convinced that a dreadful, black propaganda war was being fought. From the wealth of evidence that he had assembled over the years, Judy had concluded that Mother Earth must have become frustrated with the complacency with which the public viewed the environmental destruction of the Earth. They had therefore decided upon a most terrible course. Planning and executing a colossal double bluff, whereby the public might be shocked out of that complacency.

Judy had concluded that Mother Earth were creating

set-piece disasters in order that they might then protest against them.

Hidden agendas.

The poison convoy quickly arrived at the piazza of the Palace of Peace and Profit and came to a halt amongst the sculptures and the fountains. As the noise of the engines began to die away, Judy knew that he had to act. The plan as described to him was that, at this point, the transporter drivers would disable their tankers, and scatter into the night to take refuge in safe houses around the city. The piazza was huge and all the floodlighting had been knocked out by an auxiliary unit. Besides which, the police were keeping well clear, being unsure as to what the hijackers intended to do with all the poison. The activists would simply melt away, having proved the vulnerability of the toxic waste disposal system.

That was the plan, as Judy had heard it, but he did not believe that the transporters were going to be merely disabled. He believed that they would be sabotaged, which was why he had to act.

Judy produced the inflatable handgun which he had kept secreted about his person since infiltrating the unit (he rather suspected, in fact, that this was the source of his aggravated haemorrhoids). He held it to Rosalie's head.

'Ms Connolly. I am an FBI agent and I demand that you order the immediate withdrawal of your people from the scene of this operation.'

'Judy, you –' Rosalie blurted out, but Judy was in a hurry.

'*Now*, Ms Connolly! I mean it. I suspect that you are

intending to poison the city and I shall certainly kill you to stop that. Order a withdrawal *now* or I fire!'

Rosalie thought that Judy had gone mad. However, mad people are perfectly capable of pulling triggers and Judy looked serious. Rosalie shrugged.

'The operation's basically over anyway, disabling the transporters was just a bit of mischief.' Taking up her radio, she gave the order to withdraw. 'Take no further action,' she recited on Judy's orders. 'This operation is terminated.'

Through the window of the Land Rover, Judy watched the activists scatter.

'You too, Saunders. Run,' he said.

'I'm going to find you one day, and I'm going to kill you,' said Saunders, leaving the truck.

Once they were alone, Judy faced Rosalie in the darkness of the deserted piazza. He silently flipped on the little audio recorder in his wristwatch. What he needed now was a confession. Having of necessity stopped the sabotage before it had occurred, he wanted proof that it was to have happened. This would require very careful handling. The police would soon begin to edge their way forward, so Judy had only minutes in which to coax from Rosalie that which he already knew. He had little experience of interrogation, but he did know that the first rule was to show confidence. Lead with the presumption that everybody knows exactly what's being discussed.

'I'm curious, Rosalie. How were you going to do it?' he asked.

'I have no idea what you're talking about, you two-faced little worm.'

'It would have to look like an accident, wouldn't it? Corrosives, I suppose. Rusty tankers finally giving way?

311

Is that it? You rupture the tankers yourselves and then claim that you've *uncovered* the criminal negligence of the toxic waste industry. Of course it's quite a coincidence that the "accident" just happened to occur during a Mother Earth hijack, but so what? Coincidences happen and who would ever suspect the saintly environmental movement of dirty tricks? Not with lots of nice Natura people all set up and ready to scream about the nasty corrupt government. Do they know, Rosalie? Natura? Do all those pretty little hippies know what you do? I don't think so, they're as big a bunch of patsies as the public they preach to.'

The gist of Judy's theory was beginning to sink in.

'Are you suggesting that Mother Earth *causes* environmental pollution so that Natura can kick up a fuss about it?' Rosalie seemed genuinely flabbergasted. Sufficiently flabbergasted for a tiny doubt to appear at the back of Judy's mind.

'You wouldn't be the first to play that trick,' he said, 'the Bureau uses *agents provocateurs* all the time.'

There was a silence. It was strange to be in the middle of that great city, at the very administrative hub of a vast, international federation and yet hear a silence. Not a deep silence, there was noise in the distance as the police cleared the area surrounding the piazza, but in the cab of the Land Rover there was a genuine pause in proceedings. Finally Rosalie spoke.

'I have never been so insulted in all my life,' she said and, ignoring Judy's gun, she punched him in the mouth. Judy dropped his weapon and Rosalie produced hers.

'Come on,' she said, 'I'm going to hand you over to Saunders.'

They left the Land Rover and began to make their way

across the huge, dark, empty piazza. It was about two hundred yards to the edge and they crossed it slowly and carefully. Rosalie was nervous, lest some brave police officer had finally decided to make his or her way towards the silent convoy.

She was, however, still pretty stunned by the nature of Judy's accusation and could not resist further comment.

'I still can't believe it,' she whispered, pushing her gun into Judy's back. 'It's got to be a joke, hasn't it? Surely you're not going to tell me that the FBI actually believes *we're* causing environmental disasters?'

Judy's confidence was evaporating fast. His theory was suddenly beginning to look a bit stupid. There had, after all, been no disaster, and Rosalie's indignant surprise seemed worryingly genuine.

'As a matter of fact,' he confessed, 'it's my own private theory. Everybody else in the Bureau laughed at it.'

'You amaze me,' said Rosalie with bitter sarcasm.

Then, just as they reached the edge of the piazza and were about to disappear into the deserted streets beyond, they heard a noise. It was a sort of huge hiss. It came from the toxic waste tankers that they had so recently left. Judy and Rosalie turned to see what appeared to be steam of some sort emanating from the side of one of the tankers. Then the smell hit them, it was horrible, enough to shrivel the hair on the inside of their noses, and both Rosalie and Judy retched in disgust. Just then the steaming, hissing tanker seemed to buckle ... it just gave way in the middle. There was a splash and the ground surrounding it began to froth and burn, quite literally, as if the stone had been melted.

Anyone with the slightest knowledge of what that

buckled tanker contained could see that a major environmental disaster was about to occur. Both Rosalie and Judy had that knowledge. It was like being there at the moment the bomb doors opened.

'It's going to spread to the other trucks,' said Rosalie. 'The whole bloody lot will go.'

Judy was completely astonished. This was exactly the thing which he had just prevented, and yet here it was, happening anyway.

'Rosalie,' Judy said, 'you didn't do this, did you?'

'For God's sake, man, of course I didn't, you mad idiot!' she replied. 'This is the bloody stuff we try and stop.'

The fire and the corrosion around the stricken transporter were beginning to take hold. Pandora's Box had definitely been opened and all the evils of the world were flooding out.

'I think we should run,' said Judy. But Rosalie did not hear, she was already gone.

Chapter Twenty-Two

The penny drops

The minister replies.

Judy pushed his way through the terrified crowds and shouting policemen and away from the scene of the ruptured tankers. He would have liked to have hailed a cab but of course there were none to be had. Only endless emergency vehicles screaming and wailing, hurtling through the streets, hurrying towards yet another stable from which the horse had well and truly bolted.

The toxins were in fact heading out from the piazza more quickly than Judy himself. Within minutes, they had hissed their way across the piazza floor, poured straight down the storm drains and into the water system. In doing so, they had, as it happened, brought about one positive result amidst all the horror. They had destroyed the much loathed and completely incomprehensible symbolic mosaics which covered the whole Euro piazza. Although, interestingly, the chewing gum which covered the mosaics remained unaffected, no toxin in the universe having the power to remove chewing gum once some anti-social bastard has decided to drop it.

Even as the burning poisons poured into the storm drains, bio-suited Natura scientists were on the spot, addressing the media.

'All tap water in Belgium will very shortly be undrinkable,' the principal spokesperson stated to the robot news cameras which surrounded him.

'Now hang on, hang on, hang on, things are nothing like that serious,' said the relevant junior minister, who had been sent out to attempt a little damage control, and who was wearing a bio-protection outfit the size of a bus. 'Let's not be alarmist about this now, shall we? It isn't that the water will be undrinkable, you *can* drink it, of course you can drink it . . . and if you're a fit person with no history of liver disorders and if you remember to induce vomiting immediately after swallowing, well, then you should suffer nothing worse than a mild, or perhaps severe case of the trots. So you see? The word "undrinkable" scarcely describes the situation at all, and alarmist generalisations, of which my radical friends here seem so fond, are really no help to anyone.'

'All rivers and streams leading out of Belgium must be damned at the frontiers,' the Natura spokesperson insisted. 'Also infants and the aged must be evacuated. The atmosphere will be lethal to them and to anyone with respiratory difficulties for at least a month.'

'Now hang on, hang on, hang on,' said the relevant junior minister. 'Let's just get our terms straight here, shall we? Bandying words like "lethal" about is really no help to anyone. What exactly do we mean by "lethal" exactly? Hmm? If my alarmist friend here means that breathing the air will kill babies and grannies, well, then, yes, perhaps there is some foundation to the basis of his remarks, but really it's much too early to be counting bodies, surely? And as for sealing the borders of Belgium, may I remind my sanctimonious chum that it was his terrorist pals who dumped the damn stuff in Brussels in the first place.'

'Perhaps the Minister would rather that the disaster had happened in Lille? Or Ostend? In the English Channel, maybe?'

As it happened, the minister, who lived in Brussels, would definitely have preferred that, but he did not say so.

'The point is that the rupture of the tankers has happened. As for years we have been warning that it would. If it had not happened on this trip, then it would have been next time, or the time after. The people of Europe should be thankful to the activists of Mother Earth who diverted this deadly load into the very seat of government. At least now those whose greed, idleness or complacency have led to this terrible disaster are having to stand face to face with the results.'

'Well, now, you see that's absolute nonsense,' the relevant junior minister said. 'As I can make perfectly clear by explaining to you seventeen simple points. Let me take the second point first, because it relates partly to the first, and partly to the third. I shall, of course, return to the first point in due course before proceeding with my other points.'

The relevant junior minister was very good at damage control. He had scarcely got halfway through his points before the cameras had been switched off and everyone including the Natura spokesperson had given up and gone for a drink.

No direction home.

Puffing and panting and generally making heavy going

of it (Judy's asymmetric legs were not at all suited to this type of thing), Judy arrived at a small café which was situated on the corner of a tiny square on the crossroads of four little streets.

All the bottled water had of course been sold, so Judy had to settle for a hot chocolate with whipped cream, warm cognac and a great big double chocolate brioche. Holding a handkerchief over his face between swigs and bites, he sat down to collect his thoughts, some of which had sunk so low that he had to fish them out of the turn-ups on his trousers. Assessing his situation, he recognised it for what it was, which was not good. The crossroads upon which the little café stood offered, Judy thought, something of a metaphor for his life, for that too was at a crossroads. Unfortunately, it was a crossroads off which all the roads were cul-de-sacs. Look at it from whatever direction he might, and Judy tried them all, even standing on a table in the corner of the room to do it, he was in something of a pickle. A solitary pickle, alone, despised and unloved, the sort of pickle that is normally only found in a hamburger and which has to be fished out in order to render the burger edible.

Which road should Judy take? The road back? It would not be easy, his old colleagues in the FBI no doubt considered him a traitor and a stoolie and who could blame them? Judy had, after all, assisted in the escape of a suspected terrorist from a foreign police force, thus disgracing the entire Bureau. All things considered, the road back looked rocky. Judy searched for an alternative route.

Could he take a road forward? No obvious ones sprang to mind. His new colleagues in Mother Earth would no doubt now also consider him a traitor and a stoolie.

Again, this could scarcely be described as unreasonable. He had, after all, not only attempted to arrest their Facilitator, but had also accused them of going about their business with a callous and cynical immorality which made Machiavelli look like Julie Andrews.

How on earth had he got himself into such a fix? How had he managed to alienate absolutely everybody and achieve absolutely nothing?

Judy rehearsed again in his mind that series of suspicions and conclusions which had brought him to the lonely position in which he found himself. He had burnt his boats at the FBI because he had believed he had sufficient circumstantial evidence to conclude that Mother Earth were *agents provocateurs*. Nobody at the Bureau would take his conclusions seriously, so he had been forced to act on his own. He had successfully infiltrated a Mother Earth unit and correctly predicted that during their next mission a massive environmental disaster would occur.

After that, sadly, his theories had collapsed. Rosalie was innocent, he was sure of that. Her surprise at his accusations had been genuine, and besides, both she and her unit had been well away when the disaster occurred. What had happened? Could they have carried out the sabotage before Judy had intervened? It was not possible, the transporters had been flying along the highway only moments before Judy had made Rosalie order a withdrawal. Could there perhaps have been a second unit involved, of which he knew nothing? Perhaps, although Judy could see no obvious reason for an extra terrorist presence. Had he not intervened, Rosalie's unit would have been quite capable of carrying out the sabotage. But he had, and they didn't.

Was it sabotage at all? Could it possibly have been a coincidence that made the first tank rupture? A genuine accident? No, Judy would not credit it. He had come to Europe predicting exactly what had happened and it had happened, the fact that he seemed to have erred on who the culprits might be did not detract from the fact that, yet again, the pattern had been maintained.

Somebody had sabotaged that convoy, and since Judy no longer believed that it had been Rosalie's unit, that meant that it had been tampered with before they had seized it. What was going on? Judy did not realise it, but the clue was staring him in the face.

Soap internationale.

There was a TV on in the corner of the bar. Judy's eye was inevitably drawn towards it, reminding him momentarily of his finest hour, his achievement in getting Rosalie away from her Garda minders. Quite a stunt to have pulled off, and for what? Nothing. He had completely lost the trust he had gained and he was no further towards the truth.

The TV was tuned to the omnipresent Tolstoy system. A simucast soap internationale was playing. These were dramas that were made in English, in Los Angeles, and then simultaneously dubbed into literally hundreds of languages by means of a computerised, voice-sensitive translator. The computer 'heard' the American actor speak and then, using a synthesiser with a vast vocabulary of words and phrases, recorded by actors from other countries, it created new dialogue. Once an actor had comprehensively loaded his voice into the synthesiser it was possible for him or her to dub shows for ever, without ever being there, or in many cases even still being alive. Thus everybody in the world could now watch the same soap at much the same times, also the same news and the same chat shows. Everybody now heard and saw the same things. Even the French had all but given up on attempting to defend cultural boundaries. It was simply impossible to legislate against the myriad global ways in which information and imagery could be delivered.

The key to the mystery was about to be beamed into literally billions of homes in hundreds of different languages, just as that key had been beamed in countless times before. Somebody had to work it out some time. That somebody was Judy, who was about to make a very big discovery, although not quite as big as the consequences would be.

Global marketing.

Judy idly began to count the 'product placements' that were featured within the soap internationale drama. Soft drinks, designer clothes, cars. Some of the items, outside manufacturers had paid to have featured, others were actually made by companies owned by Tolstoy and his associates. The term 'conflict of interests' had long since become an obscure footnote in legal history. As Plastic Tolstoy himself had said during one of the last great court battles to prevent insider trading: 'Hey! If a conflict of interests bothers you, just let me buy everything, you won't see no conflict then.'

These days, product placement was considered an art form in itself. There were annual awards in which the drama directors who had most copiously featured their bosses' products were honoured. It had got subtle enough for negative placement to have become a commonly used technique.

'Did you see how every time the Slasher killed a girl with a broken bottle I used a *Pepsi* bottle?' the proud young director of *Slasher 23* would boast. 'But the *cops* only drink Coke.'

'No, I didn't notice that,' the proud young director's friend would say.

'Exactly!' the proud young director would shout in triumph. 'You didn't *see* it, but it was there, and believe me, in your subconscious, Pepsi ain't so wholesome any more.'

Judy noted that one of the groovy young characters in the soap internationale that he was watching wore a Claustrophobe T-shirt. Claustrophobe was a clothing company set up by Tolstoy to exploit the cynicism and bleak humour that young people had developed about being potentially the last generation on Earth. They marketed jeans and T-shirts with ironic slogans on them like 'Better a live rat than a dead self-righteous bastard' and 'Listening to greenies won't help you live longer, it'll just seem longer'.

It was a source of near despair to Natura that their constant appeals to adolescents to consider that the end of the world was nigh had actually served to create a 'Well, fuck that then' attitude amongst kids. In fact, that was one of Claustrophobe's best-selling lines, a sweatshirt depicting a slimy dead Earth with the simple phrase 'Well, fuck that then' embossed underneath it.

Tolstoy's clothes on Tolstoy's TV show. Judy had a vague suspicion that it might still be illegal to so blatantly self-promote one's own products but, short of shooting down satellites, the law was impossible to enforce any-way, so the matter was entirely academic.

His mind was wandering. Judy knew that he should be concentrating on planning his next move, but the TV continued to exercise its mesmeric effect on him. The adverts came on, as they did every ninety seconds at this time of the day. First up there was an ad for the very clothes that Judy had just been musing over.

'They're getting cheeky,' Judy thought to himself as the sexy Euro kids cavorted on the screen in Claustrophobe T-shirts and hats. 'That bastard Tolstoy just can't lose. The ads are just an extension of the programme. Control the information, control the ads and sell anything you want.'

Hard on this thought came a newsbreak. The terrible toxic spills in the European capital were of course the top story, and Judy forlornly watched the footage in the ludicrous hope that some clue as to the source of the disaster might emerge. He saw none. After the news there was another commercial break, and suddenly, while he watched the first advert, Judy got his clue. The penny finally dropped.

Unwelcome prodigal.

Judy now knew which road he had to take. He drained his cognac, finished his brioche and went off to make his peace with the FBI.

He did not relish returning. He had had no contact with them since absconding with Rosalie at Dublin airport, having avoided any form of communication on the not unreasonable grounds that if they had known where he was, they would have instantly arrested him. However,

Judy was pretty certain that he had finally worked out what was going on and he needed the Bureau's resources to prove it.

The preparations which Judy made before facing his old boss were both thorough and unpleasant. He dropped all of his ID down a drain, a drain now so filled with dangerous poisons that the chances of the documents ever seeing the light again were zero. Next, Judy rolled around a bit in the wet gutter in order to give himself a dishevelled appearance then, finally and most painfully, he selected the toughest looking fellow in the toughest looking bar he could find and threw a glass of beer in his face.

Crawling out into the street ten minutes later, his eyes blackened and his nose broken, Judy was soon picked up by the police.

'I am an FBI agent who has just escaped from terrorists. I demand to see the American consulate.'

And so it was that Judy made his way back to the US where the FBI placed him under arrest and asked him to explain himself.

It did not go down well.

'You're actually trying to tell me,' Klaw bellowed, 'that this *woman* dragged you on to the luggage conveyor, off the luggage conveyor, through a huge crowd full of soldiers and cops and yet you were unable to stop her!'

'That is correct, sir,' said Judy through his puffed and swollen lips.

'No, Schwartz,' Klaw insisted, 'it is not correct. I do not believe it, not even you could fail so spectacularly in your duty. I believe that for reasons of your own you helped this girl escape.'

'Reasons, sir? What reasons could I possibly have for helping a terrorist?'

Klaw hurled the photos of Rosalie down upon his desk.

'Pale skin reasons! Green eyes reasons! Cute little tits and ass reasons! You wanted to get laid, didn't you, Schwartz?'

'Sir, I –'

'Don't argue with me! You saw that you had one chance in your life to pork a really fuckable piece and you took it. Look at you! You're disgusting. A deformed, half-crippled little nerd. When did you last get any? Never, that's when. What kind of life is that? Then suddenly you're chained to some dream pussy. And I'll bet she was pushing it out, wasn't she? Baiting the honey trap? Of course she was. She knew a contemptible, inadequate piece of shit when she saw one. You weakened, didn't you, Schwartz? You followed your nasty little dick and it's going to lead you straight to the cage. Now what have you got to say?'

'I'm gay, sir.'

'Nothing! Like I thought . . .' Klaw paused for a moment as the statement sunk in '. . . say what?'

'I'm gay, sir, what's more I've been legally bound to my husband for twelve years. We were married in San Francisco. It's all in my file, sir.'

Klaw scrolled furiously through Judy's computer file. To his horror, it turned out that Judy was right.

'I didn't know we took you guys in the Bureau.'

'Sir, the FBI has been legally obliged to employ a representative quota of homosexuals for over sixty years now.'

'Oh . . . yeah, I did hear that, actually.'

'Besides, sir. Hoover was gay.'

'That's a damn lie!'

Klaw was rather shaken. He had thought he had Judy's case all sewn up, and now it appeared that he would have to think again, something he hated doing. In fact, he rather disliked even having to think the first time, let alone having to do it again. It had never occurred to Klaw that Judy was gay, nor had it occurred to any of Judy's other colleagues. He never mentioned his private life while at work, so people just made the usual presumption of heterosexuality. The bullies who taunted him as a 'queer' did so because they were dimwits, not because they had an astute eye for people's sexual preferences.

Judy seized on the moment of Klaw's confusion to press home his version of events.

'Ms Connolly managed to lift my gun, sir. She threatened to shoot both myself and any bystanders who got in the way. We were in a crowded airport, sir, I thought it best to accede to her demands.' Judy was rather hoping that Klaw had heard no reports of Judy's shouted allegiance to The Elitest Church of Christ the Crew-cut. Klaw's silence suggested that he had not, and Judy felt safe to carry on with his story. 'She had people at the airport and I was effectively a captive of Mother Earth from that point on. They kept me with them in the hope that they might learn something of Bureau policy towards them from me.' Judy paused for a moment and then remarked with casual stoicism, 'As you can see, sir, their methods of persuasion were not of the gentlest.'

Klaw eyed Judy's wounds. They certainly looked painful.

'What did you tell them?' Klaw inquired.

Judy tried to look shocked.

'I am a Federal Agent, sir. I told them nothing of either our policies or agents. In fact, they got nothing from me at all.'

Judy got away with it. Klaw had no proof of wrongdoing, could find no motive, and the fact that Judy had returned voluntarily did not correspond with the idea that he had absconded. The Bureau was forced to accept that he had genuinely been captured in the line of duty. Which meant, to their horror, that they had to give him a Purple Heart for his wounds. They made it clear in the citation however that he had utterly disgraced the whole organisation by being captured by an unarmed woman whilst he had the support of two police officers. Judy, who had never been popular in the Bureau, was now a marked man. He never ate in the canteen, never used the toilets and locked any room in which he was working.

The lonesome trail finally gets warm.

Judy had no time to get distressed about his ostracism. He cared not one jot for the opinion of the majority of his colleagues anyway. The cold, lonesome trail which he had been following for so long was finally beginning to warm up a little. Judy set himself the task of finding out which adverts had followed which news bulletins for the last twenty or thirty years. He wanted to know what products were being pushed when environmental disaster was the top story. Day after day he ploughed through the records of the broadcasting companies, the copyright libraries and indeed the FBI itself, which monitored all electronic media.

'Sounds *absolutely fascinating*,' Judy's husband Roger said to him, as he dabbed calamine lotion on to Judy's swollen eyes the evening after his return to work. 'Being a secret agent must be just so incredible.'

'I can't really tell you what it's about, Roger,' Judy apologised.

'Can't tell me about thirty years of ad breaks? How will I ever get to sleep!'

Chapter Twenty-Three

The lull before the storm

Tired and emotional.

Whilst Judy was ferreting out a truth that would shortly put both Rosalie and Max in mortal danger, Rosalie had joined her lover at the George V Hotel in Paris. She was in a funny mood.

'I want a holiday,' she told Max after the laminate had been duly stretched. 'I want a holiday a lot.'

'Cool,' said Max, who was pretty much on holiday all the time anyway.

'I'm tired and I need a rest,' she said.

'Anytime is party time for me, babe. Let's raise hell.'

'I said I need a rest and don't call me babe,' said Rosalie.

Had she been able to see into the future, Rosalie might have been even more anxious for a break. The gift of foresight would have shown her how much more limited her travel options were soon to become. She could not, however, see into the future. What is more, she had suddenly become very confused about her past.

'I don't know what I've been doing, Max. I look back and it just doesn't seem to make any sense.'

'Welcome to my world, girl,' said Max, 'I feel that way nearly every morning.'

But Rosalie was crying.

The toxic waste action had been something of a watershed. It was bad enough, having one's first action as a Facilitator degenerate into a massive environmental disaster, without the FBI popping up in the middle of it all and accusing you of the most extraordinary and horrendous things. That, coupled with the revelations that she had heard at Jurgen Thor's house, had so utterly thrown Rosalie that her idealism and determination seemed suddenly to have deserted her. She had been on active service for an unbroken five years and was entitled to some leave.

It was to be the lull before the storm.

Language barrier.

She and Max headed south-west and took a little room in a small village in Provence. Its sweet-smelling linen-covered quilt and little vase of flowers on the hand-painted dresser reminded both of them of the room in which they had first consummated their love. It made Rosalie feel a little lighter of heart. Max too felt good. A European tour with the person you love is something many a young American has dreamt of, and Max had always wanted to see the real France. He had found Paris a little snooty. He did not speak French and on a number of occasions, whilst desperate to get his bearings, he had approached a Parisian and made the apologetic appeal, 'Excuse me, but do you speak English?' only to be met by the infuriating riposte, 'Yes, of course. Do you speak French?'

Nothing irritates the French cultural elite so much as the fact that, because of American economic hegemony after the Second World War, English became the dominant world language. The *lingua franca*, as it is called, as if to add insult to injury. It is a source of constant pain to the educated French that, but for a couple of unlucky results in the battles of the late eighteenth century, the United States would have been known as *L'Etats-Unis*, MacDonald's would be selling *Grands* Macs and Rock 'n' Roll would be known as *Rocher et Petit Pain*. It is an understandable gripe for which Quebec and New Caledonia are no consolation at all.

Max had soon had enough of being patronised for being mono-lingual. His pride stung, he retreated to his hotel and holed himself up in his room, desperately cramming the French language. Virtual Reality had of course made learning the basics of a new language much easier than it had been in the past. It is universally acknowledged that the best way to learn to speak a foreign tongue is to plunge in amongst the natives. With a decent Linguafone VR helmet, it was possible to do just that in an extremely intense manner. Max spent days inside his helmet, visiting *boulangeries*, ordering *café au lait* and buying bus tickets over and over again.

A day in Provence.

By the time he and Rosalie headed south, Max was very proud of his new skills and insisted on employing them to conduct all negotiations.

'*Vous avez une chambre pour la nuit, avec une salle de bain?*' he said, giving it plenty of Gallic intonation and pantomimic hand motion. All to no avail, as it happened. Max was a very good actor, but even he could not mime a bedroom with en suite bathroom. He was met with a blank stare.

'I'm awfully sorry,' the house agent said in a plummy English voice, 'I'm afraid I don't speak French.'

Rather disappointed, Max was forced to negotiate for their pretty little room in English.

Having settled in, and then settled in again in a different position, they set off to explore the village. It was not as much fun as they had hoped, confined as they were to hot dusty little BioTubes. Provence, having long since given up any pretence at agriculture in order to concentrate on tourism, was not granted the convenience of orbital sun-screening. Since this meant that strolling outside was as hot and stuffy as staying inside, Rosalie suggested they drop in somewhere for a drink. This was an idea which Max never turned down and they made for a little cockney-style pub called The Dog and Duck.

'*Deux verres de vin rouge, s'il vous plaît,*' Max said firmly. Only to be met again with a non-comprehending look.

'Nobody speaks French here, Max,' Rosalie explained. 'This is Provence. The whole area became completely English-speaking over fifty years ago. They even drive on the left.' She bought a couple of pints of bitter and they sat together, alone in the smoky snug.

Decent proposal.

Max was looking rather uncomfortable, a bit sheepish. There was something on his mind.

'What's up, Max?' Rosalie inquired.

'Oh, it's nothing,' he said. 'Well, hey, that's not true, it's definitely a vibe, you know, if you think these things are important, which I think I do, it's a vibe . . . I was just wondering if, well, basically, if you would marry me?'

Rosalie was caught rather off her guard. Her eyes stared and her face coloured to a deep blush. Green does not, on the whole, go with red, except maybe on apples and in this case on Rosalie, at least as far as Max was concerned. Staring into her eyes, Max felt that he had never seen anyone or anything look lovelier. Feeling rather that his proposal had done little or nothing to reflect the heart-stopping beauty of its object, Max dropped to one knee and tried again.

'Rosalie, I love you. I would lay down my life for you in a heartbeat. Your eyes are like emeralds and your skin, when you aren't blushing the way you happen to be now, is like ivory . . . with freckles. You care about stuff and your voice is smooth as Irish cream or something, and you can fight and handle a gun and I love you and you've got to marry me.' Max paused, then added with a flourish, '*Je t'aime.*'

'Lord Almighty, Max,' said Rosalie, much taken aback. 'That's something to throw at a girl . . . You'll have to give me time to think about it.'

'Of course, of course. I understand.'

'I've thought about it. All right I'll marry you.'

That evening, over a celebration meal of traditional Provençal roast beef and Yorkshire pudding, followed by treacle pudding and custard, they discussed their wedding plans.

'Only close friends,' said Max firmly. 'This is going to be a real wedding, not some Hollywood stunt. We charter only *one* Jumbo sub-orbital. That's it, the limit, kapeesh? Two hundred and fifty guests from America, max. It'll mean offending some people very dear to me, but I ain't marrying them, am I? And *no press*! Just those we *invite*. Two magazines, two tabloids and any quality broadsheet that wants the story, obviously. Now, who do you want to do your dress? I think it would be a nice move if we used a Dublin designer.'

'Max,' said Rosalie, 'I'm a criminal wanted in Europe and America. If we get married it will have to be in total secrecy. We can't have any press, we can't bring anybody over from America.'

'No one?' Max asked, slightly stunned.

'No one, I'm afraid, unless you want to spend your wedding night visiting me in jail.'

'OK, so no one it is. Just my agent and my publicist then. Gee, that's weird.'

'No one, Max, not even your agent and your publicist. In fact, especially not them.'

Max chewed a ruminative mouthful of irradiated beef. The meat had been expertly reflavoured using only the finest chemicals and yet he scarcely tasted it. He was trying to get his head around the concept of doing something as big as getting married without his agent or his publicist. Who would handle the press? The fans? The cops? His mother? Then it dawned on him that none of these people would be there.

'You actually want me to get married *alone*, don't you?' he asked.

'Well, not entirely. I need to be there.'

'Is it *legal* if the press don't witness it? I mean, I kind of thought they had to be there.'

Rosalie gave Max's hand an encouraging squeeze.

'It'll be all right, Max. No need to be nervous. People do things that haven't been arranged by their agents and publicists all the time. In fact, most people don't even *have* agents and publicists.'

Max was vaguely aware that this was the case, but after eight years as a super-celebrity he found it rather difficult to imagine. Eventually though, he accepted Rosalie's argument.

'OK, there's a church in the square, let's go knock up the padre.'

'Are you out of your mind, Max? This is *Provence*!'

'So?'

'Every church within twenty miles of here is *Church of England*! Sure, I'd rather get hitched in a witches' coven.'

Nocturnal nuptials.

They left the little English carvery at about ten and headed north in their hire car. Rosalie drove, Max having had most of both of the bottles of wine they had ordered.

'It isn't always going to be me who drives, OK?' she said. 'I like a drink too, you know.'

'Fine, sometimes we'll take a taxi.'

After passing through several villages that were quite nice, but only quite, they came upon the perfect church in a little village called Donzère, about eight miles south of Montélimar. Despite it being nearly midnight (country time) they knocked up the priest.

'Father. We want to get married and we'd like to do it now if that's all right with you,' Rosalie said in passable schoolgirl French.

'Well, it is not,' the priest replied in English. 'Are you mad, coming here at this hour, I've a good mind to −'

'Father,' Rosalie interrupted him, 'I'm a wanted terrorist and I can't get married in the normal way. Now I've got a gun, and my fiancé here has suitcases full of money. Either one of these things is going to persuade you to marry us right now. Which is it to be?'

'There's nothing in the world wakes a man up like the sight of young love,' said the priest. 'How much are you prepared to pay?'

The deal done, the priest hastily put on his robes and led the expectant couple through the churchyard to his darkened church.

'You know it won't be a legal marriage, don't you?' he said. 'Without the proper papers it can only be symbolic.'

'That's all we care about,' Rosalie replied.

And so the priest spoke the marriage service in the little church, lit only by a few candles. Neither Rosalie nor Max were particularly religious people, but where Rosalie came from you got married in a church and that was the end of it. She could not imagine it any other way. Max sensibly neglected to mention his two divorces.

The road to Damascus.

Despite the fact that Rosalie was still very much wanted by the FBI, they decided to return to the USA. A new identity was a comparatively easy thing to obtain if you had Max's money and Rosalie's contacts and she entered the country without trouble.

Rosalie had decided to resign her commission in Mother Earth. Plastic Tolstoy could pay somebody else to alert the world to the need to buy more Claustrospheres. She was fed up with it. She had been fighting almost continually for five and a half years and had achieved nothing. You couldn't breathe the air any more, you couldn't drink the water, walk in the sunshine or enjoy the rain on your face, and Rosalie had no energy left to be bothered about it.

She had made the decision whilst flying the sub-orbital to LA with Max. Having got over the excitement that her first-class seat actually had an arm-rest on *both* sides, she had tuned into the news channel. She had been looking for an update on the situation in Belgium, but discovered to her astonishment that the disaster had already been dropped from the bulletins. Three days down the track and the poisoning of an entire country was old news.

Rosalie was not on the road to Damascus, she was on a flight to LA, but at that moment she saw the truth as clearly as the apostle Paul had, on his journey.

People had got used to the planet dying.

They didn't care any more, it had been lingering on for too long. The Earth was like some aged and slightly disgusting relative that just got sicker and sicker and yet refused to die. Requiring more and more attention, growing bigger tumours, bursting nastier sores and soiling its sheets ever more often. An embarrassment and an inconvenience, a constant reminder of family guilt. It was almost as if, now that people had their Claustrospheres, they *wanted* the world to die. To get it over with. Everyone had lived with the imminence of planet death for so long that they really could not get excited about it any more.

A young man was coming down the corridor from the toilets. He was wearing the famous Claustrophobe sweatshirt, slightly sanitised for general display. A picture of a slimy, dead Earth and the legend 'Well, f*** that then' embossed beneath it.

Rosalie looked at the shirt, unconsciously quoting the slogan.

'Well, fuck that then,' she said to herself.

Except, in fact, she said it to at least the ten people closest to her. Rosalie was wearing earphones in order to hear the news. She had forgotten, as so many people do, that you lose control of the volume of your voice when wearing earphones. The stewardess approached and leant across to Max.

'Would you mind asking your companion to moderate her language, please, sir. There are children on board.'

The lull before the storm.

Few people are immune to the seduction of luxury and Rosalie was under no illusions about her own delight in a bit of pampering. She did rather surprise even herself however, when she moved into a house that had a Claustrosphere attached to it. A Claustrosphere, what's more, that was the size of four or five tennis courts.

'Do you like it?' Max had asked with genuine pride. 'It has a pool, you know.'

'Max, I've spent five years blowing these things up.'

'Well, don't blow this one up or I'll divorce you. It has state-of-the-art leisure facilities and its fish cycle includes caviar. Come on, Ba . . . I mean, uhm . . . darling, we're on honeymoon.'

Max could see that Rosalie was torn; it was all very well leaving Mother Earth, but frolicking in a Claustrosphere was a big leap.

'Listen,' he said, 'husbands and wives are supposed to share each other's interests, right? Well, I've tried to get involved in your whole green thing, haven't I? Now you have to get into my stuff.'

'Which is?'

'Partying, girl. You *know* it makes sense.'

And suddenly she did. A huge weight seemed to lift from Rosalie's shoulders. It dawned on her that if she wanted to pack it all in for a while and have a good time, then she could. It was up to her.

'You're right,' she said. 'Bugger it, it isn't *my* fault the bloody Earth's knackered. I didn't do it. I'm on holiday.'

And to her astonishment, on the very first morning that she moved in with Max, Rosalie found herself lying by the Claustrosphere pool, wearing a bikini and sunbathing, something it had been impossible to do outside for over thirty years. Max suggested that since they were married and entirely alone in a hermetically sealed private world, Rosalie might like to dispense with the swimming costume.

'Maybe in a while,' Rosalie said. She was readjusting fast, but there were limits. Being inside a Claustrosphere was one thing, wandering around it starkers was another.

Slowly though, throughout that first day she relaxed. They both did, it was a honeymoon. They swam, they played tennis in the gamesuits, they got a little drunk and they made love in the soft lush grass.

'I suppose this is what life must have been like in the real world, before it all got spoilt,' Rosalie said as she lay in the quiet meadow, her hair mingling with the daisies and buttercups.

'If you were an outrageously overpaid movie star, yes. I believe it was tougher for the little guys,' Max replied.

They did not return to the house that night, but stayed where they were, outdoors but indoors, naked in a tiny meadow as the light cycle turned to velvet darkness and the fireflies in the forest area began to glow.

There was even dew in the morning when they awoke, a little chilly, at around five a.m. and Max brought cushions and blankets from the living area. They made love again and then watched the false dawn slowly turning their little private world from darkness to cold grey. Rosalie felt a fine drizzle on her face.

'It's . . . it's raining,' she said, astonished.

'It does sometimes,' said Max. 'You never know when till it happens. Just like the real thing, huh? The precipitation cycle is regulated according to seasons, but apart from that it's random. What do you think?'

'It's beautiful, Max. I had no idea these things could be so beautiful.'

Of course Rosalie knew that not all Claustrospheres were as luxurious as Max's. The vast dormitory-style municipal complexes of the English Home Counties, for instance, or those in Long Island and New Jersey or underneath the Mediterranean Sea could not boast quite such opulence, but they too had tennis courts and swimming pools, albeit public ones. They too were, in their way, beautiful.

'But it is obscene, you know that, don't you?' Rosalie said at last, trying to remember how much she hated the very idea of Claustrospheres.

'Yeah, yeah, sure, we all know that, but what can

I tell you? You have to allow yourself some time off from yourself, you have to get out of your own way.' And with that, he gathered Rosalie up in his arms, carried her to the pool and jumped in, kissing her all the while.

To start the day with a dip in your own pool is a splendid thing, but to do so in the knowledge that you have nothing whatsoever to do after breakfast is doubly so. Rosalie shrieked with joy. She had not felt so light-hearted since she had been a girl.

All that day and the next, and the next until they lost count, Rosalie and Max swam and played and made love, never once leaving the Claustrosphere. This was the beginning of their lives together and they did not want the beginning to end. Each afternoon Max worked out in his little gymnasium and watched videos, whilst Rosalie spent lazy hours by the pool with the ElectroBook. The ElectroBook was an extraordinary invention and a joy to behold. It placed all the writings of the world in the palm of your hand. Of course, it had long been possible to condense all literature on to a disc or two and read it on a screen, but people had never really taken to this method of reading, because curling up with a laptop computer was just not as nice as it was with a book. The ElectroBook solved this problem of sensual aesthetics, for it was a real leatherbound book with hundreds of pages made not of paper, but of wafer-thin, flexible, fibre optically-fed screens. On to those screens, which could be folded, bent, screwed up and read upside down in a hammock, would appear anything that had ever been written at the simple touch of an index.

One day, Rosalie and Max were lying in the meadow

together. She was on her back, while Max lay with his head resting on her stomach. She had put aside her ElectroBook, upon which she had been reading *David Copperfield*, and was staring up at the great geodesic dome above her. How splendid it looked, with its soft light and the delicate mists that floated up towards the roof. Rosalie was suffused with a wonderful feeling of well-being. All her life she had worried about the world, and now here she was in a perfect one. She had achieved that which she had always most desired: she was living in a perfect world. Outside its near-impregnable walls was the rest of the universe, filled as it was with other planets, Mars, Neptune . . . Earth. Planets that were nothing to do with her. Why should she worry any more about the dying Earth than she did about the frozen corpse that was Mars? Neither planet was her world. She had a Garden of Eden all of her own.

She found herself half-quoting some Shakespeare she had heard long ago. '"This royal throne of kings, this sceptred isle, this earth of majesty, this seat of Mars, this other Eden . . ."'

'*Richard the Second*,' said Max, who had done a lot of acting classes.

'I thought it was an old Claustrosphere advert,' said Rosalie.

'That too. Good choice, don't you think? It certainly sums up this place.'

There was a long silence, broken only by the soft buzzing of the bees, special bees that could make honey out of old toenail clippings, lived for fifteen years and had no sting.

Finally Rosalie spoke again.

'Max. Let's close it up.'

'What do you mean?'

'You know what I mean. Let's shut the BioLock.'

'It is shut, darling. The cycles don't work unless it's sealed.'

'No, let's shut it properly. Put it on the time-safe.'

'You mean . . . with us on the inside, don't you?'

Rosalie did not reply, instead she took Max in her arms and kissed him. It was a long kiss, passionate and committed, but with also just a hint of sadness, perhaps even despair.

Time-safe.

All Claustrospheres were equipped with a time-safe lock. This was because people feared the constancy of their resolve. Once faced with a lifetime inside a small shelter, they suspected that their will might crack after a while. That they might be tempted to ignore the numerous indicators and gauges with which their shelters were equipped, and open the door to have a look outside to see if things were really as bad as they were being told. If they did this while the outside environment remained poisonous, then those poisons would enter the 'Sphere and hopelessly compromise the eco-system within, killing everybody inside. It had therefore been decided that when the Rat Run finally came, the authorities would issue an estimate as to when the environment might be safe enough again for people to emerge. It might be one year, it might be a hundred. Whatever it was, the occupants of a Claustrosphere would set their timer for that duration. Once set, the BioLock would not open under any circumstances until the time had elapsed. This system was thought particularly necessary in the case of the big community BioShelters. People recognised that it would only take one crazy lunatic to crack up and open the door, and they preferred the idea of voluntary imprisonment to mass poisoning.

Adam and Eve.

Rosalie released Max from the tension of her embrace. He was a little stunned.

'You want us to lock ourselves in?'

'Sure, why not? People will be forced to pretty soon anyway, if not this year, maybe the next. I was an environmental activist, I know how bad things are.' Rosalie spoke quickly, as if fearful that having made her decision, she might, on reflection, change her mind. 'Let's do it now, forget them all. There's only us, anyway. This is our world. Let's lock the universe out.'

Max thought about it for a while.

'How long would you want to set it for?' he asked.

'I don't know, ten, maybe fifteen years. Just till our baby's grown. We can reassess the situation on the monitors then.'

'Our baby?'

'That's right. Our baby.'

'I didn't know we were going to have a baby.'

'Well, we are, and I want it to live in a beautiful world.'

Max looked at Rosalie and he smiled, a great happy smile. It was dusk in the Claustrosphere but that smile lit up Rosalie's whole universe.

'OK,' he said. 'Let's do it.'

Out of paradise.

They left the Claustrosphere for the first time since their honeymoon had begun. Max had one or two things which he wanted to put in order and Rosalie had to ring her grandparents. She knew they would be saddened at the collapse of her principles but she did not care. They were in the past, her baby was the future. She had the chance to give her baby a childhood in paradise and she was going to take it.

They went out through the BioLock and up to the house. After weeks inside the pristine environment of the Claustrosphere it seemed to Max and Rosalie as if the world was already dead. The air stank and the filtered sunlight was weak and watery.

Max made a few calls. Cancelling his subscription to *Life* magazine. Putting all his money into high-yield longterm accounts and informing his astonished agent that he was retiring. Soon they were ready. Rosalie had only to make her call, and they could go back into their little private paradise and lock the Earth out behind them.

Then the front door bell rang.

'Leave it,' said Rosalie. 'We don't live in this world any more.'

'Oh, come on, we might as well see who it is,' said Max, and before Rosalie could stop him he had flipped on the video camera that covered his front door.

Judy was standing outside.

'I don't believe it!' Rosalie gasped. 'It's that little bastard from the FBI.'

'Bad call,' said Max.

'Max.' There was panic in Rosalie's voice. 'Don't

answer the door, let's go, now, into the Claustrosphere, leave him. We were going to go, let's go.'

Max spoke gently. For the first time in their relationship it was he who would have to be the sensible and realistic one.

'Rosalie, listen, you've got yourself thinking about that Claustrosphere as if it was a whole other world –'

'It is,' said Rosalie.

The bell rang again.

'It isn't, Rosalie, it's a Claustrosphere. A building on a piece of real estate which exists in the real world. Now that man is an FBI agent, an agent who's already tried to arrest you once. The chances are he's come to do it properly this time. If we disappear, believe me the first thing they'll do is blast open the BioLock on the Claustrosphere. What you have to do is hide while I talk to him. Maybe I can get him to go away. Then we can plan our next move.'

Suddenly Rosalie saw her dream idyll fading like the dream it was. Desperately she tried to save it.

'Let's kill him,' she said.

Max looked at Rosalie, a little shocked.

'Now I hope you said that because you're hormonally imbalanced, due to being pregnant,' he said. 'Quite apart from the fact that icing people is kind of dubious in a moral sense. Practically, it would be a no-win call. If you kill FBI agents, they send more, lots more. It's a rule they have. Now you get behind the two-way mirror, and I'll let the guy in.'

'Two-way mirror?' said Rosalie, returning to the real world with a bump.

'Yeah . . . uhm . . . yeah, the guy who had the house before me was a porn king,' said Max, and, pushing

Rosalie into a recess in the wall behind a mirror, he buzzed open the door and let Judy in.

'Come on up!' he called, and Judy nervously climbed the stairs.

'I nearly went off home,' Judy said, arriving in the lounge area.

'Yeah, I was out the back in the Claustrosphere. Nice to see you again, man, what's happening?' Max replied.

'Ms Connolly not with you?' Judy inquired. 'The way you two seemed to be getting on in Ireland, I rather thought she might be.'

'No, she ain't here.'

'It doesn't matter anyway,' said Judy. 'It's you I need to speak to.'

'Me?' replied Max, full of suspicion. 'What do you want with me, man?'

'I need your help to catch a ruthless, callous, immoral viper, a man with not a single shred of compassion or decency in his body, a man who cares nothing for anything or anybody but himself.'

'Hey, man, this is Hollywood,' said Max. 'I know a lot of guys like that, you'll have to be more specific.'

Chapter Twenty-Four

The sale of the century

Waiting for the drugs to warm up.

Max had been with Plastic Tolstoy for about half an hour. He had requested a meeting under the pretext of discussing the progress of the film project which Nathan had been supposed to write, but really he was Judy's spy.

Tolstoy had readily agreed to the meeting and invited Max up to his house. Busy though Plastic Tolstoy was, Max was one of the most popular stars in the industry and even as exalted a figure as Tolstoy still understood the value of 'the money'.

They were talking in Plastic's office, Max having declined an invitation to go through to the Claustrosphere. He was carrying a tiny transmitter and he knew that nothing, not even radio waves, escaped from a closed Claustrosphere.

'I've just spent nearly a month in mine,' Max said by way of explanation. 'A guy can get too much fresh air and sunshine. I hate to feel that healthy.'

'You've been in your Claustrosphere for a month? How come?'

'As a matter of fact I've been working on the first

fermentation from my vineyard. I brought a bottle with me, I'd appreciate your opinion.'

Max had brought along a half bottle of red wine labelled 'Wine to the Max'.

'You brewed this inside your Claustrosphere? Wow! I don't have a vineyard in mine.'

'Hey, you have to have a vineyard, Plastic. What can you do with a rain forest? Nothing, hunt iguanas maybe. A vineyard will keep you occupied as many years as you have to be in there. Try it.'

'Nice. Very nice,' said Plastic, taking a delicate little sip. 'Lotta nose. I like a wine with a big schnozzle . . . So this is what you've been up to then? I heard you'd gone to ground.'

Max wondered whether Tolstoy knew that he had been at Nathan's house on the night of Nathan's murder. Had the killers recognised him in his VR helmet? Had they reported it to Tolstoy? Max had to presume the worst, so he confessed.

'Yeah, I did hide out for a while there. To tell you the truth, Plastic, I was kind of shaken by something . . . You know Nathan Hoddy? The guy who was going to write our film?'

'Yeah, I know, he died,' said Plastic with apparent indifference.

'I was there the night he got it,' said Max.

'No kidding? You were there?' Tolstoy certainly seemed genuinely surprised. 'So who bumped the poor guy off, then?'

'That's the stupid point,' Max replied. 'I was there, but I don't know who did it. We were playing a Virtual Reality game and we were both inside the helmets when they killed him. I didn't see him die. Believe it or not, what

I saw was his *thoughts* while he died, although of course I didn't know that was what they were until afterwards. It was extremely weird.'

'You saw his dying mind? Wow! Did you get a tape? I could sell something like that.'

'No way, man. When I found him, I just ran. That's why I kind of disappeared, you know? Like, I didn't feel that was the wrong thing to do . . . I had no information that could help the cops or anything . . .'

'And you didn't want to get involved.'

'In a murder investigation? No way! Would you? That kind of shit sticks. I can just hear what they'd say about me. Wild, tough Max Maximus . . . hear about him? He was in the room when his pal got wasted and he didn't lift a finger. Says he was playing a game and didn't notice!'

'Well, I guess it's all blown over now, huh? The cops have got about another thousand unsolved murders to deal with since then,' Plastic Tolstoy assured Max with a kindly slap on the shoulder. Max could not help but feel a tiny shiver at the man's touch. He hoped Plastic did not notice.

'Yeah,' said Max, 'I reckon that's history now, and so I was wondering what was happening about the film, you know? I mean, it's too bad about Nathan, obviously, but like, you know, the town's full of writers. You hear what I'm saying?'

'I certainly do, Max,' said Plastic. 'And let me tell you, I am still very interested in putting you into a picture about those Mother Earth assholes.'

'Well, that's great, Plastic,' Max said, and he knew that he could prevaricate no longer. If the drug was going to work, it would have worked by now; it took only the tiniest amount and its effects were virtually instantaneous. It was time to put it to the test.

'So Plastic,' Max said casually, 'I hear you like to watch girls go to the toilet, is that right?'

'Yeah, I like to do that,' Plastic replied, without batting an eyelid.

Max's whole body relaxed. The drug was working; it had to be working. Emboldened, he gave it another test.

'So how the hell do you manage it? I mean, do you get them to bend over you or what?'

'I lie under that glass table and they squat on top of it.'

Tolstoy nodded towards the coffee table upon which Max's drink was standing. Max decided that he was no longer thirsty. He wanted to get the job over with, and get out. Very casually he asked his last and most dangerous test question.

'So, I guess you knew that Nathan would have to die the minute he worked out that you're the guy who pays for the green terrorists.'

Baby's Mouth.

Max was smiling his gentlest, friendliest smile. Baby's Mouth was a subtle drug and it worked better if the recipient was relaxed and unaware that it had been administered. It had been originally developed by psychoanalysts after their profession had been reduced to a laughing stock by day-time chat shows. These were the daily confessionals in which every possible type of sad-act was encouraged and indeed cajoled into describing in the most lurid detail just exactly how completely and utterly screwed up they were. The sad-acts would then be confronted with other sad-acts, who either had similar problems, had caused the problems, were the victims of the problems, or, as became increasingly common, were hoping to develop the problem. An expert psychiatrist would then tell the whole lot of them that they were not to worry because the thing was far more common than they imagined, and the studio audience gave everyone a great big round of applause for 'sharing' the whole horrid business with thirty or forty million complete strangers. Now this type of TV had been fine for a while, whilst there were still some legitimate skeletons left in society's cupboard. Unfortunately, gloating over other people's private misfortune made such good television that the search for new problems and new victims very quickly became a network necessity.

'I'm not interested in decent ideas for comedy and drama,' the network chiefs would shout. 'Bring me more sad-acts.'

Teams of researchers scoured the countryside, encouraging people to think of something, anything, that might have rendered them dysfunctional. Large sections of the public racked its collective brain attempting to conjure up ever more interesting ways to glamorise their boring lives. The researcher's job was also to ensure that, no matter what problem people came up with, there was always an 'expert' ready to assure the world that this was just the tip of the iceberg. The inevitable development was of course that those watching the shows began to feel a little inadequate. They began to wonder, since all these desperate family situations were apparently so common, what was wrong with them. Why were they not attempting to divorce their pets, blaming their mothers for making them fat or trying to trace the parents who *would* have adopted them *if* their natural parents had chosen to give them up. Eventually, of course, these people also found their way on to the shows, in order to confess how dysfunctional they felt about not having anything to feel dysfunctional about. The resident psychiatrist soon put them right by assuring them that they were doubtless suppressing something absolutely fascinating, and they went away happy, promising to return the moment they had discovered what their problem was, and so the dreadful cycle continued.

One of the few desirable side-effects of this broadcast voyeurism was that it temporarily popped the bubble of the analyst industry. An industry that had been growing unchecked for decades and was out of control. At one point, the prevalence of people seeing analysts, particularly amongst the middle class, had grown to such an extent that society was in danger of grinding to a halt because everybody was sitting in small rooms talking about themselves. All this changed with the introduction of saturation afternoon discussion TV, which rendered the analyst redundant. People began to ask themselves why they should spend enormous sums talking about themselves to just one person, when they could actually be paid an appearance fee to talk about themselves to millions of people. Eventually, however, the analysts rebuilt their fortunes by playing the snob card. Enticing people back to their couches by pointing out that important people had important problems, and should not be used merely as a source of entertainment for the masses. Unfortunately, when people did begin to drift back to their analysts, they found they had become so utterly immersed in the combined problems of just about everybody else that they had lost track of what, if anything, had happened to them that would be worth talking about in the first place.

The drug Baby's Mouth had been developed in order to enable people whose brains had been filled with crap to discover some genuine thoughts and emotions. It was a truth drug. It made the person who took it say, not what they thought others wanted to hear, nor indeed what they themselves thought they wanted to say, but the truth. The basic effect of Baby's Mouth was to suppress that part of the brain which is in charge of bullshit. This of course meant that some people were rendered completely dumb by the drug. Many politicians, game-show hosts, a surprising number of poets, all had the disconcerting experience of being rendered absolutely speechless after so much as a sniff of it. For most people, however, Baby's Mouth simply gave them the unusual sensation of genuinely expressing their true feelings, of actually saying what they thought.

The drug had of course been quickly banned. Its capacity to create mischief was far too great. People need their secrets, and in the brief period that Baby's Mouth was available, dinner parties ended in gunfights, marriages foundered and even the most saintly polit-icians were found occasionally to harbour uncharitable thoughts about their constituents. No society can exist without some bullshit. It was soon recognised that if everybody told the whole truth, the whole time, we would all be at each other's throats.

Lines of communication.

Baby's Mouth had been suppressed, but it remained a valuable weapon in the world of the secret service, and it was Judy who had supplied Max with the dose with which he had spiked Plastic Tolstoy's wine. Tolstoy had only taken a sip, but a sip was all that was required, and by the easy way Tolstoy had offered details of his sexual preferences it seemed to be working. Max repeated his question about Nathan's death, this time a little more firmly. Judy had told him that those under the influence of the drug responded well to a firm hand.

'Like I said, I suppose you decided to have Nathan Hoddy killed, once he'd come up with the idea that you're the person who pays for Mother Earth?'

'It's an interesting question', said Tolstoy. 'Now let me ask you this. Where the hell do you get off coming in here and trying to hit me with a shot of Baby's Mouth, huh? Is that nice, Max? Is that fair?'

In another part of the Beverly Hills Fortified Village, Judy and Rosalie exchanged nervous glances. They were in Max's lounge room, listening to the conversation taking place between Max and Tolstoy via the tiny radio transmitter that was hidden inside one of Max's buttons. The reception was excellent and they could hear only too clearly that Judy's plan was not going well.

'You think when some guy asks me to taste their stupid wine right out of the blue, I don't smell a rat?' Judy and Rosalie heard Tolstoy saying. 'What am I? An idiot? Like you, Max? Is that it? Am I as *stupid* as you? I only pretended to drink your wine, and now I wanna know just what you tried to stick me with. It was Baby's Mouth, wasn't it?'

'Yeah,' said Max, rather weakly. Denial seemed futile. 'Should I leave?'

'Leave? No way, Max, not until you've told me why you came.'

'Because I want to know if the Claustrosphere Corporation is in the business of creating environmental catastrophe . . . You bastard!'

As the word 'bastard' barked out of their earphones, Judy and Rosalie could hear a sudden rush of movement. Max had intended to grab the drugged wine and force it down Plastic Tolstoy's throat. Instead, he found himself facing a gun.

'Max, please. No physical stuff. I hate that,' said Tolstoy calmly. 'You know what I ought to do? I ought to have you drink that wine yourself, then I could find out who's put you up to all this. But I'm not going to. Guess why?'

'Because you're a nice man?'

'No, not that, not even my best friends, were I to have any, which I don't, would call me a nice man. No, I'm not going to force you to take the Baby's Mouth because I don't need to, that's why.' Suddenly Plastic Tolstoy raised his voice. 'Do I, *Mr Schwartz*! You hear that, do you, *Judy*? I *know* who's pulling this dick's strings!' and Tolstoy laughed a loud, unpleasant, triumphant laugh.

Judy and Rosalie were nonplussed, particularly Judy. He was not an arrogant man but he had taken some pride in the trail he had followed and the plans which he had laid to bring that trail to a conclusion. Now the sound of cruel laughter ringing in his earphones told him that somehow he had been completely trumped by the object of his investigations. What was more, he was being taunted about it over his own secret radio!

Tolstoy continued to gloat.

'Hey, Schwartz, you think when some guy starts delving into my business I don't *hear* about it? You think when some little punk Fed starts checking out where

I've been placing *my* ads on *my* communications empire for the past thirty years, I don't *know*! How the hell do you think I got to *have* my own communications empire? By being a prick? Like you? Huh?'

Max was beginning to feel rather superfluous to requirements.

'Look, Plastic,' he said, 'you've clearly guessed I'm wired, so why don't I just leave you with the radio and you can talk to Judy without me standing around looking stupid. Or maybe you could just phone him, you know who he is.'

'You stay where you are, Max,' said Tolstoy. 'I want to know what gives with you. The FBI got something on you? Is that it? Is that why you did this for Schwartz? Is that why you agreed to come in here and abuse my trust? Abuse the privilege of my hospitality that I extend to so few?'

Max found himself staring at the floor in embarrassment.

'Why did you do it, Max? Let me guess again. Hah! I got it! It's a girl, isn't it? That's the only time a guy would be so stupid as to try and get the better of Plastic Tolstoy. For a girl! A *green* girl in this case, no doubt, considering the outrageous nature of Schwartz's libellous theories. The girl, I would like to hazard a guess, who tried to kill me that time in my own Claustrosphere. Am I right, Max? Yes, I think I'm right.' Tolstoy called out again, 'You listening, girlie? I can't remember your name, I'm afraid, but . . . let me see, that's it, you had red hair, I remember.'

Judy and Rosalie were ready to sink through the floor by this time. The man was positively clairvoyant.

'I have never felt so stupid in my entire life,' Rosalie whispered.

'There's no need to whisper,' Judy replied, 'he can't hear us.'

'He doesn't need to, does he?' Rosalie said angrily. 'He seems to be able to read our minds.'

'OK,' they could hear Tolstoy saying. 'Give me the transmitter, and anything else metal you've got on you. This office carries a metal scanner so I shall know if you try to cheat, and I won't be happy.'

Back in Tolstoy's office Max handed over both the transmitters which Judy had supplied him with.

'Bye-bye, G-man,' Tolstoy sneered. 'You look after yourself now, and you look after Max's cute little girlfriend too. Because you both may just be hearing from my people.'

Tolstoy smashed the little button-sized radios and Judy and Rosalie heard no more. They looked at each other in despair.

'Maybe the phone will ring,' said Judy.

They could only sit and wait.

Back in Tolstoy's office, Max emptied out his pockets, a notebook, a wallet, some cigarettes . . . a portable telephone.

'Thank you,' said Tolstoy. 'By the way, I don't have no metal scanner, who do you think I am, James Bond?'

Max smiled weakly, scarcely daring to hope that the trick which Judy had suggested he try if his transmitters were discovered would work. Tolstoy had been several jumps ahead of Judy on every point so far. It seemed unlikely that such a simple idea would fool him, but Max had to try.

'Are you going to kill me, Plastic?' he asked as he put his phone down on the table beside his other possessions. It was as dramatic an enquiry as he could muster, and Max made it in the hope that Plastic would not notice that as he put the phone down he had deftly pressed * 1, the pre-set automatic dialling code for his phone at home. Max used it occasionally when he was out and about in order to leave messages on his answering machine. He was hoping to leave a message now.

Back at Max's house the phone rang. Instinctively, Rosalie nearly picked it up, but fortunately Judy stayed her hand. There were three rings and then the machine clicked into action. First they heard Max's outgoing message. 'Ugh . . . Hi, yeah . . . OK, it's the machine, right? But you knew that. Listen, uhm . . . leave a message, don't leave a message . . . live, die, it's all the same dream, right? . . . Bye.'

Despite the tension of the situation, Rosalie grimaced slightly at what she considered to be a highly pretentious message. It did have one advantage, though, it was delivered in a lazy, quiet growl, which at the other end of the line Max was desperately hoping Tolstoy would not hear emanating from the phone.

'C'mon man!' Max half shouted, timing it to coincide with the point when he guessed his message would be playing. 'I asked if you were going to kill me!'

Tolstoy did not hear the message, and he did not spot the trick either, he had seen so many portable phones placed on desks in his time.

Tolstoy answered Max's question at the point at which, in Max's house, Max's answering machine began to record. The portable phone was a video phone, as indeed were all phones, barring the occasional chic antique one, and Max had contrived to place it with its tiny camera facing across the desk. Judy and Rosalie could not only hear Plastic Tolstoy, but also see him, and all the while he was, of course, being recorded.

The hard sell.

'Am I going to kill you?' Tolstoy said, reiterating Max's question. 'I don't think so, no. You don't know shit, and your pal Schwartz knows less. That's why he sent you here, to try and truth-drug a confession out of me. I guess the last thing I need to do right now is to give credence to his libellous hypothesis by murdering his stool pigeon, right?'

'And about his hypothesis?' said Max, trying to hide his relief. 'Is it true? Do you sink oil tankers to sell Claustrospheres?'

'What do you think?'

'I think if you can fund Mother Earth while they try to kill you, you'd pretty much do anything to make a sale.'

'You know you may not be so stupid after all, Max. How did you cotton on to the fact that I fund Mother Earth? . . . Oh yeah, I remember now, you were with Nathan Hoddy, weren't you? That's right. I guess he told you the plot of his movie, huh?'

'That's right, and when he died for it, I guessed he must have unwittingly stumbled on the truth.'

'Clever. No, really, clever. You sure the girl didn't work all that out for you? I never had you picked out as a brain boy.'

'No, I figured it out all on my own. The girl's my wife now, by the way.'

'Really? Congratulations. Like I could give a fuck about your domestic arrangements. I must confess to you though, she looked eminently screwable, nice and natural. Although to be frank, armed women with too much attitude make my dick go limp.'

Max was thinking hard, trying to conjure up the right words to suit his purpose. He knew that it was his job to coax some information out of Tolstoy about the secret Claustrosphere marketing strategy. He also knew that he was dealing with a far subtler and cleverer man than he was himself. But even clever people have weak spots, Max felt that he knew what Tolstoy's was. It was vanity.

'Plastic, does it ever bother you that what you do might be a little unethical?'

'Huh?' Tolstoy asked, as if he did not understand the question.

'I mean, I grant you it's *clever* but . . .'

'No, Max, no buts. It's clever, just that.'

Max congratulated himself. He felt that he had judged his man well, he believed that he was drawing Tolstoy in, playing on the well-known fact that Tolstoy could not resist the sound of his own voice. Unfortunately for Max, this was not the case. Contrary to what he'd said earlier, Plastic had decided that Max would have to die that day. The Mother Earth girl and the FBI man, he was unconcerned about. One was a terrorist, the other Plastic knew to be held in contempt by his own colleagues and known in the Bureau as a paranoid conspiracy theorist. Without evidence, of which they clearly had none, their voice would not be heard. Max however was different. Here was a colossal star, a man whose every word was reported in the media. True, Tolstoy owned the lion's share of that media, and Max, like his comrades, had no evidence. None the less, he was a figure of sufficient significance to be capable, in a single interview, of sparking public debate and rumour, which Tolstoy naturally wished to avoid.

Tolstoy had therefore decided to have Max killed immediately, before he had a chance to make his suspicions public. This was not a job which Plastic wanted carried out in his house and so he had therefore decided to occupy Max for a few minutes, whilst summoning his killing people. They could then be instructed to dispatch the inconvenient film star, once he had driven a suitably non-incriminating distance from the Tolstoy mansion.

Tolstoy idly pressed a button on his intercom.

'Hey, Sugar,' he said to his trusted assistant, 'I'm busy with a pal right now. When the guys from dispatch arrive, just get them to wait at the main gate, will you?'

The guys from dispatch had not, in fact, up to that point, been summoned, but they had been now. Tolstoy turned back to Max with an easy smile. Max had been right about one thing, Tolstoy loved to show off and, confident that he would not be overheard, he was quite happy to occupy a condemned man's final minutes by demonstrating what a genius he was.

'What I do is not unethical at all,' Plastic said.

'Maybe just a little bit,' said Max, pleased with himself for being such a subtle interrogator.

'No, I don't accept that. It is not unethical.'

'But you do deliberately sink oil tankers, cause nuclear leaks and hole toxic waste convoys in the middle of big cities.'

'I do that, yes. Or, at least, I have my people do it. My sabotage people.'

'And this is not unethical?'

'I don't consider it unethical. Illegal, certainly. But not unethical.'

'Look,' said Max. 'God knows, I realise you're busy, but I would love to know how you get from poisoning kids to not being unethical. I mean, genuinely, I'm fascinated. I know you're a brilliant guy, I bet you can make the leap.'

'It ain't unethical, because all the things we do would happen anyway,' Tolstoy said.

'I don't understand,' said Max.

'Because you're stupid,' Tolstoy replied, and commenced to explain what had to be the nastiest marketing campaign in history, and there had been some horrors.

'So the Second Great Green Scare is coming to an end and we're trying to offload the early model Edens, right? Eden One, Eden Two, Eden Three. You wouldn't remember them because all this was before you were born, right? But the boom's over and I'm feeling down, OK? Sure, we'd done great for a while there, sold a shitload of product, but things were dropping off. I was young and hungry and I knew that with a sure-fire item like Claustrosphere, we could do better. You getting me?'

Max explained that, though he might not be Albert Einstein, he could follow a simple narrative. Tolstoy continued.

'My problem was that I could not use negative advertising; you know the kind of thing . . . Hey! The world's fucked! Save your ass! Buy a shelter!'

'Why couldn't you do that?' Max inquired, to demonstrate how attentive he was being. 'Seems to me that would have been your best shot.'

'Yeah? Well, you're wrong. Popular research informed us that people felt guilty enough about the environment already. They took a very negative view towards a company gleefully embracing Earth death in order to make a profit from it. So I had to be clever, right? And believe me I was. I was young and I was clever.

I had ideas then! Man, did I have ideas! I used Rodin's Thinker as my principal symbol and that bit out of Shakespeare . . . you know, "This fortress built by Nature" etc.'

'"This sceptred isle, This earth of majesty . . . This other Eden,"' said Max, remembering how recently he had heard that very quote, and how happy he had been for a short while.

'You know it? Cute piece, am I right? And beautifully deployed, though I say it myself. I had a product which was basically an immoral, irresponsible, cowardly cop-out and I gave it *class*. If you give something class, then you make people think they're being clever. If you've done that, you can sell them anything. But not for ever right? You can only play the class game for so long. Engaging a customer intellectually has never been a substitute for engaging them emotionally. What I really needed was scare tactics, and like I say, I couldn't use them. So as the Second Green Scare dies down, so do my figures; plummeting would not be too depressing a word to describe the sales situation during this time. Sure, we had some good months, sometimes very good, but we were bumping along the bottom. Then I began to notice something, I noticed that those good months always coincided with –'

'Some terrible environmental catastrophe.'

'Clever kid. That chick must be good for you, Max. Of course they did. You open a paper, you see there's some province of India where no one can breathe any more. You think, hey, the future's looking kind of bleak, maybe I'd better start covering my ass here. Disaster was good for business. So I started to buy into news channels to make sure everybody got to hear about all the disasters.

If Claustrosphere itself couldn't use scare tactics, then I'd get somebody else to do it.'

'Cute,' Max observed.

'Wasn't it?' Plastic Tolstoy agreed. 'There I was, running these news channels which were getting awards and praise from greenies for prioritising environmental news, and all the time I was just doing it to scare people into buying my product. Boy, it was funny! We had all these environmentally concerned journos and researchers lining up to work on my channels. They thought, "At last somebody's taking the fate of the planet seriously." And I sure was! Claustrosphere was turning into a multi-billion dollar industry. To me, that is serious.'

Tolstoy had leapt from his chair and was pacing about the room in a manner that Nathan would have recognised, had he not been dead.

Back at Max's place this movement caused some concern.

'I wish he wouldn't do that,' said Rosalie. 'He keeps walking out of shot.'

'Don't worry,' Judy replied, scarcely able to contain his excitement. 'We've got enough of his smug mug and the voice is coming over fine.'

Indeed it was, and Plastic Tolstoy, blissfully ignorant of the phone trick, had scarcely stopped for breath.

'That's when I started to fund Natura and Mother Earth. They were my best adverts of all. Anything environmentally conscious, I promoted it . . . secretly, of course. Protest concerts, documentaries, terrorism. I was the greenest guy on Earth, and all the while, I'm selling Claustrospheres. Ha ha ha! It was perfect. But I still got a problem.'

'It all seems pretty straightforward to me,' Max ventured.

'Straightforward! It was a nightmare! Everything depended on one, non-constant factor and, in manufacturing terms, if you're dependent on a non-constant factor, that's your profit gone.'

'Excuse me?' said Max, the eager pupil.

'A non-constant factor! Which in this case was environmental disaster! Everyone was hanging around waiting for one. The manufacturer, the distributor, the retailer, the marketer, all waiting, and why? Because none of them could move without *the customer*, and the customer did not appear in any great numbers without the disaster. The tail was wagging the dog! You got Joe Soap, right? He runs a small-town Claustrosphere showroom, normal weeks he's selling one, maybe two units, right? Suddenly, there's a local disaster. The methane build-up in an old landfill that has since been built over goes pop, and wipes out half the suburbs. Bang! It's a wake-up call! A Pavlovian response. "My God, Marjorie," says every short-sighted little schmuck in town, "the world's exploding, we'd better get a Claustrosphere." Suddenly Joe Soap gets four, maybe five *hundred* orders. But he doesn't have the stock, he's geared to selling one a week. "I'll get 'em," he cries, and calls the factory which starts a rush build. Three months later five hundred units worth a billion dollars turn up in Nowheresville, by which time the explosion is forgotten, it's history, and everybody has spent the money on sending little Jimmy to college instead. A nightmare. Like I told you.'

'It certainly sounds it,' Max agreed, trying to look sympathetic.

'All the time the product was chasing the demand. You

can't run a business like that, the *demand* has to chase the *product*. I knew then that I had to rationalise my principal sales strategy.'

'Your principal sales strategy? That would be the environmental disasters, would it?' Max inquired.

'Exactly. I get to thinking, if only I knew *when* these terrible things were going to happen I could have the whole operation ready in place. The news teams ready to report, the stock ready to go and above all the tasteful, classy, non-exploitative little Claustrosphere commercials to play in heavy rotation around the news breaks that reported the disaster. That's the connection your FBI pal made, and which he tried to prove with his pathetic little plan to drug me. The breakthrough was to get the *news to fit my commercials*, in fact, to make the news itself the commercial, and the actual commercial just the pack-shot.'

'So you start creating disasters?' Max asked.

'Hey hey hey! Hold on!' Tolstoy replied, and for a moment Max thought he might be about to become cautious, but Tolstoy was waiting for his killing people and was happy to tell his story in his own time and in the right order.

'At first, I'm still trying to do it legitimately, right? Trying to work out when these genuine disasters will occur so I can be ready for them. So I get all these scientists together and ask them to predict what's going to happen next. Ask me how they did.'

'How did they do?' asked Max obligingly.

'They did shit. Never picked one, not one! They'd say, *maybe* a tanker will go down off Alaska, *maybe* a Russian power station will blow. Well, of course they would! I knew that! What I didn't know was when! Now here is where we get to the point about what I did *not* being unethical.'

'I just can't see how you're going to make that trick, Plastic,' said Max, his face a picture of concentration.

'Watch me. So I'm telling you that me and my scientists know the stuff is going to happen, we just don't know when. They're giving me all these probability charts saying ten nuke disasters a year, fifty oil spills, tigers to be extinct some time soon, all that stuff, and I'm thinking, well if it's *going* to happen *anyway*, then there's nothing wrong in me organising it to happen in a disciplined manner. It's like carrying your own bomb on to a plane because the chances of there being two people with bombs on any one plane are basically zero.'

'I'm not sure I follow that analogy, man,' said Max.

'What are you, stupid? It's like crystal. I'm thinking, if my science guys say that two tankers will sink in the Panama Canal in the next three months, then why don't I sink 'em? It's the same damage and there are huge national and international benefits to be achieved. The common good is well served.'

'It is?'

'Well, of course it is! Have you any idea how many *jobs* are involved in Claustrosphere manufacturing? Also distribution and installation? Even then, we had a colossal workforce, not to mention the associate industries. Maybe you think that millions of working men and women should be laid off while we all wait for some dumb rust-bucket to sink in the Panama Canal? A rust-bucket, I might remind you, that we all know is *going to sink anyway*! Then there's the huge investment involved. Even then anyone could see that Claustrosphere was going to be bigger than cars. In global economic terms

Claustrosphere is the difference between boom and bust. If the wind goes out of our sales, bang, recession! I had a *duty* to make the Claustrosphere operation manageable. The issue was jobs and dollars in the heartlands! That is not something that can be left drifting up to vagaries of non-specific probabilities.'

'You mean chance?'

'Exactly, I mean chance.'

'So you saw creating environmental disaster as a kind of moral thing, then?' Max really was fascinated. Tolstoy's sense of conviction was awesome.

'I saw creating a situation that was healthy for investors and employees alike as a moral thing, certainly, and if that meant creating environmental disaster, then so be it,' said Tolstoy. 'To me, encouraging growth and creating jobs is the only morality, which as it happens is fortunate, because I must admit to you, it turned out that my probabilities' theory did not hold water.'

'The one about if two tankers were going to sink anyway, you might as well be the person to sink them?'

'Yeah, what actually happened was that four tankers sank, our two and the two that were going to, anyway.'

'So the bomb on the plane theory's crap?'

'It's a cute theory. I still think it should work.'

'But it doesn't?'

'Apparently not, no.'

Plastic Tolstoy paused for the first time in a while. Max could not help but gape at the enormity of the horrors of which he had been told. Back at his house, Rosalie and Judy too were completely dumbfounded. The sheer scale of Tolstoy's crimes left them lost for words.

'Well, I guess tough decisions take tough guys,' Max said finally.

'Exactly,' Tolstoy replied. 'Personally, I see myself as a global philanthropist.'

Another job for the killing people.

Max decided it was time to leave. The danger he was in had suddenly dawned upon him. He remembered how Tolstoy had served Nathan for simply suggesting a screenplay idea. Now he, Max, knew the whole dreadful story.

'Thanks, Plastic, it's been real,' he said and ran for the door. Unfortunately, the door of the office was locked. Max turned to face Plastic Tolstoy, who was playing with his gun.

'Max, you leaving without saying goodbye?' said Tolstoy.

'Are you going to kill me, Plastic?' Max inquired.

'Oh yes, thanks for reminding me,' said Plastic and fired at Max. When the noise died away, Max was still standing, if rather paler than before.

'Just kidding,' said Plastic. 'It's a hologram. Ha ha! Like I told you, I don't want dead movie stars cluttering up my house. Besides, Schwartz and your girl know you came here. If I kill you here, it might get complicated, even for a guy with my clout. See ya, kid. Be lucky.'

Tolstoy pressed a button, the door sprang open and Max turned and ran. He left everything behind, including the telephone. He just ran, out of the office, out of the house, into his car and away.

Rosalie and Judy turned to each other in triumph. They had the whole confession on tape, this was dynamite indeed.

'We have to take it to the police,' said Judy. 'Now.'

'No way!' Rosalie replied. 'If we do that, sure we get

Tolstoy, but the tape becomes evidence, prejudicial to the trial, then the appeal, then the appeal on the appeal. We need it now! People have to see it, they have to know what's been happening to the world, what we've all let happen. This tape could be the thing that finally turns the environmental argument around.'

'I don't think so, Rosalie,' said Judy. 'Tolstoy owns the lion's share of the world's communication systems. You can't fight a propaganda war with him, even with that tape. His will be the loudest voice.'

'Maybe, but there's one voice people still listen to. One voice which will always be heard, even if not one of Tolstoy's channels were to broadcast him. Jurgen Thor has the status to get the truth about Tolstoy into the public domain. I say we take the tape to him.'

Rosalie had been galvanised back into action. All thoughts of retreating from the world had vanished from her mind. She no longer wanted to hide away in Max's Claustrosphere. She knew now that the end of the world was not inevitable, it was being manipulated, and she wanted to fight.

Just then, further discussion was cut short by the voice of Plastic Tolstoy. He was not speaking to them, but Rosalie and Judy could still see and hear him over Max's phone, which still lay, its line open, on Tolstoy's desk.

Plastic Tolstoy was speaking to his assistant on his intercom.

'Sugar, are the dispatch people at the gate? . . . Good . . . Yes, Max Maximus the movie star will be emerging in a red Porsche . . . Yes, tell them to make sure they do it well away from the house. The usual rules apply.'

Rosalie and Judy both knew instantly what Tolstoy

was saying. Rosalie grabbed the phone off the hook, thus finally ending the lengthy recording.

'Call it off, Tolstoy!!' she screamed down the phone, desperately trying to make the man at the other end hear. 'We know what you're doing! We heard you! Killing Max will achieve nothing!'

But Tolstoy got up and left his office without hearing the tiny tinny voice emanating from Max's phone.

'Tolstoy!' Rosalie screamed, 'I'll kill you if you hurt him. I'll kill you!'

But she could hear the office door close, and knew that he was gone.

Chapter Twenty-Five

The Hollywood treatment

Foiling the hit.

'Rosalie,' Judy pleaded, cowering behind the dashboard, his knuckles translucent on the armrests of his seat. 'If we get pulled for busting red lights we won't even get a chance to try and save Max.'

'Nobody's going to pull me over,' Rosalie responded tersely. Her whole body was hunched forward, willing the car to go faster, her chin nearly touching the steering-wheel. 'If we can get a few cops chasing us, all the better.'

They were driving very fast through the quiet tree-lined streets of the Beverly Hills Fortified Village, in a desperate effort to intercept Max's red Porsche.

'They can't have got to him yet. They can't,' Rosalie was repeating to herself as they hurtled across the exclusive residential area.

But they could and they had.

Rosalie and Judy skidded around a sharp corner in a leafy little road to find Max's Porsche slewed into the middle of the highway and another car, full of what looked like common hoodlums pumping bullets into it.

Much to Judy's dismay, this terrible sight caused Rosalie

to accelerate forward and she deliberately slammed her car into the side of the car occupied by the hoodlums.

'Get Max,' Rosalie cried, as they came to rest and their heads stopped whipping back and forth. 'I'll cover you.' It was only then that she remembered she did not actually have a gun. 'Shit!' she said.

'Here, use mine,' said Judy. 'I'm not very good with it anyway,' and he handed her his regulation issue machine-pistol.

By this time, the killers had regained some of their composure, and were thinking about finishing off the job which had been interrupted by the crash. They did not realise that what had happened was anything other than an ordinary accident on the public highway. They were therefore considerably surprised when the driver of the car began to shoot at them, killing one of their number almost immediately. This was not how the contract was supposed to go. There was not, as far as the killers were aware, supposed to be any resistance. Perhaps it was the cops? If it was not the cops, it would certainly not be long before the cops arrived. The killers took stock and the situation was not to their liking. The police were coming and some mad woman was firing at them for some reason, but what? Could it possibly be because she'd dented her car? The killers wondered if they should call it a day, their job seemed done anyway. Max definitely looked dead. He was slumped in his car, completely covered in blood and bullet holes. Indeed, so much blood did there seem to be that, if the bullets hadn't killed him already, he would shortly drown. Feeling their professional obligations to have been fulfilled, the killers withdrew.

Talk to my agent.

Having got the dead, or at the very least, nearly dead Max into the back of the car, Rosalie also accelerated away from the scene of the incident. She did not know where she was going, but she did know that she had to get away. Max was a celebrity and if news of his being gunned down got out there would be a media circus, and it would be impossible to keep him hidden. Rosalie felt sure that if Max was alive Tolstoy would try to hit him again.

'Is he alive?' she shouted over her shoulder at Judy, who had got into the back seat and was attempting to tend to Max. 'Please tell me he's alive!'

'I don't know, I think so. Yes, I think he is. He's twitching a little, although that could just be reflexes,' Judy replied.

'Is his hand on his crotch?' Rosalie shouted back.

'No.'

'Then it isn't his reflexes.'

Rosalie, like most women who live with men, found the male habit of constantly rearranging their wedding tackle whenever an idle moment occurred most disconcerting. On the phone, reading a book, stirring the dinner, blokes are always handling their privates and Rosalie, who had just spent nearly a month alone with Max, felt certain that if Max were dead and his muscles were going through their final involuntary spasms, somehow or other, one of his hands would end up on his dick.

'Is he breathing?' she asked desperately.

'Yes, he is, but he's a mess, that's for sure. Most of his insides are on his outside. We have to get him to a hospital.'

'We can't. If we do that, Tolstoy will find him for sure and he won't screw it up twice. We have to stay undercover.'

'Rosalie,' Judy pleaded, 'this is Hollywood and a huge star has been terribly wounded, possibly fatally. This is not something we can keep quiet.'

Max wasn't dead. His body was in total shock, but he could hear what they were saying. What is more, he knew how to deal with the problem under discussion – the same way you dealt with any problem. With a considerable effort Max managed to attract Judy's attention by tugging at his sleeve.

'Call my agent,' Max whispered into Judy's ear and gave him the number.

'Of course,' said Judy, 'why didn't I think of that,' and grabbed his phone.

Judy was not himself in that great biz called show, but he lived in Los Angeles, and he knew that when stars had problems, whatever those problems might be, they turned to their agents to sort them out.

'Koch Associates,' said a steely voice over Judy's phone. A voice which implied by its very tone that unless you had already had a featured role in at least three shows, not to even think of seeking representation. Even Judy was momentarily intimidated. Then he remembered that he was not actually an aspiring actor and had no burning belief inside him that he could make it, if only he were given the chance, nor was he seeking representation. He therefore had nothing to fear from the armour-plated voice that answered the phones at Koch Associates.

Emboldened by this thought, he said, 'Listen, my name is J. Schwartz, I'm an officer with the FBI. Max Maximus is in big trouble and I have to speak to his agent.'

There was a brief pause and another voice came on the line, this time even steelier and more forbidding than the first.

'This is Geraldine Koch. If you're some actor trying to bluff your way through to me, get off the phone now, or I shall see to it that your next public appearance will be in a Salvation Army breadline!'

'Ms Koch, this is J. Schwartz of the FBI. Now shut up and listen to me!' Geraldine was so unused to being addressed in this manner that, astonishingly, she did shut up, at least for long enough for Judy to say, 'Plastic Tolstoy has taken out a contract on Max.'

'What!' Geraldine cried, panic cracking the steel of her voice. 'Max told me he was retiring! You say he has a contract with Plastic Tolstoy! That can't be, I do his deals, not the FBI!'

'Ms Koch, will you be quiet,' Judy shouted. 'I am not talking about a film contract, I'm talking about a murder contract! They've already hit him once and he's got about a hundred bullets in him. Now we know that Tolstoy will try to hit him again the moment he finds out where Max is. He needs hospital treatment in complete secrecy and he needs it now.'

Geraldine was calm again. Things were not quite as bad as she had thought; Max was only dying. For a moment she had thought that he had gone to another agent.

'Where are you?' she asked.

'We're in a car just coming on to Sunset at the Chateau Marmont.'

'Head for 289043 Melrose,' Geraldine said. 'It's just past all the bondage gear shops and don't ask me how I know that. It's a convent hospital called The Little Sisters of the Above the Line Costs. There will be a medical team waiting.'

Geraldine put the phone down and tried to concentrate. Max may not have left her but the situation was still very serious. What could Max possibly have done to offend Tolstoy enough for Tolstoy to try to kill him? Trying to kill someone was a fairly radical step, even by the cut and thrust standards of Hollywood. Geraldine wondered if this meant that the movie deal which she had been negotiating for Max with Tolstoy's people was off? It would at least be on hold, that was certain. Max's position was clearly a delicate one. When a producer took out a murder contract on an actor, the actor's agent knew that difficult negotiations lay ahead. Geraldine resolved not to panic. She had worked in a tough town for more years than her cosmetic surgeon cared to remember and she had learnt over those years that there were very few problems, if any, which saturation lunching could not eventually fix.

'Pixie Dawn,' she snapped into her intercom. 'Clear my diary. As of now, we are lunching for our lives.'

Specialist treatment.

Rosalie pulled into 289043 Melrose to find a crack medical team on full alert. Max was whisked out of the car and on to an emergency trolley and taken straight into an intensive care theatre. Judy and Rosalie could only watch anxiously through the glass wall as Max's clothes were cut away and the dedicated surgeons and doctors began their work.

'They look like they know their business,' Judy said, attempting to comfort a tight-lipped Rosalie. Rosalie's hand stole to her stomach. She had only just become pregnant, so there was nothing to feel, but she none the less felt aware of some presence inside her.

'I want my child to know its father,' she said quietly.

Judy had not realised that Rosalie was pregnant. He did not know what to say, so he said nothing.

After about ten minutes the head surgeon emerged from the operating theatre, looking very perplexed.

'Well, we can't find anything wrong with him, I'm afraid,' he said, and there was a hint of irritation in his voice. He had been called in from a particularly tense game of VR golf against Jack Nicklaus and he rather resented the intrusion.

'Can't find anything wrong!' Rosalie gasped.

'That's right. There's not a whiff of drugs about him. We've checked his genitals and his posterior and all that's clean as a whistle. There's no overdose, no sexual disease, I've looked right up him and there's definitely nothing wedged in his backside. To be quite frank, I've absolutely no idea why you've brought him here at all.'

'Because he's dying! You stupid bastard!' Rosalie screamed in the man's face. 'Look at him.'

The surgeon turned and seemed to notice for the first time that Max was riddled with bullet holes, and had virtually no blood left in him.

'You mean *that's* what you want us to look at?' he asked, very surprised.

The misunderstanding lay in the fact that The Little Sisters of the Above the Line Costs was a private hospital, with the emphasis on private. It was not used to dealing with ailments that might be categorised as non-scandalous. People got riddled with bullets all the time in LA. Death by gunfire was a perfectly socially acceptable way to go, it could happen to anyone and could not possibly be considered in any way embarrassing or necessitating expensive cover-ups. The Little Sisters was a hospital that specialised in such cover-ups, dealing as it did with things that people needed to be kept quiet. Drug overdoses, pubic crabs, strange objects that had got themselves stuck up people's bottoms or in other orifices – vacuum cleaner nozzles, Coke bottles, small animals, etc. (Small animals were particularly common, in fact, the hospital boasted rather a fine menagerie of assorted gerbils, hamsters and possums that had been rescued from the interior plumbing of various drugged-out movie stars.)

When the Little Sisters had received an urgent call from Max Maximus's agent, demanding an immediate admission, they had of course presumed that the ailment was of a scandalous nature, which is why they had spent so long probing one of the few holes in his body that had not been caused by a bullet.

Counsel.

Whilst the doctors worked on Max, Judy and Rosalie considered a plan of action. Despite being understandably upset and anxious about Max, Rosalie was thinking clearly. She remained adamant that the only course of action was to take the evidence of Plastic Tolstoy's crimes to Jurgen Thor, the one person with the influence to get it in properly before the public. Judy, on the other hand, still wanted to go to the police and have Tolstoy arrested.

'With what we've got on that tape we could put him

away for thirty years,' Judy said. 'I mean quite apart from all the environmental stuff, we have him commissioning an attempted murder.'

But Rosalie was absolutely insistent.

'He's my husband, it's my tape, and we're taking it to Thor.'

In her own mind Rosalie had rejoined Mother Earth. She was again a green activist and Plastic Tolstoy's confessional tape was the most effective weapon the Environmental Movement had ever been given.

'If we can get this out to people, maybe we can stop the rot!' Rosalie said. 'Maybe we can show people what's being done to their world while they twiddle their thumbs. It could be the Third Great Green Scare, something to really shock people into fighting back.'

'I suppose it could,' Judy conceded.

'Of course it could. We have to try anyway, and that means getting this tape back to Europe. If we stay here we'll be dead anyway.'

That reminded Judy of something. Plastic Tolstoy knew all about him. He was in as much danger as Max was, and so, in that case, were his loved ones. He called home. His husband Roger was very upset.

'Judy! Thank goodness it's you! You have to come home right now! The house has been ransacked. I just got back, everything is –'

'Roger!' Judy interrupted. 'Are the police there?'

'Not yet. I called them but –'

'Get your passport and get out now! Come to 289043 Melrose.'

'Don't be stupid, Judy, the house is a bomb-site, I have salmon for –'

'Now, Roger! Get out now!'

Ben Elton

Agent of conflict.

For a few hours Max's condition remained critical, but as it turned out Rosalie and Judy had interrupted the killers in time. By the afternoon he began to respond to treatment.

They knew they could not remain long at the hospital, though, reasoning that on hearing Max had been spirited away, Plastic Tolstoy would be anxious to ensure that he was dead.

'The first thing he's going to do is start checking the hospitals,' said Judy. 'We need to get Max out of town quickly and into some hiding place or other that Tolstoy can't figure out. That goes for me too, for that matter. Tolstoy's going to want to clean this whole thing up properly, and that includes me.'

'Well, I really don't see how looking up old TV schedules could have got you into so much trouble,' Roger observed, but Judy assured him that it had.

'The best place to go would be my granny's place in Ireland,' said Rosalie. 'Tolstoy doesn't know my name, so I doubt that he would find us there and it gets me close to Jurgen Thor.'

'That means an air ambulance,' Judy replied, 'also European visas. Those things are difficult to organise, and we could certainly never do it without sticking our heads above the parapet. If we swan round LA trying to get air tickets and our passports stamped, Tolstoy will spot us for sure.'

There was a gloomy silence. Every second they remained inactive brought Tolstoy's deadly shadow closer. Just then, the solution arrived in the unlikely figure of Max's agent Geraldine, who burst through the door with flowers from her Claustrosphere.

'OK,' she said to Judy and Rosalie. 'Thanks for getting him into hospital but I'll be taking charge from here on in.'

'I don't think so,' said Rosalie.

'Well, I'm sorry, Miss, but I'm not interested in what you think. What you think doesn't matter. All that matters is Max needs me and I'm here for him. Excuse me.' Geraldine turned her back on Rosalie and tapped a number into her phone. Rosalie and Judy were a little nonplussed. It was not so much what Geraldine had said, but the way that she had said it. No one can put people down the way an agent can, particularly an important Hollywood agent.

It is probably not that they particularly enjoy being rude. Being rude just happens to be the principal function of their professional existence. To an agent there are two types of actor, those who are happening and those who are not. Hence there are two kinds of rudeness. There is the rudeness which is directed *at* those who are not happening, and the rudeness which is directed at others *on behalf* of and for the benefit of those who are happening. The rudeness directed at the unhappening is not normally very rude. In fact, it is really no more than the understandable brusqueness which any decent agent must develop in a world where there are a thousand actors seeking every job. The rudeness directed downwards is often tinged with affection and understanding, for agents are human beings too and it would soften any heart to be constantly surrounded by so much frustrated ambition.

Where the rudeness gets nasty is when it is delivered on behalf of a star. This is because of the great agent's dilemma, the terrible cross which all agents have to bear, that which turns young, starry-eyed enthusiasts who 'love this business' into hardened, chain-smoking attack animals.

The agent's dilemma is this: no matter how hard they work, they can never succeed. The success or failure of their clients only ever means failure to them. For an agent will never be loved or appreciated by those on whose behalf they labour. Never. Agents were born to be resented.

It starts at the bottom. When an actor is out of work and it is three months since they were even invited up for an audition, they become obsessed with the notion that their agent is crap.

'No, seriously, I really am thinking of changing my agent,' the actor will assure his or her friends. 'I mean she just hasn't got me a thing. Not a *bloody* thing! I mean, I wouldn't mind but I'm actually *quite bloody good*.'

A subtle variation of this whine is the conviction that the agent is actually capable of getting work, but for some reason does not care to do so for them. Actors conceive this latter prejudice if anybody else on the agent's books happens to have landed an audition for a soap powder commercial in the previous five years.

Sometimes, not often, but sometimes, a glint of hope peeks into the actor's life. After making two hundred calls the agent lands the actor an audition and, astonishingly, the actor gets the job. At this point there is a brief moment when the agent may bask in a thimbleful of the actor's affection. They will lunch together to celebrate the start of a great career and the agent will order good Californian Chardonnay. Even as the glasses clink, however, the actor will secretly be thinking that his or her success in getting a job was really no thanks to the agent at all. It was, in fact, entirely due to the brilliant way that he or she handled the audition. Anyone, after all, can make a phone call.

If this brief moment of glory is a one-off and the actor fails to capitalise on it, he or she will soon return to the conviction that the agent is either crap, or uninterested in them. However, if the actor's career takes off and they find themselves in demand, then the agent will have to swallow a bitter pill indeed. For the actor will now be thinking that work is available to them anyway, so what does the agent do? What skill, they ask themselves, does it require to find work for somebody who everybody already wants?

'I really don't know,' the actor will tell their friends, 'what I'm paying my ten per cent for.'

It is this terrible betrayal which truly leads agents to their joyless life of rudeness. Because they become obsessed with demonstrating to their star clients what it is that the star clients are paying their ten per cents for.

'You will not *believe* what the studio's opening offer was,' the agent will assure the star. 'No, I'm not even going to tell you. It was an insult and an offence and you should not even have to hear about it but let me tell you, it was a disgrace. I just told them to stuff it, shove it and take a hike and, believe me, I wasn't that restrained. Anyway, they've come back with a figure which is at least located on planet Earth.'

The agent's job is to make themselves appear indispensable. What they are saying to their clients is this, 'You are too important and famous to have to deal with any shit, anytime, anywhere. I will take the shit away from you. Trust me. *I will be rude for you.*'

The agent creates the impression that the star is surrounded by people who are hell bent on ripping them off, taking advantage of them, demeaning them and generally putting shit on them (shit, which, of course, the star *does not need right now*!). The suggestion being that without the agent endlessly being rude on their behalf, the star would live a life no better than that of a sewer rat.

'You mean they flew you on a *scheduled flight*? Booked you a suite with no *spa bath*? Put you in worse seats than *so and so*? The car was *how many* seconds late? . . . I don't believe it! This is simply unacceptable! Don't you worry about it, though, leave it with me. You do not need this shit! You should not have to *deal with this shit*!'

It is not just the agents of course who act in this way. The life of a star is filled with people making complaints and being rude on the star's behalf, for which they receive a percentage of the star's earnings. If many stars turn eventually into ego-monsters, they are certainly given plenty of encouragement.

Power struggle.

Geraldine, having turned her back on Judy and Rosalie, was speaking on the phone.

'Yes, thank you, I should like to speak to Plastic Tolstoy's office. Yes, now! My name is Geraldine Koch and I represent . . .'

Geraldine got no further because at that point Rosalie knocked the phone from her hand and ground it under her heel.

'Phone calls can be traced, you know, Miss Koch. I thought we'd told you. Tolstoy is trying to kill Max.'

Geraldine could not believe what had just happened. Somebody had touched her phone! In fact, not just touched it, destroyed it! That was a personal violation. Her phone was the medium of her artistry. To destroy it was like taking an artist's brush, or breaking a musician's instrument. Fortunately, she was carrying eight more. Geraldine rounded on Rosalie.

'Now listen to me, young lady, I don't know who the hell you are but I am Max's agent –'

'And I am his wife!'

This stopped Geraldine in her tracks. Wives were tricky things. They could poison the air between agent and star or they could sweeten it. You had to keep on the right side of wives. On the other hand, you didn't want to get too close to them because it left you in a very tricky position when the star dumped the wife and married the nanny. If the new wife felt that the agent was too chummy with the old wife, then the agent's life would become hell until they had ingratiated themselves with the new wife. Unfortunately, by the time they had done this, the new wife could easily be an old wife. Wives certainly were tricky things. In the long run, it was kids that were the determining factor in an agent's attitude. If there were kids, the wife had to be taken very seriously indeed.

'Well, congratulations, my dear,' said Geraldine, testing the water, 'and may one ask if we can expect to hear the patter of tiny feet?'

Rosalie was a little taken aback by the question but she saw no reason to deny it.

'Yes, as a matter of fact, we are expecting.'

'But my *darling* that's *wonderful*,' said Geraldine, thinking to herself, 'Damn, some waitress has trapped Max with a pregnancy and now we're stuck with the little bitch.'

'If there's anything I can do. Anything at all,' Geraldine said.

'Well, as a matter of fact there is,' said Rosalie. 'Max wants to recuperate discreetly in Europe. So what we need is an air ambulance and four false passports with Euro visas in them.'

Geraldine was delighted. Nothing pleases an agent more than to sort out difficult things for their clients' spouses, especially if those things are slightly dodgy. It puts the spouse in the agent's debt. Geraldine reckoned that obtaining false visas would provide her with a good deal of leverage with Max in the future. Little did poor Geraldine know that there was in fact not a great deal of future left.

Chapter Twenty-Six

Debauchery and murder

Caligula's palace.

Jurgen Thor was in the middle of an orgy when Rosalie called him. His once pristine bedroom, which had been so stylishly furnished with its single enormous bed and a few floor cushions, was now a mass of naked bodies, water couches, bondage gear and various other sexual paraphernalia. There was booze and drugs aplenty and Jurgen was a little drunk when he picked up the phone.

'Jurgen Thor? It's me, Rosalie Connolly,' the soft Irish voice said. 'I came to see you a few weeks back, I was with Max Maximus. Do you remember?'

Did he remember? Rosalie could not know it but Jurgen Thor could never forget that night. It haunted his dreams. Scarcely a night went by now when he did not awake in a sweat with the vision of a dead girl screaming at him from the bottom of a deep dark chasm.

'Yes, I remember everything. I heard you had left us, Rosalie.'

'Well, I haven't, and I need to see you again, urgently.'

Jurgen may have been drunk, but not so much that he was immune to the memory of those flashing green eyes and the pale skin. The beautiful voice brought it all back to him very clearly. The earlier part of that terrible evening, the pleasanter part, when he had still been in control and girls had still done what he told them to without having to be murdered first. Yes, that bit had been fun in its way, showing off to the lovely young woman, *soiling* her with the knowledge of her compromise. That soft voice also brought a more distant night back to Jurgen's mind. A night when it had been just him and Rosalie, alone. Now that had been a truly wonderful night. She had been weaker then, and he stronger. Then she had really been his possession. But that was in a different time, when he had still been at the height of his powers, not like now. Even so, it was fun to look back. Yes, Jurgen had fond memories of Rosalie. How nice, he thought in his alcoholic haze, it would be to see her again. He was wrong.

'You need to see me, huh, baby doll?' Jurgen breathed into the phone, trying to sound sexy but in fact merely giving Rosalie the impression that he had a cold. 'Well, come on over to my place. Hey, girl! We're having a party!'

Rosalie put the phone down feeling a little puzzled. Jurgen had sounded strange. Could he have been drunk? It seemed unlikely, his capacity to hold his booze had always been legendary. Rosalie was not of course to know just how much Jurgen Thor had been letting himself go of late. The man was slowly giving up. The process had begun even before he had found himself forced to murder poor Scout. He was weighed down with the knowledge of doom. The end was coming and he wished that it would hurry up and come. He was fed up with waiting and fed up with lying.

Scout's death had accelerated this process. Once she started returning each night to interrupt his sleep, Jurgen began to sag. It was as if a ball which had been firm and strong with tension for so long had finally been punctured. It only takes a little hole, and all the air soon rushes out, leaving the ball looking much the same, but useless for all that.

In an effort to regain his former aggressive *joie de vivre*, Jurgen had started to party, in fact, to orgy. He had jettisoned the sexual habits he had practised for decades in favour of a wild free-for-all. No more for him the private one-on-one seduction, of which he had been the master for so long. He could no longer do it. Private sex reminded him of Scout, and he had enough of Scout to contend with in his dreams without seeing her in the faces of the women he screwed. Jurgen had never imagined that such a little murder would affect him so. He had lived a rough life and seen and done many terrible things, and yet he simply could not shake the death of this one innocent from his mind. He supposed it was because she had died to protect a lie. He had killed her to defend the indefensible, and now he was paying the price. He could not even make love to a woman if he was alone with her, he had to have a crowd around him. Jurgen was scared of the dark.

Late-comer.

All the lights in the mountain home were blazing as Rosalie guided her little monocopter down through the darkness and on to Jurgen's rooftop heli-pad. She was surprised to see a number of aircraft already parked, their blades folded down to make more space. Despite this evidence that Jurgen had company, it was all strangely quiet. No one had come up on to the roof to meet her, which was very much a break with Jurgen Thor's old ways. In the past he had been extremely security conscious, never allowing people to land on his roof unchallenged.

There was no bell to ring, none had ever been needed because the occupants of the house always heard any approaching aircraft from miles away. Rosalie was forced to bang and kick upon the door in an effort to attract attention. For a while she got nowhere and began to wonder if she would ever succeed in gaining access to Jurgen's lair. There was music playing somewhere, but she could hear no talk or laughter. She became alarmed. Had some terrible gas leak or something occurred? Were they all dead?

Finally she heard footsteps on the stairs within and the door was opened by a dreamy-looking young woman, completely naked, with quite the largest breasts and the smallest pupils that Rosalie had ever seen.

'Hi,' said the very stoned woman. 'Aren't the stars amazing. People never take time to look at things, do they? I mean, *really* look at them. Come on in.'

Rosalie followed the girl down the spiral staircase and found herself yet again in Jurgen Thor's bedroom. How different it was from the other two occasions on which she had seen it. Then it had been a chic and elegant palace of seduction, now it looked like Sodom and Gomorrah must have looked on the days when the populace had decided to stop being so prissy, throw inhibition to the wind and get properly naughty.

There must have been thirty naked bodies in the room. Jurgen never had any problem assembling a decent guest-list for his orgies. People were thrilled to be invited to his legendary and, until recently, totally exclusive private home. Jurgen was one of the most important and respected people in the world, everybody wanted to know him. Society beauties flocked around, as did free-spirited Natura hippie girls . . . they always had. Jurgen was never shy of making the most of this popularity for the purpose of sexual conquest, these days he just did it in bulk, that was all.

For a nice Catholic girl the whole outrageous scene was something of a shock, and as she looked around the room Rosalie might have thought that she was dreaming, except that these were not the sort of dreams that she had.

'What on earth have you all been doing?' Rosalie asked, perhaps rather stupidly.

'We've been making good thoughts and feelings,' the large-breasted girl replied. 'They'll emanate out from this place and make the whole world beautiful again.' Which was not a bad excuse for getting rat-faced drunk and shagging a lot of virtual strangers.

The girl drifted away, leaving Rosalie alone on the stairs. Most of the company were asleep, or unconscious more like, to judge from their unnatural positions. A few couples however were still lazily making love in a distant, soporific kind of a way. One or two others were drinking and smoking, staring trance-like into the middle distance and nodding sagely, as if in agreement with some brilliant point, even though no one had actually said anything. Jurgen Thor himself lay in the centre of it all, unconscious upon his great bed, prostrate amongst no less than four women, one of whom was still half awake and sleepily blowing Jurgen's sleepy member.

Ben Elton

Jurgen was still a magnificent figure of a man, but Rosalie could not help but feel a bit queasy, contemplating the state he was in. She liked a party as much as the next girl, but to be so off your head that you could have somebody going down on you and not even notice was slightly sick-making, in Rosalie's opinion. However, she was not there to moralise, she had a desperately important job to do, and she needed Jurgen Thor.

Rosalie picked her way across the prostrate bodies stranded on the floor.

'Excuse me . . . I'm awfully sorry . . . Oh, my God! Did I just tread on your thing? Sorry,' she mumbled to the sleeping forms as she made her way to the bed.

'Jurgen,' she said, gently shaking the great man's shoulder. 'Jurgen?'

She got no further because at that moment her attention was distracted somewhat. She was standing beside the bed and the girl who had been concentrating on Jurgen's loins had reached out a hand, and was now using it to massage the inside of Rosalie's leg.

'Would you not do that, please?' Rosalie said to the spaced-out girl.

'Hey, come on,' the girl replied, looking up from the parts that she had been nibbling. 'Jurgen's rules, right? Everybody has to party. So get naked, lady, no spectators allowed.' With that, the girl moved her hand up to the top of Rosalie's inner leg, with the clear intention of unzipping her trousers.

'I said would you not do that, please,' said Rosalie, and pointed her gun into the girl's face.

'Wow! Are you the cops?' the girl asked, quickly removing her hand. But Rosalie had no wish to converse with this rampant space cadet any further. She shook

Jurgen by the shoulder and loudly demanded that he wake up. He did so with a scream that briefly roused the room.

'She's falling!' he shouted, before coming slowly round and focusing on Rosalie. 'Welcome to ancient Rome, yes, baby. My name is Caligula and the world is coming to an end. You have been designated my latest concubine.' He made a lunge at Rosalie but she backed away.

'Let's get out of here, Jurgen, I have to talk to you.'

But Jurgen had already drifted back into fitful unconsciousness and Rosalie was forced to try and rouse him further.

'Jurgen, it's urgent! It's Mother Earth business!' she said, shaking him again. 'You have to get out of bed and talk to me.'

'If you haven't come to party, don't bother knocking on my door.' Jurgen giggled and again made a grab at Rosalie. This time he found his mark and roughly took hold of one of her breasts. She hit him in the face, hard, and with a clenched fist. His hand dropped away but apart from that he scarcely seemed to notice. He certainly registered no pain, his eyes just rolled a little and he laughed again.

Rosalie could see that no sense would be got out of Jurgen for a few hours yet, and that she would have to wait. She retreated to the kitchen, which was mercifully empty of naked bodies, and made herself a cup of coffee. Jurgen's condition had shocked her deeply. True, she had long since jettisoned the adolescent hero-worship that she had felt for him as a girl, and, of course, recently his image had been further tarnished in her eyes by the revelations of who payed for his house and all the luxuries that he enjoyed so much. But he was still Jurgen

Thor, the most important and inspirational green activist there was. The Green God, the last sane man on Earth. To see him like this, a debauched and giggling wretch, was a hard sight indeed for Rosalie, particularly coming as it did on top of all the other shocking truths that she had had to accept of late.

She did not feel angry with Jurgen Thor, she felt sorry for him. Clearly the colossal burdens that he had carried for so long had finally got the better of him. The mighty and inspirational ideologue who had become an embittered pragmatist had finally taken refuge in the hollow pleasures of the dilettante. Jurgen Thor had given up, and who could blame him? Rosalie had given up herself only a few days earlier. In fact, thinking about it, drinking her coffee in that silent house, Rosalie realised that Jurgen's orgies were no more desperate or irresponsible than her own decision to hide away with Max in his Claustrosphere. She too had been planning to fiddle while Rome burned. Planning to luxuriate in the pleasures of the senses whilst the doomed world died. It had only been the knowledge of Plastic Tolstoy's marketing strategy that had galvanised her to return to the real world and take up arms again. Rosalie believed that the same thing would happen with Jurgen. He too would see that all was not lost, that once Tolstoy's taped confession was placed before the public, a new age of protest would dawn, and that Jurgen Thor would lead it.

All that would have to wait, though. For the time being, Rosalie would have to leave Jurgen to sleep it off amongst his concubines. But how strange he had looked. The mighty Thor turned into an insensitive, groping drunk. He had certainly surprised her. He was going to surprise her a great deal more before the night was over.

Another penny drops.

Before setting out to enlist Jurgen Thor, Rosalie had left Judy, Roger and Max in the care of her grandparents at their little cottage in Western Ireland. On that first evening after Rosalie had left and with Max lying in bed under sedation, Judy explained to Ruth and Sean (and indeed Roger, who was still very much catching up with things) the sequence of events that had brought them all to the current position.

'You're trying to tell us, young man, that environmental protest is basically an arm of Claustrosphere's marketing policy,' said Ruth as she produced a delicious-looking batter pudding, which she served up with a thick vegetable casserole.

'That's right,' said Judy. 'Neat, isn't it?'

'And they actually create disasters to fit in with their adverts?'

'It's unbelievable,' said Roger. 'Just so crisp and light.'

'What?' said Judy.

'This batter pudding, it's the best I've ever seen.'

'Roger,' Judy said, 'we're talking about Claustrosphere.'

'Well, I don't know why you're so surprised. The world's run on dirty tricks, isn't it? Nothing shocks me. I think the rot set in for America when the FBI killed Kennedy.'

'The FBI did *not* kill Kennedy!' Judy said firmly.

'Oh, you are so naïve, Judy,' said Roger. 'But please, let's not discuss it, I could not *bear* another Kennedy discussion.'

One of the more surprising facts about social inter-course as the twenty-first century plodded its weary course was the fact that the number of people discussing how JFK had died was actually increasing. Elvis had peaked long before, but the Kennedys went from strength to strength.

'I'll tell you what is unbelievable,' said Roger, sticking to his preferred subject. 'This ratatouille, Ruth, is quite simply gastronomically orgasmic, and let me tell you, I know. Oral orgasm is my speciality.'

There was a slightly uncomfortable pause.

'Roger's a chef,' said Judy, feeling some sort of explanation was necessary.

'Well, I thought he must be,' said Ruth disingenuously.

'You know what surprises me?' Sean said, looking up from his pipe. 'That you're still alive, Judy, after accusing Rosalie of spreading that toxic waste all over Brussels. I'm surprised she didn't kill you there and then.'

'I think she wanted to, but we had to run away from all the poison. I still can't figure out how I got that so wrong. I was so sure, you see. It all fitted.'

'Well, we can't be a genius the whole time, can we?' said Roger. 'This is called a Yorkshire pudding, isn't it, Ruth? We use batter in the States, but it's usually much heavier. How in heaven do you get it so fluffy?'

'The most important element is the fat, dear. The fat has got to be absolutely smoking hot. Also, the mix has to stand for at least an hour.'

'Well, it's yummy,' Roger assured Ruth. 'Would you like me to do this for you sometimes, Judy? . . . Judy, please don't daydream at the table, we're guests here.'

But Judy was not daydreaming. He was thinking very

hard. Yet again rehearsing in his mind the circumstances which had led him to the conclusion that Mother Earth were provoking their own disasters.

'Natura were always there, you see. It was as if they knew where and when the disasters would occur. That's why I thought Mother Earth were causing them and tipping Natura off.'

'Yes, you've *said* that, dear! But they weren't, were they?' Roger reiterated wearily. 'You were wrong. Plastic Tolstoy was doing it, which is why we've had to flee America like criminals.'

'But that doesn't change the fact that Natura are always there! Somehow they get sent into areas where the disasters occur. If Mother Earth isn't pointing them in the right direction, then it must be Tolstoy. He's causing the disasters and he's the one who profits most from Natura protest. He's giving the orders.'

'But Tolstoy isn't the leader of Natura,' said Sean.

'No,' Judy replied, and he was suddenly very afraid. 'Jurgen Thor is.'

There was a pause. Sean wondered if Judy could truly be hinting at what he seemed to be hinting at.

'What about Brussels?' Sean said hurriedly. 'We know why Natura were there on that occasion, to cover the Mother Earth protest, not because they were expecting a disaster.'

'That's right,' said Judy. 'But the disaster occurred anyway. Tolstoy had sabotaged the tankers, which means . . .'

'That he knew the action was going to take place,' said Ruth.

'So Natura get told to go where Tolstoy's sinking boats, and Tolstoy gets told where Mother Earth are creating opportunities for high profile sabotage. It seems to me that there is a rather unhealthy level of co-operation here,' Roger observed.

'Who authorises Mother Earth actions?' said Judy.

'The Number One Equal Person, of course,' Ruth replied.

'And the Number One Equal Person is –?' asked Judy, but of course he already knew the answer.

'Jurgen Thor,' said Sean.

'They're partners,' Judy said quietly, as if trying to diminish the enormity of his suspicion. *'Tolstoy and Thor are partners.'* He leapt to his feet. 'Rosalie is in terrible danger. She's only been gone a couple of hours, it may not be too late. Is there anyone you can call who has access to a helicopter? One of Rosalie's colleagues, for instance? One we can trust.'

Ruth crossed to the dresser and, opening the bread bin, she took out a tiny two-way radio.

'Rosalie's old unit are back in the Partry Mountains. They have a new commander. Sean and I have known him for years. He's a good fighter, and loyal to Rosalie, although she never liked him. The poor fellow was terribly injured and it's made him rather moody.'

Judy feared the worst.

'This guy's name . . . it wouldn't by any chance be Saunders, would it?'

Rude awakening.

Rosalie must have fallen asleep because she woke up with a start to find Jurgen Thor standing beside her, gently running his fingers through her hair. He was still stark naked and it was quite clear that he was pleased to see her. Rosalie had slumped forward in her chair and had been resting her head on her arms on the table. Hence Jurgen's erection was the first thing she saw when she opened her eyes.

'Congratulations, Jurgen. If I had a medallion I'd hang one on it, now put it away. I have something quite incredible to talk to you about.'

'I don't want to talk, babe, OK?' Jurgen replied, his words still slightly slurred with sleep, booze and pills, 'I want to make love.'

'Jurgen, this idiocy has gone far enough,' Rosalie said firmly, 'I have to talk to you about Plastic Tolstoy.'

Jurgen Thor looked at Rosalie for a moment, and even in that moment his eyes became a little clearer. He took up a robe which had been dropped upon the kitchen floor and covered himself. He did not reply until he had made himself a cup of coffee and cleared his head a little.

'What about Plastic Tolstoy?' he said finally. 'I hope you're not thinking of bringing up that stuff about the funding again, OK? If you don't like what you hear then you shouldn't ask questions. We discussed it, right? It's a secret we can never tell, and the subject is closed.'

'No, it's not about the funding, Jurgen. Something much, much nastier than that. Believe me, Plastic Tolstoy's pragmatism goes a deal further than funding a few greenies. That man will do anything, and I mean quite literally anything, to sell a Claustrosphere.'

'And what do you mean by that?' Jurgen asked.

'I mean that Plastic Tolstoy has been wreaking his own private environmental holocaust, Jurgen, and I have proof.'

Jurgen stared at Rosalie. She was so young and pretty. Just as Scout had been. It seemed that now there would be two beautiful innocents to deny him rest and haunt his dreams.

'This sounds most fascinating, baby,' Jurgen said. 'We should not discuss it here, anyone might come in. They are fools, but even fools can tell tales. Come down to my study.'

'The dead menagerie?' said Rosalie, recalling all the animal heads.

'Yes, that's right. The dead menagerie.'

And, taking Rosalie gently by the arm, Jurgen Thor led her out of the kitchen and down the stairs into the bottom floor of the house, to his study, with its stuffed animals, antler chairs and its trapdoor.

Unlikely comrades.

Even above the sound of the helicopter blades beating at the air, Judy could hear the sound of grinding teeth emanating from inside the bag which Saunders was, of course, wearing over his head.

'I don't mind telling you,' said Saunders, finally giving his teeth a rest. 'When I walked in and found out that it was you that I was supposed to help, I nearly shot you there and then. In fact, it was only out of deference to Rosalie's gran that I didn't.'

Saunders, it must be remembered, was a scouser and there are certain codes on Merseyside, one of which is to try and avoid upsetting people's grannies.

'That was very nice of you,' Judy said, attempting to sound ingratiating. Even though Saunders appeared to have accepted Judy's story, he still made Judy nervous.

'It's a pretty incredible theory, Schwartz,' Saunders said. 'If it's the truth then everything's shit, you know that, don't you? The whole world's pointless and we might as well give up because it's all a fucking joke.'

'Yes, I suppose that's true,' Judy admitted.

'Well, I just hope you're right, that's all, because this is the unit helicopter and let me tell you I'm breaking a lot of rules just taking it like this.'

Judy found Saunders's attitude strange, but he did not say so. He found most things about Saunders strange and if he had started mentioning them all he would have been at it all night. Besides, Judy was too anxious to want to make conversation. It had taken two hours for Ruth to get hold of Saunders and another one and a half for Saunders to get to the cottage. What with the start Rosalie had on them in the first place, that put her about six hours ahead. Judy could only hope that somehow she had got delayed, or had put off confiding in Jurgen for some reason. If she had not, then she was probably already dead and the vital Ansafone tape, which was their only proof against Plastic Tolstoy, lost for ever. There was no copy, the recording was contained within a micro-chip inside the machine, not the easiest thing to reproduce. Judy had been hoping to make a copy of sorts at Ruth and Sean's by playing back the message and videoing the playback, but to his amazement Ruth and Sean had no video. Rosalie had said that she would make a copy of the tape at Jurgen Thor's place.

The message is murder.

'I think we should make a copy of this right now,' said Rosalie to Jurgen. 'Do you have a video camera?'

'What? Oh, yes . . . Of course I have.'

Jurgen was distracted. He was more than distracted, he

was stunned. Taped evidence of Plastic Tolstoy confessing to poisoning seas. Taped evidence of Tolstoy attempting to organise a film star's murder. This was dynamite indeed. Jurgen had expected nothing so spectacularly damning when Rosalie set up Max's little answering machine. Indeed, for a moment, he thought that the whole thing must be a joke.

'This is the most important bit of recording you will ever see in your life,' Rosalie said with deadly earnestness. 'It's the ultimate smoking gun.'

She pressed playback and immediately a very beautiful woman in a tiny, skintight mini-dress appeared on the screen.

'Max. Haven't seen you in a while. Call me,' the stunning beauty said, adding, 'I had the hammock repaired, by the way.'

Jurgen looked at Rosalie and grinned. She, of course, coloured bright red.

'Hang on a minute,' she said, 'this isn't it.'

A second and third girl appeared on the little screen, wearing similarly minimal clothing and leaving similarly seductive messages. Then Geraldine, Max's agent, popped up.

'Max? Are you back yet? You will not believe the *shit* I've been fielding for you while you've been away, but you don't need to hear about that. Leave it with me, OK?'

There were more girls, one even wearing a bikini, despite clearly being indoors. Jurgen grunted appreciatively, Rosalie chewed her lower lip. The bikini girl pouted that she had heard about Max's divorce from Krystal and guessed he must be lonely.

'How about dinner?' she breathed over her cleavage.

'I haven't had a really good nibble for ages.' She then began to move her video phone all around her body, offering close-ups of her artificially tanned flesh. Just as she was about to drop the phone down into the briefs of her swimming costume, Rosalie got up and hit fast-forward.

'It's obviously further down the tape than I'd realised,' Rosalie said crossly. Of course Max could hardly help who phoned him up, but those girls seemed awfully familiar, and what's more, he must at some point have given them his number. It is never any fun for a husband or wife to bump into evidence of their partner's past. Rosalie felt particularly hot under the collar, since her own past consisted of exactly two affairs (not counting Jurgen). If Max ever came across an old Ansafone tape of hers, he could play it at the next Sunday School fête, a fact which Rosalie found herself resenting.

'I was enjoying that,' Jurgen Thor complained as the tape whizzed on.

'Never mind that, Jurgen,' Rosalie assured him. 'This will really grab your interest.'

And of course it did. Although not in the manner that Rosalie had presumed.

Having watched the tape, Rosalie suggested that they video record it, as that was the only means they had at present of producing a copy. Jurgen pondered a moment and then agreed.

'Certainly we must video record it, baby,' he said. 'I have a camera here in my desk. Would you be so kind as to carry the machine over to that far wall, the light is better there and there are no distractions in the background. Just put it on the floor.'

405

Somehow Jurgen felt easier about it this time. Yes this girl was young and she was innocent, but not like Scout had been. Nor was she so naïve. This girl was a tough fighter, just like he was. She knew the stakes and had voluntarily chosen to bring the battle to him.

Jurgen Thor did not think that he would cry this time.

Rosalie picked up her husband's Ansafone and began to cross the floor with it. Walking the same condemned walk that Scout had walked before her.

Chapter Twenty-Seven

The End

The trapdoor opens.

Judy and Saunders did not have quite so long to wait up on the roof as Rosalie. Most of the party-goers in Jurgen's bedroom had roused themselves by the time the two men arrived, and a single knock had solicited a response. It was morning and the girl that opened the door for them had donned a sarong.

'Hi. You're just in time for breakfast,' she said. 'Hot croissant and drugs, want some?' The girl did not say so, but she felt that Jurgen had rather let the side down with these two. It was just presumed that anybody coming to one of these functions would be beautiful, and the two men on the roof were most definitely not. At least the nerd wasn't and the other one had a bag over his head which did not bode well at all. The beautiful girl in the sarong made a mental note not to get stuck anywhere near either of them if things began to get going again, which they just might, once the breakfast drugs had kicked in.

'Where's Jurgen Thor?' asked Judy, as he and Saunders pushed their way past the girl and into the house.

Standing at the top of the spiral staircase, the scene which greeted them was slightly less decadent than the one which Rosalie had encountered on the previous evening. However, slightly less decadent than that still meant pretty decadent, especially to the likes of Judy and Saunders. They were momentarily lost for words, finding themselves faced with a room full of half-naked people nibbling at drugs, drink, brekky and each other in an extremely spaced out manner. Trying not to stare, Judy cast his eyes around the room. Neither Rosalie nor Jurgen were anywhere to be seen.

'Uhm, excuse me everybody,' Judy mumbled, 'sorry to burst in on you like this, but does anybody know where Jurgen Thor is?'

'He was here a few minutes ago,' said the girl in the sarong.

'Yeah.' A voice came from the bed. It was the girl who had tried to touch up Rosalie in the night. 'He went off to find that uptight redhead chick. I don't think he'll get very far there.'

The suggestion that Rosalie had possibly been alive as late as a few minutes ago spurred Judy on and, followed by Saunders, he ran down the spiral staircase, past the bedroom and further into the house. They passed the ablutions floor where jolly squeals of glee were to be heard emanating through the steam of the spa baths and power showers. They passed the kitchen, where a couple of slightly more together souls were making coffee.

'That's Rosalie's coat!' Saunders shouted, spotting the combat jacket that was hanging over a chair.

A floor below them, in the study, Rosalie herself had crossed the floor and was now standing on the trapdoor, the answering machine in her arms.

'Where do you want me to put it it?' she inquired.

'I want you to take it with you, baby. Ciao, good

looking,' Jurgen replied and his hand moved towards the deadly lever.

Just then, the door of the study burst open and Judy stood in the doorway with Saunders behind him. Jurgen paused, his hand hovering over the switch which would consign Rosalie to the chasm below.

'Rosalie!' Judy said. 'Thank God, you're alive!'

'Of course I'm alive, you fool,' Rosalie replied. 'Why wouldn't I be? More to the point, what are you doing here?'

'That bastard there is Plastic Tolstoy's partner!'

Rosalie looked at Jurgen. His face showed it all. Judy was right. Then she saw his hand move. A warning bell rang inside her. Somehow with that hand Jurgen Thor was attacking her, she knew it. Her whole body knew it. Every muscle suddenly tensed as she instinctively readied herself for the attack which she knew was coming. The attack, whatever it might be, that Jurgen's hand was somehow initiating.

That moment of knowledge saved her. When the attack came, the tension in her body gave her the power with which to reach for safety. As the floor dropped away beneath her feet, Rosalie's arms shot out like bolts from a sprung lock. Indeed, her whole body seemed to twist in mid-air as she lunged for the edge of the bottomless tomb that Jurgen Thor had attempted to consign her to. The Ansafone, of course, leapt from her grasp and fell away into the darkness, but Rosalie found a grip and hung on, her fingertips all that remained visible from inside the room.

During her Mother Earth training days, Rosalie had been taught to rock climb, a sport in which the last joints on the fingers are the most crucial part of the body. The climber is instructed to exercise these joints constantly, and the preferred method for doing this is to perform chin-ups, whilst suspending oneself from the tops of door-frames. Rosalie had never lost the habit and seldom went through a door at home without pulling a couple of fingertip chin-ups on the frame. Her granny had often lamented the damage done to her door surrounds as they slowly cracked and pulled away from the wall, not having been built to withstand the hanging weight of an adult person, even a small one like Rosalie. Had Ruth been able to see her granddaughter now she would have counted those door-frames cheap and a million more like them. For Rosalie was hanging on, quite literally by her fingertips, whilst hundreds of feet below her, inside the terrible granite jaws of the chasm, poor Scout's rotting corpse lay awaiting company.

All this had, of course, happened in one stunning moment. Nearly as stunning for Judy and Saunders as it had been for Rosalie, since they had not expected to see their comrade suddenly drop through the floor. Jurgen Thor was able to capitalise upon this second or two of shock to produce a gun from his desk, fit a silencer to its muzzle, out of deference to his guests upstairs, and level it at the two men.

Keeping the gun trained firmly upon Judy and Saunders, Jurgen walked around his desk and towards the hole in the floor where the eight white points of Rosalie's fingertips were flattened on the edge. It was clear what his intention was. He was going to stamp on Rosalie's fingers.

'Please remain exactly where you are, OK, guys, yes?' Jurgen said. 'Once I have said farewell to Rosalie, I should like to know how you came upon the wild idea that I hang out with Plastic Tolstoy, OK?'

It was Saunders who acted. He had a plan, not a very good one as it turned out, at least not for him, but it saved Rosalie's life anyway. Also it meant that Saunders got to die the way he had always wanted, in the defence of the planet, so perhaps it wasn't such a bad plan.

Saunders's plan was to remove his bag. The idea being that the shock effect of his gruesome visage upon Jurgen Thor would be enough to make Jurgen throw up his arms in horror, thus giving Saunders the crucial split second in which to rush him and, if possible, hurl him down into the chasm.

'Aaargh!' shouted Saunders and tore off his bag, revealing, as he had done so many times at parties, his absence of face. Sadly for Saunders, Jurgen was a big boy and had seen many horrid sights in his time. He remained unmoved and, as Saunders leapt towards him, Jurgen fired, killing poor Saunders with a single shot to the head, or what there was of the head anyway. Saunders hit the ground with a thud.

Judy now had to face Jurgen Thor alone, but not for long. Hanging in mid-air as she was, Rosalie heard the commotion of Saunders's lunge and subsequent death. She did not know what these noises signified but since her strength was already ebbing, she judged it a good time to attempt a chin-up and try to scramble to safety. She hauled her head above the edge and managed to slide one elbow over on to the floor before the sound of her movements made Jurgen turn. Seeing Rosalie clawing her way back into the land of the living, he launched a huge kick at her, catching her full in the face. Had he been wearing shoes, that would have been the end of the matter, but Jurgen was of course barefoot, and despite the pain, Rosalie was able not only to hang on, but also to grab hold of his foot.

In order to avoid being toppled forward into the trap, Jurgen was forced to throw himself backwards to the floor, dropping the gun as he did so. He was about to try and kick Rosalie away with his free leg, when Judy made a lunge for the gun. Reaching backwards, Jurgen was able to grab Judy by the trousers and, despite being flat on his back with a desperate woman using one of his legs as a climbing rope, he easily pulled Judy over. The little agent crashed down on top of Jurgen and bravely started trying to bang Jurgen's head on the floor. It was a futile gesture, considering Jurgen's physical superiority, but Judy did at least distract the prostrate giant for a moment while Rosalie, still pulling on Jurgen's leg, was able to drag her chest up over the edge of the precipice. That was all the breathing space she had, for Jurgen, quickly tiring of having Judy on top of him, hurled a mighty hammer-like fist at the side of Judy's chest, thus punching him away and also breaking most of his ribs and knocking all the wind out of his small body.

As Judy lay in agony, retching beside him, Jurgen turned his attention back to Rosalie, raising his free leg in order to kick her back down into the chasm once and for all. But the respite caused by Judy's tiny attack had been enough. Rosalie had her other elbow up over the edge, thus momentarily freeing the arm with which she had been hanging on to Jurgen's leg. As Jurgen raised his other leg to kick her down, Rosalie's opportunity lay stretched out before her. Jurgen was, of course, wearing only a gown, and by raising one leg to kick Rosalie, he revealed his meat and two veg to her in all their glory.

Rosalie threw her free arm forward and grabbed Jurgen's mighty dick.

'Don't kick me off, Jurgen!' she shouted. 'I swear I'll never let go of it, no matter how hard you kick. If I go, it goes.'

Jurgen looked down at Rosalie in amazement. This was not a development that he had expected. In fact, he was at a loss to work out how in such a short space of time he had managed to move from being in complete control, to lying on the edge of the precipice from which his enemy was climbing, using his prick as a rope.

At that moment, the door of the study opened and one of Jurgen's guests poked their head in.

'There's been a monsoon warning, Jurgen. People are thinking about heading off before –' The visitor stopped mid-sentence and took in the scene: Judy retching, Jurgen prostrate on his back, his gown thrown open whilst a girl hung on to his dick halfway out through the floor. 'Well, excuse *me*,' she said. 'Wow, you people are *wild*! Ciao, Jurgen baby, thanks for a great party.'

The woman left, shutting the door behind her. Rosalie got a leg up over the edge and, leaving hold of Jurgen's penis, lunged up and over him, trying to make it to the gun. Jurgen was too quick for her, though, and grabbing Rosalie in his mighty arms he rolled over on top of her, his hands upon her throat.

'Now I will finish the job,' he shouted. 'It seems that I must kill you before I throw you into the precipice, depriving you of the final exhilaration of terminal free-fall. So be it, Rosalie. Bye bye, baby, bye bye!'

He began to throttle her with his huge hands. So big indeed were they, and so small was Rosalie's neck, that Jurgen could probably have choked her with only one of them. Within seconds Rosalie began to lose the plot, his grip was crushing the life out of her before she even had a chance to suffocate. Her legs flailed about, her arms flailed about, she was helpless. Judy, who could see what was happening, tried to come to her aid but he could move only very slowly in case his broken ribs punctured his lungs. He was helpless, knowing that Rosalie would be dead long before he reached the gun.

Her face was turning blue, her limbs were now twitching more than flailing. She was definitely dying. One of her hands fell upon the pocket of Jurgen's gown. She could feel herself gripping something, the only item in the pocket. She recognised it, something stirred the memory in her fast-darkening brain . . . That was it! She knew what she was holding. What else would she find in the pocket of a dressing-gown at an orgy but a condom spray?

At this point, Rosalie probably only had one voluntary act left in her, but it was a beauty. With one movement she swung her arm upwards, the spray in her hand, and let Jurgen have it full in the face. Within seconds his head was completely laminated. Now it was Jurgen Thor who was suffocating. His grip relaxed almost instantly as he realised the danger he was in. There was no solvent in the pockets of the gown, he had to get to the bathroom. He staggered to his feet, leaving Rosalie on the floor gasping life back into her desperate body. Blinded, for he had on reflex shut his eyes as the liquid rubber hit him, Jurgen bumbled his way across the room and felt his way to the study door, bursting through it as Rosalie was beginning to drag herself to her feet behind him.

Staggering up the stairs, naked but for the open gown, Jurgen presented a shocking sight to those guests who had not yet ascended to the heli-pad, his head encased in rubber, the black hole of his mouth tugging at the merciless laminate stretched across it. A great heaving and wheezing was emanating from his mighty chest. Behind him came a girl, a wild, dangerous-looking girl. She too was staggering, her chest was also heaving with the pain of breathing. She was still blue in the face, and the livid marks of strangulation were yet bright red upon her neck. In her hand was a gun. The remaining guests mumbled their apologies and retreated upwards. This was rough stuff indeed. Much too rough for them. What they liked was to take designer drugs and make love to people who were as beautiful as they were. Indeed, the simple fact of being beautiful was the biggest buzz, and this was not beautiful, this was positively horrid. Pain, strangulation, guns and rubber were things that they wanted no part of. If Jurgen was pushing the party that way, then they were definitely leaving.

Jurgen kicked open the bathroom door as the last of his guests jumped out of the spa bath and slipped past him. He crashed up against a basin and, hurling open the cupboard above it, groped blindly amongst various creams and lotions, spraying his face with various scents and aftershaves before, finally, he found what he was looking for . . . the solvent. Turning it on himself he sprayed and sprayed, gasping and retching with relief as the tight-as-a-drum skin that had enveloped his mouth dissolved and he was at last able to suck in great gusts of air. Collapsing to his knees, he coughed and burped as little bits of melting rubber found their way into his lungs. He scarcely noticed, though, for he was breathing again . . . that was all that mattered. It did not even matter very much that Rosalie was standing at the bathroom door, leaning against the wall and pointing the gun at him. For the moment, Jurgen was simply happy to be alive.

Rosalie stared at him for a long time. That once mighty man, a man who had been an inspiration to a generation, and was now revealed for what he really was and had been all along, a contemptible, double-crossing wretch. Rosalie stared and stared, trying to recognise in this low figure the hero of old, but she could not. Instead she asked a question, a single word, in fact.

'Why?'

Death of a salesman.

'Why?' Jurgen spoke not to Rosalie, but to the basin which he still held on to for support. 'Because I may be many things, Rosalie, you dig? But I am not a wally, OK? The world is dying and nobody can stop it.'

'That's not true,' said Rosalie.

'It is bloody true!' Jurgen replied hoarsely. 'It's always been dying, ever since man began to take from it more than he needed. *This planet is a finite quantity, logic dictates that it cannot be consumed indefinitely.* I tell you, Rosalie, Earth as we know it is finished, because man rules it and man is incapable of acting responsibly! Of thinking in anything other than the short-term.'

'That's just a pathetic generalisation to justify your –'

'Is it, Rosalie? Is it? Let me ask you this. What politician, facing an election next year, would be prepared to make laws, the benefit of which would not be felt until the following year! I will tell you. None. There is no *profit* to be had today in protecting tomorrow.'

Jurgen Thor had said his piece. He sat down on the

floor, brushing aside the various toiletries that had fallen from the bathroom cabinet. He took another great breath and leant back against the plinth of the marble wash-basin. He was still coughing from the rubber in his throat, and there were great strands of semi-dissolved latex hanging from his eyelashes, hair and nose. He looked like one of the living dead . . . which in many ways was what he was.

'So you've always known what Plastic Tolstoy has been doing?' Rosalie asked.

'Not always, but nearly always. I joined the board of Claustrosphere as Tolstoy's number two about a year after I founded Natura.'

'But that's nearly thirty years ago! You've been on the board of Claustrosphere for thirty years?' Rosalie gasped.

'Yes, my attitude changed very quickly,' Jurgen replied. 'Like any good greenie, I could see the way the wind was blowing. The industrialised world's blind obsession with "growth" meant death, that much was obvious. The human race was going to self-destruct and take the planet with it. That would happen whatever anybody did, despite me, despite Tolstoy, despite Claustrosphere. I knew that then and I know it now. At least Claustrosphere offers people some kind of future.'

'Have you got one?' Rosalie inquired.

'Of course. I am not a fool. My Claustrosphere covers the whole of a small Pacific atoll. It is very beautiful.'

'How come they tried to kill you with that bomb?'

It was Judy who asked this question. He had collected himself sufficiently to slowly follow Rosalie up to the bathroom and had heard most of what Jurgen Thor had said.

'Believe me, man,' Jurgen said. 'If they'd wanted to kill me they would have succeeded. It was just a marketing strategy. Claustrosphere sales have been down for a while, Plastic was planning a relaunch and I volunteered to be a part of it.'

'That was good of you,' said Rosalie bitterly.

'Get real, baby, I'm no philanthropist. I have nearly as many shares as Tolstoy does, it's my profits too. I must admit to you, though, I was pretty annoyed that my dick got blown off. The blast was only supposed to singe my hair. Our sabotage people said there must have been other bombs planted in the building which ours set off. That's European democracy for you, for every delegate, an assassin.'

They made a strange triumvirate. Judy was on his hands and knees, the only position he could sustain without fainting. Jurgen sat against the basin amongst the broken bottles. Only Rosalie was on her feet and she was mightily bruised about the head and neck. It was a sorry scene, but a fitting one in which to learn how careful and meticulous was the marketing of the end of the world.

'You seem kind of happy to talk about all this. You've kept your secret carefully up until now,' Judy gasped between breaths.

'I once promised myself that if I could, I would one day tell pretty little Rosalie here the whole truth. The whole truth about her life and her world. Crueller than killing you, eh, baby? Don't you think? Your tape of Tolstoy's confession has long since vanished into the depths of my mountain. The only evidence you possess now is your word, and let me tell you, OK? Dead people speak neither truth nor lies.'

'Dead people?' Rosalie inquired.

'Yes, I'm afraid so, baby. I know Plastic Tolstoy, you see, and if you attempt to tell your story, you will be dead almost before you have uttered the first sentence.'

Jurgen spoke no further. He could not, for he himself was dead. Rosalie shot him through the head. She did not plan to do it, she just did it, without even saying goodbye. The world's second best Claustrosphere salesman was no more.

The end of the world.

Shortly after which, the Rat Run started.

It began quite slowly. One morning, about a week after the incidents described above, all the news bulletins were suddenly full of stories describing the Claustrospheres of the rich and famous. Also detailed reports about the preparations which those people were making for their own personal Rat Runs.

'These days, I have a chopper on permanent standby wherever I go, man. Hey, you're looking at one mother who ain't gonna get left out with the garbage.'

There was nothing new in stories like this, except that the reports seemed to indicate a slightly disturbing sense of urgency about the preparations being made. Almost as if the elite were in possession of information which was denied to the general public.

On the second day, these dark hints had become the top story, gaining weight with each repetition. Was there something which the people did not know? Had the pestilence and hunger so long predicted, in fact arrived, and were those in authority refusing to admit it for fear of mass panic? By late that afternoon there were widespread reports that a large, unspecified number of important people had *already* retreated into their Claustrospheres. The bulletins reported that the US President and the Chairperson of the European Federation could not be contacted for comment, the scarcely veiled suggestion being that their staff did not actually know where they were. Both the White House and the Palace of Peace and Profit quickly issued detailed statements about the whereabouts of the two key figures, but these were only sparsely reported. The suspicion had been planted and it was widely rumoured that the leaders were jumping ship. These rumours were of course immediately picked up and re-reported, gaining credibility as they did so.

'Is government on auto pilot? Who's driving the bus? I'm Dan Bland coming to you live, as it happens.'

The story had become self-perpetuating. Those channels that had not run with the original rumours soon found themselves reporting the fact that the rumours had been reported.

By now fear had gripped the world community. Those people who found themselves away from home began to try to get back. Flights were booked out, roads were clogged. Footage of packed airports and colossal traffic jams played heavily on the news media, causing more people to rush to the airports and jump into their cars. Every official denial that there was a problem served only to heighten the suspicion that there really was one. If not, why were they denying it? Smoke was being wafted about and everybody was looking for the fire.

The rumours were turning to fact.

The President of the USA announced that he would make an emergency statement on television. This he did, appearing dressed in a chunky cardigan, standing in front of a fire, and assuring America and the world that there was no need for panic. The exercise backfired badly. The statement was broadcast but so, almost simultaneously, was the news that the majority of people considered it a hoax. They felt that the President looked younger, his hair shorter, his teeth whiter than had been the case of late. The idea that the broadcast had been recorded a year or more earlier quickly gained ground.

Panic now set in in earnest. People spoke of nothing else. Everybody knew someone who knew someone who had already retreated to their Claustrosphere. Ships were returning to port. Airlines and other transport services faltered as staff took holiday in order to avoid travelling too far away from their place in a shelter.

The question was no longer if, but when, and for how long?

'If we must go,' people asked each other in anguish, 'how long must we set our timers for? When will we be released?'

The answer was forty years. Nobody knew quite how it came about, but that figure was suddenly on everybody's lips. It seemed that some scientist or other on the news had been pressed to take a guess, and scarcely before the words had left his lips, it had become the truth.

'We're hearing forty years,' reporters endlessly asked experts. 'How accurate do you think that is?'

'That certainly seems to be the figure we're hearing.'

'Four decades!' The cry went round the world and with every repetition the accuracy of the prediction became more inalienable.

Then it happened. The panic dam burst. Ten billion television sets seemed to broadcast the bad news simultaneously. The Rat Run had started. People had decided that the Earth was giving up. It was being reported that the planet could not and would not support the human race any longer. 'Don't drink the water!' the TVs said. 'Don't breathe the air! Get in your Claustrospheres and set your timers for forty years! Everybody else is.'

And everybody was. They all ran at once. Newsreaders turned around, having read their last bulletin, to discover that they were sitting alone in empty studios. Their colleagues had already gone.

As people rushed for their shelters, it was almost as if they were embracing the Rat Run, as if it was in some way a relief to be done with the Earth at last. To be done with the waiting and the uncertainty. To be done with the guilt, and that constant, nagging feeling that one really ought to be *doing* something, and never really knowing what. Now there was nothing to be done. It was over and nobody had to worry about it any more.

There were of course doubters, those who wondered for a moment if what they were hearing could be true, but they did not wonder for long. The panic was its own proof. People needed no further evidence that Eco-Armageddon was truly upon them than to see their neighbours disappearing into their Claustrospheres. There was no question of holding back, once others had begun to run, particularly for the majority of people who were destined to spend their remaining years in communal shelters. The prospect of being left outside once the BioLocks had been closed and the timers set was too horrible to contemplate.

It was all over in a day. The human race simply disappeared. Not quite all of it, of course. There were those in the poverty nations who had no access to Claustrospheres. They remained outside, scratching away at the dust upon which they lived. Perhaps not even noticing that anything had happened, except that from that moment on, their lives began slowly to improve. To all intents and purposes, however, people just vanished, the only evidence that they still existed at all being the millions and millions of geodesic domes which dotted what had up until recently been the industrialised world. The human race was hiding from its own nightmare.

This Other Eden.

Plastic Tolstoy had saved the Earth, and ironies do not come any more ironic than that. Judy pieced together the sequence of events as he sat outside Ruth and Sean's cottage, peeling the potatoes with which Roger had promised to make a shepherd's pie.

It had happened this way.

Judy and Rosalie had returned from Jurgen Thor's mausoleum to discover Max sufficiently recovered to inform them that he did not, for God's sake, possess only *one* Ansafone. There were, in fact, machines in every room of his mansion and on every one would be a copy of Plastic Tolstoy's confession.

'I'm a big star, you know?' he had whispered from his sick bed. 'I get a lot of important messages.'

Rosalie decided to wait until Max had recovered a little before telling him that she had seen the type of messages that he received, and that he'd better never receive any more. Meanwhile, Sean paid his first and only trip to Hollywood, collecting all of the incriminating tapes from Max's Beverly Hills home.

Judy sent one tape to the FBI, one to the LA Police

Department, one to the US President and one to Plastic Tolstoy.

That was the day that the Rat Run started. Tolstoy, faced with the certainty of ending his life in a cell, had chosen instead to serve out his sentence inside his fabulous Claustrosphere. It was not difficult to arrange. Panic is an easy thing to provoke, particularly if you own a large percentage of the world's media. In order to escape the justice of the law, Plastic Tolstoy used his power to sentence the rest of the world to serve time with him.

The extraordinary side-effect of this entirely selfish act was that Plastic Tolstoy ended his wicked life by saving the world. For the Earth, cured temporarily of people, soon began to recover. Free from the exploitative, parasitic human virus that had infected it for so long, the planet was able to cleanse itself. With no further poisons being produced and no further natural resources being destroyed, the process of renewal actually began with the Rat Run and when, forty years later, the human race reappeared, it was to a fresh start and a whole new view of the planet. For as far as this new generation were concerned, the Rat Run had been for real. A genuine response to a genuine global emergency, which of course in many ways it had been. Only a strange little group of aged, weather-beaten people in the west of Ireland knew the truth and they would never tell. It was better that the people who emerged from the Claustrospheres believed that the lonely exile of the human race had been a necessary punishment for its sins, that they had survived the flood and it was time to start afresh, resolving never again to practise the selfish planetary vandalism that had led their forefathers and mothers to the day of the Rat Run.

Of course, some Claustrospheres were destined never to open again, those into which only the old or the lonely had gone. One such shelter stood silent in California and inside it, under a false sky at the foot of a mountain on the edge of a rain forest, lay a slowly decomposing body. Lasting proof of the fact that whilst the planet may survive, all people, no matter how powerful, must surely die.

Popcorn

Chapter One

On the morning after the night it happened, Bruce Delamitri was sitting in a police interview room.

'Name?' said the interrogating officer.

It wasn't really a question. The officer knew Bruce's name, of course, but there was a procedure and he was required to follow it.

On the morning before, Bruce had been sitting in a television studio. Opposite him, across the sweeping curve of the presentation console, were two Ken-and-Barbie-style presenters of indeterminate age.

'His name' (pause) 'is Bruce Delamitri,' said Ken, employing the sincere, plonking tone he reserved for really big guests.

'Occupation?' said the policeman on the morning after, as if he didn't know.

'He is probably the most celebrated artist working in the

429

motion-picture industry today. A great writer, a great director. Hollywood's golden boy.'

'I heard he makes a great pasta sauce too,' interjected Barbie, by way of adding a little human interest.

It was the morning before, and the last day on which Bruce would hear himself described in such terms.

'Marital status?' the cop enquired.

'But career excellence takes its toll, and Hollywood was recently saddened by the news that Bruce's marriage to actress, model and rock singer Farrah Delamitri was in big trouble. We'll be talking about that also.'

The red light on top of the camera facing Bruce lit up. He adopted a suitably sardonic 'shit happens' expression. The next twenty-four hours would prove him right about that.

Bruce tried to look the policeman in the eye. Marital status? What a question. The whole world knew his marital status.

'My wife is dead.'

'Tell me about last night.'

'Tonight is Oscars night,' Ken beamed. 'The big one. Numero Uno. Nights don't get any bigger than this. The night of nights. The nightiest night of them all. The night which, according to all the forecasts, promises to be the greatest night of Bruce Delamitri's life.'

'Last night?' said Bruce, who had given up trying to make contact with the cop and now spoke almost to himself.

'Last night was more terrible than I could have imagined possible.'

'You're watching *Coffee Time USA*. We'll be back after these messages,' said the male presenter, whose name was not Ken but Oliver Martin. The studio lights dimmed and the *Coffee Time* logo came up while Oliver and his female colleague, Dale, stacked their papers in an important manner. There was of course nothing on their papers, but maintaining the fiction that TV presenters are proper journalists, as opposed to people who read whatever comes up on the autocue, is one of the principal duties of current-affairs broadcasting.

Bruce watched on the monitor in front of him as Oliver and Dale disappeared and were replaced on the screen by four bikini-clad babes clutching soda bottles and tumbling ecstatically out of an old VW Beetle.

'A girl, a beach, it's happening, it's real.
It's a boost, it's a buzz, it's the way you should feel!'

The studio controller killed the volume, and the bikini babes were left sucking on their bottles in muted delight.

'One and a half minutes on the break,' said the floor manager.

This was the signal for the make-up girls to rush in and pat gently away at all available faces. Oliver turned to Bruce, addressing him through a flurry of powder and pads.

'I think what we need to concentrate on here is the fact that our industry is not a dream factory any more. We deal in gritty realism. We show it like it is.'

The make-up lady applied another layer of slap to Oliver's already heavily caked features. The gritty reality was that anyone who had acquired such a deep and lustrous tan would long since have died of skin cancer. But Oliver was of the old school of TV presenting: he believed that sporting a thermo-nuclear tan was a mark of respect to the viewer, like wearing a nice shirt and tie. You had to show you'd made the effort.

'One minute to the break,' said the floor manager.

Across the vast pastel-coloured desk, Dale's voice could be heard from the midst of a cloud of hair-spray. 'I mean, surely the big issue, Bruce, has got to be this whole copycat killing thing, hasn't it? I mean, that's what America is concerned about. As an American woman, it sure is what I'm concerned about. Are you concerned about that, Bruce? As an American man?'

'America's population is not as young as it was, and soon the number-one issue concerning the majority of Americans will be adult incontinence.'

This was not Bruce. It was the TV. The studio controller had pumped the volume back up preparatory to going back on air. It was after nine, and the network advertisers were beginning to switch their focus from workers and schoolkids to a 'coffee time' audience, which meant young mums and old lonelys. Soda-sucking babes were giving way to nipple pads, denture fixative and nappies both infant and adult.

'No, I am not concerned about copy-cat killings,' said Bruce, speaking with difficulty because a young woman was painting some kind of menthol-flavoured grease on to his lips. 'I don't believe that people get up from the movie theatre or the TV and do what they just saw. Otherwise the people who watch this show would all have their hair set in concrete and their brains sucked out along with their cellulite.'

It was scarcely a comment calculated to endear him to his media colleagues, but that was Bruce. Tough, sarcastic and a bit of a stirrer. If you wore a leather jacket and shades on TV at nine in the morning, you were almost duty-bound to be abrasive. In fact, Bruce had guessed that Dale would not hear his answer anyway. He could see she was the type of interviewer who used her guests' answers as quiet time in which to consider her next question.

'Good, good, you should make that point on air,' said Dale absently, checking her eye-liner.

'Fifteen seconds on the break,' said the floor manager. Four, three, two, one . . .

Oliver's face lit up. 'We're talking to Bruce Delamitri, the hot tip for tonight's "Best Director" Oscar. But amidst all the glory and the adulation there lurks very real controversy.'

Dale picked up the ball. 'Bruce Delamitri's movies are hard, tough, witty, sassy street-wise thrillers, where the life is low and the body count is high. Remind you of something?'

'You tell me, Dale,' said Ollie, deploying his serious and thoughtful face.

'How about America's streets?' said Dale, looking equally portentous. 'That's right, the streets of America, hard, tough and dangerous, where the kids grow up fast and dying is a way of life.'

'You're saying that the movies of Bruce Delamitri reflect the streets of America?'

'Some say reflect, some say influence. America, it's your call. We'll be back after these messages.'

The studio lights dimmed again. Oliver and Dale went dark and shuffled their papers.

'Do you have sensitive teeth? Does ice-cream make you go *ow!* when you should be going *mmmmm*?'

Chapter Two

O n the morning after it all happened, a young
woman, hardly more than a girl, stared across
a bare formica-topped table at an interrogating police
officer. She was being interviewed in the next-door room
to the one in which Bruce was being questioned. Unlike
Bruce, however, the young woman was considered
highly dangerous and was therefore in chains, her thin
wrists manacled to her almost equally thin ankles. In
fact, so petite was she that it looked as if she could have
slipped off the steel bracelets if she had wished and just
floated away on the next breeze. She was indifferent to
whether they chained her or not. She had nowhere to go
anyway.

'Name?' said the policewoman.

On the previous morning, this same skinny creature had
been asked the same question in the diner of a truck-stop
motel just off the Pacific Highway, about a hundred miles
north of Los Angeles.

'I been called a lotta things,' she had replied.

The short-order chef with whom she was conversing gave her a knowing wink. 'I'll bet one of them things wuz beautiful.'

The chef was right. She was beautiful, with her big eyes and thin face. If ever Disney decided to do a stage version of *Bambi* they would be looking for a girl like her.

The young woman accepted the chef's compliment with a giggle. 'Are you flirting with me?' she asked, twisting her purse in her hands like a nervous girl.

'Ain't nuthin wrong with talking to a pretty thing, is there?' said the chef.

'I guess not. 'Cepting you're lucky my boyfriend cain't hear ya. On accounta he's real mean when it comes to flirty guys. Specially Californian guys, who he reckons is just a bunch of no-good faggots.' The young woman picked up her change, which was lying on the counter.

'His name' (pause) 'is Bruce Delamitri.'

It was Oliver Martin's voice. A TV hung from a bracket in the corner of the room, and the waitress had turned up the volume. She liked *Coffee Time USA*.

'He is probably the most celebrated artist working in the motion-picture industry today. A great writer, a great director. Hollywood's golden boy.'

'I heard he makes a great pasta sauce too.'

Oliver and Dale were working their morning magic. Their guest, Bruce Delamitri, smiled sardonically out of the TV set. The girl at the counter turned to look. For a moment she and Bruce stared into each other's eyes. Much later, the girl would wonder whether she had felt something at this point.

The chef was not interested in *Coffee Time USA*. 'You say your fuckin' boyfriend says I'm a faggot?'

'He don't mean nuthin by it,' the scrawny girl said apologetically as she gathered up her Cokes and burgers and fries and headed for the door. 'It's just he's so tough and hard 'n' all that I guess pretty much everybody looks like a faggot to him.'

'You come back soon, little girl. I'll show you who's a faggot,' said the chef. 'Bring your boyfriend.'

'He'd kill ya,' the girl remarked casually over her shoulder as the screen door slammed behind her.

'Tonight is Oscars night,' said the television set.

'So tell us about last night,' said the policewoman on the following morning.

'Well, I guess he kinda got the idea when we was having breakfast and Bruce Delamitri was on *Coffee Time* with Oliver and Dale. We wuz in a motel, see. I like motels. They're so clean and nice, and they give you soap and stuff. If I got the chance, that's where I'd live all the time, motels.'

The girl walked across the parking lot from the diner to where the line of chalets stood. There had been a summer rain storm and she was barefoot. She sought out the puddles. Warm water on warm tarmac was a lovely sensation. She had very sensitive feet. Sometimes, if they were touched just right, it could make her entire body shiver. She was always trying to get her big tough boyfriend to give her feet a massage. She might as well have asked him to crochet a toilet-roll cover.

'I don't believe in no New Age, faggot, hippy bullshit,' he would say, 'which in my opinion is eating away at the soul of this great nation and turning us all into old fuckin' women. Now get me a beer.'

437

There were certain subjects on which he was entirely intractable, but that didn't mean that he couldn't be tender and gentle when he wanted to be, and when he was, oh how she loved him.

She entered their little cabin with the food. He was lying on the bed where she had left him, a gun resting on his chest and another at his waist.

'Here's the food, honey. Seeing as how it's breakfast, I got you a bacon burger. I told him to be sure to grill that bacon good. I know you don't like eating no raw pig.'

'Quiet now, honey. I'm watching TV here.'

On the television Bruce Delamitri was working on his indulgent smile. 'Copycat killing? Pur-lease!' he said. 'I mean, *come on*! The whole thing's a media beat-up, the story *du jour*. Four networks in search of a controversy.'

Bruce could be his own worst enemy at times. You didn't sneer at the presenters of *Coffee Time*. Not if you wanted to win the hearts and minds of Middle America, which was the purpose of Bruce's appearance. Many of *Coffee Time*'s viewers saw Oliver and Dale as their closest and most loyal friends, and did not take kindly to clever-clever, sneery film-school grads acting like these friends were dumb.

Oliver sensed the atmosphere of the interview souring. He knew that 'atmospheres' of any kind were not good morning TV, and he always desperately sought common ground with his guests.

'C'mon, Bruce, cut us some slack here,' he appealed. 'This is a very serious situation. There are two genuine psychos out there, shooting up malls and killing just about everybody they meet, right? Now, in your Oscar-nominated movie *Ordinary Americans* there's a very similar young couple who do exactly the same stuff. These two genuine lunatics have blazed a trail across three states massacring innocent strangers.'

'And every time these crimes are reported in the media,' Bruce interrupted, 'the story gets illustrated with a still from my movie. Now who's making the association? The psychos themselves? Or is it the news editors of America, desperate to get an original angle on yet another boring news bulletin about murder and mayhem?

'Copycat murders, for God's sake! Human beings aren't Pavlov's dogs. You can't just ring a bell and make them salivate. They don't simply do what they see. If it were that easy to manipulate people, no product would ever fail and no government would ever fall.'

In the motel chalet the scrawny girl was getting bored with watching Bruce on the TV.

'Baby?' she said.

'Quiet, honey. I'm thinking 'bout something.'

There was a knock at the door.

In an instant the man was off the bed and across the room. He clamped himself against the wall beside the door, naked save for his tattoos and the guns he held in either hand. He put one finger to his lips, instructing the girl to say nothing.

They waited. Inside the TV Bruce continued to pontificate: 'Our industry's in danger. It's under attack. We're the scapegoats, the whipping-boys. Every time some kid lets loose with a gun, who do they blame? They blame Hollywood. They blame me. They don't like my movies – they say they're wicked. Well, they're entitled to their opinion. What they're *not* entitled to do is foist their craven and reactionary opinions on to everybody else. Censorship is censorship and it sucks!'

g:829e829e=829e Ben Elton

'Provocative? Thought-provoking?' From inside the TV Oliver addressed the room where the two fugitives waited. 'You betcha sweet grandma it is. You're watching *Coffee Time USA*. We'll be back after these messages.'

'Now you can eat what you want *and* stay trim.'

There was another knock at the door of the motel room. Still the young man and woman did not answer.

Then they heard the rattle of keys. The man nodded to the girl. She was still lying on the bed, although she too now held a gun, which she had produced from under her pillow.

'Who is it?' she called out.

'Please, you want I make up your room now?' a small Latin American voice asked.

'No, that's OK. It's fine,' said the girl.

'OK,' said the maid. 'I just give you fresh towels.'

'We don't want no towels.'

'OK.' There was a pause. 'You want soap?'

'No.'

'OK.' Again a pause. 'How about some sachet coffee and milks? Or maybe you got plenty.'

'Yeah, we got plenty. We don't want nuthin.'

'OK, that's fine. Thank you.'

The man, whose every muscle had been taut and every vein pumped full, relaxed a little.

But then the small voice came again. 'So I just check mini-bar, please.'

Suddenly the door of the chalet burst open and the maid found herself confronted by a furious and stark-naked man. She would scarcely have been more taken aback if she had known that behind the cover of the door-frame he was holding two automatic weapons.

'No fuckin' disturbo, comprende? We fuckin' honey-moono. We make amoro like Speedy fuckin' Gonzalez, OK?'

He slammed the door and returned to the bed. His girlfriend was not pleased. 'There was no call to –'

'I am trying to watch TV here!'

She knew she must not cross him further, and slumped into a sulk instead.

Bruce was still holding forth on the television. 'You can't ban a movie because you don't like it. Today it's sex and violence that get banned, tomorrow who knows? Homosexuality? Blacks? Jews?'

Oliver and Dale shifted uneasily in their seats. Words like 'blacks' and 'Jews' were not really *Coffee Time* words.

'I've heard a lot said these past weeks about the Mall Murderers,' Bruce continued, 'so let's talk about them. I made a movie about two sick maniacs, and lo and behold we got two real sick maniacs out there. Hey, what d'you know? Put two and two together and it's *my fault*! I am responsible. Oh *yeah*! Weren't there any maniacs before I made my movie? Weren't there any sickos and psychos around before movies were even *invented*? Did Bluebeard and Jack the Ripper get in a time machine and come forward in time to see my picture? Did they think, "Hey, great idea! When I get back to my own era I'll start murdering people"?'

'But you can't deny –' Dale began in a brave attempt to stop the flow. It was useless: this was a subject on which Bruce felt strongly.

'We are scapegoats! This nation is facing a law-and-order crisis of cataclysmic proportions and someone must be blamed. The politicians don't want to take the heat, so who gets it? Us, the entertainers, the artists. Well, I've got news for you. Artists don't create society, they reflect it. And if you don't like that, don't change us, change society.'

Oliver threw to another ad break, and in the motel room the naked man got himself another beer.

'Well, you gotta accept,' he said, knocking the top off a Budweiser with the butt of his Smith & Wesson, 'the guy has a point.'

'I think he sounds like a jerk,' his girlfriend replied grumpily.

'Hey, everybody's a jerk, baby, one way or another. Cain't hold that against a man. One thing's for damn sure. Bruce Delamitri makes the best fuckin' movies in the world, and if they don't give him that Oscar I for one will be extremely pissed.'

There was another knock at the door.

'Please,' the maid said, 'I must just check the mini-bar. Sorry.'

The man got up off the bed. 'I'll handle this, honey.'

'Tell me about him,' the policewoman said.

'I just used to sit there looking at him,' the young girl said, 'just thinking he is the coolest, most beautiful guy that ever was. Better than everything. You could take Elvis and Clint Eastwood and James Dean . . . and I don't know . . . all those other cool guys, and mix 'em up, and you wouldn't get no one half as cool as him.'

In the other interview room, Bruce was responding to a similar enquiry. 'You have to understand that he was a psychotic monster,' he told his interrogator. 'Do you hear me? A monster, the devil . . . a monster.'

Chapter Three

'I stand here on legs of fire.'

It was after eleven on the morning after the Oscars, and the police had left Bruce alone for almost two hours. They had given him some breakfast, which he had surprised himself by eating, and since then he had been sitting drinking cold coffee (institutional blend) and watching himself on the various morning news shows. He did not watch *Coffee Time*: that would have been too much to bear. He could just imagine how happy Oliver and Dale would be to see him brought so low after the mugging he had given them the day before. What crocodile tears they would shed over his bloodied remains. No, that he could not watch, although he found no better comfort on any of the numerous other channels that were covering his story.

Over and over again he accepted his Oscar. On ABC and CBS and NBC. On Fox and CNN and about a million other cable channels, there he was, grinning like the idiot he had proved himself to be.

'I stand here on legs of fire.'

Legs of fire? Horrible. Ugly, mawkish, inept, meaningless.

They loved it.

'I want to thank you.' Of course he did. 'Each and every person in this room. Each and every person in this industry. You nourished me and helped me to touch the stars. Helped me be better than I had any right to be. Better than the best – which is what you all are. What can I say?'

Here Bruce's voice began to crack slightly, and over a billion people had wondered whether he was going to cry. He didn't. Even though he had turned into the creature of the mob, he was not so far possessed by them as actually to blub on cue.

'I am humble,' he lied, 'humble and small . . . but also proud and big, big in heart, big in love, big in head' (for one eerie moment it had seemed as if an unheard-of moment of veracity was about to intrude on the proceedings. 'Did he just say "big in head"?' the glittering throng were about to ask themselves. But Bruce had merely stopped mid-word in order to gulp down his emotions) 'big in headstrong dedication to being the best artist I know how,' he continued, 'the best American human being I can be, and to improving my one-on-one relationship with God. Thank you, America. Thank you for giving me the opportunity to be a part of this great industry. Because this is a great industry, a great American industry full of wonderful people. People whose extraordinary, awesome, monumental, towering, Heaven-sent talent has made me the artist I am. You are the wind beneath my wings and I flap for you. God bless you all. God bless America. God bless the world as well. Thank you.'

Bruce watched himself on the television screen and felt ill. He actually gagged at the horror of it. A tide of nausea welled up inside him, as if an air-bag had gone off and was pushing the contents of his stomach up his neck. He swallowed hard, and his throat burnt with gastric acids. How sick could a man feel? Very. He'd been awake for such a long time, and his police-issue breakfast sat uneasily on top of the fifteen-hour-old soup of party canapés and booze he'd consumed in his previous life.

How *could* he have made such a dreadful speech? No wonder bitter gall was surging up his gullet. It was the acrid taste of shame. After all, the man on the screen holding the golden statuette represented Bruce at his zenith: this was how he would be remembered in his moment of glory.

I stand here on legs of fire!

The sound of sirens jerked Bruce out of his reverie. There were police cars on the TV now. The same footage of his home being surrounded by the forces of justice that had been playing endlessly all morning. There again was his garden, full of cops. His drive, full of cops. His roof, covered in cops. How many cops could swarm round one house? All the cops in Los Angeles, it seemed to Bruce. And TV people. TV people everywhere. In his flower beds, outside his four garages, milling round his pool.

Bruce wished they hadn't put him in a room with a TV. He could switch it off, of course, but somehow he didn't.

The news story arrived once more at the limousine jam. Slowly the stars and big shots got out of their enormous cars. Bruce had watched the same footage so often that he knew the order by heart. There they were again. The long, slow stream of tuxedos, polished chins, magnificent bosoms and ridiculous gowns. Absurd gowns. Ludicrous gowns. Every one of those women was like a drowning swimmer desperate to attract attention. I'm over here! Look at me!

There was the purple one now, slashed up to the armpits. Such thighs! Hollywood thighs. And nipples. Nipples like thimbles. 'She's just iced those in the car,' Bruce had thought approvingly at the time. He always appreciated professionalism, an actress's dedication to her craft.

Now it was the turn of Bruce himself; he always came after the purple one with the thighs and nipples. The cameras of the waiting paparazzi began to flash before his car had even stopped. He was the star of the show, the hot tip for 'Best Director' and 'Best Picture'. What a night! What a moment! The star of the show.

Now it was the morning after and he was still the star, though of a rather different show. Whoever said all publicity was good publicity was an idiot.

The old Bruce stepped out of his limo and on to the red carpet, just as he had done twenty times already on every channel that morning. Turn, smile and wave. Check the bow-tie. Tug at the ear-lobe. Nervous, humble body language. Tiny little moves that screamed, 'Love me, you bastards! Look! Look! This is my night. I am the greatest director in the world, and yet I have the grace to pretend I'm just an ordinary guy.' Bruce knew every ingratiating little twitch by heart. How they cheered. How they loved him.

Except that they didn't really love him, any more than he believed he was a regular, ordinary guy. Everyone was just acting in the manner expected of them at such an event. Television has taught the whole world how to behave. Except, of course, for the protestors: prophets as they now appeared to be, illuminated by the deceptive light of hindsight.

The pickets. Mothers Against Death. Wouldn't *they* be pleased this morning. 'Mr Delamitri,' shouted the anonymous woman who had now become a TV star, 'my son was murdered. An innocent boy, gunned down on the streets. In your last picture there were seventeen murders.'

Bruce sat in the small, bare police interview room and watched his past self, thinking, 'Yeah, and there was plenty of sex in my movie too, but I bet *you* haven't had any for a while.'

That was what he had been thinking. Why hadn't he said it? He couldn't suppress the uneasy feeling that things would have been different if he had told the truth. It was completely irrational, of course, but ever since the police had left him alone he had been tortured by the thought that somehow honesty might have saved him from the terrible fate that had overtaken him.

'I stand here on legs of fire.' Jesus! Legs of fire? Just for that, he almost deserved what had happened to him.

He couldn't have been honest, of course, particularly not to that picket line. Not in his old life. He'd had different priorities then. It was one thing haranguing Oliver and Dale about the absurdity of blaming a film-maker for some murder that had happened in a place he'd never been to, and quite another to do it to the anguished relatives. It would have been the most terrible thing he could have done. Imagine the headlines: 'Bruce Delamitri Insults Bereaved Mothers'. It would have been the number-one story from the ceremony, a terrible, terrible scandal. Bruce found himself actually laughing at the thought. As if he'd care now. Funny how one's sense of proportion changes when the cops have been swarming all over your lawn and a SWAT team has smashed its way through your roof.

Bruce muted the TV. He knew by heart what the anchors were saying. What else could they say? This had to be the most spectacular reversal of fortunes they had ever had the ghoulish pleasure of reporting. The catastrophe that had overtaken Bruce had (in his opinion, anyway) the stature of a Greek tragedy – with, he was forced to reflect, all its attendant ironies.

Hubris, pride, comes before a fall. When a person is so big, so bold, so beautiful, that they come to believe that the rules that govern others no longer apply to them, that's when fate sticks the boot in, and you can't get any bigger, bolder or more beautiful than winning the 'Best Director' Oscar.

Bruce's house was back on the screen. No cops now: it was the 'before' shot, serene, tranquil, to make it absolutely clear to morning America just what Bruce had lost. A gorgeous piece of footage from a video guide to the homes of Hollywood's élite. He remembered the helicopter coming over taking the shots and what an outrageous invasion of privacy he had thought it. Again, proportion. He was a man for whom the notion of privacy no longer existed. He was public property. His lawn was on the TV and there were cops all over it. Every news agency in the world owned him. They could fly a helicopter up his backside and say it was in the public interest. Bruce stared at the beautiful home where his life used to be. He glanced around the bare room where he now sat.

What a journey he had made.
In twenty-four hours.

For the manacled young woman in the adjoining inter-view room her current surroundings were something of a step up. There were no cockroaches in the room, no flea-bitten dogs poking around trying to get at the food. There were no abandoned cars and no burst-open plastic sacks of garbage with rats fossicking about in them. This young woman did not hail from a mansion in the Hollywood hills. Her home was a beat-up RV in a trailer park in Texas. She, too, had come a long way.

But her surroundings left her completely unmoved. She didn't care. She didn't care about the cops and she didn't care about Bruce. She didn't care where she came from or where she had ended up. Wherever it was, she'd rather be dead. He was gone and she was alone. She'd known him such a short time and now it was all over and she was alone.

Chapter Four

'All I said was that it's like trying to find a needle in a haystack.'

If it hadn't been so serious, a casual observer might have laughed: the almost Gothic nature of the scene was in such stark contrast to the banal conversation that accompanied it.

It was early afternoon on the day of the Oscars, and the captives were being held in a dark and dingy cellar. Toni, a woman in her early twenties, lay on her back across a table, her ankles and wrists chained to its legs. Her boyfriend, Bob, hung from a chain on the wall. His clothes had been cut away, and he looked rather sad dangling there in the tatters of what had once been an Italian suit.

The man who had made the remark about haystacks was called Errol. He and his companion, who answered only to the title of Mr Snuff, were gangsters. They carried enormous pistols wedged under their arms, which must have been very uncomfortable, and their conversation was continually punctuated with the word 'motherfucker'. Errol and Mr Snuff were of the opinion that Bob was holding out on them in the matter of some missing drugs. Bob denied the suggestion, of course, and a search had been conducted, unsuccessfully, prompting Errol to draw the age-old comparison with the needle in the haystack.

A comparison which irritated Mr Snuff not a little. 'And I'm saying it's a dumb thing to say,' he snapped unkindly. 'There ain't no haystacks any more. Leastways, not in the experience of the average individual.'

'That's just being pedantic,' said Errol.

'Listen, man, if the stone-cold truth is pedantic, then I guess that's what I'm being, because I'll bet if you was to ask every person within one hundred miles of where we're standing if they'd ever *seen* a haystack, let alone left their works in one, they'd say, "Get the fuck outa here, motherfucker."'

Errol spotted the point of confusion. 'It don't mean no works,' he said.

'Say what?'

'The needle which is referred to in the expression "a needle in a haystack" does not mean no drug parapher- nalia. It means a needle for sewing.'

Mr Snuff seized upon the point like the practised debater he was. 'It don't matter what kind of needle we're talking about here, you dumb motherfucker,' he explained. 'The point is that no one is going to lose it in no haystack. You need to bring your metaphors into the twentieth century, man.'

Bob, still hanging from the chain, groaned a little. The two gangsters ignored him.

'How about if you was to say it's like trying to find

a line of coke in a snowdrift? Now there's an image a person can understand.'

Now it was Errol's turn to be contrary. 'No, man, that's bullshit,' he said angrily. 'The whole point about a needle and a haystack is that they are very different things, and although it would be difficult to locate the former within the latter, it would not be impossible. Cocaine and snow are basically identical. You could never tell one from the other. One concept is improbable, the other is impossible – which is an entirely different thing.'

'Less you snorted up the entire motherfucker. You could sure tell them apart if you was to stick them up your nose.'

Errol laughed. It was a relief for both men. The discussion had been in danger of turning acrimonious, but now the tension was broken. For the two gangsters, that is; for Toni and Bob things remained stressful.

'That's right,' Errol conceded with a grin. 'If you snorted up the entire snowdrift, when you got to the stuff that made you talk bullshit at three o'clock in the morning, that would be the cocaine.'

Mr Snuff, having scored such an effective point, was in the mood to be generous. 'I don't want to make no Federal case out of this,' he said kindly. 'I just think that language ought to reflect the lives of the people who are speaking it. Not some rural bullshit like needles and haystacks or . . . or . . . the early bird catches the worm. I don't want no fucking worm, man. What is more, if I had a horse, which I don't, I wouldn't waste no time taking the motherfucker to water when it wasn't thirsty in the first place.'

Bob groaned again. 'Let me go. I didn't rip nothing off, man.'

He might as well have appealed to a couple of concrete gangsters for all the good this was going to do him.

'Don't insult me, Bob. You think I can't count? You think me and Mr Snuff here are so dumb that we can't count?'

Bob quickly assured Errol that he had intended no such slur.

'In which case, how come I ain't supposed to know the difference between one hundred kilos and ninety-nine kilos, you sewer-rat? A one-hundredth part is a substantial differential. Suppose I was to cut off a one-hundredth part of you? Do you think you wouldn't notice?'

It would have taken a more stupid man than Bob to have misunderstood the meaning of Errol's question, but nevertheless Errol rubbed that meaning in by grabbing at Bob's crotch. It is said that men who practise the ancient Chinese art of kung fu are capable of retracting their testicles at the first sign of danger. They probably couldn't do it if the testicles in question were held in the vice-like grip of a large gangster.

'I gave you what Speedy gave me,' Bob protested. 'I didn't steal nothing. I'm not a thief.'

Errol released Bob's hundredth part and turned his attention to Toni. So far she had made no contribution to the conversation, and perhaps Errol felt some social pressure to include her. He and Mr Snuff were, after all, in a way the hosts.

'Toni?' he enquired. 'Is your boyfriend a thief?'

'Listen, Errol,' Toni said, attempting to sound calm and considering – no easy task when one is lying prostrate and securely bound across a table – 'we ain't getting nowhere here.'

'I know that.'

'If Bob tells you what you want to hear, you'll kill him.'

'I'm going to kill him anyway.'

'But you can't kill him till he's told you where your damn hundredth part is. So he won't tell you. We'll be here till Christmas.'

It was a valiant effort. That she could think at all, considering the horror of her situation, was a miracle, but to have put Errol's problem so clearly was impressive indeed.

'OK, Bob,' Errol said, levelling his gun at Toni. 'If you don't tell me right now, I'll shoot her.'

This was a hopeless ploy. Bob was, after all, a heartless drug dealer. The chances of his being moved by appeals to his chivalry were small. Toni knew this too, but before she had time to request that she be left out of it Errol shot her.

It was a powerful gesture: the smell of gun-smoke, the echoing report in such a confined space, the scream, the blood. All this might have moved a lesser – or indeed more honourable – man than Bob to speak up and save Toni further discomfort. But Bob was, of course, not a lesser man; nor was he a more honourable one. Nobody ever is.

'I didn't steal your drugs,' Bob said.

Errol sat down at the table, oblivious of the dying woman who lay across it. He was at his wits' end. He and Mr Snuff had searched Bob's apartment, his car, his clothes. Where on earth could the missing drugs be?

'Could a person get a kilo of heroin up their ass?' he asked.

'Maybe,' said Mr Snuff. 'People get all sorts of things up their asses.'

A pair of plastic gloves lay on the table next to a set of scales. Errol had been wearing them earlier on when weighing out the heroin. He picked up one glove, shook Toni's blood from it and put it on.

'I don't have no heroin up my ass, man' said Bob, hoping, perhaps, to save Errol the trouble of further investigation.

'Well, I wish I could trust you, Bob,' said Errol. 'To tell you the truth, I am not relishing the prospect of probing your butt with my finger any more than I imagine you relish the prospect of having your butt probed. But I cannot trust you, Bob, which is what all of this unpleasantness is about.'

Errol stuck his hand down the back of Bob's jockey shorts and executed his investigation. 'No drugs up here,' he said.

'Maybe she's got them,' said Mr Snuff, peering up between Toni's legs. 'No drugs here, I think,' he said from beneath her skirt, 'but a very nice –'

Then suddenly a voice from nowhere said, 'Thank you. Stop right there.'

And they stopped.

Errol froze. Mr Snuff froze. They all froze. There was not the slightest movement. Mr Snuff's head remained under Toni's skirt, Errol's expression remained one of bored indifference, Bob's grimace of pain seemed to have been painted on. Everything had stopped – not just stopped but *really* stopped. Nobody was doing *anything*. Toni was not bleeding any more. Nobody was even breathing.

Chapter Five

The voice spoke again. 'Go back, but slowly, nice and slowly.'

Mr Snuff removed his head from under Toni's skirt and Errol put his finger back up Bob's backside.

Toni's body began to suck back into itself the blood it had lost. The red stain shrank across the table. She even appeared to revive slightly.

Errol removed his finger from Bob again and returned to sit by the table. He seemed to be in pain: he made sad, guttural noises. He took off the glove, got up again and, backing away from the table, addressed Bob in the same strange, incomprehensible sounds. He drew his gun and pointed it at Toni.

A miracle was affecting Toni. Her wound was healing. Almost all the blood she had lost was back in her body, and all that was left of the gaping blast was the bullet.

Then Toni shot Errol.

Or at least shot *at* him. A bullet emerged from her body and hurtled towards the gangster. Fortunately for

Errol his gun was in the way, and the bullet Toni's body hurled at him disappeared straight up the barrel.

The disembodied voice spoke again.

'All right. Thank you. Let's leave it there for a moment.'

And suddenly there was darkness. Bob, Toni, Errol and Mr Snuff all disappeared. It was if they had never been there at all. For the moment at least, they had ceased to exist.

'I just wanted you to see that last sequence backwards,' said Bruce Delamitri, 'because I think it's easier to deconstruct the shots when you're not being distracted by the narrative flow. Remember that trick when you're checking your edits.'

What a sentence! Calm, commanding, all-knowing. Bruce could feel the sap rising – deep within his Calvin Kleins. The good feeling he had got earlier that morning from obliterating Oliver and Dale on *Coffee Time USA* was as nothing to the buzz that now surged through him as two hundred fresh-faced, puppy-like college kids hung on his every word. They were sitting there, awestruck, scarcely able to believe that the main man, the *mainest* man, the mainest, mainiest, most main *mongous* man of them all was really there, talking to them!

Bruce loved showing off in front of students. Especially the girls. Punky ones with great big Doc Marten boots on the end of slim, delicate legs. Preppy ones in smart little jumpers and cute John Lennon glasses. Goth types swathed in black, with pale skin and purple nail varnish. Tough, vampy ones with pierced belly-buttons and who knew what else. It wasn't that Bruce was a dirty old director. In fact women liked working with him: he was a recognised non-predator. But this was different. This was a treat. When Bruce had attended college he had been something of a dork and had had to work extremely hard to get anywhere at all with girls. Oh, they certainly *liked* him. They all found him funny, with his perfect impression of the sound effects in *The Texas Chainsaw Massacre*, and his plastic space-gun, stolen when he was an extra on *Star Wars*. His contagious enthusiasm for absolutely anything and everything to do with movies had always been attractive. But being funny and enthusiastic does not get you laid. Nor does it get you respected by the other guys – who had all been into Kurosawa while he was into James Bond.

'Of course *The Magnificent Seven* is a better movie than *The Seven Samurai*,' he used to say. 'For one thing it doesn't have subtitles.'

Bruce had been popular at college but no kid had ever stared at him the way these kids were staring at him now.

He was home. The film studies course of the University of Southern California where he had spent three happy but sexually frustrated years. He had returned at last to the one place in the world where he *really* wanted to show off. This was why he had agreed, on Oscars day of all days, to drive clear across LA from the *Coffee Time* studios to address his Alma Mater. To spend three precious hours viewing and discussing clips from his movies. To show off. What other reason would anyone have for going back and addressing their old college? When the heads of student committees write and ask famous old boys or girls to return and speak, they imagine they are asking an enormous favour. They themselves think the place is crap and can't wait to get out of it. But for the old boy or girl, that invitation represents acceptance at last, an opportunity to finally come to terms with the gawky nerdiness of their late adolescence. A rare chance to reach back across the years and – in thought at least – consummate all those glorious student flings that had never been.

So there Bruce sat, a king on his podium, puffed up with pride and eagerly anticipating a splendid hour or so humbly making it clear to these fine young people exactly how brilliant he was.

Opposite Bruce sat Professor Chambers, a sad-looking, dusty old Mr Chips whom the students had asked to chair the occasion. A teacher in the chair! In Bruce's day it would have been an ace king of teenage cool doing the job, but times had changed. The two-decade sixties hangover, when youth still seemed full of infinite promise, had finally evaporated. A colder wind blew now, and students had become much more timid, more conservative. Hence their decision to invite a professor to chair this major event: they felt safer with an authority figure around.

'So,' said Bruce, 'any questions or observations about the clip we just saw? Let's hear what the future's got to say.'

This was, of course, greeted by silence. Fear of looking stupid or uncool is a powerful censor, particularly if you've just been referred to as the future.

'I would like to ask something if I may,' said Professor Chambers.

Bruce cursed inwardly. Surely this old turd was not going to have so little style as to try and grab some reflected glory for himself? Bruce had not given up three hours of Oscars day to discuss the finer points of postmodern *film noir* bullshit with an anal academic. He had done it in order to strut about in front of nymphs.

'Go right ahead, professor,' he said, throwing a half-smile at the kids in the audience as if to say, 'Let's humour the sad old goat.'

'Do you feel that the same effect could perhaps have been achieved in your scene without delving into the female protagonist's private parts?'

Bruce was somewhat taken aback. Was this guy *criticising* him? Surely not. Bruce was Oscar-nominated, for Christ's sake.

'Say *what*?' Bruce demanded.

'Ahem.' Professor Chambers cleared his throat, uncomfortably aware that all eyes were most definitely upon him. 'I was just wondering whether you feel that the same effect could perhaps have been achieved in your scene without delving into the female protagonist's private parts.'

There was a pregnant pause while Bruce debated whether to crush the professor like a small, bearded insect beneath his super-cool pointy-toed boots. A moment's reflection convinced him that this would look uncool. He didn't want to imbue the man with more significance than he deserved, which was none. Instead Bruce opted to wither him with a look of hip bemusement.

'The girl's private parts are not shown,' Bruce said. 'Didn't you watch the piece, *professor*?'

'I realize that the girl's private parts are not actually shown,' said Professor Chambers rather nervously. 'Nevertheless, they seem to play a disproportionately central role in the proceedings.'

The guy *was* criticising him. As if he was the subject of some essay. Bruce decided that this had already gone on too long. He wanted to talk to cool kids not old jerks.

'I do not make exploitative pictures,' he said with an air of finality, and turned away from the professor to feast his eyes again on the sea of adoring and expectant young faces before him.

Professor Chambers sighed. He looked older than his years, with his lined face and grey beard. He felt like a schoolmaster forced to confront a brilliant but wayward pupil. A genius boy physicist who spent his time making stink-bombs, or a gifted young writer who insisted on putting swear-words into all his creative-writing assignments. He did not consider himself old-fashioned or a bore; he had once written an appreciation of Jim Morrison's poetry for the *Boston Literary Review*. There was however, in his opinion, a limit. Eroticism was one thing, pornography another. He felt that the place for delving into people's private parts was a doctor's surgery or in the context of a loving relationship. Not while searching for cocaine.

'Nevertheless,' he said to the back of Bruce's leather jacket, 'the character Mr Snuff does stare up the girl's private parts. That is the case, is it not?'

'Ironically,' Bruce replied without turning round.

'Ironically?'

'Yes.'

'I don't understand.'

Bruce drew upon all his reserves of patience, which was almost no patience at all. 'The character Mr Snuff,' he said, as if addressing a man who had donated his brain to an organ bank, 'stares up the character Toni's private parts in a manner that will imply an ironic juxtaposition to the audience. Didn't you get that, *professor*?'

461

'No, I'm afraid I missed that. Any ironic juxtaposition entirely passed me by. Am I being terribly dense?'

Bruce threw a look of tolerant exasperation at the audience, but the sympathetic response he anticipated was not forthcoming. The students were a bit lost: most of them thought that ironic juxtaposition was something dirty you did in bed. Some of them giggled nervously.

'With respect,' the professor added quietly, 'I thought it was just rather rude.'

Things had suddenly become a little tense. Bruce, like most people, hated tension. His whole pose was one of laid-back street cool. He was the grown-up teenager in the Ray-Bans who just didn't *give* a fuck. The naughty thirty-something genius who broke all the rules. It was his job to needle authority figures like college professors, not the other way round. And on this day of all days, Oscars day, when he should have been luxuriating in the sweet ecstasy of fame, basking in a hormone-packed wave of adolescent admiration, this dusty old fossil was pissing on his parade.

Bruce struggled to stay cool. He reminded himself just how far above the old turd he was. Only that morning the *New York Times* had published an adulatory two-thousand-word profile of him, using phrases such as 'cultural icon', '*Zeitgeist*' and 'defining images of the last decade'. Cultural icons did not let bearded gnomes with pens in their breast-pockets wind them up.

'You remember that the next shot is the POV of the girl's snatch, right?'

This got an easy laugh, as Bruce had calculated it would. Using rude words in lecture halls showed just how much of a fuck he did not give.

'POV?' asked the professor.

'Jesus! I thought you ran a film course here. POV. Point of view, for Christ's sake, point of view.'

'I know what POV means. I just don't –'

'We see Mr Snuff's face from the point of view of Toni's vagina.'

'The vagina's point of view?'

'Yes, the vagina's point of view.'

This was an entirely new concept for the professor. He wondered how a vagina could have a point of view and, if it could, what its attitude would be.

'I'm sorry, but I don't –'

'Mr Snuff stares at the vagina,' Bruce snapped, 'and in a subliminal way the vagina stares back at Mr Snuff.'

'And that's ironic, is it?'

'The irony is in what we take away from the image, professor. I want to show that this is all in a day's work for Mr Snuff. I need to see his face in these extraordinary circumstances, so that I can show his expression of casual indifference. He's almost bored. This is just a job, an American job.'

This bland assertion was too much for Professor Chambers. A faint note of irritation crept into his voice; you would have needed a sharp ear to spot it, but it was there. The students, who knew their tutor, shifted nervously in their seats.

'Is shooting women in the stomach and then rummaging about in their vaginas for drugs a common occupation in your experience?' the professor enquired.

'Killing is, pal. Being a killer is a career option in America, like teaching or dentistry.'

'Perhaps not quite as common.'

'Ha! You wish.'

'Statistically, I think you'll find I'm right.' Professor

Chambers decided to drop the point and move on. 'Mr Snuff's next line is perhaps one of my least favourite moments in your motion picture, Mr Delamitri.'

'I'm heartbroken.' Bruce smiled wearily at the students and they rewarded him with a laugh.

'Hmm, yes, well, I understand that taste is subjective and that you are indifferent to mine. Nevertheless, Mr Snuff's observation "nice pussy" seems to be beyond the bounds of taste altogether.'

Bruce groaned audibly. He was genuinely offended now. He no longer cared what the pretty young things thought. It was between him and this pathetic man who seemed to be going deliberately out of his way to apply an attitude of archaic prurience to Bruce's brilliant, startling and challenging images.

'"Nice pussy" is an important line, a pivotal line – the keystone line of the movie! I put it there so that even dummies wouldn't miss the point I'm making.'

The audience was becoming genuinely uncomfortable. Confrontational debate like this was a rarity on campus these days: the consequences of giving offence to one special-interest group or another were too severe. Bruce sensed the nervousness and attempted to moderate his anger.

'Look, Mr Chambers, I am not insensitive to the fact that some people might find this sequence unsettling. I am also not blind to the possibility that other people might be titillated by the images I present. The woman has been brutalised and violated, tied down, shot, had her clothing removed, and as she breathes her last she finds herself being intimately inspected by a strange man. I do not offer up these images lightly.'

'I am delighted to hear it.'

'I am aware of my reponsibility to place all this in a suitable editorial context. That is why I took the vagina's POV of Mr Snuff's reaction.'

'Which was to smile and observe that the character Toni has a nice pussy.'

'Exactly!' Bruce exploded. 'Listen to how he says it for Christ's sake! He doesn't say, "Wow, get this! I am searching a dying girl's private parts. Is that amazing or *what*! Am I going totally *insane* here?" He shrugs and he says it's "a very nice pussy". It's a throwaway. He is relaxed, he is indifferent. He's at work. Like I say, to him, it's just a job, an American job. That's what I want people to take away from this scene.'

The professor sighed. He was sick of studying film. Drugs, bullets, vaginas, this never-ending use of the term 'motherfucker' – it was all so very depressing.

'Perhaps we should take the next clip,' he said, nodding at the student technician.

The film rolled and the scene began. It was set in a low-life roadside bar and grill. A near-naked woman was dancing seductively to slow country music playing on a jukebox. Two aggressive and unpleasant truckers were leering at her from the bar.

'Now,' Bruce thought, 'the old swine can't possibly object to this one.'

Chapter Six

The young man and the scrawny girl were still lying on the bed in the motel chalet. *Coffee Time* had long since concluded and now they were watching videos.

There was a woman on the screen, dancing to the juke-box in a roadside bar and grill.

'I'm sick of watching the tube, honey,' the girl said.

'Quiet now, baby,' the man replied. 'This is important. What I'm doing here right now, hon, is researching.'

'Researching what? You ain't doing no researching. You're just watching dumb movies which you seen a hundred times already. I want to go out.'

'What I am researching, sugar,' the man said, his tone hardening slightly, 'is our salvation. Y'hear me now? Because what I have here is a plan to get us saved. You want to be saved, don't you, precious?'

'Sure I want to be saved. Everybody wants to be saved.'

'In that case, honey pie, shut the fuck up.'

He fixed his eyes on the TV and cranked up the volume. Slow, sugary country music filled the room, music recorded thirty years ago, which had been utterly and terminally uncool for every one of the intervening years. Music that had become briefly hip. Everything gets credible if you wait long enough; one generation's cringe is another's kitsch cult classic.

The woman kept on dancing. And such a woman. A truck driver's dream. A cowboy's fantasy. Poor white trash, but what poor white trash would look like had it just descended from Mount Olympus. Tanned, shapely legs stretching up for ever from the glossy painted toes on her bare feet to the jeans cut down to a tiny pair of shorts that inadequately covered her buttocks. A naked, undulating stomach, writhing to the rhythm. A perfect navel, like a cup, a bronzed abdomen contrasting beautifully with the white cotton of perhaps the smallest vest a woman might wear and still hope to keep her breasts from public view. Breasts which knew nothing of Sir Isaac Newton or his absurd gravitational theories. Above it all a cloud – no, a mane – of impossibly blonde hair crowning sleepy eyes and a fat mouth. A fat, wet mouth that never closed but hung lazily ajar, lips slightly parted, ready, one might easily imagine, for anything.

There is a children's movement exercise in which the kids are told to dance 'in the manner of' an abstract concept, like hunger or the wind. The girl in the bar was dancing in the manner of an orgasm. Her hips, her behind, her shoulders, her bare feet sliding on the floor, all seemed to suggest that dancing on her own to a juke-box in the middle of the day in a shit-house bar was to her the ultimate in sexual excitement. As she danced her hands even stole occasionally to between her legs, brushing at the little concertina of denim that disappeared below the zip of her jeans.

If this woman wasn't masturbating to music in a public bar she was by way of doing a very good impression of it. An impression that was not lost on the two large good ol' boy cowboy trucker types who were leaning against the bar resting their beer bottles on their beer bellies. They were, of course staring at the dancing woman, leering in fact. Dribbling would perhaps not be too strong a word. Their jaws were dropping, their erections were rising. Had it not been for the vast expanse of gut between the two, jaw and erection might well eventually have met.

'Hurrr hurrrr,' said one good ol' boy.

'Hurrrr,' replied the other and despite the poverty of their language it was clear that they were discussing the young woman's charms. Perhaps she was flattered by their obvious attentions, because she seemed to be directing her dancing towards them. A rough translation of her body language might have read, 'Should either of you two gentlemen feel in any way inclined to screw me rigid, you would not find me an unwilling collaborator.' That, at least, was how the bigger and uglier of the two good ol' boys interpreted her look, for he released the bar stool that he had clamped between his vast buttocks and, pausing only to spit some tobacco on to the floor, grunted his way towards the near-naked siren dancing before him.

What a contrast they made. One so beautiful it was almost unbearable, a walking, talking, living doll, a sex puppet, achingly seductive. The other a repulsive slob, beer bottle in hand, so many chins it looked as if he had rested his face on a stack of crumpets, his belly so vast that one side of it was in a different time zone from the other. The woman's chest might defy Newton's laws, but this colossal gut seemed to exercise it's own gravitational pull. At least, the woman certainly appeared to be drawn towards him, and it was hard to imagine that this had come about through any sort of desire.

And yet everything about her demeanour suggested that it had. It really seemed as if she was attracted to this man. She pouted at him, wiggled at him. His lumpy movements and phlegmy grunts seemed to excite her and spur her on to greater displays of lithe sexuality. She took his beer bottle from him and, even though there was only an inch or so left in it, took a pull. The man had clearly been nursing that bottle for some time and one could only guess how much of the beery dregs was made up of his spit, yet the woman sucked greedily at it, her fleshy lips pouting round the bottle neck as if to say, 'Normally, of course, I prefer to do this to a fat, ugly truck-driver's penis.'

The woman emptied the bottle but instead of putting it down she rolled it around on her tummy, apparently so hot that she needed to take any opportunity to cool down. Having rolled the bottle around for a while she turned it upside down so that a small dribble of the remaining foam ran down over her belly-button and into the top of her tiny shorts, drawing attention (as if this were required) to the fact that the waist button was undone and it was only the zip that was holding the shorts closed.

'Hurrr,' said the good ol' boy, as well he might.

The woman put the bottle down on top of the juke-box and closed the gap between herself and her new companion. Now her body was against his, her hips grinding back and forth. The trucker, clearly feeling that some gesture was required on his part, put his arms round her and in lieu of a formal introduction gripped her buttocks.

'My name's Angel,' she whispered at two or three of his many chins.

'Who cares what your name is, honey?' the trucker said. 'Pussy is pussy.'

He had struck the wrong note. Whatever Angel had hoped to hear from this disgusting man, it was not that. Her mood changed even as he gripped her more tightly.

'Loosen your grip, buddy,' she said. 'I like to keep my tits on the outside of my rib-cage.'

Her appeal fell on deaf ears. Digging his huge, fat banana fingers into her behind, he dragged her body harder against his.

'Honey, if you dance like a whore you're going to get treated like a whore,' he growled. 'Now, how about you pucker up for daddy?'

'I'd rather kiss the stuff I cut off my dog's ass,' Angel remarked in a forthright tone. With that she reached out an arm, grabbed the beer bottle from the top of the juke-box and brought it down on top of her dancing partner's head, shattering the base of the bottle. This gesture was understandably enough to make the man do as he was asked and disengage himself, but he did it with no good grace and indeed seemed ready to draw back his big pudgy fist and punch the woman. She was, however, ahead of him. There was a heavy glass beer jug on the counter. Somehow or other it got into Angel's hand and she swung it against the side of the big man's head. Down he went, semi-stunned, to the filthy bar-room floor, where he lay prostrate in the mud and the blood and the beer. At the bar his pal began to release his stool from the buttock-clamp in which his ass held it. Angel dropped the jug and, reaching into her tiny shorts, produced – by some kind of miracle, for it certainly could not have been there before – a little snub-nosed pistol.

'Sit the fuck down and shut the fuck up,' this woman of strange emotional contrasts shouted, levelling her weapon at the second trucker. You could almost hear the fear as the terrified fellow reinserted the stool into his enormous lardy backside and shut up.

Meanwhile Angel turned her attention back to her ex-dancing-partner, who still lay semi-stunned upon the floor.

'Cocksucking son of a bitch!' she screamed in wild, uncontrollable, unbalanced fury, kicking the stricken man in the head and face. 'Still want me? Still looking for pussy, you goddam faggot bastard? Well, you've had your last piece, you rat turd!'

The broken bottle with which she had begun her assault was still in her hand. Dropping to her knees, she rammed its jagged edge into the stunned man's loins. Blood geysered out of his fly.

The man touched the video remote control and the image froze, the blood stopping in mid-air as it hurtled towards Angel's face.

'I wuz just starting to enjoy that, honey,' said the girl.

'Got to take a leak,' said the man. 'Don't you mess with that control, now, girl. 'Cos' I'm working here. What I got is a plan.

Chapter Seven

A hundred miles south, in the university lecture hall Bruce and Professor Chambers sat beneath the same frozen image of blood geysering from the fat trucker's loins. There was applause from the students, which Bruce graciously acknowledged. He felt back on safe ground. Surely the senile, bearded old back issue sitting opposite him could not object to such a vigorous and empowering piece of film-making. It transpired, however, that he could.

'Don't you think that's rather a clichéd scene?' Professor Chambers enquired.

Bruce could scarcely believe the effrontery of the odious little gnome. Who did he think he was? In fact, and more to the point, who *was* he? A teacher. What did he do that was so great?

'Have you any idea how much I *earn*?' Bruce wanted to shout. 'Are you aware that the Académie Française has given me a dinner?'

He didn't say that but he might as well have done.

He hit the tweedy old jerk with everything he had.

'Cliché? *Cliché?*' he said, jumping to his feet. 'Well excuuuuuse me if I opine that the meanest, most derivative cliché I ever produced is more original than everything you have ever said plus everything you have ever done.'

It was a mistake. It was meant to be a joke, sort of, but it didn't come out that way at all. Bruce had hoped to look sarky and disrespectful, the street punk in a leather jacket and pointy-toed boots thumbing his nose at authority. He forgot that he was not a punk but an impossibly rich, Oscar-nominated director, whereas Professor Chambers was a public servant on forty grand a year. Bruce was Goliath and the professor was David, not the other way round. The kids in the hall began to whisper to each other. Sweat trickled down Bruce's back and into the top of his black 501s. He had let himself get angry; getting angry was uncool and he knew it. He was supposed to be the guy who didn't care. He realised that he must get a grip, bite the bullet, chew the carpet, go home later and kick the dog.

'Just kidding,' he said, with a little-boy smile. 'You don't "dis" the prof, right?'

The students relaxed a little. Bruce had concentrated all his considerable personal charm into this jokey semi-apology and it worked – for the students. Not, though, for the professor, who was looking at the screen again and shaking his head sadly. The woman in hot pants was still astride the trucker, the broken bottle was still embedded in his loins, the geyser of blood still hung in mid-air like a cruel red spike.

'I'm supposed to feel all right about this piece of violent soft porn because the woman triumphs, am I?'

'Well of course,' said Bruce. 'It's immensely important that the female protagonist is shown in a befittingly empowering light.'

This provoked a smattering of applause from some of the young women in the audience. Bruce was even gratified to hear a couple of whoops.

'Right on!' shouted a girl with a ring through her nose.

'Hmmm.' Professor Chambers sucked on his pen as if it was a pipe. 'You can have no idea how tired I am of film-makers like you cynically cloaking their salacious, smutty entertainments in some laughably two-dimensional anti-sexist agenda.'

This was getting silly. Bruce was a *guest* for Christ's sake! When was this nasty old man going to give him a break? Bruce took further refuge in self-righteous feminism, the modern equivalent of hiding behind a woman's petticoats. 'Maybe you find images of strong women threatening?'

'Right on!' shouted the girl with the nose-ring. Bruce wanted to kiss her. Fortunately he didn't; had he done so she would have brought a civil action against him for rape. Professor Chambers did not seem even to have heard her.

'I do not consider a woman who deliberately titillates some ignorant and unpleasant oaf merely to bury a broken bottle in his private parts, strong, I consider her psychotic.'

'Listen, pal, a woman can dress and dance any way she wants.'

'Any way *you* want. This is your fantasy, Mr Delamitri. The whole scenario is a fiction created by you, and the actress playing the role dressed as you wanted her to and did what you told her to do.'

The young woman with the nose-ring kept quiet. They all did. The debate was getting out of their league. They liked things simple, and an uncomfortable suspicion was dawning on them that what their professor and their hero were discussing was not simple at all.

'Yes, I created it,' Bruce admitted, 'but what did I create it from? These things are going on out there.' He was no longer concerned with looking cool. He had a point to make, a position to defend. He wanted to get through to the professor in the same way the professor had got through to him. 'The connection between sex and violence is for real. It's out there and it's happening, USA-wide. That isn't my fault. I didn't start it and I didn't kill anyone. I just hold up the mirror.'

'Rather a flattering mirror, isn't it?'

'Excuse me?'

The professor let him have it. 'Why do your murderers and psychopaths have to be so attractive, Mr Delamitri? So cool? It seems to me that if the scene we have just watched had involved the near-rape of a plain woman, a fat, boring woman, then you would probably have let her get raped. Except there never would have been such a scene because the whole purpose of the entire grubby business was to show us a beautiful woman in a state of provocative near-undress –'

Bruce did not let him finish. Chambers had walked into a trap. Bruce had heard this ancient, puerile argument many times before, and he was in a position to crush it with the utter contempt it deserved.

'You ever see a Greek statue of an ugly chick? You ever see a painting of a battle when the guys didn't look cool and noble? Where the blood didn't look exciting and seductive? Artists make pictures and stories. That's what we do. Dull, ugly people leading boring lives devoid of sex and adventure do not make good stories. I'm not a journalist. It is no part of my duty to report life. I am an artist. My duty is to my own muse, my creative self. I take what I want in order to create what I like.'

'Really? I thought you said you were a mirror.'

'I'm ... I'm ...' Bruce knew when to throw in the towel. 'Actually, I'm running kind of late here.'

In the motel cabin the tough-looking guy had returned from the bathroom, grabbed a beer from the mini-bar and lain down again beside the girl.

'That sure was a fine motion picture,' he said. 'I may just have to watch it one more time.'

'Oh, honey,' said the girl, 'can't we go out now? *Do* something?'

'You want to go to prison, sugar pie?'

'No, of course not.'

'You want to burn in the chair? You want to feel your eyeballs melting before you're even *dead*?'

'Don't go saying stuff like that!' Suddenly there were tears on her pale cheeks.

'Then just you go get me another burger and let me watch my movie. Cos what I am working on here is our salvation.'

Chapter Eight

D usk had fallen.
　　The searchlights that explored the sky above the theatre could be seen from miles away. The crowd was getting thicker and Bruce's limo slowed down. It's a funny thing about stretch limos: you can usually hire them for no more than twice or three times what an ordinary cab would cost and yet they remain a potent symbol of colossal wealth and celebrity. It crossed Bruce's mind that he ought to be able to extrapolate some great truth from this observation, but he couldn't think what it was.

The great car crawled forwards a few yards, clinging to the number plate in front, a pink number plate which read STAR. Bruce smiled. If there was one thing he knew about stardom, it was that if you had to stick it on your fender you hadn't got it.

A limousine jam. Only in Hollywood could you have a genuine limousine jam. An entire traffic snarl made up exclusively of stretch limos. Here was another observation from which a pithy and illuminating irony could surely be gleaned. No matter how long your car is, in traffic they're all the same length: they stretch from the one stuck in front of you to the one stuck behind. Not bad, Bruce mused. He might trot it out to the press tonight to show that he still had his feet on the ground despite being so very special.

The car stopped altogether.

Bruce leant back in the baby-soft black leather, his wrap-round Rays between him and the world, a drink in his hand and an Oscar very nearly in his pocket.

His mind began to dwell on a particularly gruesome and pointless murder that he was planning. He had it in his head pretty clearly now. A run-down Korean drug store in the Valley. Two white kids enter the store. White trash kids. Better still, middle-class white kids pretending to be trash. Talking dudespeak, of course, or whatever other hellish dialect the generation with no brain affected these days. ('Generation X? Generation X-tremely fucking stupid,' Bruce would say at parties.) The two kids approach the counter and ask for a quarter of Jack plus some Pepsi Max to mix. But the old Korean lady knows the law and doesn't want to lose her liquor licence, so she asks for some ID.

'Here's my ID, bitch,' says one of the boys and hauls out a machete. Not some stupid little knife, but a *machete*. Obviously the old lady tells the kids to forget about the ID, in fact she reaches down a whole pint of bourbon and offers it to them on the house. But it's too late. She has crossed the line with these kids. She has 'dissed' them. They have been pushed too far and they ain't gonna take it any more because, quite frankly, they are sick of the bullshit. So the boy swings his weapon towards the terrified woman in a huge arc and cuts her head off. Blood starts spurting out of the dead woman's neck, which so excites the two kids that they hop over the counter and hack her up into a million pieces.

Bruce would do the whole thing to music, heavy-duty rock 'n' roll perhaps, or maybe something witty and ironic like 'Happy Days are Here Again' or 'All You Need is Love'. He would make it look like a pop video. Maybe he could have a TV on in the background, with a Tom and Jerry cartoon showing. That way, while the two kids were slicing up the old Korean woman, Jerry could be ironing Tom with a steam iron, or dicing him in the lawn-mower.

'What were you trying to tell us by juxtaposing your brutal murder with cartoon mayhem?' assholes like Professor Chambers would ask.

'I was telling you that the Korean woman had Tom and Jerry showing on her TV,' he would reply enigmatically, and hundreds of film students would write essays about irony.

'Bruce Delamitri is trying to tell us that America is now starring in its own animation,' they would write. 'We are all Tom, we are all Jerry, locked in a perpetual cycle of almost surreal violence.'

The limo driver barged in on Bruce's thoughts. 'There's a hell of a queue to drop, Mr Delamitri. We're going to be stalled for a while here.'

A limo jam. A jam of stretch limousines. It was faintly embarrassing.

Outside there were thousands of people, all staring. Faces everywhere, a wall of them. Bruce peered through the darkness of his shades and tried to focus on a pretty one but was disappointed. Despite their excitement, they all seemed drab and sad. Trash. Poor white, black, brown and yellow trash.

He glanced at the locks on the car doors. It was not that he thought he was in any danger – the crowd was well ordered and the cops were keeping it firmly behind barriers – but you could not help but feel a little exposed. All those people wanting something they would never get.

Maybe one day they would just grab it anyway. It crossed Bruce's mind that the princes of old Russia must have stared out of their carriages at faces much like these just before their world got torn to bits in 1917.

But what did they want, craning their necks by the side of the street like that? It certainly wasn't peace, bread and freedom. So what? They couldn't see anything: all the limos had mirrored windows, so all they could see was themselves. Another irony; Bruce was full of them today. The harder those people tried to look into his world the more intensely they saw their own images staring back at them. That was it! The whole truth in one startling image. Why were Bruce's movies so successful? Because people saw themselves reflected in them. Maybe better-looking and a little cooler but none the less themselves, with their fears, their lusts, their most secret desires and fantasies. That damned professor had been wrong and he, Bruce, had been right. He *was* a mirror. He did not create a world for people to watch; they created a world for him to film.

They were his muse, these *lumpen* gawpers, staring at his car, trying to guess who might be inside it. Pointing, pointing their fingers and yet all they could see was their own images, pointing right back at them.

'That's right, point,' Bruce said aloud. 'Point the finger, accuse yourselves, because you and you alone are responsible for what you see. For what you are. For what you do.'

Up ahead the starlet in the purple dress had done her twirls, making the most of her thighs and her nipples.

Then it was his turn on the red carpet.

He stepped out of his limo intending scarcely to acknowledge the crowd, merely to stroll languidly into the theatre as if he was entering a bar. Perhaps he would allow a brief, cool nod towards the throng, but certainly no more than that. The sort of stroll and nod that said, 'Am I the *only* person here who realises that this is all bullshit?' That was what he had intended, but instead Doctor Showbiz appeared as if from nowhere and gave him a shot in the arm. The crowd cheered and he couldn't resist a stolen moment luxuriating in their attention. He turned, he waved, he checked his bow-tie, he tugged charmingly at his ear-lobe.

'Love me you bastards,' he thought. 'Look! Look! This is my night. I am the greatest director in the world and yet I have the grace to pretend I'm just an ordinary guy.'

'Why, he's just an ordinary guy,' thought the crowd and the cheering redoubled. Except, of course, for the pickets. They did not cheer – well, why would they? As far as they were concerned, Bruce had murdered their children.

Their banners said, 'MAD (Mothers Against Death)'. It was extraordinary the lengths to which people would go to come up with a suitable acronym, the tortuous linguistic paths they were prepared to navigate in order to arrive at something they imagined sounded neat.

Ben Elton

These mothers weren't against death, they were against violence and murder. But that would have spelt MAVAM which was not neat, so they had had to become Mothers Against Death (by violence and murder), or MAD. Bruce knew some of them by sight. They had been with him for months, these mothers whose sons and daughters he was supposed to have killed.

'Hollywood glorifies murder', said their placards. 'Bring back family entertainment'.

'Like incest,' Bruce thought, but fortunately he did not say it. Even cool mavericks in pointy-toed boots had to recognise the limits.

'Mr Delamitri,' shouted one of the MAD mothers, 'my son was murdered. An innocent boy, gunned down on the streets. In your last picture there were seventeen murders.'

'Yeah, and there was plenty of sex in my movie too, but I bet *you* haven't had any for a while.' Again he thought it but didn't say it.

These people were beyond rational argument. Bruce turned away from them and waved at the rest of the crowd.

'Where's the old lady?' one tasteless wag shouted.

Funny how some people seem to think it's perfectly all right to be rude to the rich and famous, as if having a lot of money meant that breaking up with your wife was not a painful experience. Bruce had not got married in public, and he certainly wasn't getting divorced in public, but the whole messy business was none the less public property.

'Where are your manners, you pathetic little no-life?' was what Bruce wanted to reply, but he didn't, of course. He merely smiled a 'what can I tell ya?' sort of smile and for this small capitulation he was rewarded with a thumbs up from his interrogator and another ragged cheer.

The mirror Bruce held up was a two-way thing. Occasionally he caught his own reflection in it. He wanted that crowd to love him, to appreciate him. So he smiled and waved and in their faces were reflected his weakness and his dishonesty.

It began to rain. A summer storm was coming in. Bruce hurried up the red carpet and into the theatre. He was wearing the genuine original tux that had been worn by Bogart in *Casablanca*, but it was only borrowed and he didn't want it to get wet.

North of LA the storm had already broken. The highway shone like black patent leather, the lights of the traffic shimmering on its surface.

Inside the 1957 Chevrolet the young man and the even younger woman peered out at the road as the ancient wiper blades struggled with the downpour.

'Ya gotta sacrifice comfort for style,' the man had said, explaining his choice of which car to steal. 'Even broke down and with its engine up on blocks, this car is a better car than every heap of foreign tin between here and Los Angeles.'

'Leastways the radio works,' the girl said, and found a hard-rock station. Personally, she liked her music a little softer and sweeter, but she knew his tastes. Besides, what she liked to hear was the news. She liked being famous.

'Latter day desperadoes . . . Bonnie and Clyde for the millennium . . . a Mexican chambermaid found dead in a chalet room, clutching clean towels and soap . . .' The girl thought how strange it had been, watching movies all that time with the dead maid lying there in front of the TV.

'. . . motel short-order cook shot fourteen times . . .'

She should never have told him about that guy flirting. She'd known what would happen and it had.

The radio moved on to showbiz news.

'. . . live from outside the Oscars . . . I see Bruce Delamitri acknowledging the crowd.'

'Way to go,' murmured the man as he peered into the rain. 'You make sure you win, now, Bruce. Just you make damn sure you win.'

Chapter Nine

'Bruce Delamitri! Yeah, way to go! All *right*!' the impossibly cute blonde model-turned-actress almost shouted, making the most of her last syllable in the spotlight.

On the whole the people brought on to do the presenting at awards ceremonies are divided into two groups, the big names and the small. The big names are those who have been nominated for an award themselves and have been persuaded to muck in elsewhere during the evening to help things swing. They do not want to do this of course, since it considerably lessens a star's impact when they finally appear themselves as a recipient if they have only recently been welcomed on stage to give some nobody or other the gong for 'Best Foreign-Language Lyric'. Nevertheless, big stars often agree to do the required chore because they are unable to avoid the tiny, unworthy suspicion that a refusal might somehow affect their own chances. Traditionally, big names who have not been nominated refuse requests to present. They are happy to turn up, of course, and sit in the stalls observing proceedings with a bemused tolerance, but they are not prepared to play John the Baptist to some hated rival's Messiah. Which means that the organisers of these events are forced to fall back on the second group: small names, people who have been around for either a very short time or a very long time. The former are not yet famous enough to cause much excitement, and the latter are destined to provoke excitement only once more in their lives and that, paradoxically, will be when they die. It is these people who fill the gaps between the genuinely important names.

Bruce scored a not-yet-famous-enough.

It should not have been that way, of course. 'Best Director' is one of the jewels in the Academy's crown, and under normal circumstances one of the press-ganged biggies would have presented Bruce with his statuette. But Hollywood is a scared town. Nobody wants to be connected with any controversy, and with his placard-waving band of MAD camp followers Bruce was highly controversial. His presence on the list of nominees had been enough to cause all the glittering superstars originally approached to get headaches.

'Bruce Delamitri! Yeah, way to go! All *right*!'

Bruce leapt out his seat like an eager puppy at the sound of his name. He had intended to arch his eyebrows in surprise and then rise slowly and rather reluctantly. Instead it looked as if his backside was spring-loaded. Recovering slightly, but still grinning like a lunatic, he set off towards the podium. Behind him a tuxedoed extra slipped into his place; the Oscars ceremony is, when all is said and done, a television programme, and no seating gaps are allowed to mar the perfect picture.

The cute starlet beamed at Bruce as he approached

her. Held firmly in her grip and pressed hard against her impossibly, absurdly perfect body was the twelve-inch golden icon. If Bruce's mouth hadn't been so dry he would probably have dribbled. This felt *good*. All through the interminable earlier part of the proceedings his mind had been a jumble of possible things to say. He would speak out against the New Right and its creeping censorship, condemn the way hysterical outrage had replaced reasoned debate, call for freedom of speech, proclaim the sacred individuality of the artist in a democracy. Basically, just be a complete and utter hero.

In front of a billion people.

That was what he had been told: a billion people were watching. A *billion*. On the long walk up the aisle towards the beaming starlet, he tried to conjure up some kind of image of what that meant. He thought of all the faces outside the theatre, the ones staring into his limousine; he imagined the whole sky filled with those faces, a big sky, a desert sky, filled with gawping faces from one horizon to the other, all staring at him. He couldn't do it. It didn't mean anything. A hundred people, a billion people – either way it was a lot of people if they were all staring at you.

Now Bruce was on the stage, standing alone in a single spotlight, the Oscar in his hand.

Now was his chance. To tell it like it was. To rise above the sanctimonious emotional manipulation that had characterised the evening thus far. Like the 'Best Actor', who had won his award for playing a person with brain damage and who had actually carried a brain-damaged child on to the stage and presented her with his award. Or the 'Best Actress', who had won so many hearts by accepting her award dressed in a gown designed in the shape of an enormous Aids-awareness ribbon. Like the 'Best Supporting Actor', who had pointed out that Hollywood's duty was the 'inspirationalisation' of the world; and the 'Best Supporting Actress', who had made an emotional appeal from the podium for more understanding of everything. The endless list of thanks to Mom, Dad, 'my creative team', 'the many, many people whose dedicated work goes into enabling me to be me', God and America.

Now it was Bruce's turn. To tell it like it really was.

'I stand here on legs of fire.'

Legs of fire?

It just came out. Despite his best noble intentions to say what he really felt, the awesome scale of the event possessed him. The billion people in the mirror possessed him. Suddenly he was no longer his own man. He had become an automaton, an unwilling conduit for mawkish, sentimental drivel.

'I want to thank you. Each and every person in this room. Each and every person in this industry. You nourished me and helped me to touch the stars . . .'

What could he do? He could not rain on the parade. Nobody loves a griper, particularly if that griper is holding in his firm, manly grasp the one thing that everybody in the whole room covets the most. Look at Brando. He wasn't the only person who was sorry for the Indians or Native Americans or whatever they were called. Everybody felt bad about them, but bringing them up at the Oscars? It just looked smug and rude. Besides, the people who were outside protesting had lost loved ones. Nothing to do with him, of course, but nevertheless it ill behoved a man of his splendid achievement to piss on the bereaved from the Olympian heights of the Oscars ceremony.

'... You are the wind beneath my wings and I flap for you. God bless you all. God bless America. God bless the world as well. Thank you.'

The room erupted into rapturous applause. It was an ovation of relief. Bruce Delamitri had acted like a grown-up. When his name was announced, many people had wondered whether he would seize the opportunity to be rude and controversial. Bruce did, after all, represent the young, thrusting, cool, cynical Hollywood which simply did not *give* a fuck. It had been eminently possible – indeed probable – that he would seek unworthy notoriety by being unpleasant and abrasive. A few of the more timid souls feared he might even mention those dreadful pickets outside the theatre who were trying to spoil everybody's big night. But what a pleasant surprise. Bruce's speech had been a model of Oscars-night grace and good manners. Textbook stuff: sincere, self-effacing, patriotic and very, very moving.

Hollywood welcomed one of its own into the fold. Bruce walked from the podium and into the welcoming arms of the upper echelons of the entertainment establishment.

Back up the coastal highway, they were finally clearing away the bodies of the Mexican maid and the short-order chef, two people who had come into contact with a moral vacuum and who had paid the price. The State Troopers shook their heads. The detectives shook their heads.

'Jerry made me a steak only this morning,' said one Trooper as the trolley upon which Jerry's corpse lay was wheeled out into the parking lot. From the front Jerry had still looked like Jerry. He had taken any number of bullets, but modern high-velocity weapons make very neat entry wounds. Not so the exit wounds. Each bullet pushes an expanding cone of flesh in front of it on its journey through the body, and when it blasts its way out the damage is horrific. From the front Jerry was merely slightly perforated; from the back he was just so much pulp.

The maid had been strangled.

'Why'd they do that?' the Trooper wondered. 'I mean, why the fuck did those bastards have to do that? Weren't no call. No money nor nothing. So why'd they do that?'

Contrary to popular mythology, American police officers do not spend all day every day scraping corpses off walls and floors. Perhaps the Washington DC Homicide Department do, but not the average cop. Death is not uncommon in their job but it is not the norm either, and the two State Troopers weren't so familiar with murder as to be indifferent to it.

'Ain't no reason why,' one of the detectives answered. 'These kids are just doing it for kicks. Maybe they was high on drugs, listening to some damn Satanic heavy-metal music, or else maybe they just watched another movie.'

There were still a few news reporters left on the scene.

'So you definitely think this is another copycat killing, chief?' one said eagerly. 'It's got to be the Mall Murderers, hasn't it?'

'Well, this ain't no mall, is it? Although, hell, those psychotic bastards ain't particularly choosy where they perpetrate their mayhem. I don't know, you tell me. Maybe they was copying something they saw, maybe it was two other fuck-ups copying them.'

'A copycat copycat?' asked the reporter, scribbling furiously.

'I don't know. Maybe it's a copycat, copycat, copycat. All I know is that two innocent, ordinary Americans are dead.'

'And that's the point isn't it?' said the reporter, seizing on the detective's words like a dog with a bone. 'That's what this is, just one more ordinary story of *Ordinary Americans.*'

'Well, I don't know what you'd call ordinary,' the cop replied. 'I've been coming to this diner for over thirty years now and nobody ever got shot here before.'

But the reporter had stopped scribbling.

Chapter Ten

The Governor's Ball. *The* post-Oscars party. The glitter, the glamour, the *bosoms*! There were bosoms as far as the eye could see, a great soft undulating shelf of bosoms that stretched from one side of the vast ballroom to the other. If anything was going to snap Bruce out of the irrational but uneasy sense of failure that his speech had cast across his great triumph, it was the Bosom Ball.

He stood at the top of the stairs that led down to the dance-floor and wallowed in the glorious display. From his vantage-point he could admire the thousand or so best cleavages in Hollywood, which of course meant the best in the world. What an admirable thought! Laid out before him were the planet's two thousand top tits, creamy white, coffee-brown, sun-kissed olive, all rising and falling to the rhythm of the night. The best that Mother Nature could build, the best that money could buy. Heaving against the silk and lurex and velvet and rubber of a thousand million-dollar dresses. Bosom upon bosom upon bosom, struggling to escape the surly confines of the gowns that bound them. For the second time that day Bruce felt the sap rise within his Calvins. Was that an Oscar in his pocket or was he just extremely bloody pleased with himself? The winner! The man of the hour. The best director in town.

Intoxicated by the heady atmosphere of sex and success, Bruce forgot his private sense of failure. Everybody made awful speeches at the Oscars: it was a tradition.

Sure.

Absolutely.

In a way it was cool to be kitsch. Look at Elvis.

Right.

Buoyed up by this thought, Bruce waded into the sea of bosoms.

'Thank you, thank you very much,' he heard himself saying over and over again, struggling to address his remarks to faces not bosoms. Cleavage etiquette was something he had never been able to work out. Clearly, a woman who was presenting her tits like the centrepiece in some glorious bouquet would be saddened to think that nobody had noticed them. On the other hand, if you did stare appreciatively it looked a bit tacky. Bruce thought about putting on his shades, but decided against it. Instead he concentrated on being magnanimous in victory.

'Personally, I thought so and so should have got it,' he lied. Personally, he thought so and so's movie had been an over-sentimental piece of crap which nobody would have looked at twice if so and so hadn't been a woman. But he was trying to be nice.

'No, really, I think she deserved it more than I did.' Like hell.

'I'm just happy if someone goes to see my picture.'
Like double hell with mashed potatoes.

'Great to see you, pal.' Bruce pumped some handsome
star's hand fervently. 'I loved that cop thing you did. We
should meet. I'd like that. That would be fun.'

'Did you see the cop thing he did?' Bruce con-
fided to another firm-chinned wonder. 'Directed by
a moron, performed by a retard. I'm trying to be
nice here, but the guy has had a total talent trans-
plant.'

More bosoms. More congratulations. A couple of
drinks.

'I'm just glad for the cast, that's all. It's really their
movie . . . I just thought up the idea, raised the money,
wrote the script, cast it, directed it and told everybody
involved exactly what to do.'

More drinks. More bosoms. He was happy to address
them directly now.

'You are the wind beneath my wings and I flap for
you. God bless you all. God bless America. God bless
the world as well. Thank you.'

Bruce's voice wafted through the trees. The young
couple were lying on a blanket spread on the wet
ground. They had just made love in the warm but
drenching rain.

'Quiet, honey,' said the man, and he held his finger
to his lover's lips.

'Surely the most controversial Oscar choice in recent
times,' the radio said, 'particularly in the light of yet
another irrational murder thought to have been perpetrated by the notorious copycat killers known as the
Mall Murderers.'

The girl giggled with nervous excitement. 'Notorious!' she whispered into her boyfriend's ear.

'That's right, honey. No-fuckin'-torious.'

She lay back on the sopping rug and the rain splashed down on her fragile-looking body, forming shining beads on her white skin.

Notorious.

They laughed together at this reminder of their infamy. He ran his hand across her stomach and on to her breasts, collecting a ridge of water as he did so. Then they made love again, while the radio pumped twenty minutes of advert-free rock through the dripping trees. No chit-chat, no hard sell, just pure one hundred per cent heavy-duty rock cumminrightatcha!

'Well,' said the man, when they had finished for a second time, as he got up and pulled on his jeans, 'I guess the engine'll be cool by now. We'd best be moving on. We have some stuff to do.'

Bruce was drinking and he'd stopped trying to be nice.

Although he was something of a style junkie, the abstinence thing was one Hollywood fashion Bruce had never cottoned to. He was one of the new breed of 'Hey, I smoke – you gonna call the cops?' hard guys.

'I like to drink,' he would say. 'I like the taste and I like the packaging. It is an indisputable fact, aesthetically speaking, that a bottle of Jack or Jim on a dinner-table looks considerably more pleasing than a bottle of Évian. Trust me, I'm a movie director.'

Under normal circumstances Bruce was a happy drinker, not one of those sad Jekyll and Hyde characters who turn into social psychopaths with the third glass. But on this night, although (or perhaps because) it was supposed to be the biggest night of his life, the bourbon was not giving him that familiar warm glow.

It was all the people in his face.

His face was completely full of people – friends, admirers, job-seekers, gold-diggers – and yet suddenly, all he actually wanted was to be alone. He would have liked nothing more than to lean against a wall in solitary, half-drunk splendour, watch the bosoms and forget about himself. But he couldn't because people kept coming up and talking to him. Congratulations would have been fine, but they always wanted to justify their gushing praise with a conversation. Why couldn't they just tell him he was great and fuck off? Instead he had to be nice to them. He didn't want to be nice. He'd been nice on the podium, nice enough for a lifetime. That was enough nice; he was niced out. He should not be expected to spend the whole evening, *his* evening being nice.

'Thank you, that's kind, thank you. Well you know that's very kind.'

It couldn't go on for ever and it didn't.

'Look, I just made a movie. I didn't find the cure for cancer!' That shut them up.

'This Oscar means nothing,' he added grandly, warming to his theme.

'It's a tainted trinket.' . . . 'A statue without status.' . . . 'A bauble with no balls.' . . . Bruce loved that last one.

'Take a look at it.' He held up his Oscar, waving it about and pointing at the golden sword which coyly covered the relevant part of its anatomy. 'It's a bauble with no balls.'

People laughed – but nervously. You didn't come to the Governor's Ball and take the piss out of the Oscar statuette. It was like going to church and sneering at the cross. The Oscar was the most coveted glittering prize of them all, potent symbol of the greatest entertainment industry on earth. Cynicism was not only bad form, but utterly deceitful. Everybody knew that, balls or no balls, the Oscar was the ultimate goal and Bruce had wanted it like life itself. To grab it and then try to be smart after the event was appalling behaviour. Bruce knew this too, but he didn't care. Having failed to speak his mind in his speech, he was making up for lost time.

'Look, if a picture's good it does not require the approbation of a twelve-inch eunuch to legitimise it!'

It was the memory of the faces in the mirror pointing their accusing fingers at him. It was the dreadful, deluded MAD mothers with their sad stories of loved ones lost. It was Oliver and Dale and that smug little professor.

All of them lingered in the back of his mind, niggling away, trying to call him to account, to spoil his fun. Apparently it wasn't enough to make cool, slick, exciting movies that people got off on. No, he was also expected to try and second-guess some unknowable repercussions that his work might or might not have.

Absurd. Puerile.

Yet he'd had his chance to speak out and had said nothing. Worse, he'd made out that everything was fine. He felt such a hypocrite himself that he saw hypocrisy in everybody else. He couldn't bring himself to believe that any of the gushing praise people kept heaping upon him was sincere. Why should they be telling the truth? He hadn't. He'd cravenly failed to use the platform that the Oscars had given him to take on the censorship debate. To nail, publicly, all the dangerous, reactionary talk of copycat killings, protecting kids from themselves and whatever happened to Andy Hardy. He'd had the chance to take that famed twelve-inch golden statuette and shove it right up the collective ass of Professor Chambers, the Senate Committee on Taste and Decency, the Concerned Mothers of American Dimwits and every other God-bothering, mealy-mouthed, Moral Majority moron in the USA. He'd had the chance, but he'd blown it.

'Legs of fire', for Christ's sake!

'Give me another Jack Daniels.'

'Give me another Jack Daniels.'

The terrified storekeeper reached down a second bottle of whiskey and added it to the box of booze and provisions that stood on the counter. The scrawny girl watched proudly as the pathetic man leapt to do exactly what her boyfriend ordered. Her boyfriend had such natural authority and command. She loved that about him. She felt that, even without the Uzi machine-pistol with which he was threatening the storekeeper, his commands would still have been obeyed.

They were in the process of robbing the store of a small country caravan park, which they had stumbled across after leaving the main highway.

'There'll be road-blocks,' he'd said, swinging the big, saggy old car on to a gravel road, 'and we ain't gettin' caught till we're good and ready.'

'Ready to be saved?' she'd asked eagerly.

'That's right, baby, ready to be saved.'

She slid across the big bench seat and put her head on his shoulder. The vast redwoods slid past the windows, and for a while she indulged in the fantasy of staying in the forest for ever. The trees looked so thick and friendly in the Chevy's lights that she thought maybe they could build a secret cabin among them and live off berries and venison.

It was a delicious thought, and as she peered out through the wet windscreen and deep into the dark shadows she could almost see the two of them, standing in the doorway of their little fairy-tale home, he with an axe in his hand, she with a tray of fresh-baked fruit scones. All alone in the world.

When the caravan park hove into view it seemed to her that perhaps they had chanced upon a halfway point between fantasy and reality.

'Let's rent a trailer, baby,' she'd pleaded. 'We could stay a few days. I'll bet they haven't even heard of us out here.'

For a moment the trees and the night and the smell of the rain had tricked her into imagining that she lived in some other age, one when people still hid out in woods, when you could still run and hide. When a person could still start again.

'Honey, we ain't more'n fifteen miles from the Interstate. You think they don't have TV and a phone?' her boyfriend said. 'Besides, everybody in the whole United States has heard of us.'

'Well, couldn't we just stay one night? Y'know, like a holiday?'

'Tonight ain't jus' any ol' night, hon. Tonight is *the* night. Shit or bust. We'll just pick up some stuff and move on.'

So they had pulled in off the gravel road and forced the old storekeeper to open up his shop. They should have been out again in a couple of minutes. It should have been the simplest thing in the world. After all, they had turned over country stores a hundred times before.

But this time the robbery was going wrong. This time there was a problem.

The storekeeper had no Twinkies.

No Twinkies? Every store had Twinkies.

'I *want* some Twinkies,' the girl said, and she actually stamped her foot. 'You *said* I'd get some.'

'I know, I know, baby, but I can't just make 'em up outa dog food, can I?'

The sound of television commercials could be heard from the back room. The storekeeper had been watching TV when the robbery began.

'You're a modern girl. You know what you want and you want it now!'

'Don't take no for an answer.'

'Why wait, when you can have it all today?'

They could have been ads for anything. Even Twinkies.

'You get everything you want!' the girl shouted. 'Whiskey and pretzels and cigarettes and I don't even get no Twinkies!'

'I know that, honey, but what can I do? I'm sorry.'

'Don't shoot me, please.' The storekeeper could scarcely speak for fear.

'For me, freedom is about doing what I like to do when I like to do it' said the TV in the back room.

'What d'you say?' the young man asked the storekeeper.

'I . . . I said please don't shoot me . . . I just ran out yesterday. We're a small business. We can't carry no huge stock.'

'You think I'd shoot a guy for not having *Twinkies*?'

'I . . . I have Pop Tarts.'

'For Christ's sake, what kind of person do you think I am?' The young man was so offended that he shot the storekeeper anyway.

'C'mon, honey. We'll stop by a 7–11 when we hit LA.'

Chapter Eleven

There was a crowd of people round Bruce now, sensing scandal. Some kind of critic guy was in his face, a big noise, art editor on the LA *Times*, or maybe gardening editor, something he was pretty proud of anyway. Great Caesar's tits, the man was a pompous little pecker.

'I must say,' the pecker said, 'I found *Ordinary Americans* a wonderfully seductive piece of film entertainment.'

'Film entertainment'. What a phrase! Not 'work of art', not 'cultural benchmark', not 'celluloid reflection of the spirit of the age', but 'film entertainment'. As if Bruce made daytime soap or something.

Bruce did not consider himself conceited about his work. He was the first to admit that it was popcorn – but only if other popular and corny works like *Romeo and Juliet* and Beethoven's Fifth were popcorn too.

'And I will go to the wall,' the pecker continued, as Bruce's eyes glazed over, 'to defend your right to kill as many people as you like in your movies. The only question I ask is – that age-old bugbear – is it art?'

'Is it art?' said Bruce. 'Well, let me see now. That's a tricky one. Is shooting a whole bunch of people in a movie art? I think the best way I can answer that is to ask you not to be such a complete fucking jerk.' Not brilliant, perhaps, but it got the pecker to go away.

It brought Bruce no relief, though. One jerk was replaced by another. At least this time it was a lovely young actress. Lovely to look at, that is, not to listen to. She was a whiner, a spoilt brat. Her conversation had a banal self-assertiveness which was the result of rarely being contradicted, on account of the fact that she rarely spoke to anyone who wasn't trying to sleep with her. Bruce did not want to sleep with her and so listened to the young woman's conversation with a less indulgent ear than she was used to.

'No, actually, as a matter of fact I don't think I was emotionally abused as a child,' he said through gritted teeth. 'Well, I think I would know . . . Really? Is that so?'

According to the young woman, it was not necessarily the case at all that a person would be aware of having been emotionally abused. She herself had been blissfully ignorant of the appalling truth until it was uncovered via hypnotherapy.

'And what did he say to that?'

It was the following morning and the girl (whose name was Dove) was recounting the story of her party encounter with Bruce to Oliver and Dale on *Coffee Time USA*, the events of Oscars night having by that time turned anyone who had been with Bruce during the previous twenty-four hours into an important character witness and a sought-after celebrity. All across the air waves, hat-check girls and drinks waiters were offering their opinion on Bruce's state of mind during the five or six seconds they had spent with him 'one on one'.

'He said that I must be very relieved,' Dove replied, looking beautifully earnest and careworn.

'Hang on, let me get this straight here,' said Oliver, putting on his glasses. Oliver's glasses did not actually have any lenses, because if they had they would have reflected his autocue. Nevertheless he always kept them close by and put them on whenever he felt it necessary to make it clear that he was feeling deeply sympathetic and extremely concerned.

'Bruce Delamitri said you must be *relieved* to have uncovered hidden memories of emotional abuse?'

'Yes, he did.'

'How d'ya *like* that guy!'

'He said that it meant I was off the hook. That I could do what I liked – take drugs, sleep around, steal stuff, be a total loser – and none of it would be my fault because some hypnotherapist had granted me victim status. Can you believe somebody would say that? I cried all night.'

Dove twisted a handkerchief between her dainty fingers in anguish at this painful memory.

'Camera Four.' Deep within the control suite the editor issued his instructions. 'Extreme close-up on Dove's hands.'

Dale saw the shot cut up on her monitor and put her hand on top of Dove's.

'You're saying that Delamitri didn't believe your very real heartache was anything more than a ploy?'

'That's right. He asked me how much I'd paid my hypnotherapist and when I told him three thousand dollars he said it was peanuts.'

'Peanuts? Three thousand dollars?' said Oliver, who earned eight million a year. 'Well, I guess those Hollywood types never pretended to live down here in the real world with us ordinary folk, did they?'

'He said that a hundred thousand dollars would have been cheap. He said what price could you put on getting an excuse to screw up your life.'

'These guys just don't think the rules of common decency and good manners count for them, do they?'

'I guess not.'

'So what did you say?'

'I told him I had uncovered a deep and painful wound.'

'Way to go, Dove. Feisty stuff,' said Oliver. 'We'll be hearing more about Dove's deep and painful wound and millionaire Delamitri's cold indifference to her suffering after these messages.'

'Excess wind can blight your life,' said the sweet old lady standing in the park with her dogs.

'I have uncovered a deep and painful wound,' Dove said, attempting to fight her corner but making a pouty, sulky hash of it. She felt exposed and out of her depth. She did not really know how to handle men when they were not trying to sleep with her. Bruce just laughed. People were listening now but he didn't care. Having personally spouted bullshit to a billion people earlier in the evening, he was not going to put up with it from anyone else.

'Oh, I see,' he said. 'A deep and painful wound, but

not quite deep and painful enough for you to notice until you paid some guy thousands of dollars to point it out.'

'He didn't say that!' Dale said as Dove relived her terrible experience on the following morning.

'He did say it,' Dove protested. 'Everybody heard.'

'Let me get this straight here.' Oliver adjusted his glasses and peered at the imaginary notes he'd been making. 'He utterly denied the validity of the terrible emotional abuse you'd suffered? He accused you of making it up?'

'Yes, he did, Oliver.'

'Is that legal? I'm not sure that's even legal.' Oliver glanced about a bit. He liked to give the impression that behind the camera was a crack team of lawyers and researchers who would leap into action at the merest nod from the great man. In fact, behind the camera were a woman holding a powder brush and a woman holding a plastic cup full of water.

'So what did you do?' asked Dale. 'What did you say?'

'I said, "Mr Delamitri, just because you have made a lot of money exploiting the pain and suffering of others, that does not give you the right to exploit mine."'

'Way to go, girlfriend,' said Dale.

'Right on, sister,' said Oliver. 'We'll be back after this.'

'As a woman you have a right to firm, uplifted breasts, no matter what your age.'

Dove lied on *Coffee Time*. In reality she had not been so courageous. Actually she had just stood there, tears of confusion forming in her eyes, wondering why this man was being so *mean*.

'Anyway, what's a little pain?' Bruce said. 'I mean, what would you be without that pain?'

'Excuse me?' Dove sniffed.

'I'll tell you. You'd be the same pointless and self-indulgent idiot that God made you, but you wouldn't have anyone to blame it on.'

Dove was fighting back the tears now. What had gone wrong? People were supposed to cluck sympathetically when you told them about your emotional abuse, not emotionally abuse you.

'Take it easy, Bruce. You've had a couple.' An old friend of Bruce's tried to lead him away, having decided that both Bruce and the company that distributed his movies might regret this behaviour in the morning.

'And I shall tell you why I've had a couple,' Bruce answered triumphantly. 'Because I have an addictive personality, that's why. You know how I know? A court told me so. Oh yes it did, when I got busted for drink-driving. That was my plea. That's what I said. Not "I'm sorry your honour, I'm an irresponsible shit" but "I can't help it. I have an addictive personality". *I* drank the booze, *I* drove the car but it *wasn't my fault*! I had a problem you see and it saved me a prison term . . . Hey, Michael!'

A huge movie star was passing. He turned at Bruce's call, delighted to be hailed by someone of equal celebrity.

'Getting any at the moment?' Bruce enquired.

It was a cheap shot and it touched a nerve. The star had recently been exposed in the press as a serial adulterer. He turned away without further acknowledging Bruce.

'Addicted to sex,' Bruce explained to Dove. 'Did you read that? He said it to *Vanity Fair* after being caught in bed with various ladies to whom he was not married. He said he was addicted to sex. Not just a gutless, cheating little fuck-rat, you notice. No. A sex addict. He had a problem, so it was *not his fault.*'

A little crowd had gathered by now, which was a considerable relief to Dove. She was extremely pleased no longer to be the sole target of Bruce's anger.

'Nothing is anybody's fault. We don't do wrong, we have problems. We're victims, alcoholics, sexaholics. Do you know you can be a shopaholic? That's right. People aren't greedy any more, oh no. They're shopaholics, victims of commercialism. Victims! People don't fail any more. They experience negative success. We are building a culture of gutless, spineless, self-righteous, whining cry-babies who have an excuse for everything and take responsibility for nothing . . .'

'He mentioned shopaholics?' Oliver asked on the following morning. 'Do you think that possibly, in some weird, uncanny, unconscious way, he was connecting there with the Mall Murderers? After all, what are malls full of? Shops, right?'

'Right,' said Dove, but slightly hesitantly.

'And what are shops full of? Shopaholics!'

'And murderers,' Dale added helpfully.

'Exactly,' said Oliver. 'Maybe, in some weird, uncanny, unconscious way, Bruce Delamitri knew what was coming.'

'I am threatened by your attitude,' said Dove.

She could not have said a worse thing.

'Threatened? My God! So what? Who cares? I'm

crying here. We all feel threatened, babe. You should be threatened with a baseball bat sometime and get things into perspective. There was a time when if someone said something you didn't like you told them to shove it. Now you go to court and say you've been conversationally harassed.'

'Bruce, please.' His friend was still trying to calm him down, but Bruce wasn't talking to him, or to Dove. He was talking to Professor Chambers and Dale and Oliver and the MAD mothers and the two mad psychos who were out there somewhere, stealing his plots.

'Victims! Everyone is a fucking victim these days, and we've all got our victim-support groups. Blacks, whites, old, young, men, women, gays, straights. Everybody looking for an excuse to fail. Well, it'll kill us all, that's what it'll do. A society which defines its component groups by their weaknesses is going to die. We are losing more kids a year to violence than we did in the Vietnam war. But do we blame the violent people? No, we blame my fucking movies!'

'Go home, Bruce,' said his friend.

People were already drifting away. Dove had turned on her heel in disgust. His friend was right. It was Bruce's night but he'd spoilt it. He was bored and boring. He decided he should go.

Then he saw Brooke.

Through the glittering hordes, way, way out across the bosom shelf he saw her: Brooke Daniels. Coincidence or what? Synchronicity surely. Everybody has some special fantasy figure, a particular pop singer or actor that comes number one in the 'if you could have anyone for a night who would you have?' party game. Up until a couple of days before Bruce would probably have answered

Michelle Pfiefer in her Batwoman costume. Then he had happened to be glancing through a copy of *Playboy* magazine at his agent's office. Brooke had leapt instantly to the top of Bruce's league. And now here she was, in the flesh, looking even better without the creases and the staples.

'Excuse me,' he said to anybody who cared to hear it, and plunged into the crowd, pushing his way through to where the woman of some of his more recent dreams was talking to a small man in a hired tuxedo.

'Hi, pardon me for butting in but I won "Best Picture", so I can do what the hell I like.' All Bruce's angry petulance disappeared instantly and was replaced by his more familiar charm.

'Not at all, Mr Delamitri, and congratulations. I'm Brooke Daniels.' Brooke smiled, pulling back her shoulders the tiniest fraction in order to add further lift to her magnificent figure.

'I know who you are. I saw the *Playboy* spread – it was wonderful.'

'Thank you. I don't seem to be able to get away from that. I do acting too, you know.'

The little fellow in the borrowed tux shifted from one leg to the other, which was not a long journey.

Brooke remembered her manners. 'This is . . . I'm afraid I didn't catch your name.'

'Kevin.'

'Oh yes, of course, Kevin. This is Kevin. He's from Wales, in England. This is Bruce Delamitri, Kevin.'

'I know,' said Kevin. 'I saw *Ordinary Americans*. Bloody hell, I'm glad I didn't take my gran.'

There didn't seem to be an obvious answer to this, so Bruce didn't offer one. Brooke hastened to fill the silence that followed, feeling for some reason that the responsibilities of playing hostess lay with her.

'Kevin's a winner too, Bruce. "Best Foreign Animated Short". It's about a boy called Midget –'

'Widget,' Kevin corrected her.

'Yes, that's right,' said Brooke. 'And he has a pair of magic Y-fronts. What are Y-fronts, Kevin?'

'Underpants. They're called Y-fronts because they have an inverted Y on the front, which provides an orifice through which a bloke can poke his old fella.' Kevin hoped she'd find his British bluntness charming.

'Oh, I see.' It didn't look as if she did.

Bruce decided it was time to get rid of the Welshman. 'Wait a minute, you mean *you're* Kevin?' he said, light apparently suddenly dawning. 'The guy that makes the animated shorts? Jesus, are you a lucky guy! Sharon Stone is looking for you . . . Yes, that's right, she wants to talk about your Widget . . . No I'm not kidding . . . I don't know, maybe she likes Welsh guys, but she told me that when she saw your movie it made her nipples hard . . . That is what she said, word for word: it made her nipples hard . . . You'd better go talk to her.'

In a pub back home Kevin might have spotted that he was the victim of a less than elaborate hoax, but at the Governor's party? Talking to Bruce Delamitri? He *had* just won an Oscar, after all, so surely anything was possible, even the notion that the work of the Welsh Cartoon Collective (in association with the Arts Council of Great Britain, Channel Four Wales and some high street bank's Youth Initiative) could make Sharon Stone's nipples go hard. He thanked Bruce for the tip and scurried off.

'That was a little cruel, wasn't it?' Brooke enquired.

'No way. How many guys get to spend five minutes of their life believing Sharon Stone is interested in them?'

Bruce felt much better already. 'Great dress,' he volunteered, and of course what he meant was great body, the dress, such as it was, being merely what might be called garnish, or figure-dressing.

'Thanks. Bold, I'll admit, but it's tough to make an impact these days. Did you see the Baywatch Babes make an entrance? It was like silicone valley in earthquake season. It's getting so that the only women who get noticed are the tattooed lesbians from New Zealand.'

A little later they danced. It caused quite a stir, Bruce being nearly at the end of a very public divorce.

'Can I say something embarrassing?' Brooke asked.

'Sure.' Bruce hoped desperately she wasn't going to comment on the fact that he had been pushing his erection against her stomach for the past five minutes.

'I didn't see your picture. The one you got the Oscar for, *Ordinary Americans*.'

For some reason Bruce was pleased. 'That's OK, I don't insist. It's probably just as well, anyway. Maybe you'd have gone out and shot up a shopping mall.'

For a moment the bitter memory of his speech intruded on Bruce's burgeoning seduction. He forced such unhappy thoughts from his mind and concentrated on the extraordinary body he held in his arms.

For her own part, Brooke seemed to feel that some apology was called for. 'I can't imagine how I didn't get to see it.'

'Well, I guess you just never visited a movie theatre when it was playing . . .'

They danced for a moment in silence. Bruce had a thought. It was so long since he'd asked a girl to leave a party with him he'd been wondering how to broach the subject. Now Brooke had offered him the perfect opening.

'Maybe you'd like to see it now?'

'Now?'

'Sure. I have a print at the studio. We could grab some beers and dumb bits of cracker with blobs of caviare on them and go watch it on my editing machine.'

'My God, I've had guys ask me to the movies before, but this is the first time the guy with the Oscar offered me a private view. Quite a date.'

'So you'll come?'

'No, I have netball practice. Of course I'll come, for Christ's sake.'

'Great. I think you'll like the picture. One word of warning though: it does contain scenes of graphic violence.'

Chapter Twelve

INTERIOR. NIGHT. A 7–11 STORE.

A robbery is in progress. Terrified customers and staff lie on the floor with their hands on their heads. Standing over them are WAYNE and SCOUT, poor white trash murdering hoods on a killing spree. They are both heavily armed. Wayne is in his early twenties. He wears work boots, jeans and a torn vest, and has tattoos on his muscular arms. Scout is a waif-like girl in her late teens. She has on pink Doc Martens boots and a girlish little cotton summer dress. Clearly, there has already been a terrible incident: there is money scattered about everywhere, and two or three dead or dying people lie among the cowering customers. Wayne and Scout are both hysterically elated. He grips her to him.

WAYNE
(SHOUTS WILDLY)

I love you, sugar pie!

SCOUT

I love you too, honey.

They embrace. A customer, a fat man lying face-down on the floor, still holding a half-eaten hamburger near his mouth, steals a glance at Wayne and Scout. Wayne is chewing on Scout's ear. Close-up on Wayne's face as he turns away from Scout's head to notice that the fat man is looking at him.

WAYNE
You like to watch, fat boy?

The terrified man says nothing. His answer is to bury his face in the floor as hard as he can and wrap his arms around his head. Wayne's POV is now just the top of the man's balding head with his pudgy hand pressed against it, holding the half-chewed burger. There is a loud bang and a hole appears in the top of the bald head. Blood runs out as if from a tap, not a spurt but a silent, almost gentle, welling-up, a small flood, so to speak, which quickly forms a large pool, soaking into the hamburger and turning it completely red.

Cut back to Wayne, who is ignoring his victim completely, and is grinding his hips against Scout.

WAYNE
Oh Sweet Jesus! Killing makes me horny! I'm going
to screw you till your teeth rattle, baby.

Wayne's strong hands clutch at Scout's buttocks. It is almost as if his fingers will push through the flimsy cotton.

Cut to close-up of the dead fat man's hand gripping the blood-soaked burger. (NOTE: The impression should be that the burger and Scout's backside are just two different pieces of meat to be devoured by men.)

Cut back to full-length two shot of Wayne and Scout entwined in lust. Rock music is pumping in their heads and they seem almost to be dancing to it. If they are, it is a primitive, sexual dance, the dance of two wild animals caught between the two great life forces, survival and sex.

WAYNE

C'mon, sugar.

Wayne pulls Scout's dress up round her waist, revealing her panties, which are decorated with little hearts or cute cartoon characters. Despite her obvious sexual passion, Scout remains coy and childlike.

SCOUT

We are in a store, Wayne, a public place! We cain't do no lovin' right here now. There are people. They might see.

WAYNE

No problem, baby doll.

Wayne releases Scout and turns his machine-gun on the prostrate forms. They jolt like puppets as the bullets thud into them. Screams fill the air.

We cut to a series of close-ups.

A mother hugging a child hugging a doll, all suddenly riddled with bullets.

A businessman weeping as he dies.

A poster featuring a happy family shopping and saying, 'If you have a problem please ask our staff if they can help.'

A very wide shot of the whole store, a scene of bloody carnage with Wayne in the middle of it all, triumphantly spraying bullets. The muscles and veins on his brawny arms are taut with the tension of controlling the spitting machine-gun.

Close-up of Scout. She is staring at Wayne, transfixed with adoration. The shooting finally subsides.

WAYNE

Ain't no people now, cotton candy, leastways not any going to get offended none.

SCOUT
Oh Wayne, I surely do love you.

Scout embraces Wayne. One slender, coltish leg, fragile-looking and vulnerable despite the big boots she wears, winds about him as she reaches up an arm to draw Wayne's face to hers.

Chapter Thirteen

INTERIOR. NIGHT. THE LIVING AREA OF A RICH CALIFORNIAN HOME.

A beautiful but rather impersonal interior of vast white couches, glass and steel tables and shelves. Clearly whoever lives here had the place designed for them. Wayne and Scout stand in the middle of the room. Their cheap, dirty, blood-stained clothes are in stark contrast to the cold pastel colours that surround them. They are hot and high with excitement. They have recently broken in and Scout is staring in wonder at this opulence. They both carry machine-guns and have more weapons hanging from them.
Cut from the wide to a mid two shot as Wayne kisses Scout tenderly on the forehead.

WAYNE
(Sudden exuberant shout)
Ain't nothing like killing, Scout. I done it all in my time, stock cars, broncos, gambling, stealing and I am here to tell you that there ain't nothing to touch the thrill of killing.

Close-up on Scout. Her eyes are closed; she is drinking in the
atmosphere.

SCOUT
Don't shout, Wayne. I was just enjoying the peace.
Isn't it a beautiful home? Don't you just love the silk
cushions and glass coffee tables and all?

Scout kicks off her shoes and walks about.
Close-up of her feet luxuriating in the thick carpet and rugs.
Pan up her legs. Her hands are against her thighs, playing nervously
with her dress. She absently pulls the skirt up a little. We see bruising
on her thigh.
Two shot. Wayne and Scout.

WAYNE
You know why they have those glass coffee tables,
precious? You want to know why they have them?

SCOUT
So's they can put their coffee down, Wayne.

WAYNE
No it ain't, baby. It's so they can get underneath and
watch each other take a dump.

Close-up on Scout, her jaw dropping in astonishment.

WAYNE
Yes it is, honey. I read that. It sure is.

Wide shot of room. Wayne has thrown himself on to a vast couch,
his big booted feet up on the table under discussion. His comments
have completely deflated Scout. She is very volatile; tears show in
her eyes.

SCOUT

That is not so, Wayne! It is just not so and I do not want to hear about it. Just when everything is nice, you have to start on about people going to the bathroom on their coffee tables.

WAYNE

That's the real world, honey. It's weird. People are weird – they ain't all nice like you and me. Aw c'mon, sugar, don't feel bad. I feel good. Do you feel good, baby doll?

Scout's moods change with alarming speed.

SCOUT

Yeah, I feel good, Wayne.

WAYNE

I always feel good after I kill a whole bunch of muthas. It's like a pick me up, you know. They should make a commercial ... like for Alka Seltzer.

Close-up on Wayne.

WAYNE

Feeling low? Dull? Shitty? Don't waste a minute. Burn some muthafucka's ass. You'll feel great.

Pull out to two shot. Wayne is laughing at his fantasy.

WAYNE

You know what Dr Kissinger said, baby?

SCOUT

You didn't tell me you'd seen no doctor, honey.

Scout flops down beside Wayne on the couch. Her dress rides up; again we see the bruising, this time from Wayne's POV. He cannot avoid seeing it. Embarrassed, Scout quickly pulls her skirt over it.

> WAYNE
>
> He wasn't no real doctor, he was the Secretary of State. A powerful man, killed a whole lot more people than we ever will, no matter how hard we try. Well, you know what he said? He said that power was an aphrodisiac, which means it gets you horny.

> SCOUT
>
> I know what an aphrodisiac is, honey.

> WAYNE
>
> Well, you ain't never gonna get more power over a person than when you kill them, so I guess killing is an aphrodisiac too.

> SCOUT
>
> I guess so, honey.

A joke occurs to Wayne. He sits up in excitement, which means he has to move the gun on his lap. Moving it makes a harsh metallic sound.

> WAYNE
>
> And get this, baby doll ... if you kill a black guy, it's an Afro-American-disiac!

Wayne falls back, laughing, into the thick cushions. He makes himself more comfortable on the couch.

                              SCOUT
I don't know what you're talking about, honey, but
you keep your dirty boots off that couch and be
careful of all that blood on your pants. This is a nice
house and I'll bet the people who own it are real
nice people and we don't want to get no blood on
their couch.

                              WAYNE
The blood is dry, pussycat. Blood dries real quick
on account of it congeals. You know what, honey?
If your blood didn't congeal you could die from just
one little pinprick.

                              SCOUT
I know that, Wayne.

                              WAYNE
And you would be what is known as a homophobic.

                              SCOUT
Honey, a homophobic is a person who does not
approve of carnal knowledge between a man and
a person of the same sex. I believe you're thinking
of a haemophiliac.

Sharp zoom in to close-up on Wayne. His change of expression is
as fast as the camera movement. His face has turned from happy to
sullen and sinister. Scout knows the signs.
Close-up on Scout, she attempts a casual smile.
Close-up on her hand, which is shaking.
Two shot.

                              WAYNE
                    (With ill-concealed menace)
         Is that so?

SCOUT
(A pitiable attempt to be casual)
Yes, honey, it is.

WAYNE
Is that so?

SCOUT
(Shaking now)
I believe it is, honey.

In a sudden lunge Wayne grabs Scout by the neck with one hand and, dropping the gun, pulls back his other hand, clenched into a fist and ready to strike.

WAYNE
And what d'you call a woman whose mouth is too
damn smart, huh? A woman with a busted fucking
lip, that's what.

Wayne pushes Scout off the couch and on to the floor. She screams.

SCOUT
No! Please, Wayne, don't!

Wayne drops off the couch on to Scout, straddling her on his knees. Again he grabs her neck, ready to strike. Close-up on his fingers digging into her neck.
Pan up from Wayne's fingers on Scout's neck to close-up on her face, mouth gasping for air, eyes making a terrified mute appeal.
Scout's POV of Wayne's face directly above her, staring down, face contorted with fury.

WAYNE

You think I'm dumb, sugar? Is that it? Maybe we'd better see if your blood congeals!

Scout screams in terror.
Two shot. Wayne sits across Scout. It seems that he will beat her. Instead he kisses her passionately. After a moment Scout returns the kiss and embraces him.

SCOUT

Oh honey, you scared me.

WAYNE

I know that, cotton candy. I love to scare you, because you're just like a little bird when you're scared.

Now it becomes sexual. Wayne stretches out on top of Scout and begins to kiss his way down her body.

WAYNE
(Through his kisses)
You like to live in a house like this, cotton candy?

SCOUT

Oh yeah, sure. Like I'm ever going to get the chance.

WAYNE

We're living in it now, ain't we honey? I'll bet they've got a real big old bed up them stairs. Stairway to heaven.

Wayne is beginning to undo Scout's dress.

WAYNE

How about it, cherry pie? How about we go upstairs
and make some noise?

Scout pulls herself away and sits up.

SCOUT

I ain't doing no stuff in no stranger's bed, Wayne ...
Could be we'd catch Aids or something.

WAYNE

You can't catch Aids offa no sheets.

SCOUT

If they're dirty sheets, if they're stained.

WAYNE

Honey plum, these people are millionaires, billion-
aires even. They ain't going to have no stained sheets.
Besides which, even if they did you couldn't catch no
Aids offa them 'less you put them in the liquidiser
and injected them directly into your body! Now
I bet these people have satin and silk, and I do
not often get the chance to fuck my little girl on
satin and silk.

SCOUT

We do not ...
                    (She spells it out)
... F–U–C–K, we make love, and I don't care if
you're coming at me from behind in the restroom
of a greasy spoon, it's still making love and if it ain't
making love we ain't doing it no more because I do
not fuck.

Wayne nuzzles up to Scout. Close two shot.

WAYNE

You're right, honey, I stand corrected. And right now
I'm just about bustin' to make love your brains out.
So come on, honey.

Wayne draws Scout to him. Her resistance is weakening. His lips are
now at her ear. Close two shot.

WAYNE

Let's have us a party. I'll bet they've got a water
bed and a mirror on the ceiling and everything ...
You know something, baby girl? When I get a hold
of your ass, I guess I wouldn't let go of it to pick up
a hundred-dollar bill and a case of cold beer.

SCOUT

Oh Wayne, you know I can't resist your sweet-
talking.

WAYNE

Well, you don't have to, honey.

Wide shot. Wayne gets up and slings the various weapons over his
shoulder. Then he gathers Scout up in his arms. We linger briefly on the
tension in his impressive muscles. He carries her out of the room.

Chapter Fourteen

The first thing that struck Brooke as Bruce ushered her into the lounge of his fabulous Hollywood home was how designed it looked. It was beautiful but completely impersonal with its vast white couches, glass and steel tables and shelves sparsely decorated with extremely costly *objets d'art*. Like an enormous and incredibly expensive hotel. Brooke loved it.

The truth was that in the previous three or four years Bruce's workload had been so high and his ascendance so meteoric that he had had no time at all to arrange his personal life. He still owned his old apartment off Melrose Avenue, and in it were all his old framed movie posters and stuff like his *Star Wars* space gun. But it was just gathering dust. Perhaps one day he would move it all and re-personalize his world, but for the time being he was happy simply to decide upon a price and purchase a lifestyle appropriate to his rising status. Farrah, his nearly ex-wife, who had previously provided Bruce with the semblance of a private life, had long since tired of being married to a workaholic movie nut. She had retreated from his world, taking most of their stuff (which was hers anyway) and their daughter with him.

Bruce had never been very interested in personal lifestyle. Even as a student he had been famous for owning only one pair of jeans and one saucepan. He had always put all his huge creative energies into his work. There was none to spare for picking out cushion covers or visiting kitchenware shops. All Bruce required from a home was somewhere to wash and sleep. Of course, the more luxurious it was the better, and with his current abode he had pretty much reached the pinnacle of luxury. As far as he was concerned, he would be happy to stay exactly where he was for ever.

He was not going to get the chance.

The first thing he should have noticed as he followed Brooke into the room was a pair of pink Doc Martens boots lying on the carpet, boots that had not been there when he had left the house that morning. He should have spotted them instantly; there should have been a fast zoom to a close-up on the boots, and a sinister musical sting to inform him that things were terribly and dangerously amiss. But there was no sting and no close-up. Bruce scarcely registered the boots and remained oblivious of the fact that their presence indicated he was in very big trouble.

In the brief moment of thought he gave them, he imagined that they must be the property of his fourteen-year-old daughter, left under a couch on some past visit and only now dislodged by the cleaner. He kicked them back out of sight. The last thing a man wants in mid-seduction is to be reminded that the object of his lust is only a few years older than his own child.

Mid-seduction? Hardly. He hadn't even started yet and the sun was already up. He would have to get a move on.

A boyish grin, a nervous half-smile.

Extreme close-up on girl's lips.

Lips part slightly, revealing white teeth teased by tip of tongue.

Fuck music plays. Bang, they are at it like rabbits on E.

Not quite. Even Oscar-winning directors can't edit reality. The dull pre-sex preamble had to be gone through, and there was not a great deal of time to do it in. It was Bruce's own fault that they were so late. It was he who had suggested that they watch *Ordinary Americans*, a two-hour picture, and they had sat through the whole thing.

It had been worth it, though, there was no doubt about that, a real ego buzz. There is nothing quite like having a gorgeous girl gasp at your masterpiece. Brooke had loved his film, or at least she had professed to – and done so with sufficient conviction to satisfy Bruce. It had been a very curious sensation, sitting beside this girl, all wound up to make a move on her but not wanting to disturb her enjoyment of his great work. Which would be more exciting, hearing her gasp at his powers as a director or at his powers as a lover? Every time he had got himself ready to chance brushing a gentle kiss along her delectable bare shoulders, those same shoulders shook with mirth at one of the many dazzlingly witty ironic juxtapositions of image and dialogue with which the movie was peppered. Every time he was ready to slide an arm round her or 'accidentally' lay his hand on top of hers, the movie arrived at another of his favourite bits and he had to stop to let her concentrate.

Bruce had lots of favourite bits and vanity had been stronger than desire. He had let her watch the whole movie unmolested. Hence the lateness of the hour, the coldness of the approaching dawn and the fact that he was not even at the proverbial first base. He cursed himself for not having made a shorter film. He had always thought about cutting the discotheque sequence; after all seventies kitsch had been done and double-done. On the other hand, it was such a funny scene, the way the guy kept getting more and more stains on his white Travolta suit, first food, then wine, then puke and finally his own blood. Classic stuff. You couldn't cut it; it would have been a crime. Still, it had added eight minutes to the movie. Eight minutes in which he could have been making love to his favourite ever *Playboy* centrefold.

The movie had finally come to an end, however, and they were back at his home. It was time to make a move.

'It really is a wonderful picture,' Brooke said.

She had said it a hundred times already. She knew it and he knew it. The awkward pre-sex atmosphere had led them into one of those circular conversations in which nobody can think of anything to say and so instead they continually retread ground already covered.

'I can't believe you sat and watched the whole thing on an editing machine. That shows real dedication.' Bruce, too, had ploughed this furrow many times.

'Well, you know, like I say, it's such a wonderful movie,' Brooke said again.

'Well, I'm delighted you think so, but it still shows

real dedication to have watched the whole thing like that . . . and on an editing machine.'

Brooke simply could not bring herself to comment further on the wonderfulness of the movie. They lapsed into silence.

Bruce looked at his watch. 'Shit! It's nearly four a.m.' It wasn't meant to come out like that, but he hadn't realised it was quite so late. 'I thought it was about two thirty.'

'Is that a problem?' Brooke enquired. 'Did you have anything planned?'

'I'm afraid so. My wife will be here at nine.'

This was disappointing news. Brooke had not been one hundred per cent sure what she wanted when she accepted Bruce's invitation to come home, but meeting estranged spouses certainly wasn't it.

'I thought you said your divorce came through.'

It is true that Bruce had said this, in the car, as they left the Governor's party. It hadn't really been a lie. The whole world knew that he and his wife had parted irrevocably, and the thing really would be final in a day or two.

'We are, practically. That's why she's coming round – money stuff.'

Brooke shrugged. 'Oscar at night, alimony in the morning: life in the Hollywood fast lane.'

There was an uncomfortable pause. How could there not be? Two strangers already dealing with the difficult problems of whether to go to bed together and if so how to get to it, and now this. As chat-up lines go, 'My wife will be round in a couple of hours' is only one step from 'I am a regular drug-user and I always share needles'.

'Oh well . . .' said Brooke. 'It's been a lovely night.'

He had not even offered her a seat. They were both still standing, looking at each other across a vast couch.

'You really think so?' Weak, so weak. He had meant it to sound boyishly anxious, nervous and attractive, but it hadn't. How much better to have said, 'It could get lovelier' or 'Not as lovely as you' or even 'Never mind that, how about a fuck?' But no: 'You really think so?' Pathetic. For a moment Bruce recalled 'I stand here on legs of fire', and the erection that had been straining in his trousers for the previous three or four hours took a momentary dive.

Brooke was beginning to feel a little out of sorts herself. This big man, this Oscar-winning king of cool wearing pointy boots and Bogart's tux was just standing there. What did he expect? Was she supposed to offer herself unasked? Was it a power thing? Maybe he thought a bit of polite small-talk was beneath him. Maybe babes were expected just to climb aboard.

'Yes, I do think so. It's been a lovely night.'

This was absurd. She said something dumb, he said is that so? and she said yes, it was so. How long could they keep this up?

Brooke summoned up all her powers of imagination in an effort to advance the dialogue. 'Kind of like a first date. You know, we had a dance, we saw a movie . . .'

'That's a nice thought. It's been a long time since I had a first date.'

They were getting there.

'Me neither,' Brooke agreed, and then, after a tiny pause, she looked him in the eye and said, 'Brings back the old first-date question, doesn't it? How far do you go on them?' Well she couldn't do any more than that.

Not without actually taking off her clothes. Now it was up to him.

'So . . . What's the answer to that, then?'

She was annoyed. She certainly was not going to beg him to make a move on her. He had picked her up at the party, he had brought her to his home. He had to make some of the running, if only for form's sake.

'Well the rule in school was the boy gets a feel of the boobs but only from outside the bra.' Her voice showed traces of the irritation she felt. 'These days I tend to think the rule depends on the guy.'

She sat down. Bruce had still not offered her a seat but she sat anyway. Elegantly, beautifully, a vision. She crossed her legs and Bruce took a personal close-up on the slashed skirt of her dress falling either side of her knees.

'Nice table,' she said, studying her reflection in the shiny glass.

'I like it.'

'I can think of a good use for it,' said Brooke.

'Help yourself.'

She took some cocaine out of her bag and began to chop it up on the table. 'Just to keep you bright and cheery for your wife,' she said pointedly.

Belatedly Bruce recalled his duties as a host. He put on some music and fixed a couple of drinks. Now he was getting somewhere. He sat down beside her.

'It's so great that you liked my movie.'

Back on the damn movie. How the hell did that happen?

'It really means a lot to me.'

He said it quickly, trying to coat his boring platitude in a cloak of sincerity. It sounded *so* lame. After all, he'd only known this woman for four or five hours and here he was trying to suggest that they had some kind of intellectual bond. 'It really means a lot to me.' Oh yeah? Why? He'd just won an Oscar, the entire industry had come together to honour him, and here he was trying to tell a nude model he'd picked up at the party that her opinion was of particular significance to him. Of course, Brooke knew he was bullshitting, and he knew she knew.

'There was one thing I didn't like about your movie,' she said.

Bruce sighed to himself. He had provoked this gorgeous creature into feeling she had to justify herself intellectually. He'd told her that her opinions mattered to him and they both knew she'd had offered no opinion at all beyond 'neat movie'. Now she was obliged to think one up. He would have to sit through some desperate, second-hand, pseudo art-babble about derivative imagery, or some such thing, culled from the cover of last month's *Premiere*.

'Here it comes,' said Bruce trying to affect good-humoured indulgence. 'I knew your enthusiasm was too good to last. What's the beef?'

'I didn't like the sex scene.'

That surprised him. 'What are you, a nun? That was the sexiest scene I ever made. I edited it with a permanent erection.'

Brooke shrugged and took a sniff at one of the little white lines on the table. 'Sure it was sexy, sort of. But it wasn't true. Everything else in the movie was so real – the guns, the attitude, the blood all over everything, the guy's skull exploding when that big statue of Mickey Mouse fell on his head . . .'

'That's my favourite scene, by the way, because it's all about irony.'

Brooke handed Bruce the straw and he too took a sniff.

'So why couldn't the sex be real too?' she asked. 'The only place overacting is still encouraged is in sex scenes. Did you ever see *Nine and a Half Weeks*? Jesus, you only had to tap that woman on the shoulder and she had an orgasm. Why can't the sex be convincing? Convincing is sexy. Girls wear pantyhose, you know, not stockings. When they get laid they have to take off their tights. I never saw a girl take off pantyhose in a movie.'

'That, I'm afraid my dear, is because pantyhose is not sexy. It is impossible to remove pantyhose in a sexy manner.' Bruce rather regretted the 'my dear'. It was verging on rude and Brooke was, after all, his guest. But really! Trying to tell him how to make movie.

Brooke snorted up the last of the lines and stared at Bruce for a moment. He wondered if she was going to ask him to call a cab. Instead she got up off the couch, stood before him and, to his astonishment, began to dance. The music was sexy and the lights were low and she was dancing. In fact it was more an undulation than a dance, a kind of slow shiver that seemed to go up her body from her toes to her head and then slowly down again.

'Wow,' said Bruce.

The standard of his conversation was actually deteriorating, but Brooke no longer seemed to care. She was into her own agenda. Her hands were on her thighs now, slowly massaging the exquisite creamy material of her dress, her long fingers gently clawing at the cloth, ruffling it up against her legs before letting it fall back into place. Except it did not fall quite back because she retained a little of the dress beneath the palms of her hands, pressed as they were against the splendid outline of her thighs. Bruce realised that bit by bit, a centimetre or two at a time, Brooke was drawing up the long skirt of her dress, very slowly revealing her legs. And such legs. Bruce was entranced as shapely ankle gave way to shapely calf, then delightful knees and on, up past her equally exquisite thighs. It must have taken her more than five minutes to bring the skirt up to her panty line. Somehow she contrived to collect the folds of the material about her hips in a bouquet-like cluster, and it looked for a moment as if she was wearing a ra-ra skirt, or a rather flamboyant tutu. Then in one quick movement, almost a jerk, she brought the handfuls of cloth right up high, pulling the folds of skirt to just under her breasts, revealing all of her pantyhose and some of her bare midriff besides. Her hose was, of course, of finest quality. No ladders or frayed gussets here. High-waisted, covering Brooke's whole stomach (such as there was of it), ending a few inches below her ribs in a wide black, delicately embroidered waistband. Her whole lower body was now on show, from diaphragm, down past her navel to the shadowy half-hidden panties, her long legs and on down to the silver stilettos she wore. All encased in sheer black nylon splendour. Above all of which she held her dress in great silky folds. Not necessarily a very elegant pose, but undeniably sexy. The look on her face was slightly sullen, almost indifferent. Her legs were four-square, feet about nine inches apart. She seemed to be saying, 'This is what I've got. Do you want it?' A bad little girl showing you hers.

Now she had her thumbs under the waistband of her

hose and was pulling the material slightly away from her soft skin. Still contriving to hold up her dress, she began slowly, fold by fold, to wind her pantyhose downwards, not pulling, or tugging, but neatly peeling them floorwards, with elegant thumb and finger, one fold over another. The whiteness of her belly appeared first, followed by more black, the black of her panties, then white again as the very tops of her legs appeared, and then more perfect skin as the hose descended.

She stopped for a moment.

'Go on, please!' croaked Bruce. He couldn't remember the last time he'd seen anything so erotic.

Brooke raised one glorious limb and put her foot on the glass table. This caused the hose, which were now pulled down to a few inches below her crutch, to stretch out taut between her thighs, lending the tiniest suggestion of bondage and constraint to her sultry pose.

Her stiletto heel made a sharp tap on the table top. 'Unbuckle it,' she instructed Bruce. Her voice was cold and firm: it was an order. Bruce leant forward, his stomach pushing down on the top of his frankly spectacular erection, and did as he was bidden. The movement brought him so close to the partly revealed tops of Brooke's thighs, crowned as they were by the bouquet of her dress, that he wondered for a moment about kissing the exposed flesh. He resisted the urge. She was in control. She would tell him what to do. Brooke brought the unbuckled shoe back to the ground, and with equal balance and elegance raised her other leg.

'Again,' she snapped. Again he obeyed.

She kicked off her silver stilettos and stood for a moment on the rug, holding her dress and the folded top of her pantyhose before folding the latter a little bit further towards her knees. Her arms were now at full stretch, so she could lower her hose no further by this method.

She sat down. In one athletic movement, she lowered herself to the floor, simultaneously pulling her tights down to her knees. As her bottom touched the soft carpet she continued her movement, rolling over on to her back, and bringing her knees up to her chest. Keeping her thumbs in the band of the tights all the while, she released her dress, letting its folds fall back on to her and on to the floor around her. Her backside pointed straight at Bruce like the centre of a silk flower. For fully fifteen seconds she let him stare at the triangle of black panties that separated the flesh of her rear upper thighs from the flesh of the small of her back as it curled down into the folds of her dress on the carpet.

Then the endgame. Still lying on her back, and keeping her knees close to her chest, she rolled the tights down past her calves to her ankles and along her feet until they covered only her toes, which pointed seductively at Bruce above the eye magnet of her knicker-covered bottom. One final push on the tights and they fell down past her backside and lay crumpled on the carpet beneath the black triangle. In the same movement her long white legs shot upwards until they pointed straight and true towards the ceiling. Still lying on her back Brooke gently parted her legs to make a glorious upright V through which, by raising her head, she could see Bruce.

She smiled, lowered her legs and, picking up the tights, got to her feet. Her toes clenched at the luxury of the carpet. She took a step towards Bruce and dropped the still-warm hose into his lap.

'So?'

Bruce did his best to say something cool and classy. 'So I hope you don't expect me to be that good with my socks.'

It was certainly better than might have been expected on the basis of his previous form.

Bruce drew Brooke towards him on to the couch and they drifted into an embrace. Within moments all the pent-up sexual tension of the evening seemed to explode. Their mouths writhed against each other. Cool seduction was replaced by hot, lustful passion.

Then Brooke broke away. 'Let me get some protection.'

She reached down to her handbag and for a moment Bruce imagined himself in love. What a woman! He had just been wondering, himself, how to bring up the subject of protection, and here she was, all ready and prepared, doing it for him.

However, when her hand emerged from the chic little bag it was holding not a packet of condoms but a small hand gun.

Chapter Fifteen

'Touch me again you bastard, I swear I'll kill you.'

Bruce leapt away from Brooke as if she had pulled the trigger and it was a bullet rather than sheer shock that thrust him backwards against the arm of the couch.

She glared at him, he glared at the barrel of her gun. What the hell was going on? Had he transgressed some new pre-sex rule? Was he guilty of attempted date rape? He had heard of such things of course, horror stories of college boys who had attempted to follow a goodnight kiss with a hand up the jumper and the next morning had found themselves the subject of a poster hate campaign all over campus. But come on. The woman had just removed her pantyhose in front of him. That had to be an invitation, hadn't it? Maybe not. Oh Christ, maybe not. If a woman hoicks up her dress and flashes her knickers at you, does it mean 'yes' or 'perhaps' or even 'no'? Should he have waited for a formal invitation? Should he have asked her to state her sexual requirements, if any, clearly and concisely? Should he have got it in writing?

'Listen, Brooke . . . please, I'm sorry, but . . . but . . . what's going on?'

'You think just because I'm a model I'm some kind of whore?'

'No! My God no! Of course I don't. I . . . I . . . Look, if I've misunderstood the situation I'm very sorry. But really . . . I mean . . . I thought –'

'I know what you thought, prick-for-brains!' Brooke's trigger knuckle whitened. 'You looked at me and you saw sex, right? From the first fucking second we met I've been just a piece of meat as far as you're concerned. Well, you're going to pay, you bastard.'

She was mad, Bruce knew that. Not just angry or hysterical, not just perversely politicised in an aggressive and unpredictable manner, but stark raving *tonto*. Unbalanced like the global economy was unbalanced, or a seesaw competition between a mouse and an overweight elephant. She must be mad. It was the only explanation. Their whole evening had been one of mutual compliance, Bruce knew there was no way he could be accused of forcing the issue. He hadn't got her drunk or used his superior body weight to coerce her or done any of the other things that were apparently unacceptable to do to a woman unless you were a lesbian. No, this woman was crackers. A mad bitch of the 'seduction is just rape with champagne and chocolates' variety. But what do you do when a lunatic is pointing a gun at you? What do you say?

'Please, Brooke, please, this is not necessary.'

He was trying to turn his eyes into limpid pools of calm and compassion. It didn't seem to be working.

'Kiss my fucking feet, muthfukka!' she shouted. Screamed, in fact. Her voice cracked with forced volume so that the 'fucker' ended up a rasping squeak – which in no way diminished its furious power.

Kiss her feet? Bruce had to concentrate. Of course he must kiss her feet immediately, but how did she want them kissed? Hard? Soft? Should he take one gently in his hand and turn his lips into tiny butterflies fluttering all over them from toe to ankle? Should he prostrate himself before her and suck her toes like a hungry animal at its mother's teat? If he let his tongue explore between the digits, would that make her melt and lower the gun or would it add flames to her fury and cause her to lose what was left of her fragile self-control?

'I said kiss my fucking feet!' Brooke demanded again.

Bruce dropped to his knees without any particular plan of approach in mind and nuzzled vaguely at her toes.

'I said kiss 'em, not wipe your nose on them,' she barked.

He attempted to raise his game. He kissed her big toe, then her little toe, then he kissed them all in a row, one by one. What next? Back again? He kissed back down the row. Then maybe repeat the whole process on the other foot? He did that. Then he did the whole thing again.

That was it. He had kissed her toes. He was at a loss how to proceed. 'Would you like me to lick them?' he asked tentatively.

'Don't make me puke.'

Bruce's neck was beginning to ache. He went through his kissing routine again but after that he did nothing. What could he do? He listened to Brooke's breathing, trying to get a clue to her mood. Was it getting calmer?

Could she be reasoned with? Could he somehow win her confidence, her trust, ingratiate himself? He had to be very calm and kind. Flattering even.

'What do you want, you mad fucking bitch?'

It wasn't meant to come out that way. Fear had blocked up his brain. He cringed on the floor, waiting for the punishment which must be his.

'Are you scared?' he heard her say.

What a question. 'Yes, I'm scared.'

'How scared?'

'Very' – pause – 'fucking' – pause – 'scared.'

'Good' was all she replied.

Bruce's neck was really aching now. 'Look, Brooke, please tell me what you want.'

Brooke removed her foot from under Bruce's lips. He could sense her kneeling down in front of him. Her hand appeared under his chin and gently brought his head up until he could look her in the eye again. What now?

'I . . . want' – her eye was steady but he could feel her hand shaking under his chin – 'a . . . a part in your next movie.'

It took a moment to sink in. It wasn't until he took an extreme close-up on the nervous look in her eyes that he started to believe it.

'Put away your gun,' he said, by way of a tester.

Brooke put her gun back into her handbag. It was obvious that she really was nervous now: her hand was shaking.

Bruce was nearly speechless. Not quite, however. 'You mad, crazy fucking bitch!' he shouted.

It was Brooke's turn to be scared. Bruce's fury was only just beginning, but clearly when it erupted fully it would be mighty indeed. She had to talk fast.

'Your pictures make people horny and scared. What did I just do to you? Come on, be honest. I did it all in half an hour, first horny, then scared.'

'Pamela Anderson makes me horny, Pat Buchanan makes me scared. I'm not going to put either of them in my movie.' Bruce couldn't believe he was even bothering to debate with this outrageous woman. 'You made me kiss your feet! At gunpoint! I ought to call the cops!'

'I've sent you fifty letters. Fifty! Did you see them? Did you read them?'

'Have you any idea how many actresses and models write to me? I don't see any of that stuff. I have people.'

'Yeah, I guessed you didn't. That's why I decided to do what I did. I'm just a dumb model. Nobody would take me seriously as an actress.'

It dawned on Bruce that he had been playing patsy for the last five hours. 'Have you been planning this all along?'

'No. It occurred to me while we were watching *Ordinary Americans*. I had seen the film before by the way, five times, but I said I hadn't because I wanted to look cool.'

'Well you don't, you look fucking insane. I ought to throw you out.'

'I made you horny and I made you frightened. Be fair – I did. Give me a chance.'

Bruce looked at her, barefoot, scared, breasts heaving with the tension of her own audacity. It was true. She had made him horny, she was, after all, spectacularly attractive, and she sure had frightened him.

'Supposing I said it depended on your sleeping with me?'

'No,' Brooke replied. 'I don't screw on a professional basis.'

'Pity.'

Bruce was not a dishonourable man. Having made the pass, he knew he had in a way committed himself. Besides he didn't want to look cheap.

'OK, I'll give you a screen test anyway. Maybe you're half as good as you think you are. Have your agent call me next week. Believe me, there is no chance that I will forget you.'

'Thank you, Bruce, thank you very much. I promise I won't disappoint you.'

'You can't disappoint me any more than you already have. I'll call you a cab.'

'What's the rush? We still have some hours before your wife gets here.'

'But you said . . .'

'I said I didn't screw on a professional basis. I already got my screen test.'

Bruce wondered for a moment if it was another trick. You don't get over the kind of shock he'd had in a moment. If he embraced her, would he suddenly find himself with a knife at his throat? Brooke could see he was hesitating. She stepped forward, took his arms, folded them behind her and turned her face up towards his. Bruce hesitated no longer and within a moment they were welded together like an old steamboat. It was a great relief for both of them finally to reach the point towards which the whole evening had been heading. Bruce crushed his chest against hers, she crushed her thighs against his. Inevitably they lost their balance, but they didn't care because the huge couch was ready to take their fall.

Now their lovemaking could begin in earnest. Bruce was on top of Brooke, his hands kneading her breasts through the delicate fabric of her gown. He could feel her nipples hardening and slipped his fingers beneath the silk in order to tease them further. Brooke had one hand on Bruce's behind and one thrust down between their bodies, struggling at his fly zipper.

Close-up on Brooke's face.
Her expression changes from passionate lust to shock mixed with horror. (She is staring upwards, past Bruce's head, the back of which occupies the corner of the shot.)

BROOKE
(Struggling to maintain her calm)
Bruce ... Bruce ... For Christ's sake, Bruce.

Whip pan to take in Brooke's POV. Bruce's face is in the foreground of shot. Over his shoulder we can see Wayne standing behind him, an automatic weapon balanced casually on his shoulder. Bruce is unaware of Wayne.

BRUCE
Listen, Brooke, I really don't think I can handle any
more of your games. Are we going to make love
or do I call you a cab?

Bruce's head drops out of shot as he leans down to kiss Brooke's bosom. Wayne stands alone in the vacated shot which is Brooke's POV. He smiles and gives her a little wink.
Overhead three shot. Bruce on top of Brooke, Wayne standing over them both. Bruce is the only thing moving. Brooke is staring at Wayne, Wayne is looking back. Bruce's back and back of head writhe about a little as he nuzzles into Brooke's cleavage. Brooke finds her voice.

                    BROOKE
        Bruce. For Christ's sake. Behind you.

Bruce raises his head to address Brooke. Close-up on his face, chin
and cheeks, framed by Brooke's cleavage.

                    BRUCE
        Sure, honey, sure.

A voice intrudes upon his complacency. It is Wayne's.

                    WAYNE
        Morning, folks.

Chapter Sixteen

B ruce swung round and recoiled. In doing so he dug
an elbow into Brooke's stomach. She yelped in pain.
Despite the terror of the situation she could not help but
protest: 'Be careful, for Christ's sake.'

Bruce didn't apologise – he was too surprised, too
scared. He allowed himself a momentary crumb of hope.
'Brooke, do you know this guy? Is this part of your joke
thing?' But even as he said it, he knew that this was
no joke.

'I do not know this man, Bruce.' Brooke's voice
betrayed her status as his partner in terror.

Neither she nor Bruce could think of anything more to
say. The three of them just stared at each other. Wayne
brought the gun down from his shoulder so that it hung
casually from his hand, pointing towards the luxurious
rug. He had a pistol stuck in the waistband of his jeans
and another machine-gun slung across his back; he also
had a huge hunting knife at his belt. So heavily armed
was he that it would not have surprised a casual observer

to be told that he had a hand grenade clamped between his buttocks, a bazooka lodged behind his ear and the nuclear button hidden in the holdall he carried in his non-gun hand.

Wayne took a step towards the couch and, leaning over, stared hard at Bruce. He put his face right into Bruce's, drinking in every detail at extremely close quarters. Bruce held his ground, but he had never in his life felt so uncomfortable or so intimidated.

After what seemed like a whole minute (which it was), Wayne whistled slowly, as if unable to believe what he saw.

'I don't believe this. I do not be-fuckin'-lieve this! Sheeee-IT!' Wayne exclaimed, shouting the final expletive as he turned away from Bruce in his wonderment. 'I mean I knew it was the right house 'n' all on account of the scripts and stuff in your bathroom, but I still can't believe it . . . I am actually here, I am actually meeting Bruce Delamitri. Bruce Dela-fuckin'-mitri. The man! I am talking about the fuckin' MAN here!'

He dropped the holdall and shook Bruce's hand hard. Bruce was still sitting half on top of Brooke, so all three of them shook slightly with the force of it. 'I cannot tell you what a pleasure it is to meet you, sir. Scout!' Wayne shouted. 'C'mon in here and say Hi. Oh yes, this is a real thrill, sir. This is awesome. Scout, get your dumb ass in here right now! Don't make me come get you, now!'

Scout appeared nervously in the doorway. Her hair was tousled at the back from having just had sex, her cotton print dress gaped open a little at her breast from hurried dressing. Her bare toes were twitching again at the carpet, still unused as they were to such a luxurious sensation. There was a pistol at her hip, a huge pistol, a Magnum or something like that. It seemed to have been chosen deliberately to accentuate the smallness and birdlike, girlish quality of her body. Scout also carried a machine-gun, hanging from her hand as a little girl might hold a teddy bear. If she was trying to look like an innocent but sexy, childlike but womanly, vulnerable but dangerous, slightly imbalanced cutie pie, she was succeeding. If she wasn't trying, she was a natural.

She stared at Brooke and Bruce with what seemed to be something approaching awe. It was almost as if she was more scared of them than they were of her. This was naturally not the case, but that was how it looked. Her big eyes were sad and troubled, and there was a hesitant, almost ingratiating, smile on her lips. She wanted them to like her. She raised a hand and nervously tried to arrange her hair.

'Hi!' She giggled nervously, embarrassedly even, as if she knew she'd been naughty but hoped they were pleased to see her anyway.

Bruce and Brooke could only stare.

'C'mon in, hon. Join the party.' Wayne was as brash and confident as Scout seemed reserved. She stayed where she was, rubbing one bare foot nervously against the opposite calf.

'We messed up your sheets some,' she said, 'but you know, with modern detergents there shouldn't be any problem.'

Wayne did not feel that this was the right note to strike. You do not introduce yourself to your new hosts by owning up to having just stained their sheets. 'It don't matter about no sheets, sugar. We can buy more sheets. This is Bruce Delamitri. You are looking at the man here. *The* man.'

Wayne gestured flamboyantly towards Bruce. He seemed to mean it friendly enough, but since the hand with which he gestured was holding a gun it was something of an alarming movement nevertheless.

Seeing Bruce recoil in terror, Scout hastened to reassure him. 'Wayne's a real big fan of your pictures, Mr Delamitri. He saw you on *Coffee Time USA* with Oliver and Dale yesterday, and he's seen all your movies dozens of times . . . Me too, I like them for sure, but Wayne, he just loves them.'

'Hey, Scout, quit it. I'll bet Mr Delamitri gets real tired of people telling him all that stuff.'

A glimmer of something which, if not hope, was at least a positive and coherent thought crossed Bruce's mind. There was a great deal in Wayne and Scout's behaviour that Bruce recognised, that he had dealt with before. They were basically acting like a couple of fans, Scout shuffling her bare feet and casting shy sidelong glances at Brooke, while Wayne stood with his head held high in a 'Hey, I know you're famous but you're just a regular guy like me' pose. Bruce had met these couples a thousand times. The girl is all embarrassed, while the guy struts up to you and says, 'I guess you really hate being bothered,' and then proceeds to bother you. As if by 'being bothered' the guy means Bruce would hate to be bothered by schmucks and assholes, not by regular guys like himself. Bruce's work had always attracted these chippy, arrogant male fans, the sort of person who asks for an autograph and then says, 'You can have mine if you want,' adding with a sneer, 'Except you wouldn't want it, would you, because I'm not famous, I suppose.' As if Bruce had gone out and become a celebrity simply in order to score a cheap and easy point over a person who is clearly his equal if not a slightly better person than himself.

Oh yes, Bruce knew Wayne's tone of arrogant approbation; he had found the same thing in his face many times. What he was not used to was finding it heavily armed and having broken into his house.

'Do you want money?' Bruce found a voice of sorts. 'I have money, about two thousand dollars in cash, and there's some jewellery . . .'

Wayne raised one booted foot on to the coffee table and leant his weight upon his knee, bending towards Bruce, his boot crushing the residue of the white powder that Brooke had placed upon it. It would have made a good close-up for one of Bruce's ironic moments, symbolising virile, honest mayhem kicking aside pretentious decadence.

'Mr Delamitri . . . May I call you Bruce?'

Bruce nodded. He hoped the nod was firm and dignified, politely showing that he was following events closely and considering his options. In fact he nodded like a toy dog on the rear shelf of a family saloon, a panicky movement which suggested that Wayne could call Bruce anus-breath if he wished, so long as Wayne refrained from killing him.

'Bruce, we don't want no money. We got money, we got more money than we can spend, and we don't spend nothing anyway because we steal all our stuff. We just came around to visit with you. Is that OK? If we visit with you? How about we all sit down? Maybe we could have us a drink? Would that be OK? I like bourbon and Scout here'll take anything sweet.'

Wayne stepped back to the couch opposite the one on which Bruce and Brooke still sat, and collapsed casually on to it. Scout joined him, but with none of his showy confidence. She perched on the edge of the cushion, as if anxious to show that she did not wish to intrude or be the cause of any inconvenience. Bruce got up and went to his drinks cabinet, leaving Brooke alone on the couch. She had been half lying on it since being disturbed in mid-embrace, and she seized the opportunity to sit upright and adjust her clothing. Brooke, like Scout, was barefoot and Bruce had been on the point of liberating her bosom from her dress when they were interrupted. She put her shoes back on and did her best to cover herself up. A highly revealing evening dress is not the most comfortable garment in which to confront armed intruders.

There was an embarrassed pause. Nobody knew what to say. Socially the situation could not have been more difficult.

Scout turned to Brooke in an effort to make polite conversation. She felt, perhaps rightly, that though she was a guest, the burden of social responsibility lay at least partly with her. 'You're Brooke Daniels aren't you?'

It was like two people forced into conversation in a doctor's waiting-room. Brooke's face twitched in a reply of sorts; she was clearly in no mood for small-talk.

'Yes, you are,' Scout continued. 'I'd know you anytime from all the magazines you've been in . . . *Vogue* and *Esquire* and *Vanity Fair* . . . I love all that stuff, it's so glamorous and nice . . . I've been in a magazine too . . .'

'Sure, Scout, *America's Most Wanted*.' Wayne laughed and slapped Scout's thigh.

'It's a magazine! Isn't it Brooke? . . . Brooke? It's a magazine, isn't it? *America's Most Wanted* is a magazine, isn't it?'

'Yes, it's a magazine.' Brooke's throat was so dry she was surprised that the words came out.

'Of course it's a magazine, and I was in it and you said I looked cute, Wayne.'

'You always look cute, honey. Don't need no magazine to prove that.'

Bruce brought Wayne his bourbon. He had agonised over how much to pour. A lot? A little? Would Wayne be a violent drunk or a mellow one? If shitfaced, would Wayne start singing 'Danny Boy' and collapse, weeping, on Bruce's shoulder, swearing they would be buddies for ever? Or would he puke up on his boots and spray the room with bullets? Bruce had eventually opted for rather a short measure, which he had attempted to pad out with ice. Wayne knocked it back in one, but to Bruce's relief did not immediately ask for another.

'Hear what I said, Bruce? I said Scout here's cute enough for any damn magazine, and I'm right, ain't I?'

Bruce didn't answer, preferring to make another attempt to establish Wayne's agenda. 'Look ... if you don't want cash, I have a customised Lamborghini parked right outside and –'

'Bruce, I don't want your damn car.' Wayne's voice was calm but suddenly sinister. He addressed his reply to the ice in the bottom of his glass. 'Matter of fact, I got a car.'

'I see.'

'An American fuckin' car. Made in the motor city US-fuckin'-A, out of sweat and American steel' – Wayne's voice began to rise – 'not some fuckin' wop, faggot, greaseball-built pile of tin shit for queers! A Lamborghini! Bruce, I am surprised at you. When you drive a foreign car you are driving over American jobs.'

Bruce was silent. It did not seem the right time to discuss the relative merits of free trade and protectionism. He gave Scout her drink, thankful to have a diversion, even such a small one.

'This is *crème de menthe*,' he said. 'It's sweet.'

'I love cocktails.'

Bruce returned to the drinks cabinet and collected two small bourbons for himself and Brooke. He sat down beside her on the couch, sipping at his; she did not touch hers.

Again an uncomfortable silence descended. Having so completely misfired with his last attempt, Bruce was reluctant to have another go at establishing what these lunatics wanted. Brooke had nothing to contribute either. It fell once more to Wayne and Scout to keep the nervous, desultory conversation going.

'Why'd you do that *Playboy* spread, Brooke?' Wayne asked. 'I mean, I ain't saying it wasn't beautiful, because it was, but hell, I wouldn't never let Scout do a thing like that. I'd kill her first, and Hugh fuckin' Hefner too.'

'Oh, come on now, Wayne,' said Scout coyly. 'As if anyone would ever want to see me in *Playboy* magazine!'

She was clearly fishing for compliments. Bruce wondered about attempting to ingratiate himself by assuring her that she was certainly centrefold material. He was glad he didn't.

'Sure they would, honey,' Wayne said. 'Oh yes they would. Excepting I wouldn't let you do it, on account of the fact that my rule is that if a man even looks at you with lust in his eyes, I have to kill him. So if you was to be in *Playboy* I'd have to kill just about half the men in the United States.'

'You're getting there anyway, honey!' Wayne and Scout laughed at this.

Wayne turned to Bruce as if to explain some small private joke. 'Scout's exaggerating of course, Bruce. Why, I bet I haven't killed more than forty or fifty people.'

Again an embarrassed moment, as Scout's laughter died away into silence.

'So why'd you do it, Brooke?' Wayne returned to his theme. 'I'd really like to know.'

Brooke could only stare. It would have taken a less astute judge of character than she to have failed to notice that Wayne was unpredictable. She had noticed the traces of bruising on Scout's leg where Wayne's marauding hand had pulled away her thin cotton skirt a little. Brooke decided that the more desirable of two deeply undesirable choices was to say nothing. Scout spoke for her. She knew the answer; she had read it in a magazine.

'Brooke did it, Wayne, because being an in-control woman does not mean denying one's sensuality. Isn't that what you said, Brooke? I read that.'

Brooke nodded.

'She didn't do it for men, Wayne, no matter what you and your bar-room pals might think,' Scout scolded. 'She did it for herself because she is proud of her body and proud to be beautiful and there is nothing wrong or dirty in celebrating that. In fact, it's an assertive thing to do, a feminist thing to do.'

Scout finished her little speech and turned, smiling, to Brooke, clearly hoping to have won her approval.

'That's right, um . . . Scout, it's all those things.'

Wayne got up and helped himself to another drink. 'Well, I guess that makes me feel a whole lot better about jerking off in the john over it, Brooke. I must confess, I never realised I was doing such a fine and empowering thing.'

Scout looked as though she wanted to die with embarrassment. But before she could apologise to Brooke, Wayne pressed on. 'I want to ask Brooke something now, Scout, and I don't want you getting mad at me. OK?'

'Well, it depends on what you ask her, Wayne.'

'What I want to ask is how'd those girls in *Playboy* magazine get their hair the way they do? It always looks so damn perfect.'

Brooke managed to steady her voice. 'Well . . . you know, I guess it's just a question of styling really. They use a lot of mousse and they back-light it and sometimes they put in extensions . . .'

'Brooke, I do not mean that kind of hair.'

Scout's pale skin blushed a deep red. She could not believe what her boyfriend was asking – and them guests in someone else's house and all.

'Wayne!' She punched his ribs.

'Well I want to know!' Wayne protested. 'Ain't never going to get a better chance to find out. I mean we tried shaving yours, didn't we, sugar, and you just ended up like some kind of damn Mohican with a rash!'

Mortified, Scout turned to Brooke. 'I am truly sorry, Brooke I –'

Wayne was not going to drop it. This was clearly a subject that had always bothered him. 'But in *Playboy* magazine those girls just have a little tuft, like that was all that ever grew. It don't look shaved or nothing. These are adult women, not little girls, but all they got's a tiny little tuft. How'd they do that?'

Strangely, the turn the conversation had taken was no less embarrassing for the terrifying circumstances under which it was being conducted.

Scout stared at the carpet, clearly wishing that she could crawl under it and hide. Brooke simply did not know where to look. She tried to stare straight at Wayne to show she wasn't scared, but unfortunately she was and so she didn't have the nerve. She couldn't look at Bruce – she had nothing to say to him, even with her eyes. In the end she leant back on the huge couch and looked at the ceiling. Between the two of them, Scout and Brooke had the room covered from top to bottom.

'I said, how'd they do it Brooke?' Wayne repeated, his voice hardening.

'Well, Wayne one has a stylist.'

This was one of the funniest things Wayne had ever heard. 'A stylist! A pussy hair stylist! Now that would be one hell of an occupation! Yes sir, I guess I could get to like that kind of work!'

'Wayne that is enough!' Scout was mortified.

But Wayne did not care. In his opinion he was mining a rich comic seam. 'Oh, yes, sir! I'd work weekends and all the overtime the boss'd give me. I'd be saying, "Can I shampoo that for you madam? And how about I massage in a little conditioner?" I'd work hard and get me my own salon . . . There'd be a whole row of women sitting reading magazines with little hair driers on their –'

'I am not *listening* to this any more!' Scout grabbed two cushions, held them to her ears and began to scream. 'Aaaaaaahhhh!'

'Oh come on, honey,' Wayne pleaded through Scout's shouting and his tears of laughter. 'You cannot deny that the notion of a snatch stylist is hill-fuckin'-larious. I mean, would they talk to their clients while they worked? Say, "How was your vacation, ma'am?" and . . .'

But the more Wayne talked the more Scout screamed, adding drumming feet to her efforts to block out his comic monologue. The mad cacophony was enough to jerk Bruce out of the lethargy of terror. He strode across the room and plucked an internal phone from its bracket on the wall.

'What you doing, boss?' Wayne enquired, still smiling at his own wit.

'I'm calling my security guard. He's in the lodge at the gate. If you leave now, he won't hurt you but if you harm us, he'll kill you.'

'*He'll* kill *me*? Well ho, fuckin' ho.'

Wayne levelled his gun at Bruce. For a moment Bruce believed his hour had come.

'Bang!' said Wayne, who was still in a merry mood. 'You give that guard a call, Bruce. Yes sir. If it makes you feel better, you give that ol' boy a call.'

Bruce punched the button on the intercom and awaited a response. Scout took the opportunity to apologise to Brooke. She was still mortified over Wayne's comments.

'Brooke, I am so sorry that Wayne has gotten to prying into your personal stuff. He does not understand that a woman likes to keep her special private places special and private.'

Bruce punched the button on the wall again. He was getting no reply. Wayne looked up from the gun with which he was still playing.

'He ain't answering you, Mr Delamitri. Maybe he can't hear you . . . Here, let's see if we can't get him a little closer to the phone.'

Wayne and Scout were sitting together on the couch. The holdall he had been carrying when he entered was on the floor between his feet. Wayne reached his hand down into the bag.

If Bruce had been shooting the scene, he would probably have started on a two shot of Wayne and Scout, then taken a close-up on Wayne's hand and panned down with it as it disappeared into the bag. Perhaps he would then have covered himself in the edit by picking up a reaction shot from Scout, who knew what was in the bag; then back to Wayne's hand as it emerged from the bag pulling a severed head by the hair.

But Bruce was not shooting the scene. He was in it and his heart nearly stopped. He had to clutch at the wall to keep from fainting.

Brooke opened her mouth to scream but scarcely a sound came, only a rasping gasp, dry and painful. She felt as if in a dream, paralysed by a complete and immovable fear.

Wayne raised the head and held it next to his own.

It would have made another lovely two shot. The grotesque, blood-drained, death-head and the handsome, grinning young face beside it.

'Surprise!' Wayne said, and he laughed.

There was a sheepish grin on Scout's face too. Half pleased with the major effect her boyfriend was having, half apologetic and embarrassed, aware that they had done a very bad thing.

Wayne got up, still holding the head by the hair, and carried it across the room to where Bruce was standing. Bruce gasped and recoiled, backing himself against the wall, almost as if trying to force himself through it.

'Huh huh huh.' Bruce tried to speak but it was as much as he could do to draw breath. He still held the intercom phone in his hand, although so lifeless was his grip it was surprising that the phone had not fallen. Wayne took it from Bruce's numbed grasp and held it up to the ear of the severed head.

'Hallo! Hallo!' Wayne shouted. 'Oh Mr Security Guard! ... He don't hear so good, does he, Bruce?'

Wayne let the phone drop and held the head up so that its face was in front of his own, so close that their noses were almost touching.

'Hey! You hear me?' Wayne shouted into the dead face at the top of his voice. 'The guy who pays your salary wants to talk to you, you fuckin' jerk!'

The head swung about on its hair. Wayne turned its face away from his in disgust.

'How much did you pay this guy, Mr Delamitri? Was he expensive? Because if he was you are being ripped off, Bruce my friend. He wasn't worth shit as a guard. He just sat there in his hut with his big dog and we crept up behind him and killed him.'

Scout looked across at Brooke. 'We didn't kill the dog.'

The little caravan-park store in the redwood forest turned blue then red then blue again then red.

There was no particular call for the police car to be so garishly illuminated as it pulled up outside the shop. It was scarcely dawn yet and there had been no other traffic on the gravel road leading through the woods from the Interstate. Cops, however, will be cops. The few guests slumbering in the darkened trailers were lucky they hadn't turned on the siren.

Astonishingly, it was the storekeeper himself who had raised the alarm. Wayne had shot him only once and that had been in the shoulder. The force of the impact had spun the victim back through the open door and into the parlour behind, and Wayne could not be bothered climbing over the counter to finish the job.

The storekeeper was lucky. Such is the terrible damage done by modern weapons that even a shoulder wound can be deadly. The man's flesh, however, was old and weak and put up little resistance to the bullet as it passed through his body. In fact, the projectile had caused nearly as little damage on its exit as it had on its entry. Nevertheless, there had been considerable loss of blood, and the old man, who lived alone, had lain semi-conscious on the floor in front of the television for several hours before summoning the strength to crawl to the phone. The telerecord of the Oscars ceremony had been playing throughout, and the old man's troubled dreams and hallucinations had been further disturbed by talk of legs of fire.

While waiting for the arrival of the ambulance (which did deploy its siren and woke everybody up), the police questioned the storekeeper. They soon realised that he was another victim of the celebrated Mall Murderers, who were clearly no longer restricting their activities to malls.

'A young man and a scrawny kid of a girl,' one of the officers said into his radio. 'Same description as at that motel this morning ... All they took was some Jack Daniels, some cigarettes and some pretzels ... oh yeah, and one of those maps of the movie stars' homes . . . I don't know why. Maybe they wanted to go visit Bruce Delamitri and congratulate him on his Oscar.'

Chapter Seventeen

Wayne was still swinging the severed head about in disgust. He was clearly moved by the tawdry service Bruce was getting from his employees. He saw it as symptomatic of a national malaise, and held the head up as evidence of declining standards in general.

'I mean, shit, man! That's what's wrong with this fuckin' country. People just don't do the damn jobs they're paid for. No wonder we can't get ahead of the fuckin' Japs. Wouldn't catch no fuckin' Jap screwing up on his duty like that, man. No way! This motherfucker deserved what he got, Bruce. I did you a fuckin' favour.'

On the table stood a lava lamp in the shape of a rocket. In a gesture which amply summed up the contempt he felt for the dead security guard, Wayne impaled the head on the lamp.

Bruce gulped down his rising nausea and Brooke began quietly to weep. They stared, transfixed, as the great misshapen tumours and globules of red lava slowly rose upwards through the electric-green liquid in the lamp and disappeared into the severed neck, waited a moment and then slowly re-emerged from the head and dripped down again.

'Please,' Bruce muttered.

'What's that, Bruce?'

'Please,' he repeated. 'I don't know who you are but –'

'Oh, we're just no-count white trash, Bruce,' Wayne said, crossing over to rejoin Scout on the couch. 'We ain't nothing. Nothing at all. The only memorable thing I ever did in my whole life was kill people.'

But it was plain to see that Wayne rated himself rather highly. He was puffed up with pride like a psychotic pea-cock. He gripped Scout's thigh proudly, as if to reassure her that he was only being self-effacing out of politeness.

Scout was proud too. 'We're the Mall Murderers,' she said. 'I'm Scout and this is Wayne.'

Bruce and Brooke said nothing. Scout was a little disappointed. She had hoped her announcement would have more impact. Fearing that they hadn't understood her properly, she repeated the main point. 'We're the Mall Murderers.'

Scout need not have worried. They had heard her the first time.

They should have guessed, of course, Bruce particu-larly. Two insane murderers? A man and a woman? Big fans of his work? People whose own activities had been consistently linked with his own for the previous month and now *in his house*? It had to be them. But why? Their connection was entirely an invention of the media. In reality, Bruce had nothing whatsoever to do with the Mall Murderers. This was small comfort, though, because murdering people with whom they had nothing to do was the Mall Murderers' stock in trade.

'Are you going to kill us?' Bruce asked.

'Now what kind of question is that? Me and Scout here never know who we're going to kill till we done it.'

'It just happens,' Scout added, swinging her legs like a little girl talking about some game – although little girls don't tend to have guns lying on their laps, except sometimes in Bruce's movies and now, of course, in his lounge.

Silence returned.

Conversation was getting no easier. Again Scout felt it incumbent on her to try and oil the social wheels.

'This is so great, isn't it?' she said. 'I mean, us all here together, just sitting talking.'

Bruce was scarcely listening. His mind was racing. If these were the Mall Murderers, then he and Brooke could be dead literally at any moment. He had to do something: every second left alive with these two psychos was borrowed time. He looked at his big desk, which was positioned across the room, behind the couch on which Wayne and Scout were sitting.

In one of Bruce's movies there would have been a close-up on the top right-hand drawer and a music sting: *that drawer matters.*

Scout's voice rattled on, scarcely penetrating the edge of Bruce's thoughts.

'Because Bruce here is Wayne's hero, and I've always admired girls like you, Brooke. So beautiful and all. Except I can't deny I think it's a shame about all this cosmetic surgery you ladies get done, because these days you don't know who's really beautiful and who's just a nasty old rich bitch.'

Had Bruce moved? If anyone had been looking they might have thought he had. Before, he had been standing by the wall intercom. Now, he seemed to be a little closer to the desk.

Wayne was talking now. 'Hell it don't matter none about cosmetic surgery, does it, Scout?' he said. 'I mean, if you look beautiful, you are beautiful, don't matter how it happens.'

'I just think it was kind of nice when a girl was what she was and that was it,' Scout protested.

Bruce was definitely moving now, if incredibly slowly. He was making his way around the room towards that desk, that drawer. He glanced around to see if anyone was watching. Wayne and Scout were still concentrating on each other, their voices just babble inside Bruce's head. Brooke was staring at the floor. Only one pair of eyes seemed to be fixed on Bruce, the eyes of the security guard, popping out of his severed head. It was almost as if the head was willing Bruce on. Like some creature in an insane Frankenstein experiment, it seemed to sense a man who might avenge its bloody murder. For a moment Bruce caught those eyes and they stared at each other, sharing two extreme close-ups. For that moment Bruce half imagined those eyes alert in a living head, a head kept functioning by the great bloody globs of life-giving lava that journeyed up its neck and down again.

Bruce made a supreme effort to pull himself together. His terror was making him light-headed. The voices of Wayne and Scout, the bright eyes in the dead face and the near-certainty that death was just a heartbeat away were all crashing about his head and preventing him from thinking. Bruce was not a weak man: his glib exterior concealed a steel core. Still only in his mid-thirties, he was currently the most successful movie director in the USA. This was not something that could be achieved without considerable strength of character. None the less, Bruce's current situation was on the verge of defeating him.

'It's a movie,' a voice inside him whispered. 'Just be in a movie.'

Bruce told himself he'd seen it all a hundred times before. He was in control. He was always in control. 'It's just another movie.'

He tore his gaze away from the dead head and viewed the room in a wide shot. Nobody was looking at him. He was in deep background. Infinity focus.

'How about Brooke here? Do you reckon she's real?' Wayne was saying. He leant back into the cushions of the couch, relaxed, and clearly feeling at home. Scout cast a critical eye over the woman sitting opposite.

Brooke shrank before her gaze. An observer might have thought it strange how absurd a really sexy evening dress can look when the person wearing it is cowed and scared. One has to carry glamorous, sexy clothes off with confidence, otherwise it's possible just to look like a sad, desperate tart.

'Real? Get out of here!' Scout exclaimed. 'Why, Brooke here'll have been cut up and stretched back and sucked out and pumped up and I don't know what. Ain't that right, Brooke? . . . I said, ain't that right, Brooke?'

The star of Bruce's movie was nearly at the desk now, nearly at that special drawer. All he needed was a few more moments of inattention from his tormentors.

Bruce did not realise it but he had a co-star in his drama. It might not have appeared that Brooke was aware of his tortured journey across the room, but she was. While staring at the floor, she had caught fleeting shots of Bruce's feet moving across the back of frame. She knew that Bruce had some kind of plan and that

Wayne and Scout must remain diverted. She knew that it was up to her, that she must enter the conversation and enter it arrestingly. She raised her head and stared Scout in the eye.

'It's none of your fucking business.'

Scout and Wayne were certainly surprised. Brooke had shown little spirit up to this point, but now she was coming out punching. Her voice was hard and tough; it commanded the room. Bruce seized the opportunity and advanced a whole step.

Wayne glared at Brooke. 'Now that is where you are wrong, Miss High and Mighty fuckin' bald snatch Daniels. It is our business on account of the fact that you belong to us. You hear? You be-fuckin'-long to me 'n' my baby. Now, answer my baby's question. Unless you think you're too good to talk to her. In which case, you can talk to this.'

Wayne raised his machine-pistol to his shoulder and pointed it at Brooke. Her POV was the gaping end of the barrel with Wayne's grinning face behind it, chin resting against the stock.

But beyond Wayne's head, in deep background, Bruce was still edging through the rear of frame.

Brooke knew she must keep Wayne's attention. Bravely she met his stare, fixing on to his eyes as they hovered above the black-hole snout of the gun.

Slowly he closed one eye in a cheerfully grotesque wink. He was taking aim.

Brooke attempted not to flinch, which was not an easy task. 'All right, pervert, if you must know' – it was terrifying to risk annoying him in this way, but she knew that above all she must keep the focus on herself until Bruce got to that desk – 'I've had the wrinkles round my eyes and lips dealt with, some cellulite removed from my thighs, I have had breast implants and my navel has been remodelled.'

As she spoke Bruce opened the drawer. Wayne was never going to be more distracted than he was at that moment. It was Bruce's best chance, and he took it.

He watched his own hand in close-up, pulling open the drawer. He watched the hand disappear inside.

The drawer was empty.

As Bruce frantically felt to the very back, there should have been a musical sting. Something harsh, like a scream, or, seeing as it was Bruce's movie, perhaps something ironic, like a sit com 'wah wah waaaah' but discordant and sinister. There was no sting, however, because Bruce had stopped playing his desperate little movie game. His defeat was too real, too complete.

'Oh, Bruu-uuce.' It was Wayne's voice, nasty and sarcastic. 'Is this what you're looking for?'

Wayne had not even bothered to turn round to face Bruce. All Bruce could see was the back of Wayne's head above the cushions and his hand protruding over the arm of the couch. From one finger of Wayne's hand hung a small pistol.

'You see, Bruce, I can *smell* guns,' Wayne said, still without bothering to turn round. 'I smelt this one a while ago. I went over to fix me a drink and I thought, mm-mm, what's that smell? I like it. I do believe it's a gun. And guess what? It was! Can you believe that?'

Bruce did not answer. Not for the first time that night, he was incapable of speech.

'Also, I must confess that it is not uncommon for a man to keep his piece in the top drawer of his desk. For an Oscar-winning film-maker, Bruce, you are not very original.'

Bruce shrank a little inside. For a moment there he'd been a fighter, he'd had a plan and a chance. Now he was a fool, casually outwitted and out-manoeuvred by the dregs of a small town truck stop.

It was six a.m. and Bruce's appointment with nemesis was well under way. His old life was already over. Even if he survived his ordeal, nothing would ever be the same again.

Outside in Los Angeles, of course, and America-wide, like him or loathe him Bruce remained the lion of the hour. His Oscar triumph was still a top story on the morning news. Sadly, not *the* top story. It would have been so under happier circumstances, but the massacre at the 7–11 store was necessarily number one on all the channels. Even in California, fourteen dead while doing a bit of shopping is big news, particularly if surviving witnesses are prepared to swear that after they had committed the massacre the perpetrators actually coupled, like two wild animals on heat, against the Slurpy Pup dispenser.

'Sex and death in America today,' said the reporters, as the ambulances squealed off into the dawn. 'It could come straight out of a Bruce Delamitri picture.' An observation which coincidentally segued very nicely into the pre-edited Oscars report.

'I stand here on legs of fire,' said Bruce.

'Why'd the guy have to make such a vacuous speech?' the news editors complained. 'My God, if he'd said something about violence and censorship, would we have had *him* this morning!'

Chapter Eighteen

W ayne did not bother turning to Bruce even now. He was more interested in the conversation he'd been having. He put the little pistol he had taken from Bruce's drawer on Scout's lap, and strolled casually round the glass table to stand over Brooke. As he passed the severed head, it seemed again for a moment as if it might rotate on its gory plinth in order to follow Wayne's movements with its bulbous dead eyes. It didn't.

'You know something?' Wayne said, standing over Brooke, leering at the curiously unnatural semi-circular definition of the top of her breasts. 'I've always wanted to know what fake tits feel like. Well, I guess there ain't a working man in the United States who hasn't thought the same thing. Like, you know, are they hard? Soft? Can you feel that bag of stuff they put in? Do they move around?'

Wayne's right hand had been resting casually on the butt of the pistol stuck in his waistband. Now, he let go of the gun and blew on his fingers to warm them, clearly making ready for an inspection. Brooke did not look at him. She brought her knees up to her chest, clasped her arms round them with her shoulders hunched forward, and stared straight ahead, her chin on her knees.

'Don't you dare fucking touch me.' Her voice was quiet and shaky; she was almost muttering.

'Pardon me, ma'am,' Wayne replied, 'but I guess I didn't hear you right.'

Wayne placed the barrel of one of his guns against Brooke's forehead and with his free hand ready, fingers outstretched, he slowly bent forward, clearly intent on investigating inside the top of her dress.

Across the room Scout took up her gun. 'Wayne, you leave her bosoms alone, now. I don't want you touching her bosoms none.'

It was a stand-off, Wayne pointing a gun at Brooke, Scout pointing a gun at Wayne, Wayne's hand hovering above Brooke's cleavage.

Wayne cracked first. 'Jesus, there ain't nothing more irritating than a jealous woman,' he said, returning to his seat.

Brooke remained hunched up in her defensive position, breathing deeply. 'Just hold on,' she said to herself, 'just keep it together.'

She knew that the number-one enemy of survival was panic. The moment one gave in to that oxygen-consuming, energy-sapping, adrenalin-pumping surge of blind fear, one was done for. Only the day before, she reminded herself, she had been swimming off Malibu and had got caught in a rip. It had been a sucky one, and without warning Brooke had been pulled under, turned over, filled with water and dragged out to sea about twenty metres.

'You nearly died then,' Brooke told herself concentrating on her breathing. 'Only yesterday you were as close to death as you are now, but you made it.'

It was true. Brooke had been in mortal danger, although it would not have been the rip which killed her. Rips don't kill people. Panic does. The first instinct of the swimmer caught in a rip is to try to head back to shore. This is disastrous: no one can swim against the sea and the mildest undertow will defeat the strongest swimmer. But this suicidal instinct is strong and, although Brooke had been swimming in the Californian waters since girlhood and should have known better, she succumbed momentarily to the desperate desire to get back to beach by the shortest route possible.

Even at the first stroke, as she raised her arm over her shoulder and thrust her fingers into the foam, she could feel her panic rising. She was a very strong swimmer, but her efforts got her nowhere and within seconds she was exhausted. It happens that quickly. A couple of mouthfuls of salt water, a few flailing strokes and suddenly the toughest mind becomes clouded with despair. It is at this point that swimmers either pull themselves together or drown. Brooke had pulled herself together.

She knew the rules. Never head into your trouble. Head out of it, sideways along the shore, or, if necessary, right out to sea. Rips are always relatively confined and once the swimmer is out of them, no matter how far from shore they may be by this time, they have the opportunity to recover their energies, consider their position and calmly make their way to safety. Brooke, like any decent swimmer, was capable of keeping herself afloat for hours and yet panic could have killed her in two minutes.

That was the lesson she reminded herself of now. Rips don't kill people (breath), panic does (breath).

In his own way Bruce had drawn the same conclusion. By pretending to be in a movie, he had so far avoided being consumed and defeated by the horror of his surroundings. He had avoided panic. Just.

'What's this guy's weakness?' he said to himself, no longer in a movie, but in a script conference, reading over Wayne's character breakdown, which had been prepared for him on Popcorn's headed notepaper. 'Why does he kill?'

'He kills irrationally,' Bruce answered himself.

Inside his head, Bruce leapt to his feet, the cool, decisive producer, waving the studio memo about triumphantly.

'Here's how it is, right? The guy's stock in trade is murdering strangers, right? Well then, surely safety lies in forming some kind of relationship with him. Maybe these guys don't kill people they know.'

All this had been running through Bruce's head while Wayne was attempting to investigate Brooke's breasts. In the hiatus that followed the silicone stand-off, Bruce made his pitch.

'I'd like to ask you something if that's OK, Wayne. May I ask you something?'

'I would be honoured, sir.' Wayne appeared genuinely pleased.

'Well, I guess I'm interested in what it's like to kill someone.'

'You want to kill someone? Hell, man, do it, it's easy. Kill Brooke.' Wayne took his pistol from his belt and opened the chamber. He removed all but one of the bullets from the drum and offered the weapon to Bruce.

Bruce hesitated. One bullet. Could he achieve anything with that?

Wayne read his thoughts. 'Take it, man. You don't have to kill Brooke. You could kill me, or Scout here – 'cepting, of course, if you did vengeance would not be a long time a-comin'.'

'I don't want to kill anyone, Wayne. I just wanted to know what it's like.'

Wayne put the gun back in his belt and thought for a moment. This was a tough one. He'd never really thought about it before. It was like asking what's it like to eat or to make love, it was just stuff you did.

'You might as well ask what it's like to make a movie, Bruce. It depends. On the circumstances, on the victim. I can tell you what it ain't like. It ain't like you show it. For one thing, there ain't no music playing.'

'No, I imagine not.'

Despite the terror of the situation Bruce felt slightly annoyed at this. People were always pointing out to him that in real life nobody died to a sexy backing track. Like they were saying something really original and astute. It was one of the Moral Majority's favourite points. They always took particular exception to the rock soundtracks Bruce assembled to accompany the mayhem he depicted. They said it was manipulative. Well of course it was. Bruce put fuck music behind his love scenes too and nobody minded that.

'I'll tell you another thing,' said Wayne. 'It ain't witty.'

Witty? It seemed a strange word for a truck-stop hick like Wayne to use.

'Like in *Ordinary Americans*, when the two guys put

the little short-order cook's hand in the food-processor. You remember that scene?'

Of course Bruce remembered it. It had been a triumph of dark, brittle humour. 'Film-making for a new generation', he seemed to remember somebody saying, and if they hadn't they should have done.

'Now that was witty,' Wayne said. 'They put the guy's hand in the blender and it whizzes up blood and stuff all over their suits, and one of the tough guys says, "Shit, this suit is Italian," which was so funny because, like, the poor little cook's screaming on account of he's only got a spurting stump on the end of his arm and this guy is worrying about his suit!'

Wayne howled. 'Neo-Gothic', they'd called it, 'post-modernist pulp noir'. Wayne just thought it was cool.

'But that was only the start, right? It got better, because we knew that the boss man had told the two heavies to go to some real swank hotel to waste this black dude and they know that there is no way they are going to get into no swank hotel with all blood and pieces of bone and skin on their suits. But if they don't make the hit, the boss will burn them. So they have to go to the dry cleaners and strip off to their underwear and the dry cleaner guy is this little faggot in tight shorts and he says, "That's OK fellas, I'm used to shifting stubborn stains from delicate fibres. I have satin sheets," which is a very funny line in itself, but it's even funnier because we know that one of the killer guys just hates faggots, he hates them like a fuckin' religion, so he just digs out this huge Magnum from his underpants and wastes the faggot dry cleaner guy completely, like half his head comes off. But then the other killer guy is real annoyed and says, "Shit, man, how we gonna clean our suits now?" So they have to try to figure out how to work the machine and when they get to the swanky hotel to kill the black dude their suits is all tiny like kids' suits, because they shrunk. Now that was one classy scene, Bruce. Like I say, witty.'

Bruce did not reply. Normally when people enthusiastically repeated his work back to him, as they often did, he would say, 'Thank you, that's very kind,' at the earliest opportunity to try and shut them up. But this time he said nothing. There was an awful fascination in just how well this terrible man knew his work.

'I don't know how many times Wayne watched that movie,' said Scout.

'A shit load of times, let me tell you,' Wayne added. 'It said on the poster that the *New York Times* reckoned it was ironic and subversive. I just thought it was classic the way everybody got wasted. It was so witty.'

Bruce was getting nowhere. He had been attempting to get to know his persecutor, to get inside his head. All he got was his own imagination quoted back at him.

For a moment Bruce remembered something from before. Mirrors. Something about mirrors. Then that thought, too, was interrupted.

Buzzzzz . . . Buzzzzz.

They all jumped, even Wayne. After all it was only seven a.m.

Buzzzzz. The entryphone intercom on the wall was not going to shut up.

'Now who's that coming calling, Bruce?' Wayne took up his gun. 'It's Oscars morning. Everybody knows you're liable to have a head sorer than a hog's ass on a country farm. You ain't pushed no alarm button or nothing, have you, Bruce? Because if you have, I'll kill you inside'a one single breath.'

'No, Christ, no!' Bruce said quickly 'I think it's my wife, my ex. We have a settlement to discuss. Christ, she's an hour and a half early.'

Scout squealed with excitement. First Brooke Daniels, now Farrah Delamitri. It was like being in her very own edition of *Entertainment Tonight*. 'Farrah Delamitri! My God, I'd love to meet her. Didn't I read somewhere you wished she was dead?'

'It's a figure of speech,' Bruce replied 'I was quoted out of context.'

The buzzer sounded again, more insistently this time.

Bruce turned to Wayne. 'So I leave it, right?'

There was very little love lost between Bruce and his nearly ex-wife, and on occasion he had wished many horrid things upon her, but inviting her in to visit with the Mall Murderers went beyond any desire for revenge he might have had. Unfortunately the decision wasn't up to him.

'You've made an appointment, you keep it,' Wayne said. 'I guess she can see your big old Italian Lamborfuckin'-homosexual parked out in the drive. She knows you're here and I don't want her getting suspicious about nothing.'

Again the buzzer.

'Look, surely we don't need to bring anybody else into this. I mean . . .'

Wayne was trying to be patient. 'Ain't going to drag nobody into nothing, Bruce. You just have her come on up here, do your business like you would anyhow, and then she can go.'

With great reluctance Bruce crossed again to the wall intercom and picked it up. There was a harsh New York voice on the other end.

'For Christ's sake, Karl,' said Bruce, 'have you any idea what the time is?' He put his hand over the receiver and turned to Wayne. 'It's not my wife, it's my agent, a guy called Karl Brezner. He says he has to see me right now. It's urgent.'

'Now if me 'n' Scout wasn't here, Bruce, and it was just you and Brooke here, would you let him up?'

'I . . .' Bruce knew he had hesitated too long to lie. 'I guess I would, if he said it was urgent.'

'Tell him you're sending someone down,' said Wayne.

Wayne put all the bigger guns behind the sofa cushions where Scout was sitting. He put one handgun in his pocket and Scout kept one ready under a cushion on her lap. 'I'm going to go down to the gate and let Karl in so we can visit with him for a while. Now he don't have to see no guns or nothing but Scout and me are going to be ready, and anybody who tries to mess around with us is going to get very dead, d'ya hear? So you all just sit tight till I get back. Like I say, this guy don't need to see nothing suspicious.'

He was about to leave when Scout stopped him. 'Wayne, honey, what about the head?'

He laughed. Turning back, he plucked the head from its stand on the lava lamp and dropped it into a wastepaper basket.

Chapter Nineteen

'Did you see that movie *Ordinary Americans*?' the detective, whose name was Crawford, enquired through a cloud of blueberry-muffin crumbs.

'*Please* close your mouth when you're eating,' his partner, Detective Jay, replied. 'It makes me sick to my stomach.'

'You make me laugh, Frank. Most days you get to see the insides of some poor fuckin' dead guy or a smackhead drowned in his own puke and yet still my spit offends you.'

'Just because we work in a pigsty doesn't mean we gotta act like pigs.'

'So did you see the movie?' Another deposit of muffin crumbs.

'Yeah, I saw the movie.'

'And?'

'And when they finally blow me away, I hope I look half as good. Look, I don't care about any movie right now. I'm thinking, OK? Working. Remember work? Or maybe the city pays you to redistribute food.'

'Oh my God, that's funny. I can't wait to have grandchildren so I can tell them how funny you are.'

Detective Jay ignored his partner. 'These two psychos, they're in LA, you know that?' He was looking at the map he had made of Wayne and Scout's most recent atrocities, plotting their course. 'Look, they were heading straight down the interstate. Sure they left it after they did the motel murders, but if you plot a path between the caravan park and the 7–11, they are clearly heading for town.'

'Maybe they turned around.'

'Sure they did. They're in LA, I'm telling you.'

'Like we didn't have enough psychos in LA already, for Christ's sake,' Crawford said. 'You think they're looking to go to ground?'

'I doubt it. These wackos are attention-seekers. Serial show-offs. I mean, for Christ's sake, making out against a Slurpy Pup in front of a bunch of bullet-riddled shoppers! They think they're some kind of twenty-first-century Bonnie and Clyde. I don't see them wanting to lose themselves in a big city.'

'Maybe they're visiting relatives.'

Detective Jay looked again at the crime report on Wayne's attempted murder of the old storekeeper.

'Bourbon, smokes, pretzels . . . and a guide to the movie people's homes.'

On the desk in front of him was a copy of the LA *Times*, the front page cover of which carried a picture of Bruce holding his Oscar, alongside a picture of a corpse-strewn 7–11 and the obligatory piece on violence influencing kids and copycat killings.

'Movie people's homes,' Detective Jay repeated. 'Hey

Joe, that picture, *Ordinary Americans*. Who were the stars?'

'Kurt Kidman and Suzanne Schaefer, although there were a lot of cameos. Anyhow, I thought you didn't care about no movies.'

'Yeah, well, I changed my mind.'

Chapter Twenty

How much time did Bruce have? His was a very big house and the drive was a long one. If Wayne intended to go all the way down to the gates, he would be gone perhaps ten minutes. If he let Karl come up the drive, and met him at the front door, the whole thing would take no more than five. Either way, not really long enough for much delicate negotiation.

'All right, young lady,' Bruce barked, trying to summon up the voice with which he cowed cinematographers and hordes of extras, 'this has gone far enough. If you hand over your gun now, it is just possible that I may be able to speak on your behalf at your trial.'

Scout did not look at Bruce but she slid the cushion from her lap, revealing her gun. 'I don't want to have to kill you but I will.' She said it quietly, almost sadly, but she clearly meant it: both that she didn't want to kill him and that she would.

Bruce was at a loss to know how to proceed. He hadn't really hoped that schoolmasterly authority would bear much fruit, but it was the only idea he had.

Brooke had completed her programme of breathing. She was centred now, in control and ready to attempt a different approach. She stared at Scout. Her face wore a strange expression; she looked interested but slightly perplexed. She tilted her head one way, then the other, all the time looking at Scout as if trying to get a better angle, trying to work her out. Scout knew she was being studied, and reddened. She stared down at the cushion, which she had now put back in her lap to cover the gun.

'Scout,' Brooke said, 'may I do something?' Almost without waiting for an answer, she leant forward, took a lock of Scout's hair which was hanging down in front of her face, and gently pushed it behind her ear. 'You're a pretty girl, Scout, you know that? Real pretty.'

To Bruce this seemed such a transparent ploy that he expected Scout to shoot them both on the spot, but she didn't. She just kept on staring at the cushion in her lap and said, 'Oh I don't think so.'

'Oh yes you are, Scout,' Brooke insisted. 'A very pretty girl. Except you don't make as much of yourself as you could. Like, for instance, you have beautiful hair, but you've done nothing with it.'

Scout shyly explained that there had been all blood and bits of brain and stuff in it from a regrettable incident which had occurred recently in a 7–11. She had been forced to rinse out her hair in the ladies' room, which was why it was such a mess.

Brooke knelt on the carpet in front of Scout. 'Well, I'll bet I could help you with that kind of thing, Scout. Maybe we could do a little make-over on you. I have

Ben Elton

my beauty bag and I'll bet Bruce's daughter has left some great clothes in the house – we could pick something out. You could look like a movie star. Don't you think so, Bruce?'

Bruce was amazed. Scout seemed to be taking Brooke's interest seriously. At least, she hadn't shot her.

'Yes, Scout is very pretty,' he answered stiffly.

Scout's attention still appeared to be riveted to the cushion.

Brooke addressed the top of Scout's head. 'You could have so much going for you. I bet any agent would love to have a cute little girl like you to look after.'

Scout raised her head a little. 'You think so?'

'Of course I do. You said yourself how nice you looked in that magazine.'

Bruce was stunned at Brooke's audacity. Was it possible that this pathological murderess could be taken in by such an obvious ploy? Quietly, he began to pray that it was.

'Why would any agent notice me? I mean, I ain't saying I ain't pretty, because I know a lot of men have taken a shine to me from time to time, including my own father. But there's a heap of pretty girls in this town.'

Bruce's heart sank. His prayer, scarcely delivered yet, was already being returned to sender, unanswered. He had been foolish to allow himself to hope. Scout was not an imbecile: just because you're psychotic does not render you moronic. The woman would have to have had her brains sucked out with a bicycle pump to believe that a bit of make-up and a borrowed dress were going to turn her from a sad, sick psycho into a glamorous celebrity.

But Brooke was a lot smarter than Bruce gave her

credit for – and braver. She took Scout's chin and gently but firmly raised her head so that she could look her in the eye.

'OK, Scout, I'll be straight. You're right, ordinarily why would anybody notice you? Just one more pretty girl in a town that's full of them. But you know very well that you're not just one more pretty girl. You're a killer's girl, already famous . . .'

'I'm a killer too,' said Scout.

Brooke conceded the point. 'Well sure, but the world is going to know that he made you do it and meanwhile, if I make you as pretty as can be . . . who knows? You wouldn't be the first person to get away with stuff just for being cute.'

Scout had a faraway look in her eyes. Her toes were twitching at the carpet harder than ever. 'You really think I could be a star? You mean you'd help me?'

'Of course I'd help you, Scout. I like you and I think you like me. We could be friends.'

Scout finally raised the point that Bruce had been nervously awaiting from the outset. 'That's easy for you to say while Wayne's threatening to kill you.'

Bruce cursed inwardly. Brooke's progress thus far had been so astonishing that he had dared to think she might actually win Scout's trust. This remarkable woman had got from nowhere to serious buddy-talk inside two or three minutes. Now, however, it seemed that Scout had finally spotted the rather obvious point that Brooke's affection might be influenced by an ulterior motive.

But Brooke was a fighter, and hit back. 'Maybe you're right, Scout, but think about it. Seems to me that Wayne is always going to be threatening to kill somebody or other. So how you ever going to make any friends, huh? Y'ever think 'bout that, now?'

Not very subtly, Brooke's voice was going both down-market and in-country. It had left the upper echelons of West Coast society and was meandering gently along Route 66 towards the Heartland.

'I don't know,' Scout replied softly. 'Sometimes I do wonder about it.'

Brooke took Scout's hand. 'Listen t'me Scout. If ever a person needed friends right now, it's you. We could help you, but you have to help us. Don't you want friends?'

'Sure I want friends. 'Course I want friends. I ain't a freak, I'm just an ordinary American.'

A loud New York accent intruded on the scene. Instantly Scout's demeanour hardened. She pulled away from Brooke and her hand tensed under the cushion. For the time being at least, Brooke's heroic efforts to divide the enemy would have to be suspended.

Chapter Twenty-One

The unmarked police car pulled up outside the Beverly Hills mansion. The sun was out now, and the automatic sprinklers hidden beneath the perfect lawns had sprung to life. As he looked about him, Detective Jay could see a hundred rainbows shimmering in the spray which hung above the deep green grass. Everything looked so peaceful and so *rich*.

Jay wondered if inside that glorious colonnaded house unspeakable mayhem had already been perpetrated. It was just a hunch, after all. On the other hand, nobody had cut up a major Hollywood star since Manson.

'You know,' said Crawford as they approached the vast front door, 'this guy was a daytime soap star for years, started as a kid. That's what's so clever about Delamitri. He makes weird moves, like, you know, doing the unexpected, casting against type. Making uncool cool.'

'What, like murder?'

'You don't buy that copycat crap, do you? What? Are

we all going to have to go and watch Doris Day movies?'

Buzzz. Buzzzzzzz.

At first Kurt didn't hear it. The pounding of the treadmill and the Van Halen in his headphones blotted out any outside sound. He rarely answered the intercom himself, anyway. The staff arrived by public bus at nine, and nobody ever visited before that.

Except today.

If he hadn't stopped for a swig of salinating energiser drink and five minutes under the sun-lamp, he'd never have heard it at all.

'LAPD,' said the intercom. 'Sorry to call so early, sir.'

In contrast to the characters he played, Kurt Kidman was as dull as old brown paint. Like many people in LA these days, all he ever did was work and exercise. He had certainly never been visited by the police at six fifty in the morning.

'The *police*?' said Kurt. 'But . . . but why?' The receiver actually shook in his hand.

He had never done anything illegal in his life (although some of his acquaintances considered that squandering his huge wealth and fame on a boring, healthy lifestyle was something of a crime). None the less, Kurt was a nervous sort of fellow and anybody suddenly confronted by the police tends to feel an irrational sense of guilt, particularly at so early an hour. Had he done anything wrong? Was it possible that he'd gone over the speed limit when he drove back from the Oscars on the previous night? Or else maybe, like Dr Jekyll, he had a terrifying subconscious alter ego, who roamed the night committing terrible murders of which his conscious self had no memory in the morning.

'Good morning, officer,' Kurt said, attempting to sound calm, as he answered the door. He had tried to communicate with them only over the intercom, but they had asked him to come down in person. He half expected to be brutally handcuffed the moment the door was open.

'How can I help you?'

Should he have said even that without his lawyer being present? Kurt couldn't remember the rules. Was saying hullo incriminating? He longed to tell them that his copious sweating was the result of an hour on the treadmill, not because he was desperately attempting to cover up some guilty secret. But would that sound like protesting too much? Probably.

'Just a routine enquiry, sir,' said Detective Jay. 'Have you been visited or contacted during the night? Have any strangers attempted to speak to you?'

'No,' said Kurt.

'In that case we won't bother you further. Sorry to have interrupted your work-out, sir.'

Detective Jay gave Kurt his card and asked him to call if anything out of the ordinary occurred, and then he and his partner departed.

Kurt worried about it all day.

Chapter Twenty-Two

In the doorway to Bruce's lounge stood Wayne and Karl Brezner, Bruce's agent. Karl was a tough, hardbitten operator from New York. He had been in the business for thirty years, but judging by his manner it did not seem to have made him happy.

'Here's your man, Bruce,' said Wayne.

Karl threw a questioning glance at Bruce. Understandably he was wondering who the lowlife might be.

'Hi, Bruce. Sorry to call so early,' he said. 'Coupla real important things. So, having a party?'

Karl looked round the room. Brooke was still kneeling on the carpet in front of Scout. Wayne was also taking in the scene. Both he and Karl were surprised to see the two women in this position.

Brooke got up from the rug with what dignity she could muster and returned to her seat on the couch.

'Yeah, a party, kind of,' said Bruce. 'This is Brooke Daniels.'

Karl had eyed Brooke appreciatively as she crossed

the room. He would have had to have been made of stone not to. She was extremely beautiful at any time and if anything she was even more fascinating now, looking sad and vulnerable in her increasingly absurd evening gown.

'Brooke Daniels!' said Karl with delight. 'Well, well, well. Miss February, I didn't recognise you with your clothes on. Great spread, by the way. I'll bet the nozzle of that gas pump was cold, am I right? Who're these two, Bruce?'

Karl spoke as if Wayne and Scout did not exist. He was not actually quite as rude as he appeared. He came from a brusque culture, in which good manners were commonly interpreted as bullshit and prevarication. His style would not have gone down well in Japan or over tea at Buckingham Palace, but in New York show-business circles it had served him well.

Bruce struggled for a reply to his question.

'A couple of . . . actors. I saw them in an improv' night out at Malibu . . . thought I'd talk to them. Might be right for *Killer Angels*.'

Killer Angels was the project that Bruce and Karl currently had in development. It was again to be about people who killed strangers, but this time for a reason, anti-abortion, the environment, wiping out a sporting rival, whatever; the idea being to show that all murder is in fact arbitrary. Or something like that, anyway. They intended it to duplicate the enormous success of *Ordinary Americans*.

'Seeing actors in the early morning after Oscars night? That is dedication.' Karl turned to Wayne and Scout. 'No offence to you guys, but for me talking to actors is only one step up from visiting with the dentist.'

As with most agents, being rude about actors was Karl's favourite joke. He patronised them behind their backs, calling them childish and mad. He was, of course, just jealous. No matter how rich and powerful an agent gets, he still finds it difficult to jump queues in restaurants.

Bruce pursued his hasty improvisation, in the hope that detail would make it more convincing. 'I just thought they had, you know . . . maybe they had the right look.'

Karl cast a doubtful glance at Wayne and Scout. 'Well, I'm just the schmuck who counts the money, but these kids look about as much like psychopaths as my grandmother, God save her soul.'

Bruce was pleased at this response. The less interest Karl showed in Wayne and Scout the better.

'You want a drink, Mr Brezner?' Wayne asked.

This gave Bruce further cause for relief. Wayne appeared to be prepared to play along with the fiction.

'Are you kidding?' said Karl. 'A drink? At seven fifteen in the morning? Have you any idea how much my current liver cost me? Body parts do not come cheap, my friend, particularly those of which the donor only had one and was hence reluctant to part with it . . . Only kidding. Since we're celebrating, get me a scotch, kid.'

Karl sat down on the couch beside Brooke, taking the opportunity as he sat to cast an appreciative glance down the front of her dress.

His mentioning the time reminded Bruce that Karl had no business being there at all. 'That's right Karl, it's only seven fifteen. What do you want?'

'Lemme get this drink, then maybe we can talk down in the snooker room.'

'We'll talk here. I'm busy.' Bruce hadn't meant to snap. The last thing he wanted was to raise any suspicions in Karl that something was wrong. Wayne caught the wrongness of the tone too and shot a warning look at Bruce from where he was standing at the drinks cabinet. Had there been a musical sting at this point, it would have suggested that Bruce had better be damned careful.

'Well excuuuuse me,' said Karl. Even tough New York agents with skin thicker than an elephant sandwich can be offended. 'I forgot for one moment that you just won an Oscar and therefore are professionally obliged to treat with contempt those whom formerly you have loved and respected.'

Bruce knew he must remain very calm. If Karl's suspicions were even slightly aroused he would never leave the room alive. 'Karl, I didn't sleep yet.' He attempted a weary matter-of-fact tone. 'Could we do this another time?'

'Another time? Maybe you didn't see the papers today.'

'Of course I didn't see the papers – it's seven fifteen in the morning.'

Karl took his drink from Wayne without even glancing at him, let alone thanking him.

'Well, I don't want to be the shit-delivery boy here, Bruce, but yours is not a popular Oscar choice. Frankly, the editorials would be kinder if they'd given it retrospectively to *Attack of the Large-Breasted Women*.'

Bruce shrugged and he meant it. 'Who gives a fuck what those parasites think?'

Just a few hours earlier he would have been obsessed with what they thought, but that was a few hours earlier. Things had changed. Changed for ever. Karl, of course, was still living in the old world.

Or at least he thought he was.

'We give a fuck, Bruce,' he said. 'It's the violence thing. It's the big deal of the moment and it's getting a little serious. These fucks are talking up *Ordinary Americans* like it was some kind of training manual for psychos. Newt Gingrich was on the *Today Show* this morning –'

'All politicians are scum,' Wayne interjected. '*Ordinary Americans* is a fuckin' masterpiece.'

Again Karl ignored him. 'He says you're a pornographer and you shouldn't get honoured for glamorising murderers.'

Scout was bored. She didn't like Karl and she didn't care what Newt Gingrich thought. She had been having a much more interesting conversation before Karl arrived. She turned back to Brooke.

'Brooke, will you put my hair up like you said you would?'

Rather nervously Brooke nodded and, taking her handbag, she crossed over to where Scout was sitting and started to do her hair. Karl was not a little surprised to be interrupted in this way by out-of-work actors, but he let it go. That he should care if this little runt showed him disrespect. In his life she did not even exist.

'I think the Republicans want to turn it into a mid-term election issue. We need to make a plan.'

Again Scout barged in with her own agenda. 'You know what I love? I love the way hair mousse comes out of the can. Like, how do they get it all *in* there?'

'It expands, honey,' said Wayne.

'I know it expands, dummy. Because it's bigger when it gets out. But I don't know how it happens. It's the same with cans of whipped cream. How do they *do* that? I mean cream is cream – you can't crush it up.'

Karl looked at her, astonished. He hadn't been ignored like this in twenty-five years.

'Excuse me,' he said, 'did I become invisible? I'm talking here.'

Scout seemed suitably admonished. 'Sorry,' she said.

'You are very far from welcome,' Karl replied with ill grace, before turning back to Bruce. 'They're thinking about reclassifying for over-eighteens. That's half our box office gone at a stroke, to say nothing of actual bans, particularly in the South. In retrospect, I think the crucifixion scene was a mistake.'

'Awesome scene, man,' said Wayne.

Again Karl ignored the interruption. 'It's these fucking Mall Murderers, Bruce. Those two little punks are in danger of getting our picture pulled, Oscar or no Oscar. Do you know they just shot up a 7–11? Christ, what kind of pointless sickos are these people?'

Brooke and Bruce froze. Karl's conversation had suddenly taken an unimaginably dangerous turn.

'Well, you know,' Brooke said casually, while teasing at Scout's hair, 'I mean, you have to try to be a little understanding, see things from their point of view.'

Karl was not an understanding type of person. 'What, you mean the point of view of a socially inadequate jerk-off? *Please*.'

'I really don't think you can dismiss them that easily.' Brooke was doing her best but it was a hopeless task.

'Pardon me, miss, for appearing rude, but that I should give a fuck what you think. Wayne Hudson and that weird, scrawny little bitch he drags around with him are screwed up trailer-park white-trash nobodies who have mashed potato instead of brains. The sooner they get burnt, fried, decapitated, castrated, lobotomised, liquidised and generally fucked over, the better. I would gladly take a mallet to the little fucking scumbags myself.'

Bruce and Brooke braced themselves. Surely now the mayhem would begin. Wayne had moved to behind the couch where Scout was sitting. He had only to reach down into the cushions at her back to produce a machine-gun, and this appallingly provocative man would be dead. Scout herself need merely brush aside the cushion on her lap. Surely it was all over for Karl?

'You talk big, Karl, but you'd never do it.' Bruce's laugh was wooden as a daytime soap. 'You always end up on the side of the underdog.'

'Underdog? Those scum?' Karl replied.

Bruce was now convinced that Karl had a death wish.

'Like I would waste my tears on such syphilitic maggots? I would puke on their graves and those of their mothers, who no doubt were whores.'

Shut up! Every fibre of Bruce's being willed this loud-mouthed oaf to shut up. Brooke, too, was desperately trying to reach somehow into his mind and stop this fool from digging all their graves with his violent language.

How often had Brooke spoken in the past about auras and third eyes? While not actually holding a season ticket on the New Age Traveller bandwagon, she had always claimed to have a palpable connection with the mystic. She believed firmly that thought-transference was possible. She was getting a painful crash course in Old Age reality.

Wayne's voice was cold, although in comparison to his eyes it was positively balmy. 'You think the Mall Murderers are fucked-up white trash, Mr Brezner?'

'He does not think that!' Bruce almost shouted.

'You can't just dismiss them' was Brooke's desperate plea.

'Weird, scrawny little bitch?' Scout said to herself, a faraway look in her eyes. 'That weird scrawny little bitch *he drags around with him*?'

'Karl didn't mean that!' Bruce forced himself to laugh again; it sounded like a razor-blade cutting through a tin can. 'You should hear the way he talks about his wife.'

Karl, oblivious of the terrible agenda swirling around him, was mystified by Bruce's attitude.

'Excuse me? What is this right now? Oprah? Are we having some kind of *debate* about these fucking filth? Of course they're fucked-up white trash. What else would they be? I'd like to take that pair of pointless, gutless, no-brain, no-dick, asshole insults to the intelligence of a wet fart and –'

'Karl! What do you want?' Bruce leapt to his feet. 'I'm busy here. I have stuff to do and you are getting in my face.'

He had not wanted to confront Karl quite so bluntly. If he acted too strangely, Wayne would know that Karl's suspicions must inevitably be aroused. On the other hand, he had to shut Karl up and get him out before he talked them all to death.

Karl studied Bruce for a moment, but decided not to rise to him. Karl was, after all, an agent and Bruce was his top client.

'OK, Bruce, OK. You're the artist. I just negotiate the obscene and disgusting amounts you get paid. Now, like I say, I think we have real trouble here. This is an important moral issue and we can't be seen to duck it. We have to react to this thing responsibly. What we have to do is get out there immediately, say fuck you, and announce a sequel to *Ordinary Americans*.'

'Everybody died at the end of *Ordinary Americans*,' Bruce replied.

'Bruce, yours is not a pedantic audience. Look, you have to rise above this thing. Get out there today and work the chat shows. You did great on *Coffee Time* yesterday. Tell the world that these killers are not your responsibility and –'

Wayne walked across the room and plucked Karl's whisky glass from his hand. 'OK Bruce. I'm sick of this guy now. We have things to talk about. Get rid of him.'

Bruce jumped out of his seat in his eagerness. 'Right, good, OK. Karl, I appreciate you coming round and I'm going to think over what you said, but right now I'm busy, OK, so . . .'

Karl was astonished. He had known Bruce for years. They were friends. 'You want me to go?'

'Yes, I do.'

'Because you have stuff to do with these people?'

'Yes.'

Karl looked from Wayne to Scout and made no attempt to conceal his distaste. He was very worried. These types were clearly no good. There was trouble here. He had no idea just how much trouble there was, or indeed what kind.

'Look, Bruce' – Karl lowered his voice – 'if you want something rough to mess around with, you should talk to me and I'll get it for you. This kind of thing is dangerous. You're going to end up blackmailed.'

'Karl, go,' Bruce replied. 'Now.'

Karl turned away. He could do no more. 'OK. See you.'

WAYNE

See you.

Wide shot, taking in the whole room. Karl is walking towards the door. Wayne reaches down behind Scout and pulls out a gun.

BRUCE
(Shouting)

No!

Almost simultaneously, before Karl even has time to realise that something is wrong, Wayne has shot him in the back. Karl begins to fall forward, dead.
Two shot of Brooke standing over Scout, doing Scout's hair. Brooke screams.

SCOUT

Ow! You pulled my hair!

BROOKE

I'm sorry.

Wide shot. Everything is happening at once. Karl is still falling to the floor. Slow motion. An expulsion of blood and guts flies out from the front of the falling body as the bullet explodes through.
Close-up. On the wall in front of Karl's falling body, a framed print, a poster for *Ordinary Americans*. Karl's lifeblood impacts upon the poster in a bloody splat. A buzzing sound is heard.
Whip pan from bloodstain on the poster, across the wall to a close-up on the wall intercom, which is buzzing again.

Chapter Twenty-Three

Detectives Jay and Crawford stood on another sweeping drive outside another gorgeous colonnaded mansion. As before, all around them the false rainbows shimmered above the lawns.

'You know, if your theory's right,' Crawford said, 'this door's going to get opened with lead.'

'Hey, you get paid, don't you?' Jay replied, and he rang the bell again.

Inside the house there was panic.

Susan Schaefer had only recently arrived home, having spent the night with a new acquaintance whom she had met at the Oscars. But it was not this that had thrown the movie star into a frenzy of confusion. She was a forthright modern celebrity, and press revelations about her latest boyfriend held no fears for her. In fact, if anything she was rather proud of her exhausting private life. That was not the reason that the sound of the buzzer had created this agony of indecision in her.

The problem was simply what to do with her breakfast.

She had arrived home famished, and had instantly stuck six streaky rashers under the grill. When they were perfectly crispy, she put them on a plate, added maple syrup and some double choc ice cream from the freezer, and wolfed the lot. She had been on her way to the bathroom to puke it all up again when the buzzer buzzed.

This was the reason for the panic. Every moment that the food remained in her stomach her traitorous gastric juices would be digesting it. She had to get to the toilet and hurl.

But the buzzer kept buzzing.

'Later. I'm busy,' she shouted into the intercom.

'Police,' Jay shouted into the microphone.

'Police?' A shaky voice asked.

'That's right, Ms Schaefer. We need you to come and speak to us.'

Susan rushed down the stairs and flung open the door in an agony of haste. She could almost feel herself getting fatter as she faced the cops. Six rashers, about a barrel of maple syrup and two scoops of double choc! She *had* to get it out of her stomach! Already half of it must have attached itself to her hips.

'Yeah?' she said, looking so panicky that the detectives believed immediately that they had scored a bullseye.

Carefully they asked her the same questions they had asked Kurt.

'Look, I've only been back half an hour,' she answered breathlessly, 'and I have not seen any psychos.'

But she was sweating, shaking even. She was clearly not happy. Jay tried to keep her talking. He asked her where she had been, where she would be going later in the day. Had she checked her answering service?

'A friend's. The gym. Whadaya think? Of course I checked my messages.' All the time Susan could feel the fat caking on to her thighs, swinging from under her chin, piling up on her bottom. Eventually she could stand it no longer.

'Look, just come in and search the fucking house!' she shouted.

'Thank you, ma'am,' said Jay.

Was it an ambush? Had this poor, terrified woman been coerced into luring two cops to their deaths? They had no choice but to risk it.

Drawing their weapons they crept past Susan and entered the house. Without a word they split up and began their search. Both were on tenterhooks, listening for the slightest disturbance which would, they were sure, be the precursor of terrible violence.

It wasn't long before their worst suspicions were confirmed.

'Ugh ugh hooor aaarrrrghh!'

Behind them, they could hear Susan Schaefer croaking and gasping in agony. The psychos were killing her for allowing them in. It sounded as if she was already in her final death throes. Both officers rushed back through the house the way they had come. There was a small door leading off the hall: it was clear that the noise came from there.

'LAPD!' shouted Crawford, and assumed the firing position as Jay tore open the door.

There on her knees before them, head in the toilet, fingers down her throat, was the female star of *Ordinary Americans*.

'What's the matter with you guys?' she shouted. 'Can't a girl finish off her breakfast in peace?'

Chapter Twenty-Four

The buzzer was still buzzing. Karl lay dead on the floor.

'Answer it.' Wayne walked calmly around the couch and sat down beside Scout.

Bruce protested that it was bound to be Farrah, his wife. He said that Wayne could do with him what he wished but that he had no intention of inviting anyone else in so that Wayne could murder them.

Wayne shrugged. 'So tell her to go away. But make it good. If she comes back with the cops, we all cross Jordan together.'

The buzzer rang again. Bruce tried to focus his thoughts. What excuse could he use to send Farrah away? It was difficult to concentrate; his mind was still ringing with the sound of the shot that had killed Karl. The insistent noise of the door buzzer seemed to magnify the memory, as if the shot was still being fired and Karl was still dying.

Bruce looked down at the body of his murdered friend.

'Why?' he asked Wayne. 'We could have got him out.'

'Why? *Why?*' Wayne's emotional barometer swung once again from casual indifference to blind fury. 'Because he called my best girl a weird, scrawny little bitch, Bruce. That's fucking why. What the fuck would you have done? What would Mr Chop Chop have done?'

Mr Chop Chop? Who was Mr Chop Chop? Bruce remembered his other life, the one that was now definitely over. He remembered Mr Chop Chop. How could he forget him? Mr Chop Chop's image was emblazoned on a million T-shirts and lunch-boxes.

What would Mr Chop Chop have done?

'Mr Chop Chop is a fictitious character that I invented. So he wouldn't do anything, because he doesn't exist, you insane bastard!'

It was not bravery that led Bruce to abuse Wayne, but fear and loathing. He was in a state of shock.

The door buzzer sounded again, this time even louder and longer. Wayne looked hard at Bruce. He did not like Bruce's attitude; he felt patronised.

'I know that Mr Chop Chop is a fictitious character, Bruce. That don't mean he don't exist, now, does it? You gonna tell me Mickey Mouse don't exist? Huh? Fictitious characters got a life inside'a the fiction and what I'm asking you is, what, inside of his personal fiction, would Mr Chop Chop do to any fucker who fucked with his baby and called her names? Now you know as well as I do that Mr Chop Chop would chop chop that fucker good, which is what I did. Now stop working yourself up into ten types of asshole and answer the fucking buzzer.'

Again Bruce struggled to overcome his panic. He had to

stay calm. Christ, how could he? He took the phone from the wall and, mastering his shaking voice, attempted to send his nearly ex-wife away.

He told her she was early. That he couldn't see her. That he had a woman with him. 'I'm partying here, Goddamnit. I just won an Oscar.'

If Canute thought he had problems, he never tried to turn back a Beverly Hills spouse intent on discussing alimony.

Bruce put down the phone, the life draining from his face. 'She's coming up. She has a key.'

Wayne shrugged, indifferent once again. He wasn't much bothered either way. He got up and began to drag Karl's corpse towards the door.

'Well, I guess I'd better move ol' Karl, then. You don't want to be having no discussion about who gets the wedding presents and the CDs over a dead body.'

'I'll get her to leave,' Bruce shouted. 'Tell me you'll let her go, tell me you won't kill her.'

Wayne paused at the door. He was holding Karl's corpse under the arms. The dead face of the ex-agent was staring straight up Wayne's nose.

'Maybe. Long as she don't call us no names. Now I'll just take ol' shit-for-brains here down into the kitchen, huh? Jes' tidy him away, so to speak. Scout, you're in charge.' He departed, taking the corpse with him.

Scout looked up at Brooke. 'I'm sorry I shouted at you, Brooke.' She was contrite. 'I didn't mean nothing, it's just you pulled my hair.'

Brooke knew she had only minutes in which to attempt to complete the task she had begun when Wayne had last exited from the room. Scout's attitude, at least, was encouraging. She seemed to care what Brooke thought of her, which was the best start Brooke could hope for. She knelt down beside Scout.

'Scout, listen to me. This can't go on. Sooner rather than later you're going to get caught, and the more trouble you cause the worse it's going to be.'

Scout's stare found its familiar focus on the cushion in her lap underneath which she held her gun.

'We know we're in trouble, Brooke. Big trouble. But Wayne's got a plan.'

'What plan can he possibly have?'

'I dunno, Brooke, but he's got one. "I got me a plan, hon," he says, "and everything is gonna be just fine." That's what he said. He has a plan for our salvation.'

Brooke had no time to be gentle. 'His plan is to get you both killed, that's what his plan is, and that's how it's going to happen. The cops will come, Wayne'll fight and you'll both be shot to ribbons. Us too.'

'He's got a plan.'

'To get you killed.'

'Well, if that's his plan, then it's OK with me. We'll go out together, in a hail of blood, love and glory.'

Brooke's mind raced. She had only minutes – maybe less – to connect. What could she say? Where was Scout vulnerable?

'Love and glory,' Scout repeated. 'Me 'n' Wayne gonna get that tattooed on us one day. It's our motto.'

Brooke plunged. 'And you do love him, don't you, Scout? You love him very much.'

She had connected. This was a subject about which Scout could talk for hours.

'I love him more than my life, Brooke. If I could pull down a star from the sky and give it him I would. If I had a diamond the size of a TV I'd lay it at his feet. I got feelings bigger than the ocean, Brooke, deeper than the grave.'

It was now or never. 'Wayne needs help, Scout. If you love him, you won't let him die. If you love him, you have to let us be your friends, Scout, let us be *his* friends.'

Brooke took Scout's free hand. Scout stiffened a little but allowed herself to be held.

'Will you help us to be his friends?'

'If they take him, they'll put him in the chair,' Scout whispered. 'They'll melt his eyeballs. That's what the chair does t'ya. I read it.' A tear began to steal its way down her cheek.

'But it doesn't have to be that way,' said Brooke, gently squeezing the small hand she held. 'Maybe if we bring him in peacefully they'll put him in a hospital. They'll try to find out why he get's so angry. Bruce is a big man in this state, Scout. He can help.'

Bruce was transfixed. Could Brooke pull it off? There could be only moments left to do it in. She was close, very close. Ask her for the gun! He wanted to scream it. Every sinew of his body was taut like a dog on a straining leash. *Just reach under the cushion and grab the gun.*

Scout raised her head to look at Brooke, her eyes as big as fists. 'You know what I think, Brooke?'

'What's that, Scout, honey?'

'I think you think I'm dumb.' She seemed to say it more in sorrow than anger, as if she desperately wished it was not so.

Brooke hurried to reassure her. 'No! No, it's not true. I don't think you're dumb, Scout. I like you, I think you're smart and you've got to be smart now. You don't want to die and you don't want us to die either. Above all, you don't want Wayne to die. One day you're gonna to lay diamonds at his feet. Give me the gun, Scout.'

Scout sighed. It was almost wistful, almost as if she was day-dreaming. 'You want me to give you my gun?'

'It's best for us all, Scout, including Wayne.'

Bruce realised he was holding his breath. He'd been holding it for quite some time. He tried to let it out slowly so as not to make a sound. If he intruded on the moment it could be disastrous. Scout was still day-dreaming into Brooke's face.

'If I give it to you, will you be my friend?'

'I said I would be, didn't I, Scout?' Brooke replied. 'And I keep my word. Give me the gun.'

This was it. Bruce stared at the cushion that hid Scout's hand. Was her hand moving? Was she going to bring out the gun? Her hand was moving.

Scout's voice was quiet and scared. 'OK,' she said, the sweetest two letters Bruce ever heard.

Close-up on Scout's hand emerging from under the cushion, holding a gun.

Close up on Scout's face, which has totally changed. No longer docile and teary, it fills suddenly with naked hate and fury.

Wide-profile two shot. Scout on the couch, Brooke kneeling before her. In one extremely fast, shockingly sudden movement, Scout pulls back her gun hand and then slams the butt of the gun into Brooke's mouth. There is a nasty crunch as metal connects with gum, bone and tooth. Brooke is propelled backwards out of shot as Scout rises.

Pull back and pan across to bring Scout fully into frame. She is standing over Brooke, hand raised to strike again. Brooke is bleeding heavily at the mouth.

SCOUT
I sure fucking gave it to you, didn't I, you bitch? You

my friend now? Huh? You always keep your word,
don't you! So now you're my friend, right?

Cut to Brooke's POV of Scout's face, contorted with fury, staring
down at her.

                         SCOUT
          Say it!

Cut to Scout's POV of Brooke, lying face up on the carpet, bleeding,
struggling to reply.

                         BROOKE
          I'm your friend.

                         SCOUT
          Well I don't want you for my friend, you whore!
          Because you tried to turn me against my man and
          that is unforgivable! Maybe you want him for yourself.
          Is that it? Are you coming on to my Wayne? If you try
          it, bitch, I'll kill you.

While Scout was working herself up over the unlikely
idea that Brooke might ever make a pass at Wayne,
Detectives Jay and Crawford, having left Susan Schaefer
to her breakfast, were pondering their next move.

'Well, I guess we drew a blank,' Crawford said sympathetically, for he knew how seriously Jay took his work.
'Don't feel bad, though. It was kind of a cute idea. I mean,
the papers have been linking our murderers with that
movie for weeks.'

'We have one more call to make,' said Jay. 'The
Oscar guy.'

'Delamitri?'

'Yeah. In fact, thinking about it, I guess we should have tried him first. I mean, the directors are the damn stars these days, aren't they? They get to be more famous than the actors.'

'That's true. Did you see Delamitri at the ceremony? He made a beautiful speech. You could see he really meant it. You know, like he'd really given it some thought. My wife nearly cried.'

Chapter Twenty-Five

B ruce had scarcely had time to assimilate the catastrophic collapse of Brooke's brave attempt at dividing the enemy when he was faced with a further and even greater nightmare.

Standing at the door were not only his nearly ex-wife, Farrah, but also his beautiful and beloved daughter, Velvet. Velvet was the apple of Bruce's eye. This had not always been clear to Velvet, possibly because Bruce habitually wore shades. None the less, it was the case. Bruce loved Velvet very much. Also, deep down and in a strange way, he still loved her mother.

What a couple they had been.

Fifteen years earlier Bruce had scored his first directorial assignment and his first (and so far only) wife on the same day. The job was a used-car commercial, one of those sad, no-budget nasties, made purely for local TV, in which the owner of the business is himself the star of the ad.

'You want bargains? I've got bargains. *Crazy* bargains!'

At which point the script called for a jump cut so that the client/star could put on plastic novelty glasses, a comedy moustache and a day-glo green bowler hat with a spinning helicopter blade sticking out of the top.

'That's right, you'd be crazy to miss 'em. And I'm *crazy* to give 'em, ha ha!'

The picture froze on the client/star's amusing grin (his laughter soundtrack continued, but speeded up: hahahaheeheehee) and the address of the used-car lot appeared across the screen.

The one bonus for Bruce as he faced that gruesome morning's work was that throughout his pitch the star was to be surrounded by a bevy of gorgeous babes in bikinis. The original script had stated that after the jump cut these babes would also suddenly be wearing crazy masks and hats. However, the constraints of the budget meant this idea had to be vetoed.

Farrah had been one of the babes, and Bruce would never forget the first time he saw her. She had arrived for the shoot on her own Harley, which roared throatily as she gunned the throttle preparatory to dismounting. All heads turned, of course, and she got off the bike as if she had just fucked it. If Bruce had been a cartoon character, his eyes would have been on foot-long stalks by this time, because Farrah had arrived already in costume and ready to work. Under her studded leather jacket she wore only a bikini and bike boots.

He was utterly smitten, and that very night Velvet was conceived.

Bruce and Farrah had had a good marriage, and a long one by Hollywood standards, supporting each other as they climbed their respective career ladders. Eventually, however, their pretensions and aspirations diverged. As

Farrah got older and could no longer do bimbo parts, she started to put on intellectual airs, attending drama classes and pitching for 'proper' roles, something which Bruce found excruciatingly embarrassing. Likewise, as Bruce became more and more the doyen of hip culture his pose got tougher and sneerier (to the point where he had even considered a tattoo), which frankly turned Farrah's stomach, knowing him as she did for the nerd he secretly was. Basically, the marriage eventually failed because she was genuine street pretending to be boulevard, and he was genuine boulevard pretending to be street. They ended up loathing the sight of each other.

But no matter how many times in recent years Bruce had wanted not to see his wife, they were all as nothing to how much he did not want to see her now. On this terrible morning when the psychopath ushered the rest of his sad, dysfunctional little family into their own private hell.

For a moment longer, though, Farrah and Velvet were to remain in ignorance of their danger. Wayne had concealed his gun and Scout had quickly enveloped hers in the folds of her dress before putting the ever-present cushion back on her lap. Was it possible that Wayne might be prepared to let these two new arrivals pass unmolested through the drama he had created? Bruce could scarcely bear to hope.

Even without the weaponry, the scene that greeted Farrah and Velvet as they paused momentarily in the lounge doorway was disconcerting.

A gorgeous woman lay on the floor in a grubby, bloodied evening gown, her lip bleeding badly. A strange wild-looking creature was just rising from where she had clearly been sitting astride the prostrate woman. And the young man hovering behind them was the worst of the lot: cocky and sneering, he had nasty, violent-looking tattoos on his heavily muscled arms and what looked alarmingly like bloodstains on his vest and jeans.

'Bruce, your old lady's here,' the man said.

Farrah raised a questioning eyebrow and stuck a piece of gum in her mouth. She didn't much care for such dismissive familiarity, particularly from so obvious a piece of rough trade, but it took more than a couple of tats and a bit of attitude to throw her.

'What the hell's going on here?' she said, striding into the room. 'Some kind of disgusting orgy?'

Velvet was equally unimpressed. 'Oh Daddy, this is so-o-o gross. I mean, you have really lost it. What're you into now, drugs or something?'

Velvet was alarmingly self-assertive for a fourteen-year-old, although to be fair, as a product of the Beverly Hills private schooling system she was no more cocksure than the majority of her contemporaries.

Bruce could scarcely speak. He was still trying to adjust to his daughter's horrifyingly unexpected arrival. 'It's just a . . . a rehearsal, precious.'

Velvet's face expressed some doubt. In fact, it expressed complete and utter contempt for such an absurd excuse.

'Oh yeah?' she laughed. 'What are you rehearsing, a remake of *I Spit on Your Grave*?'

Brooke picked herself up off the floor, dabbing at her bleeding mouth and coughing from the blood she had swallowed.

Farrah eyed her with naked hostility. 'Listen, sweetie, if this is some kind of S & M thing and he's been beating up on you, you make your claim out of his share of our property, not mine.'

Brooke did not reply. There was nothing to say.

Suddenly, without really thinking about what he was doing, Bruce grabbed Velvet and pushed her back towards the door.

'Get out, Velvet. Right now, get out.'

He didn't care if he was acting suspiciously. He just wanted his daughter to run.

'Please, Daddy, don't try and order me around. It's embarrassing. I'm a grown-up woman now. I've made an exercise video.'

This was true. *Teen Workout with Velvet Delamitri* had been something of a success, partly because as many sad old men as teenage girls had bought it.

Thus rebuffed, Bruce turned on Farrah. 'What the hell did you bring her here for? Send her away now. Get her out. She has no business being here.'

'No business?' Farrah sneered 'Well thank you, Bruce, you've just proved my point. I brought *our daughter* here to remind you that she and I are *two* and you are *one*, and that fact will have to be amply reflected in the final settlement.'

Bruce could scarcely contain himself. The woman was talking about money. They were all about to die and she was talking about money! Farrah might be unaware of her predicament but, hell's tits, what was wrong with the woman?

For the umpteenth time since the nightmare had begun, he tried to calm himself. 'Look, Farrah, you'll get a fair settlement, I swear. You can have whatever you want, just you and Velvet leave –'

Huuuurgh, glob. Wayne spat. It was a big spit. He

cleared his throat loudly, grollied up hard and gobbed
the lot into a vase. It was a spit which announced that
he was still there, and still in charge.

Bruce understood. Wayne did not like what Bruce had
said. Offering Farrah whatever she wanted in settlement
was bound to sound strange, and Bruce's job was to
be normal. That was the only way his daughter was
getting out of that house in one piece. But how? How
to be normal? Bruce could no longer remember what
normal was.

Velvet could, though, and this wasn't it. What is more,
whatever it was, she didn't like it. 'Daddy, who are these
people? Are they your friends? Can't they go now?'

Wayne strolled across the room and eyed Velvet up
and down. Velvet, as most of her contemporaries did,
wore the sexy teen version of conservative grown-up
clothes. Today it was a smart, tight little two-piece
woollen suit in pink – tiny mini-skirt and figure-hugging
little jacket – white tights, high heels, lots of make-up.
A scrummy little bundle all trussed up in pastels. Cute
and clean and shiny as a ripe cherry. Wayne whistled
appreciatively through his teeth.

'Mm *mm*, I'll bet you're proud of this one, Bruce.'

Velvet set her jaw against his leering stare, but she
was acting more confident than she felt.

Scout looked at Velvet too, but she did not appreciate
what she saw. It was strange, she thought, how rich girls
had that way of looking that was just so clean and fresh
and *undamaged*. Scout knew that Wayne would just love
to dirty up that little girl's life. He wouldn't do it, of
course, because she'd kill him if he did and he knew it.
All the same, she didn't like him leering that way, and
she didn't think much of Velvet.

'It's just like you said, precious.' Wayne was still staring at the girl. 'We're friends of your ol' man's. I'm Wayne, this is Scout and the bitch with the fat lip is Brooke Daniels.'

'Brooke Daniels?' Velvet was now convinced that she'd caught her father in the middle of some disgusting post-Oscar debauch. She was half relieved and half horrified, relieved to discover that the situation was not more sinister, horrified because it was so disgusting. Overhearing one's parents having sex is enough to traumatise some kids, so walking in on one of their orgies was a tough call, even for a diamond-hard Hollywood brat like Velvet.

She made an ugly face. 'Oh Daddy, *Playboy* bunnies? Pur-lease! That is so-o-o trashy and also just totally nineteen eighties.'

'I was never a bunny, I was a centrefold. What's more, I'm an actress,' Brooke said quietly.

Bruce had to try again to make Farrah leave, whatever the risk of arousing Wayne's anger. The alternative was to let Velvet prattle on, and Bruce knew it would not be long before she made dangerously obvious her distaste for the company she found herself in. Karl had been killed for showing disrespect, and when it came to showing disrespect tough New York agents were not in the same class as cocky little Hollywood princesses.

'Farrah,' Bruce barked, pointing his finger at her, 'I'm busy! Get the girl out. Now!'

Farrah wasn't going anywhere. It was clear to her that Bruce was worried, even flustered. This suited her; she'd rarely ever seen him anything other than calm and in control. His current mood was likely to bring forth further financial concessions in her favour. She held Velvet to her.

'Bruce, you are speaking about your own daughter. Trying to throw her out of what *was* her home. You disgust me. You'd rather be with sluts and street trash than –'

'Excuse me.' It was Scout who interrupted her.

Bruce froze, fully expecting his little family to be instantly cut down in a hail of vengeful bullets. But Scout was happy to ignore the insult. She was in a curious mood.

'Mrs Delamitri? Can I ask you something now?'

'No, you may not,' Farrah replied, with enough haughty disdain to cool a chilli pepper, haughty disdain which was entirely lost on Scout, who pressed on regardless.

'Is it true you got so puke drunk one time that you miscarried? That you retched up so hard you done lost your baby?'

For a moment, even Farrah was lost for words. Her battle with the bottle had been long and public. She was naturally aware of the numerous disgusting myths that circulated about her, but she had never been so rudely confronted with one before.

'*What* did you say?'

'Well, that's what I read in the *National Enquirer,*' Scout protested.

'Well, I heard a better one than that,' said Wayne. 'I heard Mrs Delamitri here got stopped in her car one time by the cops, and they asked her to blow in the bag and she offered to blow the cops instead. And she did! Ain't that right, Farrah?' Wayne had recounted this anecdote often before, but it still made him laugh.

'I don't know about no cops and unhygienic acts,' Scout said primly, 'but it sure did say she got puke drunk and lost her child.'

'And that Velvet here had her first blow-job when she was seven,' Wayne added.

Velvet had read the article in question. 'It said *nose* job! And it wasn't true!'

Farrah turned on Bruce in fury. 'What is going on here, Bruce? Is this some kind of pathetic tactic? Are you trying to scare me or something? Because it won't work.'

'No, Daddy, it won't,' said Velvet, standing beside her mother in fiscal solidarity. 'Mommy and I want this house, plus the New York apartment.'

'Otherwise it's trial by talk show. I'll tell Oprah you used erection creams –'

'Mommy! Don't be gross.'

Wayne roared with laughter and poured himself another drink. This was better than he could ever have hoped.

Bruce was desperate now. He threw caution aside. 'You can have what you want, Farrah, everything, the last cent. I'll sign today. Just get Velvet out now.'

At last it dawned on Farrah that something might be wrong. She was hardly the most sensitive of souls. She lived in Hollywood, and other people's problems were other people's problems. She had been born with a thick skin, and it had been pulled so taut by cosmetic surgeons that these days bad vibes tended just to bounce off it like dried peas off a drum. But when Bruce started talking about handing over everything, she knew something was very wrong. Also, clearly it must have something to do with the dangerous-looking people who seemed to have invaded Bruce's life. She decided to pursue her claims at a later date.

'I'll have my lawyer call. Come on, Velvet. We're outa here.'

But alas the penny had dropped too late. Wayne was already blocking the doorway.

'No need for them legal parasites to get involved, Mrs Delamitri. Fuckin' lawyers are eating away at the soul of this country. So fuck 'em I say. Fact is, I'll be handling Mr Delamitri's side of the negotiations from now on. Is that OK with you?'

'Come on, Velvet. We'll talk with your father another time.' Farrah took Velvet's hand and tried to push past Wayne, but he held his ground.

'Truth is, Mrs Delamitri, Bruce here wants you dead.'

He let this sink in for a moment before continuing, 'He's said so himself, and I have decided, in view of all the pleasure your husband has given me in the past, to fulfil his wish.'

With this he produced his gun and smiled a big smile.

'For God's sake, Wayne, let them go. You said you'd let them go.'

Wayne raised the gun to his shoulder and aimed it at Farrah.

Velvet screamed, shedding about thirty-five years in three seconds and turning into a fourteen-year-old girl.

'Daddy, do something!'

'Wayne, please!' Bruce shouted.

Wayne kept his eye trained along the barrel and straight into Farrah's face.

'You said you wanted her dead, Bruce. You said that. He admitted he said that, didn't he, Scout?'

'I heard him.'

'You don't go saying stuff you don't mean, do you, Bruce?' Wayne did not take his eye off Farrah.

'It was a figure of speech,' Bruce pleaded, his voice cracking with fear. 'For God's sake, man, it was a figure of speech.'

'Bruce, Bruce, calm down, buddy. It is not such a big deal. People get killed every few seconds. Listen, in South Central LA they're pleased if they make it through lunch. Man, if you live to see your balls drop, you're a survivor, you're an old man! C'mon, let me waste the bitch. I'll take the rap and you get to keep everything.'

Bruce's brain was thumping. He had to think of something, say something.

'C'mon, Bruce,' Wayne continued, 'this is the luckiest night of your life. I'm a wanted killer, dropped a hundred people. One more or less won't make any difference to me, but for you . . . Hey, you'll never have to hear this bitch's voice again, never have to put up with that scrawny fuckin' skull-head in front of your face. You *said* you wanted her dead, Bruce, you know you did.'

Wayne hadn't taken his eye off Farrah. It was still trained along the barrel of his gun, while he spoke his killing pitch.

'Look, Wayne.' Bruce spoke slowly, every syllable a miracle of mind over fear. 'I said I wanted Farrah dead because I was imagining something that in thought might or might not be desirable but in reality is obnoxious. Like, have you ever said, "I could eat a horse"? I'll bet you've said something similar. Now of course you don't actually *want* to eat a horse but –'

'Bruce.' Wayne finally looked up from his gun.

'Yes?'

'Are you patronising me?'

'No, I'm just –'

'You think I don't know the difference between a figure of speech like "I could eat a horse" and a man who's telling the truth, even though he's such a spineless, unAmerican, Lamborghini-driving faggot that he don't have the guts to admit it? You hate this bitch. If she'd got killed in her car coming here today, you'd have been dancing a jig, I know you would. If fate was to take this fuckin' fossilised Barbie doll bag o' bones out of your life, that would be just fine. Well, fate's working good for you here. The bitch has met a psycho killer. Ain't your fault, so don't fight it. Watch me drop her, and count your blessings.'

Wayne took aim again. Farrah screamed and covered her eyes.

Bruce stepped in front of Wayne's gun. 'Look, I don't want her dead, all right? I don't care what I may or may not have said in the past but I'm telling you now, I don't want her to die and I don't hate her! So if my opinion means anything to you, which you keep saying it does, I'm begging you, pleading with you, don't kill her. Just leave her alone. *Please*!'

Wayne lowered his gun. 'OK OK, just trying to do you a favour. No need to get worked up about it.'

At this point, to everybody's surprise Brooke, who had appeared to be something of a spent force, leapt across the room and jammed a pistol into the side of Scout's head.

While all attention was focused on the debate about whether to kill Farrah, Brooke had been preparing to mount a counterattack. She had reached down into her bag, which still lay on the floor beside her crumpled pantyhose – the hose which she had removed so beautifully in an earlier and happier life. In the bag was the pistol with which Brooke had scared Bruce and won herself the promise of an audition for his next movie.

Brooke's movement had been so surprising and so sudden that Scout had had no time to produce her own weapon from under the cushion and so was now very much at Brooke's mercy. The balance of power in the room had suddenly shifted considerably.

'Drop your gun right now, Wayne, you sadistic bastard,' Brooke shouted, 'or I'll blow this sick little fuck's brains clean across the room!'

Brooke was an intimidating figure, with congealed blood caked around her beautiful mouth, her glamorous gown torn and grubby, her body heaving with tension beneath the soiled satin. She had come a long way in a short time, and as Bruce could testify she had not been exactly without spirit in the first place. Now she seemed genuinely capable of anything.

Wayne certainly took her seriously. 'Don't you go pointing no gun at my baby, now.' Slowly he swung his own gun away from Farrah and Bruce in order to cover Brooke. In reply, Brooke pushed her own weapon harder into Scout's head. Scout winced.

'Brooke, girl,' said Wayne 'you do know that if you kill Scout, you and Bruce and these other two will not get to draw one more breath.'

'Maybe so, Wayne, but you love Scout, and I don't love any of these shits. What is more, killing us will not bring your baby back if I have just put a bullet through her tiny brain – that is, always presuming I don't fucking miss it altogether!'

It was a classic stand-off. Any decent movie-maker

would have spent a good two minutes lingering on every aspect of the scene. The tense trigger fingers, the narrowed, steady eyes, Brooke's heaving bosom.

Wayne smiled. 'You know, when this kinda thing happens in the movies – when two people are pointing pieces at each other and sweating and all – I always think to myself, what's the problem? Why doesn't one of them just quit talking and pull the trigger?'

Then Wayne shot Brooke.

The impact threw her backwards against the drinks cabinet like a rag doll, except rag dolls don't have blood pouring from between their ribs.

'I mean that has to be the sensible thing to do, hasn't it?'

Brooke's valiant fight back had ended as quickly and as surprisingly as it had begun. Now she really was a spent force. The gun had flown out of her hand as her body hit the cabinet, and she clearly would not be picking it up again. Indeed it seemed a good bet that Brooke would not be picking herself up again either.

Bruce wondered whether he was going mad. Two people had now been shot in his lounge inside one hour.

'When is this going to end, Wayne?' he asked.

For the moment, his sorrow was greater even than his fear. This splendid person, whom he had only just met, was dying. She had fought and fought again, far better than he had done himself, and now she was going to die before him, her only crime being to have left a party with the wrong man.

'It's gonna end soon, Bruce. 'Cos what I got, you see, is a plan.'

Wayne crossed to the window and peered out across the magnificent grounds of Bruce's mansion towards the outer gates.

'And here they come.'

Chapter Twenty-Six

Detectives Jay and Crawford got the surprise of their lives.

A few moments earlier, just when Brooke was confronting Wayne, the two officers had turned their unmarked car into Bruce's drive. The main gate was open, which aroused their suspicions immediately, and they had driven up the long gravel road slowly and with caution.

'Nobody leaves their gate open these days,' Crawford opined nervously.

As they turned the last corner and quietly halted before the vast frontage of Bruce's mansion, they both knew that Jay's hunch had been right and that they had found the Mall Murderers. There were three cars slewed casually outside the house, Bruce's Lamborghini, Farrah's Lexus, with FARRAH spelt out in silver on the numberplate, and a big old '57 Chevy.

Very gently Crawford slipped the car into reverse and pulled back round the corner and out of sight.

'Detective Jay to control,' Jay breathed into his radio, struggling to contain his excitement. 'Request urgent support.'

No sooner had he said the words than behind and above them they heard a rumble which turned almost immediately into a roar. They turned round to look out of the rear window.

'Son of a bitch!' exclaimed Crawford. 'That was quick.'

A convoy of trucks and cars was piling through Bruce's gate. Some had the markings of various TV news stations on them, some bore the badge of Los Angeles's finest. The noise of chopper blades joined the cacophony as a couple of helicopters appeared, swooping overhead. Both aircraft were owned by the media; the police had taken a little longer to scramble theirs, but they would be arriving soon.

The two detectives watched from their car, and Wayne watched from the window, as the convoy surged up the long drive and spread out dramatically on to the immaculate lawns (crushing the sprinkler system) and started to disgorge hundreds of people. Within no more than three minutes the quiet solitude that Jay and Crawford had so recently enjoyed was just an impossible memory. There was a marksman behind every wall and hedge, and a news reporter plus his or her crew on what seemed like every available piece of open ground. The only things missing were the gawping sad-acts who like to stand in the background waving and grinning whenever an event is occurring and news reports are being filed.

Within the besieged house, Bruce joined Wayne, uninvited, at the window. Suddenly, just when he had nearly given up, hope was dawning. They were no longer alone.

'They've found you,' he said, 'like they were always going to.'

'Found me Bruce?' Wayne responded without taking his eyes off the extraordinary amount of activity going on outside. 'Found me? They didn't find me, man, I told them where I was. I told them to get on up here right now.'

Wayne turned away from the window, grabbed the TV remote control and began channel-hopping.

It was not difficult to find what he was looking for. Basically, the choice was either kids' morning cartoons or Bruce's house. It divided up at about twenty channels each.

Wayne flicked through the news shows.

'. . . notorious mass murderers, Wayne Hudson and his beautiful young female companion, Scout . . .' the first channel said, its reporter standing against a backdrop of Bruce's prime orange grove.

'They never know my whole name,' Scout remarked petulantly, although secretly she was delighted to be called beautiful by a genuine Hollywood cable TV news reporter.

Wayne flipped to one of the network channels, the *Today Show*, or *Good Morning America*.

'. . . the criminals appear to have taken refuge at the home of Bruce Delamitri, the renowned film-maker, the man who is said to have inspired their brutal killing rampage . . .' The immaculately groomed young reporter was making her report from beside Bruce's pool.

'Daddy, that's our pool!' Velvet exclaimed in astonishment.

Bruce stared at the screen. He scarcely knew what to think. There were so many things *to* think. The danger his daughter was in . . . Brooke bleeding to death on his carpet . . . His murdered agent and the security guard . . . Wayne's inexplicable behaviour in telling the authorities of his whereabouts . . .

But despite all these thoughts, any one of which could have stood some considerable mulling over, Bruce's paramount preoccupation at that point was one of intellectual outrage. 'They're blaming me. Jesus! Those facile morons are blaming me!'

'I sure hope so, man,' Wayne remarked, and hit another channel.

'. . . Mr Delamitri, last seen leaving the Oscars ceremony in the company of nude model Brooke Daniels . . .' A couple of photos from Brooke's *Playboy* spread appeared on the screen. Somebody at the TV station been doing some excellent and very speedy picture research.

Astonishingly, despite the fact that Brooke's whole body was in shock and she was already semi-delirious, she was still able to take in the sense of what was being broadcast. 'I'm a fucking actress!' she gasped from her position on the floor.

'Keep it down, Brooke, I'm watching TV here,' Wayne said, and flipped to another channel, where another immaculate, hairsprayed head appeared, this time standing in front of Bruce's garage.

'. . . leaving a trail of pillage, mayhem and death, murdering indiscriminately in the manner of the fictitious anti-heroes of Bruce Delamitri's Oscar-winning movie, *Ordinary Americans* . . .'

'They're blaming me! Jesus Christ, they are blaming *me* . . .' Bruce was astonished. This reporter was in front of *his* garage, literally only yards from where he himself stood, broadcasting live from outside *his* house, where he was being held prisoner by armed killers, and she was blaming *him*. Blaming him for the mayhem going on, mayhem which, as he had been assuring people for many months, had *nothing to do with him*.

Wayne changed channel again.

'Homer, I've been reading Bart's report card,' said Marge. 'It says our boy is academically challenged.'

'Really?' said Homer, drinking some beer. 'Academically challenged, huh? That sounds good. He probably gets it from me.'

'It mean's he's stupid, Dad,' said Lisa.

'Eat my shorts,' said Bart.

'Sorry about that,' said Wayne, and flipped to another channel.

'Leave it on,' Scout protested. 'I like *The Simpsons* and I don't think I ever saw that one.'

'Later, precious pie.'

Another reporter was speaking out of the screen. '. . . and so these two "Ordinary Americans" have taken refuge in the home of the man who foresaw their coming, who, some might even argue, brought them forth . . .'

Bruce shouted at the TV, 'Nature makes killers not movies!'

Wayne turned the television off.

'Well, I guess if you're just going to keep on talking we might as well have the damn TV off. Can't hear it none, anyways.'

Farrah spoke up. It had taken her some time to recover from the terror of staring down Wayne's gun barrel, but her spirit was returning. There were already hundreds of police officers outside. Maybe they were going to make it after all.

'Look,' she said, lighting a very long, very thin cigarette, made with pink paper and a golden filter, 'if the cops are here you can't escape –'

'I told you already, lady, I don't want to escape. I asked them to come here. I called them when I came down to get you.'

Bruce could make no sense of this at all. 'You called the cops?'

'Well, no, as a matter of fact I called NBC, told 'em to get all the stations down here. I guess they must have called the cops as well. It don't matter none. Me and Scout here are used to ignoring cops.'

There were now so many cops in the grounds of Bruce and Farrah's mansion that Wayne would have had to have been Buddha himself in order to ignore them. There were nearly as many cops as journalists, and more were arriving all the time. Detectives Jay and Crawford passed them as, with heavy hearts, they themselves left the scene of the action.

'Nothing more for us to do here,' Jay had been forced to admit.

It was a bitter pill to swallow. Having pulled off a brilliant piece of intuitive police work, locating two desperate and elusive felons, he was now forced to accept that virtually the whole force had been only seconds behind him. There was nothing left for them to contribute and so, as the helicopter and trucks disgorged squad after squad of paramilitary human gunships, the two detectives retired from the scene with what dignity they could muster.

One of the helicopters swooping overhead contained the chief officer of the LAPD, and he was in a hurry. Chief Cornell had been woken with the thrilling news that the Mall Murderers had Bruce Delamitri and his family held hostage in the Delamitri mansion. Chief Cornell had immediately decided to take charge of the operation himself.

He had no choice. He desperately needed the air time.

Thirty years before, when he had joined the police, Cornell had not done so in order to turn into a showbiz tart. But that was what had happened. He, who as a boy had dreamt of catching crooks, now spent half his time having lunch with them. In fact he had become one himself. His actions were no longer governed by the need to uphold justice as laid down by law. They were governed by the necessity of balancing the various social and political consequences of whatever action he took. He wasn't a cop any more, he was a politician – and a crooked one at that. All city officials were, whether they liked it or not, because the whole sad, crumbling edifice was built on lies and half-truths. Nobody could tell it straight any more because there was no straight to tell. Every group, be it defined racially, financially, geographically, sexually, by religion or by choice of knit-wear, had its own truth. And that truth was diametrically opposed to everyone else's truth. More than that, it was threatened by everyone else's truth. The city was out of control and the police chief's number one job, like that of every politician, was to persuade people it wasn't.

For that he needed profile. He needed air time.

And today he was going to get it. The chopper landed and Cornell stepped masterfully and purposefully into a barrage of clicking cameras. He was a general in a war zone, and beyond the cameras he could see the might of his army manoeuvring into position. It felt good. This was a dream come true. Suddenly, when he had least dared to hope for it (which is to say, three months before the city elections), Cornell had a real, one hundred per cent macho, shit-kickin', butt-whippin', ass-kissin' siege to deal with. A genuine proper piece of high-rolling, high-octane, high-profile police work, which above all, above double all, above all and hallelujah, was *race-free*! A race-free crime! In election year! Chief Cornell thanked his stars. He thanked his God. He would have happily conceded that somewhere in his youth or childhood he must have done something good, because all his Christmases (or holiday seasons, as the city now referred to them) had come at once. For the first time in a long time he was dealing with a crime of city-wide, state-wide, national and international significance in which race was not an issue. He had never dared to dream he would see its like again.

Chief Cornell was himself black. He had experienced plenty of racism in his life and he hated it. But his particular private and current hatred of racism was to do not with his colour but with his job. He was the city's top cop. He was proud of that and he wanted to do a good job, but racism, from whichever hue it emanated, had made that impossible. Proper police work was no longer an option available to him. Every day he encountered what appeared to be open-and-shut cases. The man killed the woman, the gang beat the guy. Simple, it would seem, but no, then it turns out that the main protagonists are of different races and suddenly the open-and-shut case turns into an impenetrable maze in which what people actually do is irrelevant. What matters is what the jury, and ultimately the public, *feel* about it.

But now, glory of glories, he had a race-free case.

Victims and villains were the same colour. Imagine, Chief Cornell thought, if those had been black or Asian punks in there, shooting white *Playboy* centrefolds and holding little white girls hostage. Absolutely everything about the case would be different. Nearly as bad would be if the director or the model had been black and the punks white. Either way, the case would already be a political football, there would be pickets and protestors at the gates. It did not bear thinking about.

But the chief's luck was in. Fate had delivered to him the perfect case in which to do, and above all be seen to do, a bit of proper policing, and by hell, Hades, glory and damnation, he was going to make the most of it.

Unfortunately for Chief Cornell, there was another chief on the scene and he was equally excited. Brad Murray, Chief of NBC News and Current Affairs, recognised the Delamitri siege as probably the sexiest bit of news and current affairs it had ever been his extreme good fortune to preside over.

'If this one wasn't true,' Murray remarked to his gorgeous power PA as they stepped off their own helicopter, 'I'd never have dared to invent it.'

But it was true, and what was more the principal villain appeared to understand the central and overriding principle of news and current affairs: that the most important element in any drama is television.

In an armoured police command vehicle the two chiefs met: an irresistible force and an immovable object. Their quarrel was over who should put the call through to Bruce Delamitri's house and open up negotiations with the villains. Understandably, Chief Cornell felt that it was a matter for the authorities. Chief Murray, however, reminded Cornell that Wayne Hudson had called the networks, not the cops, and had been most specific that he wanted to talk to a top news man.

A decade earlier, Cornell might have had a couple of his constables throw the NBC guy off the truck but not now. Not with elections looming, not with a city perpetually on edge. The police chief knew he had to co-operate with the media every bit as much as they had to co-operate with him, and so a compromise was reached. Having instructed AT&T to block all incoming calls to the Delamitri mansion (every acquaintance Bruce had in LA was of course trying to call him), the two chiefs agreed that they would call Wayne together, on a party line.

As it happened, they need not have bothered arguing about it because Wayne did all the talking anyway.

'OK, shut up and listen up,' he barked into the phone, without even bothering to enquire who was calling. 'This is Wayne Hudson, the Mall Murderer. Now me and my baby are in control here, you understand? We got Bruce Delamitri, we got Brooke Daniels, who is an actress by the way – you tell your reporters that, you hear? Also we got Bruce's wife and their daughter, Velvet, who is as cute as a button and will make very good TV, whatever I decide to do with her. Now you just give me a number right now where I can call you back when I'm ready with my demands.'

Police Chief Cornell gave the number, and having done so began to try and negotiate. He was, after all, trained in this type of thing.

'OK, Wayne,' he said. 'I think you want to make a deal.'

'What I want is for you to shut the fuck up, OK?' said Wayne. 'I will talk to you when I'm ready, and when

I do it will be me that says what's what. Understand? You know what I'm capable of. Don't call back now. Meantime, you have a nice day.'

The police chief and the NBC chief put their respective phones down and looked at each other.

'Guess we'll have to wait, Chief,' said the cop. 'Maybe this would be a good time for them to put a little make-up on me?'

'You got it, Chief,' said the newsman.

Inside the house, Wayne too had replaced the receiver.

'What did you mean about me being good TV?' Velvet asked, her voice understandably rather shaky. 'What are you going to do to me?'

'It's OK, baby,' said her mother, though it clearly wasn't. 'Are you holding us hostage?'

Wayne poured himself another drink; he felt he'd earned it. Scout was still sipping at her first *crème de menthe*. She was not a big boozer.

'In a manner of speaking, you're hostages,' said Wayne. 'Basically, what I got here is a plan.'

'Wayne's had a plan right from the start,' Scout said proudly.

'What plan?' Bruce was angry. He shouted at Wayne, 'What are you talking about?'

'Well, I guess a plan to avoid being executed for murder, Bruce. I can't think of an agenda more immediate than that for people in the position me and Scout find ourselves in.'

Brooke was still conscious. Velvet had briefly attended the Guides during her extremely short childhood, and knew a little first aid. Showing a composure that would have surprised her classmates and teachers, she had done her best to manoeuvre Brooke into the correct position and pad her wound with cushions, so that for the time being at least Brooke was still capable of following the conversation.

'Plan? Fuck you,' she said. 'You're going to die, you bastards. You don't stand a chance.'

'Don't talk,' said Velvet. 'Your wound is real big and any physical activity at all will screw any chance of the blood starting to clot.' She turned to Wayne. 'She's got to have a doctor. Can't we ask them to send in a doctor?'

'Maybe. I don't know yet,' Wayne replied.

'But she'll die.'

'Miss Delamitri, I thought you might have understood by now that I don't mind none if people get dead.'

Bruce was still standing at the window. Media cars and trucks and police vehicles continued to pour through his gate. He had eight acres of grounds and it was all already crowded. Incredible. A veritable village had sprung up in twenty minutes. Satellite dishes, tripods, fabulous hair-dos, four-wheel-drives, a million metres of electric cable. The hum of the massed mobile generators could be heard for miles.

Bruce struggled to get a handle on what was happening to him.

His security guard was dead, Karl was dead. Brooke was dying. He'd just won an Oscar and the entire LA media community plus half its police force were camped out on his lawn. What was more, the man who had brought all these things about (except the Oscar, although even that was apparently connected, according to the TV) was standing in Bruce's lounge, calmly sipping Bruce's bourbon and covering the room with a machine-gun. How could all this have happened? And in so few short hours?

What was going on?

'What's your plan, Wayne?' Bruce asked. 'Please tell me your plan.'

'OK, Bruce, I'll tell you. As you know, Scout here and me have committed murder and mayhem across four states. We can't deny it, 'cos we done it and it's true. Now I wish I could tell you that every one of those corpses we left lying all over America deserved to die. I wish I could say it was like the movies, where rapists, rednecks, bad cops, hypocrites and child-abusers get just what the fuck they deserve. But it just ain't so.'

Scout felt that perhaps Wayne was being a little hard on himself. Why should all the burden of proof lie with them?

'They might have been all those things, Wayne,' she said. 'We never knew any of them long enough to find out.'

'Well, whatever, honey. The point I'm making here is that we are in deep shit. They know who we are and they're going to get us. We've been caught on about one hundred security videos. On top of which, Scout could not resist sending her picture to her home-town local paper, for which I forgive her, even though it was dumb.'

'They all said I was trash and wouldn't amount to a hill of beans. Well, I showed them.'

'Yes, you did, baby doll. You sure showed them. So basically what I'm saying here, Bruce, is that whatever we do we are going to get caught damn soon now, and when we do I guess we have a higher than average chance of getting fried in the chair.'

Brooke gurgled at this from her position on the carpet. A gurgle that could be roughly translated as saying, 'The sooner the better, pal.'

Wayne ignored her. 'And that, Bruce, is where you come in.'

'What do you mean? What can I do?'

'We need you, Bruce. You're going to save our lives.'

'You're our saviour,' Scout added. 'That's why we came to you. You can make it different.'

'Give them what they want, Bruce. Anything – just give it to them!' This was from Farrah, for whom hope continued to dawn. Was it possible that they would be able to buy their way out of this? And did Bruce have insurance for hold-ups?

'I don't know what they want!' Bruce shouted at her. He swung back to Wayne. 'What *do* you want? Tell me, I'll give it to you, whatever it is.'

'We need an excuse, Bruce,' Wayne said.

'What we're looking for here is someone else to take the blame.'

Chapter Twenty-Seven

D own on the lawn the news reporters were repeating over and over again what little information that they had on the situation: '. . . the Oscar-winner . . . the Mall Murderers . . . the beautiful model/actress . . . the cute teen . . . the estranged wife . . .'

Their reports were punctuated on air by re-run footage from the previous night: Bruce on the red carpet . . . Bruce, standing on legs of fire, accepting his Oscar . . . Bruce dancing with Brooke at the Bosom Ball.

Then it was 'back to the studio', where the anchor men and women solemnly repeated the whole thing 'for those of you who've just joined us': '. . . the Oscar-winner . . . the Mall Murderers . . . the beautiful model/actress . . . the cute teen . . . the estranged wife . . .'

After this, the studio anchors threw back to the reporters on the ground. 'And let's go back to the Delamitri mansion, to see if there are any further developments.'

'There have as yet been no further developments,' replied the reporters on the ground. 'All I can tell

you is . . . the Oscar-winner . . . the Mall Murderers
. . . the beautiful model/actress . . . the cute teen . . .
the estranged wife . . .'

'In that case,' said the studio anchors, 'let's turn now
to our panel of criminal psychologists and show-business
experts.'

In TV studios all over LA, and indeed all over the
country, hastily summoned 'experts' were bundled into
their seats, having been hurriedly powdered down, miked
up and handed their cheques.

'Exactly what in your opinion is going on in there?'
the studio anchor asked the experts gravely.

'Well, this is a classic case,' the experts chorused, 'many
aspects of which are discussed in my latest book, which is
of course available in all good bookshops.'

Chapter Twenty-Eight

Wayne and Bruce stood together, staring out of the window at the instant city below. There were a hundred rifles trained on Wayne, but, unless the police could be sure of hitting Scout as well, no order to fire would be given.

'Someone to take the blame?' Bruce asked. 'What the hell do you mean, someone to take the blame? Some kind of magician, who can explain that the whole thing was an optical illusion and that actually someone else shot all those people?'

Bruce was feigning astonishment, but in the back of his mind a terrible suspicion had dawned.

On the floor, over by the drinks cabinet, Brooke coughed. Maybe she was trying to say something, maybe she was just coughing.

'This woman has to have a doctor,' Velvet pleaded. 'You have to let her have one.'

Wayne swung his gun towards Velvet, suddenly angry again. 'Listen, I did not ask that bitch to threaten my baby, OK? She is in this dire situation by her own choosing, on account of the fact that she pulled a piece on my girl. So shut the fuck up, because me and Bruce are talking here. Or maybe I should shut you up. Huh?'

He advanced a step towards the girl and raised his fist. Velvet burst into tears.

'If you hurt her,' said Bruce, 'I swear that whatever you want from me you will never get.'

'You'll do what the fuck I tell you to, whether I bust this bitch's head or not.' Wayne's mood swings really were most alarming.

'Please don't hurt me,' Velvet sobbed.

'There's no need to go beating up on no little girls, Wayne,' Scout remarked. 'It's beneath you.'

'This ain't no little girl, precious pie. Kids're born old in Hollywood. Why this little slut musta spent more money already in her few short years than your sweet momma woulda earned in fifty lifetimes. She *deserves* to get slapped around some.'

'I've told you,' said Bruce, 'you'll get nothing from me if you hurt her.'

Wayne lowered his fist slowly. 'I want you to know, Bruce, that I am minding the wishes of my baby here and not yours. Because I can assure you that you will do whatever I tell you to do, whether I hurt your little girl or not.'

Bruce seized upon the point. 'And what is it you want me to do?' He was almost begging. He had to know the worst, deeply fearful of it though he was. Fearful because in truth he had already guessed.

'I want you to plead on our behalf. I want you to speak up for us and save us from the chair.'

'Plead on your behalf? You're crazier than I thought. You really think my word's going to save you from the punishment you deserve? You're guilty as Hitler.'

'Sure we're guilty, if by that you mean we done all the stuff they say we done, but that ain't the point, is it? Not these days. These days, no matter how guilty you are, you can still be innocent.'

He had lost them. They all stared at him, all except Scout, who had hold of one of her feet and was inspecting her toenails.

'For instance,' Wayne explained, 'like that spick chick who cut off the guy's pecker, right? She was guilty for sure, she never denied it. She cut off that ol' boy's manhood and threw it out of a car window. Do you see that bitch in prison, huh? Is she breaking rocks in the hot sun? No, I don't think so, because although she was guilty she was innocent too. In America you can be both.'

Scout looked up from her toenails. 'That's right, she done it, but she was innocent and I agree. That bastard beat up on her and he done raped her too. He got his, and I hope she used a rusty knife.'

Wayne winced. 'Now, Scout, you know that you and me disagree on this issue. Personally, I don't see as how no woman can get raped by her husband, on account of the fact that he is only taking what's his anyway. What's more, I think that any Mexican bitch who cuts the dick off an ex-United States Marine who has served his country should rot in a hole.'

'She was abused.'

'If you think a man's abusing you, honey, you leave him. You do not cut his dick off.'

'The court agreed with her.'

'The court was a bunch of lesbians and faggots.'

Scout made a sulky face and returned to her toe-nails.

'Yeah, well, whatever,' Wayne said, 'we're getting off the point here. What I'm saying is, right or wrong, the greaseball bitch walked free. She done it, she said she done it, she was glad she done it, but she walked. Guilty but innocent, you see. You can be both in the Land of the Free, always assuming, that is, that you got an excuse.'

'Are you suggesting' – Bruce tried to sound firm and intelligent – 'that there is any excuse for mass murder?'

'Bruce, there is an excuse for anything and everything in the USA! What about them cops who beat up on the nigger and started a damn riot? They was videoed! You see them doing time? No sir you do not. Remember O.J.? They said he killed his wife. Turned out they'd got the wrong victim. The dead chick wasn't the victim at all. No way, O.J. was the victim. He was the victim of a racist cop, who incidentally also walked. Nobody gets blamed for anything in this country, *nothing is anybody's fault.* So why the Hell should we take the rap for what we done, huh?'

In his mind's eye, Bruce suddenly saw again the beautiful idiot he had harangued at the Bosom Ball. When had that been? The previous evening? The previous lifetime, more like. Bruce heard once more his own voice rising above the banality and the hypocrisy he'd thought he heard around him: 'Nothing is anybody's fault.'

He'd said it himself.

Could Wayne actually be right? Could the bastard get away with it?

'Wayne, be serious. You have killed so many people – there can be no excuse for that.'

Wayne smiled, picked up the phone and began to dial. 'Bruce, you just won the "Best Director" Oscar. I ain't flattering you when I say that you are currently the most celebrated movie-maker in the world. It ain't no more than you deserve, mind. You worked hard and you have reaped the rewards . . . Excuse me.' He turned to the phone.

On the other end of the line Chiefs Cornell and Murray grabbed their respective receivers and began simultaneously to announce their credentials.

'Shut up and listen to me,' they heard Wayne say. 'We gonna make a statement, y'hear? We gon' announce our intentions and tell it like it is, OK? Now what we want is a small ENG crew in here, jus' as soon you can get it together.'

'Yes, yes, an electronic news-gathering crew, OK,' said the head of NBC, pleased to be able to answer the questioning look on the police chief's face.

'I know what ENG is, else I wouldna asked for it!' Wayne shouted down the line.

'Yes, I was just explaining it to –'

'Shut the fuck up! I am *talking* here. One more interruption and that's it, we do our talking with guns, OK? Now, this crew has to be hooked up to all the other stations, you understand? Cable too. We ain't giving no exclusive here, everybody gets the story. One more thing. The recordist must have a direct feed to the ratings computer. I want to know just how big a TV star I am, minute by minute. Now, if you do this, I give you my word as a freeborn American that, whoever else I decide to kill, the TV people get safe passage. I guarantee they will not be harmed, on account of you are observers, man, we are the action.'

With that Wayne put the phone down and turned to his hostages. 'Now we wait,' he said. 'How 'bout we all have us a drink?'

'You seem to know an awful lot about the workings of TV,' Bruce said, and for one insane moment it crossed his mind that perhaps in some weird way or other this whole thing was a hoax. Maybe Wayne and Scout were not what they seemed, not mass murderers at all, but journalists or students or something, out to prove a point. Was it all an illusion? Brooke had tricked him before. Maybe she hadn't really been shot. Maybe this whole thing was a set-up . . . ?

It was a sad, hopeless thought and it lasted about a quarter of a second. His agent's blood and tissue still clung to the glass-covered poster on to which they had been propelled by Wayne's bullet. Fresh gore was welling up inside Brooke's mouth, threatening to choke her before she bled to death. Bruce could smell the torn and jagged flesh. There was so much stark, horrifying reality in the room it was a wonder that there was still room for the furniture.

'How'd I know about TV?' Wayne explained. 'Hey, Bruce, everybody knows everything these days. Especially TV. Think about it. Home video shows, community cable channels – real life as it happens. Not a simulation, actual footage. We're all part of it, man. It's an electronic democracy. There ain't no "you" and "us" any more because "us" is in your face every day. Appearing on your game shows. Caught on video, robbing your banks.

Confessing our sins on *Oprah*, 'n' getting them forgiven on the Inspiration Channel. People *are* television, man, and you're asking me how I know how to use it? Well, it sure don't take a lot of finding out. You know, for a smart man you're real dumb. Excuse me, I have to speak with the cops.'

Down below, in the armoured police command vehicle, Chief Cornell was almost quivering with excitement. Wayne Hudson was playing right into his hands.

'Get me the equipment he wants,' the chief barked at Murray. 'That little ENG crew is going to be composed of armed operatives from Special Forces. We are sending in an undercover SWAT team. Two seconds after my men get in there, they will have neutralised that maniac, plus the fucking she-devil he hangs with.' The police chief was already preening himself for the press conference that would follow this heroic operation.

The phone rang again. Both men grabbed it.

'Now, I know what you're thinking, guys,' they heard Wayne's voice say. 'You're thinking 'bout putting a bunch of damn commandos on me, right? Well forget it. The crew you send me best be the smallest crew there is. I am talking one camera operator and one recordist. That is two people, OK? Two. T–W–O. What is more, they have to come barefoot and wearing only their underwear. Y'hear me? Underwear, that's all, and I ain't talkin' no baggy long-johns or old lady's bloomers here. I am talkin' 'bout the smallest, tiniest, skimpiest fuckin' bits of nothing a person can wear and still keep their modesty. I'm going to check every inch of the people you give me, plus their equipment, and if I get even the *idea* that there might be a piece, a stun grenade, even a fucking penknife, within about fifty yards of those two motherfuckers, I'm gonna holler to Scout to spray bullets into every hostage we got, and you know she'll do it, on account of how she loves me and she does what the fuck I tell her. So basically what I'm saying here is that if you fuck with me, cop, four more innocent people gonna get very dead real soon, and it will be your fault, man, and every TV station in America's gonna see it. Bye-bye, now.'

The phone went dead again.

This time it was the newsman's turn to quiver with excitement. Disaster had been averted. Police Chief Cornell had, through his crass, macho zeal, been on the verge of hijacking what was clearly a cathartic media event and turning it into a police matter. Television had nearly been prevented from taking up its rightful position at the very centre of the drama, not just covering the story but being part of it. This, the news and current affairs chief felt, was what news and current affairs had been invented for. To get cameras and, if possible, personalities deep, deep inside events, moulding them, shaping them, actually *being* the news; while the old forces of authority – the cops, the politicians, the civic leaders – could only watch impotently from the sidelines.

He had so nearly lost it. For a moment there it had looked like the cop was getting ready to grab all the glory. Thanks, however, to the villain himself having a proper sense of proportion and society's natural pecking order, the media would be centre-stage where they belonged.

Chapter Twenty-Nine

Bruce's mind was no longer reeling. It was reeling, jigging, jitterbugging and doing the mashed potato.

'You are bringing a TV crew in here? Into *my home*?'

'That's right, Bruce, and you, me and Scout are going to make a statement.'

'I will not make a statement with you, you crazy bastard. You can shove your damn statement up your ass!'

Bruce scarcely knew what he was saying. Farrah and Velvet gasped at his audacity, but on this occasion Wayne did not seem to mind being cheeked.

'That's right, Bruce, get all that profanity out of your system. Don't want to go using no lewd words on TV, now, do we? It might affect the ratings.'

Scout was absolutely thrilled. 'Are we really going to be on the TV, honey?'

'Yes, we are, baby doll, and so's Bruce here, because if he doesn't I'll kill his darling little girl.'

'What kind of statement? What the hell do you want me to say?'

'Well, Bruce, let me tell you. You are going to announce to the whole of the USA – and believe me it will be the whole of the USA because between you and us we got more celebrity right here than Elvis making out with Oprah, using Roseanne for a mattress – you are going to announce to the whole of the USA that Scout 'n' me are your fault.'

Wayne smiled as if to say, 'Great plan, huh?' Bruce had known it was coming but it was still a blow.

'You are going to say that having met us and talked to us, quietly, person to person, one on one, you realise that we are just dumb, stupid, poor white trash and that you and your glamorous Hollywood pictures done corrupted our po' simple minds.' He took up the bag which had recently contained the severed head and pulled out a bundle of bloodstained magazines and newspapers. He quoted from one: 'You're going to say you understand that your "wicked, cynical exploitation and manipulation of the lowest, basest elements of the human psyche has so disturbed –"'

'No, I won't do it!' Bruce nearly gagged at the man's audacity.

Wayne strolled across the room to where Velvet had gone to stand with her mother. 'Open your mouth, darling.'

Velvet burst into tears again. Unmoved, Wayne took his pistol and forced its barrel between Velvet's closed lips so that the metal pressed against her clenched teeth.

'I'll bet you've had a lot of expensive dental work over the years, huh, baby? Let me tell you now, a bullet going through all that is liable to do a powerful lot of damage.'

Having made his point, Wayne removed his gun

from Velvet's lips, turned back to Bruce and waved the bloodied magazines in his face.

'You, Bruce, are going to say that we are "products of a society that celebrates violence". You are going to say that we are weak-willed, simple-minded creatures who have been "seduced by images of sex and death", images *you* create, man, and for which you have just been honoured with an Oscar. You are going to say that your eyes have been opened and you are *ashamed*. In fact, I got an idea, man – oh yeah! You're going to return your Oscar. Live on TV, you're going to give it back out of respect for your victims. The people *you* killed through me and Scout.'

Bruce was not a callous man. He knew that other people had problems greater than his. He was aware that two people were already dead and that another was clearly dying. Nevertheless, at this point he could think only of the dreadful fate Wayne had prepared for him. To make the kind of statement Wayne was proposing that he make, and to make it to the entire nation, would be the most profoundly humiliating thing imaginable. Career suicide. Intellectual disgrace. The complete loss of every ounce of the credibility he currently enjoyed. The immediate end of his life as an artist. And for a *lie*.

He struggled to find an argument to sway Wayne from his terrible course. 'It won't work, Wayne. It can't. Whatever I say, it won't change the law. You're guilty and the law will get you.'

'That's bullshit, Bruce, and you know it. The law is whatever people want it to be. It ain't never the same thing twice. It's one thing to a white man, another to a black, one thing to the rich, another to the poor. The law is a piece of fuckin' Play Dough – no one knows what shape it's going to be in next. Man, after you've made your broadcast me and Scout here won't be no punk killers no more. We'll be a hundred things. We'll be heroes to some, victims to others, we'll be monsters, we'll be saints. We will be the defining fuckin' image of a national debate. A debate which will go to the very core of our society.'

Wayne's eyes shone with the glory of his idea. He assumed the deep, censorious tone of the typical TV news anchor: 'America will look at itself and ask itself the questions "Who are we? Where are we going? Did Wayne and Scout act alone? Is Bruce Delamitri to blame, or do we all share something of their guilt?"'

Scout just loved it when Wayne was on a roll. He was *so* classy. 'Defining image', 'core of society' – those were real ten-dollar sentences. She never knew how he picked all that stuff up. Like her, he'd left school at the first opportunity, which was about three years before he was legally entitled to do so. Since then all he'd done was hang out and watch TV like everyone else in the country.

Which was, of course, the point.

Wayne had been watching TV his entire life, and it had not all been sit coms and re-runs of *Star Trek*. Decades of surfing the remote had meant a million bites out of the Discovery Channel, CNN, *Oprah* and *Sixty Minutes*, a never-ending diet of 'information' and 'in-depth analysis'. With their inexhaustible supply of doctors, therapists, psychologists and 'experts' of every type, news and chat shows have introduced entire nations to the instant-coffee version of a vocabulary of words and ideas that traditionally take years of study to acquire.

An intelligent man is going to pick up an awful lot

of earnest bullshit and portentous psychobabble if he watches TV his entire life; and Wayne, as Bruce was discovering, was a very intelligent man.

Because Bruce knew that Wayne was right. Right, right, RIGHT. A villain could get turned into a hero inside a single soundbite. And, as in Bruce's case, a hero could end up a villain.

He attempted a defence of sorts. 'Oh yeah. Well, what happens when I go on the TV tomorrow and retract everything? When I tell the world you forced me into accepting responsibility?'

Scout didn't think Bruce was giving Wayne sufficient credit for his brilliant plan. 'You might be dead by then, Mr Big Shot,' she said. 'You might be dead any time.'

Wayne laughed. 'You tell him, baby. But frankly it don't matter what you say tomorrow, Bruce – always assuming you're alive to say it. By tomorrow our little story here will have a life of its own. Every talk show, every paper, will be asking the question "Who's guilty?" Whatever you say tomorrow won't wipe out today. *This* is the image, man. This is the defining moment, the one they'll all remember – bigger than the Rodney King video, bigger than O.J.'s committal, bigger than the Kennedy motorcade.'

'Hey, don't undersell yourself, Wayne,' said Bruce through gritted teeth.

'Come on, man! It doesn't get any better than this. The king of Hollywood, two mass murderers, a dying *Playboy* centrefold, a rinsed-out old hag of an ex-wife, a spoilt, sexy little weeping teen . . . blood, guns . . . we've got it all. Nobody will ever forget this. It'll be burnt into their minds for ever.'

Wayne walked up to Bruce and put his face right

up close. 'And every time anyone sees you, Bruce, they'll remember this image above all the others. They'll remember you with your arms round me and Scout, your daughter weeping, your girlfriend bleeding at your feet. And you saying, "America, wake up! We sow a wind and we reap a whirlwind. These two poor benighted sinners could be kin to any one of us. They are my kin. My son and daughter. I begot them. My sins were visited upon them . . ."

'Now, how 'bout that drink?'

Chapter Thirty

O liver and Dale had been in their studio conference room, preparing to present that morning's edition of *Coffee Time*, when the call came.

'I need high-profile personalities central to the action,' the head of NBC News and Current Affairs had demanded, 'anchoring not from the studio, but from inside the story. The nation needs a friend in that house.'

Murray had already won the battle to be the station which would provide the crew for Wayne's broadcast. 'We were the company of contact and we should have priority,' he had pointed out rather pompously to the other networks, adding, 'What's more, if you don't let us do it I shan't tell you what their demands are, so the people you send in will get it all wrong and get killed.'

Having achieved the priority he desired, Murray had only to persuade Oliver and Dale, in whose celebrity the station had so much invested, that they should be the station's representatives at the centre of the drama. He didn't have much time. Wayne had demanded only a camera operator and a recordist, there had been no talk of presenters. Dale and Oliver would have to do the work of the technicians. They would need to be told how to use the equipment and the minutes were ticking away.

There was of course much to tempt the two slap covered hairspray heads into accepting the job . . . It was a tantalising prospect, to be elevated in a moment from famous person who reads an autocue and interviews celebrities, to news hero of the decade.

On the other hand, the people inside the house *were* mass murderers.

'You're sure he guaranteed safe conduct?' Oliver asked. 'I'm only concerned for Dale, you understand.'

'Absolutely safe conduct,' the chief assured them, 'and I trust him. Why would he harm you? He needs you. The guy is feeding off the media. With our co-operation he's a star, a superstar. Without it he's just a nobody who's going to get the chair. He needs us as much as we need him.'

Dale and Oliver exchanged nervous glances. It occurred to them both that a person who craved fame could get quite a dollop of it by murdering the *Coffee Time* team on live TV. On the other hand, what an opportunity! They would be fearless seekers after truth, war correspondents, risking all to bring the number-one story of the decade into the nation's lounges.

Their boss pressed home his advantage. 'I'm telling you he's given us an unequivocal guarantee.' He lowered his voice. 'But listen, we don't have to tell the world you got that guarantee. We can let the world think you've gone in there with no guarantee of your safety at all, because that's how much the people's right to news and current affairs means to you.'

'Wow,' said Dale.

'"Wow" is right. They'll probably give you the medal of honour,' the chief added.

'And of course we do have a very real duty to the public,' said Oliver, who was ever conscious of his self-appointed status as one of the nation's premier moral guardians.

'So that's settled,' said the chief. 'The equipment is fairly simple. I'll get one of the guys to run through it with you, and after that all you've got to do is take your clothes off and we're cooking.'

He nearly got away with it. For a moment he thought he had.

He hadn't.

'Take our *clothes* off?' Dale stared, aghast.

'Yeah, yeah, yeah. It's no problem,' said Murray, trying to hustle them along.

'You mean *change* our clothes, surely,' said Oliver. 'You mean you want us to put on combat fatigues, no doubt.'

Like all news reporters, Oliver relished the idea of donning a flak-jacket and looking like a soldier.

But the Chief of News and Current Affairs did not mean change their clothes. 'I mean you'll have to take your clothes off. The guy's worried about concealed weaponry. What's the big deal?'

'Ahem,' said Oliver, clearing his throat nervously, 'I think the question is one of presentation.'

Dale and Oliver looked good and were proud of it. Their image was the classic template of the news anchor team, the standard by which all other news anchor teams were judged: he silver and dignified in his late fifties, she cute and feisty in her mid-thirties. In the studio, with their make-up, hairspray and designer power clothing they looked, quite simply, superb. The American dream behind a desk; like some splendid ambassador and his gorgeous second wife.

The problem was that underneath the story was rather different. As, indeed, it normally is.

He, for instance, wore a corset. She was midway through a cellulite-reduction programme. He had two massive and unpleasant hernia scars. She had an insane tattoo on her thigh, smudged by botched efforts to have it removed.

He suddenly remembered that his housemaid was sick and he was into the second day of his last, rattiest pair of jocks. It suddenly occurred to her that she was planning an après-show tryst with her new lover, the second assistant floor assistant. She had therefore come to work wearing a pair of lacy scarlet split-crotch panties with a heart-shaped hole cut out of the bottom.

'Hey, we can get you new underwear for Christ's sake,' Murray said. 'We can put make-up on your blemishes.'

'I don't think so, boss,' said the head make-up artist, who was hovering in the background. 'Oliver and Dale use quite a lot of foundation on their faces. If the same proportions are applied to their whole bodies, I don't think they'll actually be able to walk.'

'I really do think, Chief,' said Oliver, 'that the proper place for the nation's premier anchor team in a crisis like this is in the studio – controlling the operation from the centre, so to speak. After all, generals don't go into battle, do they?'

'I'll do it, but only with a body double,' said Dale, who had not really thought it through.

And so Oliver and Dale missed their chance at media

immortality but, much more importantly, they kept their nasty bits under cover. Considerably relieved, the two of them retreated to the studio, where their wonderful researchers had already lined up an exclusive interview for them with Dove, the actress whom Bruce had reduced to near tears at the Bosom Ball.

As it happened, Police Chief Cornell, already miffed at having his authority usurped by the news broadcasters, would not have allowed Oliver and Dale to do the job anyway. 'We've got to use an experienced news-gathering team,' he insisted, 'preferably one that's seen combat. If we send in someone who fumbles or fucks up, it could push this guy over. I want the best two journalist-technicians you've got.'

And so the call went out for an experienced operator and recordist who had steady nerves and acceptable bodies and were reasonably relaxed about the state of their underwear.

Chapter Thirty-One

The arrangements were made, and Wayne made his way down through the house once more, to await the camera crew.

Meanwhile Bruce paced about the lounge, desperately trying to think of a way out.

Scout was proud of how deeply Wayne's plan had affected him. 'Ain't Wayne smart, huh?' she said.

'I can't do it,' Bruce replied. 'I just can't.'

Velvet was with Brooke, attempting to re-dress her wound with torn cushion covers. She stared up at her father. 'Daddy, you have to. This woman needs a doctor and you heard what he said he'd do to me. He said he'd shoot me in the mouth.'

Velvet was fighting back her tears but none the less was showing a strength of character of which her parents had been completely unaware. Years of wandering round shopping malls with too much money to spend had never brought out the best in her.

'Yes, all right, Velvet. I'm sorry. I won't let that happen.

But I have to think. This is a very terrible thing for me. For us. Wayne's right, you see. Once I do this thing, my life as I know it will be over, no matter what I do, no matter what I achieve, this is all I will be remembered for.'

Brooke, whose life looked as if it was very nearly over already, tried to protest at this. Although it came out only as a gurgle, her meaning was clear: she felt her problem should be number one on the group agenda.

Bruce simply could not bring himself to agree. 'Brooke, I know you're seriously wounded, and, believe me, when I can do something about it I will, but right now I am powerless to help. And I have a problem too. Ten minutes from now the entire world is going to hear me confess to mass murder.'

'But you're being coerced. You can deny it afterwards,' said Farrah. It had begun to dawn on her just how seriously Bruce's defeat was going to affect her own fortunes.

'Oh sure, Farrah. Some plea in mitigation – a retrospective claim to be a pathetic victim, outplayed and manipulated by a piece of scum out of the lowest trailer in the Midwest.'

'You'd better watch your mouth.' Scout did not like to hear Wayne spoken of in that way.

Bruce was too scared to care. 'What? You want me to *like* the guy, Scout? Your boyfriend is a sadistic maniac, a heartless psychopath.'

'You don't know his nice side.'

Bruce actually laughed.

Now Farrah had something to say. She crossed over to the couch where Scout was sitting and sat down beside her. Scout covered her warily.

'If you're thinking of trying to make friends with her,'

said Bruce, 'don't bother. Brooke tried that, and got a busted lip.'

But Farrah had other things on her mind. She had been thinking a lot since Wayne announced his plan and now she had a favour to ask. 'Look . . . Miss . . . um, Scout? Speaking of nice sides, I would like it so much if you could do something for us. A favour.'

'What kind of favour?'

'Would it be all right if my husband made a call?'

'A call? Who's he going to call? The whole world's standing right outside on his lawn.'

'What's on your mind, Farrah?' said Bruce. 'Who do you want me to call?'

Farrah had to make her pitch. She knew it would not sound good, but she had no choice: everything she had was in danger of disappearing with the morning dew. Farrah was a woman who knew what it was like to have nothing, and as far as she was concerned it sucked.

'Bruce, think about it. This thing isn't just going to ruin you as an artist. It will completely destroy you financially as well. Once you claim responsibility for inciting murder, the family of every victim of violence in America is going to sue you, and not just Wayne and Scout's victims' families either, but everyone whose life has been touched by violence. We will be in litigation for ever. Velvet's grandchildren will still be paying. Do you understand? Overnight bankruptcy. What we have to do is transfer all your assets into my name, right now, before you make the broadcast – it won't wash afterwards. So if Miss Scout here will just let you send a little fax to our bank . . .'

It was an impressive display. Everyone was surprised.

'Mom!' Velvet protested. 'This is *so* tacky.'

'Lady, I am protecting your future here.'

Scout was laughing. 'You're something, ain't you?' she said.

'*I'm* something? I'm not the one breaking into people's homes and murdering them. I just don't particularly want some Milwaukee waitress whose husband got knifed in a bar getting hold of my daughter's money, that's all.'

'Well, no one's making any calls, and no one's sending no faxes either, so I guess you'll just have to start thinking 'bout being poor. So there!'

The room was silent for a moment.

'Besides which,' Scout added irritably, 'I reckon maybe that waitress in Milwaukee would have a point. Maybe the great Bruce "Mr Oscar" Delamitri shouldn't have gone making them films and all. Maybe all that stuff Wayne's going to make you say ain't so dumb.'

Bruce was angry now, angry enough to ignore his fear. 'I don't believe it! You are actually trying to convince yourself that you're not really to blame, aren't you? It's not just a trick, you seriously want to believe it. You actually want to dodge responsibility for what you've done. You cowardly little bitch!'

'Daddy, be quiet,' Velvet pleaded. 'She'll kill us!'.

Scout fondled her automatic weapon. 'I ain't going to kill no one, cutie, not 'less they don't do what we tell 'em. All I'm saying is that –'

'*You* are the sole perpetrators of your crimes,' Bruce shouted. 'Nobody pulled the trigger but you.'

'I know that, Mr Delamitri. I admit that. It was us done our crimes, I admit we're to blame.'

'Well, that's mighty big of you, I must say.'

'Daddy, please, be nice,' Velvet begged.

'It's just, well . . .' Scout continued, 'I don't think it

helps any that everything is so ugly all the time. That's all.' She seemed almost wistful.

'What's that supposed to mean?'

'Well, you know, songs and films and stuff. All that used to be an escape from being poor and living in fear. Now everything just seems to rub your face in it. I mean, your films are like, what's that word? . . . when someone's getting off looking at stuff that's none of their business . . .'

'Voyeuristic,' Velvet said helpfully, hoping to mitigate her father's aggression.

'That's right. They're voyeuristic. I mean, you live in a big old house in Hollywood with a pool and a security guy and all –'

'Until your boyfriend cut his head off,' Bruce said bitterly. 'Now I have a decapitated security guard.'

'I *told* you I know we done that stuff and we're to blame.' Scout was getting angry too. 'I'm just saying you got all this luxury, like a king or a president or something, and you pay for it by making films about ordinary, sad, dumb people, people who live in ghettos and projects and trailer parks, and making them look ugly and sick and violent –'

'You *are* ugly and sick and violent!'

'Yes, I guess I am, and I deserve whatever I get. It just seems to me that half of America lives in hell and the other half gets its rocks off watching.'

Scout didn't want to talk about it any more so she put on the TV. Bruce's house was still on the screen and approaching it, rather nervously, were two people in their underwear.

Chapter Thirty-Two

Wayne opened the front door carefully and let the near-naked camera operator and recordist into the house.

'I sincerely apologise for the undignified working conditions,' he said, somewhat taken aback to discover that one of the team, the sound recordist, was a woman, and wondering what Scout would make of that. 'But I'm sure you understand my position here.'

Across the lawn, behind the ring of armoured vehicles that the police had established, the forces of authority watched the scene.

'Well, yet another murdering bastard is about to get his fifteen minutes of fame,' Chief Cornell reflected. The chief had with him his number-one siege team, his top negotiator, his Commander of Special Weapons and Tactics, and his press and media publicist.

'And maybe when he takes a dump we can send someone in to wipe his ass,' said the SWAT boss, furious at the lack of direct action. 'I have Special Forces in position and ready to move, sir. Let my men take this bastard. We can be in and out again in forty-five seconds.'

The publicist was adamantly opposed to this. 'It's too big a risk, sir,' he said. 'All the hostages are in one room, and both targets are heavily armed. If the SWAT guys go in, there could be a complete bloodbath, which I need hardly remind you would be in full view of every TV camera in Hollywood.'

'Yeah, and supposing we pull it off?' the SWAT man replied. 'Stun grenade the bastards and bring 'em out in chains? How about that for the cameras, huh?'

It was a tempting prospect. There is nothing quite so glamorous as a siege broken and hostages saved, especially if those hostages happen to include teen-age girls.

'There is no way Wayne Hudson is going to let you take him out of there alive,' the publicist argued.

'Dead then. Even better. As long as we save the hostages.'

'As long as.'

In the end Cornell decided that, for the time being at least, cautionary counsel must prevail. 'I think we have to see if this media stuff works. Who knows, maybe once he's had his say he might throw the towel in.'

The head of SWAT turned away in disgust. Chief Cornell did not blame him; the decision stuck in his craw too. Even before the Uni Bomber, criminals had been showing a worrying predilection for blackmailing their way on to the media. Deep down, everyone wants to get on TV. A glance at any game show is enough to show just how far people will go to achieve that aim. Why should criminals be any different? More and more, it seemed to Chief Cornell that he and his men were becoming extras in a procession of lunatics' private movies.

'It's getting so we ought to turn ourselves into agents and start charging ten per fucking cent,' he reflected bitterly.

Of course the police were themselves partly to blame, and Cornell knew it. It is the police who supply the footage for police camera shows. It is the police who give never-ending press conferences and appear on public-involvement TV programmes, appealing for witnesses. Chief Cornell knew that he himself had staged many spectacular operations with the cameras and publicity principally in mind. If the cops wanted to be stars, why shouldn't the hoodlums?

Chief Cornell sighed. 'Just as long as the bastard doesn't throw a tantrum and keep us here all day while he sits in his trailer and sulks.'

Chapter Thirty-Three

Inside the house Wayne returned to the lounge with the little ENG crew.

Scout was still watching TV. 'Shhh,' she said.

'A camera operator and a recordist are now inside the siege mansion,' the studio anchorwoman was explaining, 'so we should be getting pictures soon. The recordist is trailing a two-hundred-metre cable feed to the control truck which is parked in the grounds . . . there you can see it there, that's the truck . . . That is the control truck isn't it, Larry?'

'I believe that is the control truck, Susan,' said her partner, 'but I can't be sure. Let's bring in Doctor Mark Raddinger, of the East LA Academy of Media Studies. Doctor Raddinger, is that the control truck we can see now?'

'Yes,' replied a bearded man in polo neck and corduroy jacket who was seated beside Larry, 'that is the control truck.'

'So you can confirm that?' asked Larry.

'Yes, I can confirm that,' replied Doctor Raddinger. 'That is the control truck.'

'Well, it's as we suspected, Susan,' said Larry, 'and we have a confirmation on that. The truck currently on our screens is, as you rightly predicted just moments ago, the control truck.'

'And we can confirm that?' Susan asked.

'Yes,' Larry replied. 'We do now have confirmation. It is the control truck. The truck to which the recordist, who is currently situated inside the siege mansion, is linked by a two-hundred-metre broadcast feed cable.'

'Thanks, Larry,' said Susan. 'And further to that, I can also confirm that the recordist is linked to the TV ratings computer.'

'The TV ratings computer?' Larry enquired. 'That would be the computer which analyses and delivers the TV ratings, right?'

'Yes, it would, Larry.'

'Let's bring in Doctor Mark Raddinger again, here. Mark, can you give us a little background detail on the TV ratings computer?'

'Yes, I can, Larry. The TV ratings computer is the computer which the TV companies use to analyse and deliver an accurate statistical analysis of the TV ratings via computer.'

'I see. Fascinating. And you can confirm that?'

'Yes, I can.'

'And the TV ratings would be how many people are watching?' Susan enquired.

'Statistically and demographically speaking, yes it would –'

Wayne turned the set off. It was giving him a head-ache.

'That's enough TV now, Scout. We got work to do,' he said. 'OK, everybody, listen up. This is Bill and Kirsten, and they are going to make us stars.' He ushered the crew into the room.

Bill and Kirsten entered rather gingerly. They were a tough pair, who had covered wars, famines and presidential elections, but their current circumstances were scarcely likely to put them at their ease. It wasn't so much the woman in the blood-soaked gown who lay gurgling on the floor near the drinks cabinet who bothered them. Nor was it really the two psychopathic maniacs who were pointing automatic weapons at them. It's just never easy to be the only people who turn up at a social gathering dressed only in your underwear.

They felt naked. Bill and Kirsten were a tough, lean young news team, and they liked to look the part. Bill missed his survival tunic with its numerous pockets, out of which he often claimed he could live and work for a month. Kirsten missed her sixteen-lace-hole combat boots, the mere pulling on of which always made her feel tougher and braver. Most of all, they both missed their trousers. There was, however, nothing either of them could do about it, so they applied themselves to the task in hand like the proud professionals they were.

'How do you want to stage this thing?' Bill asked.

Wayne looked at Bruce. 'Bruce, you're the director. Where should these people set up?'

But Bruce remained tight-lipped. He wasn't going to facilitate his own disgrace if he could avoid it.

Wayne shrugged. 'Well, I guess I can do this myself. Maybe I'll get an Oscar too, ha ha! OK, I reckon you guys should set up the camera right there in front of the fireplace.'

Bill and Kirsten did as they were bidden and began to arrange their equipment. Meanwhile, Wayne thought about his staging. 'I believe we should use this couch as kind of centre of the action, OK? 'Cos one thing I know is that whenever anybody's doing any talking on the TV there is just about always a couch somewhere. So if I push it round a little, then I guess you'll be able to include Brooke in the shot. Is that right, Bill?'

'Yes, I can see her,' Bill answered.

'Well that's good, because I think she looks just great lying on the floor like that. Like some kind of wounded swan or something.'

Scout loved it when Wayne talked like that. She firmly believed that, given an education, he could have been a poet. Bill would not have agreed. Seen through his viewfinder, Brooke did not look like a wounded swan at all. She looked like a wounded person, a badly wounded person. Bill had seen many such sights during his career as a war correspondent but he never got used to them and never found them anything but appalling.

'She's dying,' said Velvet, placing a coat over Brooke.

'We're all dying, darlin',' Wayne replied, 'from the very first day we're born. What I'm saying is that her pathetic condition kind of underlines the point I'm making here. A kind of livin', or maybe I should say dyin', example of what men like Bruce here exploit and promote. So get that coat off her, sugar. It ain't cold and that coat's spoiling my picture. Ain't nothing sexy 'bout a coat.'

Velvet did as she was bidden.

'OK, that's good.' Wayne nodded his approval. 'This thing's really coming together now. So how 'bout you?' He turned on Farrah. 'What can we do with you?'

'What do you mean?' Farrah was startled. She had

begun to imagine herself exempt from the action. She was sadly deluded.

'This is TV, honey. Good-lookin' woman like you's gonna be a big draw, particularly 'longside of your cute li'l daughter. Scout baby, take Mrs Delamitri and Miss Delamitri and cuff them to that lampstand behind the sofa . . . C'mon, c'mon, get over there, girls. We ain't making *Gone with the Wind* here, this is live action.'

Scout put her hand in Wayne's bag and produced a pair of handcuffs.

'Got these off a cop,' she explained, adding darkly, 'He don't need 'em no more.'

As Scout manacled Farrah and her daughter to the lampstand, with uncharacteristic humility Wayne asked if it would be OK to take a look through the camera lens.

'You're the director,' said Bill.

'Well, that's right, I guess I am.' Wayne dropped the humility and strutted over to the camera as if he was Cecil B. de Mille. Pressing his eye to the viewfinder, he surveyed the scene thoughtfully. He could see Bruce sitting on the couch. Behind him were Farrah and Velvet and to one side lay Brooke.

'OK now, Scout,' Wayne said, further composing his shot, 'get down there beside Bruce, 'cos that's where we gonna to be sat, OK? Right next to the man.'

But he was still not quite satisfied.

'It seems all right to me,' Kirsten commented nervously. 'I mean, it contains all the elements, doesn't it?' She wanted to get done and get out of there.

'The elements is just the basics of the shot,' Wayne replied. 'What we got to do here is make one compelling fuckin' image. I mean *compelling*. Because if we ain't good, pretty soon the networks are going to go back to their regular schedules and all we'll be left with is CNN. What are we up against, honey? What's the opposition? I guess you know more about daytime TV than any woman of your size and weight in the whole USA.'

'*Star Trek: The Next Generation*, *Family Ties*, *Cosby* and *Oprah* repeats,' Scout recited proudly. 'I don't know all the cable stuff.'

Kirsten looked up from her equipment. 'Wayne, when this goes out live, every station in the country will pick up on it. You'll be the only thing showing nationwide.'

'Y'hear that, Bruce? I'm making you bigger than you was already. Now, you sure you're going to be able to get all this in, Bill? What's your edge of frame?'

'Edge of frame'. Scout nearly cried, she was so proud of Wayne.

'We have plenty of width,' Bill said. 'I'll just lock it off and take the whole thing in a static five shot. Have another look.'

Wayne did so and then, with a thoughtful frown on his face, crossed to the two handcuffed women. He studied them for a moment and then ripped open Velvet's smart little pink jacket, causing the buttons to fly off.

Scout was not at all happy with this development. Nor, of course, was Velvet, but she was in no position to protest.

'Wayne, take your hands off that girl right now!' Scout shouted.

'You want the ratings, honey? Huh? You want people to watch this thing? Sex is important on TV, sex sells.' Wayne tore open Velvet's blouse and pulled it down off her shoulders, revealing her brassière. 'Cute, huh?' he said. 'Can't show too much. There's strict rules. Just

enough for the couch potatoes out there in TV land to
get themselves off on . . . OK, I guess we're just about
ready. Bruce, in just a moment or two you're going to sit
here on this couch 'tween me and Scout and tell America
what I said to tell them.'

'Look, Wayne, this is –'

'And if you don't, I'll kill sweet little Velvet here, and
Mrs Delamitri – not that you give a flying fuck in a
thunderstorm 'bout her. Also of course, I'll kill you. I
think you're going to do what I tell you. Ain't you,
Bruce?'

Chapter Thirty-Four

Outside they were waiting for pictures. The media, the police and, increasingly, the nation were all waiting for pictures, because the siege was now the number-one news story US-wide.

'So is this asshole going to make his statement or not?' said Chief Cornell, pacing about outside his command truck. 'How long do we wait before we hit him?'

Already the police chief could sense his splendid day getting away from him. He wasn't the only one, either. His subordinates were getting increasingly frustrated and were putting Cornell under enormous pressure to take control of the situation. Sieges, in their opinion, were a matter for the police, not the media, and a lot of cops felt pretty bad about being usurped and upstaged in this manner. Particularly the SWAT boss.

'We're being blackmailed,' he said. 'This killer has bought his piece of immortality by murdering people, and now we've brought every TV station in the country to his door. The guy is making us kiss his ass, when what we need to do is *kick* his ass. We should pull the damn plug, get in there and show that motherfucker, and every motherfucker watching, that you do not mess with the LAPD.'

That was easy for the SWAT man to say. His wasn't the uneasy head that wore the crown. Chief Cornell was the cop with whom the buck would stop, and he knew that if he crashed in now and deprived the media of its prize they would finish him. If even one hostage got killed, which in all truth would almost certainly happen, he and his force would be pilloried as gung-ho, macho assholes, Neanderthals who couldn't wait and talk like responsible adults but had to barge in like the over-excited thugs they were.

Besides which, as the police publicist pointed out, there was another way of looking at it. 'With respect, we have no right to go in now. By any standards at all, a televised confrontation between the country's top action film-maker and the country's top criminal is an astonishing event. It's genuine and important news, no matter how it may have been brought about. The police have to allow the media to do its job. It's our responsibility to defend, and if necessary facilitate, an open and democratic society.'

The SWAT commander had never heard so much pansy bullshit in his entire life. 'It's our responsibility,' he barked, 'to fuck all over these scum until we have made damn sure that they never fuck with us again. Besides which, you know damn well that if someone gets killed while we're hanging around and holding the media's hand, the media will turn right round and blame us for *not* intervening. They can't lose and we can't win, so we should ignore the fuckin' parasites and get on with our damn job.'

Ignore the media? The police publicist nearly fainted.

Even Chief Cornell knew it was a stupid thing to say. 'You might as well say ignore the traffic, ignore the buildings, ignore the public,' he said. 'TV isn't an observer any more. It isn't two hours of news and entertainment in the corner of people's lounges, in the corner of people's *lives*. It's in the middle, right alongside of food. There's two results to every event, what actually happened and what people think happened. That's a fact, pal, and if you believe you can ignore it, then you don't have no election to face come the spring.'

If Brad Murray had heard Chief Cornell speak, he would have nodded sagely. Like it or not, the chief was right. It had long been accepted that TV shaped events, that things happened because the cameras were there, that what the cameras saw was what the event became. Now, however, TV was the event. Before, events didn't get seen without television; increasingly events no longer *existed* without television.

'We wait,' said Chief Cornell. 'Let the guy have his air time.'

'It's our duty as democrats,' said the police publicist.

'Bull-double-shit,' said the SWAT commander.

Chapter Thirty-Five

Inside the house Bruce found himself sitting on the couch between Scout and Wayne. The camera was directly in front of him and he was staring down the barrel. He knew he was about to enter the national consciousness as a patsy, a pathetic loser, coerced and abused into making a snivelling, never-to-be-forgotten, cowardly confession on live TV.

He would be like those combat pilots who are shot down by foreign dictators and then trotted out the next day, drugged and bleary, to renounce the US and profess allegiance to their adopted country. Everybody knows those guys have no choice, that they have been coerced, but somehow people never feel quite the same way about them afterwards. You can't just forget it when your hero suddenly and publicly denies every principle he has ever held dear. There is a secret feeling that he should have fallen on his sword. Unfair and unreasonable, of course, but none the less there.

Bruce struggled to master his panic and anguish.

'Wayne, this isn't going to work,' he pleaded. 'You're both hated murderers and one single statement from me, made under duress, won't change that. All it'll do is screw up my life for ever.'

'Well that's a shame, Bruce, because it's the best shot I've got and we're going to try it. Bill? Kirsten? Everything ready?'

'Yes it is, boss,' said Bill, who had deduced rightly that Wayne would enjoy being called 'boss'.

Bruce decided the time had come to make a desperate pitch, one he had been considering ever since the camera crew had arrived. He turned and tried to look Wayne in the eye – not an easy thing to do when you're sitting next to someone on a deep, soft couch.

'Debate me,' he said.

'Say what?'

'Debate me.'

Wayne frowned; he didn't understand. Bruce hurried to establish his idea.

'Listen, Wayne. You're not stupid, and neither is Scout. You know that the best you have here is a long shot. You know, deep down, that me sitting here with a gun at my head, claiming reponsibility for your actions, is not necessarily going to cut a lot of ice.'

'Like I say, it's all we got,' Wayne said. 'OK, Bill let's –'

Bruce pushed on. 'It isn't. It isn't all you've got. You could take a risk. Debate me, prove your point without coercion. Establish your case live on TV.'

'You be careful, Wayne.' Scout was uneasy. 'You got a plan, you stick to it.'

'Come on, Scout.' Bruce twisted round on the couch to face her. 'Think what you were saying earlier – all that stuff about me exploiting the ugly and the downtrodden, how I get rich leeching off the suffering of the poor. That's a better argument than just using me as some kind of puppet. Put your case. Establish my guilt and let me deny it. Think what extraordinary television it would make . . . You guys could be *real* stars, not just blackmailing hoodlums but proper participants. Stars.'

'Stars?' said Scout. That had got her.

'Of course stars. It's obvious. The public loves a fighter.'

Bruce had to win them round. He knew this was his chance to snatch victory from the jaws of defeat, to turn himself from a victim into a hero, to be the man who stood by his principles even when the very forces of darkness and reaction had invaded his own home. To be the man who gave America its wake-up call establishing for once and for all that 'We are all responsible for our own actions' – particularly violent criminals.

'Think about it, Wayne,' Bruce said. 'I represent the cultural élite of this country. You represent the dispossessed, the underclass, the lowest group in society. What a confrontation, what an image!'

'Yeah, and what's in it for you, mister?' Scout was no pushover. She had already demonstrated in her terrifying defeat of Brooke that she was not to be taken in.

'I get my chance to refute your allegations. I get a chance to present you as the independently minded, personally responsible murdering maniacs that I believe you to be.'

'Daddy, be nice,' Velvet pleaded, but Bruce did not even hear her.

'That's the risk you take,' he continued. 'Put your case, see if you can beat mine. If you win, you *really* win: the nation will never forget you or forgive me. If you lose, I honestly don't think you're any worse off.'

'Don't do it, hon. Your plan's better. Just make him say the stuff.'

But Wayne was intrigued. 'Well, I don't know, babe. I mean, I think we've got a pretty good argument here. Let's face it, half the Republican Party plus just 'bout every preacher in the country reckons Bruce here's the devil incarnate . . .'

For the umpteenth time that terrible night, Bruce allowed himself a moment of hope. 'Think of your image, Scout,' he said. 'What do you want that camera to see? A couple of sullen thugs on a couch, or good-looking, articulate anti-heroes? If you survive all this and avoid the chair, you'll be on every teen T-shirt in the country. You'll be able to name your price.'

This was the right button to press for Scout.

'You really think we'll be stars?'

'Of course you will. This is national TV. Win or lose, half the country's going to fall in love with you. In actual fact you can't lose.'

'You want to be a star, baby doll?'

'Of course I do, honey, but . . . Oh, I don't know . . .'

Meanwhile the outside world was getting impatient, and poor Kirsten, the recordist, crouching in her underwear in front of Bruce's fireplace, was getting the sharp end of their anger.

'What the hell is going on, Kirsten?' The producer's voice screamed along the cable link and into her headset radio receiver. 'When are we going to see some pictures?'

The producer completely ignored the delicate nature of Kirsten's situation, demanding, as TV producers often do, that everyone be told to jump to the command of the cameras. In some ways it was not his fault. He had a whole line of senior producers, editors, section chiefs and channel-controllers crushed into his ENG truck, not to mention the chief of the LAPD, accompanied by an angry man in a flak-jacket who kept muttering, 'Bullshit. Bull-double-shit.' Outside the truck there were countless more police and media operatives milling around, and all of them, inside and out, were demanding that the producer punch up some visuals pronto.

'What's going on, Kirsten? Talk to me,' he shouted into Kirsten's headset. 'We have over two hundred stations nationwide requesting footage, and all the majors have crashed into their schedules. We can't broadcast pictures of the outside of his house for ever. The studio anchors are running out of crap . . .'

The studio anchors were indeed getting a little desperate.

'Our cameras are still located outside the Delamitri mansion,' Larry and Susan were able to confirm for the millionth time. 'And we have with us an expert on the exteriors of celebrity homes. Doctor Ranulph Tofu, of the New Age Academy of Astral Learning, will be able to give us a reading on Bruce Delamitri's state of mind, based principally on the colour of his garage doors.'

In the control truck they were tearing out their hair.

'What are we waiting for, Kirsten?'

The producer got no reply. Kirsten heard him but said nothing, so he kept on shouting, turning up the volume until Kirsten's head shook.

'How long does this jerk think we can tie up the networks on his behalf? Ask the asshole what he thinks he's doing.'

In his desire to make TV, the producer was forgetting that Kirsten was ten feet away from a mass murderer. She rightly felt that to ask the asshole what he thought he was doing was not tactically the right way to go about things. But she had to say something, if only because, after ten minutes of her producer's voice screaming directly into her brain, a bullet in the head was beginning to look like a reasonable option.

'Excuse me,' she said, trying to appear as detached an observer as possible, 'the people in vision control are asking what kind of timescale we're looking at here. Just so they can give you the very best coverage they can. They don't want to lose the audience we've built up.'

Wayne looked at Bruce and made a decision. 'You want to debate me, Bruce? Let's do it.'

'And will you let Farrah and Velvet go afterwards? Will you let Brooke get to a doctor?'

'Maybe. I never know what I'm gonna do, Bruce. It's my job: I'm a maniac.'

Kirsten finally spoke into her talkback. 'Stand by in the truck.' She turned to Wayne. 'OK, Mr Hudson, they're ready whenever.' She was desperate to get out of that room and into some clothes.

'You ready, Scout?' Wayne enquired. 'Ready to be a TV star?'

Suddenly Scout realised the enormity of what they were about to do. She hadn't checked her hair, her make-up, her clothes . . . 'Oh Wayne, I look a sight. Can they send in someone to do make-up?'

'You look gorgeous, honey. Brooke did your hair just peachy. Are you ready, Bruce?'

'Yes I am, Wayne.'

'Can I give control a picture?' Kirsten asked.

Wayne said she could, and Bill turned his camera on.

'Speed,' said Bill. Kirsten flicked a switch. In the control van ten screens jumped into life and the assembled opinion-formers finally got what they wanted.

Chapter Thirty-Six

'Jesus!' The producers and cops whistled as they caught their first glimpse of the little tableau Wayne had created.

'Stand by to broadcast,' Brad Murray shouted, forgetting for a moment in his excitement that, within the control truck, etiquette dictated that he should relay his commands via the producer.

Outside, in the grounds of Bruce's mansion, a hundred hairsprayed anchors alerted the viewing public to the imminence of developments.

'I believe we should be getting pictures from inside of the Delamitri abode any moment now. It appears there's going to be some kind of joint statement from the multimillionaire director and his captor, mass-killing Mall Murderer Wayne Hudson.'

In the studios, the anchors hurried to explain the situation yet one more time. 'The ratings computer is fed by a representative sample of the nation as a whole, whose televisions are connected to a central monitor.

This monitor can then give an instant picture of what people are watching. Wayne Hudson will be aware, quite literally second by second, how many people have tuned in.'

'We know that!' the viewers of America shouted as one. 'You told us a million times. Get on with it.'

Inside the besieged house, Kirsten informed Wayne that control had a picture. 'We can go live to air any time.'

'OK, let's do it,' said Wayne.

'Let's do it,' said the Chief of NBC News and Current Affairs.

'Yes, let's do it,' his opposite numbers at the other networks and major cable stations agreed.

'Stand ready, you guys, in case we have to pick up the pieces,' the chief of police said loudly to his senior officers, attempting to remind the media types that there were people around who didn't work in television.

'We're live!' the producer screamed into Kirsten's ear.

'We're live, Mr Hudson,' Kirsten said calmly, 'live across America.'

It hardly seemed real, sitting there as they were in Bruce's lounge. Wayne grabbed Bruce's remote control and flipped on the TV. Sure enough, there they all were on the screen, the framing exactly as Wayne had wanted it. He tried another couple of channels. There they were again, and again. Scout screamed in embarrassment, and buried her head in her hands. Wayne turned the sound down on the TV but left the vision on: he wasn't taking any chances that the bargain would be broken.

'OK, Bruce,' said Wayne, trying to look calm and collected, 'you're the professional. Why don't you just explain to people what's going on?'

Scarcely able to believe it was real, Bruce addressed Bill's camera.

'Um . . . Hullo, everybody. I'm sorry that your morning's viewing has been disrupted but I guess you all know what's going on here. I'm Bruce Delamitri, the film-maker. The two women you see manacled behind me are Farrah, my wife, and our daughter, Velvet. The wounded woman on the floor to my right is Brooke Daniels, the model –'

Brooke, whose condition had stabilised somewhat with Velvet's help, croaked in protest.

'– I'm sorry, Brooke Daniels, the actress. Anyway, we are all prisoners of Wayne Hudson and his partner, Scout, whom you see sitting beside me.'

'Hey,' said Wayne, with nervous bravado.

'Hullo, America,' Scout mumbled, her head still buried in her hands.

'So, introductions over. Let's come to the point.' Incredibly, Bruce was beginning to enjoy himself. Here was his chance, the chance he had dodged the night before, the chance to take on the censors and reactionaries. And oh, such a chance. The Oscars podium paled in comparison to his current platform. What an opportunity! To face down two vicious, heavily armed murderers on live TV and bring them to some understanding of their personal responsibility for their actions. Bruce glowed with excitement. This would be a genuine moment in the social history of the United States, and he was to be the mouthpiece. He must be careful, he must concentrate. There must be no 'legs of fire' this time.

'I make films in which actors and stunt artists pretend to kill people,' he said. 'Wayne and Scout actually kill people. Not long ago, they decapitated my security guard,

689

and they shot my agent, Karl Brezner, dead in this very room – his corpse lies in my kitchen. They have also seriously wounded Ms Daniels here. They are, of course, the notorious Mall Murderers and have over the last few weeks slaughtered numerous other innocents. Is that a fair summary, Wayne?'

Wayne thought for a moment. 'Well, Bruce, my sweet momma brought me up a Christian, so I guess I know that none of us is truly innocent, because even tiny babies are born with the original sin upon them, passed down to us all from Adam.'

'Is that why you shoot people? Because they're sinners?' Bruce enquired, a sense of huge intellectual superiority welling up inside him.

'To tell you the truth, I don't know why I shoot people. Partly, I guess, because it's so easy.'

'Well, innocent or not, I think we can all at least agree that Wayne and Scout have made something of a habit of shooting people they don't know.'

'That is the case,' Wayne admitted. 'We sure do that.'

'So what has all this to do with me?' Bruce continued, sounding more like a schoolmaster every minute. 'Well, Wayne and Scout have broken into my house and attacked my friends because they claim that I am in part responsible for their actions. They contend that in some way my work "inspired" them to do what they do. Now, I of course utterly refute this puerile concept –'

'We never said you'd inspired us, Mr Delamitri.' Scout's head finally emerged from her hands. 'Now don't you go putting words into our mouths.'

'Forgive me, I thought that was what this whole debate was about,' Bruce replied.

'Daddy, don't be so patronising,' Velvet cried out from the lampstand.

Wayne considered Bruce's answer. 'No, Bruce, Scout's right. "Inspired" is the wrong word altogether. I mean, it ain't like we saw a guy and a girl shooting people in your movie and said, "Hey, I never thought of that. That's what we should be doing."'

'So my work does not inspire you? Then I'm confused. I cannot imagine what other point you make when you seek to equate me with your crimes.'

Wayne knew when he was being talked down to. 'It ain't a direct thing, Bruce,' he answered sharply. 'We ain't morons. We didn't walk straight out of *Ordinary Americans* and shoot the popcorn seller –'

Scout had been brought up to be honest. She couldn't let this go by. 'Actually, Wayne, we did.'

'Once,' Wayne conceded. 'We did that once, that's all. I must have seen *Ordinary Americans* fifty times, and only one time did I walk out and shoot the popcorn seller. What is more, that wasn't because of no movie, it was because the stupid bastard in question was a popcorn seller who would not sell us any popcorn.'

In the control truck the producer nearly gave birth in horror. 'For Christ's sake!' he screamed into Kirsten's ear. 'Can't you tell that dumb fucker to watch his dirty fucking mouth? It is ten thirty in the fucking morning!'

'Excuse me, Mr Hudson,' Kirsten interrupted nervously, 'could you possibly moderate your language? We're picking up a massive audience share but adult dialogue is going to cause problems. The children's channel has already gone back to *Sesame Street*.'

'Yes, Wayne,' Scout scolded, 'you watch your mouth, now.'

'Well, I'm sorry, honey, and I 'pologise to you good people out there, specially if you're watching with young people. But you know, what I'm describing here was a very aggravating situation.'

'Yes, honey, it was.' Scout turned to the camera as if she was speaking to a girl friend. 'We'd just come on out of the movie and I said to Wayne to get me some popcorn and Wayne said, "Sure, honey pie. If that's what you want I'll get you a big bucket." But the popcorn seller said he only sold popcorn before the movie, and it was after the movie so I couldn't have none.'

'He was there, man.' Wayne appealed to the camera. 'With the popcorn and the buckets and a scoop and a hat on and all that stuff, but he would not sell me none.'

'So you shot him?' Bruce enquired.

'Yes, sir. Yes I did. I shot that boy, because it ain't as if the world's short of assholes, now is it? The world is not going to miss one asshole more or less. Pardon me for my language.' He addressed this last to the camera.

In the control truck, there was furious debate about whether they could continue to broadcast such an intensely unpredictable situation live. Murder and mayhem were one thing, bad language was quite another.

Eventually it was decided that they could not censor the news while it was happening, that they had a duty to broadcast. They would, however, try to bleep out the strongest bits of Wayne's language.

On the numerous screens in the truck and the many millions around the nation, Bruce was still trying to get to the core of Wayne's argument. 'So you shot the popcorn seller because he was an asshole? Not, and this is an important point, because you'd just seen a movie full of death and destruction?'

Wayne sounded almost weary. 'Bruce, like I say, you are taking all this far too literally. Does anybody shoot a popcorn seller in *Ordinary Americans*?'

'I don't believe so.'

'You don't believe damn right. Fifty-seven people get shot in *Ordinary Americans*, did you know that?'

'I knew it was a lot.'

'Wayne counted them,' Scout said proudly.

'Well, of course I counted them, honey pie, or how would I know? They don't put it up on the titles do they? Like, um, that damn film you liked, *Marrying and Dying* or something – there was some faggot in a kilt who should have died a whole lot earlier as far as I'm concerned, like before the damn film started.'

'*Four Weddings and a Funeral*.'

'That's right. Well, Bruce here did not call his movie *Fifty-Seven Murders, Plus People Taking Drugs and Screwing Each Other*, did he?'

'I guess not, honey.'

'Then don't talk dumb in front of the American people. I counted who got shot in your movie, Bruce. Cops got shot, drug dealers got shot, pregnant teenage girls got shot, an old lady got one straight through the colostomy bag – man, that was a great scene, Bruce. How do you think up that stuff?' Wayne turned to the camera to explain his enthusiasm. 'There's a shoot-out, right? And this sweet little old lady takes a stray and guess what, man? It goes through her colostomy bag, and do you know what she says? She says, "Shit." That's all, just "Shit." I mean, man, is that a good line or what? Everyone in the movie house just cracks up. Pardon my language but it was in the movie and Bruce here did get an Oscar for it, so I guess it's art.'

693

'I'm glad you liked it,' Bruce said woodenly.

'I sure did, but what I'm saying is, no popcorn seller got shot.'

Bruce was getting irritated. 'So what's your point? I thought you were claiming diminished responsibility on account of my influence over you. Isn't that what all this is about?'

'Who was the guy who rang the bell and the dogs dribbled? Pancake or whatever. I saw a thing about him on *Timewatch*.'

'I think you mean Pavlov,' said Bruce.

'That's right, Pavlov. Well, you ain't no Pavlov, Bruce, and we ain't no dribbling dogs. There ain't nothing specific here. I am talking generally. I'm saying that you make killing cool.'

Bruce leapt at the point. So far his heroic battle had not been going quite as splendidly as he'd hoped. He had allowed himself to be sidetracked. He had to regain the initiative.

'No, Wayne. I make going to the movies cool. Let me put it plainly. You are sick.' He addressed the camera directly. 'These two people are sick. They have erred from the acceptable norm. They have diseased and unbalanced minds. Did I unbalance them? Certainly not. Did society? I doubt it. No, they are simply sick. There have always been murderers and sadists. Long before there was TV and movies, people got killed and raped. Now –'

Bruce was on a roll, winding up to utterly discredit these sad nobodies with the massive force of his intellectual power. Unfortunately, Wayne interrupted him.

'Tell me something, Bruce. I've always wanted to know, do you get a hard-on when you make that stuff?' He said this with a wink at the camera. 'I'll bet you do, boy, 'cos I admit it just thrills me. What's more, I look round the movie theatre and I can see all the other guys and they're just loving it too. Every one of them is just itching to haul out a gun and blast away. Of course, they don't do it, but I can see them licking their lips and wishing, just the same.'

'That's the point, Wayne, nobody *does* anything.' Bruce was slightly shaken. He wanted to keep the debate on what Wayne did, not on what he himself did. 'It's just a story.'

'It ain't no story,' Scout protested. 'First time I saw *Ordinary Americans*, I said to Wayne to tell me when the blood and gore happened so I could close my eyes. I guess I had my eyes closed just about the whole picture.'

'That's right,' Wayne agreed. 'Ain't no room for a story in your pictures, Bruce. A story is like . . . um . . . so the dude kills the dude because of, like, this reason and that reason, and afterwards he goes away and does some other stuff. A story is, well a *story* – stuff happens. Showing the dude killing the dude, in slow mo', now, that's a fantasy.'

Bruce knew this was madness, nonsense. He made movies. These two killed people. There was no connection, and yet somehow he could not nail the debate down. It was slipping away.

'To sane people, it's a diversion,' Bruce said. 'It's an entertainment, perhaps not a very edifying one, but an entertainment none the less. It's only a fantasy to people who are sick in the head like you and your girlfriend here.'

'So we're sick, are we?'

Wayne shifted his gun on his lap but Bruce was determined to press the point. 'You're sicker than a rabid dog.'

From behind the couch in the back of Bill's picture Velvet cried out in anguish. 'Daddy, be careful. Don't make him angry.'

In the control truck they cheered. They loved it when the cute little girl chipped in. Now that was television.

'Sneak a close-up on the daughter,' the producer whispered into his microphone, but Bill ignored him. As far as Bill was concerned, Wayne was producing the show by the authority of the gun he had on his lap.

Bruce attempted to reassure his daughter. 'He isn't going to kill you, honey. We're on live TV. He's pleading for his life.'

'If I'm sick, Bruce, and you said I was,' Wayne said, 'what does that make you?'

'Excuse me?'

'Well, don't your movies exploit my sickness? Don't you use the terrible, sick, mental condition that afflicts psychopaths like me, just to give people a thrill? You never saw no Aids or cancer movie where the sick people were the bad guys, did you? But that's the way it is in your movies. You want to know what I am, Bruce? I am the exploitably ill.'

Things were beginning to go horribly wrong. The question seemed to be getting more complex. Bruce had set out to shoot down gloriously a fatuous contention, but his target was moving, putting up smokescreens.

'Perhaps you're suggesting that you committed your crimes as a protest against my treatment of psychotics as a class?'

It was a weak response. Bruce knew that this was not what Wayne had suggested at all. He was trying to buy time with smart comments, in order to collect his thoughts.

'I don't know what I'm suggesting,' Wayne replied, 'except I'm suggesting that it ain't only the criminals who create a culture of violence.'

'It's only the criminals who commit the crimes. Violent people create a violent society.' This was the point Bruce wanted to make. He needed to stick with that and not allow himself to be diverted. 'It is violent people who create a violent society,' he repeated, firmly and loudly.

'Are you sure?' Scout suddenly shouted. 'Are you absolutely sure about that? Are you one hundred per cent absolutely sure that no matter how many times you show a sexy murder to a rock and roll soundtrack you have no effect on the people who watch? Because if there's even one shred of doubt in your mind, then what right have you to make your movies?'

'I am an artist. I cannot ask myself that question.' Bruce regretted it the moment he'd said it. It was true, but that wasn't the point. He knew that claims of intellectual immunity would be unlikely to impress in the heartlands.

'Why? Why can't you? If you won't take responsibility for your actions, why should we take responsibility for ours?'

Damnation, where did this bitch suddenly learn to talk?

'Because my actions are peaceable and within the law.'

It was weak. Bruce knew it, she knew it.

'A real man answers to his conscience, not to the law.'

'And I am perfectly happy to do that. Is your conscience clear?'

Wayne laughed. 'Of course, it's not clear, man. We kill people we've never met.'

'Yes, like every king and president there ever was,' Scout added.

Bruce felt his bowels almost move with tension. This woman was pulling out red herrings like a demented fishmonger. Christ, if they were going to spread the debate that wide, he was finished. To Bruce's intense relief, Wayne himself headed this one off. 'Now I've told you before I don't want to hear that kind of Communistic bull Scout. I do not respect much in this world but I do respect the American way. And in my opinion things'd be a whole lot better if the president was to shoot a few more people, 'specially them damn A-rab towel heads who keep burnin' Ol' Glory.'

'Excuse me,' Kirsten said nervously, looking up from her equipment. 'Um, this is all very interesting, of course, and the producers are delighted, they're *very* happy in control . . . it's just that the ratings are beginning to drop – see here, it's all displayed on my monitor. The chief wants to know if it would be OK to record this and then edit it for the evening news?'

'No need for that, Kirsten. I have an idea. Hey, America!' Wayne shouted at the camera. 'Listen, phone your friends, tell them all to tune in, because in ninety seconds I'm going to shoot Farrah Delamitri. In one minute and one half, the wife of the guy who just got the Oscar gets shot dead live!'

Chapter Thirty-Seven

Farrah screamed. Velvet screamed. Even Kirsten thought about protesting, but then she remembered the sacred duty of the news-gatherer: never intervene, not even if the news is being created for your benefit.

'Please, Wayne, don't,' Bruce said.

'She's my Mom!' Velvet sobbed.

Outside, in the command truck, Chief Cornell was in agony. Should he send his SWAT teams in now? If he did, there would certainly be bloodshed. If he didn't, likewise.

Oh, how he wished that somebody else would take responsibility.

Inside the mansion, Wayne had got up and was studying the ratings on Kirsten's computer screen.

'They're climbing, aren't they?'

'Yes they are,' Kirsten replied, 'but none the less my producer is saying please don't kill the woman.'

Farrah sobbed, pulling pathetically at her manacled hand.

In the control truck a lively debate was in progress.

'We have to terminate the broadcast,' some were saying. 'He's feeding off it. It's creating his crimes.'

'He killed plenty of people before there were any cameras to play to,' others contended. 'We can't turn off. We don't choose the news. We don't have a right to censor national events just because they're unattractive.'

'But if he's creating the news for *us*?

'We can't take responsibility for his actions.'

'Can we take responsibility for our own?'

The cameras stayed on, as no one had doubted for a moment that they would, and the ratings continued to climb.

Inside the lounge Wayne showed off his guns to the camera. 'Hurry up now, y'all,' he said. 'You don't want to miss it, do ya?'

When the ninety seconds ran out Wayne shot Farrah dead.

Chapter Thirty-Eight

'OK, hit it,' said Chief Cornell, and silently, through the doors, the windows and even the roof, the SWAT teams began to enter Bruce's house.

In the siege room the shot still resonated.

'You bastard! When will this end!' Bruce had rushed over and was holding Velvet, who sobbed hysterically, still handcuffed to the lampstand beside her dead mother.

'You saw the ratings, man. They went up. Blame the couch potatoes.'

'You hypocritical swine!' Bruce shouted. '*You* killed her – no one else did! What is it you're saying? That the media, the public, is responsible for the fact that you're a murdering lunatic?'

'I'm just saying I wouldn'ta shot her if people had switched to *The Simpsons*.'

'You are responsible!'

'Yes. I'm responsible for me, but you are responsible for you and they are responsible for them. I don't see anyone doing much about that. I've got an excuse, I'm a psycho. What's your get-out?'

Kirsten received a message from the producer. She turned to Bill. 'Get down! There's a SWAT team coming in!'

'No!' Wayne shouted into the camera.

Above them they could hear the sound of the roof being breached. Wayne grabbed Scout by the hand, and addressed the camera. 'Wait! Hold it. I'll give myself up, Scout too, I swear. Stop the attack. Keep the cameras rolling. We'll give up.'

Outside, Chief Cornell signalled that his forces should pause. Was it possible that they could get out of this nightmare without further bloodshed?

Wayne continued to shout at the camera. 'But we give ourselves up to the people. The people are responsible. They decide our fate, the fate of everybody in this room.' He had hold of the ratings computer now. 'It's up to you, the people out there . . . the lives of us all are in your hands. Here's how it is. When I've finished talking, if everybody watching switches off their TV, I swear me and Scout will walk out of here with our hands up . . . But if you keep on watching, I will kill every last mutha in this room, including myself and Scout. Not a bad show, huh? Exciting, right? And to see it, all you have to do is stay tuned for another few seconds. Well, you're responsible. Are you gonna turn off your TV?'

Chapter Thirty-Nine

INTERIOR. THE LOUNGE. DAY.

Wide shot. The room eerily still. Wayne stands with Scout before the television camera. In one hand he carries his weapon, in the other the ratings computer.
Close-up on Wayne from the TV camera's point of view. Grainy, video-style quality to the picture.

> WAYNE
> (Snarling into camera)
> I said, are you gonna turn off your TVs?

Whip pan down from Wayne's distorted face to the ratings computer. Picture turns to sudden hard focus. We see what is clearly some kind of graph climbing.
Wide shot of room. Wayne hurls the computer to the ground.

> WAYNE
> (Shouting)
> No you ain't!

Cut to ...

INTERIOR. THE TV CONTROL TRUCK. DAY.

Chief Cornell and the others are watching Wayne on the screens. Fast, jagged, staccato zoom on to Wayne's image on one of the screens. Mid two shot of Cornell and the SWAT commander.

CHIEF CORNELL

Take him.

EXTERIOR. THE ROOF OF THE MANSION. DAY.

SWAT officers blast their way through.

Jump cut to ...

EXTERIOR. A WINDOW OF THE MANSION. DAY.

SWAT officers swing through windows on abseiling ropes, smashing glass.

Jump cut to ...

INTERIOR. OUTSIDE THE LOUNGE DOOR AT THE TOP OF THE STAIRWAY INSIDE THE MANSION. DAY.

SWAT officers smash door down.

Jump cut to ...

INTERIOR. THE LOUNGE. DAY.

Extreme wide shot. Wayne and Scout at centre.
Mute sound. Slow motion.

SWAT officers burst through the windows and doors. Wayne and Scout open fire.

A little later the room was filled with strange green figures. Green jump suits, green rubber boots and gloves, green face masks. The green figures were tracing the outlines of the dead. One of them tried to draw a line around Wayne. The chalk made little impression on the sticky swamp of congealing blood in which his body lay. The green man tried using some white tape but nothing much sticks to blood soaked shag pile.

The whole room was alive with flashing light, the effect was almost stroboscopic. Hundreds and hundreds of photographs were being taken for further analysis. The contorted features of the corpses flickered in brief moments of glorious illumination. Their grotesquely twisted limbs seemed almost to twitch in the jaggedly pulsating light.

Hundreds of bullets and cartridge cases were being tweezered from the floor, more prised from the walls. Hairs were plucked from clothing, bloodied thumb prints carefully preserved. The green men and women missed nothing. A pair of pink Doc Martens, freckled with a few spots of blood, were photographed where they lay then placed in a plastic bag marked LAPD. Lab. Likewise a can of hair mousse, a pair of panty hose, a tiny glass, miraculously still upright and containing a splash of *crème de menthe*.

There was little point in this forensic zeal. Everyone knew who'd killed whom, who had died and who had survived. The whole thing had been captured on television and would shortly be available on video in all good stores.

Ben Elton

There is however a process and the green figures had a job to do. A full inquiry into the events of that terrible Oscar night had already been promised. The authorities were anxious to show that, despite everything, they remained in control.

Outside Bruce's house the survivors were carried away in screaming ambulances. Other ambulances waited for the dead.

Epilogue

Bruce survived Wayne and Scout's bloody confrontation with the officers of the law but his career never recovered from the terrible events for which many felt he was partly responsible. He now makes tired, cynical movies in France. He has written a book about the night Wayne and Scout entered his life, called *Who Is Responsible?* In it he divides the blame equally between Wayne and Scout, the media, the police and the millions of people who did not turn off their TVs.

Brooke died of her wounds. Her parents subsequently claimed that by pursuing a selfish debate, rather than making the simple statement Wayne had asked him to make, Bruce denied Brooke proper medical care for the vital period in which she could have been saved. They hold him responsible and are in the process of suing him.

Bill and Kirsten both died in the police assault. Their

families now claim that as they were both employees of the television companies there was a duty of care and that the companies are therefore responsible for their deaths. Both families are currently suing the networks. They are also suing the police, whom they hold responsible for not intervening earlier. In a separate claim they are again suing the police, whom they also hold responsible for intervening when they did.

Velvet was also killed in the crossfire. During a memorial service at her school, her principal reminded the congregation that society had a responsibility to protect young people like Velvet and had failed to do so. Her grandparents are investigating the possibility of suing the estates of Wayne and Scout. In the largest single claim in history, they are also suing the millions of people who did not turn off their TVs, who they feel are also responsible.

Many of the people who did not turn off their TVs have formed themselves into action groups, claiming that they have experienced anxiety, stress and mental torment as a result of the terrible moral dilemma that the TV companies allowed them to be put in. They hold the TV companies responsible and are pursuing claims for damages.

The TV companies are currently lobbying for more specific guidelines on how to act under similar circumstances. They claim that, in the final analysis, only government can be responsible for how public amenities operate. They have announced that they will attempt to offset losses resulting from claims made against them by taking action against Congress and Capitol Hill.

*   *   *

Police Chief Cornell and News and Current Affairs Chief Murray both lost their jobs as a result of the débâcle and hold each other responsible. Murray claims that Cornell should have taken charge of the situation and ended the siege sooner. Cornell claims that Murray should have denied the killers the oxygen of publicity which precipitated the final drama. In private lawsuits they are suing each other for loss of earnings.

Wayne Hudson's family are currently pursuing the Department of Welfare. They claim that it was early neglect of Wayne's problems by social workers that was responsible for turning him bad. They assert that it was clear that they were bringing Wayne up inadequately, and feel he should have been taken into care. They are suing.

Scout's family are also suing the Department of Welfare. They claim that constant intervention by social workers when Scout was younger left her insecure and easily influenced. They claim she should not have been taken into care and are suing.

On Capitol Hill, in the aftermath of the bloodbath, the Republicans claimed that the liberal values perpetrated by the Democrats were responsible.

The Democrats blamed Republican opposition to gun control.

Scout survived the gunfight and was eventually sent to a secure mental hospital, where she has discovered religion. She feels that the Almighty does all things for a purpose, and that in the long run God is responsible.

So far no one has claimed responsibility.

Two novels from bestselling author and comic genius, Ben Elton.

POPCORN

Bruce makes movies about killers. Wayne and Scout are killers. It's Oscar night and fact is about to confront fiction in this wickedly funny media satire.

THIS OTHER EDEN

The earth is doomed, and no one wants to save it. In a mass survivalist frenzy, people buy their own biospheres in which to sit out the Apocalypse. In marketing terms, the end of the world could be very big indeed.

Praise for **POPCORN** and **THIS OTHER EDEN**

'Killer prose...viciously funny satire that also works as tongue-in-cheek thriller' *The Sunday Times*

'An abso ___ ___ of black comedy' *Daily Telegraph*

'Fierce ___ ___gly funny' *Spectator*

'Serious, m___ ___ rally rich and bitterly funny' *___ n Sunday*

'One of the most brilliantly sustained and focused pieces of satire I've ever read' **Douglas Adams**

Pocket Books
FICTION
£8.99

www.simonsays.co.uk

ISBN 0-7434-6798-1

9 780743 467988